A Haunting Connection

BOOK TWO IN THE ASCENSION SERIES

MICAH BRIARMOON

Copyright © 2026

by Micah Briarmoon

Dedications

Anne Topp and I read an early version of this book together. She helped shape the book with her passion for stories and writing, her insights, and expertise. Her spirit lives on in these pages. May she rest in peace.

For Jared Bancroft, whose careful reading, honest questions, and encouragement helped this story grow into what it became.

Henan Province, China

August 2, 1945

The late afternoon sun dipped low, stretching the truck's shadow over the rain-soaked road as it sloshed through the mud. The worn suspension groaned, and the cargo rattled as the truck swayed. Ruth braced herself against the door, flexing her muscles. Her strength, however, was an act—every part of her ached. The air further intensified her misery. The humid heat suffocated. Rank body odor, made worse by her damp, muddy clothes, saturated the cabin. Strands of her black hair, which had slipped loose from her bun, stuck to her forehead and neck.

Ruth angled away from the two men beside her and draped her arm over the metal doorframe. Her skin, a rich, sun-kissed brown, shimmered with sweat. Leaning her head out the window, she hoped the fresh air would offer a reprieve from the stench, but the wind hit her with the pungent smell of manure as they passed a farm. Her stomach churned.

I'm in hell, she thought.

She opened her mouth, letting the pooling saliva drip from her lips. Fixing her eyes on her surroundings, she hoped to calm her nausea.

Narrow dirt footpaths and low earthen ridges divided farming plots, some flooded for the growing rice, others thick with stalks of corn. The truck hit a pothole, and her belly knotted tighter. The burn threatened to expel everything inside her. She braced herself for the inevitable as an acrid liquid bubbled up her throat like foaming beer. She spit the taste from her mouth and breathed in, relieved the reek of manure had lifted. Sweet scents of ripening pears and honeysuckle now filled the air, settling her stomach.

"Ruth, are you okay?" asked the sickly, skinny man sitting between her and the driver. He laid his hand on her shoulder, which slimed down her side and curled toward her breast.

Knocking his hand away with her elbow, Ruth warned, "Focus on the hills, unless you want your cargo confiscated or you think being blown away by a tank would be fun."

The truck splashed through a deep puddle, fishtailing and spraying mud to the sides of the road. Ruth's head knocked against the metal doorframe. "Ah." Skinny's hand landed on her hip. She stiffen and flexed, ready to hit him, but his hand retreated as the truck steadied. Ruth suppressed another wave of nausea as she rubbed her head, too tired and miserable to confront him.

She glanced to the driver for help. Skinny looked his way as well. But the burly man's attention was already stretched thin. He gripped the wheel with white knuckles as he navigated the muddy road and scanned the horizon for soldiers. The stress of driving through the contested zone—a treacherous stretch between Chinese and Japanese occupied territory—was testing his limits. The driver's focus spoke to his determination to stay alive while avoiding getting stuck. Ruth wasn't about to disturb his concentration over something as trivial as subtle groping from the masher sitting next to her.

Ruth drew in a breath and closed her eyes, trying to calm her emotional distress and steady herself against the truck's unstable motion. She needed to connect with her spiritual core to access her psychic abilities. Re-examining their journey was imperative if they were to evade attack and reach Kaifeng. She turned her thoughts inward and hummed a Celtic tune to build her spiritual energy. The vibrations created a sliver of light she used to reach into the future.

Her visions revealed a fire, a roadblock, tree branches swaying along a quiet road, people running in fear. The hostile region they were traveling through was amplifying uncertainty; a multitude of unmade decisions splintered paths into countless possibilities. This was the chaos of war: split-second choices shaping the future. Soldiers, military vehicles, a skirmish, the road clear and calm—no path was stronger than the others. Ruth was sure something was happening ahead of them. But what exactly, and when?

"You should slow down," she told the driver. "We're a little ahead of schedule."

The driver shot her a stern glare. "If we slow down, we'll get stuck again."

"Can you find a place to pull over?"

"No," he asserted. "We'll run into the night patrol."

"I told you the road would be open," Ruth countered. "But our window is narrow. The timing has to be perfect."

The muscles in the man's cheeks twitched, and he turned his head, looking out the driver's-side window. His shoulders tensed, and his hands flexed tighter on the wheel. Seconds stretched. Finally, with a sharp, grudging exhale, he muttered, "Fine. I'll stop at the top of the hill."

Speeding, the truck hit the incline but strained to climb the slope. The engine sputtered, and the tires slipped, causing the vehicle to jerk as it struggled to grip the ground. The driver downshifted and hit the gas. "Come on, you bitch!" he yelled. Nearing the top, the wheels gained traction and pushed forward. The heavy frame leveled out and came to a stop. They let out a collective sigh.

"You better be right about this," the driver grumbled.

Closing her eyes again, Ruth hoped the stop had clarified the future. She saw the calm road as a strong possibility, but she still felt the turmoil of battle. Relying on earlier visions and rumors of the Japanese retreat, she interpreted the open road to be the most likely outcome. The deserted checkpoint they had passed earlier seemed to confirm this, but the driver, having made this trip before, had explained that the post was inactive while the soldiers ate dinner.

Ruth needed to feel confident, but her emotions reflected the driver's—his wide eyes and bulging veins beneath his skin betraying his fear. Rumors were often wrong, and her visions had been unreliable in war-torn China, making this calculated trip extremely risky. She released a silent plea: *Give us a clear road.*

"How long will we wait here?" Skinny asked.

"Until little Miss Princess says we can go," snarked the driver.

The truck idled. The driver lit a cigarette. Skinny kept his eyes on Ruth. The amber in the sky deepened, indicating less than an hour of light, and Ruth knew that driving through the mud at night wasn't a good idea.

"Let's go," she said.

The driver shifted into gear and inched the truck forward. As they descended the hill, Ruth reached for her visions again and saw the turmoil fading— The truck rocked and threw her thoughts off balance. A hand landed on her upper leg, fingers inching toward her inner thigh. Her jaw tightened and her eyes snapped open, fixing on Skinny. His hand retreated. If she had the energy to deal with this creep, she'd ... *ugh*. She was too tired to finish the thought. The only thing that mattered now was getting to her father.

Eight years had passed since Ruth had left him in Shanghai. Her stepmother, Suzi, had driven her to Hong Kong, sold the car, and booked passage for the two of them to San Francisco. That journey, stressful and difficult at the time, now felt like a distant luxury compared to traveling during a world war. Soldiers, guns, checkpoints, they were all dangerous. The trains and buses were not reliable because the bridges were often destroyed, and the roads had huge craters in the middle of them. Everyone was afraid and no one trusted a stranger. All these obstacles added time—time she didn't have.

The truck pitched as it rolled over a large rock, tossing the three of them in their seats. "Sorry," the driver muttered.

Ruth fixed Skinny with a warning glare. This time, he reached his hands forward for support with a nervous grin. "You're pretty," he said. "Dirty, but pretty."

Rolling her eyes, Ruth leaned her head back out the window. He wasn't wrong. Her last bath had been in Chengdu, ten days ago. Grime clung to her skin, and her muscles ached from sleepless nights on cramped trains, bone-rattling buses, and a rickety motorcycle. The bags under her eyes felt heavy, but she couldn't stop. Not when she'd felt *that* disturbance—the one that had shaken her to her core.

The war had made disturbances an everyday phenomenon for Ruth—so common that she barely paid attention to them. But some were larger, sharper, and more pronounced, meaning more people would be affected. The first disturbance she had felt was in May of 1939. She was twelve years old and had woken drenched in sweat, her skin stinging and raw, as though she'd been scrubbed with steel wool. The feeling had been so terrifying, she thought her father had died. She had scrabbled at their telepathic bond. *Dad! Please, answer me.*

I'm here, he had responded. *What you felt was a psychic ripple, a foreshadowing of a life-altering event affecting millions of people. This disturbance signals an approaching war. The decision or action behind it has already happened, and the outcome is certain—most likely the start of a second world war. When? How? I don't know yet. But it will happen in Europe, so you will be safe in San Francisco.*

She had been safe, but her father hadn't. China was at war with Japan, and Shanghai had already been defeated. His telepathic messages, once full of love and sensory detail, had become brief and cold, shielding her from the horrors of war. Ruth knew he was suffering—she could feel it. Her father was overwhelmed. With her own powers fully realized, she wouldn't sit idle while he risked his life alone. War left the dead lingering in numbers too great to count, the lost souls clinging to a world that had no place for them. Her father needed help and support in guiding them to transcend.

The road curved sharply, revealing the charred remains of a farmhouse. Its blackened timbers, still smoldering, jutted out like skeletal fingers against the darkening sky. Deep impressions of tank tracks scarred the earth, advertising danger.

"Shit," the driver gasped, hitting the brakes. "Soldiers are close."

"They're long gone by now. Don't you think?" Skinny said with a lascivious smirk. He patted Ruth's knee, each deliberate touch creeping up her leg.

She pushed him away and gripped the door handle, searching the landscape. Had she settled on the wrong truth? This burned house was a sign that trouble awaited them, but she wasn't able to see from where.

The driver cursed. "Vehicles are approaching. Are they Japanese?"

Closing her eyes, Ruth saw frightened civilians driving towards them. "No. There must be fighting ahead," she said. "People on foot won't be too far behind."

From over the hill, a tight formation of four P-51 Mustangs sped past, heading southeast.

"What should we do?"

"We're safe here for the moment," Ruth reassured. "Let's rest a bit."

With a leap from the truck, she hit the damp ground and sloshed to the back. She grabbed a handful of straw and headed straight for a tree to connect with nature's energy. By grounding herself, she hoped to answer her most pressing questions: What was ahead of them? Had their chance to safely reach Kaifeng closed?

The straw made a dry seat under the tree. She paused a moment to let the cars pass. When the last one rounded the corner, she pressed her palms to the earth and focused inward. Her center fluttered with noise. She slid her fingers into the mushy grass and waited. The earth's pulse was deep and resonant. Breathing in, she aligned herself with the rhythm of life. Breathing out, she let her stress and worries fall away. After her core settled and began to glow, she drew on her spiritual energy and let her psychic senses awaken. The visions formed, no longer fractured or vague. Critical decisions had already been made, strategies committed to, and with fewer uncertain choices ahead, she was looking at the future with more clarity. ...the road they traveled would be open, the fighting was happening south of the city, and the soldiers manning the posts and checkpoints along their route would be pulled as reinforcements. She would reach the city and cross into Japanese territory.

Letting out a slow breath, Ruth snuggled in next to the tree. She hadn't had a vision this strong in over a week. She could relax, something her body sorely needed. She closed her eyes, allowing the tug of sleep to take her. Her mind slowed, but before unconsciousness claimed her, a ghostly presence entered her space.

Ruth jerked forward, her breath catching. *Pesky spirits*, she thought. They were everywhere, drawn to her brightening spiritual core like moths to a flame. This one wasn't a threat to possess her or twist her mind; it hovered at the edge of her awareness, curious but cautious. Still, its presence was enough to set her nerves on edge. She glanced at Skinny, who leaned against the truck smoking a cigarette. His eyes were fixated on her. She was under no illusion about who was more dangerous.

Explosions rumbled in the distance, causing the ground to tremble. She turned her head, searching for the source as the soul moved closer.

Nervous? she asked, more to herself than to the ghost. *Explosions have always terrified me. The first time I heard one was in a psychic vision. I screamed.* A sad chuckle escaped her lips. *That was the day my father decided I had to leave.*

She hugged her knees to her chest and let out a sigh. *Would you have sent your daughter away?*

She imagined the spirit answering, *No, of course not.*

Ruth laid her forehead on her knees. *My father wasn't going to ... but then, just like that, he changed his mind. Was it because of my vision? A moment of fear? Or ... do you think he had known something?*

"Scared?" Skinny called. He stood, calm and at ease, which felt wrong.

Ruth didn't answer. She was tempted to force the soul next to her to transcend and absorb the dark energy. If Skinny tried anything, she'd use the energy to blast him straight into the sky and let him fall to his death.

"You kept dark energy in you again, didn't you?" Suzi's sharp, accusing words resurfaced. At ten years old, Ruth had dismissed them, convinced her father would never fall to such temptation. Suzi's words had been born from bitter

suspicion, anger, and mistrust; Ruth's relationship with Suzi had strained because of this fundamental disagreement.

But now, eight years later, surrounded by war and danger, Ruth had a new perspective. Dark energy was a powerful weapon. Suzi had known that. Too bad she hadn't trusted her father not to use— Her mind paused mid-thought. What if Suzi had been right? A slow dread crawled down her spine as realization dawned. *Oh, shit! If my father has been holding dark energy all this time, then he's addicted. And if that's the case, then he's in danger. Shamans will hunt him down.*

Her heartbeat quickened. *Please, don't let it be true.*

Ruth needed to know! Had her father been holding dark energy? If he had, this was the cause of her disturbance. She had to look back, strip away her love and idealization for him, and examine his words and actions with unfiltered eyes.

"Hey, Stringbean!" the driver shouted. "Let's see what we can salvage from that farmhouse." The sickly man held Ruth's gaze, an unspoken ick slithering beneath his stare. He slipped around the truck and vanished.

With the lech gone and the soul near her nothing more than a nuisance, Ruth was able to relax again. She rubbed the knot in her shoulder and released her tension, then returned her thoughts to her father. Had he compromised himself?

A distant bomb rumbled, a tell of the battle's ferocity. Her friends, teachers, and even Suzi had been frightened by the stories and rumors of war. Ruth remembered how the whispers had turned to preparations, and how people had clapped when reinforcements arrived, desperate for reassurance.

The clapping... She had been in the garden with her father that day. The clouds had been dark from an approaching typhoon, and rain poured later that night. That moment with her father came rushing back.

The memory took hold, pulling her into that final day in Shanghai, August 12, 1937. Had he kept dark energy in him? The truth was buried in this memory. She had to see it again to believe it.

Heavy clouds loomed over the garden where Ruth Jones and her father, Damarkus, sat cross-legged on the grass. The scent of jasmine mixed with the earthy aroma of sandalwood incense drew them deeper into the garden's rhythm as they aligned their energy. Next to them grew a cluster of chrysanthemums, attracting honeybees with fuzzy bodies dusted in pollen. They hummed briefly before retreating to safety. A single candle flickered in a lantern beside them, its flame wavering as the wind stirred with insistence. Together, the two chanted the sacred mantra, "AUM." The sound summoned ancient energy, invoking the primordial forces that birthed all things in the universe and resonated with living tissue.

Ruth's essence intertwined with her father's, forming a powerful bond that let them share each other's thoughts and emotions.

Allow your spiritual energy to expand, her father said.

She felt his telepathic message as if he were reaching out with his warm, steady hand to support her.

Connect with the life forces of the garden.

"AUM," she repeated. The vibration moved through her bones, growing her spiritual core. She extended her awareness, blending and swirling the energy around her. As she cleansed her mind and slipped into a peaceful trance, her stress from the constant talk of pending war faded.

Ruth was a strikingly beautiful child, her features a harmonious blend of her heritage, highlighted by dark, smooth skin that radiated, even under the looming storm clouds. Her black, lustrous hair was neatly wrapped in a classic chignon, secured with a jade hairpin, accenting her traditional Chinese cheongsam—a knee-length dress with a high collar and fitted bodice. Ruth's eyes sparkled with intelligence and curiosity, a reflection of her diverse education at the international school in Shanghai.

Today, they were at Mr. Chen's house, the principal of Ruth's school. He had reached out to Damarkus for help after his father had died and began haunting the garden.

"AUM," Ruth chanted, keeping a steady pitch. As she stretched her life force further, her nerves caused her heart to beat erratically. She knew the ghost would be drawn to the energy she offered; that was the point. But the last spirit had been angry and burst into their space with a violent lunge. Her father had snatched it and forced it into the realm of oneness. Ruth hadn't been hurt by the attack, only shaken. Wincing, she braced herself for the arrival of this soul, hoping it would be confused. Maybe even melancholy. Anything but violent.

Stay with me, Ruth, her father projected. *Calm your fears. You have more knowledge and experience with manipulating energy than this soul. Trust your abilities.*

Drawing on her father's confidence, she inhaled, but her breath caught in her throat. A thick, ghostly presence pushed its way into their space. Ruth's eyes widened at the bold, stubborn entity. Her nostrils flared, and her hands trembled, unsure of what to expect.

You are safe, her father reassured, then invited the soul into his consciousness.

With the spirit in her father's custody, Ruth released a breath, her shoulders going limp. After the tension in her chest eased, she slipped back into a serene calm.

Now come join us, her father said.

Ruth followed his essence into the depths of his mind, and encountered turmoil. The ghost was slamming against her father's barriers. Each relentless strike sent a shock that Ruth recognized as pain. She knew it wouldn't be long until the soul started burrowing to gain control.

This time, I want you to be the teacher, Damarkus instructed. *Pretend I am a student and guide me through the steps.*

Me? she stammered.

Yes. Explain each step for forcing a soul to transcend.

Ruth paused, but her reluctance took precious time her father didn't have. The ghost sank deeper into his mind. The urgency built a suffocating need to act.

With firm but reassuring thoughts, Damarkus added, *You've seen me do this and heard my explanations. Now, I want you to use what you've learned and tell me, step-by-step, what to do. This will show me how well you understand the process.*

I'll try my best, Ruth murmured. She stared, unable to blink. The ghost was digging, scratching, and clawing for a memory rich in sensory details. The spirit would use the memory as a pathway into her father's neural networks.

Holding a deep breath, Ruth centered herself. Then she exhaled and started with, *Offer one of your memories to the ghost. One that holds special meaning to you.* Her tone grew more confident. *The memory should include sounds, smells, things you touch, and strong emotions.*

Her father's admiration flowed to her. *You're doing wonderfully. Your instructions are clear and thoughtful. But consider the word textures instead of 'things you touch,' for next time.*

Damarkus found a memory—one that Ruth had seen before; it was her favorite. The spirit took hold, recreating the scene as Ruth relived that special day with her father.

Colorful lanterns lined the paths of the temple, casting a soft glow. The aroma of sizzling duck stirred Damarkus's appetite, causing his stomach to rumble with anticipation. He navigated through the bustling crowd to the noodle stand, passing families that were laughing and chattering. Their voices blended with the melodious notes from a floor harp and flute, which tickled his ears.

Ruth's eyes were glued to the bend in the path. She waited with anticipation for her mother to round the corner, followed by her grandmother. She missed them dearly.

Damarkus stopped in front of the food stand just as Ruth's mother appeared. "Ying, don't wander, dear. Stay close," Ruth's grandmother's voice chimed. Her call caught Damarkus's attention, and his eyes flickered to the source.

Ying wore a flowing dress that swirled around her. Her smile was brighter than the brightest lamp, and her laugh rang like a bell, pure and infectious. Ruth stared as her parents' eyes met for the first time, and in that instant, Ying stumbled, a gasp escaping her lips. But before she fell, Damarkus reached out and caught her hand, his touch igniting a spark that neither of them could deny.

Ruth's chest tightened as the ghost's icy tendrils dug into her father's cognitive network. "If you let the memory play," she whispered, "the ghost will slip into your mind. It moves through the memory pathways—what you see, smell, feel. Then it starts to take control. You get quiet inside, like you're trapped underwater, and lose yourself, lose your ability to control your own body. To reverse the attack, you have to change what happened. That confuses the ghost, and it gets lost in its own memories instead. Then we can follow it back into its own consciousness and push it toward its door; the one that leads to the other side."

"Well said!" her father gushed. "So, I'm going to alter this memory to reverse the ghost's trajectory. Are you ready?"

"I'm ready," Ruth said.

Damarkus pulled Ying to him and kissed her. Then he spun her in a circle, turned, and punched a man standing next to him.

The absurdity of how he altered this pivotal emotional moment shook the very foundation of the memory and sent a shockwave that broke the ghost's concentration. The world around Ruth began to blur. Colors and shapes ran together, mixing into a kaleidoscope of hues, creating a dizzying effect.

The memory morphed and shifted, pulling Ruth through a tunnel of light and shadow. Discordant musical notes plucked on a piano prodded her. Turning her head, she became briefly nauseous before settling into a dark environment peppered with light conversation and laughter.

Piano music mingled with the chatter of patrons in a cozy pub. Ruth's stomach churned at the strong bitter scent of beer. But the rich, smoky aroma of grilled meat wafting in from the kitchen settled her. Waitresses moved between tables, balancing trays of food and drinks as they served the guests. The atmosphere was calm and convivial with laugher and clinking glasses.

Ruth and Damarkus spotted Mr. Chen's father just as a drunkard stumbled into a waitress, knocking the drinks from her tray all over Mr. Chen. He stood abruptly and shouted, "Hey! Watch where you're going."

The drunkard puffed his chest and matched Mr. Chen's tone. "Watch where you're putting your feet! You tripped me."

Ruth explained, "We are inside the soul's consciousness. Look for the door to transcendence, the one with religious symbols on it."

In the pub, the two men began to fight. Punches were thrown, and patrons backed away.

Ruth's voice reverberated. "In this realm you can do or create anything from your imagination. Picture what you need and force the soul to the door. Remember, you must exit this consciousness before the soul transcends, so choose your methods with this in mind."

"Good," her father praised. "You're guiding me through these steps really well. I have a method in mind."

Damarkus whirled a rope over his head and lassoed the soul. Then he tossed the end of the rope through the door. The rope snapped tight and began dragging Mr. Chen's father towards it.

"This is the most important step," Ruth emphasized. "If we leave too soon, there's a chance the soul will escape. That will make it more powerful and give it knowledge and ways to resist future attempts. We need to stay long enough to ensure the spirit transcends, but leave before that happens. Timing is everything."

The rope shortened bit by bit as it disappeared through the door, pulling the soul closer and closer.

"Dad, I need help. I'm not sure when to leave."

The soul's essence dwindled away, as if it were made of sand steadily blown by wind.

"Dad?" Ruth pleaded.

As the man disappeared, the entire memory began to fade.

Ruth choked. "Dad! We have to go*!*"

The sudden jerk of being snapped back shook Ruth, causing her to gasp. Her muscles tightened from the jolt, and an ache settled in, leaving her feeling stiff and sore. She caught a faint phantom aroma, a burnt smell that tainted the sweetness of the garden and clung to the smoke of the incense. The foreboding energy made her shiver.

"Dad! Why didn't you say anything? I could've gotten sucked through the door too," Ruth exclaimed, her breathing rapid and uneven.

"It was last-second, yes," Damarkus admitted. "But you did an excellent job, and this experience will make you wiser." He leaned forward and kissed her forehead. "Now. What's next?"

After taking a moment, Ruth said, "You have to drain the dark energy. Don't keep it inside you."

"Why?" her father asked. "It can be a powerful weapon. I can use it to make me stronger and faster."

She knew the answer by heart. "Dark energy is extremely addictive. It alters your emotions, making you irritated, angry, and gives you the desire to murder."

"How does one release the energy?"

"There's a dark lump in your chest. You relax it and allow the energy to flow. You said it's like trying to pee when my bladder isn't full. And you keep making me go to the bathroom, so I can practice."

Nodding, Damarkus continued, "And if I'm distracted or can't release it, then what?"

"Become angry. Make the energy a ball of tension and blast it from you. But that can hurt people, so you have to be careful."

"Is there another way to release it?"

"There is a darker emotion—the satisfaction of causing someone pain. That feeling lets it go, but causes the people around you to become confused and dizzy."

"Good." Damarkus said. "Now tell me, have you been doing the exercises I gave you? How are you at controlling your emotions?"

"I think I'm getting better. Yesterday, when Meek stole the swing from Monica, I made myself angry. But it didn't feel the same as before. I saw my anger in my hand, like a bat I could swing. Then I let it go and calmed myself easily."

Damarkus beamed. "I am so proud of you, Ruth." He reached out and laid a hand on her head. "You have learned so much so quickly."

A giant smile crossed her face. This was her first time leading a transcendence, and it was exhilarating if not a little scary. But now she had questions. "Dad," Ruth began, "why do we sometimes meditate and chant 'AUM,' and other times pray to Jesus, or praise Allah and bow during sunset and sunrise?"

With warm eyes, Damarkus said, "We need to build our spiritual energy. Every tradition, every religion, every path to spiritual understanding offers different ideas. Each has its own ways to connect with the divine. Your goal is to find the path that best resonates with you, so you can connect to the higher realm."

He plucked a piece of grass, a petal from a flower, and a stem off an herb plant. "I take bits and pieces from different religions, the parts that ignite my spiritual core." He bundled the elements together in a tiny floral arrangement. "The merging of these fragments creates harmony, providing a connection to my spiritual self and to the mystery of life. It's not about choosing one ritual over another; it's about finding what works best for you, so you can be close to the creator."

Ruth nodded, absorbing his words. Then with a spark of understanding, she said, "It's like when I speak English or Chinese to my friends. Sometimes English works, but other times there is no English word for what I want to say, and Chinese is better."

"Exactly," Damarkus replied. "I'll keep introducing you to spiritual ideas, but ultimately, it's up to you to choose your own path. Find what works best for you."

She raised her eyebrows. "So, I get to choose how I build my energy?"

"That's right," he confirmed.

Ruth inhaled, feeling a sense of weightlessness. *I'm free to choose.* Her thoughts drifted to her friends, bound by tradition, who had no choice but to follow their parents' beliefs. By exploring her own spirituality, Ruth would grow stronger.

Tilting her head to one side in a quizzical manner, she asked, "Dad, when I talk to my friends about growing my spiritual core, they don't understand. They don't even know what energy manipulation is."

Damarkus paused, hand to his chin, as he chose his words carefully. "Ruth, what you did today is far beyond what most people can do, even as adults. Only special individuals with a strong spiritual core understand what we do. The concept seems like magic or make-believe to most people. Shamans and Banishers don't typically begin to master their abilities until they are adults."

"How old were you when you started?"

"Thirty-five."

Ruth gaped. "That's old."

"Effective energy manipulators are guided by wisdom. That's why Banishers don't begin serious training until they're forty or fifty."

Her eyes widened even more. "But I'm only ten."

"Yes. You are exceptional." Pride filled his voice. "But you must be cautious. Our neighbors, the shopkeepers, your teachers—they know of my work, but they don't fully understand it. If they did, they might be frightened. History hasn't always been kind to people like us. Many of our kind were persecuted, even burned alive. Times have changed, but it's crucial to be discreet. Don't boast or show off."

Ruth shook her head vigorously. "I won't. I promise."

Damarkus ran a finger over her cheek. "I know you won't."

"I think I understand why they used to burn people like us alive."

"Why is that?"

"They kept dark energy and wanted to harm others."

"Yes," he chuckled. "Ruth, there's something else you need to know. Shamans and Banishers have often been at odds. We sometimes fight each other, especially if a Shaman becomes corrupted, or a Banisher becomes addicted."

"Shamans are our enemies?"

"They can be. There's little tolerance for a Banisher who embraces dark energy, even though we can cleanse our souls."

"At the temple."

"Yes, precisely. And there's one Shaman in particular you must be wary of—the leader of the Shamans, Yoona. As you grow more powerful, you may encounter her in your visions. She is not your friend. But if you stay clean, drain your energy, and cleanse your soul, you won't need to fear her."

"Is Yoona like the devil?"

"No, no. Nothing like that. But she opposes Banishers who absorb dark energy. So, mind your training and keep your abilities hidden. There's no need to draw attention to yourself."

"I understand." Then Ruth gave her father a curious look. "Are you going to marry Suzi?"

Damarkus opened his mouth and blinked. "Uh..." He paused. "We already got married, two weeks ago."

"No, I mean for real."

Taking Ruth's hands, he leaned in close. "You mean, are we going to have a ceremony?"

"Suzi said you had to get the papers in case the Japanese invade. So we could stay together."

"That's right."

"Do you love her? Like you did Mom?"

Ruth noticed the shift in her father's expression as shouts of excitement and applause swelled from the street. She glanced over her shoulder, hearing the rumble of military vehicles coming from beyond the garden wall.

Damarkus took her hand and said in a grim voice, "It's time to go, sweetheart."

They had a polite conversation with Mr. Chen over tea and cookies before heading home. The wind had become stronger, and it began to rain. Suzi met them at the door and sent Ruth to bathe.

As she sat on the small wooden stool in the washroom, sponging herself clean, she couldn't help but listen to a heated argument between Suzi and her father.

"Ouch! Let go of my arm," Suzi's voice cut through the thin walls. "You're hurting me."

Ruth frowned, her small hands pausing mid-sponge. Her father wouldn't hurt a fly. Suzi could be so dramatic at times.

"We need to leave," Suzi insisted, her voice strained with urgency. "The shooting of two U.S. Marines at the airfield, and then the Hongqiao Incident, scares me. My friends are leaving, and I don't want Ruth anywhere near war. You know it's coming!"

"We're not leaving," Damarkus's voice rumbled, a deep, threatening tone Ruth didn't recognize as her father's. "My place is here, especially because war is coming."

Ruth cracked the door open, just a sliver, and peeked out, seeing ... anger.

Stepping back, Ruth created distance between her and the foreign expression pasted to her father's face. Was the man standing in the living room really him?

"I'm packing my bags," Suzi declared. "And I'm taking Ruth with me."

The statement shook Ruth. Her pulse spiked, and she went straight back to the door. She wasn't leaving her father.

"No, you're not!" Damarkus's voice thundered through the small apartment as the rain pounded the window. He squeezed Suzi's arm and shoved her against the wall. "Stop being irrational."

Ruth's panic curdled into unease. Why was he being so mean?

Suzi grunted in pain and shook Damarkus off her. "I'm the only rational person in this house." She walked in a circle, huffing. "You do know that Emperor Hirohito removed protections for the treatment of Chinese prisoners. Can you imagine what that means for Ruth and me if we are taken? The Japanese soldiers can do anything they want to us."

"I won't let that happen!" he roared. "You think running away will keep you safe? There's nowhere to hide from what's coming. You're safest here with me. The Japanese won't dare attack the international settlement and risk provoking the U.K. and America."

Suzi's voice filled with frustration. "In the short term, maybe. But there is nothing safe about war, and the Damarkus I first met in San Francisco knew that." She stood taller, confronting him, her tone bitter. "You kept dark energy in you again, didn't you?" She put her finger to his chest and pushed. "You anger easily. You become physically aggressive. You refuse to see the danger that stalks us."

Ruth watched as her dad clenched his fists. She didn't feel uneasy now—she was scared. But Suzi's voice turned sweet, and she laid her hand on her husband's chest, gently petting him.

"Honey, tell me the truth."

Damarkus exhaled and lowered his head, his hands relaxing.

Ruth's whole body sagged. She let out a long, deep breath and leaned against the wall, steadying herself. Suzi had overreacted again. Her father would never keep dark energy in him. Peering back out, she kept observing.

Suzi pulled Damarkus in close, hugging him. "I think it's time you went to the temple and cleansed your soul."

Nodding in agreement, he said, "First thing tomorrow morning. I promise."

Ruth closed the door. Why did Suzi argue? She didn't understand his abilities. She couldn't connect or manipulate energy; she had no idea what she was talking about. He'd never hold dark energy.

But seeing her dad grab and push Suzi had frightened her. She wished things would go back to normal. She hated the Japanese! She hated talk about war! She hated seeing everyone so scared.

Later that evening, Damarkus called Ruth to dinner. The comforting smells of cooking rice and steamed buns filled her with joy. Scooting her chair closer to the small wooden table, Ruth glanced at her father, who was reading the paper and sipping jasmine tea, before turning to see Suzi approaching with a bowl of congee, a simple rice porridge. She picked up her spoon in anticipation and said, "Thank you."

Suzi nodded and set the plate of buns in the center of the table, joining Ruth and Damarkus.

"Additional reinforcements for the 88th arrived today," Suzi commented as she reached for a bun.

"We heard them marching in the street," he remarked, as if that were a normal thing.

In a curt voice, Suzi pressed, "And that means nothing to you?"

Ruth gripped the edge of the table as the mood in the room soured. Her father lowered the paper. "The fighting won't come into this area." His voice was hard and resolute.

With an edge of sarcasm and disbelief, Suzi shot back, "Why not? This area wasn't special enough to avoid the fighting in 1932. You think the bombs will magically avoid us this time?"

Damarkus curled his lips into a patronizing smirk. "The British and Americans have more troops here now. The Japanese aren't looking to start a war with other foreign powers."

"The Japanese are demanding reparations for the death of their soldier, which they claim was an attack ... and the Chinese respond by bringing in additional military personnel?" Reaching out, Suzi took her husband's hand. "This battle won't be like Beiping. The Chinese are prepared to defend the city. And with nothing but contempt, the Japanese won't differentiate civilians from soldiers." She squeezed his hand and emphasized, "We cannot stay."

Ruth sunk into her chair. This wasn't normal. If it weren't for the Japanese, Suzi and her father wouldn't be fighting. No one would be worried. Her friends and teachers spoke about the invasions in Manchuria, the Marco Polo Bridge Incident which led to the capture of Beiping, and the 1932 Incident with fear and anxiety. Was what Suzi said true? Were they really in trouble? War was supposed to happen in fields and far away places, not here in cities where normal people lived. She sat up and sipped her water to clear her throat. "Dad?"

"There's no need to fear. I'll protect you."

The color drained from Suzi's face. "You agreed to go to temple. You know what will happen if you don't. You can't keep absorbing that energy to 'protect' us. You'll end up hurting us!"

Damarkus's eyes darkened, and he flung her hand away.

"Dad!" Ruth gasped.

Softening his eyes, Damarkus peered at his daughter. "I'm sorry." He turned his palm up and held it out to Suzi.

"How many refugees stream into this area?" Suzi asked. "Food? Water? Goods? How scarce and how expensive do they become?"

Damarkus pulled his hand back and resumed reading.

"Please think about what's best for Ruth," Suzi insisted. "Do you really want her to witness death and destruction?"

"We're a family. We stay together. And as I've said before, I cannot leave."

Suzi shoved her chair back with a harsh scrape. She huffed and exited the kitchen.

That night, Ruth dreamed. She was running to the school, sirens blaring, people crying and shouting. She tossed and turned in bed, moaning. The shelter was full, and it was difficult to breathe. The ground shook and the sounds of explosions banged in her ears. She screamed, her cry spilling into the night as she bolted upright, straight into her father's embrace.

"It's okay. You're okay."

"It was so scary." A tear slipped from her eye as she clung to her dad. "I was in a dark room, and it felt like everything was falling apart. I breathed in dirt and coughed—I thought I'd be buried alive."

"You had a psychic vision of the future."

"But you said we were safe."

"We are. The bombs land in the city, not in our district."

Suzi entered the bedroom. "How is she?"

Damarkus's eyes drifted, and he spoke in a low, monotone voice. "You won't be able to leave by ship, air, or rail."

Suzi gasped. "What? Since when?"

"The fighting will start this morning, around nine a.m."

"But we're safe here, right?" Ruth blurted. "You said, so. We don't have to go."

Suzi's gaze was unfocused, her expression distant and troubled. "Hong Kong," she muttered. "We'll take the car. I'll sell it and use the money to book passage to San Francisco."

"You must leave by sunrise and be out of the city by nine a.m." Damarkus turned to Ruth, his eyes now brimming with tears.

Sensing the gravity of the moment, Ruth's nostrils flared. She clenched her jaw, and her own eyes filled. "No, Daddy. Don't make me leave. You said we would be safe. You can protect me," she implored.

"I'm sorry, sweetheart."

The ache in her heart choked her as she begged, "But I'm learning how to manipulate energy. I can help you send the souls on." Tears flowed down her face.

"We are connected," Damarkus said. "You can talk to me whenever you need."

"But Dad!" Her voice trembled through sobs. She wrapped her arms around him.

"It's only for a little while." Tears spilled from his eyes, and his voice broke. "We'll see each other again soon."

Ruth shook her head and tightened her grip on him. "No."

"Reach out to me with your thoughts, and I will hear you, no matter the distance."

"I can't leave you."

"You have to. Suzi is right. War is no place for a child." He took her hand. "Come. Let's pack your bags."

At six the next morning, Damarkus went to one knee and pulled Ruth into his embrace. He kissed her cheek and said, "I love you, sweetheart. Be good and keep practicing your meditations."

She hugged him tight. "I will. And when I'm strong enough, I'll come help you."

Holding Ruth's hand, her dad carried the suitcase to his black 1929 Austin 7. The rain continued to fall, creating ripples in the puddles that dotted the streets.

Though the sun had been up for nearly half an hour, its light was barely noticeable through the thick, overcast sky.

He kissed Ruth's forehead, then handed her to Suzi. "I'm here always. Reach out to me anytime."

Ruth's tears streamed down her cheek, mixing with the rainwater dripping from her hair. They got into the car and Suzi started the 747-cc engine. It purred steadily. "You should be able to get six hundred Yuan for her. Two tickets to San Francisco will be between three and five hundred." Damarkus handed Suzi an envelope. "Three hundred and fifty Yuan. Take it. Be safe." He stepped away and blew Ruth a kiss. "Stay connected."

Ruth stared at her father, seeing him for who he was: a hero.

The truck roared to life, waking Ruth. The rest made her mind fresh, but the revitalized feeling didn't last. Her sore muscles protested as she stretched, and her thoughts went straight to her father. His hoarding of dark energy didn't make sense. He knew the sweet, addictive fumes would rot his mind and attract Shamans to him. So why?

Skinny cleared his throat, reminding Ruth exactly why her father would hold dark energy. In the dim light of the waning crescent moon, Ruth saw a vampire that needed to be vanquished.

"The fighting stopped two hours ago," he murmured in a low, oily voice. "We need to leave."

Ruth pushed herself off the ground and strode straight for him, his gross smirk betraying his intentions.

"You sit in the middle. Let me have the window," he said, leering.

Without a word, Ruth wrapped her hand around his throat and slammed him against the truck. Her grip tightened as she met his eyes, their connection flaring to life in her mind. She could feel his fear, taste it even, and for a moment, she savored it.

Skinny's hands shot up, flat against the side of the truck, trembling as he struggled to breathe.

Ruth forced her way into his mind—laying bare his memories, his fears, and his pain.

—The pit was damp and suffocating. A crude lattice of bamboo and barbed wire formed the ceiling. Soldiers stood and squatted overhead, sending human waste splashing into the murky muck. The man next to him heaved, but there was nothing in his stomach to throw up. His heaving and crying made him weak and sick, something Skinny refused to succumb to—

—A chicken leg, stripped clean of its meat, was tossed into the pit like a scrap meant for dogs. Skinny watched as the men clawed, kicked, and punched. Above, the soldiers watched, laughing uncontrollably. Once the others were bloody and broken, Skinny snatched the morsel, beat off the final contender, and rinsed the meal in the muddy sludge before sucking the small pieces of meat clinging stubbornly to the joint—

— The paper in his hand detailed the goods he was to smuggle into Japanese-controlled territory. Happily, *he thought. Anything to escape the prison camp and the pit. The door opened and two soldiers brought in Skinny's brother, hands bound. "Succeed, and he works in the kitchen. Run or fail, and your brother loses his hands and gets thrown into the pit—*

—Ruth Jones, the young, voluptuous woman, sent his heart fluttering uncontrollably. His hand brushed against her skin and his body exploded to life. The desperate need to feel alive, to feel the rush, consumed his every thought and action. He needed more. She was ripe and sweet. To feel her bare skin, to lie with her would be heavenly. He would take her—

—Should I betray my friend and give the goods to the Japanese to save my brother, or sell the goods and keep the money for myself and my mother? Either decision meant death if caught... by the Chinese for his treachery or by the Japanese who would cut off his arms and legs before beheading him—

Ruth retreated from his mind and the two stared at each other. The horrors she had seen and the decisions he had faced made her want to comfort him, tell him he was human ... but knowing he planned to escalate his groping was abhorrent.

"I know your pain. I've seen your struggle to survive, but that doesn't give you the right to take whatever you can get." Projecting her thoughts straight into his mind, Ruth formed a ghostly image of her face and spoke in a low, booming voice. *If you ever touch me again, I will make you feel every inch of that pit. I will bury you in it!* She released his throat and stepped back.

Skinny swallowed hard, his terror-filled eyes stuck on Ruth.

"After you," she said, her hand gesturing to the cab door.

He nodded but didn't move. She cocked her head and motioned for him to move. He shuffled along the truck and climbed in, taking the middle seat. Ruth followed, giving a satisfactory nod as he sat on his hands.

They drove the remaining distance in silence. Ruth's thoughts went to her father. Who would be hunting him? Yoona? If Damarkus could get to a temple before they found him, he'd be safe.

The truck slowed as they neared the city. The men drew in long, heavy breaths as their eyes scanned everything. In the dusk, they spotted fortified positions and strong points—all of them empty.

"I can't believe we made it!" Skinny exclaimed. "We didn't have to bribe a single soul. We're going to be rich!"

The sky lightened as they stopped at the edge of town. Ruth handed the men the rest of the money she owed them, and the driver took it, his eyes still darting around at his surroundings.

"Take care of yourself," he said as he shifted the truck into gear and eased forward.

Ruth slung her bag over her shoulder and watched the truck rumble away, its cargo rattling as it swayed through the muddy road. "Good luck," she whispered.

She lifted her eyes to the rising sun and gazed at the orange light spilling over the buildings. With one foot forward, she headed for the Japanese—and her father.

As she wound through the alleys and roads, Ruth was mesmerized by the dark, devilish eyes of the bullet holes staring at her, crying in fear. Buildings with collapsed roofs and broken windows wilted like battered wives with broken teeth, each shattered pane punching her in the gut. Her heart sank as she took in the piles of rubble where houses had once stood. Remnants of a barricade that had blocked the road smelled of death, with dark brown stains of blood clinging to the surfaces. But what affected her the most was the damage to the people, who milled about, lost.

The dull shock in her countrymen's eyes stung. The beggars were thin, their cheeks colorless and hollow and their faces gaunt and skeletal. A gang of orphans surrounded Ruth, pulling at her shirt, pleading for money, food, anything. A girl, no older than seven, sat next to a wall holding a toddler, barely able to lift her own head to stare. Tears threatened to fall, and Ruth turned away, taking in a quick breath to settle her emotions. But an amputee with a dirty rag wrapped around his stump kept her emotions raw. He sat with lifeless eyes, staring at nothing. The sights, sounds, and smells were like those in several other ravaged villages she had seen, but each place was unique, never failing to have an impact on her. Suzi had made the right choice to take her away.

Ruth simmered with burning anger, her hatred of war stronger than ever. What had this destruction accomplished? What was the purpose of war? She passed desperate scene after desperate scene, her heart hardening, and her conviction strengthening to use her abilities to rid the world of war.

She came to a heavily guarded checkpoint. A stern Japanese officer with sharp, unyielding eyes barked orders at the people in line, his harsh, grating voice intimidating. The people kept their heads low, avoiding eye contact. The officer shoved a man who hesitated, causing him to stumble. A woman with a small child handed him her papers. She pleaded and wept as he scanned them. He backhanded her, then yelled and cursed. Two soldiers dragged her out of line, pulling her into a detention center.

Ruth stepped forward and the officer scanned her from head to toe with a gaze that made her skin crawl. He eyed her breasts and made a full circle around her. Ruth was young and healthy in a place that was desolate.

Why were some men like this? So lecherous, so ugly in their behavior.

The officer called for two soldiers to join him. They were taller, one with glasses and the other with a wart on his cheek. They undressed Ruth with their eyes, wide grins broadcasting their desires. The officer stepped closer and took in her scent. Then he ran the back of his hand across her cheek. As soon as he touched her, Ruth connected and reached for his mind.

Instantly, she began to manipulate his thoughts and emotions, erasing the lustful, predatory impulses from his mind and replacing them with the memory of his older brother shielding him from bullies. Next, she softened his aggression by pulling his grandfather to the forefront of his mind. Respect and obedience, drilled into him since birth, flooded his consciousness.

With the officer in a more subdued state, Ruth handed him her papers. As he took them, she altered his perception, making the documents appear not only legitimate but also of great importance. He straightened and saluted. The two soldiers, watching the transformation, glanced at each other and quickly followed suit. Ruth looked at them, but they avoided her eyes, bowing their heads.

The officer handed her papers back and glanced at the two soldiers. He spoke with authority and waved his hand. The two soldiers escorted Ruth past the checkpoint to a military jeep that was parked nearby. In broken Chinese, the soldier in glasses asked, "Where can we take you?"

"I'm going to the Japanese mainland. Take me to Tsingtao, where I can secure passage to Nagasaki."

Opening the door, he motioned for her to get in and then rushed to the driver's seat. The engine knocked a few times before whining to life. Ruth felt a fleeting sense of relief. She was on her way to Japan. With three or four full days of travel ahead of her, she had to believe she could reach her father before the disturbance happened.

That disturbance, much like the very first one she had experienced, had left her body ragged and limp. The world itself had exhaled in anguish—and then nothing. Silence. Hundreds of thousands of lives snuffed out in a single breath. None of which made sense to Ruth or her father.

As horrific as that disturbance had been, it was the one that closely followed which seized her attention—an intimate, inescapable disturbance that fractured the core of her being, unraveling everything she was meant to become and weaving her into something unrecognizable. Somehow, her future shift was tied to Japan, where her father had gone to uncover the mystery behind the silencing disturbance—the event that would leave the world gasping in horror.

I know my life will change because of something that happens in Japan, Ruth had told him. She poured desperation into her words. *Please, don't go.*

Her father had tried to reassure her. *We don't know what a personal disturbance means. Not all of them are bad.*

Now, after having revisited her past, she was sure that her personal disturbance had something to do with her father absorbing dark energy. What that meant—whether it was leading to his death, a quiet life in a Japanese temple, or something else—was still uncertain. She prayed for something good, content to live with her father in isolation and nurse him back to health. Latching onto that hope, she strained to bend the future to her will.

The ride to Jinan felt endless, the roads sloppy and the tension constant. Once there, the soldier checked her into a hotel and left her with a train ticket to Tsingtao. The hot bath and quiet night were heavenly. The train ride the next day lulled Ruth into a peaceful trance, the smooth movement over the tracks magnifying the harshness of the past seventeen days.

The city of Tsingtao, a main embarkation port, was alive with trade and hostility. Stepping off the train, the first thing Ruth heard was how good the local beer was—a remnant of the city's German heritage. But Ruth needed to secure passage to Japan before she could allow herself to indulge. Japanese soldiers were everywhere, roaming the streets like fat kings. They lounged at the food stalls, enjoyed tea, laughed over mugs of beer, smoked, and harassed women with the entitled ease of conquerors. With a clenched jaw and a hard stare, she cursed their indifference to the extreme poverty around them. Thin, colorless faces hurried past the soldiers with downcast eyes, while kids, dressed in rags, scrounged for scraps. Her time to change all of this would come.

The next morning, August 6, Ruth stood in line to board the ship bound for Nagasaki. Guards patrolled the line, randomly re-checking papers and luggage. The morning air was filled with smoke and noise as dock workers unloaded military equipment from cargo ships.

Ruth felt giddy, knowing she'd be by her father's side in a few days. Tempted to reach out to Damarkus, she told herself to be patient. He'd have a full-blown meltdown and berate her for making such a reckless and dangerous trip, insisting she remain where she was.

The line moved forward. Ruth glanced at the large, round clock, which showed 7:15. Reaching for her bag, her body collapsed.

Ruth clutched her chest as she fell to her knees, her other hand hitting the pavement in support. She couldn't breathe. The shock through her body spoke to indescribable destruction.

"Miss, are you alright?" the young man behind her asked, offering his hand.

Ruth looked around, seeing a woman vomit, a stray dog tuck its tail and run, and an elderly man slump on the bench, a single tear rolling down his cheek. The noise and commotion of the port seemed to pause, as people looked nervously around at each other. The closest soldier placed his hand on his head, wincing in pain, before shaking the discomfort away and shouting orders to keep the line moving.

The disturbance.

The shattering silence was so fierce it stunned Ruth into an emotionless daze. She stood and moved along with the others, feeling lost. Her blank face broadcasted her lack of emotions; she had no idea how to feel. With the larger disturbance having happened, how far behind was her personal one? Would she reach Japan in time, or was it already too late?

Her father's voice trickled into her mind. *I know you felt that.*

Ruth dropped her bag, her whole body unclenching in a wave of relief.

Please don't worry about me; I'm okay, he said.

Where are you? Ruth asked, quickly erecting barriers in her mind to keep her surroundings a secret from her father.

I'm near Saeki, about ten miles from Hiroshima. I'm sorry, but I can't talk now. Just know I'm okay. His voice vanished.

Hiroshima was two days from Nagasaki. Ruth straightened. *Four days!* She'd be with her father in four days.

On August 8, 1945, Ruth arrived in Nagasaki. The large industrial city was similar to Tsingtao in many ways—a port city with soldiers everywhere. But unlike its Chinese counterpart, they did not roam like fat kings. Many of the shops were shuttered, and the remaining carts offered little: small, bony fish and overpriced rice. School children walked alongside siblings or mothers, while factory workers shuffled back and forth—some dirty and heading home, others clean and starting their new shift, a few older children in tow. The weathered faces showed years of stress and hardship.

The following morning, August 9, Ruth boarded the 5:30 train for Okayama. Service to Hiroshima had been suspended. At 11:02 a.m., a second disturbance rippled through her—bigger, heavier, and impossibly more consuming than the one she had felt in Tsingtao. The sensation left her lightheaded and cold; her eyes burned, momentarily blinding her. When the train pulled into the next station, Ruth stumbled off, her legs weak beneath her, unable to comprehend how or why she was feeling this again. *What is happening?*

Dad! she called, using her psychic connection. *You have to tell me what's going on. What is this disturbance? What does it mean?*

It's a weapon, he replied, his words slow and slurred, as if he were drunk. *One that will end the war. I can't... I have to go.*

Wait! she cried. *I need to understand. Are you in danger?*

No, he responded in a harsh tone. *I'm with two other Banishers. We are going to Nagasaki.* She felt a sigh. *You'll learn what happened soon enough. Hasn't the* San Francisco Chronicle *reported the incident?*

Nagasaki? I thought you were in Hiroshima, she pressed.

Ruth! he shouted, his thoughts slamming into her, triggering the image of the Japanese officer backhanding the woman at the checkpoint. *Stop pestering me! I can't...* He paused, then muttered, *It's not a good time.*

Before she could respond, he cut the psychic communication, leaving her cold and empty.

After returning to the ticket counter, Ruth was unable to buy passage, and finding a way back to Nagasaki proved difficult. But by the early evening of August 11, she had finally located an aid bus scheduled to leave the following morning. She helped load medical supplies, food, and water onto the bus, then settled into a cracked and faded vinyl seat. The hot, humid air caused her skin to cling to the smelly seat, making the uncomfortable journey drag through the day. The rumble and monotonous drone of the bus's engine lulled her into a fitful sleep.

By late afternoon, Ruth was jolted awake by the rough bumps that jostled her to and fro. She sat up in a half-dazed state as the bus came to a halt, noticing the clouds were an eerie pink. Then... *What the hell!* She blinked and rubbed her eyes, staring again, mouth agape, unable to comprehend what she ... wasn't seeing. The city... It was... No, it ... wasn't.

The landscape lay in complete ruin, with debris scattered everywhere. Skeletal remains of buildings, twisted metal, and charred remnants of what were once bustling streets ripped at Ruth's heart. The ash and cinders, the smoke and dust, the smell of burnt materials, chemicals, and death rotted her insides. Small fires were still burning in rubble piles off in the distance.

Outside her bus window, a man with severe burns hobbled on a broken ankle. Pus dripped from large boils, and the left side of his face, melted away, was covered in blood from a large gash in his head. A makeshift hospital was full of people with similar injuries—skin raw and red, charred, blistered, and sloughing off. Clothes were fused to their bodies, and many were blind. The sounds of crying, vomiting, and moaning would haunt her for years to come.

Ruth's eyes burned with tears. The sight before her was beyond comprehension. Her initial shock gave way to a surge of anger directed at the senseless violence and devastation wrought upon innocent lives. Rage seethed at the injustice, at the sheer scale that defied belief.

Getting to her feet, she stumbled out the door and around to the back of the bus to help unload the supplies. As the sun began to set, Ruth snuck away and headed towards the center of town, where she was sure to find her father sending souls into the next realm. Pausing, she crouched down and stared into the sky with her mouth hanging open.

How can he stand this? Eight years of seeing the torrent of agonizing memories from souls. Eight years of hearing the cries and smelling death. Eight years of fearing for his life. Eight years of gunfire, explosions, starvation, hopelessness, and despair. The sheer volume of suffering and terror... And he experienced it all again in the memories of the souls he forced on. Tears flowed from her eyes. This could never happen again. How had her father done it—enduring the ceaseless onslaught of such raw, unfiltered pain without a break? How could she have left him alone?

I'm here now!

Ruth stood, took a step forward, and stumbled along. She would help carry the burden and be someone her father could lean on. She would nurture him back to health.

As she made her way through the street, a group of six people caught her eye. They moved with incredible speed and strength, their motions almost too fast to follow. The man in the middle unleashed a burst of energy, blasting another man into the lone wall standing in a ten-block radius. Ruth's breath caught in her throat as she witnessed the raw power on display. What was she seeing? It looked like circus performers, but that wasn't right. Awe and fear struck her as a man was thrown so far into the air, he looked like Superman leaping over a building in a single bound. Ruth's own words slapped her: *I'll blast him straight into the sky and let him fall to his death.* These people were Shamans and Banishers, using their powers in broad daylight. "Dad!" Her heart pounded. He had to be among them, fighting for his life.

"No!" Ruth's breath came in short, desperate gasps as she took off toward the fight. But the utter devastation around her was a hellscape of rubble and ruin, making every step a calculated risk. The ground was uneven, littered with debris and the shattered remnants of buildings, cars, and people. Maneuvering through the wreckage along the cracked and scorched pavement, Ruth forced herself to move quicker, her blood coursing through her veins. Stumbling, she cut her arm. She pushed forward, desperate to reach her father.

A loud screech pierced the air. Ruth stopped and stared. Two priests held a man in suspended animation. It was her dad! His voice, calm and loving, entered her mind. *I love you.*

The words were more than syllables strung together; they carried his essence, laced with memory, conviction, and hope. His affection vibrated through her entire body as if he were physically holding her. A gentleness wrapped in pride and faith slid down her cheek before fading into nothing.

His body dropped to the ground. Their unbreakable connection dissolved, vanishing without a trace.

Ruth froze, staring across the shattered remains of Nagasaki at her father's lifeless body. It lay just fifty yards from her. The stench of death and decay sank into her lungs. The pale haze of dust and smoke blurred her vision. She couldn't move—waiting for some sign of life. A flicker, a movement, some proof that what she felt wasn't real, but she was standing in a graveyard, surrounded by ghosts.

Dumbfounded, Ruth refused to accept what this meant. Her father hadn't just died; his soul had been shredded to pieces, his fragments drifting in the wind, searching for a stranger with whom to bond. That union would spark creativity and ignite inspiration, gifting the world with new art and innovations.

Her heart plummeted, heavy and hard. He couldn't be lost to her! Had someone truly erased him from existence? Was he really gone, unable to nudge or guide her again? The thought was unbearable. The truth, even worse.

She gasped for air, the ground beneath her feet seeming to shift as her body threatened to collapse. She was a mere fifty yards from her father's body but forever separated from his soul.

"Nooo!" she cried out. The word tore from her throat like a wounded animal. She had to reach him, to touch him, to do something to stop this nightmare from being real.

Ruth staggered forward, but her steps faltered. Obliterated lives blocked her path, separating her from her father. She couldn't be too late. Her journey to save him would not end in failure.

With a frantic gaze, Ruth scanned the ruins. Souls wondered through the wreckage, some aimlessly, others oblivious to what had happened. Seizing the nearest one, Ruth forced it to transcend.

Dark energy surged through her veins, raw and unrelenting, feeding her rage and grief. She shaped it into a pulsing sphere and unleashed a blast that ripped through the debris, sending it flying aside. Sprinting forward along the clear path, she dropped to her father's side. Her trembling hands found his face, his skin still warm. She pressed her palm to his chest.

Nothing.

She choked on a sob.

Her father was gone. She would never hear from him again. His right to exist, to transcend, to guide his loved ones had been taken. The theft left her shaking with uncontrollable rage.

Ruth clenched her fists, her muscles bulging. Her red-rimmed eyes blazed as she lifted her head. She would invade the murderer's mind and rip them apart from the inside until there was no sanity remaining.

Breathing hard, Ruth locked eyes with the figure towering over her.

Yoona!

This was her disturbance—the murder of her father. And she couldn't have prevented it. Not because she was late, but because Yoona—the strongest Shaman alive—had made the decision to kill him. Her father's location hadn't mattered; Japan, China, or even San Francisco, Yoona would have hunted him down and eliminated him.

But Ruth could have healed her father. She could have cleansed his soul, if only given the opportunity.

Yoona had stolen that from her.

The fury inside Ruth screamed for release, but it was useless. She was powerless against Yoona. Justice and vengeance would have to wait.

Swallowing the bitter taste of helplessness, Ruth made a silent vow. She would stop this witch, if it was the last thing she ever did.

A Haunting Connection

Book Two

Lake Valley, Oregon
Late Spring—2025

A Targeted Aura

A sleek black Cadillac SUV rolled to a stop across from the Education Center. Mr. Anderson stepped out of the vehicle, removed his sunglasses, and assessed the gathering of people attending the celebrations and ceremonies to bless the building.

A knot formed in his stomach. *Damn, I should have arrived earlier.* Everyone in attendance radiated spiritual energy. These were religious ceremonies, after all.

Ruth had given clear instructions: find and recruit a new energy manipulator—an individual whose power would rival her own. Mr. Anderson had hoped to mill through the crowd and spot the one person gifted in manipulating their spiritual power, but this event had drawn worshippers connected to a higher purpose, which made it harder to distinguish someone's faith from their abilities.

Striding across the street in his tailored black suit, he eased the scowl from his face, knowing it only emphasized his receding hairline. He passed through security and began the laborious process of scrutinizing each person's soul.

Energy manipulators had serenity and focus. They had a calm confidence and were spiritually wealthy. The individual Mr. Anderson sought would be imbued with a kind of mystic divinity, glowing with regality and courtliness.

He scanned the crowd, reading people's auras, judging their movements, and noting their gestures and expressions—a young man with a yarmulke held a guitar to his chest, tuning the strings; two women, both sporting twin ponytails and light makeup with ankle-length dresses, chatted together; and an elderly man in loose cotton robes and shoulder-length dreadlocks carried a box of incense into the Center. Their auras shimmered, their expressions neutral. None of their energies attracted his attention.

The aroma of grilled onions, peppers, and lamb drifted his way, momentarily distracting him. The food smelled delicious, and he regretted having already eaten. Reaching the stairs to the Center, he paused and swept his gaze back over the sparse crowd one last time before heading inside.

When Mr. Anderson stepped through the door, a spectral entity flashed in his mind, stealing his breath. His gaze swept the room, assessing the walls, the ceiling, and the floor. A ghostly presence surrounded him, the energy thick and soupy. The hairs on his arms stood on end, and he backed away, one slow step at a time, until he slipped free from its sphere of influence.

Ruth had told him the building was haunted, but this ... this was something beyond a mere haunting. The Education Center was possessed, oozing with this ghost's essence.

The panic gripping Mr. Anderson's chest screamed, *Run!* He stepped backwards down one stair but couldn't leave. Ruth was counting on him. The world was shifting under her hand, and she needed this new manipulator to ensure her vision of a single, unified world became reality.

With a slow, deep breath, he calmed his thoughts and relaxed. After a moment, he moved forward, feeling ... excitement; the spirit occupying the building was looking forward to the events about to unfold. Others were sure to feel this anticipation, and those were the ones for whom he was searching.

Peeking inside, Mr. Anderson observed the clueless people mingling and smiling at the front desk.

It's not hurting anyone, he thought.

Stepping over the threshold once again, he slipped into the ghost's bubble, moved through the waiting area, and headed down the hall toward the classrooms. He had to find this new user and get out of the building as quickly as possible.

When he reached the atrium, he stopped. The large common area was full of people. They gathered near a pond fed by a natural stream that flowed in from the mountain, sat on benches situated between bushes and trees, chatted near the soaring three-story pillars, and conversed with monks near a wooden stage. He opened his senses. *Let the hunt begin.*

His eyes drifted across the congregation of bodies, waiting for one to stir. *Where are you hiding?* He dipped his chin and circled the throng. Then, from the corner of his eye, he spotted a woman exit a classroom. Her soft violet aura glittered with flecks of gold, indicating spiritual insight and psychic abilities. He moved with purpose, closing the distance between them. His insides prickled as a sweet intoxication came over him. He was going to enjoy bending her will until her only desire was to travel with him to New York. He imagined Ruth beaming with pure approval.

The woman stepped into the art room, the gray strands in her long dark hair catching the light. Mr. Anderson followed, and when he entered, a white ball of pulsating energy greeted him. Here, the spirit inhabiting the Center manifested its strongest presence. He squinted, seeing what looked like silhouettes. Five figures and a child. *More ghosts?*

Needing to ground himself, Mr. Anderson staggered in a slow circle and focused on the tangibles: tables, shelves of clay figurines, paintings on the walls. His gaze ended on the window with its stunning view of the valley, and the orb, scintillating with energy as if it were a battery crackling with raw power.

The woman inched toward the sphere, the sunlight coming in through the window illuminating her light brown skin. In her hand, she clasped a rosary, her fingers tracing each bead with reverence.

Mr. Anderson made his way closer, eager to hear what she was whispering. Was she communicating with the ghosts? Positioning himself a few feet to her side, he waited patiently, building his spiritual energy. Intruding into her mind might prove more difficult than he had anticipated. The challenge thrilled him.

She finished her prayer and turned to face him, her dark eyes holding his.

"You think they're ghosts, don't you?" the woman said. "I'm not so sure."

"You're a psychic," Mr. Anderson said, extending his hand to introduce himself.

She paused before taking it. "Cynthia. And you are?"

"Mr. Anderson," he replied.

He connected, feeling certain he'd found her. She didn't prevent the connection, nor did she seem aware of it. Reaching into her mind, he gauged her strength, savoring the subtle resistance. She understood her power, could tap into it, but didn't manipulate it. He placed a thought—his mind pressing hers like fingers into soft clay—*Are you the one for me?* He watched the question take root and coil through her mind, making her shift uneasily.

He forced himself to retreat, weighing whether she truly was the one. He waited for her response, which might be recognition or even anger for intruding.

Cynthia, however, furrowed her brow and blinked rapidly. She touched her forehead and asked, "Have we met before?"

She could be trained, but she wasn't the one who had sent ripples through the ether of life. In a cold, emotionless tone, Mr. Anderson responded, "I'm sorry," and turned.

Refocusing, he hardened his gaze, determined to find this new user. The sooner he did, the sooner he could leave.

Back in the atrium, the crowd gathered around a priest. Mr. Anderson recognized him as Father Joseph. The man had been in the news, having just awakened from a coma and proclaiming that an angel had saved him from hell. Mr. Anderson watched as the father circled the rotunda, bestowing blessings upon the classrooms as his hand moved in a steady rhythm, flicking holy water. The droplets landed—*pl.. plop, pl.. plop*—on the surfaces, mimicking the pulse of a heartbeat. His words spoke of hope and purpose.

"May those who learn here find their hearts open to God's call, so their hands can be guided to serve through skill and craft."

"Amen," the group chimed.

Spiritual energy swirled; intention and devotion connected the worshippers with their higher power. The resonance grew with every prayer, every affirmation, and every whispered invocation, feeding the presence that inhabited the building. The ghost drew in the current the way leaves absorb sunlight to make food.

Mr. Anderson's scowl returned. *What is happening?* He couldn't take his eyes off the anomaly. He thought back to the excitement he had felt earlier—the ghost had been anxiously awaiting these ceremonies. Could It harness this power? Mr. Anderson considered dark energy, how Banishers wielded the power as a weapon. Spiritual essence, however, was meant for connecting, healing, and glimpsing future events. What could a spirit do with this kind of energy?

Father Joseph exited the atrium, and the crowd followed. Mr. Anderson took a moment to glance at the walls, the floors, and the pillars, wondering how this ghost had infused itself so distinctly with the building. The last of the group filtered through the doorway, and Mr. Anderson followed them down the corridor toward the front entrance.

In the main lobby, the priest met the rabbi. They exchanged a respectful embrace, and the rabbi took the lead. He spoke in both Hebrew and English, his voice rising and falling with careful cadence. The rabbi promised a place of safety, family, growth, and devotion. The energy in the room was deliberate and grounding. The current drained into the floors, and the ghost absorbed it like roots drawing water from fertile soil.

Mr. Anderson's gut clenched. *This can't be good.*

"Where the Eternal dwells, inspiration blooms. Where the Creator laid foundation, we soar. Here, we find both."

"Amen," the group responded.

Cynthia caught Mr. Anderson's eye and maneuvered through the crowd towards him.

"Isn't this wonderful?" she asked. "I can feel a transformation happening."

A guitar player strummed a gentle melody while a group of ten sang a prayer. "Oh Lord, my God, I pray that these things never end..."

Some onlookers joined in the singing. Cynthia turned and hummed along, throwing Mr. Anderson a quick smile.

Two men presented the Torah to the rabbi, and they held it aloft as he read passages aloud. Once finished, the men stepped back, and the rabbi affixed a mezuzah to the doorframe, declaring that this building was now a sanctuary where God resided.

The music started again, and the guitar player led a procession back down the hall to the arboretum. Mr. Anderson stepped aside, letting everyone pass. He noticed strong auras from two others, both women. One of them had to be the energy manipulator. Stepping forward, he shuffled along, keeping his eyes on his prize.

The crowd re-entered the atrium and kneeled on the floor in front of the stage where the monks sat cross-legged. Mr. Anderson listened as the elder monk spoke in a voice as calm as dew forming on a leaf. He told a story of shared meals, of knowing your neighbor's laugh, and of hugging your grandparents. "Home is not a gallery for possessions, but a place to find love and understanding."

He transitioned to travel, explaining it wasn't for collecting t-shirts and photographs of distant landmarks, but for walking the streets of our brethren—to share in their days and to gain their perspective. "Life," the monk said, "is more than what we display, it's in the relationships and connections we form."

He folded his hands and lowered his gaze. "As we bow and touch our foreheads to the floor, let these truths seep into the quiet places within us, until they are no longer words but the way we move through the world."

The monks chanted. The people bowed. The energy resonated, vibrating under Mr. Anderson's skin. The frequency made the air dance and the glass buzz. Then he felt the shift. The ghost that lived in the walls of the Center, with its heavy, encompassing presence, suddenly melted away.

Mr. Anderson stood very still, waiting. But couldn't sense the ghost. It had dispersed.

Where did it go?

The spirit hadn't transcended. If it had, the after stench of dark energy would have filled the room. Had the ceremonies ejected the ghost from the building? Mr. Anderson had never heard of such a thing. This certainly wasn't an exorcism. The ghost hadn't been shredded. But the ghost was no longer. There was, however, a distinct hum, a pulse. Was he feeling *life*?

Shaking his head in wonderment, he decided to tuck this question away for later consideration. He had to find the energy manipulator and get back to New York.

He pushed his way through the husks to the two women he had noticed in the procession. After connecting, he left the ceremonies disappointed. The new user he was looking for was not here.

He leaned against his SUV, steadying himself with patience as he contemplated his next course of action. Perhaps he should meditate and allow his soul to drift in the Earth's energy stream, the pulse of life moving through rocks, water, plants, and animals. The city would be a vast interconnected network where he could view the life forces. He remembered Ruth Jones's description of how she had trusted the energy stream to guide her when she had found him. It wasn't an action he could easily perform, but it would be a starting place.

Ruth Jones.

He would never forget the night he met her. His whole life had transformed that evening. He crossed his arms, closed his eyes, and let the sun warm his body. This was how it felt when she entered his mind. He had become hers that night.

July 10, 1983, his seventeenth birthday. He and his friends, itching for some fun, had jumped into his 1974 Dodge Dart Sport to cruise around. Lip sat in the passenger seat, letting his only friend with a clean license drive. At the stop light, his buddy in the back seat, smoking a cigarette, reached forward and smacked Lip on the head.

"Hey, Lip. Check out the old guy."

In the parking lot of a fast-food restaurant, a man struggled to juggle several bags while trying to open the door to his Buick Estate Wagon.

"You hungry?"

"Fuck, yeah," Lip said. He elbowed the driver. "Let's go."

With his kids in the car, the father gave up the food without a fight. The gang shoplifted beers from a convenience store and then beat up two kids walking home in their baseball uniforms, stealing their gear and heading to the ball field.

The sky darkened and the streetlights glowed. Lip's buddy pitched the ball, and he smacked it, aiming for the light.

The police spotted them in the park. The boys scattered, one into the woods, the other over the fence into the neighboring yards. Lip made a beeline for his Dodge, going around the restroom building and right into a cop who laid him out on the ground.

The police officer pressed his knee into Lip's back and pulled out his cuffs. "You're under arrest for theft, underage drinking, assault, and battery. You have the right to remain silent..."

A surge of confidence filled Lip as the officer gripped his hands. "Wait, you got this all wrong." He had always had a knack for talking his way out of tough situations, earning him his nickname. "You can handle this differently." Lip's magic lay not only in the color of his skin but in the way people reacted to his voice. They seemed to relax and succumb to the conviction in his words, which came from his core and passed through his touch. So, when the cop laid his hands on Lip, he knew he'd be able to bend the officer's will and walk home a free man. He cajoled, "We can both leave this behind us in a better way, as better people."

"Listen, kid," the officer began, his voice softening almost against his will. "You have to understand that there are consequences for your actions, that there's a price to pay when you mess up."

Lip, feeling the shift, poured all his energy and sincerity into his words. "I understand, Officer, and I agree. But what's the best way for us to face those consequences? Is it through punishment, or through a chance to make things right on our own terms? Consequences come in many forms, and the manner in which we face them shapes who we become. If you allow me to make amends on my own, you're giving me the chance to become a better person, to learn and grow from my mistakes."

The officer removed his knee from Lip's back and helped him sit up. "I can't just let you go. There's a system, rules..." He glanced down, a flicker of doubt in his eyes. "It's not up to me to decide your punishment."

Lip seized the moment, every word coming from the depths of his soul. "I know it's a tough call. But think about the impact you can have. The greatest act of justice is showing mercy and believing in someone's potential to change. As a father, a leader, and a mentor, you have the chance to see beyond the crime and peer into a young man's heart. I'm ready to right my wrongs, become a better citizen, and heal those I touch." He placed his hand on the officer's chest.

Lip whispered, "See me not as a troubled teen, but as a soul reaching out for redemption."

"All right, kid," the officer said with a gentle, almost fatherly voice. "Go prove you can be the man you say you want to be."

A second patrolman came around the corner, startling Lip and the officer. "Hey, Weasel. You talkin' again? It's not going to work this time. Fucking punk."

The first officer shook his head, blinking rapidly.

Lip slumped, exhaling in exhaustion. The bond had been broken; the control he had established lost.

"This is Wesley Anderson?" Narrowing his eyes, Lip's captor dipped his head as if dispelling a headache, then pushed the kid against the wall. "You little shit." Turning to his partner, he said, "I almost let him go."

"You wouldn't have been the first. Cuff 'em."

That's when she emerged from the shadows. Ruth Jones stepped into the light with otherworldly grace, drawing everyone's attention. Her warm, rich complexion hinted at her mixed heritage, and her tall, unyielding posture emanated power.

"Ma'am, stay where you are. Can we help you?"

She smirked and shook her head—almost amused. Her black hair, streaked with gray, was pulled tight into a high knot, the kind Lip had seen in old Japanese warrior movies. Fine lines around her dark, cold eyes spoke to her age, yet she had a youthful glow. Lip's fear overpowered the respect she commanded, and he found himself looking for something he could use to defend himself.

Ruth raised her hand and unleashed an invisible force that slammed both officers into the brick wall with grunts of pain. The policeman who had knocked Lip to the ground pulled his gun and leveled it at her.

"Hands where I can see them!"

With a flick of her wrist, the gun flew from his grip and sailed into Lip's hand. Before he could react, it fired, killing the patrolman.

Lip's eyes bulged. His breath came in ragged gasps. *Oh God!*

The second officer drew his gun but stumbled to the side, tripped, and fell. His weapon skittered unnaturally across the pavement. Raising his palms, he begged, "Please, don't shoot."

Lip stared at the blood pooling beneath the dead officer. He had murdered a cop. There was no returning to his old life. The gun slipped from his trembling hands and smacked the pavement. His chest tightened like a vice, each breath more labored than the last.

"No. This can't be happening."

He staggered backward into Ruth. She spun him around, her hand gliding from his cheek to the back of his neck. At her touch, a tingling sensation cut through the haze of panic, and her voice slipped into his mind: *You have a gift.*

With an inhuman grip, Ruth pulled him close. The breath from her lips was an intoxicating poison that both terrified and mesmerized him. Her eyes, dark and fathomless, held wisdom that penetrated the depths of his soul. His body shook with a new kind of fear—a primal, instinctive dread, as if he were a mouse caught in the clutches of a hawk.

Then, unexpectedly, she ran her fingers through his hair, leaned in, and kissed him. His body went rigid followed by a jump in his pulse so hard he felt it in his throat. The tight surge of exhilaration softened into a warm, rising tide. He closed his eyes and floated in the sweetness blooming against his lips.

He wanted her.

She turned and walked away, but her presence remained in his mind, her hands running down his body, electrifying every nerve. *How would you like to learn the true meaning of control?* Her voice was firm and sultry, undeniable in strength.

In a melodic voice, she whispered, *Are you coming? We have lots of work to do.*

Stunned and disoriented, Lip stumbled forward. His heart had been collared, and he momentarily forgot about the dead officer.

A burst of applause shook Mr. Anderson from his memory. He straightened, straining to see what the commotion was all about. He spotted six individuals parading through the crowd, their faces familiar from recent news reports: Jared, the father, stood tall and thin, his short brown hair tousled from the breeze; Leah, his daughter, young, stylish, and striking; Nong, the architect and landlord, her long, silky black hair swaying as she walked; Ploy, Nong's daughter, small and watchful; Barb and Dan, the orphaned siblings—Dan had broad shoulders and his sister, Barb, was solid and curvy. All six had been recently abducted from this very place. *How had they managed to return?*

The question barely finished forming when Barb, Dan, and Leah tugged at his awareness like a magnet. Their auras suggested latent abilities. Mr. Anderson stepped forward, watching closely. Barb nudged Leah and pointed. She had spotted another priest who had just arrived. The man glared at the building before turning around and leaving. The girls smiled.

Mr. Anderson studied the exchange as it unfolded. He felt certain the priest had come to exorcize the spirit that had possessed the Center. The girls had recognized this and were happy to see him go. Did they know a ghost had been at the Center?

His thoughts drifted back to the ball of white pulsating energy in front of the art room window. He had thought there were six shapes inside. Silhouettes. He recounted the abductees. *Five and a child.*

The number sat in his consciousness, his mind unwilling to make the connection. The idea was preposterous. *Could these six be the same— No.* He refused to even finish the thought. The six had been missing for a week. A serial abductor had taken them with the help of a police detective—the one he had seen a few days earlier with the FBI: Detective Brandon Spencer. What he was trying to conclude was impossible.

He turned his attention back to the people gathered outside, seeing lots of commotion. Two security guards created space for Barb and Dan who were speaking with reporters. Nong and Jared were holding hands as they parted ways, their fingers linked until the last second. Nong then whisked Ploy away as a woman ran from a parked car and straight into Leah's embrace. A blue pickup tore into the lot and skidded to a stop.

Mr. Anderson focused on Leah. Her aura brightened as the woman held her. Leah's shine was unmistakable. She was the one he was here to find. Had the abductees been able to escape because Leah, being a user, was able to manipulate the abductor and secure their release? If so, she would indeed be powerful as Ms. Jones suspected.

The chaos built as the driver from the blue pickup, a blonde-haired man with a beer belly, ushered Barb, Dan, Leah, Jared, and the woman who had hugged Leah back to his truck. They piled in, and the driver sped out. Mr. Anderson locked eyes with Leah as they passed. He recognized her as Leah Davenport, granddaughter to Mr. Bill Stillen, CEO of Extended Life.

After the truck turned the corner, Mr. Anderson took out his phone and called his boss at Extended Life in New York.

"What did you learn?" Dr. Smith asked.

"I believe I've found her." Mr. Anderson paused before adding, in a slow, measured response, "The user is Mr. Stillen's granddaughter."

"The CEO's granddaughter? You can't be serious! She's too young. We're looking for an energy manipulator—a powerful one," Dr. Smith objected.

"Yes. Her aura is strong."

"Lots of people have strong auras," Dr. Smith retorted. "Did you connect with her?" Without waiting for an answer, she asserted, "I need proof. Solid proof. If we're going to recruit Leah, there must be no doubt in her abilities, and our need for her." The doctor paused. "Leah? Ms. Jones's apprentice?" she scoffed. "I don't believe it." There was a second pause. "Shit! Mr. Stillen will never allow us to recruit her. Give me indisputable evidence, Anderson."

"I understand. I'll procure it."

"Are you sure the manipulator wasn't the detective?" Dr. Smith asked.

"The FBI swept him away before I could connect to him. If he is the user Ms. Jones wants, she's too late. Yoona has him."

"Confirm or eliminate Leah as a possibility, and then we'll find a way to get to the detective."

After hanging up, Mr. Anderson climbed into his SUV and opened his computer. He searched Airbnb, VRBO, HomeAway, Couchsurfing, and others, finally finding a room three houses down and across from Leah's. Booking the room for the month, he then friended Leah on social media, went to the school district website, and applied to become a substitute teacher. He also needed to break in and place listening devices inside her home. Finally, he would sift through her garbage, to better understand her. Mr. Anderson's plan was to know Leah better than she knew herself and to provide ample evidence for Dr. Smith. If he failed, Leah was sure to be recruited by the Circle. If Ms. Jones's plan was to succeed, they needed Leah.

Marked

Miley, Uncle Tim's battle-tested Chevy, rumbled out of the parking lot of the Education Center with its dented sides gleaming in the high afternoon sun like scars from the multiple collisions. Tim, broad-framed, thick-armed, and beer-bellied, looking like a scruffier version of Zeus himself, had named the truck after Miley Cyrus, because of her song "Wrecking Ball". Like its owner, the truck kept coming out of accidents relatively unscathed, still standing strong, no matter with what it had collided.

Leah sat in the backseat wedged between the door and her mom, Stacey. She pushed a curl of dark brown hair behind her ear and stared out the window. A strange man dressed in a black suit locked eyes with her. He wasn't just looking at her—he was *seeing* her. The way his eyes narrowed before widening and how his face lightened in recognition sent a creepy chill down her spine; he knew exactly who she was and what she could do. Who was he? How did he know about her? Leah was certain she'd never seen him before.

Closing her eyes, Leah fixed the man's face into her memory and ran through possible explanations. He could be a Banisher or a Shaman—someone drawn to Bellevue's spiritual energy. Maybe he was here for the training manual. Her heart sank at that thought. She glanced at Barb, who was clutching Grandma Carol's book in her lap, her wavy brown hair falling into her face. Letting out a breath of relief, Leah's thoughts returned to the mysterious man.

How did he know who I was? Did Bellevue leave some invisible mark on me that he could sense? Leah shuddered at the thought but knew it was possible. The training manual was a big book, packed with information, instructions, meditations, warnings, and dos and don'ts. She'd have to skim through it to learn more about identifying other Shamans. Rereading the book and starting her training were imperative; she would never be a victim again. With Barb by her side, the two would grow their powers and become unstoppable allies. She couldn't wait to begin.

Leah's mother, Stacy, squeezed her hand, snapping Leah from her thoughts.

"Ghost? Water spirit?" her mom asked in confusion. "What the hell is Tim talking about? Tell me what he means." Brushing Leah's cheek with her hand, she whispered, "What happened to you?"

Leah's gaze flicked to the rearview mirror, catching a glimpse of Tim's eyes. What had he said? What did he know? The last time they'd spoken, he was heading into the woods to search for her dad, convinced he'd been taken and locked away in some hidden cabin. Not only had Tim not known about Bellevue then, but he hadn't even believed in ghosts.

"I'm sorry," Leah said. "What were you guys talking about?"

"Bellevue," Tim repeated. Leah's brows raised and her mouth dropped open. He continued, "The ghost is actually a water spirit, and anyone who comes into contact with it is in danger."

What had happened while they were gone? She looked to Barb, who shook her head as if reading her mind.

"How do you know about Bellevue?" Leah asked. If Tim knew, who else did?

"The native tribe, Carol, and because of that book Barb is holding," Tim responded.

Questions popped through Leah's mind like exploding corn. What did the native tribe have to do with Bellevue? Who had called that second priest? Did her grandfather, Bill, know about Bellevue? Could the creepy man they'd passed earlier have been one of Grandpa's men searching for them?

"Does Grandpa Bill know about Bellevue?" Leah pressed.

Tim shrugged, shaking his head. "No. I don't think he does."

Stacey interrupted, waving her hands to pause the conversation, "I'm sorry, but can we stop the truck? I need someone to explain what this Bellevue is, and what exactly happened to you."

Ahead, a line of police cars drove toward them with their sirens blaring. Tim pulled to the side of the road as they approached. The first car zipped past. The second slammed on the breaks as it passed, and the third and fourth turned sharply, blocking the truck.

Leah strained to see what was happening. Looking out the back window and then out the front, she saw the officers surround the truck through the piercing lights. Tim put Miley in park and turned off the engine.

With guns drawn, the police shouted, "Hands where we can see them. Don't move!"

"Mom," Leah gasped, looking past her to Barb.

Jared turned in his seat, counseling, "Listen carefully. Do as they say. Don't argue. Don't talk about Bellevue. If they ask you anything, tell them you want a lawyer. Got it? We need to get our story straight before anyone says anything."

Officers ordered them to step out one at a time. Tim moved first, opening the door and raising his hands. The moment his feet hit the ground, they swarmed him. Leah sucked in a sharp breath, her heart kicking hard against her ribs. The police slammed her uncle against the hood and cuffed him. She caught his eyes, seeing a glint of amusement in them. He winked, and a cocky grin followed, so out of place that her body eased. Leah knew he'd been arrested before, and they both knew that this time he had done nothing wrong.

As Barb, Dan, and Jared left the truck, the officers escorted them to a police cruiser. The radio chatter, the lights, the instructions being shouted were overwhelming, and Leah was hesitant to move.

"Step out of the truck, nice and slow," a female officer said. Her voice was tender and encouraging. "Keep your hands where we can see them."

Leah looked to her mom before slipping out of the truck, realizing she was shaking. The officer took her by the arm and whisked her away, asking, "Are you hurt?"

Being placed in the back of a cruiser with Barb, Leah watched as her mom was cuffed and taken to a separate car. The pressure pushing outward made it difficult to breath, even though she knew this was only a formality. Her mom would be freed soon.

Patting Leah's shoulder, Barb said, "She's going to be fine."

Leah forced a grin and nodded.

"How many people do you think were looking for us?" Barb asked. "The police aren't messing around."

"I know, and it's not like no one knew what happened," Leah said. "There were three police officers with us. Detective Spencer arranged the whole thing. These officers are acting like we vanished into thin air."

"What do you think Detective Spencer said after Bellevue took us?"

"I have no idea," Leah replied. "What could he say? Not the truth, or he'd be placed in an insane asylum."

Barb chewed on her inner lip, shaking her head. "Do you think Brandon and the other two officers were blamed for us going missing? What if they were arrested?"

Leah raised an eyebrow at the thought, considering the possibility. She hoped that wasn't the reality. Detective Spencer had been tricked, the same way her dad and Nong had been. Even Leah had believed Bellevue. Pulling on a strand of hair, she twirled it around her finger. "I wish I knew, because I have no idea how we're going to explain our disappearance to the police."

The officer returned, sat in the driver's seat, looked at them through the rearview mirror, and explained, "We're taking you downtown to the FBI field office." Turning, she addressed them directly, "Unless you need to see a doctor first."

"No, we're fine," Leah replied.

She held their gazes for a moment longer before nodding. "Okay, hang tight. We'll be there in a bit."

Leaning her head against the glass, Leah wondered about Detective Spencer. Why hadn't he come inside with them? What had happened to him after Bellevue snatched them? Had he been blamed? The tightness in her chest spread to her gut. How were they going to explain where they had been and what had happened? Was her dad right? Could they simply ask for a lawyer and discuss it before talking with the FBI?

Houses, stores, buildings, billboards ... all zoom past. How much press and attention would they get? A bitter laugh escaped her before she could stop it. "Going back to school is going to be *fun*."

Barb groaned. "Tell me about it."

Seoul, Korea

Pieces in Play

Brandon Spencer sat on the edge of his hotel bed tying his shoes. He reached over to the nightstand, grabbed his badge, and turned it over in his hand. *Special Agent Spencer.* The title felt foreign. After years of teaching, he had become a cop, and then a detective, telling himself it was a way to move forward, to turn tragedy into something meaningful. The reality was the exact opposite. He had suppressed his trauma, only for it to haunt him.

Closing his hand around the badge, he thought about the detectives he had worked with—many would have killed for the opportunity to be recruited by the FBI. But for him, it had never been the goal.

A knock sounded, right on time. Brandon pulled on his jacket, slipped his badge in his pocket, and opened the door. Matthew filled the doorway, eyes cool and measured. The tall, muscular CIA officer had a bald head with a cobra tattoo that curled around his ear and down his neck. His black braided goatee and black leather jacket over a white t-shirt added to his intimidating image.

"Good morning," Matthew said, handing him a bag.

"Morning. What's this?" Brandon asked.

"Required reading," Matthew ribbed.

Brandon pulled out a thick textbook—*The Complete Anatomy of the Human Body.* He raised an eyebrow and flipped through a few pages of diagrams and labels. "I don't understand."

"Every trainee gets one." Matthew said with a shrug. "Your instructions are to learn about your organs and then meditate. You're supposed to become aware of them. Pay attention to how your body reacts to your thoughts and actions, and the chemicals and energy it produces." Tapping the book, he said, "It's your first assignment, and there must be something to it—Yoona gives it to every potential trainee." With a wave of his hand, he concluded, "Toss the book in the room and let's go."

Brandon laid the book on the bench and closed the door.

The second bag held two white paper cups with black lids. Matthew handed Brandon one. "Here, I got you a coffee."

"Thanks, but I don't drink coffee."

"Great. One more for me." With a nod of his head, he motioned for Brandon to follow.

Walking toward the elevator, Brandon stole a glance at Matthew's tattoo. The design reminded him of the one his father had gotten after earning his pilot's license. He had first seen it at an air show celebrating new pilots, where his father had flown in a formation flight.

"Look at him, Brandon," his mother had said. "The only black pilot in the group. Don't ever let someone tell you you can't do it."

That was the first time Brandon had seen race. Because his parents were of different colors, he had only seen people.

Eyeing the cobra, Brandon wondered if he'd ever see his father again.

Matthew squeezed Brandon's shoulder. "Assessment day. Are you ready?"

Brandon gave a quick smile. "Yeah, but I'm curious. Why is the CIA escorting me to see Yoona?"

Stopping in his tracks, Matthew faced Brandon, tilting his head and raising an eyebrow. His lips parted as if to speak, but he hesitated for a beat. "Do you know who Yoona is?" he asked.

Brandon wanted to say, *Officer Choi's aunt*, but Matthew's reaction told him she was someone more significant. "I know she's a Shaman," he finally answered.

Matthew rolled his eyes and continued to the elevator. "She is a Shaman," he mumbled under his breath with a sarcastic chuckle. They reached the elevator, and Matthew pressed the down arrow.

As they waited, Matthew reached for Brandon's black, curly hair and plucked a piece of lint from it. "Yoona is the head of a worldwide organization of Shaman called the Circle," he explained. "The CIA and every other government spy agency work with her in a coordinated effort to stop terrorism, catch weapons and human traffickers, and root out the worst scum on the planet. Our priorities don't always match, and she's picky about how and when she collaborates with us, but..." He allowed himself a brief laugh. "Yoona is more than a Shaman."

Yoona works with the CIA? Choi hadn't mentioned anything about spy agencies or terrorists, other than to say that if *he* were a spy, she wouldn't train him. Brandon had thought she simply helped ghosts and spirits.

The elevator door opened, and Matthew discarded the first coffee cup into the bin as they entered. Pressing B1, he said, "You must have some kind of superpower if you weaseled your way into training with Yoona. The agency has never been able to convince her to train one of our own."

"I still don't understand why the CIA is escorting *me*, though."

"If Yoona's interested in a person, then the CIA is interested in that person."

"The CIA is interested in ... me?" Brandon said in confusion.

Matthew shook his head, his eyebrows pulling together in a look of absolute disbelief. "Bro, do you know what you're walking into?" His voice carried equal parts frustration and bewilderment. "How the hell did you get this gig?"

With Matthew's brash, dumbfounded expression, Brandon found himself telling him the truth, unsure of how else to respond. "I got my brains bashed in by a ghost."

Matthew's gaze hardened with an expectant look, as if waiting for something of actual substance.

Brandon didn't know what else to say and shrugged.

The elevator door opened, and Matthew let out a disbelieving scoff as he exited. Halfway to the car, he stopped, pinched the bridge of his nose, and turned back to Brandon. "Yoona is the head of the Korean anti-terrorist organization, and a member of the Korean Elite Special Forces. She hosts heads of state. She's the most famous Shaman in the world, known for her psychic powers and abilities to communicate with spirits. You being invited to train with her is huge deal. You have potential to grow into something..." Matthew trailed off, holding his hands up and shaking them for emphasis before exhaling in frustration.

They reached the car. Matthew started it as Brandon buckled his seatbelt.

"Don't you know these terrorist organizations have Shamans of their own?" Matthew said, pulling into traffic. "The CIA is interested in you because others will be looking for you. You're a commodity." He paused, rubbing his bottom lip as they waited at a traffic light. "The day Yoona contacted you, we began looking into you and everyone you know—even your girlfriend in Mexico, Gabriela."

"You—what?" Brandon blinked, his mouth going dry. *Was he for real?* He stared at Matthew, searching for some sign of a joke, some hint of laughter in his eyes.

"Oh, yeah. We know everything about you."

Brandon's gaze hardened as if he could force Matthew to laugh and tell him he was kidding.

Matthew's expression turned cold. "I have to ask, and I'm being completely serious. Has anyone approached you about your potential abilities?" He waited half a second and then added, "Take a minute to think. Any kind of chitchat, casual remark, or question?"

Shaking his head, Brandon said, "No. No one's approached me."

"Are you sure? Because they are bound to, sooner or later, if they haven't already."

"No, I'm sure. I mean, I barely even began my training. Who would know?"

The car turned the corner. "They know. If someone does approach you, tell me or Yoona. People with your special talents are highly sought after—and often by the very people we're hunting."

"What talents do you think I have?" Brandon blurted, unsure as to what Matthew was referring.

Tapping the steering wheel, Matthew started, "Look, Yoona ... she's..." With a deep exhale, he said, "I need to warn you. When you're with her, not all your thoughts are actually yours. She has this uncanny ability to plant ideas and information into your mind. She can also read you, like everything about you. I swear she knows exactly what you're thinking."

"How does she do that?"

"She's part of a highly sophisticated intelligence-gathering organization and a brilliant psychologist. I know the CIA and FBI have people who can read body language and know what you're thinking by the way you twitch or fidget. But Yoona takes it to a whole new level. She knows you better than you know yourself, already anticipating what you'll say before you do. But it's more than that. She's ... well, she's a psychic."

"And you think *I'm* psychic?"

Matthew checked his blind spot and changed lanes. "I think being assessed by Yoona in person makes you someone of interest to the CIA."

"Is that so?" Brandon said, shaking his head. This was crazy. He hadn't realized that by agreeing to train with Yoona, he was stepping into a world of terror, organized crime, and covert operations—far from learning about ghosts and spirits. How had he ended up here? By investigating a cold case of a missing woman, which had led him to the kidnapping of a man. His commanding officer had told him to drop the case, dismissing his leads as dead ends—the house he was searching for had burned down, and the evidence pointed nowhere. But Brandon couldn't let it go. And because he was arrogant and believed his past trauma had been dealt with, he thought he could communicate with a ghost. It had manipulated him, and six others ended up being taken. Now, faced with the choice of going to jail or training with a Shaman in Korea, he had chosen the only option that made sense to him at the time. But this? He hadn't signed up for this.

"I'm not psychic," Brandon muttered.

"We'll see." Matthew stopped at a red light and turned on the radio, finding a station broadcasting the news.

Brandon's gaze drifted out the window, caught by the sight of an ancient wall surrounding a park. Beyond it, a temple stood, its trees flowering and swaying in the breeze. The quiet of the temple grounds called to him—soothing, simple—unlike the convoluted web of espionage into which Matthew was dragging him.

The car lurched forward, moving alongside the wall and toward his new destiny. *What have I gotten myself into?* The question gnawed at him as he turned his focus back to Matthew. "How long have you known Yoona?"

"About seven years now. I'm the contact person between her and our government. She says I'm easy to read." Glancing at Brandon, Matthew asked, "I get you're newly recruited, but did no one tell you about Yoona?"

"I wasn't told much."

"Well, you were right to say she's a Shaman, or Moodang. Shamans are a big part of Korean culture. They deal with spirits and ghosts, do fortune telling, and connect you with your ancestors. What's funny is that modern Korean society is skeptical of Shamanism and often dismiss it as a hoax, yet the industry is thriving, similar to palm readers in the states. A person may go to one for guidance or comfort but probably doesn't believe everything the reader says.

"Yoona isn't an ordinary Shaman though. What makes her extremely special is her fighting skills. I've seen her take out fifteen men on her own."

"She doesn't sound like the person I talked with over the phone."

"Hey, make sure you're completely honest with her. Don't try to hide information or lie; she already knows the truth, and you'll just piss her off."

The truth? Bowing his head, Brandon wondered how his meeting with Yoona would proceed. He had lied, and that lie had led to six people being kidnapped by a ghost. The deceit hadn't been intentional. But when she'd asked if he was married or had kids, probing to understand his weaknesses, he hadn't been able to admit his wife and son were gone. The words felt too raw, too painful to say aloud.

And now? How could he possibly train with Yoona? A ghost had already gotten into his mind and controlled him once. If he faced another, he'd become possessed for sure. His emotional turmoil had made him vulnerable, and he didn't have the psychic abilities or the inner control someone like Yoona would demand. Worse, he hadn't been honest—with her or himself.

No, she wouldn't take him on. Why would she? She probably didn't even have the time for someone like him, especially when she was busy meeting with heads of state and stopping terrorists.

Matthew cursed, "This fucking traffic." He turned the volume up on the radio. "News about the special election. The challenger is endorsing the proposal to give the United Nations governing power. There's a push to unite the world under one government, The United Federation of States, in order to avoid another world war. What do you make of that?"

"It'll never happen."

"I'm not too sure. War is closer than you think, and this next one will kill us all. Anyway, what was I saying? Yoona. This being your first physical meeting with her, you should understand that this is an assessment of your abilities and your potential; you may be turned away. The other possibility is that she gives you a task first to see how you do. While the job may seem unrelated to training, don't be fooled—it will be an integral part of your development. If you're lucky, she'll admit you directly, and I won't see you for a few weeks."

"Does she reject many people?"

"Many?" Matthew laughed. "She might assess one person a year. You have potential, or she wouldn't have invited you. But potential doesn't always translate into acceptance."

The radio announcer caught Matthew's attention, and he raised a hand for Brandon to wait.

"Something interesting?" Brandon asked after a pause.

"There was a zombie attack in a village near the Demilitarized Zone two days ago. Have you heard about this?"

"No. A zombie attack?"

"Apparently, the North is experimenting with ways to create super soldiers. These guys are literally zombie-like, wandering around trying to attack people, but they aren't dead. Well, the body isn't dead—just, nobody's home upstairs; they're brain dead. The North has been sending one of these goons over the border every other month for the past year. Yoona handled this last one. The news reports that he claims to have been a soldier from the North subjected to horrific experiments and somehow managed to escape. However, they note his distinct Southern accent and familiarity with South Korean customs, speculating that he may have been a Southern spy who infiltrated the North and is now returning." Matthew took a breath and shook his head. "It's a bad time to be living in the North."

"Dictators are scary people. The way they treat their citizens and suspected spies is terrible. I'm so glad we don't live in a fascist state," Brandon expressed.

"Here's hoping we can keep it that way," Matthew added, finishing his second cup of coffee. "Do you want to know what they're talking about? I can translate for you if you want."

"Sure. I'd love to know what's going on." As Matthew delivered the news, Brandon gazed through the window at the people on the street and in the shops, remembering his first trip to Seoul four years ago. He and his wife, Hina, had come on vacation with their one-year-old son and had walked along similar streets. Brandon stared at the entrance of a passing alley, and a tear threatened to rolled down his cheek as an image of his wife and son lying lifeless on the concrete returned to him. Wiping his eyes, he shook the memory away.

Matthew turned a corner and drove over a bridge. Sunlight danced on the water, lush greenery blanketed the river islands, and high-rise apartments along the riverbank gave way to distant mountains. When they reached the other end of the bridge, Matthew turned the car into a park.

The sign at the entrance read "National Cemetery." A wall of trees and bushes separated the quiet, green space from the loud, fast-paced world of the city. A man in military dress stood in front of a large monument depicting police and soldiers protecting citizens.

Matthew drove through a security checkpoint. Two stone dragon cats—regulators of energy and authority—sat on either side of the walkway that entered the cemetery. The white Korean flag with its red and blue yin-yang symbol at the center flew next to the military flag, a single gold star and a white anchor lodged in a sea of red.

The road climbed the mountain. Korean flags flew from lampposts between shrubs blooming in white and purple. Beyond, rows of tombs stretched out—graves of those who'd fought and died for Korea.

"This is Seoul National Cemetery," Matthew explained. "The building ahead holds the cremated remains of those who served, and their spouses. Yoona works out of that building. She also has a shop near your hotel, but she wanted to meet you here, for some reason."

The cemetery grounds were immaculate. Ornate stone walls separated plots of graves. Cherry trees shaded picnic areas along a stream. Statues of priests, monks, turtles, dragons, and lions stood along the paths as wards providing moral order, protection, and stability. Brandon admired a large memorial made from white marble engraved with images of those hon-ored—freedom fighters who had opposed the Japanese during the colonial era, and lovers, musicians, and families living together in harmony protected by a soldier with a large sword.

Matthew parked, and they made their way to Yoona's building, passing a steep path that led to a Buddhist temple. As they approached, Brandon glanced through the window; cubicles, each holding an urn, were decorated with photos, notes, and tokens of love. Entering, Matthew gestured to an office door labeled "Employees Only."

"Here she is. Go on in, she's expecting you. I'll wait under the gazebo across the way." Matthew pointed to a waiting area. "Good luck—and keep your wits about you."

"Thanks. If she accepts me, I won't see you again, right?"

"If she takes you on as a trainee, that's right. But I'm sure we'll run into each other down the road." Matthew patted Brandon's shoulder and walked toward the gazebo.

Brandon took a deep breath and stared at the door in front of him. "Here we go," he whispered, pushing it open. Bells jingled. To his surprise, the interior had the look and feel of a Buddhist temple. He removed his shoes and stepped into a candlelit room. Three-foot-high wooden shelves lined two walls. The shelf on the right held books with titles written in several languages—Chinese, French, Arabic, and Russian. The other was filled with glass bottles—elixirs and potions in every size and color. Small bowls of crystals, thick wax candles, and bundles of dried herbs sat between them.

Above the shelves, posters of past festivals held long ago decorated the walls along with a portrait of an ancient Chinese warrior who embodied honor and evoked emotions of a protective father. A low table sat in the middle of the room surrounded by floor pillows. In a wall niche, a Buddha sat amid incense, flowers, a plate of food, and a glass of clear liquid. A yellow curtain draped over a doorway in the far corner.

Brandon wondered how much of this was necessary—the candles, incense, crystals. Were these items essential for channeling spiritual energy? Or were they simply used for mood-building?

The energy here was unmistakable. His skin tingled. His chest buzzed. A subtle, electric pulse ran up the back of his skull, reminding him of when Bellevue had invaded his mind. But this was much gentler.

After a few minutes, Brandon called out, "Hello? Is anyone here?"

Clunk, clunk. The sound of wood knocking on wood came from behind the curtain.

Brandon waited. Choi had said a spiritual connection required touch—but he felt a connection, already formed. Maybe some beings didn't need touch. That was unsettling, so he reminded himself to stay calm.

The room's quiet suggested meditation. Brandon had an urge to mirror the Buddha—legs crossed, palms open, back tall. He hesitated. This idea wasn't his. Someone unseen had connected to him. He didn't know when or how, but the connection didn't hurt or demand. It just ... suggested.

Brandon obeyed and seated himself. He slowed his breathing and focused his mind on a single image—the candle. With eyes closed, he held the flickering light in his mind. The flame cast out all thoughts and emotions.

.

.

.

"Welcome, Detective."

Opening his eyes, Brandon saw an ageless woman sitting in front of him. She could have been twenty-five or sixty-five. She sat still and poised, her face emotionless—not a single muscle twitched. Her sleek, black hair inched past her shoulders, with a few gray strands highlighting and accenting her features. Her jet-black eyes twinkled, reflecting the candlelight. Her brown skin gathered the glow of the room and radiated it back as if light itself bent to her quiet presence.

"It's nice to finally meet you in person," she bestowed a greeting.

Brandon was speechless. He bowed his head to show respect. "Yoona?" he managed to say, sitting upright.

"You may call me Yoona, yes."

"You look so different in real life. I mean, from the video chats."

"Cameras cannot capture who we truly are." Yoona studied Brandon. "You've done well. Being aware of what's happening in and around you is a promising sign. However, the revelation of your secret has shaken your confidence." Her voice was sweet, mesmerizing, able to send a person into a trance.

"Do you know what happened in Lake Valley?" Brandon asked. "What did Choi tell you?"

"I am aware of the outcome. Your energy is telling me the story."

"Did you really agree to train me?"

Yoona smiled. "Go to the shelf with the bottles. Open one and smell the fragrance inside."

Brandon rose and stepped to the shelf, studying the bottles. "Which one did you want me to smell?"

"You choose. Any one is fine."

Brandon saw a bright purple vial. *My mom's favorite color*, he thought. So he chose that one.

"Stop. Think about your mother. There is something of importance there."

Setting down the bottle, Brandon recalled the last time he had seen his mom. Her hair was gray. She had cooked so much food for him. He felt bad knowing that he was going to miss her engagement party.

"Yes. That last thought. Hold it."

The engagement party. His mom had fallen in love with a professor who taught architecture at the university. Brandon had met Professor Yun just once—the meeting was all business. Brandon had wondered when the wedding would be. *I won't miss it for the world.* Those were his famous last words.

"Come. Sit. Give me your hands," Yoona instructed.

Brandon sat down, holding out his hands for Yoona. She turned them palms-up, running her fingers along the lines, reading them. Brandon's arms shivered. Pulling him closer, she reached out with one hand and touched the side of his head. Closing her eyes, she walked her fingers from his left ear to his crown. Her touch relaxed his muscles while simultaneously stimulating his thoughts. Pictures of people and places flipped through his mind as if she were a secretary fingering through a Rolodex—his desk at the department, Choi, Rodriguez, Captain Crandle, his mom's house, her fiancé Jae, the Education Center, Leah, Barb, and Bruce.

"Interesting," Brandon heard from the breath that left her lips.

Taking out a deck of tarot cards, Yoona asked Brandon to touch them, shuffle them, and spread them on the table. "Run your hand over them and draw the card that is drawn to you."

Brandon turned over the Emperor and faced it upright.

"You were right. Go. Let her know he's coming. This is the person for whom you've been waiting." Yoona wasn't talking to Brandon. As she spoke, his energy level suddenly decreased, and he realized the connection he had felt earlier had been made through a spirit.

Yoona put her hands on top of his. "I will connect to you now." The connection was gentle and smooth, like a mother running the back of her hand down his cheek. His body welcomed it.

"Should I connect to you?" Brandon asked.

"No," she whispered. "Brandon, you are not ready for training. Your energy is in turmoil. You need to find the answer to your question. Do you know the one to which I'm referring?"

"I do." He was happy to know that being a spy and fighting terrorists wouldn't be in his near future, but he had hoped to work with the FBI and help supernatural entities. At least Yoona hadn't rejected him outright. Now he had time to find his wife, Hina—if her soul were still here.

"If you are unable to overcome your trauma, I won't train you."

Brandon exhaled slowly and nodded, accepting her warning.

Yoona squeezed his hand. "So to help you work through this, I am sending you to a woman who owns a law firm. Her name is Su-Bin Moon. She'll be opening an international law division in six months and is looking to hire an English teacher to help her staff become proficient. I need you to be the firm's English language teacher."

Teaching? Brandon's chest tightened. He hadn't stepped in front of a classroom since his son had died.

"I'll know you're ready to start your training once you've connected to everyone in the firm. You'll need empathy and compassion to make those connections. If you still harbor pain, it won't be possible."

Brandon lowered his gaze. He didn't understand how his pain could prevent him from forming connections. He'd made connections with several individuals already.

"You will have to interview for the position," she went on. "I'll let you know when and where. Matthew will find you housing near the office. As you know, the situation in Lake Valley has been resolved; let go of that guilt. Take your time and heal."

Jared, Nong, and company clawed their way into his mind. The agony of what he had caused still clung to him. Did they blame him for what had happened? He hoped not. Bellevue had been stronger and more manipulative than anyone could have anticipated.

"The six are fine, Brandon. Don't worry," Yoona reassured. "Focus on resolving your trauma, so nothing like that happens again."

He clenched his hands in his lap before releasing the tension. His shoulders sank and his expression softened. He had acted with good intentions, and that mattered. He could do better. And with Yoona's guidance, he would.

"Bathe in new experiences and relationships. Rediscover yourself. Allow the people you work with to help define who you are." Yoona let go of Brandon's hands and stood. With a nod of her head, she concluded, "Be present in each moment," then turned for the exit at the back of the room.

Brandon watched as she passed through the yellow curtain, but before she disappeared behind it, she added, "Failing to hold the connections you make at the law firm means a ticket back home." The curtain closed.

Brandon sat still, contemplating her words. He was beginning to understand that her warnings about connecting weren't in the mechanics, but in the sustained longevity. His trauma was the real obstacle. Yoona wanted him to reach out and lean on others, to allow others to help him overcome his loss.

He stared at the wall with unfocused eyes. His mother's voice rang in his mind, *Avoidance.* How did one heal from such a horrid event? He was sure teaching would help. He hadn't taught since the accident, and avoiding the pain had only caused more.

Brandon pushed himself up off the floor and took one last look around the room. How powerful was Yoona? She obviously had ghosts working for her; he was sure one had been attached to him, and she'd used it to influence his thoughts and retrieve information from his mind. This was power in its purest, most dangerous form. To connect to others through spirits and nudge them toward choices they believed were their own blurred the line between guidance and control. Who questioned her? Who challenged her? Was there anyone who could?

The warrior's image hanging on the wall gave him a chill; death awaited anyone who dared hurt his daughter. With a bow of his head, he offered his respect before leaving the office.

Outside, Brandon found Matthew sitting in the gazebo observing families paying their respects. "Well, you weren't wrong," he said with astonishment.

"Yeah, I told you. She's something special. Let's go find you a place to stay," Matthew said, rising.

"How did you know? Are you connected to Yoona?"

Matthew looked confused. "How did I know?" He took out his cell phone and shook it. "She texted me."

The Assignment

Attorneys Su-Bin Moon and Min Yun drove to the Incheon Women's Correctional Center to visit Su-Bin's mother, who had been convicted of murder. Twelve years before, Su-Bin had come home, finding her father dead on the kitchen floor and her mother sitting against the living room wall, badly beaten, holding a knife. Because her father was a high-ranking official in the government, the legal proceedings were rushed, and Su-Bin had always felt that her mother never received a fair trial. As a result, Su-Bin had changed her major and attended law school.

After graduating and working at a small firm for a year, she opened her own law firm. Her first case had garnered national attention, and her firm grew quickly. Now she was in a position to attempt to free her mother. She had hired Min Yun specifically to pursue her mother's case.

"Can you check to see if anyone has responded to the offer-to-purchase ads?" Su-Bin asked.

"Sure." Min logged into several sites that had ads looking to purchase a handcrafted gold and platinum necklace with a red ruby in a dragon eye that had been woven into the chain linking. The piece had been designed by Su-Bin's mother for her father and given to him on his sixtieth birthday.

"No responses," he said. "Do you want me to continue running them?"

"Yes," Su-Bin responded. "Whoever has that necklace is either the murderer or someone who has had contact with the murderer. I'll keep running the ads until I get a response or my mom is freed. I know it's a shot in the dark, but it's worth the cost."

"It's my opinion the necklace is a trophy. You're never going to find it."

"There is always a chance someone will recognize it," Su-Bin said. "You never know how these things play out. But I know this: if you don't put the energy out there, nothing will happen."

"Don't worry," Min said. "We're making progress." He reached over and put his hand on Su-Bin's leg.

She glanced down, understanding that the sensual act was meant to offer reassurance and comfort, but these touches stirred emotions. She removed his hand and placed it on his lap, wishing he would respect boundaries. Giving his hand a squeeze, she let go.

Min continued, "If your mom can identify the type of knife used in the attack, I can use that to my advantage while questioning suspects."

"You've done a great job," Su-Bin said. "I'm feeling hopeful."

Arriving at the prison, they completed intake with security personnel, who conducted a search of their possessions. Then they sat in the waiting area until they were called.

"Moon, Su-Bin. Yun, Min. This way, please," a guard said, holding a door open.

Su-Bin followed first as Min trailed behind. She already knew the path—a right at the first door, then two lefts. Their footsteps echoed through the hall, sounding as cold as the walls felt. The clanking of keys, the sharp buzzing as doors unlocked, the grey, dehumanizing feel of the institution had only gotten harder to bear over the years. Every visit Su-Bin made came with worry. Was this the last time she'd see her mom—her real mom—the one who had doted over her and apologized in advance for packed lunches that went cold before she could eat them?

Glancing back at Min, Su-Bin gave a hopeful smile. This visit felt different. They had a plan, new testimony, and evidence that would get her mom a retrial. The guard led them into the interview room, saying, "Stay on your side of the table. No touching. The prisoner will be here shortly." Su-Bin and Min sat down, waiting.

When the door opened, Su-Bin's heart launched, forcing her to stand. She braced herself for the quiet woman with soft shoulders and downcast eyes, but the figure who stepped in carried herself with a steadiness that seemed foreign.

Hye-Kyoung Moon stood tall, her eyes meeting Su-Bin's with a proud smile. Her arms and shoulders had muscle, and she moved in a relaxed, casual manner. Flashing a defiant smirk, she acknowledged the guard's instructions and sat with her head held high.

Hye-Kyoung pointed to Su-Bin's hair, a modern, asymmetrical bob with one side slightly longer than the other. "I love this style. Edgy, sophisticated—a perfect reflection of your confidence and professionalism."

Su-Bin only stared. A response wouldn't form. This wasn't something a Korean mother would say, least of all her own. She caught a tear and brushed it away. *Prison has finally carved away the woman who had raised me.* Her chest threatened to cave in on her, even though the change had been inevitable. This final transformation meant she no longer knew who her mother was.

"Hi, Mom. How are you?" Su-Bin asked.

"I have a new cellmate," Hye-Kyoung said. "We've become quite close. She's a fighter."

"Like ... a professional fighter?"

"She fought professionally in mixed martial arts. She's lived abroad and has been teaching me. How do you like my new persona?"

Su-Bin's shoulders relaxed. She took a deep breath and nodded. Prison hadn't hollowed and hardened her mother; it had given her support beams and steel cables.

"You look amazing." Su-Bin's voice cracked, "This new you is good, but ... I miss my mom."

Min clutched Su-Bin's forearm. She patted his hand, accepting his support with a broad smile.

"Well, I feel incredible," Hye-Kyoung said, her eyes flicking back and forth between them. "Who is this?"

Su-Bin straightened. "This is Min Yun, your new lawyer."

"You won't represent me anymore?"

"Min works for my law firm. As your daughter, I shouldn't be your legal counsel. I'm too biased, and I don't think it reflects well."

Su-Bin noticed her mom gawking at Min, marveling at his smooth complexion, strong jawline, and daring eyes that always held intensity and determination. "You picked a good one. He's handsome, athletic, and irresistible."

"Mom! Don't embarrass me." Her mother of old would never have made such a bold statement.

"I can see how you feel about him. Look at how you sit next to him; you two are dating. You can't fool your mom."

Min Yun suddenly stood and bowed. "I promise to take good care of your daughter, Mrs. Moon."

"Thank you. I can see you are a good man."

"Thank you for seeing the good in me." Min returned to his seat.

"How did you meet?" Hye-Kyoung asked.

"I hired him because he was the only one who had done his homework on your case. He knows everything about it." Opening her legal folder, Su-Bin turned it so her mom could see the contents. "We have a statement from a doctor who is willing to testify that the cuts were precision-made by someone with medical training, with a medical knife; the cuts weren't random slashings. This proves your original story about an intruder. Whoever made the cuts knew exactly what they were doing. Min was insistent we investigate that specific discrepancy."

"Have you narrowed the list of possible suspects?" Hye-Kyoung asked.

Min scooted his chair closer to the table, saying, "We've eliminated several suspects, yes, but we think this evidence opens the door for new ones. Your husband had stomach surgery the year prior to his death. Perhaps something happened at the hospital. I'll begin by interviewing the doctor."

"His doctor was polite and professional," Hye-Kyoung said.

"Mrs. Moon, I found a form from your previous lawyers, detailing a piece of evidence collected at the scene." He paused and looked straight into Hye-Kyoung's eyes. "A flask."

Hye-Kyoung lowered her head.

Su-Bin sank with her.

"After examining the photos, I noticed the initials engraved on the flask weren't your husband's. I've submitted the paperwork to have that flask tested for DNA. This will give us definite proof that another person was in the house. What I don't understand is why the flask wasn't already tested, and why your attorneys hadn't mentioned it at trial."

Su-Bin's stomach turned. She had always assumed the flask had belonged to her father and had even told the police as much. The day Min pointed out the engravings, she'd nearly lost her lunch.

Mrs. Moon leaned back in her chair, cleared her throat, and lifted her chin. "Perhaps we should go through the events of that night. I'll answer specific questions as they arrive."

"Of course," Min replied. "Let's start with your husband's drinking."

"After his surgery, he had to limit his drinking, so we developed a system that helped him. We had alcohol delivered to the house—it was cheaper, and we could get what he wanted. Since the alcohol was delivered during the day, I was able to unpack the case, keeping the contents out of sight, always making sure there were only a few bottles that were less than half full in the liquor cabinet. This system worked fairly well. The problem that day was that the delivery driver left the box on the doorstep without knocking or getting a signature—I didn't know he had come. When my husband arrived home, he opened the box and started drinking right away. I knew it was going to be a bad night because he angered easily when he was drunk. I didn't dare try to take it away. Instead, I made him a big meal, but he didn't want to eat, so I thought soup might be better. I was afraid for Su-Bin. If she came home late, he would have beat her."

"How often did he become violent?"

"Only when he got extremely drunk. Maybe two or three times a year."

Su-Bin interrupted tersely, "Two or three times a month."

"Not after the surgery. He was getting better," her mom retorted.

"He was murdered ten months after that surgery."

Min touched Su-Bin's hand. "Let's continue."

Su-Bin leaned back in her chair.

With a quick exhale, Min continued, prompting, "When you served him the soup, he hit you."

"Yes. I should have waited for it to cool down. It was too hot." Hye-Kyoung closed her eyes and raised her hands. "Ahh! Sorry. I'm not to blame." Opening her eyes, she gave a weak smile. "I am breaking old habits and thought patterns." She took a breath and continued. "The soup was hot, and he burned his mouth. He cursed me, striking my face several times with an empty bottle he snatched off the table."

Su-Bin stiffened and tried to push away the multiple memories assaulting her—screams, cries, bruises. The worst was the fear—watching the door, wondering when it would open. She pressed a knuckle to the bottom of her nose and took a steadying breath.

"There are conflicting statements as to what happened next," Min said. "The police report indicates you said someone stepped in between the two of you. But at the trial, your lawyers argued you grabbed a knife off the floor to defend yourself."

"My attorneys said there was no evidence to support my initial story. You have to understand that I was in shock and had a concussion. Everything happened so quickly, and I had no one to help me. My husband had cut me off from my friends and family early in our relationship. So when the investigators and my lawyers were telling me no one else was in the house, I started to believe them."

"What do you believe now?"

"That another person *was* there. He stepped in between us, and I was afraid for him. I didn't want him to get hurt. I felt guilty for causing so much trouble. Because of my foolishness, someone felt the need to intervene. But that all changed when I saw him cutting my husband."

"We have some stock photos taken from the internet of different knives that I want to show you. But first, tell me how the kitchen knife ended up in your hands."

"The man put it in my hands as he left."

"Did he say anything? Did you get a good look at his face?"

"No. I was partially blind at that point, and the light was behind him, making his face dark. He put the knife in my hand, took a swig from a flask, and tossed it across the room. Then he tapped my forehead with the knife he had used to kill my husband and held it in front of my face."

"What happened next?"

"Nothing. I crawled to the wall and just sat there."

Looking at Su-Bin, Min asked, "And that's what you saw when you came home—your mom sitting with her back against the wall and your father lying on the floor?"

Su-Bin nodded.

Turning back to Hye-Kyoung, Min asked, "Why didn't you call the police?"

"I was badly hurt. My eye was swollen, my jaw was fractured, and my nose was broken. I was in pain. Shock. I couldn't move. I couldn't think. I just kept asking myself, 'What had I done?'"

"Why didn't you mention the flask to the police?"

"I had a concussion from the blow I received, and I had forgotten about it. The facts and events were blurry at first. I didn't remember the intruder doing that until halfway through the trial. My lawyers didn't feel the detail was important because they had already planned and argued that I acted in self-defense."

"Which brings me to my biggest question. Why did you suddenly insist on testifying and then say that you didn't kill your husband, going against all the evidence that was brought forth by both sides?"

"I woke up," she said, her shoulders rising in a small shrug. "I felt ... angry. Frustrated." She sat forward and rested her elbows on the table. "I couldn't admit to doing something I didn't do. People were telling me what I had done and why I had done it, when the truth was, I loved my husband and would never have laid a finger on him." She lowered her head and shook it. "I groveled at his feet and took the blame for everything." A faint, almost amusing huff escaped her. "Even for serving the soup too hot."

Letting out a slow breath, she added, "The trial was a lie. I couldn't accept that." She gave a small knowing smile, meeting Su-Bin's eyes. "Anyway, look what happened because of my testimony. You became a famous attorney. I wouldn't change any of it." Her expression warmed, and she straightened. "I'm so proud of you. I'm glad to exchange my life in prison for your success."

"Mom, don't say that."

"It was true for a long time," she expressed. "But I've come a long way since then, and I'm ready for you to get me out of here."

"Good." Su-Bin took out several photos of medical knives—scalpels, amputation knives, surgical knives, military range medical knives, and a dental knife. "Can you identify the type of blade you saw? Did it look like any of these?"

Hye-Kyoung's face went white. She touched a photo, running her finger along a white unicorn symbol. "It was this one," she said, pointing to an emergency medical EDC folding knife.

"It looked like this one?" Su-Bin asked.

Hye-Kyoung shook her head. "No, it was that exact knife," she clarified.

Min reached over, taking the photo. "Popular brand. I'll talk to the medical examiner, see if we can have him confirm that this type of knife could have been the one used."

"I'll type up a witness statement and have you sign it the next time we come," Su-Bin said.

"We'll get you out of here," Min said in a confident voice.

With a twinkle in her eye, Hye-Kyoung responded, "Soon enough to attend your wedding?"

The guards came. Hye-Kyoung stood and mouthed the words, "I love you."

Su-Bin responded with a warm smile and a nod. "You'll be home soon," she said.

On the drive back to the office, Su-Bin's hope grew, confidence building with every passing mile. Min had been prepared from the start—the flask, the cuts, the missing expert testimony. He had seen what others had overlooked. He knew exactly what he was doing, and that certainty was hypnotic.

"You're quiet," Min said.

"Thinking. I felt so helpless for so many years. Every time I tried to find some way to prove my mother's innocence, I kept seeing her sitting there with the knife saying, 'What did I do?' I couldn't get past it. I'd try to think objectively, but kept running into dead ends. And now here you are, and it's finally happening."

"You were too close to the case. I can see it more clearly than you. Also, I'm emotionally attached to you, which gives me motivation to find the truth." Reaching over, Min pet her cheek.

"What do I need to do next?" Su-Bin asked.

"Nothing. Focus on preparing your closing arguments for tomorrow."

"Thanks. I still need to finalize them."

With a nod, Min exclaimed, "I can't believe the trial has some relevance to your mom's case."

"Me too. I almost didn't take it because of that."

"I'm glad you did," Min said. "Your win will be poetic justice."

"Whoa. Thanks for the confidence, but this is a tough case. The law isn't on my side."

"But the evidence is. Drive that point home tomorrow."

"I will," Su-Bin said, flashing him a smile that was both professional and personal.

Min's eyes darkened with hunger, and the corner of his mouth lifted in a sly, almost naughty grin. She could feel his stare, traveling over her strong, slender figure. He reached over, sliding his finger through her hair.

"What?" Su-Bin said.

"Your mom was right. You look stunning with this hair style."

Eyeing him sideways, she gave a knowing, playful smile. "You want something."

"I want to come over tonight."

"It's drama night." She caught his eyes roll before his head turned away. "Also, Jong-In and I are going over teacher applicants."

"With everything that's on your plate, why are you interviewing English teachers?" Min asked. "You have an HR department. Tell them to do their jobs. Or even better, get someone from an agency. Don't waste your time trying to hire someone yourself."

"I'm looking for a specific person. The two people I have in HR don't need me to burden them with this. We're trying to launch an international law division in six months. That means hiring attorneys, preparing internal exams, managing compliance, training staff, and keeping everything running—payroll, benefits, taxes, leave. Pulling them off that to recruit an English teacher would slow everything down.”

“And that’s why you go through an agency.”

“Except Yoona tends to send me people in situations like this. She sent me you. Jong-In is doing the screening and first interview, and I trust his judgment.”

Min held up a defensive hand. “Okay,” he said, then changed the subject. “Well, don’t worry about your mom’s case. I have it under control. I am confident we’ll free her.”

“Your confidence is contagious. I feel it in you, and I know you are going to succeed.”

Min smiled. “Your mom doesn’t seem weak or timid to me, by the way. She’s pretty strong and forthright.”

“She’s changed. I agree.”

“I like her.”

“I’m glad. But don’t get any ideas. I agreed you could move some of your things in. That doesn’t mean we’re getting married.”

Later that night, Su-Bin cooked while Jong-In Park sat at her kitchen table scrolling through email responses and résumés for the English teaching position.

“Find any good candidates?” Su-Bin asked.

“I thought I had found someone—Korean-American, raised in the States, father’s a lawyer, mother’s a law clerk. Five years teaching English with corporate experience.”

“Sounds perfect. What was the issue?”

“All lies. A simple background check revealed that she was born and raised here and that her parents are bankers.”

“I’m sure there are plenty of other teachers that will fit,” Su-Bin said as she flipped the frying zucchini.

“A few teachers have corporate experience, and several have taught in multiple countries. I’ve set up appointments with five prospects for tomorrow. You better appreciate my hard work; I’m using vacation days to help you,” Jong-In teased.

“I appreciate nothing, slave. Get back to work,” Su-Bin mocked, laughing.

"I rather enjoy doing this, *actually*. I love being able to speak English. I hope they don't think I have too strong of an accent."

"You've always been good at English. Head of our class since—when? Eighth grade? Your English is great," Su-Bin reassured.

"Thanks to you," Jong-In said. "Remember when we inserted the curse words into Mr. Chung's flash cards?"

"Oh, my gosh, that was so funny. And he didn't even catch them. The principal was the one who noticed. What ever happened to Mr. Chung?"

"Are you kidding me? He was transferred. You don't remember?"

"Oh, yeah. That's right," Su-Bin said, nodding. "I should feel terrible."

"You should!" Jong-In burst, grinning. "Especially for talking me out of writing an apology letter."

Su-Bin lifted her chin and gave a fake snarl. "Get back to work," she hissed.

Jong-In continued emailing as she finished cooking. Then he closed his laptop and declared, "Finished." Sitting back in his chair, he admired the food. "Mmm, smells great."

"Let's eat," she said.

They placed the various food dishes on the table—scrambled eggs, seaweed, bean sprouts, pork strips, kimchi, and fried zucchini.

"I'm dying to know what happened today," Jong-In said. "Tell me everything."

"My mom has changed. She's not a docile, little wallflower anymore. Her new cellmate is teaching her how to fight. She figured out Min and I were dating, and came right out and said so. I was embarrassed."

"You? Embarrassed? Good! You should be. A Korean mother deserves this rite of passage—especially yours. Let her have this one."

"I didn't have a choice. Anyway, she likes him."

"Does she know that he'll be staying here on the weekends?"

"No! I could never tell her that."

"Maybe she'd accept it. You did say she has changed."

"I couldn't possibly. Not in a million years."

"He's sleeping on the sofa." Jong-In laughed.

"No one would ever believe that," Su-Bin giggled, blushing. "Besides, she already has us married."

"Of course she does. So ... no reason not to tell her everything now."

"Stop it."

"Okay, what about her case?" Jong-In asked. "Was she able to identify the type of knife she saw?"

"She did, from a photo. And she said it was the exact knife. Min is confident that he'll be able to narrow suspects and begin to find a motive."

"That's great."

"Yes, it is." Su-Bin looked at the time. "*Extraordinary Attorney Woo* starts in five minutes."

"I can't wait for the moment when Lee Jun-Ho and Woo Young-Woo become a couple."

"I'm afraid you might be disappointed," Su-Bin said. "I mean, Woo Young-Woo is autistic. Physical affection and emotional intimacy are difficult for her."

"But Lee Jun-Ho is perfect for her."

"They will most likely become best friends."

"And in these dramas, the best friends always end up together."

"I get that the show is leading us to believe they will become a couple, but I don't see how it's possible."

"Oh, come now. The lady always gets the handsome hero," he said, nudging her and pointing to Min's hoodie lying on the side of the couch.

Su-Bin glanced at the sweatshirt, her stomach twisting in a sick, silent way that warned, *Are you safe with Min?* Of course she was. But still ... something about the pace, the pressure... She remembered how *she* had been the one to close the distance that first night. Min's eyes, his touch, his steady confidence had pulled her in until she had lost her guard and given herself to him. But now, she wanted their relationship to grow organically, not be forced or rushed. She wanted something that could breathe.

"Hey, I'm only teasing," Jong-In said.

"Yeah, I know." She shifted in her seat. "After the show, can I ask for your help?"

"Anything."

"I'm preparing my closing arguments for tomorrow. Will you listen and offer suggestions?"

"Sure."

They finished dinner, watched their drama, and washed the dishes together. Afterwards, Su-Bin performed her closing arguments while Jong-In questioned and suggested changes.

By the third run-through, her voice had grown firmer, her confidence rising as the words became more familiar. By the fourth, she moved more freely, pacing in short strides, one hand slicing the air as if she were already in front of the jury.

Her voice gathered heat and her conviction edged toward anger. Nearing the end, her shoulders locked, and her words seared. "Would we be here if the driver had been sick that day and a different driver was working? Yes!" she snapped, her hands balling into fists.

"Hold up," Jong-In said. He laid his hands on her shoulders and pushed them down. "Look at your hands," he whispered. "I know how important winning this case is to you. I love the passion in your voice, but don't let your anger toward the company show. Otherwise, it looks like you want revenge."

"It's really important to me that I win. This company is partly responsible for my dad's death and my mom's suffering. And now a kid is dead! I—"

"I know," Jong-In interjected. He pulled her close and hugged her. Stepping back, he placed his hands on her shoulders again and looked her straight in the eyes. "This is a great closing argument. Keep the passion. Lose the anger. You're going to be phenomenal. Your mom will be proud."

After Jong-In left, Su-Bin lay in bed, exhausted. As she was about to fall asleep, her skin tingled, her chest buzzed, and a tickling sensation stirred in her brain. She rolled over, trying to ignore it, drifting into sleep. Half-dreaming, half-aware, *she saw a man with dark, curly hair walk into her living room. Standing in front of a whiteboard, he grabbed a marker and wrote the word, "Arraignment."*

Lake Valley, Oregon

A New Normal

In the FBI building downtown, Special Agent Bruce Duchovny entered a sterile, fluorescent-lit conference room. He was tall and commanding with a composed demeanor that exuded authority. His dark hair, streaked with silver at the temples, framed a face marked by years of experience. His blue eyes scanned the group, known as "the six," who had been abducted. They sat at the table, their eyes hard and unyielding, ready to execute the cover story they'd rehearsed. Bruce was happy about that, because he didn't want them talking to anyone else about what had truly happened.

Setting six folders on the table, Bruce picked up the first one labeled "Nong Ekamai." He knew what he needed to do: press them, test them. What would they offer and what would they hold back? He couldn't risk them slipping up with the press, family members, or even other officers. The truth stayed in this room.

Opening Nong's file, he scanned it and addressed her. "You moved here from Thailand," he said.

Nong parted her long, silky, black hair, revealing a small mole under her right eye. "That's right," she replied. "I was three. My father worked with Ford. We lived in Michigan for twelve years before moving here."

Looking back at the file, Bruce summarized, "Graduated from Portland State. Opened your own architectural office." His eyes rose to meet hers again. "And invested in real estate. That's quite impressive."

Nong smiled. "Thank you."

"I know you've been through a lot these past four years," Bruce said. "It must have been incredibly difficult being taken away from everything and everyone you knew."

Nong gave him a secretive smile with a twinkle in her eye.

The confident glint told Bruce she was ready to play this game.

With a nod, Bruce said, "Right. I'm so sorry we weren't able to find you sooner."

He set Nong's file down and opened the next one. Tapping the papers, Bruce eyed Jared, giving him a consoling smile. Jared ran his fingers through his light brown hair.

"It says here you were born in Wisconsin."

"Green Bay."

"Your parents own a cheese and sausage shop near Lambeau Field. I imagine that was quite the scene on Sundays."

Jared's smile warmed. "Yes. Lots of fun."

"You went to school in New York, architecture as well. Owned your own business. Seems you and Nong have a few things in common."

Jared and Nong glanced at each other, grinning.

"I see you won an award for a project expansion on a museum originally built by the Carnegies. That's remarkable. You also had several successful years designing buildings for Bill Stillen with Stillen Corp. and Extended Life. How did you end up as a delivery driver with Go Express?"

Jared leaned forward. "Isn't it all there in your file?"

"The file doesn't give the full context or the benefit of the doubt."

Jared leaned back in his chair. "After Leah's mother divorced me, Bill fired me. I was distracted and overwhelmed. I signed off on flawed architectural plans for a suburban housing project. During a stormy night, one of the houses partially collapsed, injuring an occupant. I was sued, found liable, and although my insurance covered the damages, my policy was dropped, making it impossible for me to continue my work."

Bruce sympathized, "That hurts. Did it hurt to be taken away from your daughter?"

Jared's blue eyes glared back at him. "Do you have an actual question for me?"

"I will. But for now, I'm just trying to feel you out."

"Maybe you should buy me a drink first."

Bruce's lips twitched, almost a smile. Turning to Leah, he opened her folder. "Model UN, theater, youth group, debate, horseback riding, golf, straight A's... You're certainly busy."

"I enjoy living."

Leah's confident posture said she was self-assured and strong. The slight lift in her chin said she had all the answers he needed.

"It must be nice to have Bill Stillen as a grandfather."

"It has its perks," she replied.

"Where did you go the day you found your dad?"

"You mean the day the police took me to the Education Center where I ended up being abducted? That day?" Leah countered.

"Yes, that day."

"We didn't go sightseeing, I can tell you that."

"I'm sure you saw some sights, though."

Leah smirked with a subtle shake of her head.

Opening Barb's folder, Bruce saw she was no stranger to tragedy. "Your father built the Bellevue House."

Barb narrowed her eyes and pursed her lips in anger. "And my mom burned it down and killed him. Yes. Thank you for that wonderful reminder."

"I'm sorry," Bruce offered. "I also see that you're a talented singer and participate in theater."

"That's right."

"I met your grandmother, Carol. You're very fortunate to have such a caring and loving person in your life."

"I think so."

"Did she know where you were?"

Barb lowered her head and stared into her lap, her bottom lip caught between her teeth.

Dan slapped his hand on the table and said, "You met her. What did she say?"

"She said you're a wrestler and play baseball. You attend community college and work at the movie theater."

Dan's light brown eyes were steely cold, showing his determination to stay silent.

"She didn't tell me that you were dating Leah. I found that out from Leah's friends at school."

Dan turned and looked at the wall.

Bruce turned to Ploy Ekamai, Nong's ten-year-old daughter. Her youthful innocence seemed unmarred by the ordeal she had been dragged through. He smiled, and she waved.

"Good afternoon. I'm Special Agent Bruce Duchovny." He folded his hands on the table and let the silence stretch. "I specialize in cases involving the supernatural—ghosts, spirits, and entities like the one who abducted you."

The tension in the six faces across from him eased. Jared's head tilted upwards, and he let out a sigh of relief. Nong stared at him, shaking her head, lips curled into not quite a smile. Barb looked up in surprise, Dan dropped his shoulders, letting his eyes relaxed, and Leah gave a light chuckle.

Ploy asked, "You know about the ghost house that's in the Education Center?"

Bruce nodded. "I do. I haven't met Bellevue, but I've heard a lot about It." He paused. "Let me catch you up on what happened after your abduction." He told them that Detective Spencer and Officer Choi had both played crucial roles in helping him understand the nature of their abduction. The FBI then recruited Brandon to train with a Shaman in Korea named Yoona. Brandon was initially going to return in ten days to reengage with Bellevue, but now that they were free, his training would be prolonged.

The group exchanged glances, smiles of relief passing between them.

Bruce crossed his arms. "Can you tell me how you were captured?"

Dan placed his forearms on the table. "The house was my imaginary friend as a kid. When I went to the Center, we reconnected, and It messed with my brain. With all of our brains. That's why we went back willingly."

The room became eerily quiet. Bruce glanced at each of them, stopping at Barb. She nodded in confirmation.

Ploy jumped in, "Can I tell my story?" She started with the day her mother didn't show to pick her up from school and ended with seeing her mom at the Education Center before Bellevue appeared. "I was afraid and told my mom I didn't want to go. The policeman said it was fine and that he was going too, but he didn't."

Bruce cleared his throat and said, "What I need to know now is, how did you get free? And what happened to Bellevue?"

Jared straightened in his seat, but Leah put her hand on his arm. "Let me, Dad." She explained how she had saved Father Joseph and convinced him to hold the ceremonies at the Center, which infused Bellevue with life. "The Education Center has been transformed into a living, breathing entity."

Bruce contemplated the information. He was sure Leah was mistaken in her assessment of the building. In all of his years working with the supernatural, monsters, and bizarre happenings, he had never heard of a living building. He was tempted to ask Leah to explain more, but they were expected at the hospital soon, and he still needed to go through their cover story. He also knew that the Catholic priest in the next room could offer some answers.

Tapping his fingers on the table, he said, "I don't want you anywhere near the Center. I've called a professional, who will handle Bellevue." He looked into each of their eyes, receiving a short nod or bob of the head in understanding.

Bruce straightened and said, "Ghosts and spirits are not widely accepted realities. If you tell people the truth about what happened, they'll think you're crazy. And we can't afford that kind of attention on this case or on you. Are we in agreement?"

Each of them nodded.

Bruce gazed at Ploy. "You can't say anything about being captured by a ghost. Not to anyone. It's classified. Top secret. Do you know what that means?"

Ploy nodded. "I know."

Bruce continued. "Now, let's go over your cover story. When speaking to the press, your friends, and even your family, you need to keep it simple and believable."

Bruce then laid out a story for them to practice. After they rehearsed, he added, "Emphasize your relief at being free and your desire to move forward. If a question catches you off guard, say you don't remember because of the trauma and fear. Finally, you can say that the FBI are still investigating, so you can't answer that question."

The room fell silent as the words settled over them. "Here's what's happening next: I'm taking you to the hospital so they can examine you. After that, we'll take you home to rest." His jaw tightened, and his voice turned deliberate, carrying a commanding edge. "I want the kids to go to school tomorrow." He turned to Leah and Barb. "I know today has been hectic, and you'll want time to readjust after an insane week, but falling into a familiar routine will help. Sleep in tomorrow morning; I'll inform the school you'll be in late, but I need you to go." He held their gazes, his eyes hard with determination, urging them to comply, before shifting his focus to Jared and Nong. "It's important to show the community that everything is back to normal. The sooner we clear that hurdle, the better."

"Fine," Leah announced before her dad or Nong could object. Leah nudged Barb, who said, "Yeah, okay."

"We have a press interview tomorrow with Channel 7 News. I'll have a car pick you up at four o'clock. The interview will air in the evening, and then it's life as you once knew it."

Bruce stood, saying, "Sit tight for a minute. I need to sign some papers to release you and get the vans ready. I'll be back in a minute."

Stepping into the hall, he closed the door behind him and made a quick call, arranging for the vans to take Leah, her father, and the others to the hospital for evaluation. Then he made his way to the next room, where the Catholic priest he had called in from Portland to exorcise Bellevue was waiting.

"Father," Bruce said, taking a seat across from him. "What happened at the Education Center?"

The priest rubbed his thumbs together and took in a slow breath. "When I arrived, the ceremonies were already underway. Another priest, a rabbi, and monks were performing rituals. The energy they created touched me in a way I've never experienced." His voice softened, and he spoke the next words with clear reverence. "The breath of God passed through the building."

"And the ghost?" Bruce pressed.

"I stepped toward an undeniable presence—a powerful and dangerous force. I questioned whether I could handle it, but it transcended without me having to do anything."

"Are you sure it transcended? What if the ghost didn't move on but became part of the building itself—fused with the materials by the 'breath of God' you felt? Could the soul make the structure ... conscious in some way, transforming it into a living entity?"

The priest blinked, caught off guard. "A living building?" he said with skepticism. "Inanimate objects can't be alive. They can be possessed—that I've seen. But alive?" He shook his head. "No, I don't believe that's possible. At least ... it's beyond my knowledge."

"So, the building isn't alive, and the ghost is gone."

"After the ceremonies, I felt a shift—a surge of sorts—something I can't fully explain." The priest interlocked his fingers, resting them near his chin. He spoke

in a slow, deliberate tone. "This transition, the transcendence was…" He lifted his eyebrows. "Beautiful." He paused, seemingly collecting his thoughts.
"There are different kinds of transcendence. Most spirits move on naturally.
Banishers force them violently. A Shaman will guide them peacefully. Manipulation and trickery can also be used. Each method feels distinct—the
energy resonates differently. But the transcendence I witnessed today…" His
eyes drifted in thought. "This was something new. The love and acceptance
bestowed upon the spirit gave it fulfillment, validation, peace. Absolutely
remarkable. I need to learn more about what they did."

"Just so I understand, there are no longer paranormal entities at the Education Center?"

"Whatever was there isn't there anymore. There are no ghosts left to
exorcise. The danger is gone."

Rising from the table, Bruce thanked the father, and the two men exited
the room. The secretary signaled that the vans were ready, so Bruce went back
to the first room.

"Ready to go?" he asked the group.

Leah glanced at her dad, then back to the FBI agent. "We are. Thank you
… for everything."

Bruce offered a small, reassuring smile. "You're not alone in this," he
reminded her. "Whatever comes next, we're here to help. Call me anytime,
for any reason."

As they filed out, Bruce watched them go, a flicker of unease still tugging
at the back of his mind. The priest had reassured him, but something about
Bellevue's "unique" transcendence didn't feel right. He would have to bring
the subject up with Yoona the next time they talked.

Later that evening, Leah parked next to the curb and turned off the engine.
She glanced at the darkened outline of Barb's house, seeing the Lincoln
Nautilus her mom had rented idling in front, waiting for her. Sighing, Leah
pushed open her car door, slipped her backpack over her shoulder, and
walked across the street, pressing the button on her key to lock the Audi.
She was sure the chill she felt had to be from the cool night air.

Leah hopped into the passenger seat and glanced at her mom. Stacy sat in silence, eyes fixed on the dashboard. The motor hummed, but it failed to smooth her mom's disappointing posture.

Looking out the passenger window, Leah saw the warm glow of Dan's bedroom light calling to her. "I need to stay at Barb's tonight," she said. "My stuff is here." She turned her gaze to her mom. "It feels safe."

"I just got you back." Stacy took a breath before faced her. "I want to keep you close and make sure you're okay. The hotel—"

"The hotel isn't home, Mom," Leah interrupted. "I walked into the house with Dad, and I could barely breathe. The last time I was there was when he went missing, and going back shook me. I need to be here." What she said was true, but her reason for staying here was impatience. The book was in her backpack, and Leah needed to start her training with Barb. Now, tonight.

The lines of concern on Stacy's face deepened. She reached out and took Leah's hand in hers. "We've all been through hell," she said. "Tim filled me in on everything that happened while you were with the FBI and at the hospital. Carol fought to get you guys free. She deserves some private time with her grandkids. We should give her that space."

Leah lowered her gaze. What her mom said made sense. She knew it was probably best to let Barb and Dan reunite with their grandma and reorient themselves before school tomorrow. But the need to connect to Barb and learn how to use telepathy pulled at her. They had planned to acquire these skills before they were abducted, and Leah knew that if she had already learned how, her interactions with Bellevue would have been much easier.

Staying at Barb's tonight was necessary—for her sanity. Was Leah being selfish? Yes, but part of her didn't care. She understood Barb, Dan, and Carol needed time together as a family, but Leah felt like she was part of that family. And while her mom needed her, especially after everything that had happened, Leah couldn't deny the stronger desire to study the book. Desperation took over, and her mind raced for an explanation. "I know you've been through a lot," she said. "I went through the same thing when Dad went missing." She took a breath. "When I walked out of that building and saw you, I was so happy." She turned in her seat, bringing her knee to rest in front of her. "I want to stay with you, but ... Barb's house is a refuge. Grandma Carol is practically my second mom. I've already called, and they're expecting me." She looked at the ceiling and sighed. "Just this one night. I need to be grounded in a place that is safe and comfortable. I'll be with you tomorrow. I promise."

Stacy shook her head. "You are so headstrong," she said with a deep sigh. "Okay. You can stay here tonight, but make a real effort to be with me tomorrow?"

"I will." Then a thought hit Leah, and she chuckled.

"What's so funny?"

"I finally understand why the FBI guy wanted us to go to school tomorrow. He said he wanted the public to get a sense of normalcy as soon as possible, but he really wants that for *us*."

"Make me your normal tomorrow."

"Absolutely." Leah leaned over and hugged her mom.

"So, prom in three days," Stacy said in a light tone. "We need to get you a dress. And then it's graduation, and off to Stanford. I'd love to help you move."

A smile pricked at Leah's lips. "You better. Could you help me choose my classes for first semester?"

"I would love to. Should we make that part of tomorrow's agenda?"

"I have the Channel 7 thing tomorrow."

"That's right. We'll fit it in somewhere."

"How long are you staying?" Leah asked.

"We need to talk about that. Before the whole 'love—obsessed water baby' ordeal, I had planned to fly in on Friday and leave Sunday afternoon. But now I'm thinking about staying until you graduate."

"Can you afford the time? What about the New York office? Your gig in Canada? The farm?"

"You are the only thing that matters to me."

"But Mom, it's going to be crazy here. I still have school, and exams are coming up."

"And your boyfriend," Stacy offered in jest.

Leah blushed and turned away.

"I get it. It's just that *my* priorities seem misaligned. You are the most important person to me."

"I think your priorities match perfectly for both you and me. The whole reason you left Dad was to realize a dream and to love life. You remind me that"—she straightened and met her mom's gaze—"my life belongs to me."

"Are you saying you don't want me to stay?"

"I'm saying I love you. I'm saying you'll be back for graduation, and I'll be with you for a month over summer. Keep doing what makes you happy."

"I'll sleep on it. We'll talk about this again later?"

Leah smiled in agreement.

"It's getting late. You should head in."

Leah leaned in and gave her mom another hug. Stacy kissed her on the cheek.

"I'll see you tomorrow. Sleep well and try not to dream."

Groaning, Leah said, "Tell me about it." She opened the car door and stepped out. "Love you, Mom."

"I love you, too, sweetheart. Good night."

Leah walked to the front door and waved. Her mom waved back and drove away.

Barb shuffled down the hall, her shoulders slumped and eyes heavy. She pushed her bedroom door open and stopped, frozen at the threshold. Her journal lay on top of her unmade bed. The laundry basket sat half-full in the corner. The pages to "Feeling Good" by Nina Simone lay open on her music stand, waiting for her to resume recording.

Her room had been a cocoon of safety—a sanctuary of music, books, and journal entries, where she'd found freedom in her thoughts and expressions. But now, her room was a box that dictated who she was and how she was to behave. If she stepped back inside, she'd return to that version of herself—the girl who had been cautious, withdrawn, and predictable. She couldn't be trapped like that again.

Drawing in a shaky breath, she stepped inside, careful not to disturb a single thing. The stale air was thick and heavy with an old comfort that burned the inside of her nose and left a vile taste in her mouth. She remembered feeling safe here, but now she only saw confinement. Drifting toward the table, she stared at a thin layer of dust that had collected along the edges of her computer. She ran her hand above the keyboard but didn't touch it, as if doing so would pull her completely back into her old life.

A tap came at the door. "Barb? Leah's on the phone. How do you feel about her spending the night?"

Barb spun and faced her grandmother. "Yes, please," she said. "I need her."

Grandma Carol nodded. "I thought you might. Take a shower, and then we'll eat. She'll be over in an hour."

At the dinner table, Barb finished the last of her casserole when the knock they'd been expecting finally came. She began to stand, but her grandma told her to stay and finish eating.

Grandma Carol opened the door and held her arms out wide. Leah stepped into her embrace, and the two clung to each other. She pressed Leah's head against her shoulder and rocked her back and forth.

After a full two minutes, Grandma Carol took Leah's face in both hands and wiped her tears with her thumbs. "Barb and Dan told me what happened."

Barb stopped chewing, straining to hear. She caught Leah's quick glance before returning her focus on Grandma.

"You were the one who got them out," Grandma Carol continued. "Leah, I don't have the words to express how proud and thankful I am. You were so brave." She wiped her own tears, her voice now trembling. "You came home and brought them with you. I really can't thank you enough."

Leah shook her head, but grandma stopped her, brushing a strand of hair from Leah's cheek. "You've always had a strength in you, Leah. I saw it long before all this." She squeezed her shoulders. "And I knew in my bones you'd use it for something good." Turning to Barb and Dan, eyes shining, she continued. "All of you ... you did this together. I'm so proud and grateful—" Her voice broke. "I don't know what I would've done if I'd lost you."

Grandma's wobbled words wrapped around Barb's chest like climbing ivy, and she couldn't stand still anymore. Crossing the room in three quick steps, she pulled her grandmother into a hug. Dan came up behind her and the three held each other.

"Alright," Carol said. She wiped her eyes and flashed a smile. "Go finish eating and rinse your bowls in the sink."

Barb nodded and backed into the kitchen, still watching.

Grandma took Leah's hand and asked, "Do you have the manual? Barb said she left it in Tim's truck when the police took you downtown."

The glare Leah shot Barb felt accusing. "You left the book in the truck?"

"I'm sorry," Barb responded. "I didn't think you wanted the police to know about it."

Leah shook her head. "I don't know where it is," she told Carol. "I'm sure my uncle has it, though."

"Make sure you find it," Carol said. "And give it to the FBI agent you talked with today. He'll know what to do with it."

Leah nodded. "Okay."

Carol kissed Leah's cheek, and the two of them made their way to the kitchen. Leah smiled at Dan, then took Barb's hand with a no-nonsense look in her eye. She had come for a purpose. Waving to Dan, she pulled Barb to her bedroom and locked the door behind her.

"Okay," Leah said, glancing around the room, not wasting any time. "We need to connect."

"How? Without the book—"

Leah pulled the manual from her backpack.

"Leah! What the hell? You just told my grandma you didn't know where this was?"

With a grin and a shrug, Leah laid Grandma Carol's treasured find on the floor. "We need to learn how to connect."

The plain cover bore no title but inside was a wealth of knowledge about the supernatural—a training manual for Shamans and Banishers. The shopkeeper who sold it to Carol had claimed that it held rare and guarded information and was the property of the Circle.

Leah began flipping through the pages, saying, "I am never going to play victim again." She bypassed whole chapters and sections.

"Whoa," Barb said. "I get that you're fixated. But if we're going to do this, don't you think ... oh, I don't know ... we should start at the beginning?"

"Later," Leah replied. "The beginning is stuff about growing your spiritual center and your core—meditations, diets, biology, Tai Chi movements. It's all about learning how to build and manipulate your energy. But you can already grow your spiritual energy."

Barb let out a dry, incredulous laugh. "I'm not exactly the spiritual type."

Leah stopped turning pages and lifted her eyes. They were wide with disbelief. "I beg to differ." She gestured toward the music stand. "When you sing, you're connected to a higher power. Everyone around you sees and hears it. You radiate. That's the energy you need to build."

"By singing?" Barb scoffed. "When? *Now?*"

Leah's face dropped into a blank stare before she turned back to the book. "By going into your memories."

Barb lowered herself to the floor. "My memories?"

"Hmm," Leah voiced as she continued flipping pages.

Singing had always been the one thing that lifted Barb out of her shell. Onstage she fed on the hush of anticipation. Then, when her voice rose and the awe from the audience hit, she soared, untouchable.

"Here we are," Leah said. "Connecting." She ran her finger over the text, speed skimming passages that explained the purpose of connecting, what happens if someone is possessed, how to use a connection to read someone's future, and the dangers and warnings. She went straight to the step-by-step directions for making a connection.

Leah turned the book and pushed it toward Barb. "Ready?"

Barb glared, about to complain that she had skipped too much, but Leah spoke first.

"Yes, yes. We need to read it all. But I've already read it once, and neither of us is possessed, so, let's just connect first." She grabbed Barb's hands, pleading, "This is important. I need you."

Barb chewed on her bottom lip. She understood Leah's urgency; they didn't know how long they'd have the book. But learning only the bits and pieces they wanted couldn't be good. "You do know that you're borderline obsessed, right?"

Leah's eyes brightened and a smile overtook her face. "I do." She pointed to the passage and said, "Read this part here."

Barb read as Leah closed the shades and removed two candles and a small plate from her bag. She lit the candles, dripped wax onto the plate, and, once they were in place, took her rosary from her pocket and sat cross-legged in front of Barb.

When Barb finished, she didn't feel confident. The instructions talked about visualizing the bond, moving your energy, and inviting the connection. She had no experience with any of this. "I'm not sure I'll be able to do this."

"You can," Leah insisted. "Close your eyes and be open. I'll connect first. When you feel the connection link, I think you'll recognize it. You and Dan had this with Bell…" Leah paused. "I don't want to say Its name."

"With my imaginary friend, Bella," Barb said.

"Yes."

Barb nodded. "Maybe you're right."

"Ready?" Leah said. "First we build our spiritual energy."

Barb straightened her back and rested her palms face up on their thighs. She drew from memories of her past performances, envisioning how she had pushed the notes with her diaphragm, strong and sustainable. They had resonated with power, vibrations booming pure and crisp.

Warmth unfurled in the depths of her core and expanded through to her ribs. She had belted out the lyric, *I'll always be enough,* as the crowd cheered with delight. She hadn't just sung; she had let her spirit fly. That feeling was with her now.

Leah took her hands, saying, "Look at me." They locked eyes and explored each other's soul.

Barb felt Leah's energy enter her body and drift to her heart. The feeling was familiar. She had felt this lying in bed the night Bella had first talked to her, the night after the ceremonies to bless her house. She instinctively understood how connecting worked.

"Now," Leah began, "send your energy into me, forming a cord that binds us together."

Barb didn't need the explanation. She simply connected without thinking about it. A closeness developed between them, like a flower welcoming a bee. Barb's heart quickened as the connection took hold, and Leah's smile grew big and bright.

"We're connected," she whispered in wonderment. Tears welled in her eyes. "I so needed this."

Barb reached forward, her thumb wiping a tear from Leah's cheek. Then she rose to her knees and offered Leah a hug. The two embraced and rocked back and forth.

They stared at each other and then laughed.

"What's next?" Barb asked.

Leah picked up the book and found the step-by-step instructions for sending a telepathic message. "Let's try this."

The joy Barb was feeling suddenly soured as her stomach pitched. She had communicated with Bella using telepathy. This was the way one spoke to ghosts.

"We can do this," Leah urged. "It'll be fun. And once we've developed this skill, the others will be easier to learn." She held the book out in front of her.

Barb hesitated to take it. She didn't want to become a Shaman or a Banisher. She didn't want ghosts in her life.

"You and me, together," Leah urged. "Do this with me."

Forcing a smile, Barb decided she could use telepathy with Leah, just not with the dead. She took the book and stared at the pages. *Okay. I can do this. With Leah.* Placing her finger on the passage, she read the instructions.

Leah jumped to her feet and waited. When Barb nodded, Leah turned off the lights. The candles glowed, setting the mood.

"Keep your mind open and silence your inner voice," Leah said.

Taking a deep breath, Barb sat in a meditative position and closed her eyes. The distant rumble of the dryer and the faint sound of the television threatened to disturb their concentration.

Leah whispered, "Ignore the sounds. Focus on me. I'll send you something first."

As Barb waited to receive a telepathic message from Leah, she couldn't help but think about the connection she had just made with her best friend. The closeness was so similar to what she had shared with Bella that she felt startled. And yet, this was entirely different. The warmth that surrounded her wasn't needy; the bond didn't pull or demand. The link felt... How to describe it? Barb was wrapped in a radiance that soaked into her chest, a comfort that said she was safe, appreciated, and wanted. She had a sense of peace that hadn't existed since before moving into the house her dad had built. This connection seemed to fill every pool of sorrow and hurt inside her, pushing the putrid waste out, and leaving something pure. Her heart was so full of—she struggled to find the correct term—love, life, energy, being?

Barb thought about her connection with Bella, how it had been effortless, how Bella had lived inside her mind. Barb had been so young, and the line between their consciousnesses had been blurred. Her bond with Leah, however, was a spiritual closeness, and this newfound tether to her friend felt unbreakable.

A thought popped into Barb's mind. *I need to call Leah.* The words came with a sense of urgency; the same feeling that came when she suddenly remembered she had forgotten to do something. Barb opened her eyes and saw Leah staring in anticipation.

"Did it work? Did you get something from me?" Leah asked.

"You want me to call you?" Barb questioned. "But you're right here..."

"It worked! Holy shit! I did it!" Leah exclaimed. "What did it feel like? What happened?"

Even in the darkened room, Barb could see Leah's eyes sparkling. Her face was as bright as a lighthouse beacon. Barb felt her own astonishment spread across her face; her friend had just communicated with her via telepathy. It was crazy. As crazy as learning that her childhood best friend had been her house.

Barb explained the sensation of receiving the message. Leah hung on to every word. When Barb finished, Leah shared that she had chosen this particular message because it was a simple thought she often had.

Slapping her knees, Leah exclaimed, "This is awesome!" She beamed. "Okay, it's your turn."

Repositioning herself, Barb closed her eyes. Leah's message mirrored the way she and Bella used to communicate, with full conversations and images. Barb had never questioned how; it had happened naturally. But trying to send a message to Leah wasn't the same. She struggled to find the flow, the stream of consciousness that allowed for effortless understanding. Although the connection between her and Leah was similar to the one she'd had with Bella, it paled in comparison. Bella had existed within Barb's mind—an extension of her own thoughts. That intimacy, while magical, had also been invasive. The roots of this new bond with Leah would need to deepen before telepathy became a true way for them to communicate.

Falling back on the manual's instructions, Barb reached into her being and built her spiritual energy. A swirling contentment rose and expanded within her. This energy felt like a magical cool breeze during a full eclipse of the sun, flowing through her with a gentle, serene pulse. The soothing feeling brought a deep sense of peace. As satisfaction and happiness filled her, she focused on Leah, thinking about prom and how neither of them had a dress. She pictured a midnight blue, sleeveless gown, envisioning Leah wearing it. The deep, mysterious hue highlighted Leah's clear, radiant skin. Combining the image with her energy, she released it.

"Anything?" Barb asked.

Leah scrunched her face. "I feel a pinch," she replied. "A color came to mind."

"Which one?"

"Dark blue? I think. Maybe the sky," Leah ventured.

"That was the color!" Barb burst. Relief flooded her. She had found a thread in which to send her thought. She was happy she didn't let Leah down. Telepathy was certainly exciting—a chance to explore new realms of understanding. Yet, at the same time, a nagging fear tugged at her. Telepathy meant delving deeper into the world of ghosts and spirits. This power carried responsibilities and duties to help spectral entities, like Bella, who had kidnapped them. She sensed that Leah saw this as a game, a novelty to be toyed with, and didn't understand that the abilities they were fostering came with profound implications.

"Is that what you were trying to send me?" Leah asked excitedly.

Barb explained the image she had attempted to send—the dress.

Leah described the image she received—dark blue waves, like it was a painting of the sky. She commented that Barb's image may have been too complicated but was glad she received part of it.

"Why that image?" Leah asked.

"Duh! Prom is Friday. Do you have a dress?"

"No. Do you have a date?" Leah asked.

Barb sighed. "I was going to ask Eric, but then we got snatched. I'm sure he already has a date by now."

Leah shook her head. "I still can't believe you see something in him."

Barb hadn't seen anything in him at first. Eric was a popular jock; she wouldn't have even considered being friends with him. He also had a reputation for using girls, and girls often used him to climb the social ladder. She heard the endless gossip, saw the fights in the hall, the icy glares between former friends, and felt the unspoken competition for his attention. Barb had no interest in that. But Eric had taken notice of her.

Once she began to truly see him, her perception changed. A gentleness appeared. He wasn't arrogant or mean, but rather straightforward and honest. Whether hanging with his buddies or talking with underclassmen, even those considered geeks, he had a subtle, polite kindness in his words, which drew everyone to like him. He thrived at making people feel at ease around him. The odd contrast was how people trusted him for his warmth and effortless charm, even though his reputation suggested otherwise. That reputation, however, came from people expecting something he never offered. Barb saw his true nature: he never promised more than he meant.

When his attention had shifted toward her, she began to reconsider. He had opened the door for everyone in choir but smiled specifically at her, said hi when he saw her in the hall, and caught her eye as he passed her classroom. His gestures, and the focus he gave her, had left her feeling seen and valued. She smiled at the thought of him—happy to be noticed and wanted. Combined with his good looks, Barb had found herself hoping.

With a shrug, she said, "He saw something in me. At least, I think he did."

Leah's half-grin came with a curious stare. "Have you dated before?"

Barb shifted uncomfortably. The truth was, she was seventeen and had never dated, let alone been kissed. She hadn't discussed this with anyone, and the idea of revealing it made her chest heavy.

"Um, no, not really," Barb replied, her voice barely above a whisper. She cleared her throat, attempting to regain her composure. "I've..." She paused. "I haven't exactly been in the right mindset, the accident and all." She took a breath and exhaled. "I'm kind of known as the girl whose mom went mad—murdering her husband by burning down their mansion and then committing suicide. There was a dark shadow over me that the other kids didn't understand. When you came along, you didn't know anything about me or my history. Becoming your friend felt easy."

For a moment, Leah just sat there, pity, or maybe, sadness flickering across her face. Barb dropped her gaze feeling rather pathetic.

"Hey," Leah whispered.

Barb looked up to see a tender smile.

"We are getting you a date." A mischievous grin tugged at the corner of Leah's lips. "Connect with every boy you meet and send them the feeling of love."

The statement confirmed Barb's suspicions; Leah viewed telepathy as a gimmick, a tool for manipulation or a party trick. Of course, Leah was teasing, but the ability to penetrate a person's mind wasn't a joking matter. Giving a half-hearted chuckle, Barb said, "This is supposed to be used to help souls transcend, not get me a date." She paused, then added, "Besides, we're going to be famous. Maybe someone will ask me tomorrow."

"You are beautiful. I know you'll get a date." Leah grabbed Barb's hands. "And then my mom will take us dress shopping. She'll make us look amazing."

Barb wasn't feeling confident. She knew she wasn't ugly, but she wasn't exactly a Margot Robbie either. Plus, who knew what was going to happen when they arrived at school, or how they were going to be received. She wanted to go to prom, desperately wanted to go, but it was only three days away. "Can I join you and Dan if I can't get a date?"

"You are getting a date, and we'll all go together. Tomorrow we're asking Eric. He's going to say yes. Remember, you and I are the Banisher Women of Lake Valley! Be confident."

"Leah, are you sure you want to be a Banisher? I mean … ghosts, spirits, trauma, heartache. This power is for a profession, to help those who are possessed."

"I feel strangely drawn to it, like it's calling me. You don't feel it?"

"Not really," Barb murmured. But she had to admit, it was intriguing. "Do you want to keep training?"

"Yes," Leah responded.

They practiced for another hour before calling it quits. Leah had been able to send Barb two other impressions, an image of Dan and the feeling of hunger. Barb tried unsuccessfully to send the taste of chocolate, an image of a cherry blossom, and the need to sleep. She was finally successful sending the feeling of sadness.

"We'll get the hang of it," Leah encouraged. "It just takes practice."

"I'm not sad. This is kind of amazing, but…" Barb paused, chewing on the inside of her lower lip again. "This was how I talked with … you know who, and I'm not sure this path is for me."

Grandma Carol knocked on the door. "Time for bed. It's a school night."

Leah stood, pressing the manual into Barb's arms. "Read the book but keep it secret. The meditations and exercises will help you. You'll find peace, and then we'll start from the beginning together." Leah peered into her eyes. "No one will be able to hurt us again."

Barb gave a weak smile and nodded.

Leah pulled her into a hug and said, "We're asking Eric to prom. Be confident that 'yes' will be his answer."

After Leah went to her borrowed room, Barb could hear her through the wall, talking with her grandfather on the phone. They seemed to be arguing about bodyguards to protect her. Barb shuddered at the thought.

Lying in bed, Barb's thoughts turned to Eric, and she wondered if she could allow herself to hope. Who was she kidding, Eric could have anybody he wanted; he'd never choose her. He was sure to have a date already. Dread seeped into her chest—dread for going to school, dread for appearing on TV, and dread for knowing Eric would probably reject her. But as she closed her eyes, a soothing sensation enveloped her like a gentle embrace, washing away her tension and settling into her heart—calmness.

Leah ended the call with her grandfather, the two of them settling on making her uncle Tim her bodyguard. Her grandfather was certain the abduction was a plot to extort information and money from him. He had formed that opinion based on news reports and what the police had told him, not on what had really happened. Leah almost shouted that it was a ghost that had taken her. Her grandfather was so obstinate, always insisting on his way.

Letting the frustration drain, she plugged in her phone and stared at the familiar family photos on the walls; Barb, Dan, and Grandma Carol smiled back at her. Barb's house had become Leah's sanctuary after her dad had been abducted. Sitting on this bed, in this room, Leah could breathe easily. Her rosary hung from the dresser handle, her books *Pachinko* by Min Jin Lee and *The Energy of Prayer* by Thich Nhat Hanh were next to her bed, and her clothes had been neatly folded and placed in the closet.

Laying her head on her pillow, Leah re-examined her use of telepathy. She had power and learning how to hone it would guarantee protection for herself and those she loved. She would never be helpless again.

Exhaustion pulled at her, but she needed to try one more time to send something to Barb. This time it would be an emotion, one they both needed: calmness.

Leah could feel Barb's dread through their connection, so she closed her eyes and pictured Barb enveloped in a gentle energy that coaxed her as she stood in a field of sunflowers. The golden faces swayed in the cool warmth of a perfect sunny day. A nearby waterfall sang the relaxing melody of cascading waters, which sparkled in the sunlight. The air was sweet, the breeze caressing, and her toes sunk into soft soil. This emotion was Barb. It lived in Barb. Barb's mind was clear, drifting lazily like fluffy white clouds in the clean blue sky. Her lungs filled with pure, refreshing tranquility. The flow of water and the twittering of goldfinches created a harmonious backdrop inviting her to simply be. For Barb, and now Leah, calmness wasn't an absence of stress, but a vibrant, living experience, soothing every part of their being. The images and the feeling were strong. They built their own spiritual energy within Leah, and she sent the calm emotion to Barb.

Feeling a wave of peace wash through her, Leah turned off the light and snuggled into her pillow. The darkness, however, bit and snarled. She could feel herself on the edge of the void—a place of absolute nothingness where Bellevue had trapped her. Panic surged. Leah's heart pounded, and her breath came in short, rapid gasps. Memories of *The Magic Flute's* "Queen of the Aria" echoed in her mind, a haunting refrain that played over and over.

"No!" she shouted, placing both hands on the bed and pushing herself up. She covered her face, which dripped with cold sweat. The void receded, but the fear remained—the debilitating pain that Bellevue had delivered fresh in her mind. She touched the scab on her forehead, tracing the mark Bellevue had left while reclaiming her. Paralyzed, Leah had crashed to the floor. The powerlessness she had experienced that day drummed through her. Leah couldn't sleep alone, not tonight.

She slipped out of bed, tiptoed across the hall to Dan's room, and paused at the door. Her heart raced as she pushed it open and moved to his bed. Sliding under the covers beside him, she kissed his cheek.

"You okay?" Dan asked, his voice slurred with drowsiness.

"Yeah. Just need you to hold me."

Dan pulled Leah close to him and laid her head on his chest. His strong hands rubbed her back, his warmth chasing away the chilling emptiness of the void. In Dan's arms, she knew she was safe, not because he held her, but because she had newfound powers that were growing. Her breathing gradually slowed, and she began to think about the future—prom, graduation, Stanford. She wanted to study cognitive science. Maybe the power she had was somehow connected to that field of study. Having a deeper understanding of the human mind should provide some answers.

Leah wondered if her relationship with Dan could survive the transition to college. Would they drift apart? The thought made her heart ache. She didn't want to lose him, not after everything they had been through—their first kiss in her kitchen, and then their second first kiss inside Bellevue. She turned her head and kissed him again. A warm, tingling sensation spread from her skin to her very core.

Dan squeezed her tight and whispered, "I got you. Don't worry."

Leah moaned softly against his chest. *Should I teach Dan telepathy?* Maybe that would make their bond inseparable. Her fingers brushed the edges of his ear. He stirred and kissed her forehead. She wanted to connect, but ... not yet. Not without his permission.

Beyond safety, what could this power mean for her future? Could she use it to help others? To remove hate from people's minds? To gain Barb a date?

Questions suddenly swirled into Leah's mind—questions her Language Arts teacher would be asking her right now. Whose hate is justified? Can any hate be legitimate? Hate for a rapist, for a murderer, an abusive parent—are these feelings necessary for justice or healing? And what about the hate people hold against a political party, immigrants, or trans people? Does erasing this hate erase their prejudice or the reasons behind it? Does hate serve a purpose, helping us grow and learn? If she took away someone's hate, would it change who they were, or rob them of something vital to their identity?

She could see the issue being debated on stage. Did hate propel societal progress by challenging injustices, or was it always a destructive force? Could removing hate from someone's mind hinder their personal growth or resolution of their trauma? Leah had confronted Father Joseph, a priest whose entire career had been built on a foundation of hate. He had finally denounced his toxic beliefs publicly. But now, as she pondered the broader implications of her power, she found herself questioning the morality of her actions. Leah knew the answers were not simple, but these were thoughts for another time.

Nestling closer to Dan, Leah breathed in his scent. Whatever this power brought, she was ready to master it. For now, though, she allowed herself to simply be—a girl seeking solace in the arms of someone she loved.

Jared lay on his side, half-asleep, staring at the empty space beside him—the place where, until this morning, Nong had been. Inside the walls of Bellevue, they had shared a room and, for a while, even believed they might have been married. But after leaving the place, their memories had returned, and the reality of what had happened, of who and where they were, came crashing down on them both. What were their true feelings for each other? Nong needed space, and Jared had thought maybe he did too. Reaching out, his hand brushed the cold sheet, the ache of her absence settling deep in his chest. Alone in the silence, he felt hollow, as if a part of him had been left behind with her.

Closing his eyes, he drifted into a dream-like state, breathing in Nong's scent and feeling her smooth skin. Her upbeat, positive nature and caring spirit filled his thoughts as he reminisced about their past few days. They had been relaxed, happy, and in love. That couldn't have been all Bellevue, could it? If it had, why was he feeling so lonely and lost without her?

Opening his eyes, he found Nong there, her gaze meeting his, pulling him towards her. He maneuvered himself next to her, pressing his body against hers, stroking her forehead and hair. He leaned in to kiss her, but she giggled, placing a hand to his lips.

"Whoa, Jared, wait ... this isn't a dream. This is me. I'm here."

Jerking back, Jared blinked hard. "Nong?" he whispered. Rubbing his eyes, he asked, "But how?"

She reached out her hand and placed it alongside his face, her thumb brushing his cheek. "We are still connected."

"But," he stammered, "we're not inside Bellevue anymore."

"I know," she replied. "I don't quite understand it either, but here we are."

He traced his finger over her temple and down her cheek with a tender touch. "You feel so real."

Her smile glowed. "So, you miss me."

"Very much."

Her eyes searched his. "But...?"

"No buts," he replied, shaking his head.

She scrutinized him. "How? How can there be no buts after what I did to you?"

"It's not your fault," Jared stressed. "You are not to blame. We've had this conversation already."

"I know, but you're free now," she murmured. With thick, raw guilt, she added, "I tricked you."

"You were doing what you needed to do to get back to your daughter."

"A person should be judged by their actions, especially in the face of adversity."

"Then I judge you as a dedicated mother who loves her daughter fiercely. When someone loves like that, I know they're good."

"You think I'm good?" she repeated in disbelief, as if testing the words on her tongue. "Tyler did to me what I did to you, and I hated him with every bone in my body."

"Nong," Jared whispered, cupping her face, "none of this was your fault. You are not to blame."

She took his hand and placed it over her heart, which thrummed hard and fast.

Jared felt the bold, steady pounding, her skin warm against his palm. "Is that for me?" he asked.

"Jared," she breathed. "I need to know ... do you love me?"

Looking deep into her eyes, he replied, "I love you, Nong Ekamai."

"Then show me. I need to feel that love."

Jared ran his hand down her side, grabbed hold of her shirt, and pulled it up, over her head.

She helped him remove his shirt and pulled him on top of her as they locked lips. Her legs wrapped around his waist, drawing him closer. They fell into a rhythmic beat, both releasing the angst that had come between them after their captivity. The truth was happening now, and they were rebuilding what they'd had inside the walls of Bellevue.

Mr. Anderson closed the door and surveyed his new quarters, a modest space with a bed, a desk, a couple of chairs, and a closet. The room was functional, nothing more, but suited his needs perfectly. He placed both his suitcases and a camera bag on the bed and began to unpack.

First, he pulled out his listening devices, small and inconspicuous, and set them aside on the desk. Next came his computers—two laptops, each equipped with specialized software. Then his gadgets, used for hacking into security systems. Unpacking the second case, he hung his suits in the closet. His mind drifted to Leah. He felt certain she was his target, and his excitement for getting into her mind and uncovering the depths of her abilities left him wide awake.

Leah wasn't just any girl. Recruiting her was going to be a challenge. He couldn't simply manipulate her mind as Ruth had done to him. For one, he didn't know the extent of her powers. Additionally, other forces would be against him: the Circle, Stanford, and her grandfather. First, he needed to document her abilities, proving she was vital to the company so that Dr. Smith could showcase her value and necessity. Once this was achieved, the actual recruiting could begin. He'd need to understand her dreams, her fears, and her ambitions. If manipulating her through a connection wasn't possible, knowing this girl inside and out would allow him to influence her through more traditional means.

Sliding his empty suitcase under the bed, Mr. Anderson went to the window and looked at the Davenport's house, three doors down and across the street. Jared's Honda Civic sat in the driveway, but Leah's Audi was nowhere to be seen. Maybe it was in the garage. Maybe she was with her mom at the hotel. After tonight, though, he'd be sure to know where she was at all times.

His phone buzzed. The caller ID displayed "Dr. Smith," and he answered immediately, anticipating a new order. "Mr. Anderson," he announced.

Without preamble, Dr. Smith delivered the news: "Bill Stillen hired two bodyguards to shadow Leah to ensure her safety without her knowledge."

Mr. Anderson's stomach dropped. Two bodyguards? "Fuck…" If those two idiots got in his way, or worse, if Leah discovered them, his task would become exponentially harder.

"Calm down," Dr. Smith said. "Ruth intervened. She convinced Bill that you'd be a more effective option, and now your being in Lake Valley has an official purpose. Nothing has changed, however. Get your proof, and make sure she stays safe."

Exhaling slowly, Mr. Anderson said, "While I have you on the line, I need documents to procure a substitute teacher position. I'll email the list."

He ended the call and opened his computer, sending the email. Then, lying on his back in bed with his hands clasped over his chest, he allowed a giant grin to cover his face. This was fun. He loved the hunt.

Prom Date

The next day, a whirlwind of activity began when Leah and Barb left the house at 10:30 for school. Photographers took their pictures, and the press bombarded them with questions. As they approached the school, a news camera filmed them entering the building beneath a vibrant banner stretched across the entrance, with bold letters welcoming Leah and Barb back.

Leah turned to Barb with a broad smile. "Wow, they went all out!"

Barb gave a sheepish grin. "They really shouldn't have."

The bell rang, marking the end of third period. They entered the school and were greeted by their classmates with warm smiles, friendly pats on the back, and acknowledging nods.

"I'm so glad you're okay, Leah!" one student exclaimed, giving her a quick hug.

"Leah. Missed you. Glad you two are back," a boy from her humanity's class said.

Everyone stared. Leah noticed on more than one occasion that someone wanted to offer some words of support but was either too shy or unsure of what to say.

A boy with shaggy hair and a shirt stained with paint stopped them dead in their tracks, staring with glassy, unblinking eyes. "Missed you guys."

A teacher patted the boy on the shoulder and said, "Let them pass, Luke."

The boy shuffled to the side, an awestruck grin on his face.

"So happy to see you again," the teacher told the girls. "We're holding a special assembly in your honor. Put your things in your locker and head to the gym."

After the teacher left, Barb rolled her eyes. "I hope they don't make us give a speech."

Leah grinned. Being back and walking these halls felt strange. The comfort of familiar faces and routines was juxtaposed against her new self. The old normal now screamed artificial.

Squeezing Barb's hand, Leah said, "I'll see you in the gym."

Leah and Barb parted ways, each heading to their respective lockers. Turning the corner, Leah caught sight of hers and stopped, taking in a quick breath. It stood out among the others, adorned with an array of colorful notes, drawings, and small tokens of friendship. Her chest warmed as she looked upon a small stuffed anime owl, a tiny duck magnet, an embroidered heart, dried carnations, a rosary, and a tassel laced with jewels, accented with a golden feather.

"This is incredible," she murmured under her breath as she approached.

Reaching out to touch the notes, she traced the words of encouragement with her fingertips. "You're amazing," "I miss you," and "Dear Leah, stay strong and come back to us. We love you," were written in vibrant colors. These words were meant for her former, naïve self. That person didn't exist anymore.

"Leah!" Yells came from down the hall. A small group of her friends rushed her—Jane, Cindy, Becky, and Tay. Hugs, kisses, and touches.

"I've missed you."

"I can't believe you'll be on the news tonight."

"You were cut. Does it hurt?"

"What happened?"

"How did you get free?"

Leah closed her eyes for a moment, letting the noise wash over her. But it was them. Her girls. Her constants. She opened her eyes and her heart, offering them a brilliant smile. Maybe that old version of herself wasn't entirely gone.

"It's good to see you guys too. I'm okay."

They held hands and made their way to the gym.

Barb wandered down the hallway, her steps steady as she grappled with the stares and nods the others gave her. Whispers and murmurs, real and imagined, drifted through the hallway. She focused on putting one foot in front of the other and holding her head high as she made her way to her locker.

The first thing she noticed was the balloons and streamers. As she got closer, she saw some flowers, a few notes, leaflets of school plays she had been involved in. She also noticed a news article about her winning the Lake Valley vocal competition. Attached to the article was a piece of paper with hand-drawn animals, stars, and a rainbow, with a note saying, "Your voice ignited my soul. We miss you and we're so sorry for the continued trauma you face. Hope you're safe." It hadn't been signed. The other notes offered generic words, wishing her well.

Barb turned and looked down the hall. Silent glances, smiles, and waves came in return. "Welcome back," she whispered. Her heart sank, but she wasn't surprised. This distance, this invisible barrier, had always been here, separating her from the rest of the world. Her thoughts went back to Eric. She had dreamed the whole scenario. She only wished he'd been paying attention to her.

Taking a deep breath, Barb straightened her posture. Her calm confidence was her armor—gained through storybook adventures, the power of her singing, and now, her secret skills. The magic she had conjured last night gave her strength; she would use it to step out of her box.

Turning around, she saw a girl across the hall close her locker. The girl glanced at Barb and gave a weak smile.

"Hi," Barb said. "Do you want to walk to the gym together?"

The girl's smile brightened. "Yeah, I'd love to."

Barb's chest unraveled, letting her breathe.

"I'm Lyla. We have chemistry together."

As they headed to the gym, Barb's steps took an assured grace. She could wield magic. She wasn't necessarily embracing this ability, but knowing that she could was all that mattered.

In the gym, Leah and Barb sat in chairs next to the principal and a few teachers, facing the bleachers. A microphone stood in front of them for the speakers.

The assembly featured the stirring melodies of the school's marching band, with drums pulsating and horns blaring. Leah found herself tapping her foot and nodding along to the beat.

The choir's angelic voices soared as they sang a heartfelt rendition of "Touch the Sky" from the movie *Brave*. Leah gave them a well-deserved applause.

A student poet took the stage. "Your absence felt like a shadow's touch. An agony, a fear we didn't dare clutch. Your smiles, a beacon in the darkest night, brought warmth and joy, a guiding light. Through trials faced and challenges won, you've returned to us, now let's have some fun!"

The cheerleaders dazzled with their spirited routines, executing flawless flips and jumps. They definitely had talent, Leah thought.

The chant started in the corner by a few students but quickly picked up until the entire student body was shouting, "Speech, speech, speech!"

Leah stepped to the microphone. "You guys are the best!"

Cheers and claps erupted.

She gathered her thoughts, remembering the coaching Bruce had given her. "Being drugged and held captive in a dark place was terrifying." The assembly room turned silent. Leah had everyone's attention, and, as she scanned the bleachers, she realized she was lying to them all. "Not knowing where we were or what was going to happen was..." She paused. "It's a special kind of horror. But knowing that you were here, that my friends and family were not going to give up, gave me hope. I heard your prayers. They gave me strength to endure. I love you all. Thank you."

Stepping back from the microphone, Leah felt guilt gnawing at her chest. This lie, the cover story, didn't feel right. Why? It wasn't all a lie.

Barb opted not to speak, and afterwards, Leah made her way to class, recognizing Eric Sorenson strolling boldly down the crowded hallway.

"Hey, Eric, wait up," she called.

He stopped, modeling perfect posture, with his broad shoulders pulled back and his head held high. An undeniable ease gave him natural charisma. His eyes met Leah's, and a charming smile lit his face.

Leah's inner voice laughed. He was the quintessential high school heart-throb, and he knew it.

Just as Leah reached him, a boy wearing a varsity jacket stepped in front of her to talk with Eric.

"Boardwell ran a 0:48 four hundred yesterday. I think we got a real shot at making state. If Fitzsimmons can get his time down to 0:52 or even 0:53, we could place."

"Wut? 0:48! The dude's a freakin' speedster. Look, it's simple. Fitz needs to take off sooner. I'm practically running into him during the exchange." Eric looked at Leah. "We'll talk later, Mike."

Mike turned to Leah. "Hi, Leah." Then he did a double take. "Oh. See ya at practice."

"Hey, Leah," Eric said. "Welcome back. You guys going missing really shook things up around here. You okay?"

A group of girls giggled as they passed. "Hi, Eric."

He gave them an acknowledging nod, his blue eyes twinkling.

Leah watched them pass and one of them gave her a curious look. Turning back to Eric, she said, "I'm fine." She mustered her most charming smile and asked, "Any chance you can join me for lunch? I've got something I want to talk to you about." She hoped her approach would pique his interest enough that he'd agree. Barb wanted to go to prom with him, so she was going into *Mission Possible* mode to help make that happen.

Swiping his blond hair, Eric gazed into her eyes in a flirtatious manner. "Lunch with the famous Leah? How could I say no? Will Barb be joining us?"

"Yes, she will. She wanted to talk with you, actually."

"Count me in!" Eric laid his hand on her arm.

Leah placed her hand over his, looked him in the eyes, and sent her energy to connect— A sudden jolt of electricity bit her. Instinctively, she pulled her hand back. The surge caused the muscles at the base of her neck to tighten. Had she just felt a ghost?

"Did I shock you?" Eric asked.

Leah opened her mouth to respond but paused. Her thoughts were racing through what she knew about connecting. She vaguely recalled what would happen if someone were possessed—she would receive emotions, thoughts, and memories from the soul who possessed that person. Her breath was uneasy. If she connected to him, she'd be battling a spirit. Was she ready to do this again?

Shaking her head in disbelief, she chuckled. *I'm being paranoid*, she thought. Eric must be right; he had just shocked her. "Yeah. You zapped me," she said.

"Sorry about that. I got a new computer that makes my head buzz. I'm thinking there's a loose wire or something."

"You might want to get that checked out," Leah suggested. She was hoping Eric was right, but she didn't think so. Still wanting to connect, she calmed her imagination and asked, "Can I see your hand?"

Eric turned it over before offering it to her.

She reached, but hesitated. *Please don't be a ghost.* As Leah placed her hand in his, she moved her spiritual energy to connect, mentally bracing herself. The connection solidified, and she felt a hum. The subtle vibration left her puzzled. It didn't feel like a haunting spirit or a malevolent ghost. Was this Eric's aura? Was this the energy used to manifest a psychic impression? Did Eric know what it was? Opening her eyes, she searched his face for signs of recognition, any hint that he, too, felt the anomaly. But his eyes had turned toward onlookers, who whispered as they passed.

Eric dropped her hand. "So, lunch?"

"Yes. I'll see you in the lunchroom," Leah replied.

When lunch time rolled around, Leah informed Barb that Eric would be joining them. Barb let out a long sigh, followed by a nervous smile, and picked at her sweet corn and country fried chicken. Leah watched and waited. When he enter the lunchroom, the clicking of trays, hum of chatter, and bursts of laughter seemed to suddenly fade. With a sense of purpose, Leah rose from her seat and intercepted him before he reached their table.

"Eric." She touched his arm and looked him in the eyes again, making sure their connection was strong. "Barb's waiting for you. I'll be right back."

He nodded and continued towards Barb.

Leah watched him carefully, and when his gaze met Barb's, she sent him the feeling of lust. Leah had chosen that emotion because she remembered it so vividly. Dan in her room, her body surging. Lust was a simple, primal emotion that she could easily convey, whereas love was complicated. The question now was, did he receive it? And would it work?

When Eric Sorensen entered the lunchroom, he turned heads. Whispers rippled through the room as he made his way toward Leah's table. He was used to the attention, but today his head had a nagging, persistent fog that made it hard for him to think, and the attention made it worse.

Leah stood and walked toward him. He couldn't help but admire her—confident, fashionable, popular. He had wanted to date her once and would have if she'd showed interest, but it was Barb who had recently grabbed his attention.

She had this voice—sweet and majestic, one that made flowers bloom in winter. Barb had sung a solo in choir class that left him spellbound. She was a siren, enchanting the world around her and captivating everyone in her presence. Eric had stood speechless, unable to move, feeling his heart thrum. Since then, he had found himself watching her from afar, wanting to approach but unsure of how to bridge the gap between their social circles. Who was this woman?

Barb had been an enigma to the entire school. Her mysterious past and trauma isolated her. Unlike many of his peers, she was unconcerned with superficialities and avoided the trappings of popularity, instead valuing deep, meaningful relationships. Eric studied her, noticing her authenticity and calm confidence that commanded respect, which, oddly enough, made others unsure how to approach her. She was the ghost everyone knew about, but nobody understood. He had attempted to be her lab partner, to show her he was more than a jock and a socialite and to unlock the mystery of Barb, but she had rejected him. With Leah's invitation, this was his chance. He felt a surge of excitement and anticipation as he neared, wishing his head felt clearer.

As he leaned over to set his tray on the table, he looked into Barb's eyes. His body warmed. He had a deep yearning to touch her hair, to kiss her neck, to run his finger down her chest and touch her breasts. He caught his breath and glanced at Barb anew, seeing her in a different light. Where had these feelings come from? Was it his proximity to her? Was he truly this shallow? He acknowledged his tendency to pursue girls for superficial reasons, but Barb was different. He hadn't been attracted to her for that reason, and the cafeteria wasn't the place to be thinking such thoughts. Blushing, he quickly sat.

"Hi, Eric," Barb managed. Her glossy, full lips, smooth and inviting, formed a shy smile.

He looked away, trying to calm his racing mind and his stirring heart, then glanced at Barb's plate. She had been picking at her food, a clear sign of nervousness. "Ah, the mystery meat. Not a fan?" he asked, trying to make light conversation.

Barb's cheeks flushed. "Oh, um, no. I've had a crazy day."

The day had been full of activity, but not unlike the past week, with news vans parked outside the school, reporters prowling for interviews, and investigators questioning students about the abduction. "I'd say," he acknowledged. "These past few weeks have been crazy."

Barb smiled, and she dipped her head, eyes flicking up to meet his through her lashes. "Yes, you could say that," she murmured. "The whole experience has been..." She paused. "Intense."

"I'm glad you're okay. I was worried about you. The entire school was."

Barb's eyes warmed. "That's kind of you to say so." She quickly dropped her eyes as the room became quiet, and all eyes turned on them.

A shadow loomed over their table when Eric's date, Ashley, approached, a sly smile on her face. She wore a long-sleeve white crop shirt with a light grey pleated mini skirt carrying a designer leather purse. Her long slender legs and hourglass figure, plus her full lips painted a shade of rose, were striking. If Eric was a woman's dream, Ashley was his counterpart.

"Well, well, what do we have here?" Ashley purred, her eyes flickering between Eric and Barb. "Eric, I was wondering where you disappeared to. Seems like you found some new company."

Eric's jaw tensed, but he maintained his composure. "Hey, Ash," he greeted, trying to keep his tone casual. "Yeah, just catching up with Barb. How's it going?"

Ashley dropped her smile, replacing it with annoyance. "Oh, you know, same old. But seriously, Eric, prom's coming up, and you've ditched me to have lunch with *her?*"

Eric raised an eyebrow at Ashley's accusation. "Ditched you? Really, Ash?" he retorted. "I thought you'd have a little more empathy, considering this is Barb's first day back. She's been through a lot and deserves some support."

Ashley's lips twisted into a smirk. "Oh, sorry you had to go through that," she said sarcastically, her tone dripping with insincerity. "Must have been a real crappy time." She bent over and ran her nails up the back of Eric's neck, attempting to kiss him. Eric adjusted his position, avoiding her lips. "Not here, Ash," he whispered.

Her disappointed huff was warm against his cheek. "Come on. Let's go," she urged, grabbing his hand.

He pulled away. "No, I'm going to have lunch with Barb."

Ashley scoffed, "Barb? Seriously? She's, like, invisible." Her stare went past Barb. "Ah. I see what's happening."

Eric followed her gaze and saw Leah, who stood next to the window with her head bowed as if in prayer.

"This isn't about Barb, this is about Leah. Are you thinking about taking Leah to prom instead of me?"

Barb slunk into her seat, small and silent, like a mouse hiding in the corner.

Eric shook his head, returning his gaze to Ashley. "It's not about Leah, Ash. Barb's a great person." A touch of irritation crept into his voice. "Maybe if you could open up a bit, understand people better, you'd see that."

Ashley's expression hardened. "Don't give me that line of crap. I heard about you and Leah holding hands in the hall. A couple of love birds reuniting."

"It's not what you think. We're just having lunch. You know, with the two celebs." Eric reached for her hand, but this time she pulled away. "Come on, Ash. I'll hook up with you after practice tonight."

"Don't bother." A mixture of frustration and hurt flickered across her features. "I understand people just fine. You're choosing to spend time with *her* instead of me, with prom around the corner." She paused, her gaze narrowing. "Maybe you should understand that if you can't prioritize our relationship over some girl you barely know, then maybe you're not worth my time either." With a scowl, she turned and strolled away.

Eric placed his hands on the table and pushed himself up. He needed to go after her, to smooth things over, to salvage his opportunity to sleep with her. He was going to showcase her as his prom date, to bask in the envy of others, and then consummate their partnership later that evening.

No! A desperate panic stung him. The thought had come out of nowhere, stopping him where he stood. He touched his head and grunted, then sat back down and thought about Ashley. She was shallow and superficial. Barb, on the other hand, was someone special, someone he had been thinking about before her disappearance.

Taking a deep breath, Eric shook his head, dispelling the allure of Ashley's beauty. She wasn't worth it. He'd been with several different girls similar to Ashley, and although he enjoyed the sex and wanted it with her, in the end, it would mean nothing. He covered his eyes and tried to relax. The stress was making his headache worse.

Turning back to Barb, he offered her a genuine smile. "Sorry about that. Drama seems to follow everyone before prom."

"I hear the gossip," Barb said. "And I've only been back a few hours."

Eric leaned his head toward her, getting a better look at her eyes. "How long have you been singing?"

The question was genuine, but his current thought was: would he take her to prom instead of Ashley? He could hear the scandalous nonstop wheel of talk turn already, and wasn't sure Barb would accept a proposal from him. He wasn't her type. He had too many jealous contenders and was too popular. His thoughts went back to Ashley. Maybe her storming off was simply a test. He could make up with her. Her fabulous body reappeared in his thoughts, and an ache stabbed at his heart. *She was almost mine.*

Barb spoke in a tone so soft, Eric wasn't sure he heard her. "Would you consider holding off on my answer until we dance? I mean, since you don't have a prom date, maybe we could go together."

"Umm..." The question was unexpected. Eric was stunned. Barb had charm, and definitely had more substance and personality than Ashley. He nodded, admiring her boldness. With a heartfelt grin, he said, "I'd be honored to hear your story as we dance at prom."

After lunch, Barb walked through the hall to her next class. Her steps were slow and dazed. Just last night she had refused to allow herself to hope, and now... What had just happened? A giant smile formed, broke, and then reformed. She clutched her hands together and raised them to her forehead. She had to breathe. No. She had to slow her breathing. Sticking her knuckles in her mouth, she spun in a circle and gave a silent apology to hope. *I swear, I'll never give up on you again.*

She mouthed the words: *Eric Sorensen. My prom date.* A giddy giggle escaped her lips. Would he kiss her? Would he try to take advantage of the special night and want more? She could allow herself to dream, but what did that dream look like? Her mind was racing through scenarios that she had read about in books and seen in movies—the perfect gentleman, the spontaneous and assertive kiss, and the heartfelt declaration of love. This was her senior year of high school, and she wanted to be kissed, to be swept off her feet and drowned in a feverish passion. But having no experience to draw on, and only her novels as a guide, she'd have to rely on Eric to do his thing.

Barb's lips stretched into a wide, unstoppable smile. She was chiseling a new shape for herself, and it felt good.

Deep in her core, power surged.

Leah closed her locker and leaned back, resting her head against the cool metal. She stared up at the ceiling tiles with a euphoric sense of accomplishment. Her little stint had worked. Connecting to Eric had allowed her to help Barb get a date to prom with freaking Eric Sorensen! She hadn't been sure she could do it. But the thrill of the challenge had bolstered her ability to send an emotion and give a thought in real-time. She had changed Eric's mind mid-thought. The moment was nothing short of incredible.

She had to calm herself. Standing straight, she shook her hands while noticing students' renewed looks at her. Some passed their phones, showing their friend some mysterious contents before they returned their gaze. Could social media already be buzzing about Barb and Eric going to prom together?

Rushing to class, Leah sat at her desk just as the bell rang. The girl next to her leaned over and whispered, "Can you say a prayer for my grandmother? She's suffering from osteoarthritis and diabetes."

Leah gave a puzzled stare, unsure she had heard her correctly. "Sorry?"

"My grandmother's in pain, and if you have a direct connection to the div—"

A loud, wailing alarm swallowed the student's words. Leah's hands gripped the desk as her body seized in place. *The lockdown siren!* Its piercing blast assaulted her ears, and she covered them to steady herself. The merciless, persistent ring pushed everyone to move. Chairs and desks scraped across the floor and students rushed to huddle in the corner. The alarm stopped, but the flashing red light continued to pulse, splattering the walls in the color of blood.

Leah's skin prickled, her heartbeat thudded in her ears, and her muscles were so tight she could barely breathe. She watched the teacher lock the door, the click echoing like a death call. After Mr. Eastman covered the windows, he demanded silence, snuffing out the last panicked whispers.

Each second felt like an eternity, the quiet haunting.

Minutes passed in silence, but this didn't mean safety; they were counting down. How soon until the sound of gunshots shattered nerves, and screams flooded the school? Social media and news images flashed through Leah's mind. *Deadly Attack. Twelve Massacred. Grieving Parents.* Leah looked to her peers, seeing they wore the terror she felt.

Time ticked. Her chest knotted tighter. This wasn't a drill.

A metallic *ting* from the air vent caused heads to snap and bodies to jump. A boy scrambled to the trash can and threw up. A girl gagged in response. Whimpers rippled through the group.

"Shhhh..."

The student next to Leah grabbed her hand and whispered in prayer. Leah took a boy's hand and bowed her head. She felt a touch on her shoulder, a second one on her back, followed by a third. A fourth hand lay on her elbow. This was her opportunity to build spiritual energy. The book had mentioned other abilities, but they were far beyond her. Could her subconscious somehow find and use that knowledge?

"Dear Lord, hear our prayer," Leah began when the intercom crackled. All eyes turned to the speaker. Leah held her breath with the others, waiting for guidance, for reassurance, for any shred of information to alleviate their fears.

"All clear. Teachers, please check your emails and brief your students."

A collective sigh of relief filled the room. Leah let out her own breath and turned to the girl beside her. They wrapped each other in a quick, shaky hug, and her muscles eased from the warmth. The boy next to her offered his hand and helped her stand. A sharp, sour smell stung, and she recoiled.

"Oh my God," a girl groaned. "Did you really have to throw up?"

"Hey," the teacher responded with a raised voice. "We all handle stress differently. Let's give each other a little grace, okay? Take a deep breath and relax. We're safe."

Leah placed her finger against her nose and went back to her seat. The intercom crackled a second time, silencing the room.

"Mr. Eastman, can you send Leah Davenport to the office, please?"

Curiosity and speculation spread through the class. Leah began to shake. The last time she had been called to the office, her dad had gone missing.

"What happened?"

"Her dad again?"

"Her mom?"

"I'll go with her," came a voice.

"Me too," said another.

Mr. Eastman agreed. "Leah, don't let your imagination run wild. I'm sure it's nothing, but whatever it is, we're here for you."

Leah wiped the blur from her eyes. "Thank you."

The walk toward the office was kin to a death march. The two students with her tried to joke, but Leah heard nothing. Tunnel vision hit her, and her surroundings turned black. She stumbled but was caught by the two next to her.

Was the lockdown her fault somehow? *Is someone trying to kill me? Who would be after me? And why?*

Seoul, Korea

<u>Puppets and Strings</u>

Brandon unpacked his bags and situated himself into his tiny one-room apartment a block from Su-Bin's law office. Aside from a bed, the room held a wardrobe, a kitchenette, and little table.

Yoona's voice entered his mind. *Brandon, go to the coffee shop on the ground floor of Moon Law and Associates. There you will find a man interviewing for the English teaching position. Introduce yourself and sit for an interview. The man's name is Jong-In Park. He's not expecting you, so be insistent.*

Brandon remembered Choi telling him that his aunt had the ability to talk using telepathy, but he never imagined experiencing the sensation firsthand.

Washing his hands and face, Brandon wondered why he wasn't expected. Couldn't Yoona simply announce him as a candidate? He grabbed his jacket, scooped up his laptop, and headed for the coffee shop.

The café was located on the ground floor of the law office. Brandon ordered a chocolate drink and a cookie, then sat at a nearby table, where a Korean man was interviewing an Australian fellow for an English teaching position. While eavesdropping, Brandon reminisced of his days teaching in Mexico, Thailand, and Japan. Faces of students he had taught filtered through his mind, eliciting a warm smile before a pang of regret colored his thoughts. A bittersweet memory nudged him—the souring of a past romantic entanglement with Gabriela. Had the CIA really looked into her? She was a striking woman, fun and energetic, but the foundation of their relationship was built on flirtatious lust and raw chemistry. Brandon chortled, recognizing that he hadn't quite learned his lesson.

In Thailand, he had gotten involved in a second ill-fated relationship. Because of those experiences, he had been hesitant to pursue a romance with Hina. They remained friends, taking time to learn and discover each other. His growing feelings for her had driven him to learn more Japanese. He had a desire to communicate fluently with her parents should they ever meet. That commitment demonstrated his dedication to her. Brandon felt thankful that they had waited to transition into dating. When they finally did, it felt like a masterful chef had allowed a dish to simmer until it reached the pinnacle of flavor and perfection. He quickly shook away the memories before he began to cry.

The interview ended and the applicant left. The guy leaned back, letting out a tortured sigh.

"Hi," Brandon said.

The man glanced at him, and flashed a smile.

"Are you looking for an English teacher?" Brandon asked.

"Yes, I am interviewing applicants all day today."

"My name is Brandon Spencer."

"I'm Jong-In Park. Nice to meet you."

Brandon shifted in his seat, squaring his shoulders to him. "Jong-In Park. I'm supposed to interview with you."

"Oh? What did you say your name was?" Jong-In looked at the list of candidates on his computer.

"Brandon Spencer. Yoona sent me."

The bells above the door jingled and two girls entered, loud and giggly.

"Yoona?" Jong-In questioned.

"That's right," Brandon replied.

"I'm sorry. I don't have you on my list. Who is Yoona?"

"She's..." Brandon paused, unsure how to answer. *This is so silly.* He pulled his badge and ID from his pocket. "I'm a special agent with the FBI." Brandon handed his ID to Jong-In. "I'm in Korea for training. Yoona is my supervisor. She sent me here to work with Moon Law and Associates."

After studying Brandon's badge, Jong-In stood, handing it back with both hands. "I'm Jong-In Park, IT specialist with Graphics Corp." Jong-In handed Brandon his card.

"IT specialist," Brandon acknowledged. "Big money in that field. You're not part of the law firm?"

"I'm helping my friend."

"I see." From behind the counter, a grinder whirled to life, drawing Jong-In's attention. Brandon took the opportunity to move tables. "Shall we begin?"

"Uh, wait. You are an FBI agent. Why would you teach English?"

"I have a teaching degree from the University of Oregon and six years of teaching experience. I have all my information—résumé, degrees, and such—on my laptop. I can email them to you."

"That's fine. But I still don't understand why you are here. What interest do you have in our law firm?"

"I was told to interview, so that's what I'm doing."

Jong-In furrowed his brow. "Yoona sent you? Do you know Yoona's proper title? Do you have her card?"

"I don't. I'm sorry," Brandon said. "I'm sure I can get it for you. In the meantime, why don't we begin the interview?"

The two girls slid into the table Brandon had vacated, coffees in one hand, phones in the other, snickering at some shared gossip.

"We are looking for a full-time teacher," Jong-In said, "a minimum six-month contract. If you are working for the FBI, then I don't think it's possible for you to do both."

"I see your point. But I won't be working with the FBI while I'm working with you. My supervisor sent me here specifically to see you. She told me you would be here interviewing for the position. I was instructed to meet you and interview."

"I'm sorry, but I wasn't informed. My email is on my card, go ahead and send me your credentials, and I'll take a look at them. If you are a fit, I'll get in touch."

Yoona's voice entered Brandon's mind. *Jong-In's next interview isn't for another two hours, buy him lunch.*

"I'm here now. Let me buy you lunch, and we'll talk. I'm only here to interview. You don't have to hire me."

Glancing at his watch, Jong-in nodded. "Okay."

After they ordered, Brandon told Jong-In about his family and how many of them were teachers. He explained his teaching philosophy and how he structured unit plans and individual lessons.

At first, Jong-In nodded along with a polite smile while jotting down a few notes, but as Brandon talked about different teaching methods and learning styles, Jong-In set his pad on the table and fixed his gaze on Brandon's lips.

Brandon shared his excitement for inspiring students and how he, himself, learned languages. Then he transitioned into his recent positions as a police officer, a detective, and now an FBI agent, skipping over the supernatural aspects of the story.

After lunch, he emailed his documents and thanked Jong-In for his time. As he shook his hand, he stared him in the eyes and connected. Brandon left the coffee shop and sent Jong-In feelings of accomplishment and success.

Yoona's voice returned, but this time she scolded Brandon. *Manipulating one's mind for personal gain leads to corruption. Reflect on that when you meditate tonight.*

Brandon tapped his head, taking note of what she had said.

At the table inside, Jong-In sat for a moment, sorting through his thoughts and emotions. *Confidence? Success?* Those feelings didn't belong to him, and that made him feel unsettled. In truth, Mr. Park was conflicted. On one hand, Brandon was the perfect candidate. He had the experience, knowledge, passion, and the resources to assist the firm. Being in law enforcement was an advantage. He could speak several languages and had a great personality. On the other hand, he was mysterious. His whole situation seemed odd and out of place. Why would an FBI agent, who was currently employed, want to teach English at their law firm? Was Brandon a spy? Was Su-Bin under investigation? It would be ridiculous for the government to send an agent to infiltrate the law firm in such an open way.

Jong-In Park couldn't wait to tell Su-Bin about Brandon. He wondered what she would think.

Su-Bin faced the jury with her notes in hand, ready to deliver her closing arguments. After three months of investigation and preparation, plus a week and a half of witness testimony that involved examination, cross-examination, and presenting evidence, the trial was nearly over. The prosecution had finished their closing arguments, and they were convincing. On paper, the company was not liable, and the driver was guilty. However, in practice, the story was different.

Winning this case now hinged on Su-Bin's ability to convince the jury that her client had been doing his job as asked of him by the company. That was going to be a tough sell, even though it was absolutely true. Jong-In's words rolled through Su-Bin's mind, *Keep the passion, lose the anger*. With that reminder, she began.

"Ladies and gentlemen of the jury, this has been an arduous trial. We all know why laws around alcohol exist—it's a dangerous drug and must be kept away from children. If children drink this poison, death is a real consequence. We lost a young teenager due to alcohol poisoning. We are grieving. Our hearts go out to the parents who will never recover from this loss. We ask ourselves, 'Why did this happen? Who is to blame?'

"The prosecution presented a compelling argument for why the delivery driver is responsible for this tragedy. They told us what the law says. They talked about the systems and procedures that the company has in place. They reminded us of the testimonies from the director, supervisors, and managers regarding driver training. They bombarded us with the fact that drivers receive constant and consistent reminders of how to properly deliver alcohol. The argument was neat and tidy and true ... on paper.

"As I listened to the argument, though, it reminded me of fast food—the pictures always look so good, but what I actually get is very different. The paper truth you heard from the prosecution is not the reality of what happens at Delivery, Inc."

Su-Bin paced a few steps, raising the suspense of her assertion.

"The prosecution's argument is a mere Halloween costume that is brought out and worn once a year, for the inspectors and authorities to see. After they say, 'Good job,' and sign the forms, the costume is put away. Delivery, Inc. needs this costume so they can profit from breaking the law."

She paused to let this metaphor sink in.

"The decision you are about to make is not just a guilty or not-guilty verdict. Your judgement carries far more weight, with implications that extend beyond this courtroom. You are about to tell every single company and corporation whether or not it is okay for them to deliberately break the law to make a profit—and then simply brush off the consequences like a flake of dandruff for someone else to sweep up. By reviewing the evidence and testimonies from the workers, trainers, and an administrator, we can uncover what really happens at Delivery, Inc."

She made eye contact with one of the jurors.

"Let's start with this question: would we be here if the defendant had been sick that day and a different driver was working?

"To answer this question, we need to first understand the motive of the crime. The company pays the delivery drivers only for packages that are delivered. If the customer is unavailable and the package has to be returned, the drivers make no money for their time and effort. Therefore, the company has created a motive for the drivers to deliver every package.

"Drivers who return with undelivered packages are ridiculed. A manager will badger and harass them. Other drivers will laugh at them. Why? From a driver's perspective, returning a package creates more work. The packages that are brought back must be redelivered the next day with all of the new packages. For the company, undelivered packages mean they must hire additional workers to unload, sort, and store the packages. Storage space is tight, so if every driver brought back packages, the company would need to invest money in more storage areas. By shaming the drivers who return packages, fewer are brought back. The company saves money on wages and storage space, and thus Delivery, Inc. profits when the law is disobeyed."

Again she paused, looking from one juror to another.

"Next, the company values speed. Drivers are measured by how fast they can finish. If drivers leave a package at its destination instead of following the proper procedures, they save an average of five minutes per stop. The faster a driver delivers, the more packages can be on the truck. For drivers, this means they can make more money. For the company, this means they need fewer trucks on the road. Fewer trucks means money saved on gas, maintenance, insurance, etc. Therefore, Delivery, Inc. profits when the law is disobeyed.

"The slowest drivers with the most returned packages are doing their job correctly. Yet, several employees have testified that administrators not only ridicule these drivers but also punish them by giving them fewer days to work, pushing them to quit, or even firing them outright. Because of this, drivers began to talk about unionizing, which the corporation quickly abolished. We have presented news clips and interviews of this as evidence."

Several jurors nodded, recalling those videos.

Su-Bin went on, "Because the company is anti-union, drivers have no way to fight back. However, several drivers did file complaints with the Department of

Labor, but to no avail. One driver sued the company, unsuccessfully, for wrongful termination. In all of these cases, drivers complained that it is physically impossible to deliver the number of packages in the time frame the company desires without breaking the law. That includes traffic laws, like obeying the speed limit and stopping at stop signs, in addition to properly delivering alcohol. Drivers are forced to make unconscionable decisions. Do they disobey the law, or risk being fired?"

She let the jury consider this impossible dilemma, then continued.

"If the defendant were fired, he and his family would be homeless. The conflict drivers face every day about whether to leave a box or not is incredibly stressful and outrageous. The company should be on the side of the law; however, Delivery, Inc. *profits when the law is disobeyed.*

"The prosecution stressed that all drivers go through rigorous training. Let's review that process. Several trainers testified about standard practice—leaving a package if certain conditions apply. The defendant's trainer listed three such conditions. The first was if the customer had agreed that a box could be left if no one was available. The second was if there was a good hiding place for the box. The third was if the house or business couldn't be viewed from the street. And as we heard from the witnesses who were there that day, the box was hidden. These conditions, known as standard practice, break the law. The defendant was trained to break the law, which means Delivery, Inc., in turn, broke the law.

"You heard the prosecution reiterate that drivers are given constant reminders. However, the reminders are in the form of a small sticker adhered to the box and a tiny pop-up screen that appears on the driver's scanner each time they scan a box. The first time the defendant saw that screen, his trainer dismissed it, saying, 'Oh, don't worry about that. It's nothing.' The employees who testified all agreed that they had never read this pop-up screen, only clicked the accept button to make it go away. Drivers are being trained to view the reminder as 'nothing to worry about.' Do the drivers receive reminders about policies for alcohol delivery in other ways?

"No! The defendant received no additional training and no other reminders. There are no posters or pamphlets outlining procedures or consequences for policy violations. The website doesn't list the procedures. The company doesn't have a video. These things cost money and go against standard practice. Of the employees who testified, more than half of them were unaware of the consequences for violating approved procedures. Yet, every single one of them knew they could be fired if they didn't follow standard practice, which means breaking the law."

Su-Bin moved in front of the jury foreperson as she drew near her conclusion.

"Finally, we heard from an administrator in the head office who testified that the company knows drivers are not following procedures. She testified that the company actively refuses to address the problem. The company could not produce a single piece of evidence that disciplinary actions were taken against drivers for following standard practice. Not a single meeting, letter, note, call, message—nothing. But drivers who obey the law have been fired because Delivery, Inc. profits when the law is disobeyed.

"Would we be here if the driver had been sick that day and a different driver was working? Yes! That box of alcohol would have been left in the same place by any number of drivers because that is what the company expects and how drivers are rewarded. The defendant wasn't lazy or negligent—he was following standard practice. He was doing what he was trained to do. Children, right now, today, can find a box of alcohol at a number of locations around the city left by Delivery, Inc. drivers. If the defendant followed the proper procedures, he would have been fired; however, we would still be here today, asking these same questions: Why did this happen? Who is to blame?

"Delivery, Inc.'s practices are not approved by the authorities. Delivery, Inc.'s tactics would not allow it to be certified for business. Delivery, Inc. has broken the law through its training practices. But when asked about this, the company takes out its rule book that covers up these facts. They dodge the consequences of their actions, a dead child, with their stacks of legal papers, procedures, and pop-up screens. Delivery, Inc. has made killing children 'standard practice.' If we punish this driver—the defendant, my client—then another child will die, because Delivery, Inc. profits when the law is disobeyed. This murder trial should bring justice and change. Neither will happen here today. That is because the company, Delivery, Inc. is not on trial; but make no mistake, they are the true criminals here. What will you say to Delivery, Inc. and every other corporation that does business in Korea? Will you punish the scapegoat, the driver? Or will you tell the company, 'You cannot brush away the consequences.'"

Her eyes roamed the jury box as she homed in on her final points.

"Put yourself in the drivers' position. The company wants you to break the law. And if you refuse, they will replace you with someone who will. If you are caught, then it's your fault for breaking the law. You cannot win. Drivers for Delivery, Inc. are in a helpless, hopeless situation. They are not allowed to unionize. Their formal complaints with the labor department have gone unanswered. Their lawsuits have failed. If drivers can't afford to lose their jobs, then what other options do they have? The only option left is to submit to the company's wishes and break the law. The company has maximized its control. They have all the power, take all the benefits and rewards, and suffer none of the consequences."

She paused, retreating slightly to take in all of her target audience. "Your verdict of not guilty will tell everyone that this kind of business practice is unacceptable in Korea. We, the people, will not take the fall for greedy, profit-driven corporations.

"Based on the evidence, I ask that you rule in favor of the defendant and return a verdict of not guilty. Thank you."

Su-Bin sat down.

After reading the rules for the jury, the judge dismissed them to deliberate. Su-Bin left the courtroom and called Jong-In Park.

"How do you feel?" Jong-In asked.

"Nervous. The prosecution has a strong case. We made a good argument, though. Thank you for helping me last night."

"You're welcome," Jong-In said. "And you're right. Your argument is solid."

"Thanks," she responded. "I called to find out how the interviews are going. I'm hoping the news will calm my nerves."

Jong-In chortled. "There is one person who intrigues me, but you are going to have to talk with him yourself."

"Really?" Su-Bin said. "Well, if he's captivated you, then I'm sure to like him."

"Oh, and he's totally your type—dark curly hair, solid build. If you hire him, Min will be jealous."

A chill settled in Su-Bin's chest. "Black curls?" She exhaled slowly, remembering the man in her dreams. "Tell me about him."

"He's an FBI agent from America. Showed up unexpectedly and insisted on interviewing for the job. Said he was sent by Yoona. The only Yoona I know is the superstar-singer; I'm sure she didn't send him. Do you know a Yoona?"

Su-Bin hesitated. She hadn't shared with him the whole truth about how she was able to get into law school. Pressing the phone to her ear, she shut her eyes and let the words tumble out. "Yes. Moodang Yoona."

"A Shaman?" Jong-In blurted in disbelief. "Wait. Not the woman who came to you after your father was murdered. The one who claimed your dad possessed her and was speaking through her."

Sighing, she said, "Yes, that one."

She heard Jong-In chuckle. "Okay. We can cross Brandon off the list then."

"No," Su-Bin interjected. "I want to talk to him."

With an incredulous tone, Jong-In asked, "Why?"

"Yoona has approached me several times. She's the one who helped me get into law school, advised me to open my own firm, and gave me the case that propelled my success. She told me to hire Min to free my mother and pushed me to open the international law division."

There was a long pause. Silence.

Su-Bin waited for him to say something. When he didn't, she asked, "Are you hurt?"

Jong-In's voice was low. "You switched schools because of her? Why didn't you tell me?"

She remembered the day—undistorted. And apparently, so did Jong-In.

Yoona had offered her a single chance. "If you want this opportunity," she had said, "you have to apply today. The scholarship will come through. Don't worry about the test or the admission process. Just apply and I'll take care of the rest."

Her grandmother had stood in her bedroom doorway, shaking her head, her voice sharp and certain. "You can't just decide to become a lawyer. Your high school didn't prepare you. What about Ethics? Logic? Humanities? How will you pass the university exam without having taken those classes?"

Su-Bin breathed, nice and slow. Jong-In had been the only one not to criticize her decision. And that had meant the world to her.

"I needed your support," she said. "I needed you to tell me I wasn't insane for doing this, that I wasn't making a mistake. My grandmother said I was being rash. My friends said I was crazy. My mom was in prison. My dad was gone. And you..." She paused. "You were the only one who said, if this is what I wanted, we could find a way to make it happen. If I had told you Yoona was involved, I thought you'd freak out again, and I couldn't risk that."

Silence.

"Jong-In?" Su-Bin called in a gentle voice.

"Yeah," he said. "Yeah, I get it. So, do you want me to call this FBI guy back?"

"Yes. Please. And Jong-In ... thank you."

"You're welcome." He cleared his throat and asked, "Are you expecting the jury to reach a decision today?"

"I hope so. I'll call you when they do."

"Sounds good. I have one more interview. I'll stop by your place later tonight."

"Great. See you then."

Min Yun had two appointments. The first was with the doctor who had performed Ki-Tae Moon's autopsy, and the second was with Dr. Kim, who had performed his stomach surgery. Min entered the doctor's office, exchanged greetings, and explained the purpose of his visit. Taking out the autopsy report and a photo of the knife Hye-Kyoung had identified, Min asked, "Do you think this knife could have been responsible for the cuts the victim received?"

The doctor opened the report and read through it. He examined the photos. "I remember this one. I was really nervous about performing his autopsy."

"Why?"

"He was a high ranking-official. There was a lot of press coverage. I had never had an official before."

"Do you remember the cuts?"

"I do. I remember thinking I would have to testify, but no one contacted me."

"Why did you expect to testify?"

"They arrested the wife. I remember thinking that if she weren't a doctor or a soldier, she couldn't have murdered him."

"Why do you say this?"

"Let me show you." The doctor's finger hovered over the image. "These are ... unusual wounds. A kitchen knife used in panic usually leaves erratic marks. Here, though"— he tapped the tendon near the wrist— "this cut disabled the hand completely. The placement feels ... deliberate. And here"— he pointed to the upper arm—"The blade caught the brachial artery. He lost a lot of blood by the time help arrived. Strange, unless she had some kind of training."

"Would you testify to this fact?" Min asked.

"Of course."

Min left and drove to his next appointment with Dr. Hyun Kim, who had performed stomach surgery on Ki-Tae Moon. The doctor welcomed Min with a slight bow.

"I know it's been many years," Min said, "but I'm sure you remember Ki-Tae Moon. He was a member of the National Assembly, a high-ranking official."

After thinking for a moment, Dr. Kim finally said, "Oh, yes. He had complications with his stomach. We had to perform surgery."

"I'm representing Hye-Kyoung Moon, his wife." Taking out the knife, Min stared at it before handing it over to Dr. Kim. He then placed the autopsy report on his desk. "We believe this knife was used in Mr. Moon's death by someone with medical knowledge."

The doctor put the knife down, opened the report, and read it. After examining the photos, he concluded, "It seems you may be right. Did you come for my medical opinion?"

"No. I came to ask you about Mr. Moon. How was his behavior? Did he upset anyone while he was here? I'm wondering if he made enemies during his stay."

"I'm not exactly sure where you're going with this, but like you said, it was many years ago. I can tell you that Mr. Moon was an arrogant man, but he had power and social status. People respected him."

"Do you remember the murder trial?"

"I do. Mr. Moon was a heavy drinker, and the trial made it clear that he was prone to violence, especially against his wife. She defended herself but refused to take responsibility for killing him. They never should have convicted her of murder."

"Do you understand why I'm investigating this, then?"

"With a man like that ... of course. It was clearly self-defense. Honestly, I was surprised his wife fought back. I didn't think she had it in her."

"She didn't kill him. Someone with medical knowledge did."

Dr. Kim looked at the photos of the autopsy again. "Right. Interesting."

"I need to know about Mr. Moon's stay here." His gaze fixed on him as his voice hardened. "Did he upset you while he was here?"

The room fell deadly silent. The doctor narrowed his eyes, his tone cold. "What are you implying, sir? Nothing Mr. Moon did here would have provoked murder. You should look into his political enemies."

Min took a step back and smiled. "You're right. Of course. Tell me what you remember about him."

With a breath, Dr. Kim said, "Mr. Moon's situation was quite dire. I had scheduled his surgery for the end of the week, but he insisted on having it as soon as possible so he had time to recover before the campaign. I had to rearrange my schedule in order to accommodate him."

"Rearrange. That is a polite way to say you canceled or postponed other patients who were scheduled for surgery at that time."

"That can happen in a situation like his," Dr. Kim said.

"Did someone have to die for him to live?" Min accused.

Dr. Kim hardened, red coloring his face. "If a patient was that critical, another surgeon would have taken over. We save lives here! We don't bury them."

"Assuming the other doctor's schedule wasn't already full."

Squaring his shoulders, the doctor stood straighter, then grinned. When he spoke, his voice carried a cool detachment. "I think you are referring to television dramas. Don't worry. We make sure everyone is treated here."

"I'm sure you do," Min retorted with an unyielding gaze.

A nurse entered the office. "I'm sorry to interrupt, Doctor." She glanced at Min and quickly bowed, apologizing. "Mrs. Lee in Room 402 is asking for you."

"I'll be there shortly," he responded.

She bowed again, then left.

Dr. Kim moved toward the door, and Min followed him. They bowed to each other.

"I'm sorry I couldn't be of any help," Dr. Kim said.

"No, no. You were a great help. Thank you for your time, Doctor. I hope we can meet again."

"Let me think about Mr. Moon. If I remember anything, I have your card. I'll contact you."

"I'd appreciate that."

Looking at the items on the desk, he waved a hand, reminding Min not to forget his things. "If you'll excuse me, I have to see to my patient." The doctor left the room.

Brandon sat in front of the textbooks he had received after signing up for Korean language classes. The TV was on, and he listened to the sounds and rhythm of the language, trying to pick out individual words to repeat as he paged through his workbook. Making flashcards to learn the alphabet was going to be a priority.

A knock came at the door. From the other side, Brandon heard Matthew say, "It's me. I'm coming in." He had left the door unlocked, so Matthew opened it and waltzed into the room.

"I brought you some presents—bank book, debit card, and residential card." Looking at the TV, he added, "You know, you have cable. There are English-speaking channels."

"I signed up for Korean lessons today. I'm listening to get a feel for the language," Brandon explained.

Matthew nodded. "Cool. But don't forget about your biology meditations." Handing Brandon his things, he asked, "Did you hear back from the law firm?"

"I did. They want to meet me again for a second interview."

Matthew turned to the TV. "Speak of the devil. The lawyer you'll be working for made the news."

"Oh, yeah?"

Matthew listened for a bit, then began to explain, "Closing arguments were given in a case against a delivery driver facing murder charges." He paused. "Oh man, this will turn some heads. A senior member with the Department of Labor was arrested on corruption charges for accepting bribes in exchange for not pursuing investigations. The reporter believes that this arrest is connected to Moon's case, because two hours after that arrest, Delivery, Inc. announced that it would be requiring their drivers to scan IDs for all alcoholic deliveries. Because of those developments, Moon Law and Associates will be nominated for the Social Achievement Award. Wow! This is crazy."

"What's the Social Achievement Award?"

"It's like the Academy Award for law firms," Matthew said, opening the fridge. "The award is given once a year to a firm that took on and rooted out corruption, forcing changes in policy or law that have a positive benefit to society." He closed the door and looked around the room. "The winner receives money, lots of press coverage, and is given special consideration for government contracts." He sighed. "No beers?"

"Sorry."

Picking up one of Brandon's textbooks, Matthew continued, "Moon Law was being considered for nomination for a case they had back in February. Looks like this case pushed her over the edge."

"She's a star lawyer, then. A good person to know."

"Yeah, but it's Yoona who's been guiding her." He put the book down and wandered toward the door. "She needs Su-Bin to open the international law firm for some future plans."

Brandon gave a short laugh. "It all makes sense now."

"Don't be too sure. When is your next meeting with Su-Bin?"

"Tomorrow afternoon."

"Nice," Matthew said.

"I still can't believe the bureau is allowing me to take a teaching position."

"This isn't a teaching position. You're training."

"Wait a minute. Yoona said I wasn't ready for training, and you just said she needs an international law firm for some future plan."

"Like I told you before, some jobs are, in fact, training. You'll figure it out."

Lake Valley, Oregon

Silent Voices

In the school district office downtown, Mr. Anderson stood at the counter waiting. Phones rang incessantly while staff members shuffled through paperwork and engaged in hushed conversations. He listened as one of the secretaries on the phone explained, "Yes, there was a lockdown at Lake Valley High School." After a pause, she added, "No, no one was hurt. The individual is in custody. Classes have resumed as normal."

A woman stepped to the counter, drawing his attention. "How may I help you, today?" she asked with a practiced smile.

"I applied to be a substitute teacher," Mr. Anderson responded. "I received an email to report here."

She took out a clipboard and scanned it over. Then she read from a list. "You need two forms of ID, fingerprints—the police department will do that for you—university transcripts, three letters of recommendation, and health and immunization records. If you have teaching credentials, teaching experience, or have completed any training courses, we'll need proof of those as well."

Mr. Anderson handed her a folder. "I read the requirements. All the documents are here."

"Great." She handed him a pen and the clipboard. "Fill out these forms. Mr. Hadley will meet with you for a quick chat, then we'll do a background check. If everything comes back satisfactory, you'll be able to start in two weeks. Are you interested in working summer school as well?"

Mr. Anderson reached for the forms, brushing his fingers along her hand while looking her in the eyes. He implanted the idea she needed to expedite this application and grant him emergency status, so he could begin as soon as tomorrow.

The woman stammered for words, her face contorting into confusion. "Although ... umm. I—"

Her mumbling tasted so sweet.

"I think that, well."

He watched her reason crumble as he twisted her thoughts.

"I believe you'll be granted an emergency pass. Will you be able to start work tomorrow?"

Leah sidestepped into the principal's office as the police escorted a man out in cuffs. He looked worn and wired, his hair wild and matted like he hadn't slept in days. Rough stubble—gray and brown—shadowed his jaw.

"Is it true?" he asked, "How you saved the priest and yourself?"

Leah froze, her face tightening into a knot of confusion. "What did you just say?" The words burst out, caught between shock and disbelief. She couldn't have heard him right. Only a handful of people knew what she had done, and they wouldn't have said anything.

The officers pushed him forward into the hall. He twisted his neck back, shouting with a crooked laugh, "You're gonna be on the front page of every newspaper."

Leah stared at the space the man had occupied, her heart skipping unevenly.

"Leah," Principal Morrison called. "Come in and have a seat."

She stepped inside and sat across from his desk.

He leaned back in his chair, tapping a rolled newspaper against his hand. With an empathetic smile, he began, "The lockdown was called because a photographer sneaked into the building." He sighed and leaned forward. "A teacher mistook his camera for a gun. The man was trying to find you and take your photo."

The principal handed Leah the newspaper. "The article came out this morning and has stirred up the already high interest in you. You can expect plenty of press here when school lets out."

Leah read through the article. Father Joseph claimed that she was the angel who had saved him. In the same article, her own father said she was responsible for saving "the six." It painted her as a hero with divine superpowers.

"How can they write this without talking to me first?" she asked. Once the initial shock and surprise from the article faded, she was left feeling angry and confused. She knew Father Joseph believed she was an angel, and up until this point she was happy to allow him to think that. But for him to say something so ridiculous in public was unbelievable. She knew some people would believe this and see her as some divine being. The sudden spotlight squeezed her insides. How could her dad single her out like this? When had he given this interview? While she was at Barb's? Her uncle Tim was sure to have some words. And with their news interview tonight, how was she going to address this? Her private life was over. She'd be scrutinized and hounded for more comments, photos, and statements than she dared to give. If she thought she hated the attention she got after her father was first abducted, well, she was in for a real treat now.

Handing the newspaper back, she said, "I'm leaving early and won't be back until Monday. I need to sort this out."

"I think that might be a good idea. Let's call your father."

Back at home with her dad, Leah got ready for the television interview. She had showered and dressed and now sat in front of her mirror, blending her eyeshadow, thinking about what she would say tonight. The story she was supposed to tell during the interview, the one Bruce had her practice, made sense. It kept her hidden, protected the group, and grounded the events in rational, earthly terms.

She had been relieved to have a narrative that would avoid any sensationalism. But the gnawing guilt from earlier, accompanied by the news article's publication and Father Joseph's calling her an angel, a person touched by God ... was the cover story still needed? The whole city would be watching, and this was her chance to reveal that ghosts were real, that spirits could possess people and abduct them. But if she talked about the water spirit, then she'd confirm everything in that news article and would be openly inviting a brighter spotlight.

Her rosary hung on the corner of her mirror. She reached for it and clutched it in her hand. Closing her eyes, Leah prayed, "What should I do? Please help me understand what you want from me."

Her thoughts drifted back to the library, to the hours spent with Barb and Dan reading about spirits after her father was abducted, and she finally realized why lying about this felt wrong. If the authorities and institutions had been honest about spectral entities, she might have recognized the signs of possession and could have prevented her dad from being taken. Tonight, she could warn people. She could be the one to educate the public, to speak up. Did she want to be that spokesperson? She stared at her reflection. The question didn't need to be spoken. The answer was already in her eyes. No, she didn't want to be that person.

"Leah!" Jared's voice called. "It's almost time. Come out, please."

She took a deep breath to steady her nerves. With one last look in the mirror, she examined her outfit; the *Back to the Future* t-shirt and jeans were comfortable. Dan had gifted her this shirt, and she was looking forward to his smile when he saw her wearing it. Slipping on her sneakers, she headed out of her room to meet her father.

Jared was pacing in a navy-blue suit. His eyes widened when he saw her. "You're not wearing that," he said sharply.

Looking down at her outfit, she adjusted her shirt. "What's wrong with it?"

Jared ran his hand through his hair. "This is a press interview, not a casual hangout with friends. Go change."

"People know me; they'll understand," Leah retorted.

"No!" Jared shook his head firmly. "Put on a sweater or a nice blouse. Go!"

Leah sighed. "Fine." She headed back to her room as Jared added, "And wash off that makeup. They have people at the studio who will do that."

Her shoulders tensed as she rifled through her closet. She changed into a simple blouse and knee-length skirt, then grabbed her rosary beads and went into the bathroom. She stared back at herself. *What to do?* Denying the public knowledge of the supernatural events she had experienced would only ensure the truth stayed hidden. Bruce had insisted it was for her own protection, saying no one would believe her true story, adding that the unwanted attention would make the whole situation more complicated.

"Divine powers?" she questioned under her breath.

If she spoke the truth, would she save someone from the fate she had been through? Thumbing the beads of her rosary, Leah prayed again, "Dear God, give me the courage I need to share my story, or the wisdom to stay silent if that's your will. Show me the way."

She waited, half expecting an answer, a whisper, anything. But the room stayed still. With a sigh, she washed her face and returned to the living room.

Her father gave an approving nod. "Thank you," he said. "I need them to see how strong and mature you are."

The insipid news article slapped her. Leah clenched her teeth as heat crept up her neck. "Oh, so they'll believe that I'm some divine angel sent from heaven?" she snapped.

Jared put his hands on his hips and gave his daughter a hard glare. "What is that supposed to mean?"

"Are you playing dumb now?" Leah shot back. "What the hell was that news article? I thought we agreed to only do the Channel 7 interview."

Jared rubbed the back of his neck, looking uneasy. "I know, but the reporter's niece was the first person abducted by Bellevue and—"

"Please don't say Its name!"

Jared took a breath and stared at the ceiling. When he returned his gaze, he spoke in a deliberate manner. "Amanda Bowman was the first person taken from the Education Center. Her aunt, Brenda Calderwood, is a reporter with the *Lake Valley Sun Times* and needed to talk. We had a heart-to-heart."

Leah narrowed her eyes, her glare able to cut through stone. "You put a giant spotlight on me, and now paparazzi are breaking into my school to steal photos!" She clenched her fists as the lockdown replayed itself—the piercing alarm, her class in a state of panic, her heart pounding as she crouched in the corner. The fear had been suffocating.

"The idiot's in jail now. Serves him right," Jared muttered.

She couldn't believe he had talked to a reporter on his own. What had he been thinking? "Dad! We all agreed this was the only interview we'd be doing. Agent Duchovny warned us about talking to the press."

Jared squared himself to Leah. "Brenda needed to hear what happened. I had to talk with her."

"Did you tell her everything?"

"Of course not."

"So why did you single me out?" Leah demanded. Jared saying she had been the sole person to save them all angered her most.

"You negotiated with that ghost and saved our lives. You're a hero. I want people to know that."

"But at what cost?" Leah's voice wavered, her anger giving way to hurt and fear. "The person interviewing us tonight is going to ask me questions I'm not ready to answer. This isn't fair."

Jared moved closer and placed a reassuring hand on her shoulder. "We'll get through this."

She exhaled loudly. "I wish you would have talked to me first."

"I know. And I'm sorry."

The doorbell rang. Their ride was here. Jared kissed Leah's forehead. "Come on. We'll feel better once this is over."

Later that night, Eric Sorensen sat down on the sofa and set his laptop on the coffee table as his mom came in with a bowl of popcorn.

"Popcorn? Seriously?" Eric said.

"I'm excited to know what happened. This is epic true drama."

The music cued. The news anchor started. "Up next, a special hour-long report featuring exclusive interviews with the six who were abducted. But first, these headlines."

The screen cut to images of missile strikes, smoking cities, and tanks on desert roads. The announcer reported that Iran had nuclear capabilities. Israel vowed full-scale retaliation if they deployed. North Korea was seeking a formal alliance with Iran.

"Now I know why the market crashed so hard today," Gab said.

"Dad told me he liquidated everything last month."

"Yeah, good thing too."

The anchor concluded by announcing that Iceland had officially joined the United Federation of States, bringing the total to thirty-six nations.

"Full coverage of all the global tensions will appear after this special episode."

Eric's heart skipped a beat when the camera zoomed in on Barbra Mills. *Wow!* She was beautiful, talented, and mysterious. The others were also there: her brother, Dan; her best friend, Leah, with her dad, Jared; and Nong, with her daughter, Ploy. The interviewer pushed and prodded for details, wanting the former abductees to share everything. The incident had made national news, bringing reporters from all over the country, creating a buzz in the city that swept everyone up in the drama, including Eric's mom who sat next to him, more interested in Leah Davenport than any of the others.

Barb spoke. "Leah explained to me how she escaped, but she cut her head in the process and then was recaptured. That escape route didn't end up being an option for us."

Eric remembered when he first became aware of Barb, the sound of her smooth, sweet voice. He opened his computer, the one he had recently purchased on Craigslist, and scrolled through her social media posts. Not much was there. She rarely posted.

In the TV interview, Dan recalled, "Barb had no interest in going back to our childhood neighborhood. She scolded both Leah and me for even talking about it. Our parents had died there. But we were going to look for Leah's dad, and Barb wouldn't let us go without her."

Eric searched online for news articles about Barb's old house. He scanned through details about the fire, her parents' deaths, and her grandmother. He found Dan's social media posts and browsed them, learning that he was dating Leah.

He scrolled through Dan's photos, stopping to study the ones with Barb in them—her on stage singing, playing Jenga at the kitchen table, and at an Escape Room, stealing the Mona Lisa. As he went through the posts, his head began to ache. Ever since he got this computer, every time he opened it, he felt a pain, like a sliver embedding itself into his head.

Eric's mom turned up the volume on the TV. She listened as Jared told the reporter, "My daughter, Leah, was the one who communicated with the kidnapper. She kept us calm and working together as a group while she negotiated for our release."

The reporter turned to Leah, asking her about Father Joseph's claim that she had saved him. Eric's mom clutched his arm in excitement and listened intently.

"I've read what Father Joseph said, and honestly, I think it's more a case of his mind playing tricks on him," Leah said. "After my dad was kidnapped, I ended up in the news. So, when Father Joseph went to the Education Center to perform his exorcism, it's possible that he had me on his mind. I mean, that was some dream he had. I was locked up with everyone you see here when he woke from his coma."

A congratulatory smile crossed Eric's lips as he nodded, approving of Leah's answer. He went back to his computer, hearing a voice say, *Open my email. I need to send my daughter a message.*

Eric jerked upright and whipped his head around, scanning the room.

"What are you looking for?" his mom asked.

"Um ... nothing," he responded. Pressing his hand to his forehead, he rubbed his temple with his thumb.

"You look pale. Are you feeling okay?"

"Fine."

His hand inched for the pad, but he stopped just shy, afraid to touch the computer again.

"Did you learn anything?" his mom asked, looking at the screen.

"They're Leah's social media posts about her and Barb's adventures in New York last Christmas."

The pain in his head slowly increased, and he squeezed his eyes shut. A recent memory played in his mind like a movie, starring himself.

Eric opened the garage door. The dimly lit space likened to a canopy of trees with thick leaves. The dense aroma of gasoline mixed with the thick scent of motor oil, filling the air like the humidity of a jungle. With each step, he navigated his six-foot frame through and around the mechanical foliage and undergrowth of car parts, tools, wires, buckets, and exhaust pipes like a seasoned explorer, forging a path to his father.

Two lights hung on the hood of a jeep as his dad torqued bolts, securing the cylinder head. Eric cleared his throat, and Alan glanced up. "Pass me a 9/16 socket wrench, will ya?"

Eric grabbed the tool and placed it in his dad's outstretched hand. "I found a laptop on Craigslist. Jess is swinging by; we're going to pick it up."

"What kind?"

"A sixteen-inch Lenovo 2-in-1 Yoga 7i. Thirty-two gigabytes of memory."

"How much?"

"Three hundred."

Alan came out from under the hood of the jeep and studied his son. "Why is it so cheap?"

"Her husband's in the hospital and she wants to get rid of it. Today."

"Sounds suspicious. Better make sure it works, first." Alan held his son's gaze until he nodded in agreement. "You got the cash?"

"I do, but I need it for prom. I was hoping you could spot me fifty."

Alan cleared his throat and then found a clean peachy spot on the back of his wrist and wiped his forehead. "My wallet's on the workbench," he said, nodding his head in its direction.

Eric glanced and spotted the wallet. "Thanks, Dad."

Alan grunted and returned his attention to the jeep.

Opening the wallet, Eric removed three twenties. "I'm taking sixty," he called back.

"Yep," his dad replied.

Eric's heart warmed with appreciation. His dad might not be the buddy-buddy guy or the take-you-under-his-wing teacher, but Eric knew his dad loved him and would always be there if he needed.

A hand landed on his shoulder. "Hey," Eric's mom murmured. "Do you need some aspirin?" She leaned closer, studying his eyes while reaching for his forehead.

"What?" Eric said, feeling confused and disoriented.

"Do I need to take you to the hospital?"

"No. Give me a second. I'll be okay." He closed the computer and set it on the coffee table. Slowly, the pain subsided, but the fogginess persisted, thicker now than before.

The television camera zoomed in on Ploy. "I had to wash all the pans and bowls before I was allowed to eat. The others sat at the table and waited for me to finish."

Eric pinched the back of his neck, trying to loosen the ghostly grip on his mind. He returned his attention to the interview. Would their story include being violated? He imagined they had all been locked in a dark, dirty dungeon and brought into a room one by one, made to do unspeakable acts. He watched and waited, cursing himself for wanting to hear about it. Then he finally realized that part either never happened or wouldn't be discussed. Eric felt relieved but also curious to know the truth.

The interviewer asked the group how they had ended up at the Education Center. "The FBI has asked us not to elaborate on several aspects of what happened because they are still investigating," Nong answered.

The interviewer turned to Barb. "Would you like to add anything?"

Barb glanced at the others and took a breath. "We returned ... greatly changed."

Eric's mom asked, "That's the girl you're taking to prom?"

"Yes," Eric answered.

"Could you invite Barb and Leah to the house for dinner? I would very much like to meet Leah. This might be my only chance to be in the presence of someone with divine powers."

Eric rolled his eyes. "Mom, she doesn't have divine powers."

"She's downplaying her gifts, Eric. That girl is something special. With all the attention she's getting, she probably doesn't want people hounding her."

Letting out an incredulous sigh, Eric said, "You can meet her when we take our prom photos. We're going together as a group."

Gab brushed her fingers over his cheek. "She's being hailed the hero—she's truly an angel."

"Mom, please." Eric was unable to understand why she was so fixated on this idea. She had gotten herself caught up in some kind of fantasy. He did think Leah was beautiful, and she certainly fit the role of hero. But he was going to prom with Barb. His heart swooned at seeing her on TV, and he found himself dreaming about her laying her head on his shoulder as she cried from her harrowing experience. That led to kissing, cuddling, and a loving connection.

Returning his computer to his lap, he opened it back up and continued to read all of Leah's posts that had anything to do with Barb. As he scrolled, he heard the voice again, louder and clearer, the sound of an old man: *Open my email.*

Eric turned to his mom. "Did you hear that?"

"I did. I can't believe they won't give the identity of the abductor. How can they not tell us who it was?"

"No. Not the television." Before he could elaborate, a sharp, splitting pain drilled into his skull, whitening his vision. He screamed—and blacked out.

Tim Davenport woke the next morning to the phone ringing. *Damn reporters,* he thought. He rubbed his neck, which was stiff from sleeping on the sofa. Leah, Stacy, Barb, and Jared were in the kitchen making breakfast. He snuck to the bathroom and showered.

For the next few weeks, Tim would be living with Leah and Jared. Bill Stillen had hired him to keep his granddaughter safe, and the pay was more than generous. This was a compromise Tim knew Bill was already regretting, so he'd make sure nothing went wrong.

When Tim finished washing, he went into the kitchen, only to find a plate of food waiting for him. Everyone had already left.

He rubbed the back of his head, wondering if there had been a misunderstanding. As Tim ate, he considered calling to meet up with them; however, a better idea came to him. Swiping his keys off the coffee table, he headed to Best Buy.

When he returned, the house was still empty. He called Jared, who told him to call Stacy.

"Tim, thanks for calling," Stacy said. "It's been a total nightmare." She explained that she had taken Leah and Barb to the mall to buy prom dresses, and that strangers had been approaching Leah and asking her to touch them. Parents had asked her to bless their babies, and a few handed her cards that had prayers written on them. Then the press learned where they were and hounded Leah for comments and interview requests.

"Where are you now? I'll be right there."

"No, that's all right. We're at the country club. We'll be home once their dresses are ready."

Tim flopped onto the sofa and opened the bag that held his newly purchased items. He opened the package and synced the devices to his phone. *She won't be able to slip away from me now.* He placed the items in his shirt pocket and picked up his outdoor magazine. Reading, he drifted off to sleep.

The ground trembled. Tim turned toward the hill, joining the onlookers to see what was approaching. Dread consumed him. Was it an attack, and if so, by whom? Then the sound of horses, maybe a hundred or more, thundered through the air, confirming his worst fears. He rushed to grab his bow, arrows, and an axe. Friends and loved ones ran for safety as uniformed soldiers appeared over the top of the hill. They wore dark blue wool coats with brass buttons and light blue trousers with a yellow stripe down the leg. Tim froze. There had been no warning of their coming. No demand for surrender. And they showed no mercy.

The charge—hard walls of horses' hooves pounding with their sharp edges—trampled innocent women, children, and elders. The grotesque violence that unfolded before Tim—soldiers shooting indiscriminately, swords flashing brightly before dripping with blood—stunted his immediate ability to react. In front of him, a baby was ripped from his mother's arms as a sword slashed down, splitting the mother. She fell to the ground, praying with her last breath that the soldier would keep the baby safe, but he threw it into the stream like a bag of garbage as he turned to face Tim.

The sword the officer wielded snagged Tim's attention, holding him in place. He knew that sword. It hung in his living room, refurbished, on display, a piece of history he proudly showcased to all his guests. One of his great-greats, a Union officer during the Civil War, had wielded it. Tim had always felt a sense of honor and pride, imagining the bravery and heroism it represented. But now, in the midst of this horrific dream, he saw it differently. The blade, once a symbol of family legacy, was stained with the blood of Native Americans from a brutal massacre. The violence he witnessed clashed starkly with his previous reverence, transforming his pride into a sense of disillusionment. War was not something to be celebrated; it was a haunting reminder of humanity's capacity for cruelty.

He readied himself, eyes burning red. If his life were to end today, this man, his relative, was going with him.

The sword that entered Tim's back was icy cold. His body arched, his chest pushed outward, as the tip of the blade appeared. The soldier in front of him snarled, turned, and rode away. Tim fell to his knees. The world around him fell quiet, with the exception of the baby's cry as it struggled for air, splashing at the edge of the stream.

Tim jerked awake when the front door opened, accompanied by loud bursts of chatter. Disoriented and confused, he grabbed his gun and turned before realizing it was Leah and her mom, Stacy.

Returning the 9-millimeter to his shoulder holster, Tim cursed under his breath, trying to pull himself together. He went into the kitchen to get some water and wash away the horror. Was the soldier on that horse really related to him? Was that his great-great-great-grandfather? Grief, heavy and solid, coagulated in his chest. To witness the dark beginnings of his homeland shattered his understanding of history, cracking his pride. The women's laughing and giggling, oohing and aahing, drew him back. The ugliness receded into his subconscious, lying in wait to strike again.

Tim heard Leah say goodbye to the others and returned to the living room. She rushed in, proclaiming, "I got my dress! Do you want to see it?"

"Yes," Tim said.

Leah retreated momentarily and then returned with a midnight blue, V-neck, satin gown. She held it up to reveal its A-line shape. The backless style had pleats broken by a ruched slit.

"Wow. That dress is absolutely gorgeous," Tim gushed. "You are going to look amazing. Has your dad seen it?"

"Not yet. He's hunting for office space with Nong."

"He's going to love it." Tim stepped closer to Leah and lowered his voice. "I know you're excited about prom, but please don't ditch me again. The attention you attract is serious."

"That I *attract*?!" Leah scoffed. "I'm not the one blabbing to reporters!"

Tim nodded and held his hands up. "I know it's not your fault. But people are—"

Leah cut him off. "Crazy! I totally experienced that." She sighed heavily. "I'm sorry, but Barb and I needed dresses, and you would have been bored. Besides, we were with my mom; we were safe. This whole bodyguard thing is ridiculous."

"I know you understand," Tim said solemnly.

She draped her dress over the back of the sofa and then grabbed two handfuls of her hair, giving them a frustrated tug. "Yes, I do. I'm sorry. I'm feeling overwhelmed."

"I know," Tim consoled. "It's tough. I don't envy you."

Leah forced out a breath. "The press, the police, school, the interview... Why do people believe such stupid shit? I'm an angel?!"

Tim shook his head and shrugged. "How long is your mom staying?"

"Until after prom, but she's flying in again for graduation."

Tim nodded, then handed Leah a small pouch. "Here, I want you to sew this into your dress."

"Why? What is it?" she said, examining the tiny pouch.

"It's a tracking device. This way I'll know where you are. I'll put one in your purse, too."

"Wait. I said it was okay for you to drive us, not to stalk us. Besides, Mom will be at the dance." Leah held out her arm, the device resting in her palm.

Tim stared at it, then folded his arms and locked eyes with her.

The refrigerator motor hummed to life, breaking the tension.

"A bunch of people will be at the dance," he said. "Who knows, a creepy weirdo obsessed with you could slip in and snatch you."

"For crying out loud, you sound like Grandpa. I was *grabbed* by a ghost!"

"You're a celebrity. These are the precautions you need to take."

Rolling her eyes, Leah groaned. "I can protect myself."

"There are crazy people out there," Tim stressed. "It's my job to minimize the risks."

"I think this bodyguard idea has gone too far."

"Maybe. But it won't be for long. Bask in the glory, kiddo. You'll soon be a nobody at Stanford."

"I hope so."

The phone rang. They both groaned and waited for the answering machine to kick in.

Leah turned the tiny pouch in her hand. "What if I..."—she hesitated— "connect to you instead?"

Giving Leah a sideways look, he asked, "What do you mean?"

She sat down and her uncle followed.

"It's kind of a secret," she began. "Barb is the only one who knows I can do this, so if I tell you, don't advertise this to anyone."

He eyed her suspiciously. "Do I ever advertise?"

"Promise."

Uncle Tim studied her face for signs he could keep this promise. "I give you my word that keeping you safe is my only priority," he finally said.

"Connecting isn't bad; it's similar to telepathy. I don't want people in my face, asking how I learned how to do it."

Tim would have laughed at Leah two weeks ago, but now... "I'm intrigued. Tell me more."

"I'm connected to Barb and can communicate little things, like asking her to call me."

"You can tell her telepathically to call you?"

"Yes. And if I connect to you, I can do the same."

Tim winced. His instincts told him this was a joke, but he knew better. "Shit. That article in the paper was true."

Leah's glare hit Tim like the flat of a shovel, forcing him to lean back. "Come on," he muttered. "Telepathy? This is nuts."

Exhaling sharply, Leah continued, "If I need your help, you'll get the urge to call me."

"Then it'd be a great idea if I knew where you were, so I could help."

"Fine!" Leah sighed. "I'll sew it on my dress. Give me your hand."

Tim held his hand out and Leah took it, staring him straight in the eyes. The tingling sensation started in his arm and went straight to his heart. It beat rapidly for a brief moment before settling back into a regular rhythm. The tingle dissipated.

"It's done," Leah declared. "Now we're connected."

"That means you can use telepathy with me?"

She didn't answer. Her body had gone statue-still.

Tim's brow crinkled as a thought popped into his head from out of nowhere. In a slow, half-dazed voice, he said, "I have to call you." He stood motionless staring at Leah's triumphant gaze, proclaiming her newfound ability. "Wait. You sent me that thought?"

She answered with a cocky grin.

"But ... how?"

Leah chuckled. "That's why I want you to keep this a secret. Everyone will be asking me that."

"I get it. I won't tell a soul."

Leah took a second to think. "After spending time inside that ghost, energy has become tangible. I'm able to shape it to carry information, the same way we use light or radio waves. But I can only communicate through a connection, which we now have."

"So, is this connection permanent? Can I send something back?"

"It's not permanent. I have to keep it active," she explained. "And you'd have to connect to me to send something back. Right now, I'm plugged into you, but you're not linked to me."

"Got it. And this is how you talked to the water spirit."

"Yes. Through my spiritual core," Leah said. "I form the bond from the same energy that ties me to the living pulse of the universe—the stream of life, our higher power." A timid smile crossed her lips, as if she expected Tim to push back on the idea. But he didn't. He listened. This was all too new.

Leah continued, "I can communicate with spirits, ghosts, and our ancestors. Healers, psychics, Shamans, counselors, religious leaders—they all draw on this energy."

"You know, this reminds me," Tim said. "Barb was holding a book in the truck after you escaped the Education Center. Carol said it was used for communicating with and battling ghosts."

"Oh?" Leah said, with a confused look on her face.

"A lot of what you're describing sounds like it probably came from that book." Tim paused a moment judging her expression. "Did it?"

Leah pressed her lips together, hesitating. Then she nodded. "Yes."

Tim gave a cautious grin. "You do know books like that come with a cost."

"It's just energy," Leah countered. "Lots of people use it, knowingly or not."

"Okay," Tim said. "Have you ... talked to our ancestors?"

"Great-Grandma came to visit me. She helped free everybody. I say something to her in my prayers every night now."

"That's something. I participated in a prayer circle, and afterwards my grandfather appeared to me in a dream. He spoke directly to me."

"So you have the ability, too!"

"Yeah, no. I wouldn't say that. But I understand this concept."

A knock came at the door. Tim signaled for Leah to stay seated. He answered it and stared at a tall, black-haired kid straight out of college holding his phone. Opening his jacket, Tim revealed his weapon and then pointed to the signs on the door and in the yard that read "Attention Reporters: No Interviews. Please Respect Our Privacy." The reporter nodded, holding his hands up as he retreated. Tim shouted, "Can't you read? Fucking cockroaches!"

Returning to the sofa, he exhaled. "I don't envy you."

"Make sure you yell at Dad for me," she muttered.

"Sure. So, can you read my mind? Do you know what I'm thinking?"

"I don't need any special powers to know what you're thinking now," Leah giggled. "But I will sense strong emotions. If you're elated or grief-stricken, I'll know. And when I get stronger, I should be able to speak directly into your mind. But that won't happen for a while. I need to make my energy attractive, eliminate wants and desires, not let fear control my thoughts or actions—stuff like that—before I can really do anything."

"Eliminating wants and desires? That doesn't sound possible." Tim put his hand to his chin. "I have another question that's been bugging the hell out of me. The water spirit is now the Education Center. It's not part of the building or inside the building but *is* the building. And that building is alive? How can a building be alive?"

"Inanimate objects can be possessed. A soul can occupy a hairbrush or a house. The objects hold the soul's energy."

"But being possessed and being alive are not the same thing."

"Aren't they? Our body is simply a vessel for our soul," Leah held.

"Our body requires energy. We have a brain," Tim countered.

"That's because our body is a machine, the same as a car, which carries our soul around. The brain operates that machine."

Uncle Tim had nothing to say to that. He raised an eyebrow, trying to wrap his mind around it. How could a building be considered alive? It was just bricks, mortar, and wood. Was Leah suggesting that the Education Center had a consciousness, a will of its own? The idea seemed preposterous, yet he could see the conviction in her eyes. She truly believed it. And if buildings and objects could be alive, where did that leave them? How could they ever feel safe again? He had to push back.

"Even if a building could be possessed, it still doesn't explain how it could be ... alive," Tim finally said.

"Maybe a house can be alive because electricity runs through It. Our brains are made up of neurons firing electrical impulses," Leah stated.

"Electrical currents running through wires don't perform the same task as firing electrical impulses. Anyway, wouldn't that mean the building would die if there was a power outage?"

"Maybe the soul can draw energy from the currents, the same way it absorbs energy from a body." Leah shrugged. After a brief pause, she added, "I think we are so accustomed to using our body to communicate and gather information that we've forgotten how to connect with others in our natural state."

"Our natural state being energy?"

Leah smiled, nodding. "That's my understanding. I imagine this world as a place where we gather knowledge and experience to carry into the next life."

"Let's focus on this life," Tim said. "When your dad told me the water spirit had become alive, I thought he meant the thing was crawling around somewhere inside the building, but then you told me the spirit had become the Education Center. I don't understand how."

"Life is mysterious. I know it has something to do with this energy. What resonates the most for me is that a higher power is able to create life. The priest, rabbi, and monks each connected to a different aspect of that power and, together, created life."

Tim nodded. "That land is tied to the spiritual world. The Sukiya go there to communicate with their ancestors. That might have something to do with it as well."

"Maybe. Some cultures believe rocks, water, and trees all have an essence, a soul. The Education Center has one now, too."

"Hmm. If It's alive, can It communicate?" Tim asked.

"According to my dad, communication happens through your inner voice. The building connects to you, the way I just did. You might think you're talking to yourself, or that a random idea popped into your head, but the building gave you those thoughts."

"The Center isn't alive in the sense that It can move and eat people—like that cartoon movie where the house is a monster, right? The water spirit can't lock doors or close windows." Tim wanted reassurance that a living building couldn't trap anyone the way It had as a ghost.

"It's alive, so It can learn to manipulate energy, the same way you or I can. I think it could learn to close doors and such, but maybe not without..." Leah trailed off, her words catching in her throat. Her face paled, and she clutched her gut as she finished the sentence: "...a teacher."

Tim stiffened. "What?"

She swallowed. "The water spirit saw all of my memories. Everything I know about this subject—It knows."

A crease formed between his eyebrows. "And *you* read the book."

She nodded, her eyes dark with worry.

Tim sat unmoving, the implications heavy on his mind. The "living" Education Center could connect, use telepathy, and manipulate energy. Bellevue had powers. A sick feeling slid over him.

"I don't know what it can or can't do," she admitted.

"Hold on. Let's think this through," Tim said. "The Sukiya told me that hearing a water baby cry is a sign that death is coming. Seeing a baby and picking

It up means disaster—a catastrophic event. Native Americans use those warnings to prepare themselves. But you said the water spirit has transformed. It's alive. Does that change things?"

Leah thought for a moment. "You told me I made a mistake by bringing It back to life. You may have been right. The house had turned Barb and Dan's family against each other. It pushed John to become an asshole so the kids would seek out the house for love and comfort. It did the same with their mom, but she fought back. We know how that ended."

"Right. That building is dangerous. If it bonds with someone new..." Tim became lost in thought. "We need to somehow stop people from going there. No one else can connect with that monster."

"How can we stop people from going there?" Leah asked.

"The land is on sacred land tied to the spiritual world that once belonged to the tribe. If we can get the land transferred back to the Sukiya, then they can control access to it."

"How are you going to do that?"

Tim had an idea but wasn't ready to tell Leah about it. The plan was dangerous, illegal, and probably immoral. But he was determined to make sure the city transferred the land back to the Sukiya Nation. "Tell me everything you know about that water spirit."

As Tim listened to Leah, his resolve to deal with this spirit hardened. If he didn't take action, who would?

"Olivia, let's go, or you'll be late!"

Olivia hurried to brush her teeth. Today was her first day at the Education Center, and she couldn't wait to start her new art class. As she brushed, she glanced at the mirror, catching her reflection. Rich hazel eyes stared back at a mess of red hair that curled and tangled around her face. She paused her brushing and ran her fingers through the strands, trying to tame the unruly locks.

Her red hair stood out, and kids at school called her "Firehead." But they also liked her drawings, and if she could get better, maybe more kids would like her and give her a better nickname.

"Coming, Mom!" she called as she rushed down the stairs.

She bounded off the porch and ran straight for the car, excited for the chance to make new friends, become popular, and rekindle her joy of drawing. She loved the "oohs" and "ahhs" she sometimes got, especially from her teachers.

In the car, Olivia stared out the window, her mind drifting back. This flicker of normal reminded her of when her mom and dad used to spend time with her, jumping on the trampoline or reading bedtime stories. That was before all four grandparents and her Aunt Mary had died, changing everything. Her parents had become distant, wrapped in their grief, leaving Olivia to feel like an afterthought. Fun had been sucked out of her life. But today felt different. Her mom seemed different. Olivia bounced in her seat with an exaggerated smile.

"Mom? Maybe I should take swimming lessons too. I don't want to drown like Aunt Mary did."

Her mother sighed, glancing at her through the rearview mirror. "I'll talk with your father about it tonight."

Olivia nodded, her thoughts shifting back to the Education Center. She hoped she'd see Ploy there. Ploy was in her school, and people talked—about how her mom had been kidnapped and hospitalized. Then Ploy got kidnapped, and the whole school had learned about "Stranger Danger." Olivia believed her and Ploy could understand each other in a way no one else could. If Ploy was at the Center today, maybe they could become best friends.

When they arrived, Olivia jumped out of the car and hurried inside. She entered the art room and immediately recognized two classmates from school. "Hi. I didn't know you came here."

One of the boys glanced at her, gave a quick "hi," and then returned to his conversation with his friend.

Olivia took a seat next to them. She was ready—ready to feel normal, to make friends, and to become better at drawing.

The teacher stepped in front of the class. "Welcome, everyone. I'm Mr. Bowlby." He scanned the room and flashed a smile at Olivia. "Today, we're going to create a name poster. But this isn't just any name poster—I want you to think about what makes you unique as an artist. Your poster should show who you are, what inspires you, and how your art reflects your personality. Think about the things you love, the colors you like, and the ideas that make you excited to create. This is your chance to share a piece of yourself with the world."

Olivia grabbed a blank sheet of white paper and began to doodle. As she drew, she lost herself in the creative process. She let her imagination grow and decided to dedicate this drawing to Grandma Tina, remembering all the things they had done together.

On her paper, she sketched a unicorn in a stained-glass pattern, a pair of knitting needles creating a sweater, clay figurines of a turtle and a bear, colored pencils drawing a rainbow, and a marker writing out a name.

The boy next to her suddenly leaned over and frowned. "You're supposed to use your own name, dummy."

Startled, Olivia re-examined her drawing. Her heart sank. The name on her paper wasn't hers—it was *I'm Bella*. A rush of confusion and frustration hit her. She had wanted to impress, belong, fit in. That wouldn't happen now. The boy would go to school tomorrow and tell everyone she was a "dummy." Before she knew it, she crumpled the paper and threw it in the trash.

But as she returned to her seat, the crumpled paper seemed to call to her. She stared back at the garbage can, unable to peel her eyes from the invisible tug. What had she just thrown away?

Dr. Lynn Mathis stood from her desk and walked past her framed certificate in neurological health and brain surgery that hung prominently on the wall. Eric Sorensen's brain scans lay on the table, and she collected them as she headed for the waiting area to speak with his mother. The images matched those taken from the first three Education Center abductees: Amanda Bowman, Tyler Jiles, and Nong Ekamai. They had been diagnosed with unresponsive wakefulness syndrome after mysteriously reappearing. Eric, however, was conscious. After he had passed out from a severe migraine, his mother rushed him to the emergency room. Staff transferred him into her care after his brain scan revealed unusual neurological disorders.

Lynn took a deep breath and let her shoulders relax. For years, she had been reviewing scans similar to Eric's, all coming from patients connected to the Education Center. Her frustration was at a tipping point. She'd long tried to convince the health board to close the building and label it a health hazard. When the six had been freed and found at the Center, she was sure their scans would finally shut the place down permanently. But all six had been completely healthy. With Eric's scan in hand, though, maybe she could bolster her argument and try again. She headed for the waiting room to see Eric's mom and confirm he had been visiting the Center.

Soft jazz music filled the lobby. Gab sat beside a table stacked with magazines, her leg bouncing with nervousness.

"Mrs. Sorensen," Dr. Mathis called.

Gab stood abruptly as she approached.

"Eric's pain has subsided, and he's resting," Dr. Mathis explained.

"Oh, thank goodness. Did you find out what was wrong?"

"You said he's been experiencing migraines for the past few days?"

"That's right. He bought a new computer and every time he used it, he complained of a headache. He's never had a problem before and can use the computers at school just fine. That machine must be causing these migraines, right? Do you want me to bring it here? Should I call the company?"

"I don't believe it's the computer, but you could bring it in. We'll take a look. We know it's not tumors from the tests we ran. However, the brain scan does show some unusual activity."

"What do you mean?"

"There's no cause for concern," Dr. Mathis reassured. "The scans show several active areas in Eric's brain."

"I don't understand."

"It's like he's doing a chemistry exam, skydiving, and painting a picture all at once. I'd like to keep him one more night for observation and to run a few more tests."

"It's that bad?"

A couple entered the lobby and passed them on the way to the counter. Lynn put her hand on Gab's shoulder, and they moved toward the patient rooms.

"You should cancel Eric's classes at the Education Center," Dr. Mathis said as they walked.

Gab jerked her head and stopped. With narrow eyes, she stressed, "He's never been to the Center. That place is evil."

Lynn tilted her head in confusion. "He must work near there or have friends in that neighborhood, then."

"No. He has no reason to go that way."

Lynn wasn't sure she believed Gab. Every person who had produced a scan similar to Eric's had somehow been connected to the Center. But if it were true, and he hadn't gone there... One theory for the cause of the unresponsive wakefulness syndrome in the three who had been abducted was drugs.

"Is Eric on any medication?" the doctor asked. "Do you know if he's using drugs?"

"He's a good kid, a track star. He worships his body. He wouldn't dare use drugs, and he's not on any medication. I know that."

"You may want to search his room to be sure. Ask his friends."

"All right."

Not wanting to alarm Gab, Dr. Mathis said, "The migraines might be caused by prolonged exposure to his computer. The blue light, bright flashes in the videos, and loud sounds can overwhelm his senses. Stress is also a known trigger. Considering prom and the relationship issues noted on his intake form, that could explain what's happening. I'll know more tomorrow afternoon."

"Will he be able to go to prom?"

"Yes. I'll discharge him tomorrow evening."

"What can we do if the headaches continue?"

"Limit screen time. Try sitting in a dark, quiet room with an ice pack on the back of his neck and a caffeinated drink. Walking the trails would be beneficial. Get him out in nature and fresh air."

"Thank you. Can I see him?"

"Sure. This way." Lynn led Gab to Eric's room.

As they entered, Eric straightened. "Another specialist?"

Lynn stopped, glanced at Gab, and then returned her gaze to Eric.

Gab took a sharp breath. "You don't recognize your own mother?"

Eric turned his head and rolled his eyes with a huff. "Mother?" he said, as if he were inconvenienced. He lifted his head and gave the worst fake smile Lynn had ever seen. "Hi, Mom."

Lynn had a new theory. Dissociative Identity Disorder, or multiple personalities.

Seoul, Korea

<u>Between Two Hearts</u>

Adjusting his necktie, Brandon stared at the sign on the door: *Moon Law and Associates*. He told himself he didn't know why he was nervous, but that wasn't true. Teaching had been his life, and he was now walking back into it like everything was normal. Yoona's warning pushed him. He had to overcome his trauma in order to retain new connections, or his training would end before it began.

Matthew had said this job would be training. He was wrong. The position was a placeholder—a way to develop new friends and make peace with losing Hina and Jaime. But confronting that loss would hurt; he wasn't ready. Packing his bags and going home, however, wasn't an option. He closed his eyes, took a deep breath, and braced himself to re-enter the world he had abandoned—teaching. He could do this.

As he entered the lobby, he found the reception desk abandoned and the workers' desks and offices deserted. Puzzled, Brandon glanced at his watch. *Where is everybody?* Music caught his attention, and he stepped further inside. Down the main hall, he saw a group mingling in a large conference room. He eased his way toward the gathering.

The room was full of people engaged in lively conversations. Food and beverages lined the table, and Brandon quickly understood this was a celebration. He scanned the room, taking in pats on the back, handshakes, and joyful camaraderie. Which one of them was Su-Bin?

A magnificent smile stopped his search short. The woman stood near enormous windows, the sun spotlighting her as if nature itself chose her as its focal point. She moved with grace, light on her feet and generous with her gestures of gratitude. The small group around her clapped, and she raised her hands above her head and twirled in a circle. Her dress filled with air, and her hair danced with her movements. Each playful sway radiated joy, and he found himself staring at Hina. Was it her? Was this the real reason Yoona had sent him to this place? Hina was possessing this woman.

His heart pounded, every nerve alive with anticipation and hope. *Please! Please let it be her.*

He trembled forward, each step as impossible as the last. His eyes widened, brimming with love and an aching yearning, the kind that swallowed every thought except the prayer that this could truly be her. With his chest nearly bursting with faith, he stared, ready to wrap his arms around her and hold her for eternity.

Walking into the offices of Moon Law, Su-Bin was met with excitement and cheers. Her staff and colleagues gathered around, clapping. She silenced them before giving a small speech.

"This victory comes from the hard work and dedication that each and every one of you has shown. I am so proud of you for the countless hours you put in without complaint. This win was a team effort, and I only see us growing bigger and stronger because of your selflessness and belief in our ability to be the best."

As calls of congratulations flooded in from clients, friends, and well-wishers, Su-Bin thought the major victory and prestigious award nomination deserved proper recognition. She hired a catering company to set up in the large conference room. With an array of beverages, food, and music, she invited her staff to celebrate.

Making her way around the room, she shook hands and patted shoulders. Her paralegal smiled as she approached. "Kim Joon-Ho shi, your discovery of the complaints to the Department of Labor really made a difference. I appreciate you."

"Moon nim, don't be modest. Take a bow—you deserve the credit."

With a brilliant smile, Su-Bin raised her hands and twirled in the sunshine coming in through the window. As she turned, her gaze locked with a stranger across the room. The intensity of his stare froze her in place but sent her heart into a dizzying spin.

"It's him," she whispered to herself. "The man from my dream."

His eyes held her with unspoken depth, as if he had known her a lifetime. Inching toward her, he moved as a man driven by both fate and destiny—his entire existence leading him to this moment. The world around Su-Bin disappeared, her breath stilled in her chest. He was seeing her as someone deserving of love, in its purest, most unselfish form. His pull, deep and inexplicable, made her feel naked, the essence of who she was lay bare before him.

For a moment, she entertained the fantasy of him sweeping her up and kissing her. Then Min Yun stepped between them, breaking the connection.

In the midst of the lively celebration, Min Yun leaned casually against the wall, enjoying a plate of seafood pancakes. He watched Su-Bin work the room and thank her staff. Pride swelled within him as he admired the way she commanded respect, her beauty and poise setting her apart from everyone else. This magnificent woman was destined to be his wife. The proposal would come the day he freed her mother.

His dream of snatching her for his own and winning the prize was so close he could taste it. He had followed her to law school, the best decision he had ever made, even though it meant cheating on his exams. After his mother died, his father had found work in America and urged Min to follow, but the allure of Su-Bin was too strong. He wouldn't abandon his dream of marrying her. He had stayed in Korea and called on his mother's soul to help him win her heart. Su-Bin would soon be his, and her success only sweetened the reward.

His eyes, hungry, tracked her as she shook hands, intoxicating him with her smile. Her every movement stirred his desires to lay with her—an ache he couldn't suppress.

"Take a bow—you deserve the credit," her paralegal said. The others near her clapped in unison.

She lifted her hands and twirled, her body angelic. The sun sparkled off her skin, accentuating her features. If he could, he would pull her into an empty office and make love to her right now.

Her dance halted abruptly, and she stared at someone across the room. Her eyes, usually guarded and reserved, now reflected a spark of fascination and captivation. Min traced her gaze and spotted a foreigner, locked in a magnetic stare with his girlfriend. A throb flared at the temples of his head, and an ache gnawed at his heart. *What is happening? Who is this guy?* He wanted to step in front of this stranger and punch him in the gut. No way would he lose her, not now! Not to some ... *foreigner*.

Looking back at Su-Bin, he watched her body shift to a more open pose. She was inviting this man closer. Receptive to his advances. Min couldn't believe it. Su-Bin, always composed at work, especially with him, had become pliant in this man's presence. The interaction reminded him of the Korean dramas she loved so much. His anger swelled, hot and sudden. He hated those shows—the perfect, idolized men setting standards no one could live up to, not even him. How was this happening?

Turning to meet the person who had ignited the desire in her eyes, Min moved with purpose. His insides churned like thick, soupy lava, blurping vile contention for this piece of excrement eyeing his woman. He stepped in front of the man, his eyes burning with hate. He managed to say tersely, "May I help you?"

"I'm here for an interview with Su-Bin Moon," Brandon replied.

Min struggled to compose himself. "You must be an English teacher. I'm sorry for not calling. To be honest, we forgot you were coming." Min wanted Brandon to feel unimportant and unwelcome. "I think it's best if we reschedule. I'll show you out."

"Brandon Spencer, I presume." Su-Bin said, now standing behind Min.

The two men turned. Holding out her hand, she continued, "I'm Su-Bin Moon. Thank you for coming."

"Anyong haseyo," Brandon said, bowing.

Min chuckled. "I'm sorry. Were you trying to say something in Korean?"

Su-Bin furrowed her brow at Min in disapproval. Turning to Brandon, she said, *"Bangawoyo.* Nice to meet you."

"The pleasure is mine, Ms. Moon." Brandon took her hand.

Min's anger flared. "Brandon, is it?" he said, landing a playful punch on his shoulder, strong enough to send him back a step and release Su-Bin's hand. Laughing, Min apologized, "Oh, sorry about that. I didn't mean to hit you so hard. I understand that's how buddies greet each other in the States."

"Good friends, yes. Not strangers," Brandon said with a short smile.

Su-Bin gave Min a glare. "If you'll excuse us."

Giving a polite, affectionate smile, Min masked his irritation and said, "Oh yeah, sure." He stepped back, his eyes narrowing on Brandon with an unspoken warning to back off.

You'll have to deal with him. The thought pressed on Min. He clenched his jaw, his breathing labored as he watched Su-Bin escort Brandon into the next office. What did she see in him? How could she even consider a guy who was obviously flirting with her? If she hired this bozo... He swallowed hard, the veins in his neck straining against his skin.

Brandon closed the door to the small office and glanced at the bookshelves lining the wall before taking a seat at the meeting table in the middle of the room. Su-Bin circled the table, her eyes catching the pile of folders on the desk. With a disappointed sigh, she sat across from him.

"Sorry about the mess. This office belongs to one of my associates, and organization isn't one of his strong suits."

"It's fine."

"So, Jong-In Park tells me that Moodang Yoona sent you to interview for the English teaching position."

"Yes, that's right," Brandon answered.

"He also told me you are an FBI agent."

"That's correct."

"Would you care to fill me in on the details?"

"Sure. My government sent me here to train with Yoona. The U.S. values her craft and believes the bureau would benefit from having an agent with her skill sets. However, when we met, she said I wasn't ready. She instructed me to interview for this position and teach until she calls for me. I understand you are expanding into international law and need a teacher who has experience in that field. I'm not a lawyer, but I am in law enforcement and have been to my fair share of trials. I was also a teacher for..."

"Yes, I've read your résumé and looked over your credentials. I also had someone call to verify your records. I have to say, I'm quite happy you're here; you're exactly whom I was hoping to hire. However, I am perplexed. Yoona is a Shaman. I didn't think the FBI would have believed in fortune telling and ghosts."

"Some cases are mysterious in nature, and the FBI uses all of the resources at their disposal to solve them."

"Jong-In thinks you were sent to infiltrate my law firm and report to the government on your findings. What do you have to say?"

"Do you have any cases in which the government would be particularly interested?" Brandon replied.

"That response isn't reassuring."

Brandon shifted in his seat. This entire situation felt convoluted. From his perspective, Yoona had orchestrated Su-Bin's success and sending him played into her larger plan. So why was Su-Bin questioning it now? And for that matter, why the interview? Why wasn't he simply expected given Yoona's influence? The process felt uncoordinated, almost deliberately chaotic. Yoona's motives seemed clear: send him to help Su-Bin establish the international law division she wanted, while overcoming his trauma—a win-win. But Su-Bin's scrutiny left him thinking, *does she know more about why I am here than I do?*

Brandon decided honesty was the only way forward. Omitting the supernatural aspects, Brandon told Su-Bin his story. "My wife died here in Korea several years ago."

"Oh, I'm so sorry," she offered, reaching her hand to his.

"Thank you," he said. "We were both teachers, but after the accident I needed a change and became a detective. A recent case I worked caught the FBI's attention, and they approached me about learning from a Shaman to enhance my awareness of people. I accepted. But before I can begin training, I need to come to terms with my loss. Since you are opening an international law division, Yoona felt it was a perfect opportunity for us both."

"I see. I trust Moodang Yoona. She has advised me several times and has never led me wrong. But your role with the FBI is still concerning. Are they aware you'll be working here, and have they approved?"

"I'm under the direct control of Yoona. Matthew Gates is my superior, although he technically works with the CIA. He is the liaison between Yoona and my government. The only reason given to me for being here is to teach the English language. I don't have any other responsibilities. I am at your disposal. Would you like to review my teaching plans?"

"That won't be necessary. I trust your abilities." Su-Bin took a sip of water and continued, "You mentioned training with Yoona. Will you be able to commit to this position for at least six months?"

"I can. From what I understand, I may be here as long as a year."

"We can renew your contract at the end of six months."

Brandon nodded. "Great."

He stared into Su-Bin's eyes, his wish, his hope, slipping away. Hina wasn't here. Su-Bin wasn't possessed. She was her own person, with style, strength, and an aura that exuded confidence—traits Hina had. Yet the moment they shared in the other room clung to him—her flicker of desire and her longing to be comforted. He understood the need to be comforted. It came with great loss and pain.

Brandon blinked away the distracting thoughts and refocused on the reason he was here—secure this position, connect with the staff, and communicate with Hina. Was her soul in Korea? Or had she transcended? Would he be able to feel her presence once more? He hadn't even tried, and here he was, drooling over a woman who was about to become his boss.

"Do you *want* to teach here?" Su-Bin asked.

"I do, yes," Brandon said. "This is a nice office, and I see that you care about your employees. Being nominated for an award tells me you are passionate about your work."

"Thank you for the compliment. What do you know about Korean culture?"

"I signed up for Korean language lessons yesterday. I had my first class today. I also watched a Korean drama on TV."

"Oh, really? Are you a fan of K-dramas?"

"The show I watched was entertaining. I binged several episodes."

"That's great! Jong-In Park and I enjoy watching them. If you'd like, you could join us. The show we're watching now is called *Extraordinary Attorney Woo*. We get together every Tuesday to watch another episode. We're hooked."

"Sounds great. I would love to join you."

Su-Bin stood and offered her hand again. "It was nice meeting you, Brandon Spencer. I will have my team prepare a contract, and we'll have you sign it tomorrow. I look forward to working with you."

Shaking her hand, Brandon thanked her in return and sent his spiritual energy to connect. But a jolt returned, causing him to pull his hand back, flexing it. The surge felt eerily familiar, and his eyes widened. Was he feeling a ghost? Hina? His chest heaved. Renewed hope gushed forth, filling him with anticipation.

"I'm sorry," he uttered. "I…" He balled his hand into a fist to stop the shaking before extending it back out. "May I see your hand again?"

Su-Bin curled her eyebrows in slight confusion. Her gaze shifted from his hand to his eyes. "Are you okay?"

Brandon didn't know what to say. He didn't want to sound crazy. "I … uh. Yeah, I'm okay. You shocked me," he said with a chuckle. "I wasn't ready for that." After a brief hesitation, he turned his palm upward, saying, "I'd like to give you a proper handshake before leaving."

Su-Bin placed her hand in his.

He held her with delicate care, as if she were a borrowed memory. Every nerve in his body buzzed, amplifying the smoothness of her skin. Building his energy, he braced himself for what he thought was Hina. Would she attach to him? He remembered the pain from Bellevue, but he'd endure four times the suffering to be with his wife again. Sending his energy into Su-Bin, he connected. But what had initially felt like a ghost didn't materialize. Instead, a gentle hum pulsed, not a bit possessive, aggressive, or even spooky—just a soft buzz. What did it mean?

Returning to Su-Bin's eyes, he studied her. Did she know what this was? Could she feel the rhythm? The familiar intimacy of the connection solidified, and Matthew's words replayed: *Some jobs are, in fact, training.*

"Thank you again," Brandon said.

Her fingers tightened around his. Her voice turned soft, a slight tremble in her words. "My pleasure."

That's when it hit him. Su-Bin was receiving the reverence meant for Hina as if it were meant for her. The tension of two people drawn to each other was sweet and intoxicating, and he liked it. But this wasn't what he had intended.

"Let me see you to the door," she said with a tender smile.

They walked down the hall, stealing glances and exchanging smiles. Brandon reminded himself that this was his boss.

He stopped at the door and bowed. *"Annyeonghi gyeseyo,"* he said.

"Please get home safely," she replied.

He exited, walked several feet, but an urge to see her one more time pulled him to turn back. The sun, reflecting off the glass, surrounded her. Through the glare, he could make out her form and one other silhouette.

Su-Bin slowly backed inside, but the second figure remained, unmoving. Brandon squinted, trying to make out who or what he was seeing. Su-Bin waved, and memories of her life erupted in his mind.

A young Su-Bin sat on a swing in a school uniform, looking straight at him.

"아버지."

Brandon didn't understand, but she came running to him and took his hand. The second memory was of an older Su-Bin, dressed in an elegant evening gown. She dragged him along by the hand, urging,

"아버지, 빨리 빨리."

She handed two tickets to a doorman, and they entered a concert hall. The orchestra was warming up as they found their seats. Sitting down, he looked up to a third vision. Su-Bin stood confidently in the halls of the university, her first day.

Brandon released a slow, ragged breath as he placed his hands on his knees. Su-Bin was telepathic! He looked back at the building but saw no one. Were Su-Bin and Yoona partners? Is this why he was here?

Brandon straightened and took a dazed step forward. Was Su-Bin going to be the one to train him? She had sent full memories. Why? To demonstrate her abilities?

He kept walking, wondering what the meaning behind her display of power was. He bumped into a passerby, completely unaware of his surroundings.

"Jwehsong hamnida," Brandon apologized, bowing his head.

This was crazy. What had happened with Su-Bin? He was feeling lost—mentally, emotionally, and physically.

"Beeeep!" a screaming horn blasted.

A hand yanked Brandon back as a car sped passed, inches from hitting him. With a gasp, he spun to see who had saved his life. A young man cursed something in Korean, probably the equivalent of, *Hey, buddy! Watch where you're going.*

He thanked the man. *"Kamsa hamnida."*

Returning to the party, Su-Bin spotted Min. He approached and handed her a drink. "You're not going to hire that guy, are you?"

"Why were you so rude to him?" Su-Bin scolded.

"Rude? I was trying to be friendly. Make him feel at home," Min countered.

"You seemed rude."

"I'll make a better effort to welcome him next time. So, can I come over tonight?"

"Ask me later. Not here," Su-Bin answered with indignation.

"I'm leaving for the hospital," Min stated. "I won't be back to the office today."

"You're leaving now?"

"I am."

"I thought you already interviewed Dr. Kim."

Min nodded, his gaze lingering on her.

Su-Bin's irritation flared. She had a strict rule against such interactions at work, yet Min kept sneaking yearning glances at her, sparking rumors of an office romance she wanted to avoid. What was worse, she occasionally found herself reciprocating. His charm and confidence were a hypnotic power that melted her defenses. His appeal extended beyond broad shoulders and a solid frame; she found a comforting strength in his reassurance that her mother would soon be free.

But after feeling Brandon's angelic touch, she couldn't ignore how aggressive Min felt—how he crossed boundaries with disturbing ease, and how he saw her as an object of desire rather than a person.

"I'm interviewing one of the nurses who cared for your father while he recovered from surgery," Min said. "She knows something."

"Why do you suspect that?" Su-Bin asked.

"She had interrupted my meeting with Dr. Kim. She stared at me with a conscience-stricken expression. I'm taking her to dinner. I have a feeling she wants to talk."

"She barged in on a meeting. Her expression would be expected."

"No. What I saw was more than a reaction. She knows something." Min lowered his voice. "I was hoping to come by afterwards, so I could share what I learned."

Su-Bin hesitated to answer, knowing why he wanted to come over; it wasn't to share information. She enjoyed that aspect of their relationship, but her heart ached for more. She longed for connection, for the veneration she had glimpsed in Brandon's touch.

"I'm going to ask about the flask," Min said. "The initials on it are the same as the doctor's. I'm betting it belonged to him, and I'm betting she'll recognize it. I'll swing by tonight and tell you everything."

"Yes. All right," Su-Bin answered with a resigned sigh. This was what she hated—how well he understood his power. She wanted to scream at him for using the clues he had uncovered and the information he had gathered to seduce her. And yet, to be enveloped in the comfort of his confidence and lost in the brilliance he displayed satisfied a strange longing. She craved the progress and the excitement. "Come on over. You can spend the night."

Min's triumphant smile accompanied the excitement in his eyes. He took a step back, holding her gaze before leaving, a bounce in his step.

Su-Bin shook her head. *Such a little boy.*

Lake Valley, Oregon

<u>Exposed</u>

Barb stood with Eric in Leah's backyard. She had one hand around his waist and the other resting on his cheek. From the side, she heard Leah and Dan snickering.

"What's so funny?" Barb asked, holding her pose, her gaze locked with Eric's.

"Tilt your head back and in, like you're offering your neck to him," the cameraman said.

"Careful, you two are going to fog up the camera," Dan teased.

Barb smiled. The camera clicked. Eric sighed, eyes lifting in a display so cold he could have come straight from an ice bath.

"Now, lean into each other."

"Hold on," Stacy interrupted. She stepped in, straightening Barb's corsage and smoothing a stray lock of hair before tugging Eric's tuxedo into place. "Try to look like you're having a good time," she whispered to him.

Barb faced Eric, wanting to feel hot, to feel passion stir her heart. But Eric offered nothing. His dashing smile and confident posture were missing, the once bold man, now sheepish and shy.

"What's wrong?" Barb whispered.

Eric's lips twisted before he muttered, "I can't believe I'm a teenager."

"What's that supposed to mean?"

"A little closer," the cameraman called. "I want your noses to be almost touching."

Eric huffed and leaned closer.

So much for being swooned, Barb thought as the camera flashed.

"You guys look great," Carol praised, adding a spark of vigor for reassurance.

"Dan and Leah, you're next," the cameraman said.

Barb watched Eric turn from her and head toward his mom. She glanced at Jared and Nong, who were holding hands, and wished she could be doing the same. Nong bobbed her head in Eric's direction, encouraging her to follow.

Drifting over, she stood beside him, stiff as a mannequin, while watching Leah and Dan melt into one another.

After the shoot finished, Tim whisked them off to Anthony's restaurant for dinner in the Cadillac XT6 he had rented, while Stacy headed to the school to volunteer for the evening.

The ride to the restaurant was awkward. Eric angled away, careful not to make any physical contact. His eyes remained forward, as if glances at Barb were inappropriate.

"Your mom said you spent the night in the hospital," Barb murmured. "Are you feeling all right?"

"Apparently, I had migraines," Eric replied. "The doctors ran a few tests because my brain scan showed some abnormalities."

"That sounds serious, Eric," Leah said. "You don't remember having migraines?"

Eric looked out the window, taking his time to answer. "No."

Barb shot a concerned look to Leah, who raised her brows and glanced at Dan. Shoulders shrugged. Eric's response left no room for conversation. Barb chewed on the inside of her lip, her chest tight with unease.

Inside the restaurant, the hostess led the group to their table. As they followed, Barb noticed Dan and Leah holding hands. She reached for Eric's, but he pulled away. She slowed, letting him move ahead. Glancing around the restaurant, Barb appreciated the ambience. Then she spotted Jess, Eric's best friend. She reached forward and tugged on his sleeve. "Look. Isn't that Jess Boyle?"

"Who?" Eric responded.

Leah glanced back. "Really, Eric?"

Eric shrugged. "What?"

At the table, as they perused the menu, Jess strolled up wearing a huge grin. "Look at the celebrities!" He patted Eric's shoulder, saying, "How you doing, buddy? I heard you spent the night in the hospital."

Eric glared at the hand and slowly raised his chin until their eyes met. "What do you want?"

Jess removed his hand and backed a step. "Easy, man. I'm just curious how you're doing. I know those headaches were pretty intense."

"Headaches?" Eric gave a sigh of impatience. "Oh, the migraines. I'm fine."

Jess glanced at Barb. She scrunched her face, as confused as he was. He looked at Leah, who shook her head. "Dude, what's going on?"

Eric cleared his throat and intoned, "As you can see, we are about to finalize our dinner orders before proceeding to the evening's dance."

Jess inhaled, raising his eyebrows. "Right. Well, have fun with that. I'll see you guys at the dance." He turned and left.

"Eric, I'm sorry, but I don't understand what's going on with you," Leah expressed. "Why would you treat your best friend like that?"

Eric looked back at Jess. "Ah. Right." He paused before repositioning himself at the table. Using a calm and respectful tone, he said, "I'm not feeling quite myself. I have some work waiting for me at home, and I'm feeling a bit anxious about it. To be honest, I was pressured into coming tonight. I don't mean to be rude, but the sooner we conclude, the sooner I can get back and finish what I need to do."

Barb's mouth dropped. She couldn't believe what she just heard. Her chest twisted, and she turned away, lifting her hand to cover her mouth as tears welled in her eyes. *What an asshole.* Everything about this evening made sense now. Someone like Eric would never take interest in her. She was a pathetic fool to think otherwise.

Barb didn't want to cry. Not here. Not in front of him. She looked to Leah for confidence, for comfort, for something to steady the storm in her chest.

Leah tightened her jaw and daggers shot from her eyes. She spoke with a hard rigid tone. "How dare you! You inconsiderate bastard. We just went through hell, and you have the audacity to shit on a dream. I thought you were better than this." Leah grabbed Barb's hand and pulled her up. "We're going to the ladies' room. Dan, can you order for us?"

"Yeah, sure."

Leah dragged Barb across the room. Her pride flaked and pealed, and her tears fell. How had she allowed herself to fall for this trap? Eric had used her to dump Ashley. She had been a convenience—stupid enough to believe he had been honest. The humiliation burned.

Leah pushed Barb against the bathroom wall and told her to stop crying. Grabbing a handful of paper towels, she said, "You have to pull it together. You're ruining your makeup." She dabbed at her eyes.

Barb barely noticed Leah's hands. She was falling … into an abyss. "I'm an idiot." Her words were faint and almost inaudible.

"No, you're not," Leah shot back. "Something is wrong. Eric isn't himself. He had migraines, and now he's a different person. He doesn't even know who his best friend is. What does that sound like?"

It was the question that yanked her back into the bathroom—the sink, the mirror, the paper towels pressed beneath her eyes. Slowly, she began to register what Leah was implicating. "Wait. That's absurd. There's no way."

"Have you connected to him?" Leah asked, continuing to dab at her eyes and cheeks.

"Connected? No." Barb stood taller and took the paper towels from Leah. "The book said connecting is to discern if someone is possessed or to aid someone grieving so a soul can transcend. Why would I have connected to him?" She blew her nose and took a calming breath. "I only connected to you."

"Do you want to connect with him? Learn if he's possessed or not?"

"And be flooded with the garbage the soul is carrying with it?" Barb raised a hand. "No, thanks! What if he was murdered or feels regret for beating his kids? I don't want to experience any disturbing memories or traumas that come from connecting with some strange soul."

"I get that. I'll reconnect with him then."

Barb's expression hardened. "When did you connect the first time?" Her mind went straight to the lunchroom, followed by her dazed and confused walk in the hall as she wondered what had happened. "What did you do?"

Leah rubbed her forehead. "It doesn't matter. He's showing all the signs of being possessed. Let's focus on that."

Narrowing her eyes, Barb demanded, "What did you send him?"

Leah pulled on her hair.

Barb pressed, "Love?" Eric's behavior made total sense now—Leah's spell had worn off.

"No. That emotion is too complicated." Leah lowered her head. "It was lust."

Barb laughed. "Well, obviously it didn't work. He couldn't be more cold."

"I think it did work. He asked you to prom, but then he attracted a ghost, and it possessed him."

Barb tossed the paper towels into the bin. "Let's interrogate him, first." She wasn't in the mood to see Leah cry out in pain. "If we think he is possessed, then we'll talk about what to do next."

"What's there to talk about? I know what to do."

"We tell Bruce," Barb insisted.

"You know I've done this before. I can help him myself."

Barb lifted her chin and stared at the ceiling with her mouth hanging open. This was classic Leah. There was no talking her out of it. "Fine, but not here. Wait until the dance. It'll be dark and noisy."

As Leah opened the bathroom door, Barb grabbed her arm. "Wait."

"What?" Leah asked.

"Thank you. But please don't connect with people to exert your power over them. The book warns against connecting with the intention to manipulate or control."

Leah shook her head. "It also says to practice with a variety of people because each person is different. Connecting is a nuanced skill that takes time to perfect."

Holding up a finger, Barb refuted, "To practice with willing participants or under the guidance of an instructor."

Leah held out her arms and turned side to side. "Do you see an instructor anywhere? And this is supposed to be a guarded secret. I'm not about to ask for volunteers."

Barb pursed her lips. "At least stop messing with people's minds."

"No more mind games," Leah said. "Understood."

They returned to the table and took turns asking Eric questions about school. His teachers, projects, girlfriends, and track. Leah went to his online profile and learned he played tight end, and defensive back in football. He had scored twelve touchdowns and had 36 catches for 720 yards. Eric attempted to dodge most of their questions, and the ones he did answer were wrong.

Dan gave a questioning look and pointed his finger at Eric.

Leah nodded. Eric was possessed.

Mr. Anderson walked along the sidewalk with a black bag on his shoulder and turned into the Davenport driveway. He took a small, circular device from his jacket pocket and stuck it under the bumper of Leah's Audi. Strolling into the backyard, he glanced through the window and saw Jared and Nong engaged in a passionate kiss. He circled to the back door and waited. The two soon made their way to the bedroom, and Mr. Anderson opened the back door, which remained unlocked.

Taking his time, he strategically placed devices—under the counter, on top of the cupboard, under the coffee table, and on the bottom of the picture frame. He made his way to Leah's room and rummaged through her stuff, taking special note of the books she read, all the while photographing. When Jared walked past and entered the bathroom, Mr. Anderson stepped into the closet. Nong soon passed, following Jared. The shower ran and Mr. Anderson finished placing the listing devices, before slipping out of the house.

Back in his room, Mr. Anderson got ready to chaperone at prom. He dressed in a suit and put his school ID around his neck. His suit pocket had a tiny camera to record the evening. Every interaction Leah had tonight would bring him closer to better understanding her.

Uncle Tim sat in the parking lot of Anthony's while the kids ate dinner. He was researching ways to de-annex the land from the city so that the tribe could regain their property. Reading old articles about protests to return Indian lands and looking at the profiles on Facebook of those who had organized the protests, He learned that Roy Running Deer was one of the leaders. Tim found his number on the internet and called, hoping to recruit his help.

"Hello."

"Hi. Is this Roy Running Deer?" Tim asked.

"Who is this?"

"My name is Tim Davenport. I was hoping I could talk with you about the Education Center."

"Davenport. I know that name. Are you a reporter?" Roy asked.

"My brother, Jared, was abducted. He's been in the news this past week."

"Ah. Gotcha. Go ahead."

"I know how important the land where the Education Center sits is to the Sukiya Nation. I am looking into de-annexing the property so that it can be returned to them," Tim said.

"De-annexation is nearly impossible. The city council would have to pass a resolution calling for a special election and sixty percent of the city would have to agree. The owner certainly won't submit a petition for that to happen. Why do you care, anyway?"

"A past relative of mine was a soldier in the American Indian wars and committed atrocities similar to the massacre of your people 150 years ago. I had a vision of it after attending a ceremony with the elders. Now that vision haunts me. I must atone for the wrongdoings of my family. But more importantly, a water baby inhabits the Center. More people will die unless we stop it."

Tim waited, the silence thick with nervousness. What would Roy say? The kids approached the truck, and he hurried to conclude the chat. "Can we meet? I can share my ideas. Maybe you could give me some advice."

"Let's meet for lunch tomorrow. There's a cafe on the lake, Captain Pat's. I'll see you there at twelve-thirty."

"I'll be there."

Tim hung up the phone, got out of the SUV, and opened the back doors, helping the young women and their dates into the Cadillac.

"Channel 6 News has live coverage of prom night and updates on two special seniors."

"That's right, Chuck," said Amelia, the news co-anchor. "It was little more than a week ago when the city was on edge, searching for three missing families who were abducted. Among them were seniors Leah Davenport and Barbra Mills. Tonight, Lake Valley celebrates as they attend their senior prom. Let's go to Brenda Calderwood with a live report from the high school."

"Thank you, Amelia. The theme for this year's prom is 'Under the Stars,' and the staff has gone above and beyond to create a truly magical night. Billowing white drapes sweep across the ceiling like clouds, while deep blue and black tapestries cloak the walls creating a twilight mood. Blue spotlights and tiny twinkling lights mimic the celestial heavens above, transforming the room into a night sky that woos the romantic imagination and invites every heart to dream.

"Of course, all eyes will be on Lake Valley's most popular student, Leah Davenport, who has risen from the recent drama as a hero, described by many as an angel. We had a chance to talk with Leah as she arrived at the dance.

"You look absolutely stunning. How does it feel to be attending your senior prom?"

"Thank you, Brenda. I'm excited. The whole experience has been so fun. Dress shopping with my mom and best friend, doing my nails, hair, and makeup, putting on my dress, getting photos... We had dinner at Anthony's, and now being here at the dance—I feel like Cinderella."

"As you should. The journey hasn't been easy. Did you think you would be all dressed up, attending prom, a week ago?"

"Prom was the *last* thing on my mind a week ago. But here I am, and I'm grateful."

"Does it upset you that charges were not brought against Detective Spencer for his role in your abduction?"

"No, not at all. In fact, I'm very happy he wasn't charged. Detective Brandon Spencer found my dad and reunited me with him. If it weren't for Brandon, Dad could have been missing for years. Detective Spencer should be promoted."

"Does it worry you that the body of the abductor has yet to be found?"

"It doesn't. He's gone. That's behind me now. I'm at prom! I should go; my date is waiting."

"Of course. Thank you for talking with us this evening. Enjoy the dance."

"Thank you."

"That was Leah Davenport, and I'm Brenda Calderwood with Channel 6 News."

Leah followed Dan, Barb, and Eric inside the school. The music's pulse vibrated through the floor and Leah moved her hips to the pounding beat as she made her way over to the tables. Jess and Nancy had already pushed two of them together.

Becky rushed over, followed by a boy who stood awkwardly behind her. She clasped Leah's hands and bounced with excitement. "This is so fun! I'm glad you're here," she said, with a wide smile that shined.

Leah squinted, straining to catch Becky's words. "What?"

Becky leaned closer and spoke directly into her ear. "You remember Andrew—from youth group."

Leah nodded at the boy. "I do," she said, motioning to the tables. "Come, join us."

They dragged two extra chairs over.

"What's wrong with Eric?" Becky asked.

Eric sat slouched like a wet cat forced to endure a bath. He glanced aimlessly around the room, devoid of interest. Leah clenched her jaw, heat building in her chest. The ghost possessing him wasn't going to ruin this night. "Headache," Leah responded.

"We're going to grab drinks. You want one?" Barb shouted.

"Yes, please. Thank you," Leah replied.

Becky and Andrew went with Barb.

Leah spun in a circle, looking for Dan. He tapped her shoulder and slid his arm around her waist, pulling her close. She placed her hand over his and tilted her head back, feeling the quiet thrill of being desired. His lips nibbled her ear, and she moaned. "I need to use the restroom. I'll be back." He kissed her cheek. She watched him stroll through the crowd, sturdy and handsome.

"Leah, is what they say about you true?" Jess asked in a boisterous tone.

She turned to face him. "I don't know. What do they say about me?"

"That you have divine power."

Leah laughed, arching an eyebrow. "Really? Please, Jess."

"I know. I'm just curious what you think about the whole thing."

"It's stupid."

Nancy stepped close and asked, "Is Eric feeling okay?"

"He doesn't quite feel like himself," Leah said.

"I can't believe the doctors didn't give him any pills," Jess said. "I was kind of hoping to score a few off him."

"Seriously?" Leah looked at Jess sideways, her eyes narrowing with disdain.

Jess shot Leah a surprised look. "Don't tell me you don't dabble?"

"I don't need to. I know how to enjoy myself just fine. How long have you known Eric?"

"Since seventh grade."

"Do you know him well?"

"We're best friends," Jess said.

A group of four students tapped Leah's shoulder. "Can we get a selfie with you?"

"Umm, sure," Leah responded. They arranged themselves in a group and took a few photos.

"Thank you, Leah!" they said, looking at the shots as they left.

Barb, Becky, and Andrew came back with drinks, crackers, veggies, and dip. They sat, watching the crowd, listening to the music, and sipping their drinks. Dan returned, pointing out Leah's mom, Stacy, who was taking student information at the photo stand. Andrew and Becky left to dance.

Dan asked Leah, "Want to get a photo?"

"Not yet."

He leaned closer. "Because of Eric?"

"I'm going to connect with him, find out what the ghost wants."

"I really don't want you to do that. You were in so much pain last time."

"I'll be okay. I've learned a lot since then."

Jess touched Dan's arm. "I need to talk with Leah. Why don't you dance with Nancy for a couple songs?"

Dan hesitated. "Umm."

"It's okay," Leah said.

Dan kissed Leah. He turned to Nancy, who took his hand. They hit the dance floor while Jess moved closer to Leah.

"So, I'm really curious about what happened to you guys. All this talk about you being a hero and an angel, it's kind of crazy."

"Yeah, crazy," Leah agreed.

"Tell me what happened."

Leah paused, thinking about what to say. "Well, we were kidnapped. I don't know what else to say, Jess. I have a hard enough time talking to the therapist about it."

The DJ played Kylie Minogue's song "Padam Padam," which filled the dance floor.

Leah and Barb exchanged glances, telling each other it was time.

"Jess, if I get dizzy, can you catch me?"

"Dizzy? You need some water?"

"Just ... if I start to get dizzy and stumble, don't let me hit the floor."

Leah stepped in front of Eric and put a hand on his shoulder. She leaned in and stared him in the eyes. Connecting, she immediately felt saturated with guilt. "Oh, shit!" The emotions were heavy, and their weight made her stumble.

"You all right?" Jess asked, guiding her to a chair.

Putting up her hand, she said, "No, wait."

Leah was pulled into a vision—a memory, but not hers. It was from the ghost possessing Eric named Paul. Frustration, dread, anger, and fear flooded Leah's body. Paul had been forced to type an awful email. She couldn't make out the text but understood that Paul's daughter had made an important life decision that upset the government. An agent showed up at his house and insisted Paul stop her.

The vision continued, showing the agent hovering over Paul as he wrote. The interaction transitioned into a phone call. Paul forced anger into his voice to satisfy the man.

Jess squeezed Leah's hand. "What do you need? Should I get a teacher?"

Leah shook him away. "No." She glanced at Eric, wondering what the vision meant. Did the agent murder Paul?

Eric stood and faced Leah. "She needs to know that wasn't me. I didn't want to send that email. Let me go to the boy's home; I'll write a new email explaining what happened, and then I'll leave."

"What's at Eric's house?" Leah asked Paul.

"My computer."

Leah turned to Jess. "Did Eric buy a new computer?"

"Yeah," Jess said. "He got it on Craigslist. It was really cheap."

Eric pressed, "I need to send her another email. I need to apologize."

"Who did he buy it from?" Leah prodded. "Why was it so cheap? Did the owner die?"

"I don't know," Jess said, shaking his head. "Why does it matter?"

"I need to know who he bought it from. Was it a guy named Paul?"

"We picked it up from a lady. Her husband was sick in the hospital." Jess turned to Eric. "Who did you buy that computer from?"

"If he knew, I would have asked him myself," Leah shot back. Looking at Eric, Leah asked, "What's your name? Your full name. Paul what?"

"Once I email her, I can rest," Eric said impatiently.

"That computer's probably been wiped. Tell me who you are, so I can help."

"Who he is? What are you talking about? Who is Paul?"

Barb put her hand on Jess's shoulder. "Not now."

"I'm sorry," Eric said, "but I have to get home. I only need to email my daughter."

Leah took his hand. "No, not yet. You need to dance with Barb first."

Barb glared at Leah. "We should call Bruce."

"The FBI?" Leah questioned. "It's prom. I can do this."

"What the hell are you two talking about?" Jess exclaimed. "Why would you need to call the FBI?" Then he slapped Eric's chest. "You have a daughter?"

Barb intervened, telling Jess he didn't have a daughter. Then looked at Leah. "This is a bad idea."

Leah let out a sigh of frustration. "Keep him dancing. I need a minute to prepare myself."

Taking Eric's hand, Barb dragged him to the dance floor.

"Man, I do not understand you!" Jess shouted. "Eric has been having migraines and spent two nights in the hospital. He's totally out of it. I think Barb should take him home. She can come back and hang with us after dropping him off."

"Maybe. I need to talk with Dan first," Leah said. "Can you dance with your date?"

Jess shook his head. "Sure. But you should get Eric out of here."

Jess turned and found Dan, patted his shoulder, and pointed to Leah. When Dan reached her, she said, "Eric bought a computer that had a soul attached to it. The soul needs to email his daughter before it will transcend."

"Who is this soul?" Dan asked.

"His name was Paul," Leah said. "I can engage with him, get the email address or a phone number, and then help him ... or force him to transcend. Once that happens, Eric will be free. He'll be confused, but at least he'll be able to enjoy prom."

"And remember it."

"Exactly. So, you agree with me?"

"What did Barb say?"

"She wants me to call Bruce. But this is prom. I want her to enjoy it. I want Eric to remember it."

"Why don't you just ask for the email address or number? You don't need to take the soul out of Eric for that. You're making this more complicated than it has to be."

"I'd feel better if I freed Eric first. I want to make sure Paul transcends, and if the soul is with me, I can force it, if I have to."

"You know how to do that?"

"How do you think I saved us? I got this."

Laying his hand on her arm, Dan said, "Think about this for a minute. You could—"

"Dan! This is what I'm doing," Leah interjected. "Besides, the soul isn't exactly cooperating. I need to grab ahold of it."

"Sure. Yep."

A couple approached Leah and pointed to a cell phone. "Can we get a photo with you?"

In the corner of the gym, guarding the doors that led into the halls of the school, Mr. Anderson watched Leah and her friends. Something was wrong. Their body language told him that Leah and Barb were stressed. Dan showed concern, one of the other boys, confusion. And Barb's date was … not himself. His aura suggested he was possessed. Mr. Anderson needed to connect with him.

Moving strategically, he waited for his moment. When two students asked to take photos with Leah, he made his way onto the dance floor and locked eyes with Eric. He rubbed the boy's shoulder as he passed, making the connection and bringing a surge of emotions and memories. It was Paul! Of all the ghosts, it had to be Paul.

"Un-fucking-believable!" he muttered under his breath. He had sent an agent to Paul's house. The guy was supposed to have Paul convince his daughter, Misty, to drop her application to join Doctors Without Borders. That had been eight months ago, before Paul's death. Despite that meeting, Misty had joined anyway and gone to the refugee camp, causing trouble for Extended Life with her relentless crusade against them. Mr. Anderson should have taken care of that himself.

Paul's presence could complicate matters. But maybe, just maybe, this could be turned to his advantage. Mr. Anderson shifted his focus back to Leah.

Oh, Leah. Awe was the first feeling he had. She was already connecting, and not just to a person, but to a person who was possessed. He had trained with Ruth for over a week before he could make a strong connection, and that was after years of making weaker connections on his own; he just hadn't understood how he had done it. Another year of training passed before his first ghost encounter, and here Leah was, interacting with a ghost, with no training. Going into Leah's mind to implant thoughts was now off the table. She was aware and actively wielding her powers. She wasn't just an energy manipulator; she was a prodigy.

His mind juggled this information. This was the absolute proof he needed. But how could he document it? First, he had to get evidence that showed Eric was possessed. His parents would know something's wrong and probably take him to see a doctor. Mr. Anderson would get those records. Those documents, combined with the video footage of tonight... Mr. Anderson grinned. Leah's future belonged to him.

Seoul, Korea

<u>Closures and Clues</u>

After nearly being hit by a car while dazedly stepping into the street, Brandon decided to hail a taxi. He took it downtown to Malli-Dong district to visit the alley where the accident had happened. He couldn't put off going any longer.

In the cab, Brandon found it difficult to breathe. Heat clawed up the back of his neck. They passed a familiar corner, triggering a memory—lifeless bodies lying on the concrete, the blood winding through the bricks like a river. He couldn't hold the tears back and broke down. The taxi driver pulled the car to the curb and turned to examine Brandon. He said something, but Brandon couldn't understand. He didn't even know if the man was speaking English or Korean.

The driver got out, opened the back door, and sat with Brandon as he heaved uncontrollably. The commotion drew the attention of a college student who came close, asking Brandon if everything were okay. He calmed himself, stopped crying, and gained his composure. After a few minutes, the driver took his seat and continued to the destination.

Brandon paid double the fare listed, insisting that the cab driver keep it. Walking from the hotel, he found the alley and stood at its entrance, staring. His heart had turned into a lead rock, seeping poison into his blood stream. He couldn't move; his body refused to obey.

The alley darkened as his chest tightened. The longer he stood, the more the shadows thickened, creeping around the edges of his vision, distorting the world before him. A stranger bumped into Brandon, pushing him into the bright and lively alleyway. He forced himself to keep moving, one step at a time, hoping to find more than devastating heartbreak. He was looking for Hina's soul.

The narrow cobblestone path was littered with advertising. Signs attached to walls, propped on the ground, and hanging from rope in the middle of the alley were brightly lit in purple, yellow, and red, with arrows pointing to the entrances of a hair salon, a bar, and a noodle shop. Several other businesses could be found along the snaking path that ran between buildings and ended at the entrance to a park. Gutters, pipes, and electrical wires flanked green plants growing in stone flowerpots. Parked mopeds, puddles, and people cluttered the path, forcing him to weave through the congestion. Hina and he had walked through this alley on three separate occasions, stopping at the mom-and-pop convenience stand halfway through to buy snacks—the alley hadn't changed a bit. Brandon inched along to the very spot Hina and their son had lain, a steady stream of tears running down his cheeks. His chest ached as the paralyzing memory assaulted him.

His boy had awakened around midnight and was restless in the dry, stale air-conditioned room—a walk in the park would have him sleeping again in no time, as there was a light refreshing breeze that night. Brandon held his son as he and Hina walked down the alley toward the park. Just then, two men exited a bar.

"Hey! It's him," a stocky guy with short hair said, pointing at Brandon. The second man, taller, muscular, wearing basketball shorts and a Manchester United football jersey, grunted and cracked his knuckles.

Brandon handed Jaime to Hina. She rested their son's head on her shoulder and took a step back.

"Didn't think you'd ever see me again, did you?" the smaller guy said. "You Americans are all pieces of shit."

Brandon raised his hands, surrendering. "I'm sorry, but my wife and I are just tourists. We're in Seoul to celebrate my baby's first birthday. You and I have never met."

As Brandon spoke, the second man walked straight to him and punched Brandon in the face. Hina's scream was the last thing Brandon heard as he fell, hitting the back of his head on a plastic sign and then the front of his head on the stone pathway. There, he lay unconscious until he was shaken awake by a young man and woman.

Kneeling, Brandon put his hand in the place Hina and Jaime had fallen, the doctor's voice ringing in his ears, "She most likely tripped on the stone." He saw the raised block was still there.

"Hi, sweetie," Brandon managed before standing and stumbling back into the wall. Running his hands through his hair, he slid down into a squatting position—his eyes red, his cheeks wet, snot running over his lip. "Where are you?" He stared into the sky, knowing he had to stir his spiritual energy if he was going to attempt communication, but the raw, stabbing heat struck relentlessly. He couldn't. *Breathe. Just breathe.*

Curling into a ball against the wall, Brandon lay, looking at the spot where his family had died.

Min Yun sat on the bench in front of the hospital, waiting for the nurse, Eun Yeol, to exit. When he saw her, he approached, introduced himself, and offered to buy her dinner while they talked. She accepted, and they crossed the street to a seafood restaurant.

The cook stood on an elevated platform with an aquarium in front of him that held live crab, lobsters, and oysters. He greeted them as they entered, pointing to several empty tables. Min led Eun Yeol to the far table in the corner. While the nurse looked at the menu, Min removed a small writing pad, pen, and several photos from his suit jacket and laid them on the table.

After ordering, Min began. "Tell me what you remember about Ki-Tae Moon."

"He was a high-ranking official in the government. He had complications with his stomach, and the hospital ordered a surgical procedure."

"What kind of patient was he?"

"What do you mean?"

"Was he rude, temperamental, or argumentative?"

"He was a VIP patient. I still don't understand why you are asking about him. His wife killed him in self-defense years ago."

"Mr. Moon was murdered, but not by his wife. Someone with medical training cut him. Dr. Kim is a suspect."

Eun Yeol blinked. "Dr. Kim?" She leaned away, widening her eyes and knitting her brow. "But why? How?"

Min took out a recording device and pushed play. Dr. Kim's voice said, "Mr. Moon was an arrogant man. He had power and social status. Mr. Moon was a heavy drinker, prone to violence." Min pushed stop.

"But that's all true. Everyone knew that."

"Did Dr. Kim seem agitated or upset by Mr. Moon?"

The nurse thought for a minute before saying, "He was frustrated that Mr. Moon didn't show appreciation for being moved to the front of the line. That man didn't care that other patients got bumped; he felt entitled, believing he was afforded special treatment."

"Did that anger Dr. Kim?"

"I wouldn't say angered. We just wished Mr. Moon had shown a little gratitude, that's all."

"What happened to the other patients—the ones who were bumped?"

"They were rescheduled or seen by another doctor."

"So it all worked out? There were no problems or complications with postponing the other surgeries?"

"That's right."

Min's gaze hardened.

Eun Yeol scooted back, her breathing quickening. She swallowed and said, "One patient did die. A woman."

"Do you remember her name?"

"It was so long ago, I'm sorry. But I'm sure the hospital has the records."

Min picked up the photos, showing Eun Yoel one of them—an image of a flask. "Do you recognize this?"

She held the photo. "Should I?"

He showed her two others taken of the flask from different angles, and then a fourth focused on the engraved initials. "How about now?"

"Yes, I recognize it. The staff gave Dr. Kim that flask as a Christmas gift, ten or twelve years ago. But he lost it soon after. I remember he asked me to help him find it."

"It was found at Mr. Moon's house the night he was murdered." Showing the nurse another photo, this one of a necklace, he asked, "How about this?"

"That was Mr. Moon's necklace. He was very protective of it. He had a safe brought to his room specifically to hold it. What does that have to do with anything?"

"It's missing and has never been found. I believe the murderer took it as a trophy."

"And you think Dr. Kim has it?"

"What else can you tell me about Mr. Moon's stay at the hospital? I need to know everything."

The waiter returned, setting down their drinks and a small basket of warm bread along with a bowl of sticky rice, a seaweed salad called gim, and dishes of kimchi and dried anchovies.

Eun Yeol took a slow sip of her beer before answering. "He was grabby. Kept touching the nurses inappropriately."

"Did Dr. Kim know about that?" Min asked.

"Older rich men with power tend to do that. It's just the way it is. We're used to it."

"Dr. Kim was grabby, too?"

"No. Never. He's a decent man. A good doctor."

"So, he was upset by what was happening."

"Upset?" She took another sip of her beer. "He sighed and shook his head. What could he say? This was a member of government."

"How about the other doctors?"

"We never talked about it."

"What else can you tell me?" Min asked.

"Nothing. The surgery was performed, and Mr. Moon recovered quickly. He left the hospital four days later."

"And in those four days, he didn't upset anyone?"

"He wasn't exactly a nice man. We were happy to see him leave."

"Has Dr. Kim ever showed his anger at work? Is he the kind of man to hold a grudge?"

"I've worked with Dr. Kim for over fifteen years. He's a fantastic physician and a good friend. I really think there must be a mistake. I can't see him hurting anyone. He's not a murderer."

"I know how you feel and understand why you think that. I've heard these very words from the friends and spouses of loved ones who were found guilty."

The nurse shook her head. "I don't believe you."

Min gave a polite smile. The nurse needed time to process the information. "You have my card. Think about it. And please call me if you remember anything. Enjoy the rest of your meal." Min thanked the nurse, paid the bill, and left.

Outside the restaurant, Min made a call. "I need you to watch Dr. Kim. I'll need detailed descriptions of his daily routines. Get photos."

Standing between a judge, Su-Bin and Hina faced each other under a tree in the park. A nervous breeze came in off the lake stirring the leaves. The sky, a shade of gray, made the judge's face appear grim. The women studied each other. Hina reached out, touching Su-Bin's hair. Su-Bin, in return, touched Hina's cheek. The women smiled, then shook hands. The judge stood, congratulating them. The sky lightened as the three turned away from each other and walked away in separate directions.

The dream dissipated as a hand shook Brandon awake. He opened his eyes, finding two police officers: one crouched beside him, shaking his shoulder, and the other stood over him like the Jolly Green Giant, arms crossed with a broad smile. The officer helped him to his feet, smelling his breath for alcohol and examining his eyes. When he was satisfied Brandon was neither high nor drunk, he motioned for him to move along.

Bowing, Brandon thanked the officers and exited the alley. On the side of the street, a vendor was selling noodles. He ordered a bowl and sat at one of the folding tables, thinking about the dream and wondering what it meant. Was it a message? Had Hina met Su-Bin? He was still unsure who Su-Bin was, her role in his training, or what would become of the intense gaze they had shared.

Brandon stared into his bowl of noodles, noticing he could breathe a lot easier now. He would go home, build his spiritual energy, and focus on Hina. If he was lucky, she'd nudge him.

He opened the Naver Map app on his phone and searched for the nearest public transit that could take him home. Subway Line 4 was just a few blocks away. As he stepped onto the train, a memory stirred—sitting on the subway while holding Hina's hand. This was a nice memory, one that he could now cherish.

It had been a cool Saturday evening in Tokyo. Hina wore a light spring jacket, clutching it tight to stave off her nervousness. Tokyo's city lights flickered past as the train rattled along the tracks. He watched her twist the string of her hood. Despite her anxiety, he couldn't help but admire how beautiful she looked. Her dark hair was smooth, brushing her cheeks as she stirred from the motion of the train and her own rocking.

Brandon reached over, taking her hands. He squeezed them to offer reassurance. She looked at him with a small, grateful smile.

"Daijoubu," he offered. "It'll be okay."

Hina closed her eyes and shook her head, a light trembling in her hands.

His own nerves were surprisingly calm. He knew her father was a well-known shakuhachi player, having performed for the Imperial Family and being designated a "Living National Treasure," his shakuhachi technique recognized as an "Important Intangible Cultural Property." Brandon had taken lessons himself, so he understood the significance of the instrument—a traditional end-blown flute made from the root of a bamboo tree that followed the pentatonic musical scale. In preparation of their meeting, he had practiced "Sakura," one of Japan's most famous melodies, hoping to show some respect and acknowledgement of her father's craft.

Hina's mother was also famous. Her goldfish paintings were internationally renowned, often compared to Riusuke Fukahori's work. Her most famous piece hung in the prime minister's office, solidifying both of Hina's parents as cultural icons.

"Try to relax, okay?" Brandon said. "I'm ready. You said my Japanese was good enough. I've worked hard."

"Brandon..." she said, slowly and deliberately. "You don't fully understand. And I'm sorry I haven't mentioned this earlier, but my parents had expectations for me. Big ones."

She looked up, scanning the ads posted above the windows. Her gaze settled on the one advertising the benefits of an overseas education. "They sent me to a boarding school in Paris, thinking I'd follow in their footsteps—as an artist. But I was never good with my hands." She bowed her head. "And when I had to complete my school's volunteer requirements, I started tutoring. I love working with kids."

Brandon rubbed her upper arm.

"When I became a teacher, I became an embarrassment." She looked into his eyes, her own watering. "What saved me was teaching at an international school. This position restored some dignity for them." She squeezed her eyes tight, and a small tear formed. "But now I'm bringing home an American boyfriend... They're going to see this as another way I've strayed from expectations."

The subway car rocked as it rounded a bend. The intercom crackled, announcing the next station.

"Hina, I love you. What can I do to help comfort you?"

A hollow chuckle escaped her lips before she murmured, "You could tell them you're a billionaire, or the heir to an ancient samurai clan, descendant of the Tokugawa shogunate." She sighed, then smiled. "That might impress them."

He marveled at how lucky he was. Hina was brilliant and sharp-witted. She had the courage to follow her own path while still considering her parents' hopes for her. She didn't run from her heritage, nor let it define her. But as much as he admired her and felt grateful to be her partner, there was a guilt that slivered its way into his heart: he was the cause of this stress.

Hina must have recognized his shifting emotions because she quickly added, "Their disappointment is on them. Don't for a second think you're the cause of my worry. Their emotions and reactions speak about them. Their feelings are their problem, not ours. I chose you, and if asked to choose again, I still choose you."

He squeezed her hands once more. "Thank you." Offering her a reassuring smile, he said, "We've got this. I can't wait to meet them."

The memory faded as Subway Line 4 in Seoul came to a stop. The doors slid open, and Brandon stepped out. This was the first time he had allowed himself to remember.

Arriving home, Brandon needed to know Hina was in a good place. He sat on the bed and took the position of the Buddha. After growing the energy in his spiritual center, he sent it out with Hina in mind. He whispered her name and pictured her—meeting her for the first time in the school cafeteria, walking past her classroom to steal glimpses of her teaching, asking her for advice on lesson plans, and bringing her presents: chocolates, a thumb drive, mangoes. He remembered the first time they were passionate: sitting in the car, she climbed onto his lap, facing him. They kissed, touched, and explored each other's bodies until the wee hours of the morning, hearts racing, body parts throbbing.

Rubbing his fingertips together, Brandon let his mind go blank and invited Hina to him. He sat, waiting. Ten minutes. Twenty minutes. Thirty-five minutes. Then a vision materialized.

Hina appeared, surrounded by light, saying, "Hello, my love."

Clutching his pillow to his chest, Brandon lay back on his bed. Relief, satisfaction, and acceptance washed all the strain and grief from his body. That little whisper, "Hello, my love," was laced with memory and love, enough to let him know she was okay. This nudge gave him what he needed to move on.

Smiling, he rolled onto his side, holding the pillow in his arms. "Hello, my love," he answered. Then drifted off and napped.

In a half dozed, dreamy state, he saw Su-Bin. She was reading a news article online from the *Lake Valley Sun Times* about the disappearance of six people at the Education Center and Brandon's subsequent arrest.

He woke with a start, wondering how she would see him after reading the article. It didn't exactly portray him in the best light.

A second vision appeared, this one through his connection to her. She was watching a video, a news clip from Channel 6 News about prom. Brandon opened his phone, searched for the video, and hit play. The reported ask if she was upset charges hadn't been brought against him. He silently thanked Leah for praising him.

This was strange. The visions of Su-Bin—the energy accompanying them—didn't feel like her. He rubbed his head, trying to understand. How should he respond? Should he send an image of himself watching the same video? No. He shouldn't respond at all. If he sent her an image, how would she interpret that? He knew she liked him; their interaction together at her office was all the evidence he needed.

The spark between them was undeniable, but Brandon had no interest in starting a new relationship, especially with his new boss. Besides, he was only going to be in Korea for six months, a year at most. He didn't need any drama, particularly at work.

A third vision came to him: Su-Bin emailing the HR department to make a schedule for Brandon. That must mean his hiring was now official. *Should I respond?* he thought. Perhaps a text message would be better because it was less intimate, even cold in comparison. This way he could acknowledge her without giving her the wrong impression. Brandon texted: "Looking forward to meeting you again tomorrow. Have a great night."

As soon as he put the phone down, he regretted texting. These visions were her way of flirting. He laid back down, staring at the ceiling. This was going to be complicated. He could already feel the tension.

Lake Valley, Oregon

A Night to Regret

Tim Davenport paced back and forth in the school parking lot, talking on his phone with his buddies Big Steve, Bret, Nate, and Dylan.

"You have to trust me on this," Tim said. "The land needs to be returned to the Sukiya Tribe. It's the only way to ensure no one else gets hurt, kidnapped, or killed at that place. This plan will work. I'm meeting with a protest organizer tomorrow, a Native guy. But we need community support—at least 60 percent to make the de-annexation campaign a success. I want you guys to pick an idea and start drumming up support for the city to hand the land back. Once we get the buzz going, we'll start circulating petitions and then we'll 'rally' right before the election."

"What kind of ideas were you thinking about?" Big Steve asked.

"Anything that will make the Education Center sound bad or make people angry when they think about that property," Tim explained. "We want people to believe the city never should have annexed it in the first place."

"How about rumors?" Bret asked. "The property is currently owned by a Chinese lady. Some of my more racist regulars have already voiced distrust of the Education Center, saying the owner is using it to spread pro-Chinese propaganda."

Big Steve laughed. "The lady is a political refugee. The Chinese government literally wants to hang her."

Nate jumped in, "We can actually use that, though. You remember when people were saying that aliens were abducting the people who disappeared from the Center because they came back in a coma and couldn't remember anything? Well, we can say it was the Chinese government doing experiments on them. It'll work, too, because the FBI said the kidnapper died, but no name has been released. The U.S. government doesn't want an international crisis, so they are covering up the whole thing."

"We already have an international crisis with them," Big Steve said. "You don't think this'll stoke anti-Asian sentiment?"

"It might, but the media will be sure to address that," Nate countered. "I bet this idea spreads like covid at a super-spreader event."

"I think we could start several different rumors and disinformation campaigns," Dylan said. "Anti-immigrant, religious, conspiracy, pro-Native."

"I know a conspiracy theory that is kind of already out there," Nate said. "When the FBI were combing through the Education Center, many of them complained about getting headaches. They called in a specialist to see if it was a chemical leak, and I heard someone saying they believed toxic waste was buried there."

"These are great ideas," Tim stated. "Let's use them all."

"I'll take a religious stance," Big Steve said quickly.

"Are you sure you know enough about the Bible to make a good argument?" Bret asked.

"It wasn't too long ago that the place was possessed by the devil," Big Steve said. "Besides, I just need to get Leah to say something about how it's evil in a news article and people will believe it. The movement will build itself."

"Good luck with that, Big Steve. All those religious nut jobs just blessed that place. I'll take the easy one—the Chinese are using us as guinea pigs to test their drugs," Nate said.

"Okay, I'll go with, 'The government buried toxic waste,'" Dylan said. "That's why the owner went crazy and burned down the house."

"Good one," Bret said.

"I like it," added Tim.

"I could say that one of the teachers is gay," Bret said.

"They probably are. That's not such a big deal anymore," Tim said.

"Haven't you been paying attention to the news?" Dylan retorted. "Gay bashing is back in now that gay marriage is a thing."

"I get we're preying on the gullible idiots out there, but we need people to support returning the land to the reservation. A gay teacher isn't going to do that," Tim argued.

"I agree," Big Steve said.

"I know. I'll spread some disinformation about why we should give the land back to the Sukiya. I'll say stuff like, we signed a treaty, and by keeping the land we are breaking that contract," Bret offered.

"Did we sign a treaty?" Dylan asked.

"That's the exact response we want," Tim replied. "No one actually bothers to look that shit up."

"Is that a no?" Dylan pressed.

"Tim, you should contact the doctor who has been warning people about attending the Education Center," Bret said.

"Who is that?"

"Go online. I read the article after your brother was abducted. She's advocating for the health department to shut down the Center permanently."

"Hey, I gotta run. When are we meeting to plan this 'rally'?" Big Steve asked.

"I'll get back with you all after I meet this Roy guy tomorrow," Tim said.

"Okay. Later. Love you guys." Big Steve hung up.

The others took turns saying goodbye and hanging up as well.

Tim returned to the truck and checked the tracking device to see where Leah was. She wasn't in the gym but outside the school. *What is she doing?* Tim thought. She was probably fine. After all, she did say she would send him a telepathic message if she needed help. But what if she were unconscious?

"Dammit!" Tim had to check on her.

Spinning on the dance floor, Leah and Dan joined Eric and Barb.

"I can't make the soul transcend here," Leah said. "There are too many distractions. Let's go to another part of the school."

Barb surveyed the area. "The teachers are guarding the doors. We'll have to go outside."

"There are people out there too," Dan said.

"That's where you come in," Leah said. "Make sure no one interrupts me. I can't be distracted once I start."

"I'll be the lookout then," Dan said.

Eric leaned close. "Take me home. I'm done."

"Let's talk outside," Leah said. "Barb, make sure no one follows us."

Barb nodded.

"Come on, Paul." Leah led Eric to the doors. "What's your last name, Paul?"

"Once I send my email, I'll leave. That's all I need to do."

At the door, the teacher addressed them. "How are you kids doing? Is everything okay?"

"Yeah. We're going out for some air," Leah said.

"Leah," the teacher said. "Can you say a prayer for my aunt? Her name is Diana Bass. She has stage-three cancer."

"Diana Bass. Sure, I can do that for you."

"Thank you so much."

Going through the doors and out into the parking lot, Paul asked, "What is it with you?"

"Nothing."

Dan was on the sidewalk near the back corner of the school waving them over. Leah took Eric's hand, leading him.

"Wait. The car is over there," Paul protested, pulling back.

Leah stopped and grabbed Eric's tuxedo near his collar. She pulled him close, saying, "Listen to me, Paul. I need you to trust me. I know what I'm doing."

Leah and Eric turned the corner, and Dan stepped away.

"Paul, I'm going to invite you to me," Leah said, pushing Eric to his knees. She joined him and held his hands. Leah prayed, "Dear Lord, please give me the power to help this soul. I surrender to your wisdom and allow your strength to flow through me." She thanked her grandparents and her great-grandmother, her teachers, and, finally, her mom and dad.

Finishing her prayers, Leah went through the connection process again. With Paul in mind, she sent her energy out and invited it back, leaving her mind open.

Eric fell forward onto Leah, before rolling onto his back. He grasped his chest and breathed heavily.

A stabbing headache surged through Leah, and she snatched Eric's hand, squeezing it. The spectral being was desperate to break the barriers of her mind and seize control. The pain was visceral as Paul dug through her memories. But Leah had gone through this before.

Two options were available to her. Leah could engage with the memories Paul was digging through and transfer into his consciousness or open her mind and go completely blank. She chose to empty her thoughts and open her mind, not allowing the ghost anything to hold. Focusing on the drumbeat coming from the DJ's music inside the gym, Leah clutched Eric's hand while running her fingers through the grass with the other. The cool night air, mixed with the smell of freshly cut grass and Eric's cologne, gave her a sense of grounding and clarity. She was here. Calm. Relaxed. No worries, no problems, no anxieties. Just a beautiful night, outside. Leah breathed easily, the pain having subsided.

Why have you yanked me to you? Paul asked. *Just take me to the boy's home. I can email my daughter and then I can travel away.*

Let me call your daughter right now and we'll talk to her together. Who is she? Leah asked.

We can't. She volunteered with Doctors Without Borders. She's in a refugee camp in India.

An email then. Give me the address.

I can't remember it. That's why I need that computer.

I told you, the computer has been wiped. Just give me your password, and I'll log into your account, copy her address, and then send her the email.

I don't remember my password. Everything was auto load.

Paul, you're making this very difficult. How old were you, seventy?

Sixty-one. I had my passwords in a black book in my study, but everything is gone.

Listen, I'll send her a message through the company website. What's her name?
Misty Davis.

In a deep, throaty tone, laced with a hint of sarcasm, Leah said, *Thank you. Was that so difficult?* Her eyes rolled, and with a sense of exasperation, she added, *What do you want to say to her?*

Tell her she made the right choice, and I was wrong to challenge her. She was following in my footsteps, and I was proud. I love her. Say she has a big, wonderful heart, and I was wrong to have been bullied into guilting her away from this opportunity by using her mother's death.

Bullied by who?

It's political. That's not important. What's important is that she knows I didn't mean what I said. She's stronger than she knows. Tougher than I gave her credit. I hope she knows that.

I'll tell her.

I need to tell her! Paul shouted.

Leah could feel Paul clawing to grab hold of her mind, but the light breeze, subtle vibration of the music, and Eric's hand kept her centered and open. Paul bombarded Leah with memories, emotions, and conversations he had had with Misty. Leah knew this flood of experiences served a dual purpose: to ensure Leah fully grasped the depth of his message and remorse, and also to elicit a response from her, providing an opportunity to possess her so that he could convey the message himself. She was prepared.

Leah experienced a telephone conversation between Paul and Misty first. Leah heard Misty's excitement as she explained the volunteer position. Going overseas and helping people during their most dire and vulnerable point in life felt honorable and worthy of a mission that would make her father proud. Misty expected praise, but Paul felt afraid and glanced to the man hovering over him, listening. Making his voice sound angry, Paul told her he hadn't paid for her schooling so she could go play wet nurse in a foreign country. She needed to make money, to help support him and her brother. Debts didn't pay themselves. Then a genuine fear crept into his voice. Misty would be in war zones. The thought of losing her was compounded by the loss of his wife, and he used that against her, insisting she stop dreaming and return home.

The memory was laced with the threat to Paul's life and that stung Leah. She couldn't ponder or question though. She had to let the feeling and memory go untouched or risk Paul possessing her. Other memories and emotions quickly followed—Paul driving Misty to Boston to start college where he helped her move her into the dorm room, Thanksgiving dinner with smiles, hugs, friendly banter, politics, and a turkey drawing dice game.

Leah let those memories slide over her, not allowing Paul to stir her own memories or emotions. She could feel him digging, but she remained relaxed and open. *I'm going to disengage with you. I will pass along your message and let you know when it's done.*

Closing her eyes, Leah repeated, "Calm, be calm." The mental image she had prepared and sent to Barb, the one in the sunflower field with the waterfall that embodied calmness, replayed for her now. The music in the gym had a steady beat, and she clicked her teeth in rhythm. Leah stopped thinking and enjoyed lying in the grass. Feeling serene and at peace, her mind open, she waited patiently for Paul to leave.

Paul lingered.

Eric sat up and leaned over her, brushing her bangs from her eyes. She used his touch to remain here, open, and free, knowing it could take a minute or two before Paul drifted away.

"Leah!" Uncle Tim shouted.

Eric pulled his hand away and scooted back toward the wall.

Not now, Leah thought. Then a dull throb embedded in her mind with a thud. She felt slightly dizzy. Waves of nausea swept over her as her heart rate increased. Paul attached to her.

Uncle Tim kneeled next to his niece and held her face in his hands. "Leah, talk to me." Looking at Eric, he demanded, "What happened? What did you do?"

Eric was oblivious. "I have no idea. I don't even remember how I got here. Where are we, anyway?"

Leah moaned, "I'm fine, Uncle Tim, really."

"You don't sound fine. Why are you out here? Where's Barb?"

"Leah!" Stacy shouted as she turned the corner, brushing past a man staring at them and rushing to her daughter's side, Dan following.

"Tim, what happened? Is she okay?" Stacy pressed.

"I think so," Tim responded.

"Yes. I'm fine. Please stop badgering me," Leah said, wincing from the throbbing in her head and the tightness in her stomach.

"Eric! What are you two doing out here? Did you…?" Stacy accused.

Eric raised his hands in defense.

"Mom! Stop! He didn't do anything."

"Where's Barb? Tell me what's going on," Stacy insisted.

"We just needed to talk."

Stacy surveyed the area, Leah's dress, and Eric's tux, before saying, "Shit, I was worried sick. You can't be wandering off like that. It's not safe, Leah."

"I'm sorry, Mom. I should have told you we were coming out. I was a little worried you would have said no, and it was important."

"Did you guys sort everything out, then?" Stacy asked Eric.

"Umm. Yeah. We're good."

"Let's head back in," Stacy said, motioning the kids to walk in front of her.

Leah looked forward, her eyes tracing the path they needed to take. Ahead, standing at the corner of the building, was a man partly shrouded in the shadows. They locked eyes for an instant before he turned and left. Leah's heart skipped a beat. He was wearing the same meticulously tailored black suit he'd had on outside the Education Center. She recognized his receding hairline and got the same creepy impression. She turned to say something, but her mom and Tim were talking.

"Sorry, Tim," Stacy said. "Thanks for keeping an eye on her."

"Absolutely. She's a pistol. I think she gets it from you."

"I'm sure she does."

By the time they rounded the side of the gym, the man was gone. Who was he? A member of the press? Maybe, but why did he feel creepy? Was that his aura? Leah glanced back at Tim, her official bodyguard, feeling a bit more appreciative.

Back inside, Jess and Eric bumped fists. "Dude, you're back," Jess said. "What happened?"

Eric looked at him. "I don't know. It's all a blur."

Pressing, Jess asked, "How do you feel?"

"Great. A little confused, but shit, we're at prom, man!" He turned to Barb. "You look absolutely stunning." Reaching out, he took her hand and pulled her to her feet. He wrapped his arm around her waist and moved in close.

Leah watched Eric whisper in Barb's ear. She blushed, and a giant smile crossed her face. Leah didn't think she'd ever seen Barb this happy.

Taking Barb's hand, Eric escorted her to the dance floor.

Barb looked back at Leah, mouthing the words, *Thank you.*

Jess stared at Leah and asked, "What did you do? He's totally himself now."

Leah shrugged. "Yeah. He's all good."

The DJ started playing "Cha Cha Slide." Eric yelled from the dance floor, "Jeessss ... come on, man!"

Jess eyed Leah before leaving.

"So? What happened?" Dan asked.

"The ghost is attached to me. I feel crappy," Leah said.

"Attached? Like the first kind of attachment? The tag-along kind?"

"I'm not exactly an expert, but he's not trying to control me," Leah replied. "So, yeah, I think he's just observing."

"What are you going to do?"

"I'm going to help him. His daughter works with Doctors Without Borders, so I'll contact her through their website. Can you google Paul Davis?"

"Sure." Dan took out his phone and Leah did the same. "Tell me what happened."

"Paul was pressured to talk Misty out of joining the organization. He said it was political. Although, he was also terrified she'd be sent to a war zone. He said some awful things to her in an attempt to change her mind. He regrets those words and needs to apologize."

"Why is he attached to you?"

"I invited him to me and then was distracted by my uncle before the soul could leave. It's my own fault. I need to learn how to make a talisman. If I had one, the soul would have been drawn out of me."

"Yes, you should, especially after yelling at me for wanting to visit Bell without one." Scrolling through the search results, he added, "So, I'm assuming this soul isn't a singer-songwriter, is he?"

"Maybe. Did he die in Oregon? Was it recent?"

"Good point. Let me try a new search."

"I found the contact email for Doctors Without Borders. I'm going to type a quick message." Tapping on her screen, she wrote that she was looking for Misty Davis, a doctor who had joined the organization. She needed to contact Misty about her father, who had recently passed away. She included her contact information and added that it was urgent.

"Here. I have an obituary for Paul Davis. He lived south of Lake Valley. He died eight months ago and is remembered by his son and daughter. His wife died of cancer four years earlier."

"Which is probably why he didn't want Misty in harm's way. Is there a memorial page? How did he die?"

"It doesn't say," Dan replied. "I don't see a link for a memorial page. Do you want me to keep searching?"

"No, that's okay." Directing her thoughts to Paul, Leah asked, *How did you die?*

The question was answered with a stinging pain through her head as he tried to grab control. With a deep breath, Leah let the question go, keeping her mind relaxed.

"What do you want to do now?" Dan asked.

Leah paused a moment to look around and take in the atmosphere. "Let's enjoy prom. We can work on this later."

"Sounds like a plan. Do you want to dance or get a photo?"

"Yeah, let's get a photo and dance."

Holy shit was all Mr. Anderson could think. The music, the laughter, bodies pressed too close in the half-light as prom pulsed around him—none of it registered. His attention was solely on Leah and what she had just done. He had witnessed her extract a soul clean out of her classmate, unscarred by the procedure, a feat that had taken him two years to master. And he had it on film! He was overjoyed at having proof that she was the one for whom they were looking. The thought of her capabilities thrilled him, but then the air shifted, making his chest tighten.

A coldness pressed into his mind. Fingers swept along his hairline, down the back of his neck, then hooked under his chin, tilting his face upward. He knew that touch, the way an alcoholic knows the taste of relapse.

Ruth. She appeared, and Mr. Anderson leaned toward her. She tightened her grip and pushed him to straighten. He glanced behind her, seeing she was seated at a long table crowded with senior members of the Vietnamese National Assembly.

Hello, Lip, she said. *You're excited. Give me the good news.*

Leah is the manipulator you wanted me to find, he answered.

The corners of her lips curled into a satisfied grin, followed by a faint tremor in their connection. *I trust you can recruit her,* Ruth said.

The strain in her eyes was pronounced, and Mr. Anderson could see she was struggling to maintain the connection. The edges of her form and the room she sat in, both vibrated with static. She was weary. Leah's help wouldn't come soon enough. Ruth would buckle under the stress first. *You need help. The travel, the connections, souls, muddying the stream so the Circle can't find you… I can get Leah, but if you collapse before the Federation gains momentum, it won't matter how powerful she is. You'll have lost everything.*

Ruth inched closer, and for an instant he wished for her kiss. But she took hold of the scruff of his neck and squeezed. *Don't presume to know my limits.* Her cold words stung before lowering into a dangerous murmur. *I will end the need for war. With the Federation growing, the practice will soon be obsolete. Then we tackle hunger, poverty, and the hoarding of wealth. One by one these evils will fall. That is what I carry.*

Mr. Anderson swallowed. But he knew she couldn't continue like this on her own. *Why don't we recruit Sam Cros? He is cracking. I could feel the ambition he holds at his last press conference. He could be an ally. Let me go back to Washington, D.C. Leah isn't going anywhere.*

Her grip eased and a tired smile ghosted her lips. *You're right.* Her hand brushed his cheek. *I'll visit Sam myself when I return from Vietnam. You keep Leah safe. Find a way to bring her into the fold before the Circle realizes they have the wrong person.*

Mr. Anderson nodded, and she vanished.

Eric pushed past a cluster of dancers and squeezed his way into the kitchen, looking for Barb. The prom afterparty at Cindy's house was packed, and he had lost her in the commotion. Cindy's mom filled the punch bowl and offered Eric a drink. He declined.

Cindy's dad slipped in and kissed his wife on the cheek. "Someone brought alcohol," he said. "Keep an eye open."

Eric lifted a brow, a smile tugging at his lips. *I will. Thanks.*

He had seen Cindy's dad monitoring the activities: euchre, spades, and Texas Hold 'Em in the lounge; music and dancing in the living room; foosball and pool in the basement; darts and table tennis in the garage. But hadn't seen Barb. He had a sick feeling they were circling each other.

Eric entered the dining room and glanced over the table full of appetizers. Once he found Barb, he hoped to fall back into his rhythm—to feel confident, wanted, and real again. The past few days had blurred into a disjointed dream he couldn't piece together. His friends said he'd been in the hospital, something about neurological anomalies, but he remembered none of it. What he remembered was Barb—her full lips, her shy gaze, and her perfect voice. He wanted to kiss her. More than that, he needed to make out with her. He had to take back control.

His gaze swept the room, and he finally saw her leaning against the glass doors that led to the deck. Barb spotted him and waved. He moved straight for her, determined to make this night one he *could* remember. Taking her hand, he pulled her onto the deck and closed the door, the glass muffling the booming music inside. Barb wore a giddy smile, and she clasped Eric's hand tightly. He stared into her eyes, breaking through the haze of confusion and uncertainty that clouded his mind.

"It's a little chilly out here," Barb whispered.

Eric pressed his body to hers, his arm moving behind her back. He saw Barb's eyes sparkling with anticipation, and he knew why. She was with the charming heartthrob who enjoyed women, and she was ready for him to do his thing. He would oblige—because that's who he was.

Eric explored Barb's body, running his hand up and down her side, his fingers touching her hips, her belly, all the way up to her breasts. Barb's trembling excited him, and her quick breaths emboldened him. His hand traveled up to her chin, and he used his thumb to play with her bottom lip.

His feelings in the lunchroom the other day, the lustful desires for Barb, had confused him. But now they made him feel alive.

As his thumb toyed with Barb's lip, she kissed it, giving him permission to take her. Lowering his head, he pressed his lips to hers. At first, she didn't move. Eric guessed she hadn't kissed much. Then her lips parted. Wet. Passionate. Awkward.

He clasped her head with both hands and maneuvered closer. Tilting her head, he took control. He noticed her fumbling with her hands, unsure where she wanted them—in his hair, on his chest, wrapped around his body. He grabbed her hand and placed it on his ass. She squeezed it and pulled him close to her. He grew hard and was sure she could feel him.

With lips still locked, he pushed her against the wall and raised her hands above her head. Holding her wrists together in one hand, the other traveled down the length of her arm, gliding over the sensitive area above the curve of her breasts. He felt her shiver and saw the sweat beading on her brow.

His hand eased under her dress. He fondled her breast, his thumb massaging her nipple. Barb moaned, then bit his bottom lip.

Eric slid his tongue into her mouth and released her hands. She grabbed his hair, pressing hard against him, satisfying a long deep desire.

A tap came at the glass door. His friends were cheering, some filming. Eric shielded Barb as she put herself together. Grabbing her hand, he pulled her after him, and they ran around to the front of the house, giggling the whole way.

They stopped at the door. Eric touched his lip and saw blood. "You have a little wicked streak in you."

Barb grinned. "I had to make our first kiss memorable."

"You definitely did that."

"Can we sit and talk for a bit?" Barb asked.

Eric pointed to the stairs. "After you."

Barb sat on the top step, and Eric took the step below to face her at eye level.

"I'm curious," Barb said. "What was that back there?"

Eric nodded and took a breath. She asked a good question. He wanted to say, *Thank you. Thank you for making me feel alive and like myself.* But that felt weird.

"Was that just a moment?" Barb asked. "Did you want to take it further?"

He found her searching his eyes for answers.

"Is this going to lead somewhere?" she pushed.

Eric looked away, wondering what to say. The kiss had been him doing his thing. He was forward. Girls were attracted to him, and they liked kissing. "I thought you were into it."

"It was fun," Barb professed. "I'm glad you kissed me, but I'm feeling confused."

Eric paused. "I thought we had this vibe, that you wanted me to do that. I guess maybe I misread you." Thinking more about his feelings for Barb, he decided to be more truthful, hoping she would understand. "To be honest, I think I was trying to find myself again. To feel normal."

That reply touched Barb. He saw her eyes widen in realization, as if a puzzle piece had been jammed into place. A sigh escaped her lips, and she lowered her head. "Okay, I get it. Yeah," she said.

The tone in her voice gave him the strange feeling that she knew what had happened to him. Barb's lips curved into a smile, but it lacked warmth. She was trying to mask the underlying tension and unease she was feeling. He saw it in her gaze as well.

"You know what happened to me, don't you?"

She shook her head, biting her lip. "What happened to you?"

"For the past two days, I felt like I was trapped underwater. Everything was dark and murky, and voices were muffled." He paused. "It was Leah, wasn't it? What did Leah do to pull me back?"

Barb's eyes glazed over, and she seemed to stare past him as she collected her thoughts.

"Tell me what you know," he pressed.

"What do you mean?"

"I don't remember going to the hospital or taking photos together. Did we eat dinner? Jess says I was there, but I can't recall it. Driving to the dance and standing next to you with the reporters are a blurry haze. Then I woke up behind the school with Leah." Eric watched Barb clench her jaw and fidget with her dress. "What do you know?"

Barb opened her mouth, took a small breath, and started to speak but then cut herself off. A strained grimace followed with a brief, almost audible, "Nothing."

Eric raised his eyebrows, coaxing her to give him something.

Her lips parted once more, but she hesitated. After a moment of contemplation, she said, "You were charming and sweet at lunch, and you agreed to go to prom with me. Then you were different. Leah took you out to get some air."

Eric scrutinized Barb's eyes. There was something knowing there. "I woke up on my knees, facing Leah," he said. "She was in pain, holding my hand. What did she do?"

Barb put her hands together and pressed them to her lips. She couldn't hold his gaze. "Eric, I don't know what to tell you."

"The truth." He waited, and after she sighed, he asked, "Who is Paul?"

"Eric, please. I don't know."

Eric scratched his head. "Jess said Leah was calling me 'Paul.' He also said you two were debating calling the FBI. You know something! Please tell me."

Barb put her hands in her lap and stared at them.

Lowering his head, Eric tried to make eye contact, but she looked away.

"Right." He clapped his hands. "I tell you what. I'll be honest with you when you can be honest with me. How about that?"

Barb sat still for a long moment. Then, repositioning herself, she faced him. She reached out and touched his forearm briefly before pulling her hand back. Her shoulders sank, and with a sigh, she said, "I've always loved to sing. I used to sing with my mother when I was little. She told me I'd find my true love with my voice, like Ariel."

"*The Little Mermaid*," Eric murmured. Barb was a siren. There was a long pause as they stared at each other. "So, that's it?" he asked.

"Let's go in. I'm cold," she replied.

It was nearly two in the morning when Tim called the kids to go home. As Leah, Barb, and Dan left the party, two boys bumped into Leah. The first, in a drunken slur, said, "Hey, are you sure you're not a witch?" The other responded, "No, man. She's the good witch."

Dan pushed them away, but Leah grabbed his arm, saying, "Let's go. Come on."

Outside, as they walked to the SUV, Barb said, "Rumors are already spreading about what you did for Eric, Leah. Maybe you should have let him be until after the dance."

"It'll be fine," Leah said.

Tim dropped Barb and Dan at home first. Barb slipped into her pajamas and lay in bed, struggling to fall asleep. Raw, unrealized emotions sat heavy in her chest: part frustration, part disbelief, part elation, and part dreamy hope for what could have been. She had been kissed for the first time, and it was everything she had hoped it would be. But then Eric had seen the truth in her eyes and pressed her for answers. How could she explain that he'd been possessed? Honesty for honesty. That was his proposal.

Could the evening have gone differently? If she could have hidden her understanding of what he was going through or come up with a cover story, maybe there was a promise of a future. What if she had called Bruce instead of letting Leah handle it? The night wouldn't have ended in a kiss, but perhaps with the prospect of dates to come.

Now, all she knew was that any potential relationship with Eric seemed lost, evaporated like a dream upon waking. She never really got a chance to know Eric, but she did get to kiss him, and oh, how nice it was.

Rolling onto her side, hope tapped her heart. *Please don't give up on me again.*

Uncle Tim said goodnight to Leah before arranging himself on the sofa. As he dozed off, his haunting dreams returned.

Screams and cries came from beyond the smoke and fire. Tim ran toward the village, weaving his way around and ducking under uniformed soldiers on horseback. There, in the clearing, Leah struggled to get free from two soldiers who were dragging her into a tipi. One of the men opened the flap as the second threw her inside. Both had evil grins as they entered behind her. Enraged, Tim charged toward the tipi, but a horse appeared in front of him and reared, kicking him in the chest. He hit the ground hard. The horse reared again, and its hooves came crashing down—

Tim woke, clutching his chest. "Leah!" He sat up, gasping for air, and heard someone stumble in the hallway.

Jared rushed into the room. "What's wrong? What happened?"

"Sorry, bro. Just a bad dream."

Resting his hands on his knees, Jared took a moment. "Tim, why are you insisting on staying here? Go home."

"Leah's Grandpa Bill is paying me a pretty penny to stick close to her. He's worried about her, and so am I."

"You think I'm not? She's my little girl. I'll take care of her." Sighing, Jared gestured to the sofa. "It's your back, man. But honestly, everything is fine here. Go home to your wife."

Tim pressed his palms to his forehead and leaned back against the couch.

Jared hesitated at the hall entrance. "We're taking Stacy to the airport tomorrow. Try and get some rest."

Tim nodded without looking up. "Yeah." The room fell quiet, and he laid back down.

Lake Valley, Oregon

Oh, Fuck

A knock came at the bedroom door. "Leah, wake up, honey," her father said. "Breakfast is ready, and your mom is here. We're taking her to the airport in an hour."

"I'll be out in a bit!" Rolling over, Leah sighed, feeling groggy. Paul was still in her. *Why can't you just leave me?* she asked.

And go where? You said you would help me contact my daughter, Paul responded.

And I will. We already messaged Doctors Without Borders. When we hear back from them, we'll get her contact information. But it'd be so much easier if you could remember her email address.

I didn't have to remember it. I just clicked on the reply link, and it was there.

You don't have any brothers or sisters, someone I can call? What about your son?

I can't remember anyone's number, Paul said with a sigh.

What about your social media pages? Give me your login information and I can find everyone from there. Leah's phone rang. She saw it was Barb and answered. "How did you sleep?"

"Fine. I'm here, at your house. I'm in the kitchen with Nong, your mom, dad, and uncle. Are you coming out?"

Laughing, Leah said, "What the hell. Why don't you just come to my room?"

"Just come out. I'm eating."

"Okay. Is Dan with you?"

"He's working today."

"Right. Give me a minute." Leah got up, used the bathroom, dressed, and headed for the kitchen. When she entered, the discussion centered around the architectural firm Jared and Nong were planning to open.

"Nong showed me the office you guys got," Stacy said. "It's really nice. When will you start moving in?"

"Next week," Jared replied.

"My dad put my whole office into storage after I disappeared," Nong said, "so we've got everything we need."

Uncle Tim grabbed Leah's arm and pulled her into the living room.

"Leah, I need to borrow the book. You know the one. Just for a day or two."

"What for?"

"Does it matter?"

Leah took a step back and glanced into the kitchen. What was Tim planning to do with the manual? She lowered her voice and whispered, "It's a rare and guarded book. If you're interested in learning from it, we could read it together."

Tim chuckled. "Look, kiddo, I just want to skim through it, nothing more. But I would like it today. What do you say?"

"We'll need to stop at Barb's house."

"Great. We'll go there after we drop off your mom."

After breakfast, everyone got into the SUV Tim had rented and drove Stacy to the airport. When they arrived, Tim unloaded her bags while Leah and Stacy stood face to face, holding hands.

Her mother looked her straight in the eyes and said, "I don't want to hear anymore ghost stories."

"No more ghost stories," Leah agreed.

Stacy's eyes glistened, and she pulled Leah into a tight embrace. "I'll be here for graduation. Your grandfather's coming, too."

Leah nodded.

With a firm grasp of her shoulders, Stacy stepped back and studied her. They held each other's gaze. In that silent exchange, unspoken what-ifs, regretful decisions, and future plans passed between them. "I know, Mom. I know."

A photographer began snapping photos.

"Hey asshole!" Tim shouted, striding toward the man with purpose. "What the hell do you think you're doing?"

Stacy gathered her bags. "I'll call you tonight. Be smart, stay safe." After giving Leah a kiss on the cheek, she went into the terminal.

Everyone piled back into the SUV, and Tim drove to Barb's house. Leah followed Barb inside as she retrieved the training manual.

"Why are you giving this to your uncle?" Barb asked.

"He's just curious about it. He'll give it back. How far have you read?"

"I'm half way through it."

"Great! I'm so ready to start training with you." Leah snagged a sweatshirt from Barb's laundry basket and wrapped the book.

Back in the Cadillac, Leah slid the book under the front seat. Tim gave her an acknowledging nod.

When they arrived at Leah's house, Tim let everyone out. "You'll be okay here?" he asked Jared.

"We'll be fine, Tim. Go ahead," Jared replied.

"I'll be back in a couple of hours," Tim said, then left to return the rental.

Jared turned to Leah and Barb. "You two will be fine by yourselves, yes?"

"Why?" Leah asked. "Where are you going?"

"We have a few errands to run for the new office."

"Yeah, go. We're good," Leah said.

Jared nodded. "Okay. Lock the doors. Don't let anyone in. Just wait for Tim to get back."

Leah agreed and headed inside with Barb.

"I wanna go back to sleep," Leah said, as she plopped onto the sofa.

Barb laid her head in Leah's lap. "Me too."

Running her fingers through Barb's hair, Leah said, "I heard Eric kissed you."

Barb raised her eyes to meet Leah's and gave a sheepish grin.

Leah smiled. "Your first kiss?"

Tucking a strand of hair behind her ear, Barb asked, "What does it feel like, having a soul attached to you?"

Leah giggled. She knew that Barb and Eric had shared more than just a kiss, which was probably why her friend had just changed the subject.

"I want to know," Barb pressed.

"Sure. At first, I felt sick. Now I wouldn't even know he was here if I hadn't invited him myself. I feel normal." Leah laid her head back and thought more about it. "Actually, the sensation feels rather protective, like someone is watching over me. There's a strength in it."

"Do you talk to him?"

"Sometimes. His voice is older. He sounds gruff. But it's more like a third inner voice that's just part of who I am."

"That doesn't sound too bad."

Leah petted Barb's hair. Then, she saw her uncle's outdoor magazine and grabbed it off the end table. "Barb, I know how we can strengthen our powers."

"There are plenty of meditations and exercise routines in the book that explain how."

"I know, but beyond that. We need to go camping."

"Camping?" Barb lifted her chin and stared at Leah with a look of dread.

"Grandma's book says that the energy is strongest in the forest. I forget which chapter, but then I read this." She handed Barb the magazine. "There's an article in here about how our brain is rewired after being in nature for three days. They interviewed mountain climbers, park rangers, and hunters. The article also talks about forest bathing and how it's really healthy."

"You want me to get naked in the woods and smear dead leaves over my body?" Barb said with slight disgust.

"The term is Japanese, referring to the practice of being mindful and present in nature. Read the article; you'll find it interesting." Leah examined Barb's queasy expression as she opened the magazine. Leah pressed, "We need to go for at least three days. Connecting to the Earth through nature, hiking, and living outdoors will boost our immune system along with a host of other health benefits, including deeper access to our inner power."

"You want to go camping for *three days?*"

"Yep. We're taking Friday off from school and going into the woods. My uncle's got all the gear we need."

"Have you ever been camping?" Barb asked.

"Of course," Leah said. "Two or three times a year. And Dan said you guys went camping a bunch with your dad."

"Yeah, but that was a long time ago, before he built his house. Camping was fun, I guess. I remember staring at a line of ants that were eating the food on the ground."

"You see? You were connecting to nature." Leah smiled. "Three days is the magic number. That's when we'll be in tune with our spiritual energy."

Barb shook her head. "I don't understand your drive to learn about this."

"Are you kidding me?" Leah said. "Manipulating energy is..." She paused, stared out the window, and lowered her voice. "Power."

"And you've already abused it," Barb warned. "Sending Eric lust."

"Got you a date to prom."

"It was wrong."

"I'm supposed to practice," Leah said.

"For the purpose of helping souls," Barb retorted.

"That's what I'm doing! Paul is a soul."

Barb took a deep breath. "You should have called Bruce."

"Come with me. Connect to the Earth," Leah said, her words dancing off her tongue. "It'll be rejuvenating."

"And Dan?"

"I think it should be just you and me. A girl's retreat."

"Will your bodyguard allow that?"

"I'm a hundred percent sure he'll be tracking us. He'll probably have a drone flying overhead, watching our every move." Leah laid her head back against the sofa and groaned.

"Okay. I'm in," Barb said. "We might have some fun."

Leah returned upright with a giant smile. "Really? Thank you," she said, clutching Barb's hands.

"No problem, but I think it's time you shed Paul."

"He's not hurting me," Leah said. "He'll leave as soon as we contact his daughter."

"But, how do you shower?"

Leah raised an eyebrow. The question was a practical one.

Just then, a knock came at the door. Leah froze, the stranger from prom coming to mind. Tim wasn't here.

"I wonder who that is," Barb said, stirring.

"I don't think we should answer," Leah whispered.

Getting up, Barb went to the door and peered out the window. "It's a girl from school."

Leah followed and saw that it was a classmate. The girl had a little boy with her. Opening the door, Leah asked, "May I help you?"

"Hi, Leah. I'm Jen. We have calculus together."

"Hi, Jen. I know who you are."

"This is my brother, Max." Jen put her hand on his head and he waved. "He has severe persistent asthma. I've heard people talking about you. They told me what you did for Eric, and I thought maybe you could help Max."

"Jen, you know those are just rumors. They're not true. I'm just a normal person."

Barb stood behind Leah, leaning against the door.

Jen smiled at Barb, then continued talking with Leah. "I guess I kind of knew the rumors weren't true, but I'm desperate to try anything. Max has these terrible episodes, and it scares me. Maybe you could hold his hands, like you did with Eric. Say something to him."

"Sure." Leah knelt and held out her hands. "Hey, Max. How old are you?"

The boy took her hands, smiling, "I'm eight."

Connecting to the boy, Leah smiled back, saying, "Eight! Wow. I bet you're good at riding a bike."

"Nope. I need more practice. Usually, I'm at school, and I can't practice there. Also, I can only ride if my mom, dad, or big sister is with me." Max observed his arms. "You're making me feel tingly."

"What do you do for fun?"

"I play video games. But I also like to draw comics. I just finished reading *Wings of Fire*. It's a fantasy book."

"I love reading too. I just finished reading a book about ghosts."

"Was it scary?" Max asked, eyes wide.

Barb answered, "It's very scary. I'm reading it now, but wish I wasn't."

"Why are you reading it then?" Max replied.

"So I can talk about it with my friend," Barb said.

Letting Max's hands go, Leah stood up and looked at Jen. "I wish you the best. I'll keep you in my prayers." Turning her gaze back to the boy, she said, "It was nice meeting you, Max. I hope you get better soon."

"Yep. Thanks," Max said with a smile.

"Thanks, Leah. Sorry for bothering you. I'll see you in class tomorrow." Jen took Max's hand.

Backing inside, Leah and Barb exchanged glances. Barb didn't say anything, but her look said everything; this wouldn't be the last knock.

Mr. Anderson listened to the audio files and edited them into clips, isolating the conversations he needed. Then he labeled each clip. There were four: "The Attached Ghost," "The Book," "How to Grow our Powers," and "Manipulating Eric." He could use these to convince Bill his granddaughter was special.

Tapping his lips, Mr. Anderson wondered about this book. Could it be one of the Circle's training manuals? If so, that explained a lot. Misty also concerned him. He didn't want the two of them talking.

His more pressing issue was Paul. Soul transcendence was tricky, no matter how advanced she was. There were so many variables: knowing when to disengage, avoiding dark energy, keeping the soul from a panicked outrage. He had to take it from her. But how? And when?

The camping trip. If Tim used drones to watch the girls, following them wasn't an option, unless he could hack into the video feed of the drone. Then he could create a loop, inject a fake feed, or create a lagged response. Whatever he did, letting Leah try to force Paul to transcend on her own wasn't an option. The last thing he needed was her to fall into a coma or get sucked through his door.

He would need to act soon. The risk was too great, and she was too valuable.

After dropping off the rented SUV at the dealership, Tim drove his own truck to Captain Pete's Café near the lake to meet Roy Running Deer. Inside the diner sat a handful of people—a couple at a booth, grandparents with their grandkids at another, a businessman at a table, and two gentlemen conversing at the counter. The waitress stood chatting with the cook, so Tim sat himself at the far booth in the corner and looked over the menu. Having arrived a few minutes early, he ordered an iced tea and waited for Roy.

A man walked into the café. He was just under six feet tall, with long, black hair and golden-brown skin. He had on a jean jacket over a gray t-shirt. Two silver turquoise rings adorned his fingers, and a necklace with a single bear claw hung around his neck.

"Hey, Roy. Haven't seen you in a spell. What brings you by?" The waitress placed her hand on his shoulder and leaned in for a kiss.

"Hey, Izzy," he said, accepting her kiss. "I'm meeting someone."

She pointed at Tim. "He's sittin' over there. You know what you want?"

"I'll take fish and chips," Roy said.

"I'll bring it over in a bit."

Giving Tim a hard stare, Roy turned back and said, "Izzy. Better make it to go."

"Will do, sugar."

Roy strutted across the room, joining Tim at the table. "You got about five minutes. Tell me again what it is you want."

"Umm, yeah. Okay." Tim fumbled for words, then regained his composure. "I have a plan to return the stolen land to the Sukiya Tribe. I was hoping to—"

Roy cut him off. "Who do you think you are—John McClane? The white knight, who's going to ride in yelling, 'Yippee Ki-Yay' and save us poor American Indians? I think you've watched too many Kevin Costner movies."

"No! No, that's not it at all. The opposite is true. I need you to ride in and save me. I can't sleep at night. I wake up sweating—my sheets, soaking wet. My heart is gripped with guilt. I'm haunted by my great-great-grandfather's evils." Tim's pleas had a relaxing effect on Roy, whose face calmed. "I have a plan, but it won't work without you."

"You want to have the land de-annexed from the city. I think that's a stupid plan—it won't work! And even if it does, the land is owned by a Chinese lady who has a business there. She's not about to give it up."

"My friends own a few establishments—a bar, a nail salon, and a coffee shop. The plan is to spread some rumors, make up a few lies, and put some disinformation out there about the land. Dr. Lynn Mathis believes the Center should be closed, and we're going to amplify that message. Then we'll get petitions started and dig up some dirt on a few city council members—pressure them into adding a de-annexation measure to the next election." Tim's index finger tapped the table, punctuating his words. "I need you to lead a campaign for the true reason the land needs to be returned. Your protests were working. You swayed public opinion. The only reason it didn't work is because the guy who bought that land paid off government officials to make it happen."

Roy didn't say anything. He just sat, studying Tim.

"I'll give you two thousand dollars to start. Now is the perfect time to begin the campaign. People are obsessed with my niece. I'll get her to help you build it."

Roy let out a dry laugh. "Two thousand and your niece? And you think that will build a strong campaign?"

"Of course not, but it's a start. The press loves her right now, so we'll raise more quickly."

"And what about the business that is standing there?" Roy asked.

Tim lifted a book from the seat next to him and placed it on the table. "This is a teaching manual for communicating with souls and spirits. A water baby possessed that business, which is why all that crap has been happening there. Now, It's alive. The water baby has merged with the building. That business won't be there by the time the election comes around. But you don't need to worry about that."

Opening the book, Roy asked, "Where did you hear about water babies?"

"I went to the reservation and joined a prayer circle—a spirit calling, or something. That night, my grandfather told me about them. Said his grandfather was involved in the Indian wars and created a similar one."

"Are you sure your sanity is still intact? It sounds like I should call the police. You're talking crazy and planning crazy too."

"I know how much you love the police. I mean, you've spent enough time in their custody. Come on, you must know about these water spirits; they're part of your culture."

Roy lifted an eyebrow. "The same way Santa Clause is a part of yours."

The men looked hard at each other, judging.

"I'll make a call to the tribal leader," Roy said. "Then I'm going to take a tour of the Education Center. I hear there's a nice green space inside the building, perfect for sitting and reflecting on what you've just learned. You'll either hear back from me, or ..." Roy stood, taking out a recording device and shaking it "... you'll hear from a police detective." He went to the counter, paid for his food, and left.

Tim put his hands over the back of his head and exhaled, "Fuck."

Seoul, Korea

<u>The Unseen Link</u>

Brandon stopped by a street vendor on his way to work and bought some Korean toast and spicy rice cakes for everyone at the office. Upon arriving, he went straight to the break room and put the food on plates, setting them on the table. A thought popped into his mind: *You're a good man. She deserves a good man.* His heart swelled with feelings of affection. Turning, he saw Su-Bin.

"Here you are," she said. "The receptionist said you had arrived."

Su-Bin stood, a vision of elegance and authority. Her navy-blue blazer, fitted to her figure, highlighted her strong, slender frame. Underneath, she wore a crisp white blouse, its collar neatly pressed and slightly open at the neck, revealing a pearl necklace. Her natural beauty gripped Brandon, and he felt his emotions stir. The image of Su-Bin and Hina together, from his dream yesterday, emerged. He was still unsure if that dream had been a message or not.

Su-Bin blushed. "Brandon, are you feeling all right?"

He blinked, a sudden realization he was ogling. What was he thinking? *She's my boss!* Touching his forehead, he apologized. "Sorry."

With a gentle smile, she replied, "Nothing to be sorry about." Gesturing towards the snacks on the table, she added, "Did you bring these? Thank you. That's very thoughtful of you."

"It's nothing. My pleasure."

"I got your text last night," she said. "I'm sorry I didn't respond. I guess I wasn't sure what the intention behind it was."

The statement hit Brandon. He blinked in rapid succession, wondering how she could say this. She had sent messages straight into his mind. He should be the one asking about intentions.

"I don't follow," he said.

"Brandon, I'm curious... In your eyes, who am I to you?" Su-Bin asked.

The question felt direct. He opened his mouth but didn't know how to respond. He couldn't say, *I see you as my wife Hina*. And the truth was, it was more complicated than that, because he saw her as someone special. But his interest was not one-sided. "I could ask you the same question," he finally responded.

"Really. Why is that?" Su-Bin asked.

Brandon paused, considering his words. "After our connection yesterday, I felt—"

Su-Bin quickly interjected, "I think you got the wrong impression."

"Did I?" He was taken aback, not sure if she was playing games or if he misunderstood the whole situation. Did she not interpret the intimacy of delivering a message straight into one's mind the way he did? "I texted because I didn't want to give you the wrong impression by communicating with you through our connection."

Su-Bin knit her brows while tilting her head. Then a quick smile surfaced. "Is that FBI code for something?"

Brandon's confusion mirroring her own.

"You should know that Min and I are dating," Su-Bin said.

A vision hit Brandon—Min holding a knife, eyes burning red, engulfed in anger. The image would have startled him, but his partner Choi, back in America, had sent him an image of a burning man, twice, which was way creepier. Letting the vision go, he said, "You hold an interesting view of Min."

"Oh? What view is that?"

The question gave him pause. Was she asking him to interpret the image she had just sent him? "Angry," he replied.

Su-Bin put her hand on her chin. "Angry? Why would you say that?" She then added, "Although, injustice does anger him. I would probably use the word passionate. He's passionate about righting the wrongs of injustice."

Raising his eyebrows with a reflective nod, Brandon said, "I guess I'll have to learn how to interpret our communications better."

She shook her head slowly. "So … is cryptic-speak a prerequisite for training with Yoona? Because you got that part down."

Brandon reached back and scratched his head. *There's obviously some kind of disconnect here,* he thought. Gesturing to the table, he asked, "Would you care for a spicy rice cake?"

With an amused grin, Su-Bin said, "Sure. I'd love one, thanks."

As she picked up a rice cake, Brandon removed a paperback from his bag. "I bought this for you." He set the book on the table. "I've marked a few pages, and I'm hoping you can read them before our first lesson."

"Thank you. I'll do my best to get to it before then." She tucked the book under her arm. "I wanted to let you know that we have a staff meeting at ten. Since you're here, I'll give everyone their tentative schedules. If you could introduce yourself and give some expectations, that would be great."

"Sure, I can do that."

"Good. I'll send the receptionist in. She'll give you a tour and show you where your desk is." Lowering her voice to a sweet tone, she added, "I'll see you at the meeting." She held his gaze for a second longer before turning to leave.

Su-Bin stopped short, her shoulders tightening in a quick, involuntary twitch. Min stood in the doorway with an unreadable expression. Brandon hadn't noticed him. How long had he been there? What had he heard?

Su-Bin lifted her chin and adjusted her stance.

"I didn't expect to see you here already," Min said, his cold eyes leaving Su-Bin and focusing on Brandon.

"Su-Bin had told me she made a schedule, so I thought I'd come in early and start preparing."

"I see," Min responded. His smile warmed as he glanced back at Su-Bin. He reached for her hand, but she bypassed it and touched his shoulder.

"Have some breakfast," she said, then proceeded to her office.

Glaring at Brandon, Min said, "No thanks. I lost my appetite." He slowly backed out of the room.

After Min left, Brandon let out a long, tortured sigh. He leaned against the table and mumbled, "I'm such an idiot. What the hell am I doing?"

The receptionist knocked and stuck her head inside.

"사무실 견학 준비 되셨나요?"

"I'm sorry. I don't understand Korean."

"Excuse me." The receptionist paused, searching for her English. "May I offer you a tour?"

"Yes, please." Brandon followed the woman. Extending his hand, he said, "My name is Brandon."

The woman bowed slightly, then touched Brandon's fingertips briefly with her own. "I'm Seo-Ah."

Seo-Ah showed Brandon the two conference rooms, the strategy room, the library, copy room, workroom, and the large meeting room. Then she introduced him to a group of attorneys, the two human resource officers, the accountant, the business manager, and the rest of the staff. Finally, she showed him to his desk situated in a small cubicle with a computer and a short filing cabinet. Brandon thanked Seo-Ah and slid into his chair, feeling tired.

Connecting with everyone at the law firm wasn't easy. Making the initial connections wasn't the issue, maintaining them was. Despite forming twelve connections, Brandon lost ten of them upon attempting a thirteenth. After connecting to nearly forty people, only five had held.

Spinning in his chair, Brandon looked around the office, recognizing a man he was connected to. But when he couldn't remember anything about him, the connection dropped, leaving him with just four. Choi's advice from training came to mind: "A new connection might last a day, maybe two. It needs to be fostered." Brandon raised an eyebrow and exhaled. *More like a minute without fostering,* he thought. He was going to have to learn how to keep these connections. If not—

Choi! Brandon felt him and knew they could still communicate. Closing his eyes, he put Choi in the forefront of his thoughts. Building his spiritual energy, he pictured himself wandering in the woods, lost. He merged the image with his energy and sent it to Choi. A few minutes later, an image of a compass came back to him. Brandon smiled.

Opening his computer, Brandon emailed Choi.

Subject: Losing Connections Fast

Hey, buddy.

I'm in Korea and met your aunt. I have to say, she's something special. How have you been? Could use some advice on connecting. I have to connect with everyone at the office, forty or more people, but I've lost most of them after only an hour. How do I keep so many new connections?

Hope the family is well. Tell me what's happening at the office.

Brandon

Looking at the time, he had a little less than half an hour before the staff meeting.

Min Yun stood outside Su-Bin's office door. Her decision to hire Brandon enraged him. The way Brandon had looked at her yesterday should have been a red flag—the man lacked the social and cultural awareness required for the job. If he was already flirting before he was even hired, how long until he engaged in other inappropriate behavior? Min would be damned if it happened with Su-Bin. Why hadn't she considered Seo-Ah, so young and innocent, vulnerable to Brandon's advances? Min's blood boiled.

Then there was this morning—the flirtation continued. Was Su-Bin attracted to Brandon? Was that why she hired him? Min clenched his fists, jealousy clawing at his chest. With controlled breaths, he fought to suppress his emotions, but they churned like a slushy machine, spinning sweet, enticing ideas he knew were dangerous. One thought in particular kept circling back, and if he acted upon it, he would jeopardize their relationship.

Min rolled his shoulders back, releasing the tension. Then he knocked on the door and waited.

"Come in," Su-Bin called.

He stepped through the door and said, "Hey, sweetie."

Su-Bin raised her head from the computer and glared. "Min, not at the office. We've talked about this."

Min knew the rules. She had insisted on them early in their relationship. Min had leaned in to kiss her, but she stopped him and set some boundaries: no touching at work, no flirty eyes, no accidental brushing, no words of affection. They were to remain strictly professional.

His frustration flared back full force, and he used all his strength not to vent aloud. She had broken her own sacred rules with someone she'd just met. Someone she knew nothing about. It was a slap in the face. Especially now, in her office where no one could see them.

"It's just you and me here," he pointed out, emphasizing *you and me*. He heard the strain in his voice as he tried not to let his emotions burst from his skin.

Su-Bin gave him a stern look. "I'm serious. Not at the office."

Min forced a smile and nodded.

"Thank you," she offered in return of his acceptance. "What can I do for you?"

With a deep exhale, he explained, "My phone isn't working. I'm going to slip out and take it to get fixed."

"Now? We have a staff meeting in a few minutes."

"Ah, right. Can I use your phone for a second? I need to call and reschedule the appointment."

A hint of irritation flashed across her face at the unexpected request. She hesitated, then replied in a curt manner, "Use the office phone."

"I have to look up the number."

Her eyes went straight to his, and she probed. Min sensed her unease. He gave a small, casual shrug.

Su-Bin sighed. "Sure." She put her thumb on the phone to register her print and then typed in the passcode. The screen came to life, and she handed it to him.

"Thanks." He opened the browser and began tapping. "Are you excited? Nervous?"

"About the announcement?" Su-Bin asked. "A little. We're still six months from officially opening the branch, but I'm curious to see who puts their name in the hat to be part of the team." She removed a thumb drive from her computer, logged out, and locked her desk. "Did you find the number?"

"Yes, just now." Min put the phone to his ear.

Su-Bin rose from her desk. "I'm going to get ready. Coming?"

"Be there in a second." Then Min began to talk to the salesman on the phone.

"I'll see you there." Su-Bin left the office.

Brandon entered the meeting room and looked for an empty chair. Only one remained. A U-shaped table in the middle of the room held ten people on each side. Twenty more chairs had been arranged around the room, most situated in the back. The forty people in the room made it stuffy, even with the air conditioning on full blast. A projector sat on the table, and a screen was set up on one wall. Brandon took his seat and waited.

Su-Bin stood and began the meeting. Brandon didn't understand anything that was being said, but Su-Bin was fabulous. She spoke with confidence, had power in her voice, and seemed to charm the room with her delightful tone. The PowerPoint presentation included photos of war, protests, and celebrities. Several slides showed different industries—factories, shipping, and fishing, followed by multinational corporation headquarters. The United Nations building came next, followed by a parade of world leaders. Then there were numbers—money amounts and percentages—among others. The last slide showed office space, and when Su-Bin made some kind of declaration, the crowd broke into applause.

Then she switched to English. "That is why we have hired our very own English teacher, Mr. Brandon Spencer."

Brandon stood and waved.

"Because this new branch will bring in foreigners, I feel that it's important that the entire staff be proficient in English. A tentative schedule has been made for you to start learning. This is not a set schedule, so talk with HR if there is a conflict, and we'll get it fixed. Classes will start next Monday.

"Before I have Brandon introduce himself, I want you to know that the positions for the new team are open to current employees first. The company is prepared to pay for additional education, and the university has prepared an international law exam that you will need to pass before being accepted. We are offering a bonus to anyone who takes the exam and passes, regardless of whether you decide to join the team. That includes the janitor, if he feels so inclined." Su-Bin then spoke in Korean as the room filled with chatter.

Brandon sat, admiring Su-Bin when a thought popped into his mind. *Isn't she lovely? Truly talented.* Confused, Brandon looked at Su-Bin. *Why would she send that to me?* Brandon thought maybe he knew what was going on.

When the meeting ended, Brandon had to wait before talking with Su-Bin, so he began decorating his classroom. He hung linguistics posters showing tongue positions for making sounds, set up a vocabulary wall, and displayed photos of different settings for practicing conversation.

When it was time to go home, he stopped by Su-Bin's office and knocked. He had an idea for why they had been experiencing this odd disconnect. There was only one reason she hadn't understood his reference to communicating through their connection, and that was because she hadn't connected to him. A ghost or spirit attached to her had.

Su-Bin called out in Korean, so Brandon slowly opened the door and peeked his head in. Su-Bin was on the phone. She looked at Brandon and waved him in, gesturing for him to sit and wait.

As Su-Bin talked, Brandon admired her office. The large windows offered a beautiful view of the city, the conference table had room for six, the sofa, love seat, and coffee table made for a comfortable chat, and the liquor counter held plenty of sins to help calm anyone's nerves. On the wall was a large photo of a Korean politician standing in front of a crowd with his hands raised, waving. Below that photo, but in the same frame, was an image of the Nobel Peace Prize awarded to Kim Dae-Jung on December 10, 2000. Brandon read the quote on the bottom of the photo: "Only the truly magnanimous and strong are capable of forgiving and loving."

Brandon took a seat. He tapped his thumbs against his leg as he composed his thoughts. The memories sent to him weren't from Su-Bin. They belonged to someone else—to the person through whom the memories were experienced. That someone had admired Su-Bin on the swing, had run with her into the concert hall, and had taken a photo of her at university. He believed that person was probably her father.

Su-Bin finished her conversation and hung up the phone. "Brandon, are you done for the day? Heading home?"

"Yes. I just wanted to ask you a question before I left."

"Sure. How can I help you?"

"Have you experienced any strong headaches recently? Visions, thoughts, memories, or impulses that pop into your mind all of a sudden?"

A puzzled look came over Su-Bin. "It wasn't recent, but I did, yes. Why do you ask?"

"Did you ever find the cause?"

Su-Bin hesitated, her eyes narrowing. "Why are you asking me these questions?" Her tone had an edge to it. "What did Moodang Yoona tell you about me?"

Brandon raised his hand and shook it. "No. She didn't share any personal information about you. I have observed..." He paused, unsure how to broach the subject of ghosts. "Well, some ticks that suggest you may have had a problem in your past."

"Ticks?" she asked curiously. "What have I done or said that would make you think I have 'ticks'?"

"Ticks isn't exactly the right word. You didn't do anything."

"Try again. Don't lie."

He glanced down into his lap and pressed his lips together as he figured out how to lead her into the subject. "It's not something *you* did. May I ask if your father is still living?"

"I'm not exactly comfortable discussing my private life with you, but since my father's death was a very public ordeal, I can tell you he was murdered twelve years ago. What does my father have to do with my so-called 'ticks'?"

"You know that I am to train with Yoona. I've been introduced to her powers and have..." Brandon stopped. He wasn't ready to mention ghosts just yet. "I'm still trying to understand why she sent me here."

Su-Bin smirked. "Welcome to my world. I don't think we'll ever know her true motivations. But you are evading. Please answer my inquiry."

"Do you remember the article you read the other night about my arrest in Lake Valley? The one about the three families going missing at the Education Center?"

Su-Bin straightened in her chair and became very still. When she spoke, her voice was low and hard. "How did you know about that?"

"A ghost possessed the Education Center. I was attacked. The photo of me grabbing my head and screaming in pain was taken during that assault. I nearly lost myself. During that attack, memories played in my mind, stirring emotions.

In my attempt to understand why I am here, I thought maybe you went through the same experience."

Su-Bin folded her hands together, leaned back in her chair, and put her two index fingers to her lips. Her glare held suspicion as she studied him.

Brandon was glad she didn't laugh or label him a crazy loon.

"Is there more?" she asked.

"There is. If you'll be patient with me for one moment, I want to show you something." Brandon closed his eyes, re-creating the image of Su-Bin and Hina shaking hands in the park as the judge congratulated them. When the image was right—clear and detailed—he began building the energy needed to send it. *Su-Bin must see this image. It is meant for her.* Weaving the image into his spiritual energy, he let the connection carry the message.

He opened his eyes to find her gaze had shifted. Her attention had turned inward.

"This is the FBI coded message you were talking about this morning," she said. "This is magnificent. I've never been to that park. I don't know who those people are with me. What is this? How did you do that?"

"I've been wanting to ask you the same question. I've been receiving images, thoughts, and even memories like this from you since the day we met."

"From me? I have no idea how to do that. They didn't come from me."

"Did Yoona say you were possessed?"

"You think I'm possessed?" Su-Bin asked with a laugh. "No. She never said I was. But my father did talk to me through her, or so she claims. She said my father is close by, watching over me."

"I see. I believe he is the one communicating with me then. Your dad gave me memories of you."

Su-Bin arched an eyebrow, her expression saying, *This'll be entertaining.*

"In one of the memories you were pulling him along inside a theater. You handed two tickets to the usher and made your way to your seats just as the orchestra was warming up."

Su-Bin's expression tightened before gradually softening. "Of all the memories to choose from and he sent you that one," she said aloud to herself, then asked, "How many memories did he send you?"

"A couple. One of you on a swing and another of you in college. Your first day, maybe? He cherished that memory."

"I know the day," she remarked in a dry tone.

"He seemed like a loving father," Brandon observed.

Su-Bin exhaled sharply, scoffing at the comment. "So, my dead father is talking to you." She shook her head and grinned.

Sitting a bit straighter, Brandon said, "That's my understanding. Would you like to know what he's been saying?"

"That's okay. Let's just leave it there." Cocking her head, she added, "I would like to hear more about this ghost attack and your arrest in Lake Valley."

"The FBI recruited me because of what happened. That situation brought me here."

"Please, tell me what happened."

"I'm afraid you won't believe me."

Su-Bin laughed. "I think we're past that concern, aren't we?"

"I guess we are. Maybe I could tell you about it over dinner. It's getting late."

"Yes, very well. I know a place where we can talk and eat in private."

Lake Valley, Oregon

<u>The Liar, The Planner, and The Officer</u>

Back at the police station in Lake Valley, Choi responded to Brandon's email.

Subject: Prepare to be Enlightened

Miss you, too, brother.

Craziness happening here. The FBI arrested a few city officials, and the police chief has been pulled in for questioning. You left at the right time. Prom was the other night. I saw Leah and Barb dressed up with their dates on the news. Still can't believe they escaped on their own. So, you need my help. Well, I can't say I'm surprised.
"How to Make a Connection and Keep It," by Officer Choi.

1. Remove your wants and desires from the interaction. Be open to who they are. Listen without steering. Let go of outcomes and take in their essence.
2. Live in the moment with the person you're meeting. Nothing else matters while you're with them. They are the world to you.
3. Catch their eye and keep it. Allow an impression to be made.

Basically, focus on the person in front you—their tone, the meaning behind their words, how they hold themselves. Then when you connect, it's smooth, quick, and lasting. But remember, a connection needs to be fostered and cared for, so send a thought every now and again. The stronger an individual connection is, the more connections you can keep. Connecting isn't just about sending your energy out and inviting it back; it's much more encompassing. Hope that helps.

Keep in touch.
Choi.

Leaning back in his chair, Choi thought about Leah. Her name had been in the news a lot lately. Public attention had a way of drawing the wrong kind of people, and he didn't like the idea of her standing in the spotlight unprotected. The photographer being arrested at the school seemed to confirm his fear.

Tapping his desk, he decided to check in on her. Leah's attractive energy seemed to be growing, and the news calling her an angel and a savior raised a red flag in his mind. *Was Leah the energy manipulator his aunt had wanted him to find?* The idea crossed his mind, but he dismissed it. News stories enjoyed exaggerating the truth—and besides, she was too young.

Still, the nagging feeling wouldn't let go. Was it because she had been in the news? Partly. The other reason was Brandon's struggle to keep more than a few connections at a time. If Brandon wasn't the new user, then someone else was. Choi knew that these nagging feelings meant something, so he grabbed his jacket and headed for Leah's house. A small chat with her would give him the opportunity to connect and make sure she was okay.

Mr. Anderson stepped into his room, dropped his keys and school badge on the bed, and sat down at his computer. The hacking program he had installed in the school's computer system had been running all day, collecting login data from students accessing their accounts. When Leah logged in to her email from the library, she gave him exactly what he needed.

He brought up the program and filtered the results by name. Lines of data scrolled past, then stopped. There was Leah's password. He logged into her account and scrolled through her messages, seeing that Misty Davis had emailed. Once Leah responded, Paul would transcend. Mr. Anderson couldn't allow that. The danger was too great.

A plan came to mind. Mr. Anderson would call her, posing as a police detective or maybe a delivery driver and ask her to meet him outside. When she stepped out, he would connect and take Paul from her.

With the decision made, he went to the window and waited. Tim's blue truck pulled in front of Leah's house. She got out and rushed inside. Mr. Anderson waited a beat for Tim to leave, then headed for Leah's house. He punched in her number on his phone and was about to press call, when a police cruiser parked in front of the house. Mr. Anderson dipped his head, checked his watch, and turned back.

Leah entered the house and dropped her bag next to the door. "Dad? You home?" She poked her head into the living room, then into the kitchen. Going down the hall, she called, "Dad?"

"Yeah. Give me a minute," Jared said, his voice coming from his bedroom.

Leah slipped into her room, opened her computer, and moved the mouse to click on the Word Document tab. As she did, she noticed she had several new emails.

Did my daughter send a message? Paul asked excitedly.

"I don't know. I'll check it in a minute," Leah responded.

"You talking to Barb?" Jared asked, standing in Leah's doorway.

"Oh, hi, Dad. Will you sign a note for me to miss school on Friday?"

"Why?"

"I have to get away from people. They're talking behind my back, and it feels weird. So, Barb and I are going camping for the weekend."

"That's great. But do you really need to miss school?"

"We need to be in the woods for at least three days. Uncle Tim will be tracking us the whole time and will help us pack."

"Okay, but three days is rather specific."

"That's how long we need to realign our brain with the Earth's energies."

Jared paused, giving her a long suspicious dad-look. "This isn't a cult, is it?"

"No! We're bonding with nature, Dad. This is a spiritual connection to the Earth and to womanhood. I need this. I wouldn't ask if it weren't important."

"The stress is getting to you." Jared's shoulders sank, and he dropped his head. "I'm sorry. I'm sorry, I didn't talk with you first, before I opened my big fat mouth. I was just so proud of you and wanted you to get the credit. I didn't know my talk with Brenda would blow up like this."

"It's okay, Dad. Really. But I do need these three days."

"Okay." He gave a small, decisive nod. "Yes, I'll sign it."

The doorbell rang, followed by a series of knocks.

"Are you expecting anyone?" Jared asked.

"No," Leah sighed. "But it's probably for me. Can you answer it?"

Jared nodded. "Of course."

"I'll write the note. And thanks, Dad."

"No problem." Jared went to answer the door.

Check the email! Paul demanded.

"All right. Relax."

After logging in, Leah went to her email page and saw several from *NPR*, *ABC News*, *People Magazine*, Oprah Winfrey, and others. Scrolling through them, she found one from Misty Davis.

"Leah," her father called. "There's a police officer here to see you."

Open it! Paul demanded.

"Chill!" she told Paul. "Coming," she shouted to her dad and headed for the door.

No, wait! Paul yelled. Tiny drills burrowed into Leah's mind, dropping her to the floor. He yanked the memory of *her and Barb standing in the middle of Grand Central Terminal's main concourse in Midtown Manhattan, admiring the clock and iconic architecture. Leah immediately changed that memory by snatching a coffee from a stranger's hand and flicking it across the concourse like Rollie Fingers. The cup hit a businessman, spraying hot coffee everywhere. The screams propelled Leah into Paul's consciousness.*

Standing on the pitcher's mound in the center of a baseball diamond, Paul glared at her. "How did you get here?"

*"You've messed with the wrong mind." Leah evoked the one law every Ban-isher knew inside a consciousness—**Imagination**. Leah looked at her wrists. Spring-loaded gadgets that propelled restraints appeared. Lifting her hands, she shot handcuffs with chains attached to them that latched onto Paul. She pulled him close and wrapped the chains around his neck, his arms a pretzel across his chest. She*

spotted his door and dragged him to it. Turning him to face the exit, she pushed him until his essence slowly began to siphon through the door.

"If you ever try to take control of me again, I will make you transcend without knowing what your daughter has said. Is that clear?"

Paul nodded.

Leah spun him away from the door and dropped him. Now what? *she thought. Bellevue had always pushed her out of Its consciousness—an unwelcome guest. Giving Paul a threatening stare, she cleared her throat and said, "Send me back."*

Paul waved his hand, and Leah opened her eyes, seeing her dad stumble through the door.

He dropped to his knees, breathless and flushed. "What is it?"

"I tripped," Leah lied.

The corners of his eyes tightened. "On what?"

She looked around the floor, seeing nothing. "The carpet."

Choi stepped through the door, and Leah smiled. "It's great to see you again. Have you heard from Detective Spencer?"

"Special Agent Spencer with the FBI," Choi corrected as her father helped her to her feet.

"Right. I knew that."

"He's training in Korea and dealing with some trauma, but he'll be okay."

"Are you here to see me?"

"I am. You were on the news, so I came to make a social call—check in on you and make sure you're okay." Choi studied her, and asked, "Are you okay?"

Leah gave a reassuring smile. "Hunky-dory."

"You seem to be quite popular these days," Choi said. "That comes with some challenges. Have you felt threatened or in danger at all? Has anyone been giving you a hard time? Any stalkers?"

"I mean, it is kind of strange, but nothing bad has happened." In a playful tone, she added, "My uncle is being my bodyguard. Even has a tracking device on me."

"That's good to know. Well, we are here for you, so don't be afraid to reach out if you need," Choi said.

"Thanks. I won't."

Choi offered his hand. "It's good to see you again."

Leah just stood there, staring at the hand. Choi knew about ghosts, and with Paul attached to her—

"Leah?" her dad said.

She blinked and shook herself loose. "Uh, yeah. Sorry." She lifted her gaze from his hand and smiled. "I'd shake, but I'm, uh..." She glanced down at her palms. "I'm dirty."

"Let me give you my card." Choi took one out and wrote on the back. "This is my personal number. If you are in trouble, have a question, or just need to chat, you can call me anytime. I'm available twenty-four seven." Choi handed Leah his card. As she reached for it, Choi took her hand and placed the card in it.

A tingling sensation rush up her arm, but before she could think about how to stop it, Choi's grip tightened. *He knows.* The connection linked, and Choi let her hand go, his eyes fixed on her.

"Officer Choi. Actually, there is something you could help me with. Can we take a walk?"

"Yes, I think that would be a good idea," Choi said.

Leah glanced at her dad, who shifted his gaze from Choi to her hand. She saw her dad go cold with worry.

"What just happened?" Jared asked.

"Nothing," Leah squeaked. "I need to talk with Choi about prom."

Her dad's voice tightened and grew deeper. "What happened at prom?"

"Uncle Tim knows about it. Nothing bad. I'll be back." Leah walked to the door with Choi and then headed for the sidewalk. Jared followed, then watched from the porch.

"Leah," Choi began.

"Yes, I know. His name is Paul. He died eight months ago, and we're just waiting to talk with his daughter before he transcends."

Stopping dead in his tracks, he stared at Leah. "So your dad was telling the truth when he said you saved everyone. Are you channeling your energy? How did you learn about connecting?"

Realizing her mistake, Leah said, "It's called connecting?" She didn't want to tell Choi about the book, for fear he would confiscate it. "That's neat. When I was captured, I was able to free myself for a little while. After being recaptured, I felt the energy and figured out how to use it."

Leah held her breath as Choi mulled over her answer.

"How did Paul come to be attached to you?" he asked.

Shit, her answer had only created more questions. *What can I tell him?* A few rules about lying came to mind. *The bigger the lie, the more believable. Keep the lie tied to the truth. If you lie, tell white lies.* The second option was best. "My friend's date was possessed. I connected to him at prom."

"Okay…" Choi said, drawing the word out. "But how did that soul become attached to you? Did it attack you, or did you invite it?"

Fighting to keep her expression neutral, Leah thought about how to respond. She knew her last answer was telling; she knew he was possessed, and she connected to him knowing this. What could she say that wouldn't give away the book? Nothing came to her.

"Leah," Choi said, his voice dark. "This is powerful energy you are playing with, and without the proper training, you could be hurt. There are souls in this world that will kill you. Now tell me, how did Paul become attached to you?"

Keep the lie tied to the truth, she repeated to herself. "I invited him to me. I was going to disconnect, but my uncle distracted me. Paul just wants to let his daughter know that he's sorry and that he accepts her decision. Then he'll transcend. He's not hurting me."

"How did you learn to invite souls to you?" Choi asked.

"Like I told you. Bellevue invited me into It. I was inside Its consciousness. I felt how that happened and learned how."

Choi let out a heavy sigh. "You're not telling me the truth." His tone sharpened. "Souls don't invite us—we transfer into them. This is how Banishers work." His next question came out firm, like a command. "Who is training you?"

Leah took a deep breath. She needed to say something to get Choi off her back—something that he would believe. But how could she answer when she had no idea what he knew? She had to say something, but— "How do you know about this?" she asked.

"My aunt is a powerful shaman," he replied. "I was in training for several years." The line in his jaw hardened. "Leah, this energy is a guarded secret. There are rules in place for its use. You need to tell me who is training you. It's imperative." He paused, keeping his focus on her. "I'm not going to arrest the person you are protecting. I just need to talk with them and learn the extent of their power, to make sure they aren't using it for nefarious reasons."

"No one is training me," she insisted. What could she say that would explain her abilities? Then an idea came. "I've been having dreams, vivid ones. I'm in that house and remember how it felt. I've been re-creating those feelings."

"Tell me what happened in the house."

Leah began with how the house had shut her out of her own memories. She explained how she had prayed and given herself to God, her dream with her grandmother, and her escape. "The ghost chose a painful memory to regain control, but I couldn't relive it. I couldn't stand to see what was coming, so I changed the memory and found myself inside Its consciousness." She explained the back-and-forth, the dark void, and how they came to an agreement.

If she had said she changed her memories intentionally, Choi would know for sure she was learning from someone or something. After she finished, she looked down at the ground, acting like a kid in trouble, waiting for her punishment.

Choi leaned forward, lowering his head to catch her eye. "I'm not sure I believe you," he said. "If you're protecting someone, you need to think long and hard about that. Maybe you could find a way to introduce this person to me without saying anything. I'll know who they are when you do. That way, I can observe them without giving you away."

"No one is training me," Leah insisted. "I'm telling you the truth."

Choi smirked. "I'm connected to you, Leah. I know you're not giving me the full truth." He took out his notepad and a pen and began sketching. "I'm taking Paul from you. And then I need you to think about introducing me to this mystery person." He finished drawing and lifted his eyes to hers. "Or I'll have to use my abilities to travel your life path."

Leah's stomach dipped. "Travel my life path? What does that mean?"

"Look at your past and future, and everyone connected to you."

Her thoughts went straight to Barb and the book. Would he really be able to witness the events in Barb's bedroom so many nights ago? "You can do that?"

"Not easily," he admitted. "But yes."

Leah turned her face, trying to hide her stunned disbelief and rising panic. She swallowed hard. "You're going to *spy* on me?"

"Messing with this energy is dangerous," Choi said. "Your teacher—" He paused. "Whoever is teaching you may be far more important than you realize."

Leah lowered her gaze and nodded. *Important indeed. If he knew I had the book, he would confiscate it for sure.* "No one is teaching me," she whispered.

A long silence settled between them. A delivery truck groaned through the nearby intersection, and Leah instinctively glanced to her dad on the porch.

Choi cleared his throat. "Let me take Paul from you."

"His daughter emailed me," Leah said. "I just opened it when you knocked. I haven't read it yet, but once I do, Paul will transcend."

"That's great news. Forward the email to me. I'll take care of it."

Choi slipped the notepad into his pocket, took Leah's hands, and closed his eyes. After a minute, she felt Paul leave. She sagged, her arms and legs growing heavy. The empty space where Paul had been, created a hollow ache of longing and loss. Leah missed him. "Paul is in you?" she asked.

"Yes. He's with me."

"What did you draw in your notepad?"

Choi grinned. "You might think it's silly, but it's actually really important. I drew a talisman. I'll use it to draw Paul out of me before he transcends. I don't want him inside me when he passes to the other world."

"A talisman. You can draw one as easily as that?"

"Leah, if you are interested in this, I can have my aunt contact you. She can explain what life is like as a Shaman. What you would need to do. What you would be giving up. From my personal experience, I can tell you it's not an easy life."

"No, that's okay. I really don't want to be involved with any of this. It makes me feel sick."

Nodding in agreement, Choi smiled. "Yes, it does."

A car drove up to the house and stopped. A man got out and looked at Leah's house, checking the address and waving to Jared.

"Oh, great!" Leah sighed.

"Your fan club?" Choi asked.

"Most likely."

"I'll talk to them. Why don't you head inside?"

"Thanks, Officer Choi."

"I'll come by every now and again to check on you—for your own safety." Choi walked briskly up the sidewalk to the gentleman, who had turned the car off and made his way around the vehicle. "Excuse me. Can I help you?" Choi asked.

Leah watched Choi confront the man, feeling a little sad that she wouldn't be able to give him the comfort he was desperately seeking. But at the same time, if he was from the press, she was happy not to have to deal with him. The guy got back in his car and drove off. Choi waved goodbye, got into his own vehicle, and drove away.

Now she needed to tell her dad something. She hated lying, but she wasn't ready to tell anyone about the book or that she was developing her abilities. Leah saw her dad waiting, clearly perturbed, as she walked up the sidewalk.

"What are you not telling me?" Jared asked.

She turned and pointed to the car. "You saw what's been happening to me, Dad. I talked to Choi about it. Teachers and kids at school keep asking me to pray for their family members and stuff. They think I can help them."

Her dad didn't say anything.

"Dad, you have been perfect. I'm glad you are chasing your career. You and Nong are good together, and Ploy is like a little sister to me. You're doing exactly what needs to be done. I have to say, I appreciate the space and trust you have given me."

Jared smirked and shook his head.

Leah continued, "You know I'm dealing with a lot. Maybe you feel like you're losing me or that I can't confide in you, I can. I know that. I just really need to go on this camping trip with Barb. It's important to me."

With a stern glare, he said, "Officer Choi was worried. His face was dark, and you knew why he was concerned. May I see your hand?"

Leah held out both of her hands. Jared took the same one Choi did, turning it over and pushing up her sleeve. It looked like he was searching for a cut, a tattoo, a needle mark, something that would have set Choi off. "What is it, Dad? What are you looking for?"

Jared released her hand. "Nothing. I'm just worried about you. I need you to make good choices." He sighed. "Should I go to the school and talk to the principal about what's been happening?"

"No, it's okay. School's almost over, and it's really not that bad. I have good friends."

Jared pulled her in and gave her a big hug. "I love you." Kissing her forehead, he added, "Go write your note. I'll sign it."

Leah went straight to her room and collapsed on her bed. *Ugh!* She didn't want Choi to know what she was up to, or her dad. Couldn't she and Barb have their little secret gift? Sitting back up, she decided to read Misty's email.

Subject: Thank You for Reaching Out

Dear Leah,

Thank you for contacting me. How did you know my father? Feel free to tell me your memories of him. Please forgive me if I don't respond in a timely manner, internet isn't always reliable where I am.

Misty.

Leah retrieved Choi's card from her pocket, hit reply, and typed Choi's email address in the CC space.

Subject: About Your Father

Dear Misty,

I only knew your father for a few days. When we met, he was terribly upset with himself for sending you an awful email. He said that you had the biggest, warmest heart of anyone he knew and that he was so proud of your decision to join the organization, but that he was deathly afraid you would be hurt.

After our talk, he had planned to apologize to you personally. I just learned that he died before he was able to tell you that. Please know that he wanted to support you and always loved you.

I am sending a copy of this email to Officer Choi. He was the one who told me about your dad's passing. He may have something to add.

I'm so sorry for your loss. I can't imagine losing my dad so suddenly. I would be devastated.

Leah.

Sinking into her bed, Leah replayed Paul's attack, and how she had quickly and easily subdued him. She felt like telling Barb, but then thought better of it. Barb would scold her for being reckless. What Leah really wanted to do was read the training manual again and begin the meditations and exercises. She had to get the book back from Tim. Closing her eyes, she visualized the information in the book and let it marinate in her thoughts.

Three houses down, Mr. Anderson returned to his computer and read the email Leah had sent Misty. Then he downloaded photos he had taken of her and Officer Choi. He studied them, seeing Choi closing his eyes while holding Leah's hands, and her deflated look after Choi had taken the soul. *Disaster averted,* he thought.

But Mr. Anderson had a new problem: Choi. The Circle knew about Leah, which meant someone—either a Banisher or a Shaman—would be coming to assess her. How long until that happened, he wasn't sure. They could be here in a week or a month. But one thing was certain—his timetable had just shortened.

He'd worry about that later. For now, he needed to prepare for Leah's little camping trip. Going to his box of toys, Mr. Anderson found three devices—his HackRF, an RTL-SDR, and a CQRX. He would tap into Tim's drone feed and record what he saw, while sifting through her trash to sink deeper into the mystery of Leah. With the Circle coming soon, he'd needed to device a solid, airtight recruitment plan that would ensure Leah came with him to New York.

Uncle Tim stood in his game room with the guys—Dylan, Big Steve, Nate, and Bret. Leah's book lay on the pool table. Tim explained that the book was a training manual for communicating with the supernatural, and that a ghost had been responsible for Leah and Jared's abduction. He described how Leah had communicated with him using telepathy. He concluded by telling them the water spirit had merged with the Education Center, and that the building was now alive.

His friends stared at him. Tim knew what he was saying sounded crazy, but it was all true. He went on, listing the warnings the elder at the reservation had given to him.

There was still no response.

"We need to destroy that building," Tim exclaimed.

Bret took the initiative and laughed. "That was great. You are so serious; didn't even crack a smile." Picking up the book, he thumbed through the pages. "Sure is fat. Looks like a fun read. Why doesn't it have a title?"

"I'm not joking," Tim said. "Do you remember the news showing video footage from the day Leah was captured? It makes a lot more sense now, doesn't it? And that priest saying Leah is an angel. His soul was captured by that thing, and Leah freed him. Look at what's been happening ever since the city stole that land. The building needs to be destroyed, and the land given back to the reservation."

Dylan took the book from Bret. "I don't know about all this supernatural talk, but I get wanting to return the land. What you're asking us to do, though, could dump us all in prison."

"You mean like, when you and Nate decided to burn down that drug house run by the police, and we had to save your asses? Or when we helped you take out that teenage trafficking thug? That kind of prison?" Tim retorted.

Dylan threw the book on the table. "Dude, those were totally different circumstances. This is insane. You're asking us to destroy a legitimate business." After a pause, he added, "Tim, my brother. Jared and Leah are safe. The guy is dead."

"There was no guy! That was a bullshit cover story." Tim wrapped his hands around his head and exhaled. "Okay. I get it. Let me have Jared, Nong, and Leah tell you the story themselves. I'll have Leah connect with you all, so you know what I'm talking about."

"I believe you," Big Steve said. "I'm in."

"I'm not sure I believe you, but it doesn't matter. I'm in too," Nate added.

"Yeah, okay. I'm in as well," Bret said. "But I do want to hear Jared and Leah tell the story. You didn't give enough details. Experiencing telepathy would be pretty wicked, too."

"We're not young anymore," Dylan protested. "Big Steve, you've got a family. We got lucky last time we played cops and robbers. Let's just wait to see if anything else happens before we storm the castle."

Tim placed both hands on Dylan's shoulders and stressed, "I'm asking you to do this for the same reason we did that other shit—no one else can fix this. I wouldn't have called you here if I didn't believe destroying that building was the only way. And I'm doing this with or without you."

Releasing a long sigh, Dylan conceded, "Okay then. What are we doing exactly?"

"Nate, do you still have a copy of *The Anarchist Cookbook*? We're going to need it."

"I do," Nate said.

Big Steve put his hands on the pool table. "This is for real. Mind your texts. Don't be talking about this on the phone. And start preparing alibis."

The late evening sun shone through the kitchen window as Choi pushed a toy car back and forth on the table with his finger while holding the phone to his ear. His son's voice, bright and eager, said, "Grandma's taking us to the beach today."

"That sounds fun, buddy. Why don't you go get ready? Give the phone back to your mommy."

"Okay. Here mom, dad wants to talk with you again."

"Hey," Jasmine said.

"Hi. I know being with my mom is a challenge, so if you need a break, take the train to Busan for a week or two. You can also go to Jeju Island. I can arrange the trip for you from here."

"I'll keep that in mind. We're about to head out the door, so I'll call you again in a couple of days."

"I love you," Choi said.

"I love you too," Jasmine replied.

Choi placed the phone on the table next to the toy car and sat in silence for a few moments. There was so much on his mind that he was struggling to process it all.

First was the reason his family was in Korea. A disturbance was going to happen in Lake Valley. He didn't know what it would be, but it would bring his Aunt Yoona, and that scared him. Yoona, the leader of the Circle, the head of the Korean anti-terrorist organization, being summoned to this place meant the disturbance had to be incredibly dangerous.

He wondered if Leah Davenport had anything to do with that future disturbance. He doubted it, but the person training her certainly could. If this person were a Banisher addicted to dark energy in need of souls, then the disturbance would most likely be some sort of explosion. His priority right now was finding the person training Leah.

The other thing on Choi's mind was the soul he had taken from Leah—Paul. He had been murdered, but the official records had recorded his death as an accident. After several conversations with Paul and exploring the soul's memories for himself, the murder had all the markings of a carefully orchestrated effort to keep Misty Davis from joining Doctors Without Borders. But why? Had it been done specifically to alter future events? And if so, did it tie into the disturbance that was going to happen here in Lake Valley? The soul had found its way here, and he wasn't sure if that was a coincidence or a warning?

Choi knew he needed to talk with his aunt about Leah, the energy manipulator training her, and this mysterious murder. Yoona was sure to send someone to assess Leah and help Choi find this user.

He tapped his aunt's icon on his phone and texted: "How certain are you that Brandon is the energy manipulator you were looking for?"

Yoona's voice spoke in Choi's mind. *He has the right mindset. I know he's important and has great potential. Have you found another user?*

Choi texted: "I have, but she's too young. I believe she is being trained."

I'm afraid I can't help you, Yoona said. *The corrupt Shaman in Washington, D.C., is making it difficult for me to read future events or probe. Between the wars, political happenings, terrorist plots, and weapons trafficking, the Circle is inundated with tasks. I must trust that you can find this user on your own.*

Choi texted: "I'll try."

Is there something else you wish to tell me? Yoona asked.

Choi took a breath and then made a voice recording. "This girl, Leah Davenport, invited a soul into her—a man who was murdered. Based on what I learned from him, I believe his death was intended to alter the future." He ended the recording and sent it.

I'm listening.

He pressed record and continued. "A government agent went to the soul's house and demanded that Paul persuade his daughter not to accept a volunteer position with Doctors Without Borders. When Paul was unable to persuade Misty, he ended up dead. After running Misty Davis through law enforcement databases, I found that she has reported multiple missing persons and suspicious activities linked to a private medical facility in New York called Extended Life. The FBI did a brief inquiry but closed the case. I've tried to make out the name on the ID of the agent who visited Paul, but this ghost has a poor memory."

Choi sent the audio file and pressed record to create another. "My next steps are to get a composite sketch of the murderer and attempt to identify him that way. I'll contact the homicide division and have them reopen the case."

You said, 'You sensed this death was meant to alter the future.' What path does that altered future lead to?

Choi texted: "I have a feeling it leads to the disturbance that is coming to Lake Valley."

Then follow that thread and investigate. Begin by merging with the life stream. Tracing Paul's life path in reverse will give you answers. Do the same with Leah. She'll be connected to whoever is training her. Follow those connections.

Yoona's presence faded.

Choi washed his face, went into the garden, and sat under his cherry tree. He ignited his spiritual center through meditation, then inserted his earbuds and listened to a tribal piece of music with a strong drumbeat. Lying on his back, he breathed along with the beat. The quick, deep breaths sent Choi into an altered state of consciousness, where he was able to meld with the garden's current of energy and go straight to the stream of life.

First, he viewed Leah's connections to her Uncle Tim and Barb. He saw her natural connections with Dan and her parents. He noticed residual connections with Eric and Max. But there was no connection to a teacher. Moving on, he traveled her main life path, witnessing her meditating, praying, forest bathing to strengthen her abilities, studying for exams, and interacting with friends. She had plenty of decisions to make and the forks made it difficult to see far. The fact that he didn't see a teacher was concerning. It could mean that her teacher had the capability to hide a direct connection. This was a master-level ability, and only a few people in the city could do this—psychics.

Next, Choi directed his focus on Paul Davis's life path, tracing it in reverse. He discovered that Paul was an activist who, due to his strict nature and high expectations, had a strained relationship with his family. He found the man who had threatened Paul, but Choi wasn't able to glean any new information about him.

The tether to Choi's body tightened, signaling his need to return. He shifted his focus and found Misty Davis through Paul's connection. Moving from Paul to Misty, he traced her life path backward. Choi discovered that Paul's death had delayed her trip to India by three months. Traversing, Choi moved toward the present, observing Misty's life. He saw her settle into her new position in India where she quickly became a trusted figure. She formed close friendships with both patients and colleagues. Choi observed her take an active role in selecting refugees for resettlement in America. Then he saw her distress. A young man she deeply cared about had failed to call or write. She reached out to the other refugees he had traveled with for answers but was unable to contact a single person. Consumed by worry, she emailed, called, and wrote to officials and politicians in a frantic bid to uncover the fate of those taken from her camp.

Choi's body strained under the stress of his soul's prolonged absence. The tether tightened and yanked him back to his body.

Opening his eyes, he lay on the ground, his chest heaving as he recovered from the intense journey. The first thing he noticed was the missing soul. Paul had transcended while Choi was away. He couldn't believe it.

Choi was relying on Paul's memories to guide the murder investigation. But with Paul gone, those memories—already secondhand—were fading. The face of the agent, once a clear imprint, was a blur with the loss of its source. The composite sketch would be unreliable at best. Beyond that, the urgency he had felt was no longer present. Was investigating this murder still imperative? He wasn't sure, but he would pass the information he had gathered to the homicide department and let them look into it further.

Paul's death had delayed Misty's trip to India, and he believed that was by design. Her absence had allowed a private hospital in New York to take refugees before she began her relentless pursuit for answers. But how was that tied to Lake Valley? He couldn't see any possible connection. His intuition was telling him to focus on Leah, so he decided this information should be passed to the FBI.

Inside the house, Choi opened his laptop and composed two emails—one to the homicide division and the other to the FBI. He outlined what he knew about Paul's murder and about the refugees and what he suspected, urging them to reopen both cases. Had Extended Life murdered Paul? Was Leah's abilities tied to the future disturbance? He was going to find out.

Choi closed his computer, went into the bathroom, and took a long, hot shower.

Seoul, Korea

<u>Discovering a Betrayal</u>

Once again, Brandon arrived early for work, this time with an assortment of pastries. After leaving them in the kitchen, he headed for his work area, sorted through English test scores, and noted common grammatical mistakes. He jotted down essential vocabulary, and outlined conversation activities.

Su-Bin touched Brandon on the shoulder. "Good morning. You're early."

Smiling warmly, Brandon replied, "I wanted to make sure you had something to eat."

Returning his smile, she said, "Thank you for your kindness, but I'm afraid you'll go broke if you continue to feed the office."

"I'm receiving two salaries. I am more than happy to feed everyone."

"Do you know how I'm feeling today?" Su-Bin wondered aloud.

"I don't. You seem happy."

"So your connection to me doesn't tell you?"

"I will feel strong emotions from you—elation or depression. If you wanted me to know your everyday thoughts and feelings, you would need to connect to me."

"I feel relieved about that and yet disappointed at the same time. Funny," she mused. "You said this connection existed with siblings and lovers."

"A natural connection can, yes, and it will develop over time, especially the more you learn about each other, but it rarely becomes as strong."

"I see," Su-Bin said.

"If you are uncomfortable with my connection to you, I can sever it."

"Strangely, I rather appreciate being connected to you. I think Yoona is correct. You're a more effective teacher this way."

"I'd love to teach you how to connect with others, but I'm sure I'd be reprimanded for that. I'm not sure Yoona would appreciate me telling you what I already have."

"I am glad you did. Our relationship isn't a mystery anymore," Su-Bin said with a small smile. "Just one more question. Is my father still with me?"

"To be honest, I'm not sure. He hasn't sent me anything lately, but I am still new at this."

"Okay. I was just curious. Well, I have a lot of work, so I'll get going. Have a good day."

"Thank you. You too."

Later that evening, after work, Min Yun rushed to Su-Bin's apartment. He placed a vase of red roses, candles, and a bottle of wine on the table. He needed to win her back. She was drifting ever since Brandon showed up. So tonight needed to be special.

In the kitchen, he opened the takeout bags and placed the *galbi jjim* (braised short ribs) and *japchai* (stir-fried glass noodles) on serving platters and emptied the *kimchi jjigae* (a spicy stew), into a bowl. Spinach and spicy radish salad came next. He arranged them neatly on the table and then cleaned up, paying attention to the time. Finally, he changed, lit the candles, and put on music just as Su-Bin arrived.

"A romantic dinner? What's the occasion?"

"I have a surprise for you."

"That's so sweet. What is it?"

"Later, after dinner." Min brushed his hands along her shoulders as he took her jacket.

She turned to face him, then moved closer. "You are being uncharacteristic tonight." Her voice was soft and sweet. "Did a honeybee sting you?" She ran her fingers through his hair.

Min placed his hand on the small of her back. "I plan on integrating this sweetness into my character."

Su-Bin kissed him.

The world narrowed to the tenderness of her body. Pressing closer, he pushed her lips open, pulling more from the kiss than she offered. He thirsted for the warm wetness of her mouth and moved his tongue deeper. Her presence was addictive, and he took it all—the scent of her skin, the uneven rhythm of her breathing, the way her body reacted to his hand as he slid it lower, grasping, squeezing, claiming what he desired.

Su-Bin's hand came to his chest, and she pushed him back. "Slow down," she said, her breath unsteady.

Min took her hand and brushed the top of it, stilling his urges. Escorting her to the table, he slid out her chair and guided her to her seat. A distinct pink colored her cheeks as he served her. He caught the twinkle in her eye as he sat.

She lowered her gaze in a very shy schoolgirl manner. It excited him.

"Do you believe in fate? Destiny?" he asked.

"I'm not sure." Su-Bin regained her composure. "I believe we control our own future. I think there are powers that try to guide us, but we must listen to them and make a conscious effort to follow. Do you?"

"I think that when a string of events happens that connect us to someone, then they are the one we are meant to be with."

Su-Bin frowned.

"What I'm trying to say is, I think it was fate that brought us together. I feel connected to you, and your mother saw that."

Sighing, she turned her head away. "Min, this evening started off so perfectly," she said. "The meal, the candles. You're being so sweet and handsome. Don't ruin it by using my mother's situation to manipulate my emotions and push for something I'm not ready for." Her voice was cold.

"I'm sorry. I didn't mean to upset you. I want to understand you better. I want to hear your ideas. I'd like to build a strong connection with you."

Su-Bin's brow drew together, eyes flickering with unease.

Min reached for her hand. "Would you be willing to meet my father?"

She pulled her hand away and rubbed her forehead. "Min, I think it's a little early for that. I also remember you saying the two of you haven't spoken in some time."

"He's engaged to be remarried. I thought if we took a trip together, it'd give us time to strengthen our relationship. And I was hoping, with you by my side, my reconnection with my father would be easier."

With slow, deliberate movements, Su-Bin picked up her napkin and wiped her mouth. "I had a conversation about connections last night with Brandon," she said. "Connections form a very personal link between two people. I'm glad you want to reconnect with your father, but you should do that before I meet him."

Min took a moment to gaze into her eyes. "Our connection is special. My true self shines when I'm with you. You are the piece that fits perfectly into my life. I need you. I want my father to know the new me, as someone who is with you."

Su-Bin closed her eyes and took a breath. When she looked at him again, she seemed weary.

How could he break through her defenses? He knew she wanted more, so why was she resisting him? She couldn't be thinking about Brandon now, could she?

With sweet eyes and vulnerability lacing his voice, he continued, "I knew from the moment I saw you that I loved you. I've tried to show you through my actions and this evening. I need you to understand that my feelings are real and deep. I want us to be more—to be woven together in experience, dreams, and devotion. I'm willing to fight for us, and I hope you can see that."

"Min—"

He interrupted, knowing she was shutting him down. "Why else would Yoona have told you to hire me? She knows our happiness lies together."

"Min, I think—"

Not wanting to hear a rejection, Min shifted. "We got the DNA results back from the lab."

"I'm sorry, what?"

"From the flask. The DNA is not your father's. What's more, I know whose it is."

"You're kidding me. Who?"

"Dr. Hyun Kim. He's the doctor who performed the stomach surgery on your father. His initials are carved into the flask, and the nurse who has been working with him for the past fifteen years identified it as his. I went to his office and got a DNA sample. I sent it in. In a week or two we'll have the match confirmed. We have your mother's murderer."

Her hand shot to mouth. "You did it." She rose and stumbled back.

Min was on his feet in an instant and rounded the table. He wrapped his arms around her as she buried her face into his chest. After a moment, he tilted her head and kissed her. She froze at first, but then swung her arms around him and kissed him back. The passion built into a pooling fever, and he guided her to the bedroom, closing the door behind them.

The next day, as Su-Bin worked in her office, Brandon stopped by. "We're going out for lunch, fried chicken. Would you like to join us?

"I'd love to. I am craving fried chicken right now, but I can't. I'll eat later."

"I can bring you some back."

"I would love that. Thank you."

She returned to her work and twenty minutes later, Min came in. "I know you're busy, so I brought you lunch." He held out a small box of fried chicken.

"I thought you had a meeting with Daehan Financial today."

"I did. I just got back." Min handed her the box. "You always eat late when you have a trial to prepare for, so, I got you chicken. I know you crave it sometimes."

"Yes, but—" *You've never done this before.* "You're being awfully sweet lately. It's strange."

"A good strange, I hope."

"Yeah, a good strange."

Min perked up, flashing that silly grin. Su-Bin couldn't help but smile. The little boy had reappeared.

"I'm driving to the prison to meet with your mom," he said. "I need her to sign some forms. Is there anything you want me to tell her?"

"Oh, darn. I was hoping to go with you. Just tell her I love her, and I'll see her at home real soon."

"Will do. Would you like to have dinner at my place or yours tonight?"

"I'm going to be working late."

"Yours it is. I'll have it all prepared for you when you arrive."

The following day, Su-Bin was in the strategy room with her team when one of the witnesses called to cancel her appointment. Su-Bin convinced her to reconsider. "I need someone to pick her up. See if there is anyone available," she instructed her assistant, who promptly left the room.

Min entered a minute later. "How is everything going?"

Looking up from the table full of documents, Su-Bin replied, "This isn't a good time. Is it important?"

"No. I was just checking on you," Min explained. "I had some free time and thought maybe you would like some coffee."

"Could you pick up a witness?" Su-Bin asked.

"Sure. Where does she live?"

Su-Bin was struck by an odd thought. How did he know the witness was a woman? This wasn't the first time he had anticipated something without being told. He seemed to be suddenly one step ahead, a stark contrast to his usual behavior. Dismissing the thought, she gave Min the information, offering her thanks.

Later, Su-Bin saw Brandon heading for class and called after him. He waited for her to catch up. "Jong-In and I are watching our drama tonight. There are only a few episodes left, but I thought you might want to join us and practice your Korean."

"Absolutely, I'd love that."

"Great. I'll have a cab pick you up in front of your apartment at six."

"I'll be ready. Thank you."

As the office closed, Min stopped Su-Bin as she headed for the parking garage. "I know you and Mr. Park are watching your drama tonight, and I was hoping maybe I could join you. I'll cook dinner, and it'll give me a chance to catch up with Jong-In."

Su-Bin put her hand to her chin, considering his request. There was no way he'd be able to sit through a full episode without complaining. Why the sudden interest? "You hate dramas."

"I could learn to love them. I'm willing to try."

The statement pleased her, but they were on episode thirteen. "Maybe when we start a new one. This one is almost over."

"It's a date," Min said.

As he headed for the door, Su-Bin shook her head. This wasn't like him. Did he know she had invited Brandon?

Brandon sat on Su-Bin's sofa, feeling a bit uncomfortable. Su-Bin and Jong-In were familiar with each other and it showed. They sat together on the floor with their backs against the couch. Brandon picked at the popcorn, watching them more than the show.

During a particularly tense scene, Jong-In bit his knuckles and Su-Bin leaned into him, their shoulders touching. They chatted and commented, voices full of disbelief and frustration.

Every now and again, Brandon would catch a word or phrase the characters had said, and he repeated it, like, "*Daebak.*" Then Jong-In or Su-Bin translated it for him. "It means 'great' or 'awesome.'"

As the two love interests onscreen had their misunderstanding, Jong-In slapped Su-Bin's leg, and she elbowed him in return, their eyes never leaving the screen. Near the end, during an emotional moment, Su-Bin briefly rested her head on Jong-In's shoulder, and they both sighed in unison.

When the commercial break came, Jong-In dashed to the kitchen while Su-Bin checked her phone. With a huff, she rattled off a stream of Korean in a tone that sounded like complaining. He recognized the words "*pon baeteori*" meaning phone battery, but couldn't understand the rest of what she said.

"가빨리 없어져. 왜이래"

Jong-In returned and reached out his hand for the device. Her voice softened, and Brandon caught the words, seriously, thanks—"*jinja komawa.*" She pressed her thumb to the screen, typed in a passcode, and handed the phone over.

After a few minutes of tapping and scrolling, Jong-In's expression grew grave. His voice lowered and turned serious as he explained something.

Su-Bin gasped in disbelief. *"Mwo? Ottekhae?"* Brandon knew the phrase—what do I do?

Su-Bin's voice rose in pitch as she spoke faster and faster. A bead of sweat trickled down her temple while she fired off a series of questions without pausing long enough for Jong-In to answer.

Brandon gathered Jong-In had checked her phone—for a virus, maybe—and Su-Bin was wondering what the virus did, and if her bank information was safe.

Then Su-Bin shouted, *"An dwae!"*

Brandon didn't need a translation for that one. The term was full of meaning: No! This can't be happening!

Her eyes widened and flickered as if scanning for a threat. Brandon knew something very bad had happened, and his mind began to play through the possibilities.

His initial thought was that her phone had been hacked, but her reaction was so strong he pivoted to maybe someone in the firm had been accused of legal misconduct. Perhaps something devastating happened with her current case—her client being arrested? Su-Bin's hands were shaking though, and he knew it must be worse than that—embezzlement or fraud, perhaps.

Then silence. Su-Bin froze, cheeks burning. Her next words held contempt, and her muscles tensed, making Brandon uneasy.

"What happened?" he asked with hesitation.

Su-Bin took in a sharp breath and stared at Brandon before calming herself. "It's nothing. Jong-In will take care of it."

Brandon nodded, thinking about Jong-In's connection to the law firm. He was an IT specialist, so maybe his first guess was right and her phone had been hacked. Thinking about it more, he finally understood her reaction. Bank accounts, passcodes, credit cards, social media, photos ... and then she was a lawyer, so she had documents, emails, client names and numbers. His heart dropped in sympathy.

The ending credits of the drama played, previewing scenes to next week's episode. Brandon stood, bowed, and wished Su-Bin well. She tried to hold her anger back as she showed him to the door, but there was no denying it. Something very bad had shaken her, and she was livid!

After Brandon and Jong-In left, Su-Bin drove to Min's house. *Why had he done this?* she thought. She remembered the moment clearly, him asking to borrow her phone right before the staff meeting. She had felt hesitant and uneasy handing it to him. Why had she trusted him? Because she wanted to believe he was a good man. She needed to believe he was trustworthy, because she had agreed to date him.

Su-Bin knew she had to go to the police and report that her phone had been compromised, but that idea made her sick to her stomach. The press would have a field day reporting it; the story was click-bait. She was a nominee for a prestigious award, and if she were found to not have taken proper security precautions, her clients could sue. She felt so screwed.

She arrived at Min's house and banged on the door.

He opened it, smiling when he saw her. "Hi, sweetie. You don't have to knock."

Holding a box full of Min's stuff, Su-Bin asserted, "I've come to give you your things and to ask for your resignation."

Acting completely surprised—rather poorly—Min floundered. "Why? I don't understand. What happened?"

"Let's not play this game, Min. Jong-In traced the signal."

"Su-Bin, truly, I have no idea what you're talking about. Traced what signal?"

She ground her teeth. "We have a strong connection? Fried chicken? If you're going to spy on someone, try to be a little less obvious about it. You hacked my phone! You listened in on my conversations! Who else has access to that nanny app you downloaded? I have confidential information on my phone. I have private meetings with clients. I just laid out our whole trial strategy. Who else was listening to that? Where is that information now?"

When he didn't reply, her voice grew stern. "Under law, I must report this! And that's the last thing I want to do. Do you realize the harm you may have caused me? The seriousness of this problem? If I'm unbelievably lucky, only the three of us will know what happened—you, me, and Jong-In." Fury flared behind her eyes. "What the hell were you thinking? And this better not be because you're jealous. I swear for real."

Hopelessness crossed Min's face. He transformed into a puppy, his eyes pleading. "Su-Bin, I love you. I would never do anything to jeopardize that."

"You love me? I think the words you're looking for are, 'You want to possess me.' This isn't love. This is obsession." Laughing sarcastically, Su-Bin continued, "I am so pissed right now, I don't even know how to act."

"Can you give me a chance to explain?"

"Ohh!! What happened to, 'I have no idea what you're talking about'? Let me explain it to you. I don't want to see you. I don't want to hear from you. I don't want to run into you. I want you out of my life."

"I am worried about you. I don't trust Brandon. He's shady and up to no good."

"Trust?! I can't believe I trusted *you*. And all the warning signs were there, too. I would appreciate any and all information on my mother's case." Su-Bin's nostrils flared, and she pressed a hand to her lips, holding back the emotions threatening to spill. She turned away to compose herself. Firing Min right now was the worst possible timing for her mom. They were so close to filing an appeal. She drew a trembling breath and managed to say, "If you want any sliver of hope of talking with me again, I need everything you have on my mother's case and for you to leave the office quietly with nothing but your personal belongings." She paused and forced her voice to steady. "If you can do that, I will know there is a shred of decency in you. I'll give you two months' severance pay, but ..." her jaw tightened, and she seethed, "if you continue to contact me, or—unacceptable—stalk me, I will press charges and make sure you are disbarred." Su-Bin dropped the box and left.

Min fell to his knees. He couldn't lose her. He refused to believe Su-Bin was gone. Min leaned forward and pounded his fists against the floor. "Shit, shit, shit." He stood and walked around the room, thinking. "Flowers? Yes, lots of flowers." Punching the wall, he screamed, "Fuck!" Circling back, Min pulled on his hair, "What can I do? How do I win her back?" He stumbled to the table and then slammed his fist against the surface. "That fucking prick. Why the hell did he have to flirt with her? Everything was perfect!" Grabbing the dining room chair, Min grunted followed by a scream as he threw the chair across the room, sending it smashing into the bookcase with a loud crash. Multiple books tumbled to the floor. "Why is he so interested in my girlfriend?"

Min paced back and forth, stewing. "What the fuck is Brandon even doing here?" Because of the nanny app on Su-Bin's phone, he knew Brandon hadn't come to teach English. All that talk about connecting to people, her father, Shamans, being an FBI agent, and the other garbage spewing out of his mouth the other night had made Min anxious about Brandon's true intentions toward Su-Bin and her firm.

Sitting at his computer, Min googled Brandon Spencer. For the next twenty minutes, he scrolled through everything he could find on him and wasn't surprised to see he had been arrested. Did Su-Bin know about this article? *What else can I find on this creep?* Then Min came across Brandon's mother. His jaw dropped. "What the fuck?" Min stared at the page for a long minute. He stood, walked in a circle with his hands on top of his head, came back, and read the name again: Judy Spencer. Laughing to himself, he said, "This can't be." Min googled Judy Spencer, finding her website selling animal paintings. On the bio page was her photo. He went to the end table, opened the drawer, and took out the invitation to his father's engagement party. Opening it, he read, "Judy Spencer and Jae Yun invite you to celebrate their engagement to each other." The photo inside was of his father and his new fiancée. "I think it's time I meet my future stepmother."

India

A Perplexing Discovery

In a refugee camp on India's eastern border, Misty Davis read a second email from Leah Davenport. She had written a kind, heartfelt letter that was a total lie. The first line read, "I only knew your father for a few days. When we met, he was terribly upset with himself for sending you an awful email." Misty chuckled. Her father, self-reflecting? That was worth a laugh. Plus, he had died an hour after sending that "awful email." There was no way Leah could have known her dad for a few days. "Fucking scam artists." She moved the mouse to delete the email but stopped.

Two questions popped in her mind. First, how did Leah know her father had sent that email? Misty had deleted his accounts and cleaned the computer. Her brother had used it for work until he got sick, and his wife sold it. Second, why would Leah CC a police officer?

Misty opened a search browser and found the Lake Valley Police Department's website. She clicked the Contact Us tab and scrolled through a list of officer names until she found Officer Choi—the email addresses matched. Misty's curser hovered above the link, but she decided to google Leah Davenport first. The browser filled with information about her abduction. Misty watched news clips and read articles detailing a series of abductions over the course of nine years. Leah had been hailed as an angel for her role in freeing a group of six individuals, earning praise for her bravery and leadership. Three officers, including Choi, had been arrested for their participation in her disappearance. Misty couldn't believe what she was reading. She felt terrible for Leah. Continuing to scroll and read, she came to an article that caused her body to lock. Her eyes widened, and a gasp escaped her lips. Bill Stillen, the CEO of Extended Life, the company that had taken young, healthy refugees from her camp to America only for them to disappear, was Leah's grandfather.

"Leah Davenport, welcome to the game." Had Misty's letters and phone calls to Congress members and senators rattled cages? Had Bill Stillen recruited his granddaughter? Was the CC to Officer Choi a warning? "You better be careful; you could be abducted next."

She read the email again. "He was proud of you…" "…wanted to support you…" "He loved you…" There was no specific threat or even a hint of a threat, but she got the message. Except: How would she had known it was a threat if she hadn't googled the information? The email itself was anything but threatening.

Misty decided to write back. She could try and coax some details from Leah and use that as evidence against Extended Life. She would pretend to know nothing about her grandfather and see what she could learn. *I'll play along, for now.* Clicking the reply button, Misty responded to Leah's email.

Hanoi, Vietnam

<u>Soul Diplomacy</u>

Inside the Communist Party headquarters, Ruth Jones paced back and forth along the hall, speaking on an encrypted line. She had called U.S. Senator Jackson, reminding him how he was to vote on the motion to send a resolution to committee that outlined the proposal for the United States to join the United Nations in forming one world government—the United Federation of States.

"Ms. Jones, I must be candid with you. After much consideration and reflection, I cannot in good conscience support this motion. The outcry and backlash coming from my constituents regarding this resolution are resounding and unequivocal. They vehemently oppose it, and their voices cannot be ignored."

"We had a deal, Senator Jackson. I gave you a new, healthy body and a lot of money. In exchange, you become a senator and vote the way I tell you."

"I will be betraying my country."

"I understand your concerns, but let me be clear about the stakes involved here. If you choose not to support this resolution, I will release evidence that proves, without a doubt, that you kidnapped, raped, and murdered the Johnson girls fifteen years ago."

"Your accusations are baseless and untrue. I have never committed a crime in my life. Blackmail and threats won't change my stance on this."

"While it's true that you, personally, have not committed any crimes, the body you now inhabit has a dark history. The individual who previously occupied the body you are in was responsible for those murders. Your DNA will match with the DNA collected. I have video footage showing you with the girls. And I have the car you used to transport them. Do you really want to spend your years here on Earth sitting on death row? And let me make one more final point clear, in case you insist on remaining resolute. Your children will suffer. I have the power to transfer their souls into the bodies of those battling leukemia. Imagine the anguish your children would suffer if I were to put them into such fragile bodies. I implore you to think carefully about your next steps. Do not underestimate me, Senator."

"Fine, I'll do as you ask. But mark my words, this isn't over. Justice will catch up to you one way or another."

"Thank you, Senator Jackson, for seeing reason. I knew you would make the right choice."

The senator ended the call.

Ruth slid her phone into her purse and entered the General Secretary's office. He was with his wife and two sons.

"General Secretary, it's a pleasure to see you and your family again. I come bearing the final paperwork that solidifies Vietnam's commitment to join the United Federation of States under the United Nations. The assembly has reviewed and debated the documents and are awaiting your authorization to proceed with the final vote. This agreement will bring immense benefits and opportunities to your country."

Taking the documents, the secretary shook his head with a look of disbelief. "I'll be honest, Ms. Jones, I didn't think you could actually convince the assembly to accept this plan. They've been ... hesitant, to say the least."

Ruth smiled, unperturbed. "It wasn't so difficult. Vietnam has a lot to gain here—healthcare, education, infrastructure, and global stability. The National Assembly knows this. They're simply giving your people what they deserve."

The secretary nodded as his expression hardened. "Before I pick up the phone and allow this vote to happen, I need you to swap my soul with that of my wife's. Here. Now. Although the demonstration you gave the last time you were here was impressive, I have had time to reflect and believe your trick was nothing more than smoke and mirrors. If you cannot, or will not, prove to me that your abilities and promise of eternal life are true, then I will have you escorted to a maximum-security prison."

Ruth smirked. His offer sounded fun, but she wasn't here to play. "Of course, Mr. Secretary. Please, make yourself comfortable. I understand your skepticism, but rest assured, what you're about to experience will leave you profoundly changed, expanding your understanding of life and the universe."

The boys sat together in their father's chair at his desk while the secretary and his wife relaxed on the sofa. Ruth removed a bottle of holy water from her purse, poured some into a small bowl, and began chanting in Latin as she tied her hair up. She dipped her fingers into the water and sprinkled droplets onto the couple's heads. Then she sat on the floor in front of them.

Ruth had spent years mastering the art of soul transference, the final key to global control. She was playing chess on a planetary level, not as a piece—but as the hand that moved them all.

Energy manipulators had long believed that soul transference was impossible. To place a new soul in a body, the tether—the invisible bond between body and soul—had to first be cut. However, a living, tethered body could not survive the loss of its own soul. Yet Ruth knew better. Yoona had transferred her soul into a new body.

Guantánamo Bay had given Ruth the perfect environment to experiment. With no oversight and unlimited access to detainees, she was free to study the process. A few of the prisoners had been Afghan Shamans—energy manipulators presumed to be linked to insurgent groups. Through coercion and promises of safety for their families, Ruth had secured their cooperation. In them, she found both test subjects and teachers.

Her studies began with exorcist priests—men trained to draw souls out of bodies. But their methods had limits. Younger, inexperienced priests often mistook mental illness for possession, and in performing the ritual, removed the very soul that actually belonged to the body. When that happened, the body died. Exorcism could extract a soul, but it couldn't preserve the vessel—the outcome Ruth needed. She knew of two natural phenomena that kept the body alive: Banishers and Soul Harvesters.

Banishers confronted possession by connecting to the consciousness of an invading soul and initiating a forced transcendence. The danger was timing. A Banisher had to disconnect before the soul crossed over, but not before the process was underway. If a Banisher stayed too long, they transcended alongside the soul. When that happened, the Banisher's body remained alive, but soulless.

Soul Harvesters ripped souls from bodies and either forced them to transcend or kept them to feed off their power. If the soul was kept, the body remained in a coma, waiting for its return. But if the soul was forced to transcend, the body roamed, seeking a new soul to replace the one it lost.

In both the Banisher and Soul Harvester cases, the tether was cut, yet the body remained alive. Why? The answer, Ruth realized, was this: a Soul Harvester had no tether of its own, and a Banisher left their body willingly, transcending through a foreign door. In contrast, Ruth was an extractor already tethered to her own body.

There was no way a living person could extract a soul and keep the body alive. So how had Yoona done it? Ruth found her solution in the subconscious. She triggered a primal survival response so that once the soul transcended, the body began searching for a replacement.

Next, she had to create a new tether between body and soul. The natural process was fragile, and unobservable. Ruth spent years in frustration trying to artificially create the tether until she realized that a chemical alteration of the mind and body had to happen first. Injecting the body with psychedelic substances, she was able to observe the tether and how it functioned.

Her final challenge was binding the body to the soul she offered, an outcome that had rarely happened. Her trick to increase the success rate? Recognition. By stimulating specific muscle memories within the body and aligning them with corresponding memories carried by the soul, Ruth created the familiarity the tether sought when accepting a soul.

But what the secretary wanted—soul-swapping—wasn't truly possible. Not in any controlled, reliable way, because the tether between body and soul was never broken. A swap would only happen between two people with a natural connection, rooted in complete trust, deep understanding, and unconditional love. Ruth had only ever witnessed it once—in a desperate exchange between a father and son whose bond ran soul-deep. The secretary and his wife had no such bond. They barely tolerated each other.

Ruth could, however, force a temporary exchange by holding the souls in their new vessels through sheer focus and force. The tethers would resist, pulling the souls back to their rightful bodies, but she could keep the illusion alive for a minute or two. And a minute was all she needed.

The problem: swapping souls would strain her existing connections, and each of those connections demanded mental effort to maintain. Performing this ritual meant she would lose many of those ties. With the U.S. Senate vote approaching, she couldn't afford to lose any of the senators to whom she was connected. Ruth took a breath, solidified her hold on her most important links, and readied herself for the ceremony.

Le Tran Duc, the General Secretary of Vietnam, sat on the sofa in his office next to his wife. He had been approached by a Myanmar General over a year ago who explained that Extended Life had saved his daughter by putting her soul into a new body. He also explained that they were offering eternal life to the leader and their family of any country that would join the United Federation of States.

Intrigued, the secretary invited Ms. Jones to demonstrate her abilities and to make her case that relinquishing Vietnam's sovereignty was in the country's best interest. He wasn't disappointed.

But over time, as the awe wore away, and the opposition grew, he couldn't believe that what he had witnessed was indeed true. Le Tran, now comfortable on his sofa, waited for confirmation that he hadn't been duped.

Ruth began to chant in Latin as she wrapped her hair into a topknot. Dipping her fingers in water, she sprinkled it on their heads. After another minute of chants and water droplets, Le Tran felt a shift. His body became heavy, like a lead blanket had been laid over him. He didn't move—uncertain if he should, unsure if he could. His senses fell silent, and his body sank like a heavy bag. Yet his spirit remained still, suspended like a leaf on water. His soul had separated from his body yet remained attached. He drifted and had an urge to fly. Suddenly, an invisible hand wrapped its grip around his essence. Le Tran's soul was lifted into the air. He felt naked. The pain in his knee and the persistent, burning itch in his chest were gone. The secretary saw his body, a lifeless bag of water, lying on the couch next to his wife.

Then Le Tran was lowered into his wife's body. His soul slid into place like a coin into a slot machine. As he settled into the new body, he felt whole. He examined himself, feeling his breasts, and pinching his nipples to experience the sensation. Turning, he saw his own body moving. He tried to speak but found he couldn't. His thoughts ricocheted like pinballs in his mind. He became numb. Then, without warning, he was flung back into his own body, the whiplash reverberating through every molecule of his soul. He gasped for air and erupted into an uncontrollable cry. Tears streamed down his face, stinging his eyes. The shock had made him lose control. He lay on the sofa sobbing like a little boy who had lost his mother, until his sons came to comfort him.

Once he had regained control, the secretary stood and asked, "Why were we replaced so violently?"

Sweat rolled down Ruth's face. "You wanted proof," she said, gasping for air. "I gave it to you."

Le Tran glanced at his wife, who was still crying. His gaze returned, his scowl hardening.

"You have talked with others I have helped. You have seen a demonstration. And now you have experienced it yourself. I offer you and your family eternal life, free of sickness and suffering. I offer your people a life free from the threat of war and hunger. The resources of the world will become your resources. As a member of the United Federation of States, you will become governor. You will be able to keep your laws. Your autonomy will not be completely lost. You have everything to gain and nothing to lose."

The secretary placed his hands on his hips and turned away.

"I'm okay," his wife said.

"All right," he agreed, nodding. "I'll make the call. Then you can accompany the president when he signs the papers on national television."

"I will have the United Nations representative accompany him. This is a historic day for Vietnam. Welcome to the family."

Lake Valley, Oregon

<u>Foreboding Visions</u>

Leah glanced behind her. Barb had hooked her hands under the straps of her backpack, straining to climb the slope into the national park. Their packs were stuffed with camping gear, slowing their pace.

In an attempt to lighten Barb's mood, Leah held out her arms and spun in a circle. Her hands grazed the tops of pink and yellow wildflowers, blooming in scattered clusters along the edges of the trail. "Isn't this just beautiful?" she marveled, a smile lighting her face.

Barb grunted. When she reached Leah, she wiped the sweat from her forehead and glanced at the clouds. "The temperature's dropping. Do you feel it?"

Leah drew in a deep breath. "Yeah ... smells like rain."

Starlings squawked and swirled, catching Leah and Barb's attention as the sun peeked through the clouds. The ray of light streaked across the sky like the hand of God, settling the restless birds.

"I can't believe I'm witnessing this." Leah murmured. Her gaze lingered on the sunlight as she admired the calming effect it had. This trip was meant to be. She was on the right path. Her spiritual connection to life was already strengthening, and she felt uplifted and energized. "It's magical," she whispered.

The sun disappeared behind the darkening clouds and the starlings continued their chattering.

"Leah, I'm not sure how long I can keep going. My back is already killing me."

"Let's rest," Leah said.

"At the rate we're stopping, it's going to take us three days just to get where we're going."

"We can do anything we want," Leah said. "But let's get a little farther away from civilization before we set up camp."

"Maybe being close to civilization is better. That way we can get back easily if the storm is bad."

"Barb, I need you. Connecting to life and transforming our energy is going to be an emotional journey. I want to experience this together."

"Okay. I get it. It's just, I'm not so sure I want to dabble in this energy."

"Don't say that. You and I are a team. The Banisher sisters of Lake Valley."

A short breath, halfway between a laugh and a sigh, escaped Barb. She let her backpack slip off her shoulders as she turned and looked away. "Leah, this is probably our last summer together."

Leah dropped her own bag and took a step toward Barb. "No, it's not. I'll be back."

"But I might not be." Barb faced Leah. "I've been asked to audition for the Hawthorn School of Performing Arts. If I do well, they're going to offer me a scholarship."

Leah's face brightened. "That's great news. Hot damn, girl!" She leapt forward and wrapped Barb in a giant hug. "Why didn't you tell me earlier?"

Barb patted Leah, then stepped back and sat on her pack. "I still have to audition." With a quick shrug, she added, "And this dream might crumble away."

"No, not if you use your energy to ensure you're accepted. Tap into your core and let your magic shine."

Barb's smile melted into a scowl.

"Come on," Leah said. "This is great! I'm so happy for you."

"Do you read the warnings and dangers in the manual?" Barb asked. "'Tap into my core?' That kind of thinking eats away at you from the inside out."

Leah straightened. She had read every word in the book. She hadn't had a chance to study it, but she remembered enough. "I did read the warnings. Tapping into your spiritual core to shine won't corrupt you."

"That's not how you phrased it." Barb stared at the ground and kicked at the dirt. "You're turning into a different person before my eyes."

"What are you talking about?"

"Planting emotions into other people's minds. Lying to your dad and mom, my grandmother, the teachers, the cops. It's not like you."

"What? Am I supposed to advertise that we're learning magic?" Leah said, exasperated. "That's a fantastic way to smooth everyone's worry."

"It's not only the lying," Barb stressed. "You had the soul of some dead guy attached to you, making you sick. And that's level zero for potential problems."

"Don't you want to help people?" Leah asked. "We could be superheroes."

"I just want to be super friends."

"We are." Leah's frown deepened. "I thought we were a team. If we could work together, we'd never be vulnerable again. Nothing would ever be able to trap us, and we could protect the people we love."

"You said Officer Choi took Paul from you. That he knows all about this magic."

"That's right. So?"

"So, he's a cop. That's his job. We should let him do it."

"Can you at least learn to do the telepathy with me? It's going to be so amazing to talk with you whenever, wherever."

"That's what cell phones are for."

"Well, shit, Barb. Why did you agree to come camping with me if you have no interest in learning this?"

"I didn't say I had no interest. I'm just not sure. And I'm here because I care about you, Leah."

"What aren't you sure about?"

Barb sighed, her shoulders dropping as she looked away. "Ghosts. Trauma. Being different."

Leah took a deep breath and let it out slowly. A ghost had killed Barb's mom. Leah hadn't considered that. She stepped closer.

"Dan misses you," Barb whispered. "You've been ... distant."

"Yeah. Lots going on," Leah replied. "Still, this trip feels right. And I'm really excited for you. You deserve to win the Hawthorne scholarship." She rubbed Barb's arm. "You're going to wow the judges."

"Thanks," Barb said with a smile. "But let's keep going. I want to set up camp before it rains."

They hiked for another hour when a raindrop hit Leah. She turned to Barb, who was looking at a drop that hit her arm.

"We need to stop," Barb said.

"I know. Look, there's a flat spot over there in the middle of those trees."

A light rain started as they cleared the area of sticks. "Let's hang the tarp first so we don't get drenched," Barb suggested. They strung the tarp just as the wind picked up and the raindrops became heavier. The tarp and the trees offered some protection, but the girls knew the evening wasn't going to be comfortable.

When they finished setting up the tent and stowed their gear, they were wet, tired, and hungry. They turned on the portable heater, changed into dry clothes, ate some granola, and huddled together, laughing, as the rain began to pour.

Uncle Tim and his wife, Patty, were preparing dinner when Jared called. Setting his potato peeler down, Tim answered, "Evening, bro. What's up?"

"I called to ask about Leah. Do you have eyes on her? Is she okay?"

"They were getting ready to set up camp when I had to fly the drone back. They might be a little wet, but they're fine. I wouldn't worry about them."

"It's raining pretty hard."

"It's strong, but not strong enough to worry about. I'm cooking dinner with Patty, and she's eyeing me, waiting for these potatoes. So I'm going to let you go. Come over tonight. Have a few beers with me."

"Yeah, all right. I'll be by around eight."

Hanging up, Tim resumed peeling.

"He's worried about Leah?" Patty asked.

"Yeah. I hope the girls were able to get the tent set up before the rain started."

"They'll be fine. This trip is going to be a story they can tell their kids," Patty said, adding, "You'll be able to tell your own stories soon, too."

Tim froze, the words replaying in his head. "Are you saying what I think you're saying?"

"I am," Patty admitted with a huge smile.

He grabbed his wife and spun her in a circle before engaging in a long, passionate kiss. Then his phone rang again. "Sorry, sweetie." Looking at it, he saw it was Roy. His face went long with guilt as he looked back at his wife. "I have to take this, honey. I love you so much. Give me one minute."

Patty's face turned red. "What kind of trouble have you gotten yourself into?"

Tim sighed and answered the phone. "Roy."

"I have a name in my mind. If you can tell me what it is—"

"Bellevue," Tim said without hesitating.

Roy didn't respond.

"So, I'm assuming I won't be hearing from the police," Tim said.

"I've heard It. It spoke to me. Is that your water spirit?"

"It is."

"I talked with the elders. There's nothing you can do to avoid what's coming. They said the best course of action is to do nothing."

"Nothing? People will die."

"Maybe. Maybe not."

Tim scoffed. "That's easy to say when it's theoretical. But if that thing connects with a student, a teacher—hell, several of them—we're talking about lives torn apart. Not just the people who get caught up in It, but their families. Parents, spouses, siblings. You think they'll just move on? No. This will destroy them."

Silence. When Roy spoke again, his voice was low. "Yeah. I get it." Another pause. "There is one person It's already connected with."

Tim's grip tightened on the phone. "Who?"

"One of the art students. Olivia Rose. She drew a beautiful picture of the Bellevue House, and it's on display. You were right; that's a warning. It's supposed to signal an impending death, but it doesn't necessarily mean the girl is the one who will die. If we intervene, we will make the situation worse."

"Or we could prevent the situation from happening in the first place." Tim sucked in a quick breath. Bellevue's escalation was happening faster than he had anticipated. Now he had to play defense and adjust his timetable. "I'll find out who this kid is and talk to the parents. We can prevent that death. But more importantly, we must return that land to the reservation. As long as it stays a part of the city, people are in danger."

"I've been told that trying to prevent what is sure to happen will only cement the certainty of the outcome."

"How can you be positive? How do you know we wouldn't be saving a life?"

"Look, I'm just relaying what I've been told. I'm not completely sold on the inevitability of anything."

"Good, because I can't sit back and do nothing. I won't."

"Okay. Then I'll start putting together the campaign."

"Then you believe this is the right strategy?"

"I don't believe there is a right strategy, but I agree with you that we're not doomed no matter what we do."

"All right. We're on the same page then."

"Tim, I have to go," Roy said. "We'll talk more about this later."

"Sounds good. Bye." Tim set his phone down and sighed. He wiped his face and noticed his wife glaring at him.

"Timmy," Patty intoned, "you better start talking."

Barb woke the next morning, feeling uncomfortable. Water had leaked into the tent and pooled at her feet. She poked her friend. "Is your sleeping bag wet? Mine is soaked."

Leah groaned. "A little bit." Rolling over, she faced Barb. "But the birds sound happy, the sun is shining, and the air smells clean."

"We're not hiking today, are we?"

"It doesn't sound like it from your tone of voice. Let's make a fire, eat, and hang our bags to dry." Leah crawled to the door and unzipped the flap. "The sky is so blue!"

Barb sat up and looked at the puddle of water, her toes cold and wet. "Nature. So much fun."

"I'm not sure we can build a fire. Everything is wet," Leah said.

"Including me," Barb grumbled, unpacking some clothes and changing. "Leah, do you know if there is a river or stream nearby?"

"I know there is one where we were heading. It's another hour or two of walking, though."

"Ugh. Never mind." Leaving the tent, Barb held up her phone looking to see if she had a signal. Delighted, she exclaimed, "Yes!"

"No! Barb! No phones," Leah protested.

"I just want to double-check the weather." After a minute, Barb exhaled loudly. "Thank god, sunny skies."

"Put that thing away. Let's arrange the site."

They eventually got a small fire going, hung the sleeping bags and wet clothes to dry, and set the tent in the sun. Then they cooked breakfast and organized the campsite.

After a while, Leah took out the manual and asked, "Are you really not interested in learning this with me?"

Barb hesitated to answer. "To be honest, not really. I don't think you are ready, either."

"Why do you say that?"

"The first part of this book talks about eliminating wants, to not desire certain outcomes, to live in the now and be present in each moment—mindfulness."

"And?"

"And you have this desire for us to be the dynamic duo. You want me to learn with you. You wanted Eric to be my date and for me to enjoy prom."

"I see your point."

"Maybe you should read the chapter about controlling your emotions."

"I did."

"Really? Summarize the chapter then."

Leah huffed. "You control your emotions. Your emotions don't control you. Rise above them, catch them, label them, observe how they affect you, reframe your thoughts, gain a different perspective, and let them go. I got that."

"You read it; I'm not sure you're practicing it."

"It'd be good for me to hear it again. Would you read to me? Then I can close my eyes while listening and practice."

"Sure." Barb sat crossed legged next to the fire and opened the book. As meditations and exercises came up, they paused, talked, practiced, laughed, told stories, and read some more.

Officer Choi entered a psychic shop. The front part of the store held display tables, glass cases, and shelves lined with lavender and vanilla lotions, pink crystals, honey-pear tea, sandalwood incense, sage-scented candles, silk scarves, and more. The back of the store had two doors, one labeled "Psychic Readings" and the other labeled "Palm Readings." In between the doors were chairs, a love seat, and a coffee table with magazines. Two ladies were sitting, chatting, as Choi looked around.

The salesclerk asked, "Are you looking for something specific, or would you like to make an appointment?"

Approaching the counter, he said, "Hi. I'm Choi," and offered his hand.

The woman received him. "I'm Stephanie."

Choi connected, asking, "Are there any appointments available?"

"There are." Stephanie typed on her computer, bringing up the schedule.

"May I meet them before I decide to make the appointment?"

"Sure. Madam Caitlin will be done in about ten minutes. Lady Karen just started a session, so she may be a while—at least a half hour."

"I can wait. Thank you."

"If you have any questions, let me know."

Choi nodded and began to browse. This was the third psychic store he had visited today. He wasn't here for candles or crystals. He was here because of Leah. Someone had to be teaching her, and his money was on a psychic.

He ran his hand along the scarves for sale. The smooth silk, light and wavy, moved like a current through his fingers.

The stream of life was a living web. Every soul existed within it, linked by memory, presence, attention, and love. Psychics, Shamans, and Banishers who understood this could use those bonds, the threads that tie us together, to surf between life paths, traveling from one person to another in the stream, so long as the connection remained open and strong. And hiding a connection to someone in that stream was nearly impossible.

The most gifted energy manipulators, psychics included, could cloak a connection. Circle members could do this. But it took intention, discipline, and a familiarity with the current's swirls, backflows, and eddies. Whoever was teaching Leah wasn't just powerful—they'd learned to disappear.

This concerned Choi. The Circle existed to guide energy manipulators, to offer support, community, counsel, and accountability. Without this family, even the most well-meaning users could drift.

If Leah's teacher had grown strong outside the Circle's reach, they were walking that path alone. Choi needed to find them—to offer what the Circle was meant to provide: a place to belong, and a compass to keep their gifts from twisting into tools of control, pride, or personal gain.

Stopping at a shelf, Choi admired crystals with deep purple hues. He picked one up and turned it in the light, watching the way the rock bent and fragmented the beam. Most psychics could only skim the stream's surface, glimpsing vague impressions. But a rare few, like the crystal, could refract the current itself—shifting, cloaking, and vanishing from view. If Leah's teacher was one of them, Choi knew he was dealing with someone dangerous. And the only way to find them was by connecting to them directly. One psychic at a time.

Karen and Caitlin were strong psychics, but they hadn't been able to navigate the stream the last time he'd connected with them. The final shop in town was Cynthia's. If none of these psychics were Leah's teacher, then he would question her uncle, Barb, and finally her father. If that revealed no answers, he would confront Leah again. Was she learning about the dangers associated with manipulating energy? How to protect herself? She had seemed surprised by the talisman he had quickly drawn to dispel Paul from his body.

The door to Caitlin's room opened and Choi made eye contact. She met his gaze with a knowing look and waved him over.

Leah opened her eyes as Barb finished reading. The fire burned low and hot, the sleeping bags hung loosely on the line, and the blue tarp, strung tight between the trees, fluttered in the breeze.

"Okay, it says we're supposed to internalize the teaching and reflect on what it means," Barb said, closing the book. "You go first."

Leah thought for a second. "Let's say someone wanted a motorcycle." She glanced off to the side and pursed her lips. "Is it the thing they want or is it the activity they love? If they want a reliable bike to live their passion, then anyone will do; it doesn't have to be new or a specific brand. But if they want status—a new Harley—then desiring that specific item corrupts your spiritual core."

Barb nodded. "The passage reminded me of a vacation. The destination is insignificant. It's the journey that's important—who you're with and what you learn along the way."

"Right, good analogy," Leah said. "What's next?"

"You need to explain why learning about energy manipulation is important to you," Barb said.

Leah took a long breath and then looked at her surroundings—the trees, the sky, the dirt. She struggled to find an answer and ran her hand across her face. "At first, it was to free my dad. Then it just sounded cool and fun. I thought having a special connection to you that no one else understood would make our friendship unique. But after we got trapped, this power saved us. And once I free Father Joseph, I became hooked. I helped Eric, which made a difference in people's lives—you, his mom and dad. Helping Paul also felt rewarding. He needed his daughter to know he loved her in order to find peace. I did that. When people ask me for help, I feel their hope, which is a strong emotion. Helping people is becoming my passion—and this energy, this skill, is a way for me to do that."

"Geez, Leah. I think you are definitely in the right mindset now. How do you feel?"

"It's weird. My whole body is buzzing. I feel ... strong. Let me try to send you a thought. Something new."

"Okay."

Centering Barb in her mind, Leah pictured a tuna sandwich. The bread's brown texture, with tiny air pockets where the yeast and flour had melded together, was fluffy. The light brown flakes of tuna held the robust briny scent of the sea—a salty, fishy odor that caused Barb's stomach to growl. Mixing the tuna with the creamy, smooth mayonnaise, thick and rich, turned the meat into a delicious meal. Barb held the sandwich, smelling it, and moaning. Leah dared her to taste the soft, scrumptious treasure wrapped in bread. Barb needed to eat this sandwich. It was hers. Leah connected the image to energy and sent it to Barb.

Barb froze. Her eyes darted back and forth. "A tuna sandwich?" Her brow arched and she smiled. "Wow! I could almost taste it. Are you hungry?"

"Yeah. What are we having for lunch?"

"I packed a can of tuna, and I have mayo packets."

After eating, Leah was ready to bathe in nature. "I'm going to meditate. I'll be back later."

Hiking into the woods, away from the trail, Leah soaked in the beauty and power of life. She heard the "chick-a-dee-dee-dee" call of a black-capped chickadee and "cheerily, cheer up" warbling of a robin. Mosquitoes buzzed in her ears as she passed a cluster of sword ferns. A damp, musty smell saturated the air with moss, mushrooms, and the sinuous tendrils of stringy white mycelium. She maneuvered around a large western red cedar, the aroma filling her body with a richness older than … names. The forest pressed closer, welcoming her connection. The tranquil serenity of the woods wrapped around her, lifting her spirits and awakening an ancient alignment with the Earth.

A tall ponderosa pine came into view. It looked old and wise. Stepping over a log, she closed the distance, placed her hands on it, and circled the magnificent giant several times. A pulse emanated from the sentinel. The roots went deep, and she felt the interconnected web of life, a community of interdependence.

Sitting with her back against the pine, Leah focused on her breathing. In—*I am here.* Out—*I am one with nature.* She opened her mind and let her spirit join with the surrounding life. Images of deer and chipmunks, hunters and hikers, touched her. Splashes of the past crept in the shadows—two lovers pausing to kiss, and the strike of lightning that sparked a fire. This was the stark duality between life and death within the heart of the forest.

Time slowed. There was no need to rush or hurry. There were no pressing issues or concerns. Calmness claim her until the hum of a surveillance drone flying above the trees pulled her from the trance.

Leah imagined her uncle frantic to find her. She stood, found a clearing, and waved to the drone.

Tim let out a sigh of relief as Leah waved. He adjusted himself, taking a more relaxed position on his stool. Directing the drone, he swept the area, panning for animals or hikers. The door creaked opened, and he glanced over to see Nate holding a book.

"Whatcha looking at?" Nate asked.

"Leah and her friend went camping. I'm just checking in on them. Give me a second to land this thing."

"Sure. Here's the book," Nate said. "Please be careful with it."

"Which book?" Tim asked but then remembered. "Oh, *The Anarchist Cookbook.*"

"That's the one." He slapped it on the table, startling Tim.

"Easy, man," Tim soothed. "You all right?"

Nate exhaled loudly. "So, tell me. How do you plan to buy the ingredients to build these bombs?"

Landing the drone in a clearing, Tim set the pad down and studied Nate's disheveled appearance. His dirty blond hair was messy as if he'd been running his hands through it in frustration. He was agitated. Speaking with caution, Tim said, "Very slowly, at different locations, wearing a medical mask, paying cash, and by asking friends to get their friends to help, unknowingly. But I do need a place to build them. I can't build them here. If the police decide to look into us, I can't have any traces at my home."

"I hear that," Nate said. "Let me try to find a place. I've got time."

"Thanks. I appreciate that."

"Have you been paying attention to the news?" Nate asked.

"Yeah. I think these arrests will help us."

Nate straightened, almost as if taken aback. "Arrests?" he said, incredulously.

"The FBI arrested two city officials on corruption charges. Some of those charges go back to the annexation of the land. We can use that to bolster the claims that the land needs to be returned to the tribe."

Nate shook his head in disbelief.

Tim eyed him, wondering what was going on. "Have the guys started the disinformation campaign yet?"

"That's all the boys are talking about now," Nate said. "The rumors are flying. Big Steve's even got his kids on social media posting shit."

"Good. I talked with Roy last night, and he's on board, too."

"When are we meeting again?"

"I'll drop by and let you know," Tim replied.

Nate nodded, twisting his lip into a snarl.

"Are you having second thoughts? I wouldn't blame you if you backed out."

Nate made a fist and pounded the table. The vibration sent a box falling to the concrete floor with a resounding crash.

Tim stood, throwing his hands in the air. "Talk to me, Nate."

Nate paced in a circle. "Sorry about that."

"It's nothing. An old DVD player and some power strips." Tim waited for Nate to face him. "Something going on with your boy?"

With a disbelieving huff, Nate asked, "Do you really not know? Or maybe you don't care."

"Look man, whatever it is, I've got your back."

"The fucking U.S. Senate voted to form a committee to discuss a possible resolution that would have us join the goddamn United Nations, giving them governing powers. The proposal the European Union has offered is not good. All policing will be solely held by the UN."

"Yeah, I heard."

"You heard. That's it?"

"I wouldn't worry about it, Nate."

"Wake up, man! Forty countries have already signed on. If we don't fight this, one morning we'll walk out the door and storm troopers will be marching down our streets. It'll be something straight out of a *Star Wars* movie. Are you not pissed off?!" Nate spat.

Tim shrugged.

"We live in the greatest country in the world, and they're talking about surrendering our sovereignty? Giving up our freedom! How are you not fucking livid?"

With a small chuckle, Tim said, "We have the greatest military in the world. I wouldn't say greatest country."

"We are the freest people with the most rights."

"We have the highest incarceration rate, and let's not forget the mass shootings. We're not exactly leading in happiness, healthcare, or education either," Tim countered.

Nate's glare turned venomous, so Tim raised his hands in a placating gesture, trying to defuse his anger.

"I thought you loved our country. I thought you were one of us. What the fuck happened to you?"

"I do love our country. Always have and always will. It's these dreams." Tim paused, his expression troubled. "They keep me up at night, showing me the horrors of our history, of my family lineage. The guilt is killing me. The evils we committed to create this country..." Tim shook his head. "Nate, you don't understand the horrors of war."

"War?" Nate scoffed. "You don't understand the horrors of absolute power. A single government, a single police force—who checks that? Who stops them when they turn into tyrants? Look at what happened with the Nazis and with Stalin. Imagine that power, but global, with no one to fight back. We'd lose our rights, our freedoms, our very identities. We'd be handing the world over to the next Hitler, and there'd be no place left to run."

Tim turned away and sat back down. Shielding his eyes, he said, "I just need to get rid of that building and put the land back into the Sukiya's hands. Once that happens, I'll be back in my right mind."

"Yeah, whatever." Nate retreated toward the door. "You're still my friend. I love you, and I'd die for you. But don't fuck me from behind." He turned and walked out, saying, "See you around."

After Nate left, Tim took a deep breath. The news had shaken him when he had heard it, and he understood Nate's anger. He couldn't deny the truth in his words. But the world was already on the path to corporate tyranny, so Tim didn't really care. All politicians were bought and paid for, except for maybe that young New York chick who was smart as a whip: the bartender. She had won by pure determination. Tim had seen a few video clips of her in action, and she impressed. The others? They were put in office by corporations.

Look at the tobacco industry. In the 1960s, the surgeon general wanted a label on cigarette cartons: "Warning: Cigarette Smoking is Dangerous to Your Health." The government was aware of the risks and was planning to regulate the industry. Big tobacco mobilized, handpicked their own men, and made sure they were elected. First, they softened the language. "Warning: Cigarette Smoking May Be Hazardous to Your Health." Then, those elected officials derailed regulation plans, using their own biased findings to argue against regulation. Tim still remembered how stunned he'd been when he first learned the people in charge weren't protecting anyone but themselves.

Tobacco had learned this trick from timber and cotton, which orchestrated the government's ban on hemp. Big oil, the military complex, big pharma, alcohol, soda, health insurance ... they all saw what tobacco did and followed suit. Bush? An oil man. Cheney? A military complex guy. Biden? A corporate lawyer! Democrats and Republicans were merely two wings of the same crow. The current system wasn't working. The citizens weren't choosing who made it to the ballot, the corporations were. The war machine would forever churn. Maybe joining the United Nations was the best thing: one people living together on one planet, under one government. Tim, however, was under no illusions that it would happen, and so, he honestly didn't care.

He was tired. These dreams kept him awake, making him rethink what he believed.

Picking up his screen, Tim flew the drone to check on the girls one last time before flying it home. He had another mission: to meet Olivia Rose and her parents.

It was a twenty-minute drive to Olivia's house. Tim arrived and knocked on the door. When Olivia's mother answered, Tim asked, "Are you Jane Rose?"

"That's right. You must be Tim Davenport," she replied rather harshly.

"Yes. Thank you so much for agreeing to meet me."

Jane put her hand on her hip and huffed. "You had me worried. I don't know where you guys are getting your information, but I'm becoming frustrated. My friend was telling me I shouldn't allow Olivia to study at the Center because of some ridiculous, bogus story about the Chinese slipping drugs into the kids' water. Then you call and are concerned about her being involved with someone who's trouble. I talked to Olivia after our chat. She said her friend isn't even real. She's imaginary."

"Then how did I know about her? I've never met Olivia. Olivia has never talked to me."

"You've never met my daughter? Then..." Jane tilted her head and squinted her eyes. "How do you know her? And why are you concerned about her? What made you think her new friend would harm her?"

"I know about this friend because Olivia's artwork is displayed at the Center."

"The only thing she has on display is a drawing of a house."

"Do you know about the house she drew?"

"Olivia's teacher said it used to stand where the Center is now. It was famous, and the kids who used to live there have been in the news."

"I'm going to bet Olivia has never seen a photo of that house."

Jane laughed. "What are you talking about? I just told you the story's been in the news. If she's never seen a photo of it, how could she draw it?"

"When's the last time you saw a photo of the house?" Tim asked and then paused. "If Olivia has seen that house before, then I made a mistake, and I'll leave."

Jane glared at Tim. "All right. I'll go ask her. Wait here." Jane closed the door. Tim turned and put his hands on the railing of the porch, admiring the neighborhood. The lawns were professionally groomed, the streets and sidewalks perfectly smooth. Two or three cars sat in each driveway.

After a few minutes, the door opened again. "How did you know she had never seen that house?"

"May I come in? Can we talk, the three of us?"

Taking a hard look at Tim, the woman sighed and let him in. Tim waited in the living room while Jane called upstairs, "Olivia! Come down here for a minute."

When Olivia bounded into the room, her mom asked, "Do you know this man? Have you met him?"

Olivia stared at him. "No."

"You've never seen him or talked to him?"

"No," Olivia repeated.

Tim asked, "Olivia, who did you tell about Bella?"

"No one. Do you know her too?"

"Yes. My niece spent some time with her. Do your friends know about her?

"No. Me and Bella just play by ourselves."

"So, you haven't told anybody else about her?"

"Nope."

Looking confused, Jane asked, "Nobody? Not even your teacher?"

"Bella told me not to tell anybody about her."

"Why not?" Jane asked.

"She said the other kids would make fun of me and that if you found out, we couldn't be friends anymore."

"Bella told you that?" her mom asked.

"She talks in my mind."

"Imaginary means make-believe, not real. You know that, right?"

"Duh. I'm not stupid, Mom."

Tim asked, "When do you talk with Bella?"

"During art class at the Center."

"How about at home?" Tim asked. "Do you talk and play in your room or in the backyard with her?"

"No. Only at the Center."

Olivia's mom put her hand up, interjecting, "Olivia, why don't you play with Bella here at home?"

"I can't. She doesn't live here."

Jane looked at Tim, who raised his eyebrows. "Thanks, Olivia. You can go play," her mom said.

Olivia ran back upstairs.

Tim looked Jane dead in the eyes, saying very slowly and deliberately, "Barbara and Daniel Mills both had this same friend when they lived at the Bellevue House. You know what happened to their family."

"Stop it. You're scaring me."

"Good. You should be scared. There are reasons these rumors about the Education Center exist. There's a reason that land is sacred to the Sukiya tribe. There's a reason bad things happen there." Tim could see she was thinking. "If you haven't read the news article that was in the *Sun Times* about Father Joseph, then I suggest you do. There is more truth in that article than you may think. Don't trust that place. It's not safe."

The temperature dipped by late afternoon, the sun sitting above the horizon. Leah put the last of the wood into the fire and then sent Barb an image of herself holding a pile of dead sticks.

Barb poked her head out of the tent and said, "I can't believe how good you are at this. Do we need wood?"

"I'm going to collect some."

Heading back into the woods, Leah found a dead tree with plenty of branches. She started breaking them off and made a small pile to take back to camp. Then she heard the sharp, high-pitched warning from a crow, unlocking a memory of Uncle Tim holding her shoulder.

Listen, he had whispered. *There's a predator nearby.* He had pointed, and a shadowy figure darted away.

Leah stood silently, looking and listening for a fox, cougar, or bear. The breeze, saturated with smells of pine, carried the crow's calls further south. She turned in a circle, green grains of dusty pollen shimmering in the rays of sunshine that cut through the forest canopy. In the nourishing dampness from the rain, pollen was the ingredient of life, and the sun was the cook. Energy stirred her spiritual core.

Continuing to collect wood, Leah grabbed a large branch, and beneath it, she saw grubs, beetles, and worms crawling around. Bending down to watch, she put her hand to the ground and heard echoes of voices in her mind. Phantom forms blinked between the trees—native peoples, hunters, loggers. Leah stood and whispered, "Hello." She knew her life had taken a turn, but the peacefulness of brushing against the thin membrane between moments, where memories and possibilities lived, hadn't been the dramatic crescendo she had expected. There were no surges of power or grand bangs, just an intimate stillness that felt personal. She collected the pile of sticks and started back toward camp. Brushing against an Oregon white oak, a brief but familiar impression flashed through her mind—Bellevue.

Leah dropped the sticks. How had she felt Bellevue? Tiny pricks needled her chest. Had It left the Center? Did the transformation fail? Her curiosity to know battled against her fear of being trapped.

Leah calmed herself. If she remained opened, Bellevue couldn't take her. She inched closer to the tree and held her hands out. "Bellevue?" Placing both hands on the tree, Leah leaned into the soft current of energy and connected.

Detective Brandon Spencer stood on the drive that led to Bellevue, hugging his mom. A young girl, maybe nine years of age, stood next to her, waiting. A man meandered ahead of them, admiring the house. The man stopped and called, "Judy. Olivia. It's time." Releasing her son, Judy took Olivia's hand, and the girl skipped merrily as they made their way toward the man. Joining hands, the three of them ambled toward Bellevue together.

Leah shouted, "No! Don't go. It's a trap. Come back!"

"Leah!" Barb shouted. "Where are you?"

Opening her eyes, Leah touched her head. She was lying on the ground next to the tree that had sparked her vision. "I'm here," she called.

Barb ran over. "What happened? Are you okay?"

"I think so."

"Did you pass out? You've been gone for over an hour."

"Barb, I think something terrible is going to happen."

"What do you mean?"

"Detective Spencer. His mom is in danger. We need to warn her."

"Slow down," Barb insisted. "You need to catch me up."

"I had a vision. I think I saw the future."

Paths Cross

Seoul, Washington, D.C., Lake Valley, Diamond Creek

Accelerated Collision and a Traitor

Su-Bin hunched over her computer reviewing precedent rulings in preparation for her new case. A tap came at the door, and she leaned back in her chair, grateful for the short break.

"Yes."

Seo-Ah poked her head in. "Excuse me, Ma'am, but Min Yun just put his name plate on my counter and left with his things."

"I'm aware," Su-Bin said.

"Oh. Okay. Umm, a package arrived for you. It's wine."

"You can sign for it."

"I would, except they need to scan your ID."

"Sorry?" Su-Bin said, unsure she heard her correctly.

"It's a new policy for alcohol. Your name is on the box."

She nodded, remembering she was the one who had created that change. Digging into her purse, Su-Bin grabbed her ID and walked with Seo-Ah back to her desk.

Seo-Ah asked, "Is it true that you will pay for me to go to law school?"

"Yes. If you agree to work with the firm for five years following your graduation, we will pay for it in full. If not, you will be responsible for paying some of it back, depending on the time you've spent with us. Check with HR for the details. Are you planning to take advantage of the offer?"

"I am."

"That's wonderful. I'm happy to hear that."

The delivery driver scanned Su-Bin's ID and left. The door to the conference room opened, and several employees came out laughing and conversing as Brandon held the door for them. Su-Bin tapped one of them, asking in English, "How was the class?"

The employee responded without missing a beat. "Oh, it was enjoyable. He is a good teacher."

Su-Bin looked at Brandon. He spotted her and smiled. An image of a textbook formed in her mind. Her pulse skipped, causing her cheeks to warm. Thinking about a book had never percolated such emotions. She knew it wasn't the book, but him. His telepathic touch carried the subtleties of his essence, warming her. She had a private lesson with Brandon in two days and was now thinking about it in a new light.

Min Yun plopped his suitcase on the bed and opened it. He slipped in his earbuds and called his dad. Jae Yun answered, sounding exactly as Min imagined he might—surprised, shocked, and relieved.

"Hey, Min. It's been a long time. I'm so glad you called."

Min packed as he talked. "Hi, Dad. I'm flying into Lake Valley tomorrow evening. I got some time off and decided to meet your fiancée."

"That's great news. Judy will be so excited to meet you," Jae responded.

Min held up a slim glass vial, the fine white powder shifting as he tilted it. A slow, deliberate smile spread across his face. "I'm looking forward to meeting her, too," Min said.

"How long will you be staying with us?" Jae asked.

Drawing in a breath, Min returned the vial to his bag. "Look, Dad. Let's just play this by ear. I'm packing now. My flight leaves in a few hours. I'll text you the flight information. Will you be able to pick me up at the airport?"

"I'll be there. Thank you for coming. See you soon, Son."

"Yep. See ya, Dad." Hanging up, Min took a screenshot of his itinerary and sent it to his dad, then called for a taxi.

The next morning, Leah and Barb packed, deciding to head back home early. Leah was anxious about the vision she had. It felt real, as if it had already happened: She was standing there, looking at Brandon and his mom, staring at Bellevue. The sounds, the smells, the scenery—it was all fresh in her mind, as clear as the memory of prom just a week ago. The book mentioned that psychic abilities were often associated with using this energy, but the actual experience was intense and surreal. If this vision truly were of the future, then she needed to warn Brandon and his mom.

Barb called from behind, "Leah, slow down. The ground is wet; I don't want to slip."

"Sorry. I can't shake this feeling inside me that we need to hurry."

"You said they were looking at the house, not the Education Center. That doesn't make sense. Also, you told me Detective Spencer is in Korea. You can relax."

"I thought you wanted to go back."

"Oh, I do. But I'd like to have both legs intact when we get there."

Leah stopped. "You're right." She took a slow, deep breath. "You lead."

Barb patted her friend on the shoulder. "Practice catching those feelings and observing them."

"Thanks, Coach." Leah grabbed Barb's hand and squeezed it. "I appreciate you."

Barb nodded.

Taking out her phone, Leah called Uncle Tim to let him know they were coming home early.

When they reached the end of the trail and emerged from the trees, Tim was leaning against Miley, waiting.

Barb raised her hands in celebration. "Yes! We're back."

Leah hugged her uncle. "Thanks for coming."

"No problem. Leah, you look different. Barb, did you cut her hair or something?" Tim asked.

"No. She's just in the zone. The trip was a stress reliever for her and a stress provider for me."

"You don't go camping much?"

"I prefer a toilet and a dry bed."

Uncle Tim took their backpacks, threw them in the back of the truck, and drove them home.

On the way, Leah looked online for information on Brandon's mom. Finding her website, she took a mental photo, attached the image to her spiritual energy, and sent it to Barb.

"Really? I'm sitting right next to you."

Uncle Tim asked, "What's going on?"

"It's nothing. A private joke," Barb said.

Leah had a great meme in mind for her uncle. She combined it with her energy and sent it to him.

Tim chuckled.

"What?" asked Barb.

"An image popped into my head of Mr. Bean making one of his classic crazy faces, saying, 'Ohhhh.'"

Barb looked at Leah.

Leah's giant guilty smile made Barb roll her eyes.

Tim stopped at Barb's place first. Leah carried her backpack to the front door. "I need to borrow your car tomorrow. I'm going to Diamond Creek."

Barb stared at her in disbelief and sighed.

"I'd love for you to come with me."

"And skip school?"

"Yes."

"Why do you have to go tomorrow? If you want to meet her, we can go in the evening or next weekend."

"It feels urgent. I'm not sure how to explain it. I feel a pull in my chest, and it won't let go."

"Okay, I'll come," Barb said. "Someone has to keep you in check."

Leah gave Barb a hug. "I'll see you tomorrow."

"Do you want to say hi to Dan?"

"I'll call him later; my uncle's waiting."

"Maybe Dan could come with us."

"I'd rather not worry him. He's in the middle of exams."

"Good point. Okay. See ya."

Back in the truck, Tim said, "Leah, you look different. A real glow about you. I'm glad you had a good time."

Leah managed a quick smile, but her mind was back in the forest: the book, the vision, her abilities. If the wrong person knew she had the book, they would take it away.

"Uncle Tim, who else knows about the book? Does my dad know?"

"I didn't tell him. I assumed you did, though."

"Have you talked to him about me?"

"We've talked some. He's worried about you—said an officer came to check up on you. He asked me if I thought you were using drugs."

Leah sighed, putting her hand to her head. "Crap. Okay. What did you tell him?"

"I told him you had too much going on to be messing with that shit. Said I saw you every day, and you were fine."

"Thanks. You didn't mention my powers?"

Tim paused. "Why haven't you mentioned them?"

"This book, the magic in it, it's for real. The officer who came to see me would confiscate it if he knew I had it."

"Yeah, I get that. But you can trust your dad."

Leah leaned forward, trying to peer into his eyes. "What did you tell Dad?"

Tim licked his lips and shifted uncomfortably. "Leah..."

"Uncle Tim," Leah pressed.

He rubbed the back of his neck. "Your dad was talking about his connection with Nong and how they lay together even though they were in separate houses. I told him you had connected to me."

"Okay. Anything else?"

"We were a little drunk. But he knows you have a special gift. He still can't believe you saved everybody. I think you should be honest with him. There's no reason not to."

"I feel like the fewer people who know about this book the better. That's all. By the way, what did you do with the book when you borrowed it?"

"I told half a dozen people about it."

Leah glared at him. "You what?"

"I wouldn't worry. None of them gave it much merit. Look, Leah. You need to be honest with your dad. It's not like he won't believe you. Hell, he probably already knows."

"I need a little time yet."

"Nong and Jared are allies in this endeavor. They could help you."

"Or they could say it was too dangerous and take the book away."

"Yeah, maybe." Tim pulled up to Leah's house. They sat for a moment. "Hey, I know you'll do what's best. And no matter what you decide, I got your back."

"I know you do." Leah leaned over and hugged her uncle. Then she scooted over and opened the door to exit.

"Leah?" Tim asked. "Who wrote that book, anyway? Where did it come from?"

Weaponized Chaos

Brandon was hunched over his Korean language workbooks with pen in hand when Yoona's voice entered his mind. *Get ready to leave. Matthew will be at your door soon.*

Closing his books and stacking them, Brandon wondered if he'd ever get used to the sensation of telepathy.

A knock came at the door.

"It's open."

Matthew entered, cold and somber. Brandon could barely make out his eyes through the tight slits.

"Training is over," he said in a hushed tone.

"What's going on?"

"There's been an incident off the coast of Taiwan. The U.S. and China are on the verge of war."

"What does that have to do with me?"

"We've got some intel on weapons being smuggled to North Korea. We're going to intercept them."

"Me? But I'm not CIA. I have no jurisdiction here."

"You're part of Yoona's team. Come on, let's go."

"Shit," Brandon muttered as he stood and grabbed his coat. A storm of thoughts crashed into him as he headed out the door. This was insane. He had come to learn how to talk with ghosts, not play spy games. Intercepting weapons? North Korea? His mind struggled to catch up.

On the way to the car, Matthew said, "There are two other guys with me. I can't introduce you, so just be cool."

A sarcastic thought flashed through his mind. *Great. What's next? If you talk, you die?*

Brandon climbed into the back of the SUV, the cold leather cooling his anxiety. He nodded to the agent sitting next to him, a huge guy whose head brushed the ceiling. Scanning the agent, Brandon felt a sense of relief that the man was on his side. His solid, muscular build spoke of intense training, and his broad shoulders and thick neck added to his imposing appearance.

The second agent glanced at Brandon through the rear-view mirror. He was lean, with styled black hair. His dark eyes, framed by perfectly groomed eyebrows, were assessing.

"We're heading to Yoona's city office, located in Hongdae," Matthew said.

They drove into a lively part of town, and after parking, walked through the crowded streets. Neon lights colored the scene as the thick aroma of sizzling grilled meats and spicy *tteokbokki* rumbled stomachs. K-pop tunes buzzed through the loud conversations and livened the crowd's steps. Tourists, wide-eyed and excited, snapped photos and sampled street food, completely unaware of the pending doom. The festive atmosphere made Brandon's heart clench tighter, feeling dark and foreboding against the backdrop of innocence and naivety.

Tucked away on a quieter side street, they came upon Yoona's shop. The exterior was classic Korean architecture, with a curved tiled roof and wooden beams polished to a rich sheen. A hand-carved wooden sign, inscribed in both Hangul and English, read "Moodang Yoona. By Appointment Only," followed by a phone number.

Large windows with their curtains drawn flanked the door. Two lanterns hung from the wood awning, illuminating an imposing man standing guard. He stepped aside and the group enter.

Brandon removed his shoes, stored them on the rack, and stepped onto the polished wooden floor, which felt warm underfoot. He admired the intricate silk tapestries of traditional Korean landscapes that hung on the walls. Passing the front desk and a couple of bench sofas in a waiting area, the four made their way through a set of sliding doors and entered the main room.

Framed art pieces decorated the walls. Watercolors and charcoal sketches of mythical creatures gave the room a mysterious vibe. The bold lines and shadows held ethereal beauty, evoking the essence of psychic realms and unseen spirits. In the center of the room stood a large, round table surrounded by eight chairs upholstered in rich, red fabric. The table was the focal point of the room, seemingly used for important meetings and gatherings. Nearby, a minibar offered a selection of drinks.

Yoona entered, tall and confident. The room itself seemed to pause, drawing breath to acknowledge her. She radiated natural authority, and Brandon straightened without thinking.

"Good evening, gentlemen," she articulated.

The first agent—the huge, muscular guy—put a briefcase on the table, opened it, and extracted photos, a case description, personnel profiles, and other documents.

Yoona took his hand and studied the lines. Then she pulled him forward, put her thumb on his cheek, and looked him straight in the eye. "Good," she said, letting him go.

The personnel profiles were the first Yoona examined. She flipped through faces and names before stopping on a particular individual. "I thought you locked him away."

"Mr. Mercer was part of a prisoner swap two years ago," Matthew said.

Yoona dropped the stack and gestured for the second agent—the lean guy. He stepped forward, and she took his hand. The energy in the room became nervous. Grabbing the man's chin, Yoona turned his face left, then right, before nodding in approval.

Seeing the two men manhandled, devoid of any semblance of politeness or gentleness, seemed odd. It was almost as if Yoona was performing a clinical procedure. Her complete lack of hesitation or explanation only added to the strangeness of it all.

She went back to the documents, sliding papers around until she reached the cluster of photos. Laying a hand on a photo of shipping crates, she paused and squinted her eyes. Then she raised her other hand; her fingers danced in the air as if playing a piano.

Brandon held his breath along with the others. What was she seeing? Could a photo like this actually trigger a vision? He watched patiently as something took shape behind her eyes.

Yoona lowered her hand. "These weapons are from a supplier inside the U.S."

Brandon jerked upright. Had he heard her correctly? He took a step forward and continued to listen.

"They're prototypes. Who knows you're here?"

"The people in this room and your bodyguard outside," Matthew answered.

"Keep it that way," Yoona said. She paused, her gaze going unfocused. Then, more quietly—almost as if the thought were forming as she spoke—she said, "We need to play the game."

Matthew stilled.

"Treat this intel as incomplete," Yoona continued. "Report it exactly once, through normal channels. No urgency. No revisions. You suspect Mr. Mercer might be smuggling weapons bound for North Korea. Unverified origin. Unspecified payload. No conclusions beyond that."

Matthew turned his gaze to the smaller agent. The man nodded, opened his phone, and retreated into the foyer.

Yoona proceeded, "I need to go with you on this one."

"I understand," Matthew said. "You still don't know who the corrupt Shaman is?"

"I'm close, but there is so much noise." Yoona's face creased like a mother rejecting her son's heavy metal music. "The interference hurts my brain. Identifying this person is like trying to catch smoke with bare hands."

"I thought you had an inside guy."

Yoona's eyes dulled and tension built in her shoulders. "I do. Or at least, I did." She glanced at Brandon then back to Matthew. "General Sam Cros."

Brandon's stomach tightened. Yoona's inside guy, a spy, was a general in the military? This information made him uneasy. Did it mean that his presence here could now be considered treasonous and land him in jail?

Matthew flinched, reflecting his own disbelief. "The advisor to the president?" Matthew stammered. He cocked his head to better scrutinize Yoona.

She nodded, drumming her fingers against the table. "For him to be in his position and not have identified the corrupt shaman ... is disturbing."

"If General Cros is your inside guy"—Matthew waved his hand over the documents in a questioning gesture— "do you believe this to be a real threat?"

"The threat is real in the sense that it demands my attention."

"Does that mean they expect us to stop them?" the bigger agent asked.

Yoona gave the man a blank stare. Matthew glanced over before returning his attention to Yoona.

The big guy caught Brandon's eye. "I thought it was a valid question." Brandon shrugged and looked back at Yoona and Matthew, who continued talking.

"We're losing, Matthew," Yoona said. "The future is so muddy, I can't see much of anything now. And what I do see isn't making sense. I worry Sam has turned. I worry that the Circle has weakened, and I'm at a loss for how to fix it."

Brandon didn't like the sound of that. It felt dire.

"I'm hearing that the European leaders are gathering support," Matthew said. "If their proposal to unify the world under the United Nations with full governing power is accepted, then we win, right?"

"It feels like a trap."

"Yoona, the world is tearing itself apart."

Brandon thought about all the wars, conflicts, and potential alliances. The Iranian-Israeli war had already decimated millions. There were the Ukraine war, Afghanistan and Mexican civil wars, the Yemen and Venezuelan conflicts, and now the threat of war between the U.S. and China. Now that Iran had nukes, Brandon knew it wouldn't be long until North Korea had them as well.

Matthew continued, "A United Federation of States will ensure peace."

"No," Yoona countered. "It would ensure centralized power."

"Through a democratic system with checks and balances."

"Systems fail. Rome. Germany."

Brandon's eyes went back and forth, engrossed in the conversation.

"A year ago, the idea of a centralized world government wouldn't have seen pen to paper," Yoona said. "Not a single world power would have considered it. Now it's being debated by the U.S. Senate? Our Shaman is manipulating world leaders."

"What if we work with this Shaman?" Matthew suggested. "Then we could ensure the system worked."

Yoona shook her head. "Shamans, Banishers, psychics, astrologers, fortune tellers ... we are healers, offering comfort, perspective, and hope. We help ghosts move on. We counsel the grieving, so their pain won't trap spirits in our world.

"But our power can be twisted. Alexander the Great, Phillip II, Napoleon, Cecil Rhodes ... all touched by spiritual corruption. So when I see a movement to unite the world under a single system, and the signs point to an individual with immense spiritual power, I don't see peace. I see history repeating itself. I created the Circle to stop our kind from rising to power. And I intend to uphold that promise."

"It's not just the U.S. considering the proposal," Matthew said. "Vietnam is the latest ASEAN nation—"

Yoona held up her hand, stopping him. "I know what's happening," she said with a pinch of irritation.

Brandon gave a timid wave. "I haven't heard about this."

Matthew raised his eyebrows, and Yoona nodded. He continued, "Vietnam has joined the Philippines, Brunei, and Cambodia in signing the agreement. That makes forty nations that have united together. Several other countries are debating the possibility." He faced Yoona. "If the corrupt Shaman were behind this, that person would have to own a lot of powerful people. There's no way."

"A corrupt Shaman craves power above all else. If the world united under one government—"

"It'd be a dream come true!" Matthew interjected.

"Yes—for the corrupt Shaman," Yoona retorted.

"I can't see how one person would be able to control so many."

"This person has a special kind of leverage," Yoona said. "I won't know what that is until I can identify who it is."

Brandon shook his head. Grand conspiracies, world leaders... Why was he here?

The door slid open, and the thinner agent stepped back into the room.

"So, how do we proceed?" Matthew asked.

Yoona picked up a photo of a cargo ship. "We need to take care of this situation first."

Matthew shook his head. "The corrupt Shaman is using these situations to hide. At some point you need to tackle this person head on."

Yoona placed her hand on Matthew's shoulder. "That time is coming soon." Pointing to the pile of papers, she said, "As you probably have guessed, the information you brought me is misleading. The message you sent will result in the formation of a Korean task force to capture this smuggler. It will fail."

"Is all of the intel bad?" Matthew probed.

Yoona handed Matthew a photo of the container ship named *Artemis* believed to be transporting the weapons. "They've identified the wrong ship. We're looking for the sister ship named *Tamar*. It will arrive two days earlier than this one."

"So, I'll continue to track the *Artemis* and plan accordingly," Matthew said.

"It'll just be the five of us." She looked directly at Brandon. "Welcome to the team."

Brandon forced a grin, feeling like he'd stepped into a swamp, the mud sucking his feet down into the murky operation for which he wasn't prepared. "But—" Brandon stammered.

Matthew hit the table with his fist in a celebratory fashion. "This is going to be awesome."

Yoona gave him a stern look and scolded, "You cannot overreact. Stay calm and focused."

Matthew straightened. "Sorry."

Yoona eyed Brandon, then turned her gaze to the others. She raised her voice, addressing the three of them. "Let's meet again in six days to discuss the plan of action." Then with the look of death in her eyes, she commanded, "Say nothing of this to anyone. This will be a gun battle, so if you can, get to a shooting range."

"I never doubted that fact," Matthew responded, a bit too cheerful.

Then there was silence. Yoona and Matthew stared into each other's eyes.

Brandon guessed they were conversing about a top-secret something. He did not want to be involved in any of it, especially a gun fight. How had he allowed himself to be dragged into this? Was it too late to back out?

Matthew said, "Yes, ma'am."

The giant agent shot Brandon a confused look. Brandon shrugged.

"Of course," Matthew added. "I understand." Gripping the big guy's shoulder, Matthew asked, "Can you get the equipment and materials we'll need to make a successful raid?"

His partner answered in a deep thundered voice, "Not a problem, boss. Just give me a list."

Turning to Brandon, Yoona spoke to him using telepathy. *Can you feel the souls in this room? I want you to build your spiritual energy and probe for their presence. I will guide you.*

Brandon closed his eyes, allowing Yoona to manipulate his thoughts and actions. He took deep breaths, inhaling slowly through his nose and exhaling through his mouth. He visualized a bright, radiant light at the center of his being. This glowing ball of energy represented his spiritual core, and with each breath it grew brighter and more vibrant until his entire body filled with positivity. *I am connected to divine energy. The river of life replenishes my spirit and empowers me. I am one with the Earth.* Brandon's energy expanded outside of himself, and as it did, he caught the impression of the lean, well-groomed agent, the bulky, strong agent, the bold confidence of Matthew, and radiance of Yoona. Then he felt several spirits. One was a soldier, an expert in explosives. The other was Su-Bin's father, a politician, who seemed to smile and wave at Brandon. A third spirit was a diplomat, who had served terms in China and Japan.

Yoona continued, *This meditation gives you a great advantage over your enemies, especially in the dark or to detect where they are hiding. It will help you attract souls and feel their presence.*

Brandon opened his eyes to see the others staring at him. He looked at the smaller agent, seeing the ghost who had been an explosives expert enter his body. The man fell to his knees and grabbed his head, screaming in pain. Brandon turned to Yoona for answers.

In a smooth, calm tone, she said, *I had the special forces soldier possess him.*

Matthew held the big agent back. The second crawled backwards on his hands and knees, retreating to the doorway.

"Brandon, block the exit," Matthew commanded.

Brandon walked between the agent and the opening.

Matthew moved and kicked the man's shoulder, making him fall onto his back.

After another minute of tortured screams, the man became quiet. He rolled over and slowly stood.

Yoona said, "He is now an explosives expert. The knowledge I have given him is vital to the success of our mission. He may not be himself for the next few days, but he'll return to normal once the operation is complete."

After the meeting, Yoona sent Matthew and the others ahead, keeping Brandon behind for a moment. Placing her hands on both sides of his head, she said,

"I am going to enter your mind and implant some knowledge. I am doing this because I know you are ready and can handle it."

Brandon stepped back, freeing himself from Yoona's hold. "Wait. What are you giving me?"

"Abilities. This is not a path I take with trainees, but we are out of time. I am going to need you by my side in the coming months, and you must be ready."

Brandon's face turned white. Yoona was choosing him to be her counterpart. "Why me?"

"You are a unique individual who possesses all the potential to be a powerful manipulator. You are ready to begin training, and you carry no preconceived notion of what is truly possible. Until recently, you didn't even believe in ghosts. Your mind is fresh, a beautiful piece of clay I can mold." She paused. "And I trust you unreservedly."

A knot formed in Brandon's stomach as heat rushed to his face. He wasn't prepared for this. Swallowing, he tried to process what she was saying. What had he done to earn her unquestioning trust? He was honored to have it, but could he live up to that trust? His heart hammered in his ears as he shifted his stance. "I—I don't know what to say."

"'Yes' would be sufficient."

"I'll do my best."

"You'll do more than that," she answered with a sly smile.

"Is it dangerous—planting abilities in my mind?"

"I will be gentle at first, but as we proceed with your training, I will need to push. The experience will be..." Yoona paused. "I believe Choi said it best: 'Like a baseball bat full of nails being driven into your brain.'"

Brandon's heart quickened. Bellevue had dropped him to his knees. The pain was unbearable.

Yoona took Brandon's shoulders, pulling him back toward her. "What I am about to give you is meant to stimulate and awaken the rest of your brain. You'll feel pinpricks. Over the next week, you'll begin to understand and control aspects of your body that are currently off limits to you. You'll find the ability to create and release chemicals and control your organs, like how much water your kidneys filter out of your blood, allowing you to maintain your own hydration level. Your body will feel more like a vessel that you inhabit and less like you. As you become aware of your soul as pure energy, all energy will become tangible. That's when the real training will begin."

Brandon wasn't sure how to feel. Did he want this?

"And because you are unsure if this is the path for you, I am empowered to give it to you."

His hand sprang up, creating a barrier between them. She was moving too fast. "Wait," he said, squinting his eyes shut so he could think. Moral and ethical questions still swirled in his mind regarding this power. Choi was a good man and a good friend. Brandon trusted him and, in extension, his aunt. He knew she was on the right side, or at least, he wanted to believe that. But WWII, murder, and judgement jumped at him, not to mention the spy who was advising the president and global conspiracies. He needed more information. Needed to know that this crazy gun battle they were asking him to participate in was justified. Where to start the questions, though?

"Choi told me you were in Japan at the end of World War II. May I ask, how old are you? I didn't mean to be rude, but Choi said you have the ability to slow the aging process. You don't look much older than..." His cheeks reddened. "Thirty-five?"

Yoona's lip curled into a grin, and her eyes twinkled. "I am able to slow the aging process, but only enough to extend the life expectancy of this body by thirty years." She paused. "The body I currently occupy has been alive for fifty-three years. I, however, have been walking this Earth nearly fifteen centuries."

Shocked and confused, Brandon couldn't believe what he was hearing. "How?"

"Let me answer why, first. There are evil forces in this world that need to be confronted and held in check. I will continue to fight them until my replacement is found."

"Are you training me to be your replacement?"

With an enduring smile, Yoona said, "I'm sorry, Brandon, no. You have an important role to play, and if I am to succeed in capturing the corrupt Shaman in the White House, I need you by my side, able to manipulate energy and fight."

Brandon lowered his head. *Fight?* He'd spent his life defusing violent situations, not engaging in them. "I see," he responded. "Do you often fight?"

"No. But the fight is coming, whether we want it or not."

Leaning against the door frame, he stared at the floor. Her words touched him. He'd been an officer long enough to understand what she meant. "I'm curious. Do you train everyone who learns to manipulate energy?"

Yoona laughed. "Goodness no. I do visit the temple here in Korea once or twice a month to help with training, but no. I have Shamans and Monks who teach. There are also training manuals one can read to assist them."

"Are you not afraid a training manual will fall into the wrong hands?"

"I acknowledge the fear and am thankful for its warning, but I do not let fear dictate my actions. Unfortunately, the book has fallen into the wrong hands despite our precautions. But, learning strictly from reading the book is not an easy task. We have watchers, the community, and the Circle who monitor the flow of energy, and until recently, we could easily find a person experimenting with the book's teachings. But the world has grown chaotic. War and hidden agendas blur the future. We are having difficulty locating individuals abusing their abilities for personal gain, greed, and deception. You will become a powerful member of our community and help us keep order and balance, in addition to helping souls transcend."

Brandon exhaled slowly. "It sounds like you want me to become a mentor."

"Yes, that's exactly what I'll be asking you to do, once we have found the corrupt Shaman."

"I hate to ask, but isn't it evil of you to possess someone else's body? It's the ultimate theft."

"This body was soulless when I inhabited it. You will learn about Soul Harvesters and Banishers in good time."

Searching Yoona's eyes, Brandon looked for the truth. Was he safe with her? Did her moral code align with his? Would she ask him to use this power without questioning her authority? Yoona's eyes held nothing but wisdom and conviction. Brandon felt satisfied: she was who he believed her to be—a good person. Yet he questioned her actions of tonight. She had ordered a soul to possess a man without his consent or forewarning. That didn't sit right and was precisely why he hesitated to trust her. How could he reconcile her flagrant use of power against an innocent individual with his own ethics?

"Take your time in coming to your conclusion," Yoona said. "Weigh *all* the evidence."

All the evidence? The words circled in his mind. *Who is Yoona?* If the world's political stage were a chessboard, Yoona was the queen, aware of every-thing—grand conspiracies, spies, gangs, terrorist, and corrupt Shamans that threatened the world. She had the power to protect, guard, and attack. She considered each decision, and the consequences that came with them. Having a single man possessed for a greater purpose fit within her moral and ethical boxes, where it fell outside of his own. Brandon breathed deeply. If he remained powerless, he could do little to help her, and nothing at all to challenge her if she ever went too far.

He nodded. "Let's begin."

Yoona placed her hands on Brandon's head and pushed him to his knees.

He took a sharp breath as she entered his mind. Jerking and flinching, Brandon struggle to remain still as prick after prick stung him. He felt tired. The kind of tired that came after cramming a month's worth of new knowledge into his brain for an exam the next day. Then Yoona's voice, sweet and tender, began to sing, echoing in the halls of his consciousness, filling the space like fog consuming a forest. She left droplets of knowledge. He covered each one, like a seed in dirt. Her voice trailed off into the distance as she retreated from his mind.

"When you get home, practice the meditation I gave you earlier. Grow the light inside you and spread it out as far as you can. Feel everything that surrounds you."

Brandon rose to his feet, and Yoona patted him on the back, sending him to rejoin the others

Conditional Legitimacy

In a high-security federal office building in downtown Washington, D.C., General Sam Cros sat at his oak desk reviewing documents when a knock came at his door.

"Come in."

Agent Daniels entered, carrying three legal folders. He was slightly shorter than the general, around five-foot-nine, with a stocky build, dressed in a shirt and tie.

"Daniels, good to see you. Can I get you a drink?" Sam offered, falling into the routine of their regular monthly meeting to discuss the search for the corrupt Shaman in the White House.

"No, thank you, General." Daniels's voice carried nervous excitement as his eyes darted around the room, taking in the Persian rug covering the hardwood floors, the framed awards, bookcases, and large windows with red curtains.

Sam stood tall, letting his lean, athletic build reinforce his authority. In a smooth and purposeful manner, he walked around his desk and offered his hand. Daniels took it with a firm and strong grip.

"Have a seat." Sam waved to the leather sofas arranged around the coffee table.

Daniels sat, setting the folders on the table. He leaned back and fidgeted with his hands.

"I see you have something interesting for me."

"I do. But I need to preface this by saying, they don't match the criteria you laid out for me, but their stories are unusual."

Sam sat in his seat and crossed his arms. "All right. Go ahead."

"What do you know about the company Extended Life?"

Sam furrowed his brow, unsure what Extended Life had to do with their search. "Bill Stillen pitched me his idea for the company back in 2005. I introduced him to Larry Lynn, who was the director of DARPA at the time, part of the Advanced Research Projects Agency at the Pentagon. The company specializes in the integration of computer and biological systems, advanced nanotechnology, and cellular regeneration techniques aimed at prolonging human life and enhancing physical capabilities."

"Well, that explains why Extended Life operates at a Black Ops level—access is restricted to individuals with top-tier security clearance or those who are ultra-wealthy and thoroughly vetted."

"Yes, I'm aware."

"Okay. Follow me for a bit. I promise this all has purpose. Three months ago, the FBI received a tip from a Misty Davis, a volunteer working with Doctors without Borders in India. She sends us a list of names—refugees from the Chin conflict in Myanmar. Someone from Extended Life, sponsored by the Defense Department, issued visas to young, healthy individuals and brought them into the U.S. Those individuals have been reported as dead or missing.

"The FBI opened a probe into the matter, but direct orders were issued to cease the investigation, citing national security."

"Interesting."

"The agent investigating the case goes to the State Department, who told him the visa entries were processed under special directives from the Defense Department, bypassing regular vetting procedures under the national security exemption act for a top-secret project." Daniels paused. "Ask yourself this, what does Extended Life need with refugees? They aren't scientists or doctors. These people are farmers and manual laborers."

Sam inhaled and cocked his head. He wasn't sure where Daniels was going with this, but it was sounding a bit conspiratorial. Refugee camps weren't void of doctors or engineers. And even if the Extended Life only recruited manual laborers, every company needed them. Still, the reports of dead and missing people bothered him. Why was Daniels bringing this up?

"Stay with me," Daniels said. "I got an email from a police officer in Lake Valley, Oregon asking me to continue looking into this case. I did what I do and found a connection that may intrigue you."

Sam nodded. "All right. Keep going. But I hope this leads somewhere."

Daniels opened the first folder, displaying a photo of the late Ruth Jones. Her Chinese features prominently visible, and her hair wrapped in a samurai bun, her go-to hairstyle.

"We originally thought that she was our corrupt Shaman. What happened to her?"

"She passed away."

"Are you sure?" Daniels asked, raising an eyebrow.

Sam shot him a look that said, *seriously?* "Yeah, I'm sure."

Daniels persisted, "We know she went to the border with members of congress to spotlight the horrors of the Trump administration's policy to separate children from their parents."

Sam interjected, "She ended up in the hospital during that trip and died of heart complications."

Daniels nodded. "Think about the situation at that time along the border. The chaos, the shoddy paperwork, the overcrowded prison system—it was a nightmare. Kids were shuffled around like cattle, no proper records, no real oversight. Many of those children became lost in the system."

Sam was becoming impatient. He leaned forward, propping his elbows on his knees. "Tell me you have a point here."

"Refugees, many of whom went missing." Daniels flipped to the next photo of the young Guatemalan, Ruth Jones. She was wearing the same samurai bun. "Those refugees were from Central America, many from Guatemala."

"Let me stop you right here," Sam snapped. "I gave you a set of parameters for a reason. Ruth is too young, not ambitious enough, and frankly, too polite. We're looking for someone who can connect with and manipulate others in a significant way."

"Sam, you're not seeing it. They're wearing the same hairstyle with the same hairpin."

General Cros leaned forward and examined the photo again. He laughed. "What are you suggesting? This proves nothing." But Sam knew better. A memory itched the back of his mind: Iraq, 2002. Yoona had walked into the conference room in a new body.

Shaking his head, Sam dismissed the thought. Yoona had sworn the technique was hers alone—and he believed her. A soul could not transfer between living bodies. "Our young Ruth wears her hair this way as a bit of a joke, highlighting the fact that she shares the same name as the former Ruth Jones who used to work in the White House. It's her playful nod to the coincidence. Please tell me what this is about."

"Let's go back to Extended Life. Do you know who the Chief Strategist for the company was?"

"I have no idea."

"Ruth Jones."

Sam frowned. "Wait. The older Ruth? The former Executive Assistant to the Chief of Staff. The Ruth Jones who had worked in the White House since the Bush Sr. administration. That Ruth Jones?"

"She oversaw the company's strategic direction and reported directly to Bill Stillen. She also had exclusive access to the detainees at Guantánamo Bay and apparently spent a bit of time there. *60 Minutes* ran a piece last month detailing the tortures that happened at the prison, including an interview from an Afghan Shaman who claimed his soul had been ripped out of his body."

"That is unusual and, honestly, a bit unbelievable. But it's a moot point. Ruth died several years ago."

"It would be a moot point, except for who is currently overseeing Extended Life."

"Daniels, the drama is killing me. Get to the point."

"Our young and beautiful Ruth Jones."

Sam's heart skipped. Then his face tightened. "The young Guatemalan? The Special Assistant to the National Security Advisor? You're kidding. How old is she—twenty-five?" The realization that this young Ruth held such a significant position left Sam deeply unsettled. How could Ruth inconspicuously wield such influence within the company and simultaneously within the White House and the Pentagon? How strong was she? Who was she manipulating? Could she really be a Shaman at such a young age—and a corrupt Shaman at that? To hold both of these positions meant she was truly more important and powerful than he had thought possible. "You have my undivided attention."

"The older Ruth was born in 1927 and was part Chinese. The new Ruth was born sometime in the early 2000s and is Guatemalan, yet I have proof that these two people are actually the same person."

"I would normally laugh here, but go on."

Daniels held out a report for Sam to look at.

"A voice analysis report? You really are going to make me laugh."

"Voice analysis is more than sound and accent. It's speech patterns, rhythm, pitch, vocabulary, and idiosyncrasies. The report should reflect the stark differences from both Ruths—age, ethnicity, places where they grew up. However, their voices are a 92 percent match." Grabbing another report, Daniels excitedly added, "And look at the psych evals. Cognitive function, personality traits, patterns of response to stress, work styles, leadership capabilities ... they all are nearly identical." He removed a third report and laid it on the table. "The handwriting samples show a 97 percent probability of being from the same individual—letter size, spacing, slant."

Sam flipped through the documents.

"And here's the kicker. Look at the EEG that both Ruths took for their physical to ensure mental stability and cognitive function when obtaining their high-security clearance. The brain-wave patterns in both are exactly the same. A 100 percent match."

Sam's jaw dropped. Had someone discovered Yoona's technique? The memory from Iraq in 2002 nagged at him, barely allowing him to focus on Daniels's words.

"I believe Extended Life has found a way to map the conscious mind and transfer it into another body. That's what the refugees were brought in for."

Daniels pulled out a final report. "This is the old Ruth's last physical, when she turned ninety." He handed it to Sam. "Remarkably, she was in perfect health for her age. The report notes a slight loss of bone density and minor joint stiffness, but overall, she was in outstanding shape."

Sam studied the report, noting the near-exceptional health metrics, further evidence that she had indeed been the Shaman he had believed her to be.

"Ruth's death was 'stress' related. The medical report also indicated dehydration. I find her heart failure due to stress very difficult to swallow based on this medical report."

Sam nodded in agreement, but his mind was already back in 2002, during the pivotal meeting that led him here. The memory was vivid: Yoona, the Circle members, the nervous energy of Mosul as war loomed over the country. His focus, though, was on Yoona's shocking revelation, her telepathic communication, and her warnings. Sam felt a tightening in his chest as he recalled the day his loyalty to Yoona wavered. Were his suspicions of her then truer than he realized? He contemplated this as he explored that memory.

In the pristine, white confines of the conference room in Mosul, Sam Cros found himself captivated by the vibrant colors of the Iraqi flag—black, white, and red with three green stars and the words "God is Great" written in the center. Its bold hues broke the pale monotony, intensified by the bright overhead lights. Hushed conversations and uneasy glances among conference attendees filled the room with a nervous energy as the group awaited Yoona's arrival with news from the UN inspectors.

Glancing at the members of the Circle, Sam noticed Abena Cilla tapping her fingers, watching the hall with a furrowed brow through the large glass wall in anticipation of Yoona's arrival. Abdul Sharif maintained a focused demeanor as he explored the future, glimpsing nations' responses to the news the report held. Sam's connection to Florentine Kissinger informed him that she was engaged with political figures back home, ascertaining their reactions to the information soon to reach them. The others discussed politics quietly among themselves until a young Korean woman with striking features and an aura of ancient wisdom bounded into the room.

Her long, black hair flowed gracefully with each step, and her youthful yet intense gaze commanded immediate attention. Despite her appearance, an ageless depth in her eyes hinted at centuries of experience and knowledge. Sam's brow furrowed in confusion as he took in the new arrival.

"Who is this?" he muttered to himself, bewildered by the unfamiliar face and her audacious assumption that she could just walk into the conference room like she owned the place.

A familiar voice entered his mind, clear and authoritative. *It's me, Sam. Yoona.*

His eyes widened. The others turned, their expressions sharing his own shock as they realized who stood before them.

"I'm sorry for keeping you waiting. I just finished talking with the Director General of the IAEA. I'm sure you've sensed the report's findings—no evidence exists that Iraq has weapons of mass destruction. The inspections found that the factories in question have been inactive for over ten years. With the Iraqi government fully cooperating with UN inspectors, there is no reason for the U.S. to continue its path to war. Yet, my visions are clear; the United States will attack no matter the evidence. Has anyone here had a different vision?" Rounding the table, Yoona came to her seat and stood behind her chair.

The members of the Circle exchanged glances, their eyes dark and expressions grim as they shook their heads no, all the while questioning if the person in front of them was indeed Yoona.

"Before we delve into the United States government's problematic stance, let me address your concerns." Yoona paused as she made eye contact with each member. "I encountered a Soul Harvester yesterday outside the city of Fallujah. It created several soulless bodies, including this Korean businesswoman. I have taken this body as my own. The technique is both dangerous and morally fraught, but one I felt compelled to master."

A murmur rippled through the council, expressions ranging from concern to curiosity.

Yoona continued, acknowledging the unease and unspoken questions among the Circle members. "This technique is known only to me. And because I understand the gravity of this ability, I will not be teaching or sharing this knowledge with others."

The council members shifted uncomfortably. Sam sensed several of them wanted to voice objections, but Yoona pressed on, leaving no room for interruption. "This practice raises many questions, and rest assured, we will hold another meeting to address those concerns. But now is not the time."

Florentine Kissinger rose abruptly, her chair scraping the floor. With a sharp pivot, she squared her shoulders to face Yoona. Her eyes narrowed, her lips pressed into a thin line, and the set of her jaw foreshadowed her accusations.

"Are we to understand that you, alone, carry the secrets to eternal life? That you have somehow discovered a way to manipulate a natural phenomenon that we all know is impossible to duplicate?" Every muscle in Florentine's posture went taut and coiled with a kind of restrained energy that made her presence feel like a storm about to break. "I, myself, have studied soulless bodies and have spent years trying to understand how they capture new essences. The fact of the matter is this: any attempt to observe the phenomenon interferes with the energy's alignment. Awareness itself disrupts the process—like trying to measure a dream before it ends. A tether cannot be forced into existence through ritual or science." Her finger shot forward, pointing directly at Yoona like a blade of accusation. "It's not possible to consciously create the tether that binds a soul to a body. And because it can't be done, you are not who you claim to be."

The room turned deadly silent.

Yoona, unfazed, circled the table with deliberate grace and moved straight to Florentine. The two women stood, locked in a silent exchange. The sheer force of Yoona's calm confidence seemed to dwarf Florentine, who stiffened as Yoona extended her hand, offering it without hesitation. Her gesture was unmistakable—she was inviting Florentine to examine her soul.

Eyes widened in disbelief at the unfolding scene. Muscles froze, unwilling—or unable—to move. Everyone held their breath as they watched.

Florentine stared at Yoona's hand, then clasped it. Their eyes fused.

A moment later, the sharp edges in Florentine's face softened, and her shoulders dropped. She released Yoona's hand and sat back down.

Sam's chest rose as he took a breath and relaxed. The tension in the room stilled, thick but stale.

Yoona's gaze swept over the council. "This discussion is tabled." She returned to her position. "I await my true successor. When the time comes, I will transcend like everyone else and allow my replacement to assume leadership."

After a moment of silence, she spoke again, "But for now, we must focus on the immediate threat before us. President Bush is refusing to accept the truth that Iraq has no weapons of mass destruction and continues to lie to his people. Therefore, I suspect and fear a Shaman has paired with a Banisher and infiltrated the U.S. government."

Gasps erupted at the announcement of a second pairing, sidelining all thoughts of Yoona's soul transfer. The proclamation caused sweat to bead on Sam's brow as he sensed the Circle would turn to him for answers. If a pairing had occurred in his home country, how would that affect his standing in the Circle? He'd be seen as weak, lazy, and ineffective; his reputation would be in shambles.

To his relief, however, the thoughts he heard were focused on finding the pair. Everyone seemed to understand that if a pair truly existed, they would be entrenched in political camps, untouchable as they rose to power, protected by myriad allies in the business, media, and political worlds.

Yoona added, "I believe this for two reasons. First: the American press continues to print and report verbatim the nonsense the White House releases without verification or investigation. The administration, House, and Senate refuse to debate the issue; rather, Congress has given the administration a green light to do as it pleases. This tells me the Shaman in question has connected with and has been manipulating all of the aforementioned people. Second: because the U.S. used 9/11 as an excuse to attack Afghanistan, and because war with Iraq is the only outcome the United States will accept, this tells me the Banisher has a ravaging thirst."

"Are you certain a corrupt pairing has occurred?" Galina asked with worry. "I have not seen nor felt this."

The others nodded in agreement with hushed whispers.

Yoona raised her hand to quiet the group. "We all know ways to calm the ripples. The evidence cannot be ignored. This pair fears our retaliation, which is why they have not made themselves known. Their power comes from anonymity."

Abdul Sharif glanced at Sam, giving him a slight nod before raising his hand and asking, "The vice presidency is the perfect position to manipulate others from behind the scenes. Is it possible that Dick Cheney is either the Banisher or the Shaman?"

Abena Cilla stood, her bright yellow geometric-patterned dress capturing the eyes of the council. "We have no reports of Cheney being trained in either art. I believe his interests in this war are strictly business-related."

Abdul quickly countered, his words thick with anger, "Four training manuals have gone missing in as many years, two of them from U.S. branches—the book from Louisiana and the book from San Francisco. It's very possible he could have one of those manuals."

Abdul looked back at Sam again, their eyes locking in a silent exchange of frustration. The two of them had discussed the missing manuals and prepared a plan for recovering them. Sam turned his gaze to Yoona, shaking his head in subtle disappointment. She had denied their request, asserting that the manuals' disappearance played into future events. Sam shared Abdul's anger; the future was now, and the events were not promising. Sam's expression hardened as he questioned Yoona's leadership. Was she secretly engaged in this unfolding plot?

Florentine Kissinger rose, placed her hands firmly on the table, and scanned the room. "Our first priority must be to retrieve the manuals. As long as they are unaccounted, we have no way of controlling this knowledge."

Yoona interrupted, "The books are of little concern. Without guidance, it's very difficult to achieve any level of proficiency. Let us instead focus on finding a way to identify the Shaman and Banisher nestled inside the U.S. government. We need someone to infiltrate the White House, ideally in a military capacity. I propose we authorize Sam Cros the direct use of his powers for the specific purpose of rising in rank within the U.S. military."

The room filled with chatter as individuals debated this proposal with their neighbor. Sam's eyes widened. To use his powers to rise in rank went against the core principles of the Circle. Frightened, he contemplated what this proposal meant—his thirst for domination would grow. His immediate thought went to his hippie days, tripping on LSD at Grateful Dead concerts and getting high around campfires on the beach. He had been able to wean himself from those drugs, but could he cut himself from power once he attained it?

Chloe Moreau stood. "The threat of corruption is too great. Using his power to ascend in rank is begging for a greater catastrophe than we currently face."

Yoona's voice thundered over Chloe's final words. "A Banisher with power will do anything to attain souls. The United States will invade Iraq. We know not how Russia or China will respond. If we delay, which country will be next? Iran? North Korea? Perhaps a manipulated war between Israel and its Muslim neighbors? Think of the worst-case scenarios; they are all possible until we identify this pair."

Abena spoke directly to Sam. "Mr. Cros, how do you feel about this proposal?"

Sam cleared his throat. "I would be a fool and a liar if I denied my fear, but this proposal is not unprecedented. I agree with Yoona. The current threat is great. If this action isn't authorized, it's possible a genocide worse than the Holocaust could occur. I will submit to every precaution you subscribe to me, and I will find the pair."

Daniels coughed. "General Cros?"

Sam blinked, looking at Daniels.

"I believe this Ruth"—he pointed to the younger—"is the same Ruth who worked in the White House before. She stole this young Guatemalan's body for her own."

"You're dismissed," Sam said dryly.

"Sorry?"

"We're done for today. You may go."

"But I haven't told you about the other person. His story is just as strange."

"I'll look through the file myself. Go. I need time to think."

Daniels slowly rose to his feet and cleared his throat. "I'll schedule another appointment with your secretary for us to meet again."

Sam nodded, dismissing Daniels with a wave of his hand, then unbuttoned his collar. He stepped in front of his mahogany bar cabinet and poured himself a scotch. The glass clinked against the bottle, punctuating the silence and his unease. Downing the drink in one swift motion, he wiped sweat from his forehead before pouring himself a second drink. Sam's eyes remained locked on the files as he paced his workspace. The ice cubes in his glass rattled like thunder, broadcasting the approaching storm. He took the files and settled into his chair, its creaking leather acknowledging his apprehension. Ruth and Yoona ... were they working together?

General Cros leaned back, resting one arm on the surface of his desk as he toyed with the brown folder. He pushed it back and forth, knowing all his hard work, scheming, and investigations had paid off. The results were here, but they revealed more questions than answers. How many others were out there who had the ability to change bodies? Had Yoona allowed those training manuals to go missing, and if so, to what end? What was the ultimate plan? Had she been using him all along?

Sam swirled his drink, his expression hard, eyes dark. He ran a hand over his mouth, wiping his lips, sweat dripping down the side of his face. Setting his drink aside, he tapped the folder, unwound the tiny white string, and then wound it back into place. Why was this so difficult? He knew he had to open it. He knew relief would replace his tension once the contents of the folder were known. His mission was complete. Ruth was the Shaman. Who was the Banisher? Once he knew, he could step down and return home—General Sam Cros of the U.S. Army, a hero to the world.

Panic ripped at Sam's insides. How had he not seen who Ruth was? How had he not felt her energy? Had she been manipulating him this whole time? He swallowed hard, lifting his glass. *I'm a fucking idiot*, he thought. Why was he hesitating? What was he waiting for? He had to perform his duty!

Bringing his glass to his lips, he drank. Then he leaned back in his chair and mulled over the impending reality of leaving his position of power. He was a general, an advisor to the President, a man with immense influence. He had averted war with China and ensured Iran's nuclear capabilities remained unused against Israel and out of North Korean hands. No one else could have done that.

His loyalty to Yoona was shaken. Relinquishing his military command and returning to his former role in the Circle might be exactly what she wanted. He couldn't abandon his post.

Sam finished his drink. Was his inability to leave the corruption taking him? Maybe, but he had to stay, just until relations with China normalized. His service was indispensable. He had to believe that his motives for this decision were noble.

Returning his attention back to the folder, Sam unraveled the string to open it when a knock at his door startled him.

"Yes?" he responded.

Ruth Jones entered his office wearing a gray blazer with a white collared blouse that made her ruby-red lips stand out, her signature samurai bun in place.

General Cros stood, his chest tightening, a sick look crossing his face. "Ruth. What brings you here?" He wouldn't be able to defeat her. If she knew he had identified her, he was in trouble. There was no doubt in his mind that her abilities far surpassed his own.

"General," Ruth articulated. "I'm sorry to inform you, Lieutenant General Jill Foster died this afternoon. I know you two were close, and I wanted to extend my condolences."

"Ahh." He breathed a sigh of relief. "Yes, thank you. I've known for a few days now that she was going to pass."

"I never got the chance to meet her before she died," Ruth said. "But we became acquainted on our way here."

Sam's face paled. Ruth knew that he understood her true identity.

Reopening the door, Ruth stepped aside, and a young woman no older than nineteen waltzed into the room with the same confident swagger Sam had seen countless times from his Junior. Her skin was a warm, rich brown. Her hair, jet-black and falling in loose waves, framed a face marked by resilience. She bore a small scar on her left cheek. Stopping in front of him, she saluted. "General Cros, sir. It's good to see you again."

Sam returned her salute, not saying anything. He stepped flush against his desk and inched his left hand toward the buzzer next to his top drawer to alert his secretary he needed assistance.

"Don't you remember me?" she said in jest.

Sam stared nervously. Her striking, warm-brown eyes were intense, hinting at a depth of experience beyond her years.

"Surely you remember our last visit." She tipped her head slightly to the side in a playful manner, teasing him. "I told you I was bored. I said I was happy to be leaving all this bullshit behind. I complained about religion, saying that as long as it was allowed to thrive, we will continue to butcher one another." A slight grin pierced her lips. "I was happy to be leaving. And what was your response? Do you remember? You sat next to my hospital bed, grabbed my hand"—turning her palm up, she revealed a general's star— "and boasted, 'It's my extreme honor to have served with you, General Foster. Your duty, service, and sacrifice have saved millions of lives. You are a true hero.' Your words were so traditionally lame, I about choked. But to hold this elusive star felt good." She took a deep breath. "But I'm glad to be back. How do you like my new body?"

The young woman was lean and athletic. She stood tall, with a vibrant confidence. The general was horror stricken. "You've possessed this body? Why?" But the question wasn't genuine. Jill's aura didn't suggest a possession.

Ruth interrupted with a chuckle. "Jill isn't possessing this body. She owns it."

General Cros reached for the button to press it, but an invisible force grasped his hand, stopping him.

"Please don't. Wait until you hear what I have to offer," Ruth said.

Sam closed his eyes. "There is nothing you can say!" He reached for Yoona.

"Not even eternal life, Yoona's secret." Jill cut in.

Sam stopped and opened his eyes.

"Jill's soul is the sole occupant of this body," Ruth said. "I removed the former and inserted hers. Think about the implications. Our best soldiers can live forever. Death, old age, injury—mean nothing."

Sam held her eyes.

Ruth continued. "With the key to eternal life, you'll be the most powerful man on the planet—the rich and revered under your thumb, the criminal under-lords at your beck and call. The power to remove a soul from a body and replace it with another means you rule everyone."

"Why are you offering me this power? If you already have it, why not use it yourself?"

"I am not doing this for power. It's not about me. I haven't been corrupted. I'm not even a Shaman."

"Not a Shaman?" The words slipped from his breath, barely formed.

"I am a Banisher," Ruth said. "And I am using this power to help humanity."

Sam stared at her. This didn't make sense. "Who is the corrupt Shaman?"

With a wry smile, Ruth said, "There is no corrupt Shaman. That was something you and the Circle convinced yourselves had to be true."

Sam lowered his head, finally understanding why they hadn't been able to find Ruth sooner.

"I've been watching you for a long time, Sam. You've been using your abilities to move up in rank. You enjoy the limelight, the position of influence, and the ability to wield your will. Let me give you a true and honest reason to use your power. Together, we can accomplish what neither of us could alone—world peace."

Sam lifted his head and focused on Ruth's eyes. He expected to see traces of black, showing she'd absorbed dark energy, but there was none. Nothing about her said she was addicted. This meant Ruth was the yin to Yoona's yang. Yoona, a Shaman with Banishing abilities; Ruth, a Banisher with Shamanic abilities.

Jill interrupted. "Imagine it, Sam. We'll possess the most elite soldiers the world has ever seen. Our best men and women will be immortal! Sam, I'm living, breathing proof."

Sam gulped. "Extended Life," he stated dryly.

"You should know," Ruth said. "You helped negotiate their government contract."

"But..." He paused. "This is..." he stammered. "I had no idea. The Circle will never allow you to wield such power. They will stop you."

Jill leaned on the desk, her eyes locked onto his. "No more wars, no more suffering. We can mold the world into a peaceful home for everyone. You can lead the new revolutionary police force, the United Nation's stabilizing arm."

Sam's expression hardened as realization dawned on him. "The European Union." It all fell into place. He now knew the plan. "You're pushing for global governance. This is your doing. You have manipulated the world leaders. You made the debate on the Senate floor possible."

Ruth nodded. "We have the chance to reshape our existence and end the exploitation of our planet's resources for profit. To end the corporation stronghold. With a single governing body, we can eliminate hunger, poverty—solving problems that have plagued humanity since the dawn of time. Extended Life is simply a tool that we are using to achieve that end."

Sam dropped into his seat. "You've orchestrated the entire push for global governance?"

"Exactly," Ruth confirmed. "A centralized government with a single, elite police force. No more armies, no more wars, just one force maintaining peace and order. Yoona's secret ensures those soldiers will be unbeatable, eternal guardians of a new era. And with you as our leader, you'll have pure, unadulterated power to shape a utopia."

Scratching his head, Sam stood and turned to face his bookshelf on the back wall.

"I'll teach you how to live forever, and once I destroy Yoona, you may take her place."

Sam's jaw tightened and he clenched his fists. "No. You can't—"

"It's your leadership we need," Ruth exclaimed. "Your integrity is what's required to guide this new force," she insisted. "With you at the helm, we can ensure the transition is smooth and the world remains secure. Yoona represents everything that's wrong. She's a relic of the past, clinging to outdated beliefs and refusing to see the potential for change. We have the power to solve the world's problems, but Yoona has banned us from doing so. She's holding back progress!"

"It's time to put an end to Yoona's tyranny," Jill added. "We can move the world forward. Let's begin a new era of peace and prosperity."

"I know we can achieve this dream with you leading the way," Ruth said.

The two women stood and waited for his response.

Sam took a moment to breathe. The European Union was creating something real. The happiest countries in the world existed there, and their transition to help stabilize the world held real promise. Could this path lead to world peace?

"Are you with us?" Jill asked.

"Why don't we propose this idea to the Circle?" Sam suggested. "Many of them may agree to help."

"No! You cannot contact the Circle," Ruth countered. "If Yoona knows who I am, she'll stop me at all costs. The same way she did with my father. Without the element of surprise, our secrecy, our ability to manipulate and control others, we'll be shattered. You have to sever your connection to her. To all of them."

"What happens to the Circle in this new world you're building?" Sam asked.

"Once we've realized our vision, we bring them on as a branch of the government," Ruth said. "The Circle is still needed."

"And Yoona? What are you going to do to her?"

"She needs to transcend. I'm sure we can both agree on that."

Sam closed his eyes and shook his head. He couldn't see Yoona surrendering without a fight. Could he betray her? Should he? Was his loyalty justified? He let that question simmer. The answer that came back was no.

"Our plan is in motion," Ruth said. "The United Federation of States is now forty countries strong. There are fifteen others currently debating whether to join, and Yoona is mobilizing to stop us." Ruth leaned forward. "Ask yourself why."

Sam nodded. Why indeed? He had been using his powers with Yoona's consent and had averted devastating crises from happening. How was Ruth's work any different? She was redefining how nations interacted on a global stage, and Sam wanted to be part of that. The good he could do in such a position... The idea curled and branched, seeping into the corners of his mind. If he were a part of this, he could shape the world government into something humane.

"Yoona transcends," Sam said. "I won't let you shred her soul."

"That idea never crossed my mind."

"Okay. I'm in."

"Cut your ties with the Circle. Then connect with me," Ruth said, extending her hand.

Sam glared at the hand in front of him, feeling sick. This was happening too fast.

"Look at me," Ruth commanded.

He raised his head, expecting to see cold, ruthless eyes, but they were warm and affectionate. "I was taken from my father because of war. I've seen the death and destruction it leaves in its wake. I know the pain of losing a loved one." Ruth rounded the desk, stepping inches from Sam. "My father was a Banisher. We lived in Shanghai in 1937."

Sam recalled his history. He remembered the documentaries he had watched of WWII. The Japanese had bombed the city and killed indiscriminately. "I'm so sorry," he offered.

"I made my way through war-torn China to Japan trying to find him. I was eighteen years old, and what I saw, witnessed..." She paused. "We have learned nothing! My dad died in Nagasaki three days after the bomb was dropped. I was there. The stench, the sores, the pus..." She trailed off, inching closer. In a firm, reassuring tone, she said, "I will realize the dream of a true United Nations." She lifted her hand again, asking him to connect.

Breathing deep and slow, he raised his own, while simultaneously building walls and barriers inside his mind. Ruth had Yoona's abilities. She was angry and determined. Sam was under no illusions that his walls would keep her out of his mind and knew that she would enter if the situation called for it. But he also saw her will, and she would do anything to see her vision a reality. He severed all his connections, then clasped her hand.

Outside the building, Ruth raised her hand and hailed a taxicab. Washington, D.C. was alive with horns, crosswalks beeping, and the rhythm of feet hitting pavement. The cab stopped next to the curb. She opened the door and ducked inside. Jill followed right behind.

"The airport, please," Ruth said.

The taxi merged into traffic and stopped behind a school bus.

"I told you this approach would work," Jill said. "I know Sam."

"You did," Ruth agreed. "And he's exactly who we need—charismatic, strong. The people love him. But he's already slipping. I can't allow him to assume power after the transition."

"What will you do?"

Ruth glanced at the driver, then spoke using telepathy.

I'll remove Sam's soul and replace it with someone less corruptible.

Is he that weak? Jill asked.

The car made the light and turned onto the freeway ramp. They inched along in traffic.

I do have a backup plan, Ruth said. *I've devoted the entire eighth and ninth floors of Extended Life to my clone program. Once I'm able to grow adult clones, I can switch him out that way.*

You're able to grow adult clones?

Not yet. The clones experience neurological decay and organ failure. We need to figure out how to stabilize the growth rates after we remove them from their pods. As soon as we do, we'll have a way of maintaining a corrupt-free government and an endless supply of bodies for our soldiers.

How close are you?

The last clone aged fifty years in seven weeks. The worst part: the brain didn't support the consciousness of a soul at any stage of its growth.

Jill's phone dinged. She opened it and scrolled through the message. *I have a body for your judge—a gang member in Florida. My guy says he's left a nice paper trail: drugs, arson, assault. Shall I have him brought to New York?*

Yes, bring him. I'll replace the soul in that body with the judge's. We'll need a Texas Supreme Court member deciding in our favor. Ruth transitioned back to speech. "Then I need you to go to Geneva and present the Palestine deal. The European States have to agree. And when they do, Iran will join the Federation. That will end the war with Israel, displaying the true power of unification."

Impact Point

The baggage claim area at the Lake Valley airport was loud with conversations and noise—electronic dings, service announcements, and the rumble of circular baggage belts. Min saw his father waiting for him near an information kiosk. He strolled over and bowed. "Hello, Father."

"Min." Jae Yun said, looking happy to see him. "How was the flight?"

"It was fine," Min replied. "Where's Judy? She didn't come?"

"I asked her not to. It's been a while since I've seen you."

"That's because I don't run away from bullies, Dad. I stay and fight." Min stepped to the side, letting a family with their luggage pass.

"There was nothing left to fight for," his dad replied. "Nothing but pain and hurt remained. I wish you would have come with me."

"I couldn't leave Mom's soul alone. I wasn't going to abandon her."

"We did everything we could. Her death was not your fault."

"No, it wasn't. It was Ki-Tae Moon's. But he got what was coming to him."

"I heard his wife killed him in self-defense."

"She was falsely accused and wrongfully convicted."

Jac shook his head. "You really think so?"

Min gave a sharp exhale and nodded. The glass doors hissed open, releasing a burst of car horns and the roar of bus engines. He picked up his bag. "I'm ready. Let's go."

Opening his arms, Jae said, "I'd love to give my son a hug."

Min glared at his father, remembering the last time he'd seen him. His dad had been pale and thin. The endless hospital visits, the growing number of bills, and his fading hope had worn him to the bone. Min's mother's sickness hadn't been easy for either of them.

Min took a new look at his father and saw how at ease he seemed. The tension in his shoulders had vanished, and a soft demeanor replaced the old strain. The gray threads running through his hair, though, irritated Min; they reminded him that he should show respect.

Letting out a sigh, Min said, "Sure." He set down his bag and welcomed his dad.

"It's so good to see you, son."

Min patted his father's back, then released him.

Jae picked up Min's bag and led the way to the car. "Are you hungry? Would you like to stop and grab a bite to eat?" he asked. "There's a Korean barbecue place on the way. Or we can stop at the sports bar. They have fantastic hamburgers, and a Mexican side dish called a quesadilla."

Min stared out his side window. He wasn't here to play son. He had a job to do, one that would send Brandon running home. "How did you meet Judy?"

"At an art show." Jae said. "She paints these comedic drawings of animals doing silly things. I found them entertaining. I picked one out, and she told me the story behind it. She made me laugh. I thought I had forgotten how." Putting his hand to his mouth, Jae suppressed his emotions. "I went back to see her later that day and asked her out. She's an amazing person—kind, caring, considerate, a fabulous cook."

"If she's so awesome, why isn't she married?" Min pried.

"She was married. Her ex-husband lives in New Mexico."

"Any kids?"

"One. A son. He's three years older than you. He's actually in Korea now. Works for the FBI."

"The FBI doesn't work overseas. I think you mean the CIA."

"Maybe. I don't know. But he was promoted just a few weeks ago."

"Have you met him?" Min asked, his contempt clear.

Jae threw Min a questioning glanced. "I did. Only once. His wife and child died not too long ago, and he's buried himself in his work. Judy is giving him space."

"So, he's on the rebound," Min muttered while grinding his teeth.

"Have you met Judy's son, Brandon?"

Raising his eyebrows, Min said, "What? No, how could I?"

Jae shook his head and continued, "It's crazy. His wife and kid died in Seoul; how he's dealing with that right now is beyond me."

The secondary conference room at Moon Law was now a makeshift classroom. Brandon opened the notebook that held his plans for Su-Bin's English lesson. The door opened and he looked up to see her enter the room. She approached with a teasing smile and sat down next to him.

"Good morning, Teacher."

Brandon blushed. "Good morning, Student. Did you get a chance to read the passages I marked?"

"I didn't. And I can't stay for class. I was hoping you could come over for dinner and we could read together."

Brandon's breath hitched. The words *"over for dinner"* rearranged themselves in his head, loosening the spark that had been sitting in his chest from their first meeting. Excitement stirred, and fantasies followed: passionate kissing, ripping off their clothes, rolling naked on the bed. "Are you sure that's best? Don't you think we should keep our relationship professional?"

"Of course. We won't be alone. Jong-In will be with us." A smile warmed her lips. "I don't need you to send me any thoughts; you are wearing them all over your face." With a seductive smile, she stood. "Shall I have a taxi pick you up tonight?" She waited just a second before adding, "Let me know later."

Brandon watched her leave. As she passed through the door, she caught his eye and flashed a devilish grin.

Needing to calm his racing thoughts, Brandon rushed to the bathroom and splashed cold water on his face. He gripped the edge of the sink, staring hard at his reflection. Su-Bin's advances couldn't have come at a worse time. The upcoming raid on the illegal weapons traffickers had him worried. He already felt guilty for not being able to tell her what was unfolding, and if they became romantically involved, keeping that secret would become a betrayal.

But he couldn't deny that he had feelings for her—she was smart, confident, friendly, and very attractive. He knew something had happened between Min and her, suspecting he had hacked her phone. The worry, anger, bursts of physical outrage over her device, combined with the fact that Min quit the next day, made it fairly obvious. Looking in the mirror, Brandon muttered, "Why are you thinking about this? It's such a bad idea."

Yoona's words surfaced, as if instructions for him to follow: *Bathe in new experiences and relationships.* Brandon smiled, knowing that advice wasn't referring to having affairs, or was it? He finally decided to just live in the moment, not expecting or desiring a specific outcome but allowing whatever was going to happen, to happen. He sent Su-Bin an image of a taxi.

Back in Diamond Creek, Min stood in front of the mirror in his dad's guest bathroom. Jae tapped on the door. "Min, you ready? We're going to Judy's for breakfast."

"In a minute."

He held the glass vial, staring at the barbiturate—enough to put Judy into a coma. He'd rehearsed the whole scenario on the flight over. Checking his itinerary, he saw his return flight left in four hours, more than enough time. Soon, they'd be sitting down to eat. Min would pour the drug into Judy's drink, she'd collapse, Jae would ride with her to the hospital, and Min would grab a taxi to the airport. He'd be on his way to Korea long before his dad realized what had happened.

Min returned the vial to his pocket and took a long hard look at himself in the mirror. He was a fighter. A winner. Brandon had brought this upon his mother. Stepping out of the bathroom, Min called to his dad, "I'm ready. Let's go."

As Jae drove to Judy's, he asked Min about his life since the move. "I understand you became an attorney? Mrs. Yi told me you were working with a small firm outside of Seoul."

"I was. I've been hired by a bigger firm. They put me on Mrs. Moon's case. I'm working on getting her a new trial."

"Please tell me you told them about your mother."

"Why? That woman didn't kill Mom. Her husband did, and she never should have been convicted for his murder."

"Your mother was sick. There was no telling if the surgery would have helped."

"We'll never know, will we."

"Min, you're too close—"

"Look, Dad! It's none of your business. If you're going to lecture and complain, then I'm leaving."

Jae didn't respond. After a few minutes, he finally voiced, "I'm sorry."

"For abandoning us? You should be."

"I'm happy you came to visit."

They arrived, and Jae knocked once before opening the door. "Judy, we're here."

Min followed and closed the door behind him.

Judy pranced in with a giant smile. "Min, welcome."

"Ms. Spencer." Min bowed. "It's nice to meet you."

Judy put her hand on his upper arm. "Thank you so much for coming. Your father is so proud of you. Told me all about you being a medic in the army, and now an attorney. That's fantastic."

Min gave a shallow smile.

"What made you want to practice law?" Judy asked.

In a warm voice, he said, "A girl."

"And?" she pressed with a hint of excitement in her voice.

"And we're dating," Min said. Su-Bin—her smooth skin, tender embrace, and sweet kisses—filled his thoughts, followed by Brandon! Min's smile hardened.

"I love romantic stories. Come in, come in. Tea is ready. I have a pot of rice boiling, and I'm about to scramble eggs. Jae, take Min's jacket. Put it in the bedroom."

After handing his coat to his dad, Min walked with Judy into the kitchen. She pointed to the table, saying, "Have a seat. Help yourself to tea."

The teapot sat beside the honey and a plate of cut lemons. Three cups on saucers were arranged at the table settings. As Judy turned to stir the eggs, Min poured the contents of the vial—a concentrated dose of Thiopental—into Judy's cup and stirred. Then he slid it across the table.

"Min, could you hand me the small plate of tomatoes on the counter?"

He stood, went to the counter, and handed Judy the plate just as his dad entered the room.

Jae sat in Judy's spot. "Smells delicious." He picked up the cup of tea to take a drink.

Min screeched, "No, that's mine!" Leaping toward the table, Min extended his arm to stop the cup from reaching his dad's lips. His fingers caught the edge, and the cup tipped, spilling hot water onto the table and into Jae's lap.

"Ah!" Jae howled, standing quickly.

The cup hit the floor and broke.

"Shit!" Min exclaimed.

Judy grabbed a towel and laid it on the table, soaking up the water. "It's fine. Jae, there's a pair of sweatpants upstairs in Brandon's old room. Go change into those."

Min finished cleaning up the water as Judy swept up the glass. After the mess was cleaned up, he dropped into his seat, frustrated. Judy wouldn't be going to the hospital. Brandon wouldn't be rushing home. Min hit the table with his fist.

"Don't worry about it," Judy said in a comforting tone. "Your father's fine, and I have plenty of cups."

"Yeah," Min said through gritted teeth.

"Eggs are done," Judy announced. She put them in a bowl, wiped the counter, and then set them on the table.

Min's plan was shot. *Now what? Think... Think...*

"It feels really good to have you here, Min. You remind me so much of my son, Brandon. I think the two of you would get along nicely."

That name dug under Min's skin. Tightening his fists, he contemplated standing and punching this woman to a pulp. That would bring Mr. Shitbag home.

"How so?" he almost growled.

Judy gave a concerning look that seemed more like pity. "Brandon loves languages and learning about new cultures. He was a teacher for a few years, traveling to Mexico, Thailand, and Japan. Then he became a detective. I bet the two of you would have lots to talk about."

Min didn't respond. He sat in thought. Strangulation. Overdose on sleeping pills. A bite from a poisonous insect or animal. Was she allergic to anything?

Judy placed the rice on the table. "Do you enjoy traveling?"

Min took a second to register the question, then asked, "What made Brandon want to travel to those countries?"

"He was always fascinated with the kids who could speak multiple languages. He thought it was a superpower. It was his dream to live in another country and become fluent. He chose Mexico because he had this fantasy of meeting and falling in love with a singer, a Mexican pop star, who was from there. He went to her hometown and taught for a year. I'm not sure why he chose Thailand, but I know why he went to Japan. He often watched Japanese cartoons with his friends and used to collect the dolls and figures. Boy, those were expensive. They're up in his room now, a shelf full of them."

A sneer formed. Brandon was delusional. His obsessive fantasies were sure to be problematic for Su-Bin, especially if she allowed Mr. Shitbag to get close. It was apparent to Min that Brandon had issues with relationships and sexuality. If he could get evidence of this... "What city did he go to in Mexico?"

"It was pronounced Wa-ha-ka, but spelled O-A-X-A-C-A."

"Did you visit him there?"

"I did. Two weeks over Christmas. I'll show you photos after breakfast."

Min didn't respond. He was forming a new plan.

"How long are you planning on staying?" Judy asked. "Your father wasn't sure."

"This is a working trip. I'm playing it by ear."

Jae returned to the kitchen as the front doorbell rang.

Officer Choi pulled up to Tim Davenport's house. His hopes that a psychic was training Leah didn't pan out, so now he was turning to her self-described bodyguard to give him some insights. He rang the bell, then knocked and waited.

Music crept around the house from the backyard. Choi rounded the corner, seeing an open gate. He hesitated, unsure whether he should enter the premises or not. Pushing aside his better judgment, he walked through the opening, crossed the lawn, and banged on the shed door.

A shout came over the blaring music. "Yeah, I'm here."

Officer Choi didn't answer but knocked again.

The shed went quiet, and a moment later the door opened. Tim was surprised to see Choi. He slipped out and closed the door behind him, obviously concealing something he shouldn't have been doing. "Officer. Is there a reason you are on my property?"

Offering his hand, he said, "Hi, Tim. My name is Choi. I'm a friend of Leah's."

Tim stared at Choi's outstretched hand. "Okay. She mentioned you. What can I do for you?"

"She told me you were her bodyguard."

Tim laughed, sliding his hands into his pockets. "Yeah, she doesn't appreciate it much, though."

"Oh, I think she does. With all the attention she's been getting lately, I was happy to hear you were keeping a good eye on her."

"Yep."

Resting a hand on Tim's shoulder, Choi said, "Someone has been working with her, helping her study. Any chance you can give me a name?"

Tim looked at his shoulder and stepped back, then placed his hand over his heart. A knot formed in Choi stomach. Tim's reaction meant he knew about connecting. Which meant he knew about Leah's abilities and probably her teacher.

"Leah's a smart cookie," Tim said. "She grew up with tutors, so if anyone's helping anyone study, it would be her.

Choi nodded and pressed, "Right, but I need to know who she's been seeing."

Tim shrugged. "Leah's been reunited with her mom and dad. She's been spending all her time with them."

"When I talked to Leah, she mentioned prom." Choi hoped the reminder of her being in danger might prompt Tim to reveal the person training her.

"She had a little lover's quarrel, but they sorted it out."

"Was that with Paul?"

"No, his name was Eric."

Choi knew Tim didn't trust him and wasn't about to cooperate—his aura was dark. He had bad intentions and was clearly up to something.

"Tim, I know you're hiding something. I'm worried." Choi paused to gage his reaction. Would he glance behind him? If so, that tell would speak volumes to Tim's scheming.

Tim shook his head. "Hiding something? About Leah? What could I possibly be hiding?"

"Leah's been experimenting with something dangerous. I need to know who she's been seeing. I'm trying to protect her."

"I'm glad you care about her, we all do. But she's a good kid. Stanford is around the corner, and she's getting ready for that adventure. I wouldn't worry, officer."

Choi's heart suddenly tightened as a burst of terror hit him.

"Leah!" both Choi and Tim gasped at the same time.

Putting his hand over his chest, Choi looked Tim dead in the eyes. "What do you know about this?"

"Know about what?" Tim stammered.

"Where is Leah?" he demanded.

"She's at school."

"Are you sure? Call her."

"I'm not calling. She's in school."

"Something is wrong," Choi said. "She's in trouble."

"I dropped her at school this morning. I'm sorry, but I can't help you."

Choi turned and headed out the gate. "I'm going to the school to check on her. You should call her."

Leah reached forward and rang Ms. Spencer's doorbell.

"We should have called first," Barb said.

"Don't worry so much," Leah replied. "We need to be here. It feels right."

The door opened. Leah turned and smiled at the woman in the doorway. "Judy Spencer? Hi, I'm Leah Davenport, and this is Barb Mills. I was wondering if we could talk with you for a moment."

Judy let out a light gasp and touched her chest. She opened the door wider. "Yes, of course." Steeling a quick glance behind her, she added, "Come in. Have a seat in the living room. I'll be right back."

Leah and Barb stepped in and made their way to the sofa.

"This feels awkward," Barb whispered in protest. "It's not a good time for her."

"We won't stay long," Leah said.

Barb sighed.

The room was bright. Two large windows, set side by side with a southern view, filled the space with light. The open-air vibe made the room comfortable. Family photos and funny animal paintings hung on the cream-colored walls. The sofa, chairs, and coffee table, arranged in a circle, invited conversation. Leah didn't see a television, only bookshelves filled with novels and a few games. Two books lay open on the table, as if set down mid-read. The room felt cozy, intentionally designed for talking, thinking, and getting lost in a good story.

Judy came back, followed by two men who looked to be father and son. Leah recognized the father. He was the man in her vision, the one who walked with Judy and Olivia into Bellevue.

Judy introduced the two men, "Barb, Leah, this is Jae Yun and his son Min Yun." Putting her hand on Jae's arm, she added, "Barb, Jae helped your father build his house."

Barb's face lit with recognition, and she jumped to her feet. "Oh my gosh, I haven't seen you in since forever."

Jae blinked in surprise, then smiled warmly. "The last time I saw you, you were just yay high." He held his hand waist-level.

"My father made us dress up every time you came over."

"I remember. You always looked very nice." Jae glanced down at his sweatpants and tugged on them. "Sorry for my attire. Tea mishap." He turned to the man standing next to him. "This is my son, Min."

Min shook Barb's hand.

Turning his attention to Leah, Jae said, "I'm so sorry about what happened to you and your father. We followed the news and were relieved when you were able to escape."

Leah smiled. "Thanks. It was pretty scary."

Judy motioned for Jae and Min to sit as she sat herself. "I'm very grateful for your visit," Judy started. "I know my son was involved with your abduction, and if there is anything I can do to help you, please let me know."

Leah leaned forward, resting her forearms on her knees. She could only imagine how Judy must feel, her son being implicated in the disappearance of the six. "No, Judy. Your son was amazing. I'm grateful for his help. He tried his best. It's just, well, he was deceived. We all were."

"It was a haunting deception," Barb clarified.

"I understand. Still, I can't imagine the terror that you must have endured."

"That's the reason we're here," Leah said. "I need to warn you."

Jae spoke quickly, "Warn her? Of what?"

"Actually, to warn you both," Leah revised. "Have you ever seen the Bellevue House?"

"Of course. I helped build it," Jae said with a chuckle.

"I mean, after It burned down," Leah corrected.

Glancing at Judy, Jae said, "Brandon thought the house had been rebuilt." Looking back at Leah, he asked, "Was it?"

"Many people believe that it was. They have claimed to have seen It. But no, the house was never rebuilt. I'm here to tell you that if you ever see It, don't believe your eyes. It's a mirage. Officer Rodriguez called it a magic trick. The guy lures people in and then captures them."

Judy looked confused. "I thought the guy died."

"I just need you to understand this. Don't ever go into that house if you see It. It's not real." Pausing, Leah asked, "Does your granddaughter know about the Bellevue house?"

Judy's expression turned somber. "My grandson died two years ago. I don't have any other grandchildren."

"Who is Olivia?" Leah asked, curiously.

"Olivia? I don't know anyone by that name," Judy responded.

Min laughed, "What—did you have a nightmare and then rush over to tell us about it?"

Leah glared at Min. His energy was weird.

Barb answered, "More or less, yes. But we wouldn't be here if it hadn't happened to us. It's not a joke."

Min nodded, saying, "Okay," with a pinch of sarcasm.

Judy jumped in, "I appreciate you coming. May I have you for dinner sometime next week? I am desperate to hear everything that happened. My son was so vague about it all that I was left worried, with only my imagination and the news to fill in the gaps."

Leah stood. "I'll call you. I have your number from your website."

"Please do," Judy said, rising and giving Leah a warm, genuine embrace that made her feel like family.

Leah withdrew and turned to shake Jae's hand. "That house must have meant something to you."

"It did," he said with a nod. "I rather loved that house. Barb's dad was a good friend. I was grateful he allowed me to help him with the project. I'm forever changed by the experience."

Leah gave Min a forced smile as she reached out to shake his hand. "It was nice—" Her voice cracked into a sharp yelp as a jolt of energy bit her. She staggered back and dropped onto the couch, gaping at Min.

Barb stepped away, shaking her head. "Is he?" she asked.

Judy rushed over, fretting, "Oh, are you okay, dear?"

Jae scrutinized Min with a sharp gaze.

Min's baffled expression hardened into accusation as he faced Leah.

Leah pressed her hand to her forehead and grimaced. Min had a soul attached to him, and she was processing a stream of emotions slamming into her through the connection—anger, abandonment, and jealousy—followed by memories.

A woman in a hospital bed listened to a nurse explain that her surgery would be postponed another day. Resignation consumed the woman and her strength evaporated. She lost the will to keep fighting. With nothing left to hold on to, she simply slipped away, allowing her spirit to drift out of her body.

Next, she saw Min on his knees in front of a memorial. He was devastated. Jae knelt beside him and made a final plea for his son to sell the house and join him in America.

Then, she watched as Min Yun met a beautiful woman named Su-Bin. Her son had fallen completely in love. When Min prayed for her to help him, the spirit attached to her son and nudged him to follow Su-Bin to law school.

Finally, Leah saw Brandon, Min Yun's nemesis, flirting with Su-Bin, and Su-Bin reciprocating. This sight made the spirit's anger boil, leading her to concoct a plan. She drove Min Yun to visit Judy and pour a white powder into her tea that would send Judy into a coma. This would force Brandon to return home, eliminating the threat.

Leah sent Barb an image of Brandon. "He knows him. They've met. And they're not friends."

Jae narrowed his eyes, asking, "Have you met Min before? What's happening here?"

Leah returned to her feet. "Mr. Yun, I need to have a private conversation with your son. It's rather important."

Min scoffed. "What could you possibly need to say to me?"

"Su-Bin," Leah said.

Min's face went cold. "How do you know that name?"

"It seems we both know another person who knows that name," Leah stated.

Jae turned to Min and asked, "Son? I'm confused."

"Stay out of this, Dad."

Leah motioned to the door. "I think it's best if we talk outside."

Min's face darkened. "I don't think we should."

"Do you really want to talk about breakfast tea here?"

Now Min's face went pale, and his eyes hardened with fear.

Jae, Judy, and Barb watched anxiously, waiting for a resolution. The tension was as thick as a western standoff.

Min finally agreed, "Okay. Let's talk outside."

Barb grabbed Leah's arm, whispering, "Remember what happened with Paul. You need a talisman."

"I'm not sure how to make one yet. And this can't wait. I'll be okay."

Leah led Min out onto the front lawn. She noticed Jae, Judy, and Barb huddled at the window watching. Turning to face Min, a sudden chill crept into her consciousness.

Leave my son alone, or I will be forced to hurt you.

Leah felt the danger—desperation of a mother fiercely protective of her child. Her words weren't just a threat; they were a promise of violence. Leah straightened. *You think you can intimidate me? I'm not afraid of you, and I won't allow you to keep manipulating Min into hurting people.*

A mocking laugh grated Leah's mind, amplifying the mother's amusement. *Stop me?* the voice hissed. *You're just a child playing with forces you don't understand. I've protected Min his whole life.*

Leah clenched her jaw and grabbed Min's hands, locking her eyes onto his.

Is that a threat? the ghost taunted.

Leave him. Now. Or I'll force you out and make you transcend.

Try it! the woman intoned.

Closing her eyes, Leah opened her consciousness and set the stage for the spirit's arrival.

In her mind, she recreated the woods where her and Barb had gone camping. This is where her power was strongest, and this is where she would face Min's mother. Finding the tree that had produced the psychic vision that led her to Judy, Leah communed with the earth's energy, drawing strength and confidence. Then she invited the ghost into her.

Min's mother's cold presence crashed into her consciousness like a wall of ice water. The forest around her froze and mountains of snow replaced the trees. The air became so cold it burned.

The ghost dug for memories. Leah cried out as metal spikes sank into her skull. Columns of fiery rock burst through the frozen floor. Her knees buckled, and she dropped into boiling water, unable to move. Leah had to let go or she would drown. This was her consciousness, and she had to reclaim it, or the fight was already lost.

Breathe.

Blacking out her thoughts, Leah took several controlled breaths. She knelt and ran her hands through soft, warm soil. With her focus on the smells of the forest, she opened her mind and relaxed. Life was her savior. The trees, pollen, moss, and insects returned. Her torment subsided.

The spirit snaked through her mind, worming its way around the shadows of the woods—behind trees, through branches. A creeping chill blew in from the south, making the hairs on the back of her neck stand on end. The woman was here.

Leah backed uneasily, looking for the ghost as she breathed through the pain. This spirit was stalking its prey. Leah's gut tightened, her eyes darting back and forth, up and around, frantically searching for the woman. Without warning, a cloaked figure surged from the ferns and struck Leah like a storm. The shock sent her flying onto her back.

Groaning, Leah scrambled to her feet and faced the woman.

The spirit's pale skin was almost translucent against the backdrop of the dark woods. Her cheeks were hollow and sunken, giving her an unsettlingly gaunt appearance. Her pitch-black eyes bored into Leah, endless voids that threatened to swallow her whole. Leah saw a terrifying woman who was once beautiful, now consumed by vengeance.

A demonic, seething voice filled the air. "You should've left us alone!" The words were a psychic blow that paralyzed her thoughts and left her unable to think, let alone react.

The ghost rushed her with feral intensity, a rabid animal out for blood. Lifting her hands, she revealed jagged shards of glass where her fingers should be. Leah caught her heart in her throat. She raised her arms instinctively as the ghost's glass-like claws slashed at her. But instead of tearing into flesh, they skidded off her skin. The force of the attack sent Leah sprawling back to the ground.

The world shifted as she fell, the familiar woods vanishing. She landed hard, the earth beneath her replaced by a wooden floor. The thud from the impact sent a jolt of pain through her side. Disoriented, she scuttled backwards, glancing around. Leah wasn't in her own consciousness. She was inside a dimly lit room of the ghost's consciousness. "Fuck. This is bad."

The woman cackled as she inched closer. Her sneer deepened with every step, as if savoring the terror etched on Leah's face. Lying on her back, Leah raised her arms, replacing them with cannons. Min's mother laughed, and with a swipe of her hand, sent the cannons rolling across the floor into a door—the spirit's doorway to transcendence. It creaked open, spilling light from its edges. A sweet, haunting melody invited them both to enter.

At the sight and sound of the door, the woman roared. Smoke rose from her skin and her mass doubled as muscles bulged grotesquely. Her glass-like fingers stretched and lengthened, catching the light and shimmering with the cold gleam of death. She swiped down again, aiming for Leah's throat.

Fear paralyzed her mind. She hadn't had a moment to recover, no time to think, floundering against a power far greater than her own. But as the deadly shards came within inches from her skin, something inside her stirred—an instinct born from her battle with Bellevue. Without thinking, without even realizing, Leah thrust her hands forward.

A gust of wind exploded from her, wild and desperate, catching the woman mid-strike and sending her stumbling back. The force of the wind surprised even Leah. Her chest heaved as she blinked in disbelief at what she'd just done. If Leah could blow Min's mother through the door—

The ghost lunged again, her scream filling the room. Leah pushed back harder, channeling everything she had into a second gust of wind. The woman waved her hand and the air spun like a tornado around her. She stood in the eye, unfazed.

Leah swallowed hard. Min's mother would kill her.

Just then, the woman stumbled back. The cannons from Leah's arms had spun from the whirling wind and one hit the woman's ankle. Her foot landed on the second cannon and she slipped, falling in front of the door. Min's mother began to dissolve. She held out her arms, her jagged fingers scraping against the floor as she tried to catch hold of something solid.

"I'm not ready," Min's mother cried.

The room shuddered. The cannons vanished. The wooden walls turned translucent. Leah felt her own soul thinning. The door beckoned, and the world listened, her soul already answering.

Leah shoved herself backwards on hands and feet, looking for an escape. Her thoughts echoed the woman's cry—she wasn't ready to die either. Turning, Leah saw only the walls of the room, draining of color and form. The tug of the door intensified, and Leah began to slide toward it. She had to leave! She scrabbled upright and ran at the colorless wall, bursting through it. She landed back in the forest of her own consciousness.

Black smoke filled the woods. The phantom burnt aroma had a sweet, sticky smell that expanded and lifted Leah into the air. Pure power surged through her bones, her blood, her skin. Leah wasn't just alive, she felt immortal.

Opening her eyes, she fell to her hands and knees, struggling to contain the power coursing through her veins.

Barb stood at the window with Jae and Judy, watching Leah and Min. She couldn't believe Leah was doing this again. After admitting she didn't know how to make a talisman, Leah was still stepping into magic she didn't fully understand.

Leah took Min's hands and a tight knot twisted under Barb's ribs. *She better not die.*

A moment later, they both fell to their knees. Leah grabbed her head and curled into a ball. Min clutched the center of his chest and sagged like a wilted flower. It was happening. Leah had taken the ghost.

A cold ripple of fear swarmed without warning, gripping Barb's heart. She gasped in fright. "Leah's in trouble! We have to help her."

"Hold on," Jae said, putting his hand on her shoulder. "We don't know what's happening out there."

Barb backed from the window, her eyes fixed on her friend.

Leah's face contorted in pain. Then her body went limp. Slowly, she began to rise, effortlessly, as if floating to her feet. Her skin darkened briefly. Barb saw Min gape in awe.

Leah fell to the ground, landing on all fours. She was trembling. But a moment later, she regained her balance and sat up.

Barb wanted to breathe, but her body was too tense. Outside, the two began to talk. At first, they seemed calm and civil. But as the conversation continued, Min's facial expressions became sharp and sudden. His hand balled into a fist, and he held it up to Leah's face.

"Oh, no!" Judy cried.

Jae and Barb ran for the door and rushed outside. Jae stepped in front of Min, and Barb pulled Leah toward the car.

"You're a psychopath!" Min shouted. "Stay away from me and my family, you creepy witch!"

"Don't respond," Barb said. "Let's just go." She slid into the passenger seat. Leah started the car and drove away.

The Next Step
Diamond Creek, Seoul, Lake Valley

<u>Empowered Temptations</u>

Leah drove a little too fast for Barb's comfort. "Leah, slow down."

"My whole body is buzzing," Leah erupted. "I feel so strong." She squeezed the steering wheel as she drove. "Power," she emphasized. "I have power. It's flowing through my veins, in my muscles. It's like invisible wires are wrapped around my bones with electricity juicing them. It's the fucking bomb."

Barb ground her teeth together. The dark glow she had seen around Leah in Judy's front yard—was that dark energy? Had Leah forced a soul to transcend? "Stop the car!"

Leah didn't respond. She kept talking, the speed of the car increasing. "I bet I could cure that boy of his asthma—."

"Stop the car!" Barb demanded.

Leah glanced over. "What's wrong?"

Everything was wrong. Leah's demeanor, her language, her eyes... Barb was sure this "power" Leah felt *was* dark energy. "Stop this car, Leah. Right now!" If Leah had absorbed dark energy, she needed to release it. Dark energy was addictive. Over time, with continued use, life and death would have no meaning. An addict would easily kill for the opportunity to force a soul to transcend.

Leah parked next to the curb. Barb got out and walked to the driver's side. She opened the door, saying, "Get out," just as Leah's phone rang.

Leah glanced at the screen. "It's my uncle."

"Call him back later. You need to get out of the car."

Leah stepped out. "Barb, are you okay?"

"Let me ask you one more time. And now I'm being serious. Did you or did you not read the warnings and dangers in that book?"

"I did," Leah answered.

"I believe I witnessed you force that soul to transcend. You used the techniques associated with Banishers, right?"

"I had to. That soul was turning her son into a monster. She was crazy and tried to put Judy in a coma so Brandon would have to come home."

"Leah, the energy you get from forcing souls to transcend is like cocaine. It's a huge power rush, but after the energy dissipates, you'll crave more. You'll start hunting for souls, eventually being driven mad trying to find them. You'll end up at hospitals and funeral homes or resort to killing people."

Leah showed no comprehension.

"It's dark energy!" Barb shouted. "The smoke from a fire. The exhaust from a car. The soul transcends, and the waste left behind from that transfer is inside you."

"Okay. And?"

"Get rid of it!" Barb yelled.

"Barb, what the fuck has gotten into you?"

Barb slapped Leah in the face. Leah turned red, and an energy wave shot out of her, sending Barb smack into the car and Leah seven feet in reverse. She landed on the cement and slid into the curb across the street.

"Ouch," Leah moaned.

Barb stumbled forward, rubbing her back and wiping blood from her nose. Then she bent over, placing her hands on her knees. "Goddammit, Leah," Barb burst. "I wish you would force yourself to slow down and think."

Leah rubbed her head then pushed herself into a sitting position.

"Barb, you don't understand. That ghost—"

"Yeah! I understand. You have dark energy in you!"

Taking a slow breath, Leah rubbed her chest. "I do. You're right."

"You have to drain it."

"How do I do that?"

"Holy shit, Leah. Did you not read anything in that chapter? Put your hand, palm down, flat, on the street. Let the energy flow from you."

Leah placed her hand on the pavement and waited. "Nothing's happening."

Barb moved closer and stepped on her hand.

"Ahh! You fucking bitch." Leah tried to move her hand, but Barb pressed harder, keeping it in place. Glaring at Barb with blood-red eyes, she shouted, "Get off my hand, you crazy—" The area around her hand began to smoke.

"What the—?" Barb jumped back, the smoke had a strange texture.

After a minute, Leah let out a deep sigh and rolled onto her back. "It's gone."

Stumbling further back, Barb covered her nose. "It smells." She focused on Leah, trying to read her expression. "How do you feel?"

"Empty," Leah responded. "Spent. Exhausted." She stared at Barb. "Are you okay?"

"I'll be fine."

Leah stared at the pavement. "What happened just now?"

"I needed you to react so you would release the energy. You can't keep it inside you. God, Leah, I swear. You can't skim over anything in this book. You have to read all of it. There is a huge difference between Shamans and Banishers, the main one being that Banishers must release this energy or risk becoming addicted. It's Yin and Yang, Shamans and Banishers. This is exactly why you needed the talisman, to draw the soul out of you."

"I got that. I read the book. But a lot of shit has happened. Being captured, talking with the FBI, doing interviews, prom ... and you've had the book most of the time. I only read it once before we were kidnapped, and since then, I've only cherry-picked things to look at. Give me a little slack."

"You're the one who wanted me to read it! And you just can't help but mess with magic you don't fully understand. You're going to get hurt. Look, the book is all yours. Read it, study it, give yourself a fighting chance."

"Message received, loud and clear," Leah mocked.

Barb shook her head. "I can't believe I'm your friend." She stepped closer and offered her hand.

Leah took it, pulling herself up to a seated position.

"So, let's hear it," Barb said. "Tell me what happened at the house."

Leah stared up at the clouds. When she returned her gaze, she said, "I invited the soul to me, the same way I did with Paul, but..." She paused. Her face went dark, and her eyes glazed over. Pulling her knees to her chest, she wrapped her trembling arms around her legs and stared at the ground. When Leah resumed talking, her voice was shaky and coarse. "The lady attacked me." Leah's nostrils

flared. "She…" Leah stammered for the words. "She … entered my consciousness like a rabid beast—fast and fierce. Her fingers were blades of shard
glass, her voice was demonic, and her eyes…" Balling a hand into a fist, she
placed it over her mouth. "They were pitch-black and seemed to swallow me
whole. The attack was so sudden, so vicious, so mad in every meaning of
the word that I had no time to think, only react." Leah stared at nothing.
Her breathing labored, and her muscles tensed. She sat, stiff as a board. "She
wanted me dead. She was going to kill me. If it weren't for Bellevue, …"

"Bellevue? I don't understand."

Leah nodded and inhaled. "When I was interacting with Bellevue, It kept
pushing me with gusts of wind. So, when this soul came at me, I pushed her
back the same way. But…" Leah's forehead wrinkled as she continued, "The
woman kept coming. Barb, I was terrified, so I pushed her into the doorway
where she transcended. Then … it was just unbelievable. When she went
through that door…" Leah looked up, her face relaxed, and a wide brilliant
smile erupted. "Wow! Power and strength. It felt like the ghost had reached
into my body with jumper cables and attached them to my bones."

"When did you disengage? How did you avoid going through the door?"

"I'm not sure. I pushed her and scrambled away. But this power is real.
Shit, I blasted you."

"Yes, you did. But don't dwell on that memory. Let it pass. I don't want
you to get addicted to that feeling."

"Understood."

"You should have remained open, calm, and clear-minded so she wouldn't
have been able to attack you."

Leah nodded. "I set the scene and thought I could handle her, but her rage
was so intense that, honestly, I'm feeling lucky to be alive right now."

"So, maybe you should stop. Let's give the book back to my grandma."

"I'm not ready to give up. I just need to be more careful. Take my time."

"You're telling me. At least stop inviting souls to you until you've reread
the whole book, especially the chapter on how to make a talisman. And all
of the warnings."

"Right." Standing, Leah added, "I love you, Barb."

Barb stared past Leah, seeing an older man with a receding hairline sitting in a black SUV, staring at them. "I love you, too," she said. "Come on, let's go. I'm driving."

When they got back into the car, Leah tilted her seat back to rest. Barb checked her mirrors, making sure the SUV wasn't following.

Leah's phone rang and she answered. "Hey, Uncle Tim." She then proceeded to tell him they were in Diamond Creek and were fine. When she finished talking, Leah said, "Shit."

"What was that about?"

"My uncle. He felt my panic. So did Officer Choi and my dad. They're worried about me and called the school."

"I felt that panic, too," Barb said. "It scared me."

Leah's phone rang again. "My dad," she huffed.

Barb shook her head. "You didn't tell your dad we were coming here?"

"No."

"Umm, hmm..." Barb murmured, shaking her head.

As she drove, she listened to the conversation. Leah hawed and hummed in dissatisfaction. She played the adult card and told her dad she'd had to come; it was important. When she finished, Leah slumped in her seat. "Drive me home."

Barb chuckled.

"Oh, stop," Leah whined.

Her smile grew. All Barb could do was shake her head. "What is you dad going to do to you?"

"I don't know," Leah responded. "Ground me? I'm really tired, though. I need to sleep. Is that okay?"

"Sure. Go ahead."

Min Yun watched Leah and Barb drive away. "Who the hell was that crazy bitch?"

"They were abducted and only recently escaped," Jae said.

"She needs to be committed."

"What did she say to you? What happened?"

"I don't know."

Judy came outside.

"You don't know? What do you mean—you don't know? What was that?"

"She was just talking shit, Dad."

"How do you know her?"

"I don't! I've never seen her before."

"Su-Bin? Breakfast tea? She was awfully close to you, touching you."

Judy rubbed Jae's back. Her face was full of concern, and Min was sure she wanted to know what the two of them were saying. If Judy could speak Korean, she would probably have slapped Jae for speaking so rudely. Instead, she purred, "Hey, forget about it. Let's go eat."

Jae's eyes stayed on Min. "Well?" he asked.

"I don't know," Min repeated.

"Come on," Judy urged.

As they ate, Judy talked about her art, and Jae talked about the university. After breakfast, they went through the photo albums and Judy recounted her trips to visit Brandon.

Min took special notice of the school names, faces of those with Brandon, and the places they visited—markets, shops, restaurants. And in stalker fashion, he had taken his mom to the house where the pop singer he admired lived. What bothered Min even more were the photos of Brandon with his arms wrapped around young girls. It was disturbing.

"He's lived a fantastic life," Min said, trying not to throw up.

"Let me give you his social media info. You two should connect when you get back to Seoul."

"I'd love that. Thanks," Min replied, happy for the information. Maybe he could learn something from digging into it. "I'm feeling a bit tired. I'm going to take a nap." But what he really did was book his flight to Mexico.

Standing in front of Su-Bin's door, Brandon hesitated to knock. He had a strong feeling Jong-In was not going to show. The thought of being alone with her thrilled him more than he wanted to admit ... and worried him for the same reason. He raised his hand but couldn't bring himself to knock. With a sigh, he let his hand fall and stepped back, only to stop and returned to his original spot.

He reminded himself to be open, to live in the moment without expectations. They were both adults. They were both professionals. He was here to teach and would keep his focus on that fact. Straightening, he set his resolve and knocked.

Su-Bin answered, still wearing her business attire—black dress pants and a white blouse. She rested her head against the edge of the open door, her tender gaze meeting his.

Brandon's nerves flickered. He dipped his head in a small bow and offered a polite smile. "Good evening."

The corner of her lips curved into an endearing smile. "Come in," she crooned.

Brandon edged forward, and Su-Bin moved aside, opening the door wider. The smell of pasta filled the house. "You cooked Italian?" he asked.

"I made lasagna," Su-Bin said. "It's my third time trying it. I have my own recipe, so I hope you like it. I don't use too much cheese, and I add lots of vegetables."

"Sounds delicious."

Su-Bin went into the kitchen as Brandon hung his jacket on the coat stand.

"Is Jong-In here yet?" he asked.

"He couldn't make it. His office had a company dinner he needed to attend." Stepping back into the living room, Su-Bin added, "Our dinner's in the oven, and the timer's set. Shall we read?" She motioned for Brandon to join her on the sofa.

"You and Jong-In seem close," Brandon remarked, taking a seat.

"We are. He's been my best friend since middle school."

"How did you meet?"

Su-Bin chuckled. "Funny story, actually. I was on the swim team, and he was one of the managers. My best friend had this huge crush on him but was too shy to talk to him—so I volunteered."

"You asked him out for your friend?" Brandon asked.

"Pretty much. I said, 'My friend likes you. She wants to go out with you.'" Su-Bin paused, still smiling. "Jong-In looked back at me and said, 'But I like you.'"

"What did you say to that?"

"What could I say? My best friend liked him. I couldn't very well say, 'Really? Let's date.'"

Brandon smiled. "No, I guess not."

"But I did invite him to eat lunch with us. He and my friend ended up dating."

"And?"

"Middle school romance. They were together for a while. I ended up dating his best friend. Jong-In and I have stayed friends ever since."

"That's ... actually kind of sweet."

Su-Bin handed Brandon the book they were going to read from tonight: *20 of the Best and Worst Legislations Ever Written.*

Taking the book, Brandon explained, "We're going to read one of the worst legislations written first, then discuss the choice of language, the way it was structured, what it was supposed to accomplish, and what it did accomplish. Then I want you to guess what kind of lawsuits challenged the legislation and what loopholes it had. Finally, we'll read the author's thoughts. Next, we'll do the same with one of the best legislations ever written and compare."

He opened the book and turned to see Su-Bin staring at his hair. She reached up and touched his curls with the same dreamy eyes he had seen at their first meeting.

"They're magnificent," she whispered before pulling her hand away. "Sorry." Flashing a quick smile, she added, "Okay, I'm ready."

Brandon didn't respond. He was mesmerized by the way her fingers had tangled in his curls. Shivers ran down his spine, and he found himself trembling. He lifted his hand, and it hovered near her forehead. Her lips parted. Her eyes locked on his. The suspended pause bristled with friction. His voice came out thin. "I ... should get a turn to touch you," he quavered. The proposal hung in the air as he slowly reached over, his heart hammering and his mind racing. *What am I doing?*

Just going with it, he replied to himself as his finger rested on her forehead. Admiring her clear, smooth skin, he brushed his finger along her hair line. Su-Bin drew in a sharp, passionate breath. Brandon rounded the delicate curve of her ear, and he watched her close her eyes, a voiceless moan shaping her lips. He withdrew his hand, saying, "Okay, let's begin."

Her eyes shot open, and she gasped, "Wait!" A pause. Brandon held his breath. Vibrations stirred the silence. Su-Bin moistened her lips. "I get another turn," she whispered. The decree warmed his body. Su-Bin chortled, "You touched me longer than I touched you."

Blushing, Brandon agreed, "All right. It's your turn."

Su-Bin placed her thumb on his bottom lip and gently slid it across to the corner of his mouth. He pressed his tongue against her thumb as it passed, his breath quick and shallow. She moved her hands to his chest, resting them over his heart. Moving them up and out, she felt his pecs, his shoulders, and his upper arms, squeezing his muscles. Using her two index fingers, she ran her hand back to his shoulders and down his chest to his bellybutton. Brandon gasped, letting out a slow, trembling breath. As they stared into each other's eyes, she urged, "Your turn."

Brandon's entire body was saying he wanted her. His heart was so loud, he knew she could hear it. Placing the back of his hand against her cheek, he looked deep into her eyes, before sliding his knuckles past her ear, down her neck, over her clavicle, and down the center of her chest. There he paused. Turning his hand over, his fingertips caught the edge of her bra. He contemplated touching her breasts. The want was desperate, and from the way she trembled, he knew she shared the yearning. Waves of excitement pounded him. He traced the outer rim, letting his fingertips memorize the shape of her, savoring the anticipation as it coiled tighter. He continued over the center clasp, his finger moving downward until he reached her bellybutton. A shot of adrenaline coursed through his blood as he explored the delicate dip, the gentle rise and fall around her pearl before touching the top of her pants. There he rested his finger. She sucked in her belly, giving him space to move his hand under and in. Slipping in, he felt the lining of her panties.

The delicate lace stirred him. She licked her lips. He unbuttoned her pants, and flattened his hands, feeling her stomach. His thumbs traced the line of her underwear as he moved his hands to her sides. She lifted her hips, giving him permission to remove her pants. His fingers wrapped around the belt loops, but he resisted. Sliding his hand over her hips, he moved his thumbs to the soft dip of her pelvis and squeezed before resting his hands on her thighs. There, he paused.

"Your turn," Brandon whispered.

Leaning forward, Su-Bin laid her head against his chest, her ear just below his shoulder. Her arms wrapped around him, feeling the muscles on his back. Moving her hands over the top of his shoulders, she ran them onto his chest and pushed him back against the couch. She lifted his shirt and placed her palms on his belly. He flexed. Her fingers moved across the top of his pants, electrifying his skin. She undid his belt and pulled it off. Slipping her fingers underneath his pant line, she felt the lining of his underpants. Her fingers brushed against him; he was so hard. Her smile widened, and she pet his little brother before grabbing hold of his pants and pulling him closer.

Sitting up, Brandon put Su-Bin's leg over his own and moved closer. Pressing his cheek to hers, he smelled her hair. His fingers ran up the back of her neck, sliding through her hair. He lifted his chin and pressed his lips against her temple, not quite a kiss. He held her, welcoming the intimate warmth. His passions were reawakening. His hands tilted her head back and he kissed her nose, the top of her cheek, the edge of her upper lip, her lower lip, down to her chin, and finally the top of her neck.

Su-Bin's body pulsed. Her scent was sweet, and her sweat sweeter. She pushed Brandon back down and pulled up his shirt. Her hands gripped his abdomen. She leaned down, her teeth nibbling at his skin, while she moved her hand to his pelvis. She continued nibbling to his chest. Turning her hand, her fingers felt his size. He moaned with pleasure.

Su-Bin stopped abruptly and sat back up. Brandon held his breath, caught off guard. He stared at her, uncertain.

"Shall we read now?" she teased.

A flutter of relief washed over him. Wanting. Needing. Brandon moved to the top position, sending Su-Bin onto her back. He slid his face down between her legs, wiggling his nose up and down, back and forth against the fabric. Brandon opened his mouth and pressed, cupping his lips around her lady. He blew, wanting the warm, moist air to excite her. He massaged the area with his lips and then used his nose and rubbed again.

Su-Bin moaned. Wrapping her legs around his head, she squeezed and pressed his face snug against her. Brandon's hands went under her shirt, feeling her stomach, running them up over her bra, his fingers slipping underneath, tickling her nipples.

Knock, knock, came a call from the front door.

They both jumped and rolled upright.

Buttoning, tucking, and straightening, they took long breaths to steady themselves. Su-Bin ran her fingers through her hair, as Brandon put his belt back on. They looked each other up and down, before giving an approving nod.

He opened a notebook and set a pen on the paper, as though they'd been working. She approached the door.

Ding, went the timer for the lasagna.

Su-Bin called out in Korean, "Yes—who is it?"

"It's me, Jong-In."

She opened the door and smiled. "I thought you had to attend the company dinner."

"I did. I left early. What did I miss?"

"Nothing. We just started reading. Dinner's just about done. Did you eat?"

"A little bit. It smells great. I'll try whatever you cooked."

"Great, come on in."

Brandon stood and bowed his head slightly. "Hi, Jong-In. Nice to see you again." Looking at Su-Bin, he added, "The timer went off." Then he pulled a small, black piece of lint off his tongue. "Let's eat."

Min Yun sat in the chair in the guest bedroom, his eyes fixed on the phone in his hands. Across from him, the bed remained neat and tidy, the bright pink carnation comforter undisturbed. His thumbs tapped the screen, entering his credit card information and finalizing his purchase for tickets to Oaxaca, Bangkok, Tokyo, and Seoul.

He missed Su-Bin and wondered what she was doing. How was she handling Shitbag's advances? He clenched his fists, hoping she hadn't fallen for him.

Judy had said that Brandon went to Mexico because of some love obsession over a pop singer. That statement rang loud and clear in Min's mind. He was sure he'd find something at his former schools that would shed light on Brandon's true self—Shitbag.

Reviewing his notes, Min ran through the things he needed to do before leaving for the airport: book a room, rent a car, find an interpreter, make an appointment to see the principal at Instituto Cumbres Oaxaca. Mr. Shitbag had skeletons, and when Min found them, he'd show Su-Bin all the ways in which this guy was evil, including his arrest. Then he'd win her back.

Leah drifted back to consciousness as the car rolled to a stop and the engine died.

"Wake up," Barb said. "You're home."

Placing her hands on the sides of her head, she groaned before opening her eyes. Yawning and stretching, she sat up and readjusted the car seat. "What time is it?"

"Just past noon. How do you feel?"

The morning activities rushed back—Judy's house, Min Yun, the ghost, and dark energy. "Lucky to be alive," she responded. Her bones vibrated as if tiny orchestras were playing inside them. She felt her heart beating smooth and steady, a well-oiled machine ready and waiting to work. Her mind was foggy but clearing quickly. "Surprisingly, I feel strong," she added.

"That's good. Because look." Barb pointed at the car parked in front of them.

"Your grandma's here?" Leah asked.

"She's not the only one," Barb said, pointing across the street.

Leah leaned forward, peering through the window to see Officer Choi's police cruiser and Nong's Lexus.

"I'm sorry," Barb said. "But I can't go in with you. Lyla and I are working on a chemistry project that's due next week. It's basically our final exam."

"Lyla? That's the new girl you've been hanging with, right? Does she know about connecting and energy manipulation?"

"God, no," Barb retorted. "I need at least one person in my life that's normal."

Leah nodded. "Good." She sat tall, stretched her face muscles to wake up, and smoothed out her shirt. She glanced one last time at the cars, knowing she was in for a serious meeting.

"This isn't a job interview," Barb said.

"It's important I address them with clarity and respect."

Barb gave a quick head shake. "Something's different about you. Making that soul transcend has changed you."

Raising her brows, Leah responded, "When we touch the essence of another being, it's impossible not to be transformed. We gain a deeper understanding of life, and in that understanding, we find a part of ourselves we never knew existed."

Barb laughed. "Where did that come from?"

Leah rubbed her forehead. "I don't know." She took a breath and said, "I was trying to say that we are all constantly changing and with new experiences come new perspectives."

"Yeah, something's not right," Barb said. "Good luck in there. I'm going to school. Call me later."

"I will." Stepping out of the car, Leah looked back. "Thank you for coming with me. Your assistance was invaluable."

"Invaluable?" Barb said with wide eyes. "In other words: what would you do without me? I'll see you later."

Leah closed the car door and watched Barb drive away. Her mind wasn't only clear, it was fresh. A new awareness was taking root, one that was sharper. Turning toward the house, she took a confident step toward the front door.

The adults quieted as Leah entered the room. Choi's face went dark with recognition, Jared showed concern, Nong turned from delight to surprise, and Grandma Carol wore a subtle scowl. "Good afternoon, everyone," Leah said with a calm confidence.

"Leah—is that you?" Nong blurted. "Have you grown since I've seen you last? You look amazing."

"You do look all grown up," Carol agreed.

Leah blushed. "Thank you." Addressing Nong, she asked, "How is everything progressing with the firm?"

"Well. Thanks." Nong glanced at the others and then dipped her head as if to apologize, allowing Jared to speak.

"Leah, we felt something today. A panic. Officer Choi told us that you were deathly afraid of something. He suspects it has something to do with spiritual energy. The same kind that allowed you to free us and that connects Nong and me. He says you have been exploring and experimenting with this energy. Can you tell us about that?"

Offering a polite smile, Leah said, "Thank you for being concerned for my well-being, but I can assure you that I am quite fine. The incident to which you are referring was a misunderstanding between Judy Spencer's soon-to-be son-in-law and myself. As for the energy, Officer Choi is correct. I have been learning to control it."

A puzzled look crossed Jared's face. "Leah, what's going on with you right now? You're acting weird."

The power did seem to have split her personality—as though the old Leah, the child, was no longer the default. Reverting to her teenage persona, Leah said, "Come on, Dad. I'm not acting weird. I'm simply choosing to articulate. I'm still me." In the next breath, she switched again, calmly adding, "If you wish, I can continue to carry on in such a manner, allowing my emotions to dictate what I say; however, that doesn't seem prudent in this situation. You are worried about me, and I must show you that I am in control."

"I see." Jared looked to Carol.

"Leah, I don't think I have to remind you what happened to my daughter, to Barb and Dan's father. The power to communicate with spectral entities is dangerous. I cannot express how worried—and, frankly, disappointed and betrayed—I am to learn you've been hiding this from us." She paused to clear her throat. "Your decision to recklessly meddle with powers you don't understand risks not only your own life, but condemns us all to repeat the same heart-wrenching tragedies."

Leah gave a weak nod. "I know, Carol. I understand why you're worried. Thank you. I love you too. But I'm *not* ignoring your pain. I'm embracing it—to ensure you never feel that way again."

Carol fixed her eyes on Leah as if measuring her words.

"I have a firm grasp on this power," Leah continued. "And I have chosen to pursue this path because I refuse to let what happened to your daughter happen to Barb, Dan, or any of us. I am ensuring our tragedies are never repeated."

Carol turned to Officer Choi. "Is she right? Does she have control of her powers?"

Choi stood, stepped to Leah, and took both her hands.

Leah stared him in the eyes, built her spiritual energy, and connected. She felt him reconnect with her.

"What happened today, Leah?" Choi whispered.

Leah squeezed his hands, and the bond between them grew stronger. It felt like vines reaching out and wrapping their tiny fingers around Choi's being. She could sense his concern for her. She felt his longing to be with his wife, and the empty hole in his heart where his son lived. "Where is your family?" Leah asked.

"With my mother in Korea."

Leah traveled the vines of their connection and touched Choi's mind. She glimpsed the memory of his wife kissing him before going through the security gate at the airport. She saw Jasmine's worried expression as she said, "You're scaring me." She heard Yoona speaking to him about a disturbance that had caused him to send his family away.

"Are you," Choi mumbled, *in my mind?*

What is this disturbance? Leah did not speak these words, but rather gave them to Choi while in his mind. *What's going to happen?*

Choi's mouth dropped open.

Leah wanted to search for this disturbance, but Choi pushed her out of his memories and built walls. *Are we in danger?* she asked. The act of placing her words into Choi's mind was as easy as running her finger along the spine of a book.

Choi dropped Leah's hands, and her head spun. She exhaled with a gasp and stumbled backward, feeling disoriented. The vertigo strained the base of her neck, threatening to drop her to her knees.

Choi touched her hand, and everything came back. "Sorry," he said.

Stretching the muscles in her face, she said aloud, "Not your fault."

"Look at me, Leah," Choi directed. "I need you to tell me the truth. Who's training you?"

The question had made Leah nervous before. But now a clear and precise answer came to her. "Why are you so certain I'm being trained?" she asked. "You assume this only because you lack the ability to do what I have just demonstrated. Do you acknowledge that I have been through a unique set of experiences, different in scope from any you have had? And that these experiences could have given me the tools and understanding I needed to learn on my own?"

"I do," Choi said. "But I trained for three years, Leah. You have been playing with this for ... two, three weeks?"

"Your point being that if I were being trained, I could never have progressed to this level. I agree. Therefore, you have just proven yourself wrong. I, in fact, am not being trained."

"It's not possible," Choi insisted.

"Yet, here I am."

Choi turned to Jared and shrugged as he sat down.

Carol cleared her throat, getting Choi's attention. "She has a training manual. I bought it years ago. I told her to give it to the FBI"—Carol glared at Leah— "but she obviously didn't listen."

A lump formed in Leah's throat. Her attempts to keep the book a secret from Choi, her dad, everyone had failed. Would Choi confiscate it now?

Nong interjected, "I think what we want to know is, are you being safe? Are you making good decisions? You've been playing and experimenting with this energy behind our backs, in secret, against Officer Choi's warnings and Carol's permission. We're feeling left out, betrayed, and hurt, because we trusted you to be forthcoming and honest with the things you are doing and the people you are spending time with."

Leah tried to mollify them. "I understand your position and point of view. I apologize for the secrecy. However, you must understand that I didn't fully know what was happening to me, so by not sharing, I was being considerate. My father has been focusing on getting his life back together. Searching for office space and putting together a business plan takes time and energy. I didn't want to burden or distract him. I understand now that this may not have been the wisest choice. But you all know that I have always been strong-willed and fiercely independent."

"But you have also been open and honest," Jared pointed out.

The room fell silent.

Nong moved next to Leah and put her arm around her. "This is a really exciting time. You are learning new skills and creating new relationships. It might be scary or unknown, so we want you to trust us—trust that we won't try to control you or the situation, but rather help you succeed in the safest way possible, with as much guidance as you need. We just ask that you be more transparent about who you are spending your time with and the things you are doing, learning, and exploring—so that we can be a part of it, too."

"Okay."

"So, tell us. Is Carol correct? Are you learning from a manual? And what made you want to learn more about this power?"

All eyes fell on Leah.

"I am learning from the manual. I started reading it after Dad went missing. I needed to try and save him. And after Bellevue took us, I was able to save us because of what I knew. My endeavor to learn more about Shamanism is rooted in the need to keep us safe. To ensure we are never hurt again. My camping trip intensified the energy's strength and triggered my ability to manipulate it."

Jared dipped his chin in disbelief. "That's why you went camping. You lied to me."

"I didn't lie," Leah said. "I connected to the energies of the Earth as I said I would."

Nong shot Jared a firm glare, then turned to Leah. "Thank you for sharing."

Surveying the room, Leah saw that her audience was at a loss of words. "If you'll excuse me, I have had an eventful morning. I need to rest." She stood and walked toward her bedroom.

"Leah," Officer Choi called.

Turning, she said, "Yes?"

"I will inform my aunt of your abilities and of the manual. You can expect a call from her."

"Your aunt, the Shaman?"

"She is a Shaman, yes. But more than that, she is the one who upholds the standards and rules that govern our abilities. She authored the book you're studying."

A knot of dread formed in Leah's stomach. Choi's aunt was the enforcer of the rules? And had written the "rare and guarded book" Dan's grandmother had found and purchased?

"Will she make me surrender it?" Leah asked.

"I don't know. Maybe."

"I will have you talk with my father about that first," Leah said. "He and I can discuss it further at dinner." She turned and headed down the hall to her bedroom. When she reached the door, she rested her hand on the handle and paused, listening to their conversation.

"Your daughter is incredibly powerful," Choi said. "She's able to do things only masters have attained after decades of living and training at temple."

"Then she was right," Carol said. "She has control. We should let her continue learning."

"No," her father stated.

Nong interjected. "Now, hold on a minute. I think we need to step back a second and look at the bigger picture."

Leah slipped into her room and closed the door.

What is happening to me?

Had she really gone inside Choi's mind? Had she really touched his thoughts, his memories, and placed her consciousness there? What had absorbing that dark energy done to her? And what if Barb hadn't made her drain it?

She dropped onto her bed and looked around her room, noticing a glow emanating off the window. She stared at it, wondering what it was. Standing, she peered closer. The glow was pure energy coming from the heat of the sun. She reached out to touch it. Tangible power coiled around her fingers. She jerked back and stared at her hands, struggling to understand how this glowing force could be pliant. Dancing energy along the carpet fibers, drew her attention. She blinked in disbelief. It shimmered in her blanket. The static electricity was everywhere, even in the air. A buzz came from the wall. She heard the electricity flowing through the wires. Her phone was warm. Holding it, Leah's hand tingled. The battery was at 80 percent.

She suddenly had an urge to siphon the energy. Moving the muscles in her hand, she began taking the energy from her phone without understanding how. It felt like trying to suck a thick milkshake through a narrow straw. The battery went to 72 percent and then to 65. Setting the phone down, she slowly brought her fingertips together. Before they touched, tiny sparks arced between them.

Leah flicked her fingers, shaking away the last bits of light. Covering her face, she tried to control her breathing. *What is happening to me?*

She picked up her phone, pressed Barb's number, and texted: "Please call. I'm scared."

When it rang, her voice trembled, "Something's wrong!"

"Whoa. Calm down. What's going on?"

"I'm seeing and experiencing things I don't understand."

"You took a dose of dark energy, and it affected you both mentally and physically," Barb said. "You've got a nasty hangover, and I'm sure this one comes with a lot of consequences."

"What should I do?"

"Read the book cover to cover and go through the exercises step by step."

"Good idea. I'm going to start right now."

"You're going to be okay," Barb said reassuringly.

Leah hung up and opened the book. She read with renewed vigor and concentration, devouring the words with a newfound sense of purpose.

Later that evening, Leah was called to dinner. She slipped into the chair across from her father; the table felt unusually quiet and tense. Leah was unsure what Choi had told her dad or what he would demand of her. She wished Nong was here.

Jared's expression was stern. He cleared his throat, breaking the silence. "Can you say grace, please?" He reached his hand across the table.

She took it and thanked the farmers and workers, their creator, and her dad for preparing the food.

Her father put a spoonful of mashed potatoes on his plate and then on hers, followed by a pork chop and some beans. They ate in silence for several minutes.

After taking a drink of water, her dad finally said, "Leah, there's something important we need to discuss."

Leah met her father's gaze but found it hard to form words. Her thoughts were a jumble of apprehension and determination. She wasn't going to stop learning, even if it meant surrendering the book. Choi's aunt scared her, and she didn't know how to reconcile that.

Jared continued in a gentle voice, "Choi has told me about your abilities. I want you to know that I'm here to listen."

Leah nodded, grateful for her father's reasonable approach. But the silent, cold stare that followed flattened that reassuring thought. Leah refused to look away. She was prepared to fight.

"Do you know about the Circle?" he asked.

Leah knew the name. The book was property of the Circle. She guessed that Yoona might belong to that organization if she enforced the rules that Shamans and Banishers lived by. But she wanted to know what Choi had told her dad. "No," she answered.

"It's a council made up of twenty-three individuals from around the world who monitor and regulate energy manipulators." Her dad paused, studying her reaction.

Leah remained calm, not showing any emotions.

He continued, "What you are learning is a skill meant for a special profession, one that requires you to live your life in a specific, spiritual manner. Are you aware of this?"

Leah shrugged.

Jared's frustration finally showed, and he burst, "How did you get yourself messed up in this?" He leaned forward. "Why are you learning this, Leah? What do you plan to do with it?"

"Am I forbidden to learn?" Leah asked.

Jared exhaled loudly. "No, of course not. But Choi has hammered into me that there are real dangers associated with using this power—not just in their application but in the potential devastation if they're misused. I mean, Jesus, Leah. If the Circle deems that you've used your powers immorally or unethically, they'll annihilate your soul, for Christ's sake." Jared lowered his head and massaged his brow.

Leah reached for her dad's hand. She could see that he was stressed and didn't understand anything. She didn't understand much more and couldn't alleviate his fears with words. Choi had scared him, and he was reeling from their conversation.

Jared took her hand, and Leah connected. Squeezing his fingers, she felt the vines of her energy growing, weaving tendrils into her father's consciousness. As they wrapped and wound around his essence, their link strengthened, and soon Leah found she was inside her father's mind.

Jared shuddered. "What are you doing to me?" His face twisted, and he raised his free hand to his temple.

Leah saw a tangled ball of anxiety, embodied as a pulsating sore, raw and inflamed. With a deft touch, she cooled the feverish worry with a whisper of frost. Her ethereal touch eased the swelling, calming the throbbing ache of stress. Then she retreated and released his hand.

Her father's demeanor transformed immediately. His tense expression eased, and a slight smile crossed his lips. "Well, I'm sure you know what you're doing."

Leah gave a reassuring smile. "I do."

"Choi wants to set a time for you to meet his aunt. Do you have his number? Can you arrange that?"

"I can," she replied.

"Great. So, we've started moving into the building." As Jared changed the subject to his new enterprise, Leah tried to justify what she had just done. She was tired. Her dad was unnecessarily worried. She didn't want to answer his questions or explain herself. But although Leah knew she should feel like she had done something wrong, that she should feel bad about using her power without informing him or asking permission, she didn't. Looking at her dad, normal and happy, she felt vindicated.

Mr. Anderson sat at his desk, reading an email from Dr. Smith. She wanted the evidence he had collected and a time frame for when she should expect Leah to arrive. Compiling the audio recordings, photos, videos, and detailed notes into a zip file, Mr. Anderson emailed Dr. Smith, then opened his phone and called her.

Dr. Smith answered, "Go ahead."

"I've emailed you the evidence."

"Good," she replied. "I'll go through what you sent me and put together a proposal for Bill. I need you to get to Washington and start connecting with members of Congress."

"I don't think we should go to Bill," Mr. Anderson responded. "Let Leah do that for us. You'll understand why I say this after listening to the audio files."

"You're kidding, right?"

"I'll confront her directly. Our goals will resonate with her. I'll make it clear that her grandfather has no idea we're approaching her and that she'll have to convince him she's a valuable asset. Bill will be at her graduation, so she'll have the opportunity to discuss it with him."

There was a moment of silence. "It's risky."

"Do you doubt my salesmanship and manipulation abilities?"

"I doubt hers," Dr. Smith replied. "Bill has been bragging about her attending Stanford in the fall."

Mr. Anderson stepped to the window and looked across to Leah's house. "She's extremely headstrong. Let's use that to our advantage."

"Can we wait until graduation? Yoona is looking for this girl."

"The Circle already knows about her but haven't made a move yet. We have time."

"All right, I'll trust you on this, but I'm not comfortable with it."

"You will be. Look through the file. Her powers are raw—instinctive. She's been training from a manual. I traveled her life path through the stream to see how far through the book she's reached, but I couldn't find her reading from it. She's hidden it. Not because she knows how, but because she has that kind of natural talent. She'll convince Bill on her own. You don't have to worry."

"Very well. Call again after you meet with her."

Mr. Anderson put the phone in his pocket and smiled. This was the part he loved—exposing vulnerabilities and appealing to desires. He'd have Leah singing psalms and signing in blood.

After washing the dishes, Leah retired to her room and fell fast asleep. She woke later that night with a start. Her Uncle Tim was having a nightmare. She could feel the ache in the pit of his stomach and the racing of his heart. Rubbing her temples, she wondered if this was going to be her new reality—connections disturbing her peace at all hours. Leah was so sleepy. Her head was heavy, and her eyes didn't want to open. She bundled those feelings into a nice package and sent them to her uncle through their connection. A minute later, he passed out of her consciousness, and she fell back asleep.

In the morning, Uncle Tim pulled up to Leah's house. She got into Miley, buckled her seatbelt, and turned down the radio. He drove toward the school, not saying anything, his eyes fixed on the road in a hard stare.

"Were you able to fall back to sleep last night?" Leah asked. "You had a pretty bad nightmare."

Uncle Tim glanced over with a puzzled scowl. "How did you know about that?"

"The same way you knew something happened to me yesterday."

"You made me sleepy?"

"I did."

"Thanks for that. I crashed right away."

They sat quietly again as the radio announcer explained that the Senate was expected to vote in the coming days on a resolution to join the United Federation of States. If it passed, the proposal would move to the House, where it was expected to face significant opposition. General Cros met with members of Congress to show his support for the resolution. The commentator then mentioned that downtown traffic was congested due to anti-United Nations and anti-war protests. He mentioned that similar protests were happening all across the country. Another skirmish in the South China Sea had taken place, and war with China seemed imminent.

Leah glanced at her uncle. "Are you still going to organize protests for the return of the Sukiya's sacred land?"

"Yes? Maybe. The problem is that the world is going to shit, really fast."

"You don't think a single-world government would work?"

"I don't know, but there's no way thirty-eight states will support it. We'll never give up our own freedom."

"I don't think we'd be giving up anything by becoming global citizens."

Tim's face tightened. He shifted in his seat, resting his forearm on the steering wheel, leaning away from Leah. "Don't you?" he said with an edge of sarcasm.

Resting her head against the back of her seat, Leah twirled her hair. "What's wrong?"

Tim chortled, then hesitated before speaking. "Why am I driving you to school if you're just going to skip? Driving off with Barb yesterday, to who knows where, without telling anyone, and on top of that, leaving the tracking device at school... That was incredibly stupid."

"Are you looking for an explanation or did you just need to vent?"

"I don't need an explanation. I need to be kept in the loop. I'm here to keep you safe. And I'm feeling pretty damn unappreciated right now."

"I'm sorry. That certainly wasn't my intent. Is that all that's bothering you?"

"Oh, goodness, no. I've got lots on my mind. Which reminds me. Your grandpa Bill will be at your graduation. If I were to organize a protest, I'd do it there with two major celebrities. Would you be willing to stage a protest during graduation? With you leading, it'll get lots of attention and press coverage."

"Wouldn't it take away from the ceremony?" Leah asked.

"I think it'll add to the ceremony—young activists getting involved before they even leave high school. It's in the spirit of graduation. Besides, protests are a dime a dozen these days, so I feel like we need a special angle for it to get attention."

"What did you have in mind?"

"I don't know," Tim said. "I'll introduce you to Roy. He's the mastermind." Pulling up to the school, Tim gave Leah a thoughtful glance. "It's the only way to get the attention we need."

"I'll think about it. Let me talk to Barb, Becky, and Cindy. Maybe Eric would help, too." Leah got out of the truck. "Don't worry. I'm not going anywhere today. I'll see you here after school."

First period was physical education, but today Leah had an appointment with her counselor. She went into the office and sat on the chair in front of her desk, waiting.

The door opened behind her, and fingers touched the back of her neck. Leah jerked and glared at the person who had violated her. An older man in a black suit with a receding hairline stared her in the eyes. The creepy guy! He smirked and connected. Leah quickly formed her own connection.

"Wow. A nice, strong connection," he said. The way he lingered on the words made her skin crawl. "I'm impressed."

Leah could feel him wandering through her mind, the way she had been in Choi's and her dad's, sifting through thoughts and memories. She explored his mind in return, searching for information, for anything to tell her who this asshole was.

"Who is Lip? Is that you?" she demanded.

Walls sprang up, separating his mind from hers. Leah tried to mimic what he had just done, but her barrier was more like chicken wire. Still, it kept him from rummaging through her mind.

Rounding the desk to face her, he said, "So much power, yet so little control." Then he spoke directly into her mind. *Leah Davenport. My name is Mr. Anderson. I have been watching you for some time. You are a magnificent individual.*

Fear gripped Leah's spine. *What do you want?* she responded in kind.

I want to train you. To offer you a position in your grandfather's company, Extended Life. To give you the opportunity to help people. Mr. Anderson handed her his card.

Leah's apprehension eased a little as she formed the thought, *Train me to do what?*

For starters, how to disconnect. You would like to know how, wouldn't you?

A smirk crossed Leah's lips. Bringing the lockdown alarm to the forefront of her mind, she blasted the relentless, ear-piercing siren as loud as she could.

Mr. Anderson's reaction was perfect. "Ahh!" he cried out, placing his hand to his ear. Using his voice, he spoke, "Not bad. But not allowing an individual to connect in the first place would be easier."

"But not as fun," she retorted with a sly grin. Leah turned his card over, studying the printed name and title. "Special Initiatives Director." A small chuckle escaped her. "What is it you initiate exactly? Telepathic communications?"

A hint of a grin surfaced but never fully formed.

She tucked the card into her pocket and asked, "Did my grandfather send you?"

"Not exactly."

Why would her grandfather not know he was recruiting her?

"Leah, Extended Life recruits individuals with special talents like yours. The company works with the U.S. government and magnates of influence. We help soldiers, politicians, scientists, doctors, men and women with extraordinary minds by prolonging their life."

This was probably the shadiest explanation for a company she'd ever heard. "I don't see how I fit into this narrative."

"We live in turbulent times. War is engulfing the planet, and the Chief Stratagist of Extended Life wants to change that. She is the one behind the push to unite the world under the United Nations banner, to create a single-world government. She envisions the extinction of war and hunger, and an eternity of peace and prosperity, one in which all peoples are free to express themselves. Extended Life plays a crucial role in this push, and we need you to join us. With your abilities to touch minds and communicate with souls, your help is vital to the success of this mission."

Leah wasn't sure how to internalize this information. Was he asking her to touch minds to help build a utopian society? Barb would have a few things to say to this guy. A pit formed in her gut. Barb would have something to say to Leah, if she knew what she had done to her dad. Barb's words, *Stop messing with people's minds,* scolded her.

"We'll fly you to New York after graduation and begin your training," Mr. Anderson explained. "The position comes with a house, a car, and a starting salary of seven hundred thousand dollars."

Leah's eyes flicked up, just a fraction. Her surprise quickly smoothed over, though. He was offering her a lot, but money didn't impress her. She did wonder what, exactly, she was expected to do in return.

Mr. Anderson continued, "Your familiarity with cultures, your ability to handle the press, and your desire to help others make you invaluable to us."

That was *her* word, but it meant something different coming from him.

Mr. Anderson waved an arm, and a blue folder with the Extended Life logo floated off the table and drifted into her hands. "I will personally oversee your training until your abilities surpass my own, at which point, my mentor will take over. Once your skills have been developed, you will understand the true meaning of control."

"Who is your mentor?"

"You'll meet her in New York."

Leah opened the folder. It was full of corporate literature—promotional materials, advertisements, company goals and values, and a history of its development. Flipping through the pages, she skimmed over phrases like nanotechnology, enhanced immune systems, smart blood, A.I.-supported implants and prosthetics, psychedelic therapies, and bioengineered creams and injections to slow aging. She was searching for the director's name and a photo but couldn't find either. "Shouldn't the director be the face of the company?"

"At this point in time, we're keeping a low profile until we can solidify more support for the union of our planet. As you can imagine, there are powerful individuals who rather enjoy the perks the current state of affairs offer."

A brief thought flashed in her mind. *Does that include my grandfather?* She closed the folder and stared at the name: Extended Life. Leah knew that name. Her father had been the architect who designed all of their buildings. "Why should I work for a company that fired my father?"

"I was unaware of that. But believe me, if you would like him to work with us again, it's done. He can start the same day you do. The company will move both of you to New York at our expense."

Leah was warming to the idea until she wondered, *Are these my feelings or are they being implanted into me?* "Excuse me one moment." She closed her eyes and searched her mind. Mr. Anderson had left without a trace. She found nothing foreign in her thoughts. Reopening her eyes, she let out a sigh of relief.

"I don't think you realize how strong you are, Leah. What you have achieved in under a month took me five years. And I was assisted by a master. You could very well become the most powerful person on the planet."

Leah's inner voice giggled. This guy was playing it up, but he wasn't the only one who expressed shock and awe at how quickly her abilities had manifested. She placed the folder on the desk. "Why are you making this proposal to me? Why isn't my grandfather talking to me about this? Are you sure he would approve?"

"He's..." Mr. Anderson paused. "The two of you will discuss it at your graduation, I'm sure. We may need you to nudge him a little in our direction."

Leah shook her head, smiling. "I see."

"Think about it. To be in New York with your mom and dad, working in a company that helps people, and being an instrument that achieves world peace. I know that's something you are interested in doing."

Hesitating for a second, Leah scrutinized Mr. Anderson, wondering exactly how much he knew about her. Was he aware that Barb had abilities? That her life here with Dan was special? Leah wanted to test how far Mr. Anderson was willing to go. He clearly wanted her on board—badly. The way he was talking, it was almost desperate. Could she stretch this opportunity to bring Dan and Barb into the fold?

"How about my friends? Would there be positions for them?"

Mr. Anderson smiled. "You hold tremendous leverage, so anything is possible, especially for your friend Barb. She has a wonderful voice. Music and song are powerful tools."

"There's a singing position in the company?" Leah asked sarcastically.

"Oh, you have so much to learn."

Leah tapped the folder on the desk. "Let me talk with my parents."

"I'd be cautious about approaching them just yet. They'll have questions, and the answers aren't exactly simple. The use of energy manipulators isn't something we advertise."

"They know I have abilities."

"I would keep this proposal to yourself for now. We'll contact your father and arrange for a proper meeting with him and your mother after you convince your grandfather this is an opportunity that's best for everyone. World peace, Leah, that is our goal. And to achieve it, we need you. What do you say? Will you come to New York and allow me to train you?"

Leah didn't answer. She was contemplating his words. If Yoona made Choi confiscate the manual, then this was her ticket to continue training. And world peace. She'd seen the news about the formation of the Federation, and yes, she definitely wanted to help with that. *Maybe this is my path,* she thought.

"Before I agree, I want to make sure I understand you correctly. You want me," she pointed to herself, "to talk my grandfather," she pointed to the window, "into hiring me for you," she pointed to herself again and then to Mr. Anderson. "You're asking me to do your job."

Mr. Anderson almost grinned. "I think you, of all people, understand your grandfather."

She grinned. "You're afraid of him." With a nod, she added, "Okay, I'll do it."

At the Education Center, Olivia's mom, Jane, walked into the art room, admiring the student-made clay figurines that were waiting to be fired on the shelves. The teacher waved. "Hello again. You are Olivia's mom, right?"

Jane tucked the curls of her hair behind her ear as the young man bound toward her, his short blond hair a mess and his infectious smile glowing. His red and blue flannel shirt was stained with all sorts of colored substances—chalk, clay, paint.

"Yes, that's right," Jane said.

"I see where Olivia gets her wild curls," the teacher said with a playful grin. "I'm guessing the fire-red comes from her dad?"

Jane flashed a forced smile.

"I haven't seen Olivia for a few sessions," Mr. Bowlby said. "I hope she's not sick."

"Sick of me, maybe," Jane said, with a forced laugh. "Actually, I was going to pull her out of class, but I decided I should talk with you first."

"I'm glad you did. It's my understanding that Olivia has had a rough time lately. Her artwork was a bit dark at first, and she told me that she recently lost family members."

"My mother passed away two years ago, followed by both her grandfathers last year. My husband's sister drowned while on vacation in Florida a few months back. So, yes, we've gone through a tough patch together."

"I'm sorry to hear that. Are you alright?"

"Getting better. But I am worried about Olivia."

"She's thriving here. Her work has improved. I mean, that drawing of the Bellevue House"—he raised his eyebrows— "I've seen hundreds of student pieces, but that drawing is remarkable. The details she added... It's almost as if she had lived in that house."

"Do you know where she saw the house?" Jane asked.

He scratched his head. "She said her friend had shown it to her."

"Mr. Bowlby, is it?"

He nodded.

"Was it her imaginary friend that showed her?"

Mr. Bowlby shrugged. "That would be a little creepy, wouldn't it?" He laughed.

Jane didn't share his amusement. "I saw the drawing," she voiced. "There's no way Olivia could have drawn that house without seeing it firsthand."

He nodded in contemplation. "The image has been in the news and people have been talking about the building, especially here. She's a gifted artist."

"Aren't you worried about her imaginary friend?"

Straightening, he said, "I see her talking to herself and giggling. If she's doing that with her imaginary friend, then personally, I think it's helping her." He shifted his weight. "If the idea of her having an imaginary friend bothers you, perhaps consider having Olivia see a therapist."

Jane smiled. "She's a kid. You know how resilient they are."

"I'd still think about scheduling a couple sessions with a therapist and get a professional opinion. How does Olivia feel about not coming to class?"

"She hates not coming. She's become extremely difficult to handle—acting out violently, throwing things, and shouting."

Mr. Bowlby scratched his chin. "She was doing really well here. Every time she came to class, she was happy and excited. I'd suggest thinking twice before dropping out." Then he added, "And I'd definitely schedule a session with a therapist."

Jane's whole body slouched, and she shook her head. "So you think I overreacted by pulling her?"

Placing a hand on her shoulder, he said, "Parents make tough calls; it comes with the job." He took a moment, holding Jane's eyes. "But I do think Olivia was doing well here."

Jane took a deep breath. She was feeling so confused. Olivia loved art class, and her teacher was calm and confident. Why had she let that strange man—Tim—scare her? She looked around the room again. The space was bright, peaceful, and full of art. Laughter still clung to the walls. Olivia had flourished here. Whatever Tim had stirred up in her, it wasn't truth. It was fear.

Lifting her head, Jane's eyes remained serious. She could guess the answer to this next question, but she had to ask. "You're aware of the rumors going around about this place, right? The toxic waste, Chinese drugs in the water."

Mr. Bowlby's expression flattened before he turned his head, hiding a smile. "These rumors are complete nonsense."

"I thought so, too. Thank you. I'll have her come back then."

"I think that's the best thing for her."

Plans Are Hatched

Seoul, Mexico, Thailand

Strategies in Motion

Brandon hadn't fully woken up when Matthew banged on his door. He slipped on his shoes and glared at the clock—4:30 in the morning. *Why do we have to meet so early?* He opened the door, and they headed out.

The office building Matthew parked in front of looked unoccupied. Signs covered the doors and windows, and Brandon struggled to read the Korean. Then he saw a sign in English: "For Rent," on one of the doors.

Leading Brandon into an empty room, Matthew instructed him to hang a map of Korea and surrounding countries up on the wall, along with a headshot of a businessman and a cargo ship. As Brandon put up the pictures, Matthew dragged a table over and laid out a large map of the port, placing a red marker next to it. Moments later, the two agents Brandon had gone with to see Yoona entered. He met Kim, the giant, muscular guy, and Jeonmunga, the lean and neat guy, now possessed by an explosives expert. Matthew began the debriefing for the upcoming mission.

"As you know, there have been skirmishes off the coast of Taiwan. China and the U.S. have been battling, and although we aren't officially at war, China could invade Taiwan at any moment. The U.S. will defend it. North Korea is expected to team with China, and someone inside the U.S. is supplying them weapons." Pointing to the photos of the cargo ship and the man Brandon had hung on the wall, Matthew said, "This ship, the *Tamar,* is currently docked in Japan. It's scheduled to arrive here sometime tomorrow evening." Matthew smoothed out the map on the table and circled the wharf berth in red. "As of now, it's unclear when the weapons will be unloaded. Our job is to watch and wait. Yoona needs to catch the individuals on the inside—an American and a Korean.

"In order to succeed, we must be ready at a moment's notice. The unloading time hasn't been scheduled by the docking officials, and Yoona suspects it won't be confirmed until minutes after it's timetabled.

"Our main objective is to capture the American operative. Once we do that, Yoona contacts the Korean officials, who will arrest the other spy."

Matthew pointed to the map of the port. "To accomplish this, Jeonmunga and Yoona will rig small explosive devices in this area tonight to be detonated remotely. When the American arrives, the dock officials will schedule the ship for unloading, at which point Yoona and Jeonmunga confront the ship's officer of the watch. When they do, we set off the explosions. This will shut down the dock and clear the workers from the area.

"Jeonmunga will then interrogate the captain while Yoona takes care of the mercenaries. To prevent the operative from escaping, we'll park trucks at these three points of entry and disable them." He pointed to the areas on the map with the red pen. "This means any escape attempt will be made on foot. Brandon, you will be responsible for covering this area to the north. Kim will cover the area to the west, and I'll take the south."

Matthew paused. "Once the American is in our custody, Jeonmunga will rig the ship with explosives. Some of these weapons are prototypes, and their destruction is of the utmost importance. Therefore, we must clear the area and be far away when the ship detonates. Yoona will handle the logistics. Just understand that this is the plan and do as you're told."

Handing everyone earpieces and a monitor, Matthew continued, "We'll communicate with these. Your monitor is hooked up to the dock security system. Each of you has a view of two strategic camera angles. You are responsible for monitoring those." Pointing to the photo of the American, Matthew reiterated, "When this guy shows up, we only have minutes to act. So, be alert! He is our main target, and we need him alive. Yoona is hopeful she can give us a heads up on his arrival, but don't count on it."

Matthew looked at the guys and lowered his voice. "Yoona is in charge out there. Listen and live. All right, we will meet again tomorrow morning at the hotel near the dock. Make arrangements to be away for at least three days. Any questions?"

Brandon turned and looked at the photo of the American as the others continued to talk. The clean-shaven businessman looked forgettable—some random guy with a wife, two kids, and a dog. Yet he was a trained killer selling arms to North Korea. He would be surrounded by bodyguards and mercenaries who would shoot anyone that looked at him the wrong way. How were they supposed to take him into custody in the middle of a gun battle? It didn't sound possible, even with Yoona's help. Five of them against ... he guesstimated, twenty? Maybe more?

The room fell silent. Brandon returned his attention to the group, seeing Matthew rub his chin. "Yeah, good. It'll work."

Brandon glanced at the two Korean operatives, wondering what he had missed.

The big guy, Kim, patted him on the shoulder and said, "See you tomorrow." He and Joenmunga headed out the door.

"Help me pack this up," Matthew said.

Brandon nodded and took down the posters. He paused before rolling up the photo of the businessman. He imagined facing him with a gun shoved in his face.

On the ride back, Matthew asked, "Have you ever been in a gunfight?"

"No. This will be my first," Brandon responded.

"Ever kill a man?"

"No. And I hope I won't have to."

Matthew reached over and placed his hand on Brandon's chest. "Listen to me. It's going to be intense. These guys don't fuck around. You can't hesitate."

"I won't."

"War is a huge business," Matthew continued. "And this ship is probably carrying a billion dollars' worth of death and destruction. For every one of those dickheads you take down, you are saving a hundred innocent lives. Do you understand?"

Brandon nodded. He knew Matthew was right, but it didn't make it any easier to accept.

Matthew drove the rest of the way in silence. Brandon tried to relax and forget about the growing angst in his chest.

Back in his apartment, Brandon got ready for work. When he arrived at the law firm, he went straight to HR and canceled his classes for the next three days. Then he sat at his desk, wondering what he was going to say to Su-Bin.

Spinning in his chair, he saw her enter the copy room. She gestured for him to join her. Taking a breath, he stood and made his way to the room. As soon as he opened the door, she closed it behind him and locked her lips to his. Her hands ran through his hair, and she pressed her body against his. Then she slipped him a note, pushed him away, and left without a word.

The note said to meet her for lunch tomorrow at the Riverside Hotel. It was signed with a kiss—the paper stained with red lipstick.

What should he tell her? He couldn't give her the truth; Yoona had demanded secrecy. Doubt crept back into his thoughts. Now he would need to lie to a person he cared about. It was another negative notch in his mental log of negatives. What had he gotten himself into?

Returning to his seat, Brandon saw Su-Bin across the hall. She was radiant. She caught him staring and bit the tip of her index finger, an obvious nod to her plans for them tomorrow. Brandon's heart ached with desire and agony.

Later that day, Brandon's phone dinged. He saw Su-Bin had sent him a message.

Su-Bin texted: "I understand you canceled your classes for the next three days. Is that for us? Are you anticipating being lovesick?"

Brandon texted: "I need to take a few personal days. I was going to tell you in person, but you attacked me and then left abruptly. I won't be able to meet you tomorrow. Rain check?"

Su-Bin texted: "May I ask why?"

Brandon texted: "I'll tell you all about it when I return."

Min Yun sat in the passenger seat of the car as his interpreter, a young Mexican woman with short black hair tied into a ponytail, navigated the busy streets of Oaxaca. She was a college student named Nayeli and had barely stopped talking since they'd left the airport.

She glanced his way, her eyes sparkling with enthusiasm. "I'm so happy to be working with you. Whatever you need, just let me know." She smiled, shooting a quick look to the road, and then back to him. "Do you want me to translate only from Spanish to English? Because—if you want—I can add some Korean phrases."

Min didn't respond. His eyes were fixed on the passing streets as he tried to think. He was certain Brandon had done something sick at this school, but he doubted the principal would give up any information about it willingly. An ugly scandal would destroy the school's reputation. Min needed time to think about which pressure points he could push to make the principal talk. He had to be smart, precise, and deliberate. But this girl wouldn't shut the fuck up. How the hell was he supposed to strategize with her rattling on beside him?

Nayeli continued in a chipper voice, "I've taken two semesters of Korean but had to stop—too expensive. The conflicts and skirmishes happening across the country have scared away tourists; not much work for me. But I'm teaching myself through YouTube. If it's okay with you, I'd be happy to mix in some Korean while translating. It'll be great experience for me."

Min sighed again, louder this time to emphasize his irritation. Why had the agency assigned him this incessant blabbermouth?

She kept talking. "When I saw your name, I begged the agency to let me work with you. It's been my dream to go to Korea, so this is a perfect opportunity to learn more. I want to visit the village where *Hometown, Cha, Cha, Cha* was filmed. Are you a fan of Korean dramas? My favorite is *Crash Landing on You*. It has the most beautiful chemistry between the leads. I heard they fell in love while filming and then got married. Isn't that amazing? I think it's just so romantic."

Min's face tightened and he growled, "No. I hate dramas."

Nayeli's eyes widened in surprised. "Really? But they're so good! Have you ever seen *Oh, My Ghost*? That one is so funny! The main character becomes friends with the spirit who possesses her. It's hilarious how the other characters are so confused by her shifting personalities. And it's about cooking, too. I love Korean food. *Kimchi, bibimbap*—all of it!"

"Can you shut up?" Min snapped. "And just speak English when translating."

Nayeli stiffened. She glanced at him one last time before focusing solely on the road. The car was finally quiet. But now it was too quiet, so Min rolled down the window, letting the heat sting his skin.

When they arrived at Instituto Cumbres, Min was struck by the building's bright, modern, and colorful design. Unlike the enclosed school buildings he was used to in Korea, this campus was open, with each classroom accessible from the outside. Shaded walkways connected the airy buildings, and as he made his way to the principal's office alongside the covered play area that sat between the two buildings, he glimpsed at classrooms equipped with smart boards, projectors, and sleek laptops. Students moved between classes in neat uniforms, chatting politely and carrying themselves with an unexpected maturity. It was the kind of school Min would consider sending his future children. But he hadn't come to admire the school. He had come to uncover the truth.

Seeing how upscale the facilities were—and how well-off the student body appeared—Min understood how the school had earned its reputation as one of the best in Oaxaca. And that reputation only confirmed what he suspected: Brandon's misconduct—his promiscuity, his betrayal of trust—had certainly been buried, swept out of sight to protect the school's gleaming image.

And that's exactly what he got. His conversations with the teachers had been infuriatingly mundane. Praises flowed from their lips—dedication, generosity, kindness—all the words Min loathed to hear. The "performance" the staff gave would have certainly negated any formal complaint.

His meeting with the principal was no different. The man handed Min a yearbook and talked at length about Brandon's time at the school. Min flipped through the pages until a photo caught his eye: Brandon, mid-embrace with a female staff member. His arm curled around her back, his fingers slipping beneath her arm like a teenage boy reaching for something he shouldn't be touching. His hips angled in toward her, making the pose feel uncomfortably lecherous.

Min tapped the photo. "Here," he said to the interpreter. "Who is this girl? Do you see what's happening?"

Nayeli leaned in and studied the picture. "It's sweet."

"You don't see anything wrong here?"

"What do you mean?"

Min ignored the question. He read the caption beneath the photo and found her name—Gabriella.

A few minutes later, he had her address. Min thanked the principal and headed for the woman's house.

Nayeli drove through the narrow streets in silence. Min frowned, saying, "I'm sorry for snapping at you earlier, but I'm here on serious business and needed to think."

"It's okay," Nayeli said.

"The man I'm inquiring about, Brandon, is a pathological liar. He's the kind of guy who steals girlfriends just to prove he can." He glanced at Nayeli to gauge her reaction. She didn't flinch.

Min continued, "Brandon wasn't in Oaxaca to teach. He'd come to stalk a famous singer." He paused for a moment, then added, "The photo I showed you—did you notice how his hips were turned, angled just right so he could brush himself against her leg? And his fingers—they were sliding beneath her arm."

Nayeli's eyes flickered from the road to Min. "I didn't notice," she said. "I just saw her smiling."

Min's voice grew firm. "That smile? It was the smile of a girl in love. And I'm guessing he used her, then abandoned her."

The interpreter frowned. "I don't know. The teachers and the principal—they really praised him. They were all very positive."

"That's because they can't risk the school's reputation," Min said. "Brandon was arrested in Lake Valley, Oregon, for his role in the abduction of two teenage girls." Min quickly Googled the incident and pulled up the article. Nayeli looked at it while stopped at the light.

Min saw her finger twitching and kept explaining, "He drifts from country to country, teaching at different schools, never staying in one place for more than a year. Right now, he's in Korea. And I'm afraid whatever he did to those girls in Lake Valley, he'll do again. I need to find evidence of wrongdoing here so I can establish a pattern. Do you see how important this trip is?"

Nayeli tapped insistently against the steering wheel, then she nodded. "Okay, I think I understand."

"Good," Min responded. "This guy, Brandon—he's a slick, charming snake. Gabriella may still have feelings for him, even though he doesn't deserve them. You might have to press her. We want anything that's damaging. If you can get it, I'll give you a sizable tip. Can I count on you?"

She looked at him with newfound determination. "I'll make sure to ask the right questions."

They arrived and stepped into a concrete house tucked between a larger home and an office building alongside a shaded alleyway. White stucco walls, splashed with pink and blue, gave the place a whimsical, almost childlike vibe—one Min couldn't appreciate. Yet, the terracotta-tiled roof and small courtyard filled with potted plants offered a relaxing and cool atmosphere. Inside, the living room was cozy, with wooden furniture and faded yellow cushions. A light breeze drifted in through the open windows, carrying the faint undertones of exhaust from a motorbike idling outside. Min sat down on a worn but comfortable sofa with the interpreter beside him, while Gabriella took a seat across from them, her hands resting nervously in her lap.

"Gabriella, I'm Min Yun, a lawyer from Korea investigating a colleague you once worked with."

The interpreter explained in Spanish.

As the conversation progressed, Gabriella relaxed her shoulders. It wasn't a promising sign. Then her voice carried a note of hopefulness that Min couldn't miss. Her eyes flickered with something—a memory, maybe. The tone of her voice was almost wistful, with a hint of admiration hidden beneath sadness.

Min leaned in slightly, catching the subtle regret in her eyes and embedded in her voice. She spoke with a kind of longing that punched Min in the gut. He knew that whatever she was recalling, it wasn't bad.

Glancing at the interpreter, he asked, "What is she saying?"

"She said Brandon was kind," Nayeli said. "They met not long after he arrived in Oaxaca and started dating right away. But they didn't really understand each other. Besides the language barrier, they had cultural differences. She was glad his Spanish was improving, but she wished she had focused more on her English while he was with her. They had tried to make it work. She had hope."

Lowering his head, Min placed a fist to his forehead. This wasn't what he had come all this way to hear. He tapped his knuckles against his head, trying to think, when a young girl about six years of age waddled into the room.

Min stared at the little one. "Ask if Brandon had ever showed violent tendencies." The tiny person touched Min's leg and smiled. Her black curls reminded him of Brandon. "Who is this child's father?" he asked.

Nayeli nodded, and the two continued their conversation. Min fixed his gaze on the little girl's eyes, trying to read her heritage. If she were Brandon's child—

The mood in the room suddenly shifted. Straightening in his seat, Min observed Gabriella with eagle eyes. Her expression was somber. Her voice trembled. He saw unresolved pain. Opening his phone, Min began recording. The raw emotions needed to be captured so Su-Bin could see for herself what Brandon had done.

"Brandon se fue justo antes de que todo cambiara, justo antes de que nuestras vidas se vinieran abajo. Después del terremoto que destruyó el pueblo, tomó casi un año antes de que todo volviera a la normalidad, pero todavía hay daños irreparables. Nuestras vidas cambiaron de la noche a la mañana."

She finished speaking. Min stared at the interpreter with wide eyes, waiting for her to reveal the truth behind Brandon. The recording he had taken though, spoke for itself—Gabriella's sad expression and heavy tone was the evidence. The translation was simply frosting on the cake.

Later that night, while sitting on his hotel bed, Min uploaded the video to his computer and edited it down to a single, damning clip. He rewatched the woman closely, observing her eyes and, more importantly, listening to the inflection in her voice. As the camera shifted from her to Nayeli, Min listened again with giddy excitement.

"Brandon made me feel comfortable. His connection to me was warm, but then he destroyed my life by getting me pregnant and leaving me. I live in shame. I can't find honest work, and I can't afford to move. People look down on me and my child."

Before leaving for Bangkok, Min made a note to hire a cameraman in addition to an interpreter at his next stop.

Yoona drove into Jongno District, the official hub of several government agencies. The last time it had been this busy was during the frantic mobilization at the outbreak of the Korean War. With China and the U.S. poised for confrontation, South Korea was on military alert. She parked, stepped out of the car, and adjusted her blazer. Her meetings with military attachés and embassy liaisons to discuss troop movements and security concerns would inevitably try her patience.

Her phone rang. She dug it out of her pocket and saw it was Choi. She answered. "Talk to me."

"It's about Leah Davenport," Choi said. "She's the one I told you about before."

Yoona received a telepathic image of a young woman with long strands of deep brown hair and penetrating chocolate eyes. Stylish. Confident. These were signs of an energy manipulator. Choi's stress accompanied the projection, with it rough edges and blurred image. Along with the tightness in his voice, she knew he had been shaken.

Yoona stopped walking and took a breath. "I'm sorry, Choi. But this isn't a good time. I have several meetings today." But more importantly, she had to keep her focus on the *Tamar*—the ship that was carrying weapons bound for North Korea. Capturing the American spy involved in that shipment took priority over everything. "I must keep my energy focused elsewhere."

"Leah has absorbed dark energy," Choi pressed. "She can connect, communicate telepathically, and invite souls into her consciousness."

"Already?" This information surprised Yoona. She now understood Choi's distress.

"She is powerful, Auntie." His voice rose with urgency. "I don't understand the magnitude and speed at which she has advanced. This girl is the energy manipulator you wanted me to find."

Yoona responded in a measured cadence, hoping to settle his nerves. "Choi. Have you learned who is training her?"

"The person training Leah?" There was a pause. "I'm not sure. She claims to be learning on her own from a manual. You *need* to send someone from the Circle." Choi's words rushed out. "Nehio Mah-seet's yearly visit is almost here. Tell him to come sooner."

"Slow, calm breaths, Choi. This isn't an emergency."

"She was in my mind!" Choi burst. "Searching my memories."

"Hyun-Woo Choi!" her voice commanded.

The phone went silent.

Yoona let the quiet stretch, waiting for Choi to regain control of his emotions. When she felt his composure return, she asked, "Did you travel Leah's life path?"

"Yes."

"What did you learn?"

"I wasn't able to travel far," Choi said. "She has a lot of decisions to make in the near future. I didn't see any links to a user or a manual."

"And the absence of a guide unsettled you."

"Yes. Does Leah have something to do with the disturbance?"

Yoona considered the disturbance. She'd had several dreams and visions about its aftermath, which is why she needed Brandon, but never of the actual incident or the cause. "I haven't been able to see future events clearly, so my understanding of the disturbance hasn't changed. I do know that it'll happen within the next few weeks."

"So, Leah could be responsible for the event," Choi remarked. "Should I take the book from her?"

"No. I have embedded talismans into the books. They are meant to find a user. If she's as powerful as you say, then the book chose her."

"This girl is young," Choi protested. "Training from a manual is difficult even with help."

"I allowed the manuals to go missing, so the right person could find them."

"You let the manuals go missing ... intentionally?"

Yoona didn't respond.

"Okay," Choi said. "I trust your judgment. How should I proceed?"

"Let her keep learning. I will assess her myself when I arrive."

"And if she is the reason for the disturbance?"

"We cannot prevent a disturbance. Keep a close watch; others are searching for her, so be alert."

"I will, Auntie."

When Su-Bin arrived home after work, Jong-In was waiting on her doorstep with dinner. She was rather happy to see him, although she wasn't sure why he had come over without informing her.

"What brings you by?" she asked. "Missing me?"

"Always," he responded.

Su-Bin eyed the containers in his hands. "Takeout? Or did you cook?"

"I cooked. Only the best for my queen," he teased.

Su-Bin gave him a long, sideway look. "You should be careful. One of these days I might get the wrong impression and think you're flirting with me."

"You know me better than that," Jong-In replied.

"Mmm," she hummed. "Thank you for cooking. I was feeling so lazy." She unlocked the door, and they entered the house together.

Su-Bin went to the bathroom and washed her hands and face. Then she changed into a pair of silk pajama bottoms and a sweatshirt. When she rejoined

Jong-In, he had set the table with barbecue, soup, kaminchi, fried mushrooms, and rice.

"So, tell me, really. What's going on?" Su-Bin asked. "What's with the special surprise?" She'd seen this side of Jong-In before, overly attentive, unexpectedly thoughtful. It surfaced every now and then, vanished just as quickly. She liked this version of him and wished it would stay longer.

"I didn't want you to be alone," he said. "The whole situation with Min was crazy."

"Yeah, it was." She pulled out her chair and sat down. "I saw the red flags, but I lost myself in his charm and good looks. In hindsight, I see that. Don't worry, I've learned my lesson. I won't let that happen again." Wondering why Jong-In had truly come, she asked again, "What's the real reason you stopped by?"

Jong-In poured some wine. "You've been working late." He set a glass in front of her. "I wanted to make sure you were eating. Is everything all right at the office?"

"Everything is fine." She picked up her glass and sipped the wine. "My current case is turning out to be more complicated than I had anticipated, so I filed a motion for continuance. Oh, and on the drive home, I was thinking about my mother's case and realized the DNA results Min submitted should have come back days ago. I need to call and find out what's going on with that."

"What will you do if the DNA matches that doctor?"

"If it is the doctor's DNA, then I'll request a search warrant of his residence. If my father's necklace is there, we have a solid case against him. With the evidence, I'll be able to free my mom."

Jong-In placed some grilled beef on Su-Bin's plate. "Your nerves must be on edge."

"They are." She tasted the seaweed soup and gave Jong-In an approving nod.

He smiled in returned, tapping his chopsticks on the edge of his dish. "How's Brandon doing?"

"Great!" Su-Bin ate the strip of beef, then lifted her eyebrows in appreciation. "He's a very good teacher. He has a knack for getting people up and talking."

"I asked, because I get the feeling the two of you are close."

"You're very perceptive. We had a lunch date planned for tomorrow, but he canceled without saying why. It's making me nervous."

Jong-In set his chopsticks down. "Are you sure it's a good idea to be getting involved with him?"

Su-Bin lowered her spoon into the soup again. "He stirs something in me," she said. "He's…" She paused, searching her feelings. "…always present, even when he's not." She let out a soft chuckle. "I know that sounds strange."

"No, I get it." Jong-In said. "He has a way of getting inside you."

Su-Bin grinned. "Yes, he does." She picked up her spoon and took another sip of her soup. "I've decided to run with it. We'll see where it goes."

"Okay. I'm cheering for you." Jong-In put his fist in the air, emitting a, "Hoo, hoo!"

Su-Bin blushed. "What is it with you?"

Three hours east of Bangkok, with his cameraman and an interpreter, Min Yun stood in front of a three-story building. "I'm in Thailand at Streemanda School." Gesturing to a woman standing next to him, he said, "This is the headmistress, Sister Atchara." Min faced her and asked, "You knew Brandon Spencer. Can you tell me about him?" Min then indicated to the interpreter to translate. She asked in Thai,

"ตอนน้ำท่วมคุณ Brandon Spencer ได้อยู่ที่นี่หรือป่าว
ช่วยบอกหน่อยว่าตอนน้ำท่วมเกิดอะไรขึ้นที่โรงเรียน"

Sister Atchara answered,

"คุณ Brandon ไม่ได้อยู่ตอนน้ำท่วมค่ะ,
นั้นเกิดขึ้นหลังจากที่เขาไปแล้วแต่น้ำท่วมได้ท่วมขึ้นชั้นสอง."

The headmistress turned and pointed to the second floor of the school.

"โรงเรียนได้ปิดลงหนึ่งเดือนเพราะความเสียหายและค่าใช้จ่ายมันแพงเกินไปค่ะ"

The camera filmed the interpreter. "Brandon was initially a good teacher. The students loved him. He taught middle school on the second floor. Our school became competitive in English competitions. But then we found out…" She looked at the Sister with a shocked expression, then continued, "...that he seduced a student and had a child with her."

Later that day, Min sat in his hotel room reviewing the clip, thinking, *Su-Bin will have to fire Brandon now. He's a fucking pedophile.*

Min's phone rang, and he answered it.

"Mr. Yun, sir. We found a young woman. Would you like to meet her?"

"Yes. I'll be right down."

The interpreter drove Min through the Thai countryside in an aging Toyota pickup, the air conditioner cranked so high that Min shivered in his seat. "Does it have to feel like a refrigerator?" he muttered, rubbing his arms. "Going from searing heat to arctic cold can't be good for your health." The interpreter glanced behind him at the cameraman but didn't respond. Min sighed, folded his arms, and endured.

The truck turned off the main road and onto a dirt lane flanked by overgrown grass and scattered mango trees. When Min opened the door, he was hit by a wave of tropical heat. The shock of transitioning from the frigid air conditioning made his head momentarily dizzy. He steadied himself as he glanced at the path ahead, which sloped downward toward the river.

The house perched on wooden stilts high above the ground. Beneath the house, the ground was cluttered with large clay water pots, rusted tools, and a hammock that swayed between two beams. Min climbed the dozen steps and reached the small porch. A clay basin sat next to a faded blue plastic bowl, used for washing feet. The interpreter and cameraman both slipped off their sandals and rinsed their feet before entering. Min awkwardly followed suit, peeling off his shoes and socks as a mosquito buzzed in his ear.

The inside of the house was simple and airy. The windows lacked glass but could be closed with wooden shutters. The room's furniture carried the unmistakable cadence of Thailand—solid wood platforms built for both sitting and lying, bright cushions, and heavy carved tables and chairs. Family photos and a large portrait of the king hung on the wall. Min caught the scent of steamed rice and fried fish.

The mother greeted them with a respectful "*wai*," her hands clasped together in front of her and a slight bow. After exchanging a few polite words, she invited them to sit. Her daughter, who appeared to be around nineteen or twenty, held a small child on her hip. With permission granted, the cameraman began to record the interview.

"Can you tell us what Brandon did to you?" Min asked.

The translator asked in Thai,

"คุณ Brandon เป็นครูของคุณหรือคะ?"

The young woman nodded, answering,

"ค่ะ คุณ Brandon เป็นครูที่ดีมาก"

The translator then asked,

"คุณเป็นแม่เลี้ยงเดี่ยวหรือเปล่าคะ? แล้วคุณพ่อของลูกหายไปไหน?"

The young woman responded,

"เขาไม่รับผิดชอบอะไรทั้งสิ้นค่ะ สาเหตุที่ฉันมีลูกก็เพราะตอนนั้น
เราเมาเหล้าและได้เสียกัน จนฉันท้อง เขาก็ทิ้งฉันไป
หลังจากนั้นฉันจึงหลบมาอยู่กับแม่ และช่วยงานแม่ที่บ้าน
ทำงานพอประทังชีวิตไปวันๆ"

The camera focused on the translator. "Brandon made a connection with me. He manipulated my emotions. After I got pregnant, he just left the country, leaving me with nothing. I had to quit school. I struggle to survive, wishing he would return to take responsibility for his child."

Min leaned back in his seat, suppressing a smile. Everything was working exactly as he had hoped. The next day, he boarded his flight to Japan, knowing that Su-Bin would be horror-stricken she had hired such a monster.

Potent Forces

Seoul, Tokyo

Ambiguous Heroes

Yoona woke with a start and swung her feet over the side of the bed. Every fiber in her body was telling her that the operative was close. She rushed to the port, passing gantry cranes loading and unloading ships at the berth. Stepping into the harbormaster's office, she saw an open storage room and swiped a uniform before making her way through the container yard. Turning down a lane of warehouses to a new stretch of berths, she found the *Tamar*, a large cargo ship waiting to be unloaded. A train blared its horn off in the distance as she boarded the ship.

Yoona approached the deck officer in charge. "Your berthing window is expiring. What's the delay?"

"We're waiting on personnel. It'll be sorted soon," the man explained.

"When are you expecting to begin? I need to have the handover point logged for land-side."

"Not long."

Yoona thanked the man and disembarked.

Back on land, she made a call. "Matthew, let's get ready."

"Suit up!" Matthew announced. "It's time."

Brandon sprang to his feet and strapped on his vest and shoulder holster with two handguns. He clipped a double-mag pouch to his waist, secured the holster to his leg with extra clips, and slid in his earpiece. He checked his M4A1 assault rifle before slinging the strap over his head.

Matthew took hold of both his shoulders and looked him dead in the eyes. "Don't hesitate. You shoot, and you shoot to kill."

Brandon swallowed hard. He nodded once—tight and quick—and thumped Matthew's chest with his fist. But as he left the hotel room and climbed into his truck, he was doing everything he could not to throw up.

When he reached the port, he wove through traffic and people before parking at his designated spot and reporting. "I'm in position," Brandon radioed.

"Yoona and Jeonmunga are in position," Matthew responded.

Kim's voice followed. "I'm in position."

"Wait for the first explosion, then block the exit points," Matthew instructed.

Brandon wiped his sweaty palms along his jittering thighs and waited.

Matthew sat behind the wheel of his dump truck, thumbs tapping along with the high-energy guitar intro to *Thunderstruck* playing in his mind.

Boom! came the first explosion.

"Go!" Matthew ordered, turning his truck to block the lane and killing the engine.

The first explosion caused people to stop and look.

Boom! thundered the second explosion. Chaos ensued as everyone ran. A second later, an alarm sounded throughout the yard, indicating an active shooter was on site. The intercoms burst to life and instructed workers to take cover.

Matthew frantically eyed men, looking for the American. When the dock workers saw Matthew, they veered away and ran in fright. Then a car raced toward him, followed by a delivery van close behind. The vehicles stopped, their exit obstructed by Matthew's truck.

The van executed a multi-point turn. Matthew engaged the occupants with gun fire. The American exited the car and ran for the van. Matthew moved to get a clean shot, aiming for his legs.

Whap, whap, whap! Multiple shots hit Matthew in the chest. He fell backwards to the ground, struggling to breathe and cursing in pain. Rolling behind cover, he collected himself, thankful the bullets hit his vest.

"He's in the van," Matthew managed to say.

The first explosion roared. Brandon's body seized as his hands locked around the wheel.

"Go!" Matthew's voice rang in his ears. He slammed the truck in gear and turned into the lane, blocking traffic. Jumping out of the cab, he headed straight for the clearing.

Peopled looked south toward the explosion. A few jogged toward the sound, ready to offer assistance, when the second explosion thundered through the port. That sent everyone scattering for cover.

Sirens blared through the open air. A man froze in place, staring at Brandon. His hands flew into the air, and he dropped to his knees. Brandon's eyes swept right over him as he scanned the crowd for a white, foreign face. Gunfire erupted in the distance, and Brandon quickened his pace.

Rounding the corner, his eyes widened and his mouth dropped open. He was staring at a massive ship, his eyes glued to Yoona. She flew through the air and smashed a man's face in with her knee. Then she twirled and kicked another, sending him flying in the air. She took down four men as if they were paper cutouts.

Fool! Yoona's words pierced his thoughts. *Behind you!*

As Yoona delivered a quick chop to a mercenary's neck, she spotted Brandon. Two men had exited the building behind him and took aim. She pushed him a warning as she caught a man's arm and drove his head into the metal railing. He went limp, and she dropped him. His two buddies lunged. Yoona snapped the first man's arm and dislocated the second man's knee. Four others approached, their guns drawn and ready to fire. Using her foot to prop up the unconscious man's head, she stomped on the back of his neck, killing him. She brought the soul inside her, forced it to transcend, and channeled the dark energy. She threw the man she was holding off the side of the boat, then hurled the man with the broken knee toward the four approaching soldiers. When he landed, she clapped her hands, blasting a ball of energy that sent all five of them flying the length of the ship, off the stern, and into the water. Turning, she produced a second burst as two soldiers fired their weapons. The shock hurled the men off the bow of the boat.

As Yoona took care of the mercenaries, Jeonmunga was on the bridge holding a drill to the captain's eye. The captain told him everything. He playfully slapped the captain's cheek and left him tied to the wheel.

Joining Yoona, Jeonmunga said, "Fifty containers."

"Do you know which ones?" she asked.

"I do, but it's going to take me time to get to them and set the explosives. You're going to have to keep the police at bay until the charges are ready."

Yoona nodded.

Grabbing his bags, Jeonmunga said, "There's a present for you in the captain's quarters." Then he rushed aft.

Yoona quickly glimpsed over to check on Brandon. He was pinned behind a steel beam with two mercenaries advancing toward him. She shook her head, reached out her hand, and used dark energy to collapse the men.

Yoona's warning pushed Brandon. He spun and fired. The recoil of the gun caught him off guard; the kick sent him crashing onto his ass. The two gunmen closing in on him exchanged a glance and laughed. That half-second beat allowed Brandon to roll behind a steel beam as gunfire chewed into the concrete where he had just been.

"The American is in the van," Matthew's voice crackled through his earpiece.

The gunfire stopped. Brandon jumped up and fired. He emptied his magazine at point-blank range. Silence followed the realization that had come too late. The men he had killed had already dropped their weapons and fell to their knees. He stared at the bodies lying on the pavement, his chest going cold.

The screech of tires and the roar of an engine ripped him from his horror. A van race toward Brandon. He drew his Glock 19 and opened fire, aiming for the tires. From the corner of his eye, he saw Yoona extend her arms. An energy blast tipped the van, sending it sliding several feet.

Men spilled out of the vehicle and scrambled for cover. Gunfire cracked around them. Brandon caught sight of the American, crouching low behind the van's rear wheel. Then the shooting stopped.

The American glanced around, spotted an opening, and broke into a sprint.

Brandon holstered his weapon and met him head-on. They collided and tumbled onto the concrete. Rolling across the pavement, they scrabbled for position. The man pinned Brandon's right arm and then wrapped his leg around his neck. Brandon struggled to breathe as black spots swarmed his vision.

A knife came at Brandon's face. He raised his free arm to block it, but the knife slid into his forearm, striking bone. He cried out.

Yoona's presence entered his mind. *Create a shield. Focus on one forward point and compress all of your energy there.* He felt her guiding him, directing energy from his muscles, his gut, his chest. *Push with intent,* she instructed.

The man tore the knife from his arm and struck again. The blade stopped mid-air. The man stared at the knife, then at Brandon. He cursed, brought his other hand to the knife, and pushed down with both hands.

Brandon's pinned arm was free. He gathered his strength to punch the man, but trying to raise his fist weakened the pulsating field between him and the blade.

Stop trying to move! Yoona scolded. *Stay focused. Push your energy.*

The knife dropped, stopping an inch from his face. With his energy flowing to his shield, Brandon had nothing left for his body to use. He was immobilized.

The man squeezed his leg, tightening the pressure around Brandon's throat. He couldn't get air to his lungs. His energy waned, and its flow slowed.

Hold on, Yoona stressed. *I'm coming. Just hold on.*

The man lifted the blade and struck for his face again. The knife came down, bounced off the remnants of his shield, and plunged into Brandon's shoulder. Waves of black accompanied the pain. His focus failed and the shield dissipated. The moment his energy returned to his body, the world lurched and spun. The American yanked the blade free, splattering blood everywhere. He raised the knife once more.

Brandon didn't have enough oxygen; blood drained from his body; an avalanche of pain crushed him; he fell unconscious.

After the van tipped and slid to a halt, Yoona aimed a rifle and shot two men standing in Matthew's way. Satisfied the situation was under control, she dropped the gun and headed for the captain's quarters to see what this "present" Jeonmunga had mentioned was.

Upon entering the captain's quarters, she saw a long, slender black case. Opening it, she found a weapon—a sword or staff of some kind. Three blades protruded from an opening at one end. The round handle was wrapped in leather with two switches. Yoona had a bad feeling. This weapon was designed and built specifically for an energy manipulator. She reached for it, then suddenly stopped and gasped. "Brandon!"

Yoona reached into his mind as she ran as fast as her legs could carry her.

Matthew took aim and shot the last man standing between Kim and Brandon. Kim sprinted. The American pulled the knife embedded in Brandon's shoulder and took aim. Kim rammed the butt of his rifle into the man's head.

Brandon didn't move. Kim rolled him over and patted his back. Nothing. Flames engulfed the truck.

Matthew yelled, "Kim, run!"

Kim locked his hands under Brandon's arms and hauled him upright. He grunted as he lifted him onto his shoulder. But before he could move, the truck exploded.

Yoona sprinted across the deck, vaulted off the railing, and soared through the air. Crossing her arms, she lifted her index fingers and swept her hands in a long, smooth arc, purging the remaining dark energy. Her fall turned into a controlled glide, and she landed safely between Kim, who held Brandon over his shoulder, and the blazing truck.

Then came the explosion. The truck erupted in a storm of fire, twisted metal, and shards of glass. Yoona's shield shimmered as the flames and debris curved around her and the men, leaving them untouched.

"Set him down," Yoona commanded.

Kim laid Brandon back on the pavement. She knelt beside him and placed her hand on his chest, coaxing his heart back to life. His lungs expanded, and he gasped for air.

The next day, Matthew entered Brandon's hospital room, seeing him propped against pillows with half his body wrapped in bandages. He approached the bed, put his hand on his shoulder, and looked him in the eyes. "How you doin', partner?"

Brandon nodded. "I'm managing."

"You did a good job out there. We saved a lot of people."

Brandon forced a smile, then averted his eyes.

Matthew gave his shoulder a pat before withdrawing his hand. "We got the job done, and you're still alive. That's all that matters."

"I kind of wish I was dead. I'm not allowed any pain medication per Yoona's instructions."

With a chuckle, Matthew said, "You're a trainee; no drugs." He glanced around at the flowers, seeing cards tucked between vases. "You're a popular guy."

"They're from my students at the law firm."

"I figured." Matthew leaned closer and saw the bruising on Brandon's body. "You look like shit."

"The doctor said I won't lose the use of my arm, so that's good news. How are you? I heard you were shot."

"I'm fine. A bit sore, but it's all good." He paused and watched Brandon rub his fingers along the sheets while taking slow, measured breaths. Was it the pain, or was it the fact he'd killed someone? If Brandon didn't face the trauma and deal with whatever lingering guilt he had, his training with Yoona would suffer.

"Look at me," Matthew said.

Brandon attempted a smile and glanced up.

Shaking his head, Matthew said, "No. Don't deflect. You have to face this head on. You didn't do anything wrong. Those men made their choice and knew what the consequences could be. Get yourself right in the mind so you can continue your training."

Brandon said nothing.

Matthew nodded, knowing he needed time. He smiled. "You're missing all the fun—police interrogations, press interviews..."

"Oh, I talked with someone from Korean intelligence last night, and a CIA guy just left about an hour ago. I've had my share of fun."

"What did you tell them?"

"The truth, more or less. I came here to teach and visit a friend. That friend requested my assistance in stopping a terrorist organization. I've been asked to write a formal statement and submit a full report. You're going to type that for me, right?" Brandon chuckled, then winced as he pressed his good hand against the bandages and groaned.

"So we're friends now?" Matthew said in jest. "Well, that's news to me."

Brandon took a moment to catch his breath before asking, "Did you know Yoona had those powers?"

"Right!" Matthew said. "She totally kicks ass. The best martial artist I've ever seen. God, I love that woman!"

Su-Bin, her entire staff, and most of Korea had seen the news. The incident had taken the country by storm, and the coverage was playing on every television station. Su-Bin was initially shocked to learn Brandon had been a part of the raid. She watched the footage again, unsure how she was supposed to feel.

The news showed a fireball tearing through a container ship, body bags lining the concrete, and police escorting men away in restraints. Eyewitnesses recalled the gun battle as commentators echoed their words. Brandon and his team were being heralded as heroes for intercepting prototype weapons bound for North Korea.

Pride surfaced before she could stop it. He had been part of something dangerous, catastrophic, and significant. The thought left her in quiet awe. But how could the news be talking about the same Brandon. The man she admired, the person she had kissed, was gentle, kind, and painfully polite. She couldn't imagine him holding a gun, much less pulling the trigger.

Seo-Ah stepped beside her. "Do you think he'll recover?"

Su-Bin glanced at her, seeing her somber expression. She placed a hand on her shoulder. "They said his wounds weren't life-threatening."

"His physical wounds, maybe. What about his psyche? This will scar him for life."

Su-Bin turned Seo-Ah to face her. She lifted the young woman's chin with her other hand, seeing she was a bit emotional. "Come," Su-Bin said and pulled Seo-Ah into an embrace. Brandon's connection to her was stronger than she had imagined.

After returning to her office, Su-Bin closed her eyes and took a calming breath. The quiet in the room did nothing to stop her racing mind. How had Brandon ended up in a shoot out? Her arms were shaking. She balled her hands tight to try and starve off the tension. Hadn't he thought about anyone other than himself before rushing into a gun battle? What if he had died? She clutched her chest, the imagined loss tightening around her heart. Her emotions ripped in opposite directions as her anger hardened. Had he thought about her at all?

She shook her head. Of course he hadn't. He hadn't come to Korea to study Shamanism or to teach English. He was here as an undercover operative. The more she thought, the more her anger shifted into a sharp, painful frustration. She should have known, or at least suspected, that Brandon was using her as cover for being in Korea. *I'm so naïve.*

Later that evening, Su-Bin called Jong-In and invited him over. When he arrived, they sat and watched the news, eating snacks, and drinking soju while Su-Bin talked and Jong-In listened.

"I guess what upsets me the most is that he specifically said he was at my disposal. He didn't have any responsibilities other than teaching at the office," Su-Bin ranted. "How stupid can I be to believe an FBI agent is honestly here just to teach! Obviously, that was a lie. I gathered he needed to be in the country for a different purpose, or this ambush would have been in jeopardy ... but don't lie to me about it. Don't use me like a paper towel—handy and convenient—and then throw me away. My firm wasn't inconsequential. Give me the dignity and respect I deserve.

"And Yoona," she continued. "Does she see my trust as something to take advantage of? She abused it not once, but twice! I can maybe forgive her for using me to sneak Brandon into the country, but what about Min? Why would she send me that slime ball?

"If she would have come to me and said, 'I need a favor. A terrorist organization is plotting to create havoc, and you can provide the cover needed so our people can succeed in stopping them. Can you allow me to place an agent with you for a week?' Then I would have been more than happy to accommodate her. It would have been an honor to assist. But to go behind my back..."

Su-Bin grunted, taking a shot of soju. She looked at Jong-In. "Well, say something. Tell me I'm wrong or that I'm overreacting."

Jong-In didn't respond. He gave a half-smile, half-shrug.

"And now what?" she continued. "I suppose I'll have to find a new teacher. Perfect! So much for continuity." Su-Bin stared at Jong-In. "You don't agree?"

"Oh, I do. I never trusted Yoona from the get-go. It's one thing for her to offer comfort and support. Giving a person advice is helpful, especially when they need it. But it's quite another to manipulate them. As for Brandon, I'm not surprised at all that he was involved in that raid. His whole situation seemed contrived from the moment I met him."

Su-Bin thought about that. Yoona was helpful. Su-Bin had never felt manipulated by her, until now. "I'm upset they lied. I'm upset they used me. I respected Yoona. I trusted her, believed her, had confidence in her. And that blinded my judgment."

"Now you know. Take every piece of advice on its own merit," Jong-In said. She huffed in frustration.

"Have you heard from Brandon yet?" Jong-In asked. "Do you know if he's all right?"

"I called the hospital. He's not able to receive visitors pending the investigation. They said he was in stable condition. It may be a few days before he's released."

"How bad were his injuries?"

"I don't know."

"Are you worried?"

"I was initially. I hope he is okay, but at the same time, my anger won't go away. I'm not sure that's even a rational emotion to be having at this point. But after the whole experience with Min, I'm feeling vulnerable."

Jong-In took her hand, and she shifted to face him. At that moment, a news anchor said her name. She pulled away from Jong-In and turned to see her firm's image plastered across the screen. She covered her mouth.

"FBI Agent Brandon Spencer was hired by Moon Law and Associates. Agent Spencer, who holds a teaching degree and has six years of international teaching experience, came to Korea to instruct the staff in English. Su-Bin Moon, the CEO, has recently been nominated for the prestigious Social Achievement Award. With her firm's recent victory against Delivery Inc, a major corporation, Agent Spencer's association with the firm will be sure to boost Moon Law's chances of winning this award."

Su-Bin stared at the TV, biting her nails, a habit she broke in middle school. How many new clients would this bring? The international law branch! She'd be opening it sooner than expected. She would need to hire more HR staff, lawyers, and secretaries; her business was about to double. She could open a second branch in Seoul, one in Busan. Tokyo? Seattle? Press conferences would be abundant. She could already foresee the countless phone calls she'd need to manage. She needed a PR person. Yoona had done it again!

"I don't believe it," she gasped. Great things were on her horizon.

In Japan, Min Yun sat in Hina's parents' living room with an interpreter, asking about Brandon. He videoed the conversation, already satisfied with her emotional response. The story would play in his favor.

"娘の Hinaは Brandonに恋をした. お二人とも素晴らしい先生でした.
彼がプロポーズしたとき、Hinaはとても興奮していた.
彼らは一緒にとても幸せでした. 彼らには男の子がいました.
彼らが亡くなったとき、Brandonは荒廃しました.

The translator relayed: "My daughter Hina fell in love with Brandon. They had a son together, but he left her. Hina hired a private detective, who found him in Korea. My daughter took her son and followed. I believe Brandon hired two men to scare her away, but they ended up killing my daughter and my grandson."

Min Yun thanked the woman for sharing and left. He couldn't believe what he had—evidence that Brandon was a potential murderer who preyed on high school girls. He had to warn Su-Bin that she had hired a sick, twisted fuck. But how should he approach her? He decided to write a letter and leave it on her doorstep with the videos and wait. She would be calling him soon afterwards, forgiving him, and welcoming him back. Then, after Min freed Su-Bin's mother, they would marry.

Sitting in the airport lounge, Min glanced at the TV, seeing video of a container ship in Korea, bursting in flames. He sat straighter, reading the subtitles scrolling along the bottom of the screen. The video ended, and Brandon's face popped up next to the commentator. He was ... a hero?

Min blinked, momentarily at a loss. How had this happened? How would this change Brandon and Su-Bin's relationship? His hero status was sure to benefit her firm.

Then, as if Min had cued the camera, Su-Bin's face appeared. The commentator explained that she was a lawyer who had hired Brandon. Min shook his head in disbelief. The free publicity, the heightened visibility, and the narrative casting her judgment in the best possible light had just made Brandon far more difficult to remove.

Min curled his fingers into his palm just as the whole situation made sense. *I was right! Brandon never went to Korea to teach English.* Min could use this whole hero act in his favor. Brandon was a liar. A user. The evidence he had about his past, the arrest in Lake Valley, and now his manipulation of Su-Bin—it all fit together.

Oh, this is perfect. He checked his watch. He'd land in Seoul in three hours. He had to show her he'd always be there to protect her.

Su-Bin drove home, exhausted. The past three days had been a whirlwind of press interviews and TV appearances. Brandon and the team were national heroes. No—international heroes. His connection to the firm was mentioned in every newspaper and news report around the globe, giving her more positive coverage than she could have ever imagined. Her public announcement of opening an international law division created additional buzz. She didn't know what to think. She was overwhelmed and needed to rest.

When she returned home, she found a package at her door. Attached to the top of it was a letter from Min Yun. Her eyes burned in her sockets as she rolled them. She was tempted to just throw the box away. But inside the box were photos and a thumb drive. She decided to read the letter.

Dear Su-Bin,

I know you are angry with me, and I don't blame you. My actions were reckless, but I truly and honestly knew that something was wrong with Brandon. He lied about why he was here. I saw how he was manipulating you with his romantic gaze, gifts, and daring adventures and fantastical tales about ghosts and goblins. Did you know he was arrested for helping a man abduct two teenage girls? I traveled to the countries where he has lived and taught, and gathered evidence that shows his true nature. Please review these disturbing facts for yourself. I love you. I only have your best interests at heart. I was foolish in how I handled things, but everything I did was to protect you. I hope, in time, you can find it within yourself to forgive me.

With love, always and forever.

Min

Looking at the photos, she saw Brandon in various countries with different women and little babies. She picked up the thumb drive, then called Jong-In.

Jong-In glanced at the clock, seeing the hour was much later than he had thought. But he was obsessed with finishing these new lines of code that would make the password detection protocol loophole-free.

His phone buzzed. Jong-In continued to type, but when the buzzing finally jarred his concentration, he glanced at the caller ID—and smiled. He answered immediately.

"Hey, can you come over?" Su-Bin asked. Her voice was tense and quick. "Min left me a box of ... evidence about Brandon. I need you to check it for viruses."

Jong-In swiveled away from his computer. *Min?* The name bit him like a poisonous snake. "I thought you weren't talking with him."

"I'm not, but..." She paused. "I'm curious to know what's on this thumb drive."

"I'll be right over."

He shut down his workspace and left the office. The city passed in a blur. Was Su-Bin safe? Was Min going to be trouble?

When he arrived, the first thing he did was hug her. She patted his shoulder, saying she was fine, then gestured to the box.

His initial thoughts about the photos were that Min was trying to destroy Brandon's reputation. The people sitting with him could be anyone. They didn't know the true context of the photos. After watching the videos, however, he wasn't so sure.

The knot in Jong-In's side twisted as he remembered his first meeting with Brandon—the strange connection with him, how the man and the situation had seemed out of place. Yet he had felt successful, even though his true thoughts at the time had been suspicion.

"God, I'm sorry. I failed you," he said. "I should have been more honest about my thoughts of Brandon."

"Don't blame yourself. He connected to me, too. Made me feel comfortable while worming his way into my mind."

Su-Bin's face went white.

"What's wrong?" Jong-In asked.

"This information will wipe out all the positive press I've been getting. When the media learns about Brandon's past, they'll destroy me."

"What are you going to do?"

"I don't know. I don't think I can fire him; that'll create too many questions. I think my only option is to hope he can finish out his contract before his past is exposed." Su-Bin exhaled. "I need to talk with Yoona."

"Are you kidding me?" Jong-In shot back.

"Both of these men came to me through her. She has some explaining to do. I don't exactly trust Min. Are these videos even authentic? He's extremely jealous."

"Or he knew Brandon couldn't be trusted," Jong-In offered.

"Do you really think that? Min hacked my phone. That came from some obsession toward me, not concern about Brandon."

"I'm sorry. You're right. I don't trust Min either."

"If you don't want me to talk to Yoona, what do you think I should do?"

Jong-In hesitated. "Actually, talking to Yoona is probably the best thing to do. You also need to talk to Brandon. Get his reaction and see how he responds."

The following day, Brandon returned to the office with his arm and shoulder in bandages and a sling. He was getting lots of attention from everyone wanting to hear his story. But the experience was not positive. The quick movements, a push here or there, the thrust of a notepad for him to sign, were all triggering flashbacks. Brandon became jittery and protective of his arm. He locked himself in his classroom.

Leaning back in his chair, he cradled his injured arm against his chest as stubborn pain accosted him in waves. He rocked in his seat, wondering which hurt more—the stabbing or his anger. Yoona had allowed him to kill defenseless men. They had been on their knees, weapons on the ground. They hadn't been a threat, and Yoona was the only one who could have done that. *Why didn't she tell me? How could she let me murder them in cold blood?*

Brandon wondered who the men had been. Were they trying to provide for their kids? How many times had he heard the excuse—*I needed the money.* That had to be the reason they were smuggling weapons—a big paycheck. But he'd never know; they were dead. The Federation of States claimed life would be better for everyone under a single umbrella. They promised a world without hunger or desperation. Would that stop men from trying to illegally sell weapons? He stared at his arm, thinking, *No. Greed always wanted more.*

Change was never easy, but those men he had killed could have changed. Death, however, had closed that door forever, and Brandon had been the one who pulled the trigger. *Why hadn't Yoona stopped me?*

Su-Bin opened the door and stepped into his class. Brandon stood, replacing his deep, concentrated scowl with a warm, loving smile.

"Are you sure you should be working with that injury?" Su-Bin asked with a cold stare.

"Hi," he said, standing a bit straighter now. "It's nice to see you."

"I need to be frank with you right now, Brandon. I thought you were here to teach. You told me you were at my disposal. You lied."

Brandon bowed his head. "I'm sorry. I wanted to tell you, but I couldn't."

She crossed her arms and supported her weight on one leg, waiting for him to continue.

"Yoona is my superior. This whole thing happened so quickly, and I got dragged into it. It's cloak-and-dagger shit, with spies and sensitive information. The weapons we destroyed were being transported to the North. War is imminent, and these weapons would have killed a lot of people."

Su-Bin's lip twitched. Brandon shifted uneasily, feeling her judgment. He imagined she was determining whether he was telling the truth.

"I get that," she finally said. "But when I agreed to hire you, it was because you wouldn't be working with the FBI while in my employment. I don't appreciate being used or lied to."

"You're right. I'm sorry. This was a special situation."

"How many other 'special situations' are you planning to find yourself in?"

"Su-Bin," he pleaded.

"Right," she responded, cutting him off. Turning the photos in her hand, she shoved them in his face. "And these?"

The quick motion made Brandon jerk. He saw a knife coming at him and winced. His wound throbbed with pain.

Su-Bin pushed them forward. "Look! Who is this?"

Brandon blinked his eyes, now seeing the photos. The top one was of Hina and Jamie. He hadn't seen an image of them in years—ever since he'd boxed all their photos and stored them in the closet. He stared at their faces. The pain in his arm mirrored the pain he had felt in the alley, where he had awoken to see Hina and Jaime lying in a pool of blood, had ridden with them in the ambulance to the emergency room, and had learned they had died. Brandon was speechless. He stepped back and asked in a whisper, "Where did you get this photo?"

Su-Bin turned in disgust and stormed out of the room. She had seen his secrecy about the raid as a betrayal, just as he had feared. But why was she upset about Hina? He had told her she died. Did Su-Bin think he had lied about that? Did she believe Hina was still alive?

Lake Valley, Oregon

The Grip: Control and Fear

Leah sat across from Barb in the school cafeteria, listening to the boys at the next table talk about the Education Center. One of them was frustrated because his dad believed toxic waste was buried at the Center, and the boy had to quit his guitar class. Leah smiled.

"Earth to Leah. Are you with me?" Barb waved her hand in front of Leah's face.

"Yes, sorry. What did you say?"

"I said it feels awkward. I don't think protesting at our graduation is appropriate. Maybe if it had something to do with the school, but holding a rally to return native lands?"

"I was feeling a little torn about it myself." Laughter exploded from a group of girls sitting alongside the windows. Leah glanced over but didn't lose her train of thought. "Until I remembered why it's so important." Her eyes met Barb's again, and she emphasized, "The land has a purpose, and that purpose is not a part of Lake Valley. The water spirit living there is dangerous. You know that as much as I do."

"I do," Barb sighed. "But that building is alive now."

"Exactly. It'll find someone to bond with, just like it did with you and Dan."

Barb nodded. "You're right. Okay."

"Good," Leah said.

"So ..." Barb started, "what do you know about Officer Choi's aunt?"

"Not much. Apparently, she is a powerful Shaman in Korea. She trained Choi."

"Sounds great. I think you should talk to her. Maybe she could give you some pointers."

"About that." Leah took the business card out of her pocket and slid it to Barb. "Someone from this company offered me a job. Seven hundred thousand a year."

"Holy shit, Leah. Say yes!" Barb exclaimed. Then her brow furrowed, and she asked, "What would you be doing?"

"Using my powers. Helping people. I asked about you, and he said there would be a position available. Something to do with your voice."

"Me? Did he give you details?" Barb scanned the card. "'Extended Life.' What do they do, exactly?"

"I'm not sure. It's supposedly a biotech company that uses nanotech, cybernetics, and medical science to prolong life, none of which I know anything about. He's going to make an appointment to talk with my parents after graduation."

"That sounds ... umm. I don't know. They're offering you a lot of money."

Leah spoke in a sassy tone, "I'm a magnificent individual."

"How do they know about your powers?"

"He's been watching me. I remember seeing him a few times—after we were freed, and again at prom." Leah took a bite of her sandwich.

Barb asked, "Older man? Wears a black suit?"

"That's him."

"I spotted him in Diamond Creek. He saw the energy blast you created. I got dark assassin vibes from him." Barb paused as a group across from them stood and took their food trays to the cart. "Did you connect to him?"

"I did. But he connected to me, first."

"What are you going to do?"

"I agreed to meet with him again," Leah said. Lowering her voice, she stressed, "The guy talked to me using telepathy and can make shit levitate, like Darth Vader."

Barb grimaced. "Yeah, that's the vibe. Why are you considering working for them?"

"It's my grandfather's company."

"Ah. Your grandpa's company. Well, that make sense now. Seven hundred thousand a year is legit. How much would they pay me?"

"I'll ask at the meeting. If you do join me, we'll be partners after all."

"This can be my backup plan if I don't get the scholarship."

"When is the audition?"

"June twenty-first."

"Two weeks after graduation," Leah said. "Plenty of time to get ready. Can you ask Lyla to join us at the protest? I'm going to ask Becky and Andrew. Is it okay if I ask Eric as well?"

"Why would you ask Eric?"

"Because I know you won't, and this will be a great opportunity for you two to bond."

The bell rang, signaling the end of lunch. They stood and headed out, stacking their trays on the metal cart as they left.

"Don't ask Eric," Barb said.

"Why? You like him. Go with it."

Barb sighed. "Just, don't. Please."

They parted ways. Leah turned to face Barb as she backed down the hall, a giant smile plastered across her face. "Hey, Barb!" she called. "I'm asking Eric!" She spun around before Barb could react.

After school, Leah found Eric by his locker. She jogged up to him and said, "Eric. Can I ask you a quick question?"

Eric dropped his bag and glared at Leah. "Only if you explain what you did to me."

"What do you mean?"

His jaw tightened. "I want to know what the hell happened at prom. Why were you calling me 'Paul.' My mom says I blacked out and spent two nights in the hospital. I had strange brain scans. You took me outside, and bam! I'm back. I don't have headaches anymore, not even when I use that computer. The doctor says my scans are normal."

Eric stood tall, intensifying his glare. "I woke up, and you were holding my hands, praying or something. I want to know what happened."

"You had a headache, and we went outside to get some fresh air. Then you felt better. That's it," Leah tried.

"Bullshit! Who is Paul? How can I go from totally out of it to completely normal by you touching me?" A frantic note entered his voice. "Did you give me drugs? Are you an angel? Or maybe you hypnotized me that day in the hall—holding my hands, looking me in the eyes. I felt a strange tingle in my arm. Was that the drug?"

"Eric, I didn't do anything. You needed some air. That's all."

"Bull-shit again!" Eric said, drawing the words out. His face tightened, and his stare didn't relent.

Leah nodded, knowing she had to go into his mind. He needed peace, and she could give that to him. "Eric..." she said, reaching out to touch him.

He swatted her hand away. "Don't touch me." Squaring his shoulders, he inched closer, hovering over her. "You know, I never believed any of the crap people were saying about you until it happened to me. Whatever voodoo, witchcraft powers you have ... I want to know about it. I want you to teach me everything."

Leah faltered. She searched for a response but found none.

"I like Barb, but she and I will never be an item until I understand who she really is. I'm guessing it has something to do with your abduction. Neither of you ever talk about it." Eric looked her over. "So, how about it?" He softened his tone. "Will you teach me?"

Leah took a step back. Eric with power? More than he already had? She shook her head.

Eric picked up his bag. "When you're ready to be honest with me, you know where to find me. I want in." He turned and walked off.

Leah let out a heavy sigh. That hadn't ended the way she thought it would. *Why didn't Barb tell me he was upset?*

Leaning against the lockers, Leah tilted her head back and stared at the ceiling. Her lips curled and she gave an incredulous giggle. *Teach him? No way. He has no clue what he's asking.* Min's mother immediately came to mind. *He'd become possessed again or killed.*

She looked up and down the hall at the few remaining students milling about. The whispers, hidden glances, people avoiding her as they passed, gave her shivers. She had become someone else in the eyes of her peers, and it didn't feel good. Her being here felt wrong, like a Stephen King kind of wrong. The rumors were out of control. Luckily, school was almost over.

Heading for the parking lot, Leah was happy to be getting out of the building. She scanned for Uncle Tim but found her father instead. She hopped in the car, saying, "Hey, Dad. Tim couldn't make it?"

"I'm taking you out for ice cream," Jared said.

She buckled her seatbelt. "Cool. What's the occasion?"

Jared reached over and took Leah's hand. "I miss my daughter." He squeezed her hand and sighed.

Leah saw the melancholy look in her father's eyes. "We're going to be okay, Dad. There has been a lot going on, with both of us. But I think we've passed the worst of it."

Jared smiled. "I know. I love you."

"I love you, too," she responded, but felt her dad's uneasiness. "What is it, Dad? What do you want to say?"

"Ever since the incident, I feel like we've drifted apart." Jared paused, and a dopey look came over his face. "You've changed before my very eyes, and I missed it somehow. I want to reestablish a routine together and reconnect with you. Movie night. Long talks over dinner. I used to know everything that was going on in your life. Now I feel intentionally left out."

"Does this 'reestablished' routine include going out for ice cream every day after school?"

Jared laughed. "No. Today we're celebrating my return as an architect."

"Really?! You opened the office?"

"Not quite, but we did get our first customer. It's a simple project—single-family home on Lakeshore Avenue."

"Congratulations, Dad!" Leah leaned over and hugged him.

"This is the Leah I know and love," Jared said, hugging her in return.

Jared started the car and inched along in line to exit the parking lot. Leah felt a sense of relief and safety. Her social life was derailing, and reestablishing a bond with her father would give her the closeness she needed. Movie night—laughing, groaning, quoting lines, singing songs. She wanted that again. It was fun. But those nights seemed like a lifetime ago, when she was a normal girl and her dad was dealing with depression. They were in very different states of mind now. So what was the path forward? Maybe she should try and be honest with him.

"Dad, if you could get your old job back in New York, would you take it?"

Jared glanced at Leah. "Where is this coming from?"

"I'm just curious. If it were possible, would you?"

"Did your grandfather say something?" Jared asked.

She paused, debating how much to say. "It's a hypothetical. You loved working in New York, didn't you?"

He tapped the steering wheel. "Are you worried about me working with Nong?"

She shook her head. "I'm sure you two will be fine."

Jared turned onto the street and caught the green light.

Leah dropped her shoulders with an exasperated exhale. There was too much she couldn't say. She stared out the side window. "Final exams are next week."

Uncle Tim squeezed his wife Patty's hand as they peered into the examination room, seeing a technician at the computer next to the exam table. She looked up from the screen and gave them a warm smile.

"Come in," she said.

The room had a nursery feel—the walls painted a pale sky blue, and a shelf stocked with prenatal vitamins, baby formula, breast pumps, and diapers. The young woman with her baby face, short black hair, and tan skin could easily passed for a nanny. But the skeleton model, medical posters giving healthy pregnancy tips, a chart showing fetal development, and the distinct hospital smell failed to hold the baby room vibe.

They entered, and Tim helped Patty settle onto the exam table. He tucked a strand of her blond hair behind her ear, then sat beside her.

"Hopefully, we'll be able to hear the heartbeat today," the technician said. "Go ahead and lay down."

Patty pulled up her hospital gown and positioned herself so the doctor could easily reach her. Then Tim supported her as she laid her head on the pillow.

The ultrasound screen beeped to life. Patty stared at it, her eyes betraying the nerves she tried to hide. Tim gave her hand another gentle squeeze.

The technician applied lubricant to the latex cover of the wand. "Are you excited?"

"More nervous, actually," Patty said.

"Is this your first time being pregnant?"

"No, I've had two miscarriages. But this pregnancy has made it the furthest."

"I'm so sorry. I know how painful those losses were."

"Thank you."

"Let's get the baby's vitals and see how the precious one is doing. I'll also take a measurement and give you a due date. Ready?"

Patty nodded.

"This may be a little uncomfortable, but you won't feel any pain. It's completely safe for the baby as well." She spread Patty's legs and inserted the wand.

They looked at the screen.

"There it is," the doctor said.

"Where?" Tim asked.

Pointing, the doctor said, "Here."

"That little raisin? That's our baby?" Tim said, gripping Patty's hand tighter.

"Oh, my god, it's amazing," Patty declared.

"I'm going to do something called an M wave. That will give us the measurement." The screen showed a bunch of waves. "Length: 2.3 centimeters." Pointing to the upticks in one wave, she said, "See these? That's the baby's heartbeat. Let's see if we can hear it."

After a few clicks, another screen popped up, and they heard, *Dadat, dadat, dadat, dadat,* in quick rapid succession.

"That's our baby," Patty said, pulling Tim close and kissing him.

The doctor withdrew the wand and removed her gloves. "Everything looks healthy. Make sure you keep taking your vitamins, and call if you feel any discomfort."

When they returned home, Nate was waiting for Tim in his car. He stepped out as they headed for the door.

"Hi, Patty," Nate said.

"Nate. Are you stealing my husband?"

"I am. We have a political meeting to attend. Don't worry, I'll have him home before dinner."

Patty kissed Tim and headed inside. Tim gave Nate a hug, then hopped in his Dodge Ram.

"What did you find?" Tim asked.

Nate started the truck and turned into the street, heading towards Roy's.

"I rented a cabin on the other side of the lake," Nate said.

"Cash?"

"Yep. I got my sister to talk her friend Stan into signing the rental agreement. We've got it for two months."

"Are we going to have any issues with Stan?"

"No. He's an investment banker," Nate said. "She told him she was using the cabin for turkey hunting. I guess he's squeamish about blood."

They stopped at a red light. Nate handed Tim a piece of paper with the address on it.

"Thanks for this. I'll start setting up shop tomorrow."

The light turned green, but the car in front of them didn't move. Nate hit the horn, showing his frustration.

They drove in silence for a bit. An uneasiness hung in the air. Nate's rigid posture, eyes fixed straight ahead, and tight grip on the wheel gave Tim pause. He didn't want to argue with Nate again. Clearing his throat, he braced himself.

"I'm afraid to ask, but what's wrong?"

Nate's voice was gruff and heavy. "The resolution passed the Senate."

"Really? I didn't hear."

"Of course you didn't. Everyone's glued to the news about those prototype weapons getting intercepted in Seoul. Please. Those things were never going to end up in North Korea. This whole thing—the explosion, the arrests, the investigations—is theater to draw attention away from the resolution." He shot Tim a stiff glare. "Those fuckers have become artists at turning heads."

"We can definitely agree on that," Tim said.

"You pissed off yet?" Nate asked.

Tim ran his hand down the side of his face. "Nate. Thirty-eight states will never vote in favor of handing over government control to the United Nations. Stop worrying."

"You are so fucking blind, it hurts."

Tim stared out his side window. "I know you don't believe protesting will make any difference, so what do you want to do about it? What exactly are you thinking?"

After a long, tense silence, Nate said, "We need to be ready to fight."

Tim glanced back at him. "What do you mean?"

"Stockpile ammunition, weapons, gear, medicine, tech. We need safe houses where someone can disappear for a spell. Drop points, caches, communication protocols, tunnels. Let's get Miley off-road ready."

"You serious about this? Tunnels, caches?"

"Yes!" Nate exclaimed. "Bret's been working with me. You know about my Eagle, right?"

"Yeah, yeah, your old AMC Eagle."

"I've been working on her." He gave a small grin. "I've named her 'The Ghost.'"

"Be-cause..." Tim asked, stretching the word out.

"Because..." Nate playfully drummed the top of the steering wheel. "I bought a military grade jammer. This thing blocks drone systems and tracking lasers. The Eagle's got high-tread off-road tires, a heavy-duty suspension, and a nitrous system."

"Nate, I don't know what to say?"

"I started planning after the E.U. unveiled their grand plan. I would have said something earlier, but you had a stretch of jobs and then your brother was abducted."

"Yeah, I've been a bit distracted."

"This whole Federation thing has ballooned quick, and we need to prepare. The dark web has everything we need. Why don't you come over, and I'll show you everything we've detailed."

Tim sighed. "Alright. Once the land is back in the Sukiya's hands, I'll come over."

They pulled in front of Roy's place and saw that Big Steve, Bret, and Dylan had already arrived. After the pleasantries, small talk, and a round of beers, Roy handed everyone a stack of forms. "These are the petitions we need signed. They state that the citizens of Lake Valley would like to hold a special election to de-annex the property known as 4871 175th Street. You can only get signatures from people who live in the city limits. They must print their name in the first space, write their address in the next space, and sign in this final space. Make sure they know what they are signing so that when the opposition challenges us on signatures, we won't lose."

Roy handed Nate a pen. "You start. Fill out the first row of your form so that others can see how it's done. I usually have friends and family sign the first row of new forms and then staple them together. As you get more signatures, people can see how many others are supporting us and it builds momentum."

"How many signatures do we need to collect?" Dylan asked.

Roy chuckled. "A lot. If we get 12,000 signatures, they'll have to debate and consider the issue. But we want the initiative to be automatically added to the ballot. For that, we need ten percent of the population, roughly 30,000 plus signatures. Some of the signatures will be disqualified for one reason or another, so more is always better. Right now, we have twenty-five people collecting signatures. If we're going to make the August fifth deadline, we're going to need more people. Get your friends and family to help."

"Can I lay these out on my store counter for people to sign?"

"No!" Roy responded. "Someone needs to talk with the person signing. Ideally you would read the description on top before having them sign. And only get signatures from those who can legally vote."

"That rules out Bret," Dylan joked.

"Rally the troops. Let's get those signatures before the spirit at this place harms anyone else," Tim said.

Olivia Rose bounced in her seat, her red hair dancing along with her excitement. Jane peeked at her through the rearview mirror, trying to remember the last time she'd seen Olivia so happy. She pulled into the Education Center parking lot and asked, "You ready for art class?"

"Bella's going to be so happy to see me," Olivia said in a joyous tone.

She skipped alongside Jane into the building, through the lobby, and down the hall. Stopping in the atrium, Olivia turned and pointed at Jane. "This is my mom. She knows all about you now."

Jane took a quick breath, reminding herself her imaginary friend was helping Olivia. "What's your friends name again?"

"Bella," Olivia answered. "Say hi, Mom."

Forcing a smile, Jane said, "Hi."

Her inner voice responded, *Hi. It's nice to meet you. I'm Bella.* Jane's face cringed with confusion. Did she just think that?

"That was Bella, Mom. She said 'hi' back. She's happy to meet you."

Jane's heart quickened. *It's my imagination,* she told herself.

Olivia grabbed both of her mom's hands and swung them back and forth. "Are you going to wait here until class is over? If you do, you can talk with Bella."

"Come on, let's get to class," Jane said.

"Wait. I want to try and connect with Bella first." Olivia ran to one of the giant columns that stood three stories high and supported the glass ceiling. Hugging it, she said, "I missed you, too." Then Olivia squatted next to the column and put both her hands flat on the floor.

"What are you doing?" Jane asked.

"I'm trying to connect with Bella."

"What do you mean?"

"Once we're connected, I can talk to her anywhere, all the time." Then she whispered to the column, "Did it work?" After a brief pause, she added, "I don't know how to do that."

Tim's warnings pressed against her chest. *There's a reason those rumors existed. Barb and Dan had the same imaginary friend; look how that turned out. You should be scared!*

I think the imaginary friend is helping her, Mr. Bowbly had countered.

Jane was confused. Seeing Olivia, hands pressed to the floor, talking to a post, felt ... scary. Was this a sign that something was wrong? Or was this simply imagination?

Tim's dread. Mr. Bowbly's calm. Rumors. Protests. War. Senate Debates. Rising food prices. The market crash. Phantom voices in her mind. Jane struggled to control her breathing.

"Mom, can you go away?" Olivia asked.

Rubbing her eyebrows, Jane said, "What?"

Her inner voice spoke again. *I need a moment of privacy with Olivia. I'm going to teach her how to grow her spiritual energy.*

Jane's eyes doubled in size. *Those were not my thoughts!* Her hands trembled, and she was unable to move. "Olivia," the word was thin and breathless. "Move away, honey."

"Mom! You move away," Olivia demanded. "Go over by the water." She stood and pushed Jane to leave.

Snatching her daughter, Jane said, "I'm sorry, honey. We have to go." This place wasn't safe. It didn't matter how calm the teacher was or how bright the windows were.

"But, Mom. I haven't connected to Bella."

With Olivia propped against her hip, Jane rushed back toward the lobby. "I know, baby. I'm sorry. I forgot something."

"Mom, put me down. My art class starts soon."

"I know, sweetheart, but I can't. We have to go. It's important."

Olivia began to squirm, trying to wiggle out of Jane's hold. They reached the doors, and her daughter began a full-blown meltdown. "No! I don't want to leave!" she screamed. "Let me go!"

Dragging her daughter to the car, Jane did her best to get Olivia in without hurting her. She was kicking and screaming, flailing about, with tears pouring down her face.

Leah sat down at her computer to write her grandfather an email. What did he know about her new abilities? What exactly would she be doing at Extended Life? Was he really okay with her not continuing her education? Logging in, she again saw lots of new emails—*Fox News, This American Life, Sixty-Minutes*, and in the middle of them, Misty Davis.

Subject: Seeking Clarification

Dear Leah,

I understand you have gone through a lot of trauma. I am so sorry this happened to you. Are you reaching out to me for help? Did a friend of mine mention my name as someone who could help you? I ask because your last email didn't make much sense to me. There is no way you could have known my father, Paul, after he wrote that awful email. I'm not even sure how you knew he wrote it in the first place. I appreciate you trying to make me feel better, but I honestly thought you were a scammer. Please tell me who told you about me and what you would like from me.

Misty.

Sitting back in her seat, Leah sighed. How should she respond? Paul had already transcended, but his connection to his daughter would be difficult if Misty held a negative opinion of him. It wouldn't be easy for him to nudge her, guide her, or protect her if Misty closed herself off to him. Leah didn't know what their relationship had been like, but it didn't seem very loving from the conversation she had experienced between the two of them. However, he had refused to transcend until his daughter knew he was sorry. Leah needed to try again.

Subject: Regarding Your Father

Dear Misty,

Thank you for your concern. I am fine. I have a wonderful support group. I wrote to you because your father was overwhelmed with guilt. He needed you to understand that he was sorry. Your dad shared a few memories with me. His proudest moment was driving you to Boston to help you move into your dormitory. He also loved cooking with you and eating Thanksgiving dinner together. Seeing you laughing during the turkey dice game filled his heart with joy. I'm not a scammer. I want nothing from you. Just know your father loved you. His greatest regret was saying those hurtful words. He hadn't wanted to say them but was forced to by the government...

Leah stopped, deleted, and rewrote.

He only wanted you to reconsider your decision, and using your mother to do that weighed heavily on his heart. He couldn't bear the thought that losing you could be a possibility. If you can open your mind and your heart to him, he will whisper to you, nudge you, guide you.

Sincerely,

Leah.

Turning her thoughts back to her grandfather, Leah decided to wait. He would be here for her graduation. She'd talk with him then.

After turning off the computer, Leah moved to her bed and picked up the training manual. Her new routine was to read one section, and then do the exercises and/or meditations that accompanied it. Tonight's exercise was to be done several times a day, every day, until mastery. It involved learning how to move and control every muscle and tendon in the body. Leah took off her socks and started with her toes. For half an hour she concentrated on moving the individual digits with little success. Next, she twisted and curled her feet, then her ankles, moving her way up her legs, feeling the muscles and tendons. She was surprised by how many she felt around her rips and up her spine. An hour later, after attempting to find and move every muscle in her body, she flipped back to the first exercise in the book—stretching.

Stretching was first because it reduced tension, increased blood flow and flexibility, and released serotonin. She read over the first two meditations about being present in the here and now, and not wanting or desiring objects or outcomes. The pages outlined ways to build her attractive energy and to use different yoga poses to teach her balance and control. After that came martial arts movements, meant to help her focus, build strength, and reinforce coordination and agility.

Before Leah called it a night, she peeked at the next exercise—being aware of her organs. Turning off the light, she climbed into bed and paid close attention to her heart, her stomach, and her kidneys. She quickened her heartbeat and then slowed it down using different thoughts and memories.

The goal of the meditations and exercises was to give her total control of her body and mind. People spent years practicing these first steps. Many wouldn't progress past them. Leah had skipped them altogether, having moved straight to the back of the book—psychic visions, touching minds, and forcing souls to transcend.

Lying in bed, sleep didn't come easy. Mr. Anderson, Misty Davis, Officer Choi, and the uncertainty around the manual all lingered in her thoughts. To calm herself, she rubbed the bed sheet between her fingers and stared at the ceiling, turning the shadows into designs. The stillness in the room finally pulled her to sleep.

The next morning, Uncle Tim drove Leah to school. He handed her some petitions, paraphrasing Roy's instructions: get signatures from those who can vote and who live inside the city limits. Then he asked about the protest. "What did your friends say? Will they help us?"

"They're not sure. Exams and all."

"Graduation is a week and a half away. If this is going to happen, we need to organize now."

"I'll get enough people to help. I promise," Leah said.

"Thank you. I'll have Roy call you tonight."

"Don't worry, Uncle Tim. I got you."

Exiting Miley, Leah tucked the petitions into her bag and walked toward the school doors, strategizing her approach. She spotted Barb's friend standing at her locker and waved.

"Hey, Lyla."

Lyla didn't bother hiding the roll of her eyes as she turned her back.

"Can I talk to you for a second?" Leah asked.

"I know why you're here. And no, I'm not interested."

"You don't even—"

"You're putting together that protest," Lyla interjected, shifting her books higher in her arms. "And look, I care about the Sukiya, I do. But graduation isn't the place to protest. We've been working for years to get here. This ceremony is supposed to be about us, not you."

Leah blinked, taken aback. "It's not about me."

"It's always about you," Lyla shot back. "Rich girl with her angel persona, always grandstanding."

Leah forced a smile. "Okay. I get it. I just thought you'd be interested because Barb's going to be there. But—hey, no hard feelings." She adjusted her bag on her shoulder as if she were ready to leave. Then she paused. "Can I at least shake your hand? Just ... truce. No hate."

Lyla shut her locker and fixed Leah with a glare. After a long hesitation, she sighed and extended her hand.

Leah wasted no time. She stretched the tendrils of her energy and slid into Lyla's mind, scrabbling for her thoughts on the Sukiya. Finding them, she strengthened her urgency to help and bent her will toward joining the protest. Then she slipped out.

Lyla pulled her hand back, frowning. "Did you... Were you..." Her brows knitted together.

Leah stepped away. "I know Barb would love to see you there, so if you change your mind, let me know." Backing down the hall, she waited a beat for her manipulations to take hold.

"Fine," Lyla burst. "I'll help. But only because I know how important that land is to the Native people."

With a nod and a smile, Leah responded, "We agree on that."

Lyla spun and stormed down the hall.

Air rushed into Leah's lungs as her muscles relaxed, leaving her shaky. She'd been holding her breath without realizing. *What did I just do?* Her pulse quickened, knowing Barb would be furious. But Lyla's words still burned, poking her chest like an accusatory finger: *It's always about you. Rich girl with your angel persona.*

Leah clenched her jaw. She wasn't doing this for herself. Uncle Tim's plan had to work, or Bellevue would hurt more people. And Lyla should stand with her friend.

She shook her head. *I'm not being selfish. I'm doing what must be done.* This protest had to happen, and she was going to get the people she needed.

By day's end, she had successfully enlisted twenty "volunteers."

In the police station downtown, Officer Choi opened his computer and wrote Leah an email.

Subject: Regarding you and your abilities.

Dear Leah,

I hope this message finds you well. I wanted to touch base with you regarding the development of your abilities and to ask if you are navigating this path safely and responsibly.

I've talked with my Aunt Yoona, and she will arrange a time to assess you in a few weeks. In the meantime, you are welcome to continue training with the manual. I'll be monitoring you for support purposes and urge you to inform me of your progress. Please review the inherent risks and responsibilities that come with manipulating energy.

My primary concern is your safety and ensuring you understand what it means to be a manipulator. There are moral and ethical boundaries surrounding the abilities to manipulate energy and serious consequences for crossing those lines.

I must also warn you, be cautious if approached by others and inform me immediately if someone shows interest in your abilities.

As to your question regarding the disturbance. It'll be a dangerous event with life altering consequences for several individuals. It may also cause a political shift to happen. I am telling you this because as a user you may have or have had visions that hold insight into this disturbance. If you experience or have experienced any psychic visions, no matter how minor, please contact me promptly. This vision will be accompanied by some sort of pull or call to action. It's a warning designed to protect you.

Let's discuss these matters further at your earliest convenience.

Choi.

India

Clues and Questions

Misty Davis scrutinized Leah's email, attempting to decode its meaning. "Oh, she's been snooping," Misty muttered, scrolling through the recounted activities Leah had listed—driving to Boston, turkey dice game, their last phone conversation. Although Misty shouldn't have been surprised, the reality of it felt surreal. What was Leah planning? How did she intend to leverage or manipulate Misty with this information? Leah's revelation that Paul had exploited her mother's death to guilt her into moving home felt particularly intrusive. It meant someone had been surveilling Misty for a while. There was no other way Leah could have known this detail. Revisiting Leah's email, Misty dismissed the notion of her father feeling remorseful or offering an apology. Guilt? Whatever. Sorry? It wasn't in his vocabulary.

Rolling her finger over the mouse, Misty stared at her computer. Something was off about the email. The situation didn't add up. Misty had been a nobody; why would a powerful businessman bother tapping her phone? Nothing remarkable or noteworthy about Misty would have attracted attention before she started causing a stir.

Grabbing pen and paper, Misty jotted down the order of events that had led to this email:

1. I graduated medical school and joined Doctors without Borders.

2. I called my dad, and we argued.

3. I got an email from my dad. An hour later, he was dead.

4. The funeral. Sorting his things. The garage sale. The donations. The words unsaid.

5. I went to India.

6. The Department of Defense took refugees.

7. I checked in on them, only to learn they had been taken to a private hospital in New York called Extended Life and were reported missing or dead.

8. I contacted U.S. officials.

9. More refugees were taken and again ended up missing or dead.

10. I contacted the FBI, the New York police department, the *New York Times*, congress members, and senators. I also informed the Indian authorities.

11. Leah Davenport, granddaughter to the CEO of Extended Life, emailed me and knows details about my life and private conversations with my dad.

Sitting back in her chair, Misty digested the information. It was time to talk with Leah in person. Clicking the "respond" button, Misty pasted her video chat ID and typed her message:

Subject: Call Me

Leah,

We need to talk. Saturday, 8:30 p.m. your time. Call me.

Misty

Lake Valley, Oregon

<u>Confronting Conundrums</u>

Leah's Saturday morning was brimming with tasks and meetings, starting with a bull session with Roy for the upcoming protest. She powered up her computer to print his ideas and noticed emails from *Rolling Stone* magazine, NBC, Officer Choi, Roy Running Deer, and Misty Davis.

Opening Roy's email first, she learned that the principal and the school district had strictly forbidden the protest to take place. She would have to obtain permission from the school board. Without their approval, the risk of legal repercussions, including arrest, was a distinct possibility for everyone involved. Leah noted the time and place of the next meeting.

Opening Choi's email, Leah rubbed her forehead with her fingers. "Monitoring me?" she gasped. "Responsibilities?" These words felt like chains. Leah was happy to read that Choi wouldn't be confiscating the training manual, but the idea that someone else would be "assessing" her again didn't sit well. Ever since her abilities had been discovered, she felt like others were trying to put her in a box.

Leah's inner voice screamed, *Why does everyone think they know what's best for me?* She just wanted to keep her abilities hidden and help people the best she could in her own way. But now, it seemed like the whole world wanted a piece of her, wanted to mold her into something she didn't want to be.

Leah slammed her computer shut and seethed. "Father Joseph!" All of this had started with his declaration that she was an angel. The requests pounded in her mind: *Say a prayer for my aunt, heal my mom, cure my brother.* The reporters and photographers hounding her. And now Officer Choi's Circle! *We'll be monitoring you.* Couldn't she just be in charge of herself, a normal girl with powers who occasionally helped people?

Above all others, Mr. Anderson stood most prominently. His dig into her mind. His proposal: seven hundred thousand dollars a year, a house, a car, and a chance to make a real impact. Was she interested? You bet.

Leah closed her eyes and whispered, "I control me. I'll use this power for good, but I'll do it my way."

Brandon, his mom, and Jae came to mind. Choi's mention of a psychic vision that would "call her to action" was ominous. The future she had seen in the forest fit his description; it had pulled her to help Judy. That whole fiasco was over with, though, and telling Choi about it would only invite more scrutiny. Better to not say any more than was absolutely necessary.

Reopening her computer, Leah read Misty's email: We need to talk—a request that made perfect sense. She inserted the time on her phone so she wouldn't forget. Then she gathered the printed papers and headed out to meet the volunteers and Roy at Uncle Tim's house.

Her classmates convened in the game room, laughing, playing, and teasing. Leah saw Barb and Lyla, but avoided them. If the two talked about her, Barb might put the pieces together.

After Roy settled everyone down, Leah was the first to speak. "Just so you know, the principal made it clear, in no uncertain terms, that we are not to hold this protest during graduation." She caught Lyla's glare, her lips pressed tight. Leah held her stare, saying, "I'm going to the school board meeting to ask for permission." Then she turned her gaze to the others, concluding, "But if I don't get authorization, we could get into some serious trouble by proceeding."

The group broke out in dissent.

"He can't tell us what to do."

"Free speech!"

"Who does he think he is? We have the right to peacefully assemble."

The ultimatum only strengthened their resolve.

Roy spoke. "I'm assuming since you're all here voicing your disapproval of this news that you are prepared to move ahead."

"Damn straight," a boy yelled. The others applauded his response.

"As long as you know you could get in trouble," Roy said. "You won't be looked on as heroes or as brave. You do understand that, right?"

The group nodded, and a chorus of "yeses" rose from many.

"All right. If you're sure about this, we'll proceed. Let's go over everything we need to do before graduation."

Later that evening at 8:30 p.m., Leah went to her room, sat at her computer, and called Misty Davis. She answered, wearing her doctor's whites.

"Hi," Leah said.

Misty didn't respond. She just stared at her through the screen. The silence stretched, becoming uncomfortable.

"I asked you to call me because I needed to know who was actually emailing me," Misty finally said.

"I understand," Leah acknowledged.

"Let me get to it then. Who are you? How did you know the contents of my private conversation with my father?"

"I thought I explained that already. I met your father shortly after his email with you. He confided in me."

Misty laughed. "And as I told you, that's not possible. My father died an hour after that email was sent. He slipped and fell down the stairs, breaking his neck. So, I'll ask you again. How did you know the contents of our private conversation?"

"I can see you are upset, and I'm sorry. That was not my intention. I was simply passing along a message. I won't bother you anymore."

"Oh, well, color me surprised! For all your spying and hacking, you certainly missed the mark on my father. He wasn't exactly the apologizing type. He was more of a hard-ass who only cared about himself."

Thinking about prom and how Paul had treated Barb, Leah raised her brows and said, "I can't disagree with that. But he realized his mistakes and was full of guilt."

Misty shook her head. "I need to know what you want and why you're harassing me. What's your grandfather up to? Are you a government spy?"

Leah's brow furrowed deeply, and she squinted as if trying to decipher Misty's words. "I don't want anything. I'm not harassing you," she said in a tone of disbelief. "And why would you think I'm a government spy?"

"I've researched you online. I know about your recent abduction, and that you're still in high school. I'm also aware that your grandfather is the CEO of Extended Life, which has a contract with the Department of Defense. The military has been taking young, strong refugees and shipping them to your grandfather's hospital in New York. These individuals have gone missing or have been reported as dead. If you're attempting to intimidate me so I'll stay quiet, it won't work. My camp is not a source of bodies for the Defense Department's nefarious purposes!"

Leah's mouth fell open. "Umm..." Nothing Misty had just said fully registered. Wiping her forehead, Leah said, "I'm sorry. I really don't know what you're talking about. I only wanted to relay a message to you from your father."

"Really? Then tell me the truth. How do you know me and my family?"

Leah didn't know how to answer that question. She was still catching up after being blindsided by accusations. A government spy? Misty's words held power, which made her insides cringe. Mr. Anderson had said Extended Life was helping people, and now someone was claiming the opposite. The material she had been given made the company sound wonderful. They had discovered technology that was like ... *her.* What was Extended Life truly doing? Were the individuals taken from Misty's camp like Leah? Did they have abilities?

"Why did you say I'm harassing you?" Leah asked.

"I've been digging deep into a serious issue regarding refugees from my camp. Your grandfather is involved. The fact that you have detailed knowledge about my life and conversations raises red flags. I need answers, Leah, and I need to understand how you fit into all of this."

"I am clueless. The last time I talked with my grandfather was on the phone after I was released from my abductor. He was concerned about my safety and asked my uncle to be my bodyguard. I don't know anything else. I can talk to him. He is coming to my graduation ceremony. Tell me what happened, and I'll confront him about it."

Misty explained that on two occasions, a representative from the U.S. Department of Defense had visited the camp and handpicked ten individuals. "I felt a sense of relief, thinking they were being granted visas and flown to America with the chance to make a new life. But the more I thought about it the more suspicious it felt; visas were given by the Office of Refugee Resettlement, not the Department of Defense. It was unsettling." She continued by telling Leah that the individuals were taken to a private hospital in New York called "Extended Life," and by the time she followed up, they were dead or missing. When she asked about it, she was given lame excuses about infections, a virus, a heart attack, and running away. She knew these people. She knew their medical histories. "Something very wrong is happening. And I feel like you're in on whatever's going on."

Leah placed her elbow on the desk and rested her forehead in the palm of her hand. "I'm not, honestly." She sighed. "Email me their names. I'll do my best to find out what's really happening."

Misty nodded. "I'll email you the list of names, but I don't trust you. I'm still left with the question: how do you know me?"

"I don't know how to answer that."

"It's a pretty simple question. Answer with the truth."

"You wouldn't believe me."

"Try me."

Leah sighed.

Misty asked, "You didn't happen to buy a computer recently, did you? Maybe from a kid named Eric?"

"I know about the computer, yes."

"You knew it was my father's computer and that my brother sold it?"

"I knew it was your father's."

"Okay, you're a hacker," Misty stated, believing she had uncovered a simple truth. "That wasn't so hard."

"I'm not a hacker," Leah responded. "Eric is my friend. The computer was giving him headaches, and he ended up in the hospital. He became a different person."

Misty's face turned white. "Eric became a different person?"

"He didn't know who he was, or who his friends were."

Misty sat in silence for a long moment. "My brother ended up in the hospital. He had become my father. He had the same mannerisms, used the same kind of language, and had the same temperament." Misty paused. "After his wife sold the computer, my brother returned to his normal self."

In a soft, friendly tone, Leah said, "Your father transcended after I wrote to you. He needed you to know how sorry he was before he could move on. He won't be possessing anyone else. He's in a good place now."

Misty's expression turned to confusion. Then she laughed. "You talked to my dad when he was a ghost?! Is that what you're telling me?"

"I am studying the art of Shamanism."

Misty rubbed her face with her hand, shaking her head. "I can't deal with you right now."

"Misty, I'm sorry. I'm sympathetic to how this looks and sounds. I was just trying to help."

"Right. Well, you can help by telling me what's happening to my patients."

"I will. I'll write you after I meet with my grandfather."

"I look forward to that. Have a good night." The screen went dark.

Leah stood and paced the room. A chill ran down her spine. Was what Misty said really true? Her story was troubling, but she admitted to not fully understanding the facts. What *was* Extended Life? What did this company do? Was it good or bad?

A snicker began to bubble up within her. The absurdity of the situation struck her. Eric, Paul, her grandfather, Misty, Mr. Anderson... She couldn't believe the timing or the connections. This couldn't be coincidence, could it?

Leah spotted the book next to her bed and eyed it. *With attractive energy, people, things, opportunities, and even ghosts and spirits will come to you.* Turning to her computer, Choi's words flashed in her mind—*Understand what it means to be an energy manipulator.* She closed her eyes and Barb asked, *Leah, are you sure you want to become a Banisher? I mean ... ghosts, spirits, trauma, heartache.*

Leah grabbed a pillow and screamed into it.

She needed to meditate. To calm her mind and her emotions. To reconnect to her spiritual core and her purpose.

Slow... she closed her eyes. *Calm...* she swayed back and forth. *Breathe...* she inhaled. *Relax...* she exhaled.

The pulsing of energy returned—an etheric flow. It was an interconnectedness of the universe, and she knew that tapping into it would gain her insights into the past, present, and potential futures. If she could dive into the pond of possibilities, she could glimpse the myriad paths ahead and maybe learn about Extended

Life. Was she ready to learn how to do this? Did she want to try? Would she be able to find the answers to her questions there?

She picked up the book and opened it. The chapter on connecting stared at her. She felt the book judging her. The title at the top of the page read: The Perils of Unchecked Connections. Was the book scolding her? Leah vaguely remembered that this section explained loss of self, ethical boundaries, manipulation, abuse, physical and mental strain, and preventive measures. She was about to flip past it when she felt compelled to read. She exhaled loudly and said, "Fine. I'll read the beginning, but I already understand."

She began reading: *The dangers and risks of manipulating others for personal gain are profound and insidious. It begins innocently enough: a simple desire to sway a loved one's decision in your favor. Perhaps you implant a thought in your partner's mind to persuade them to allow you to attend a party. The success feels exhilarating, a newfound power that is harmless and justified.*

This initial act plants the seed of entitlement. The ease with which you manipulate a situation for your benefit becomes a temptation too alluring to resist. You begin to believe that your desires are paramount, that others' wills are mere obstacles to be circumvented.

As the scope of your influence expands, you will no longer be satisfied with minor personal gains. Altering others' beliefs to align with your own follows. You convince yourself that you are guiding them towards a better path, one that only you can see. The one true and righteous way. The power to shape minds becomes intoxicating, and soon, you wield it with increasing frequency and fervor.

Your ambitions grow bolder. You seek to control not just individuals, but entire groups. You manipulate public opinion to win a political position of power and secure an agenda. You shape decisions and strategies to ensure your dominance. The lines between your true self and the personas you craft in others blur, leading you down a path of deceit and corruption.

The more power you accumulate, the more ruthless you become. Opponents are not merely rivals; they are threats to your control, to be crushed without mercy. You justify these actions as necessary for maintaining order and achieving your vision. Yet, with each step, you lose a piece of your humanity, replaced by a relentless drive for supremacy.

What starts as a benign act of influence spirals into a devastating addiction to power. The path to corruption is paved with good intentions, but it ends in the complete loss of one's soul.

The consequences for manipulating an individual for personal gain include isolation to purify your soul. But beware: cleansing rituals cannot erase corruption's stain. Even after purification, you will forever feel its pull. Should your will falter, a Circle member will find you and shred your soul. Before you move forward in your training and learn to connect, ensure you have purged wants and desires from your being. Live in each moment as it presents itself.

Let's take a closer look at this progression and how to recognize the signs you are becoming corrupted. First is emotional overload.

Leah closed the book and swallowed hard.

Barb's voice echoed through her thoughts, *Did you or did you not read the warnings that are in this book? You are messing with magic you don't understand.*

Calm... Leah closed her eyes. *Breathe...* she inhaled. *Relax...* she exhaled.

Leah slid the book under her bed. *I'm not ready to learn any more.* Extended Life could wait a few days. It was her grandfather's company, and she'd have a long talk with him about it when he arrived. She went to close the computer and saw that Misty had sent the list of names.

The list stared back, demanding she put a face to each name. She closed her laptop, aware that sleep wouldn't come easy tonight.

Seoul, Korea

Paths Diverge, Souls Merge

Seo-Ah knocked on Su-Bin's office door. "Excuse me, ma'am. There are two attorneys here from Hanada Law firm to see you."

"I'm going to trial today, Seo-Ah. I'm not seeing anyone. Ask them to make an appointment."

"They said it was urgent and would only take a minute of your time."

Su-Bin exhaled loudly and straightened, fixing a hard, unpleasant gaze at Seo-Ah.

"They're quite insistent."

Clenching her jaw, Su-Bin slid her files into her leather bag. "Very well. I'll meet them in conference room one. And Seo-Ah, call the courier. Courthouse pickup."

"Yes, ma'am."

Su-Bin shut down her computer, locked her desk, and placed the lid on the banker's box of exhibits. Then she headed for conference room one to greet the two attorneys who waited.

The men stood and bowed as she entered. "Good morning, gentlemen. How may I help you?"

"We know you're in a hurry, so we'll get straight to the point. I'm Si-Wan Lee, a lawyer representing Dr. Hyun Kim." He took out a stack of papers and set them on the table, then slid them over to Su-Bin. "Dr. Kim is suing you for defamation of character, slander. Your firm has wrongfully accused Dr. Kim of being a murder suspect. These false statements have caused substantial harm to the doctor's reputation, damaging his working relationships with his colleagues.

The forms outline our demands in order to resolve this issue. If we don't hear from you by the end of the week, we will file this case with the courts."

Su-Bin flipped through the documents, catching the headings and signature lines. She didn't have time for this. She looked up and fixed them with a flat, unimpressed stare.

"Ms. Moon, our client isn't interested in tarnishing your name or negating the excellent work you have done. He is aware of your award nomination and is only interested in clearing his name. We respectfully ask that, in the interest of both parties, you agree to the terms outlined in these documents. The attorney who falsely made these outlandish claims should be the one punished, not you. We look forward to hearing from you very soon." Bowing, the two lawyers concluded, "Good day, Ms. Moon."

Su-Bin bowed slightly as the men left. *Ugh ... of all days!* Glancing at the documents a final time, she immediately thought about the DNA samples Min had sent in three weeks ago. She should have called about them days ago. She looked at the time as she headed for the car. As long as traffic wasn't bad, she would have plenty of time to touch base with her client and run through key points. In the car, Su-Bin called her secretary and asked her to inquire about the DNA results.

Nearing the courthouse, Su-Bin received a call from Soe-Ah.

"I called the lab as you requested. They were asked to hold those results until Min Yun came to collect them. He picked them up on Tuesday," she said. "I did request an additional copy be forwarded to us."

"Okay, thank you, Seo-Ah." Parking the car and grabbing her briefcase, Su-Bin wondered what Min Yun's game was. He wouldn't try to use those results as leverage to see her, would he? Surely not. Perhaps he was simply curious, or maybe he was trying to delay the advancement of the case as a way to protest. Certainly, he didn't think that his discovery about Brandon would allow him to return.

"Yoona! What kind of maniac did you send me?" Su-Bin cursed under her breath as she passed through the metal detectors. She couldn't be thinking about this now. She needed to focus on the trial.

As she hurried down the hall, she called Seo-Ah back. "Can you make an appointment for me to see Moodang Yoona? Her number is in my contact information."

"Yes, ma'am. I'll text you the appointment information once it's scheduled."

Since Yoona had gotten her into this mess, she could damn well get her out of it.

She entered the trial courtroom and found her client already seated at the counsel table. Su-Bin arranged her workspace, then reviewed the schedule and procedures for the day. Her phone buzzed, and she read Seo-Ah's text: "Next available appointment is a year and four months away."

Lifting her head in frustration, she whispered, "Of course it is." Thinking quickly, she texted: "Ask Mr. Spencer to set up the appointment. I need to speak with her in the next few days. I'm in court now, so I'll turn off my phone."

Su-Bin hated being distracted while at trial. She excused herself and went to the restroom, washed her face, and took deep calming breaths, pushing everything away except this trial. She reentered the courtroom, focused.

Brandon sat at his desk, preparing for his next class. His arm and shoulder ached from the stabbing. Yoona had instructed him to take control of his mind, his nerves, and find the cool line where pain stops. *Touch the wound with your mind. Feel the blood flow to and from the injury.*

Gently rubbing his cuts, his consciousness went straight to the area. He closed his eyes and turned inward, "seeing" the cells divide, rebuilding the damaged tissues. Blood pumped in needed materials and took away the waste. *More*, Brandon thought, and soon the vessels were packed with vital supplies. The cells worked faster. He *was* able to channel extra resources and aid in the regeneration of his own biological structures!

Brandon sat in meditation, directing his body like a foreman at a construction site, until a tap on his shoulder shook him back. A lawyer nodded toward Seo-Ah, who had apparently been trying to get his attention. Brandon apologized. Seo-Ah bowed and did the same. She informed him of Su-Bin's request for him to contact Yoona. Brandon acknowledged her and said he would right away.

Brandon missed Su-Bin. Her beautiful eyes, her confident gait, the time she nibbled on the tip of her finger. Ever since the raid, her angry eyes told him to stay away. He wasn't exactly sure why Su-Bin was so upset. The broadcast news had clearly pointed out that he and his team had stopped a terrorist plot and captured one of the leaders. Brandon was a hero, and the positive coverage Moon Law was receiving made her firm a household name. He had told her about Hina. Told her she had died. He wondered who gave her the photo, the one of him, Jaime, and Hina. But he didn't wonder for long. Min was the first person to come to mind.

Knowing it would all work out, Brandon let it go. He pressed Matthew's number on his phone and texted: "Can you inform Yoona that the owner of the law firm, Su-Bin, would like to meet with her as soon as possible?"

An hour later, Matthew texted: "She'll come to the law firm later today."

Brandon relayed the information to Seo-Ah.

Su-Bin left the courthouse and returned to her law firm. Seo-Ah wasn't at her desk. Realizing her phone was still off, Su-Bin took it out and pressed the power button as she walked into her office. Yoona stood in front of the window, admiring the view. Startled, Su-Bin spluttered, "Oh, hi. You're here. Give me a second to put my things down."

"Of course. I had your secretary show me in. She is devoted and loyal. She'll be a powerful ally for you in the future."

"She's young, still setting goals for herself." After hanging her coat and dropping her briefcase behind her desk, Su-Bin motioned for Yoona to have a seat. "Would you like a drink?"

"I don't drink, but thank you."

"I hope you don't mind if I pour myself one," Su-Bin said, opening a bottle of scotch. Drink in hand, Su-Bin sat with Yoona. "I didn't expect to see you here. I would have been happy to come to you."

"Su-Bin, you are in control. Relax," Yoona stressed. "I know you have questions and concerns. I'm here to answer those for you."

"Thank you." Su-Bin gathered her thoughts and decided to start with the raid at the port. "Moodang Yoona, I have always followed your advice, and it has led me to success. I've felt grateful to you, but am beginning to have questions. I didn't know you were in law enforcement. I didn't understand your true intentions for sending Brandon to me. This terrorist incident and the windfall from it have been crazy. What I want to say is, I'm sensing that you didn't trust me enough to tell me everything. This makes me feel used. It's unpleasant. If you needed my help, why didn't you just ask, instead of playing spy games?"

Calmly, Yoona eyed Su-Bin. "A lot has happened since Brandon has come to you. You are growing, learning, expanding your understanding of this world. You are on a journey of discovery."

Yoona's mysterious codes annoyed Su-Bin. She wanted an explanation, a straight answer. "A lot of *drama* has happened since Brandon arrived!" she snapped. "Unwanted drama. Did you know Min Yun was a jealous, obsessed, manipulative jerk? Did you know about Brandon's past? I appreciate all the attention my firm has received because of him, but Brandon's being a pedophile will put my firm in jeopardy. I trusted you and put that trust in the men you sent me. I made a mistake."

Yoona's expression hadn't changed. Nothing Su-Bin said fazed her.

"What is this journey I'm supposed to be on? Discovering I shouldn't count on the people you send me?"

Now Yoona smiled warmly. "Discovery, yes. You will discover the answer to every question you have."

Leaning back in her seat, Su-Bin downed her drink. "I cut ties with Min Yun. I warned him to stay away from me, but he is still meddling in my affairs. I'm ready to go to the police."

"I will simply tell you that Min Yun is deeply involved in your mother's case, and that by allowing him to continue representing her, you will find the best result for all parties involved."

Su-Bin lowered her brow. "Are you saying I should bring him back—give him my mother's case? Are you kidding me? He's the reason my firm is about to be sued, on top of everything else he's done."

"Min Yun is motivated to free your mother. More factors are at play than you know."

"I know he's obsessed with me. He thinks by winning my mother's free-dom, this somehow makes me his property. He played and toyed with me. Used my desire to free my mother as a way to manipulate my emotions. I allowed him to take advantage of me. I won't let that happen again."

"Allowing him to discover that truth will make you a stronger person. Min Yun is the most qualified and dedicated person for your mother's case. She will be free in a matter of months if you allow him to continue. It's time for you to manipulate him."

Su-Bin let that process for a moment—*Min can free my mom because more is happening than I know.* What did that mean exactly? She went to the bar and refilled her drink. Politics could be dangerous. Su-Bin had always suspected a political enemy had murdered her father. If that were true, was Min somehow connected? She returned to the sofa and studied Yoona. The woman's face revealed nothing.

"What about Brandon?" Su-Bin asked. "Can you tell me if his past is going to suddenly blow up in my face? The stress of knowing that I'll soon have to answer for his criminal acts is taxing. And if I fire him, I'll have to explain why."

"Brandon's past cannot harm you," Yoona reassured. "You should feel comfortable and safe with him."

Su-Bin laughed, "I guess I've been misinformed then."

Yoona didn't say anything.

Su-Bin narrowed Her eyes. Did the Shaman's silence confirm her statement?

"You don't need to worry; I'm taking Brandon from you," Yoona finally said. "He is ready to begin his training."

"Taking him? Wait a minute. I know his character is questionable at best, but he's an excellent language teacher. I have him under contract for six months. How will I explain his departure?"

"With the truth. Brandon's presence here was never about teaching." Yoona paused before continuing. "He was here to help you. He has done that. Take some time to review all that has occurred because of his presence. Then I need you to search your feelings and discover whom you truly love and why."

"Whom I truly love?" Su-Bin shuddered. "Is my life a game to you? Am I some form of entertainment? Whom I truly love!? Are you spying on me—using my life as a reality drama?"

"When your journey is complete and you have had time to reflect on everything that has happened, you will thank me."

Su-Bin glared at Yoona, unconvinced. "I doubt that. What am I supposed to do about a teacher? I spent a lot of time looking for one before Brandon arrived."

"A suitable teacher will present themselves soon. Be patient."

"Suitable? Brandon is exceptional."

"The power he uses to teach is meant for a higher purpose. I'm sorry."

Su-Bin exhaled.

Leaning forward, Yoona touched Su-Bin's hand. "Cherish the time you had together."

With a disgusted look, Su-Bin uttered, "I'd rather be thankful for the time we didn't share together."

In a soothing tone, Yoona reassured her, "Su-Bin. It's okay to be happy with the closeness that you had. It meant something to you at the time. Don't minimize that experience. Allow the happy, wonderful memory to thrive. Magical moments matter. Your instincts about him were true. Don't discount that."

"Are you saying Min's evidence against Brandon is a lie?"

Standing, Yoona informed her, "You are scheduled to come see me in four months. Your secretary has already added me to your calendar. We'll talk about all of this again and say goodbye to your father."

"Right. Apparently, he's been hanging around."

"He's been working with me as he watches over you."

Su-Bin stared hard. Yoona turned and left.

Collapsing in her chair, Su-Bin didn't want to think or spend time analyzing Yoona's words. Instead, she just wanted to be with someone who understood her—someone she could trust. Someone with whom she felt safe. She needed Jong-In.

She took another drink, then waited half a beat for it to hit. Tapping her phone, she called Jong-In. "Can you come over? I need to be with someone. A lot has happened today."

"Yes. I can be there in an hour."

"I'm leaving the office now. See you soon."

Su-Bin, feeling the alcohol, took a taxi home. Her mind wandered back to the conversation with Yoona. Giving Min Yun his job back was the last thing she wanted to do. It felt like a betrayal, like she was stabbing herself in the chest with an ice pick. And worse, she knew Yoona was right. She sensed her father whispering to her that this was the best way forward.

Call him and tell him to come back, was now the loudest thought in her mind. It also happened to be the one thought she didn't want to have. When she arrived home, she paid the fair, thinking how terrible the idea of contacting Min was. She ground her teeth as she dialed his number.

The call went to voicemail. Su-Bin was relieved not to have to speak with him directly. After the beep, she left her message. "I haven't forgiven you for what you did, but I'll reinstate you on two conditions: you take my mother's case, and you avoid me for the time being. Don't call me back. Just show up tomorrow if you accept." She closed her phone.

With a deep sigh, she headed inside, thinking she needed another drink. She didn't want to see Min again. His presence was such a strain on her energy.

Min Yun came out of the shower to find Su-Bin's phone message. He'd been anxiously awaiting this call, hoping she wouldn't yelled at him about the DNA results. He just needed her to understand that he was still available and that he wanted a chance to prove himself.

He listened to her voicemail. She was short with him but did ask for him to return. He listened to the message several times, and when he finally put down the phone, he threw punches into the air, celebrating. "Yes! Yes! Yes! I love you, Su-Bin!"

Jong-In's knuckles hovered above Su-Bin's door. This place, this moment, felt all too familiar. He'd been in this position countless times before, always the best friend, the one Su-Bin could lean on when things went wrong.

Maybe this was fate. The thought wasn't new. He'd had it after every failed attempt to profess his love. But tonight, it was stronger, more concrete. Tonight would cement his role forever as the best friend.

Jong-In had loved Su-Bin for as long as he could remember—from the very first moment he had seen her. When she had told him that her best friend, Nari, liked him, he had responded, "But I like you." Su-Bin had smiled and invited him to lunch. Later, he realized her invitation had been for Nari. He had agreed to date her, not because he had feelings for Nari, but because he wanted to be close to Su-Bin. When he and Nari had broken up, he wrote a note to Su-Bin, rehearsed the words, and waited by her locker, heart pounding. But when Su-Bin had turned the corner holding hands with his best friend, the practiced words evaporated with his hope. He was the friend.

Then there was the day he had rushed to her house with flowers, ready to finally declare his love. But when he had arrived, he found Su-Bin sobbing. Her father had been murdered the night before, and her mother had been arrested. Jong-In stood there, flowers in hand, realizing everything had changed. She needed him, not as a boyfriend, but as a brother—to be her family.

Finally, there was the day she had transferred schools. He had everything ready—the picnic, the flowers, the string quartet. Then she had called. "I'm transferring to law school. I have to apply today. Can you help me?" And he had—because she needed him. He would support her, believe in her, and help her through the chaos. Love—real love—knew when to be silent.

Su-Bin was single. The window was open to tell her how he truly felt, but here he was again, in front of her door, ready to fulfill the role he'd always played—the friend, the brother. He was ready to accept that they would never be more than this. And he now understood that's how it needed to be.

The dissonance in his heart, however, told him he was crazy. He reminded himself that she had always been there for him, ever since Nari had broken up with him. Su-Bin had chosen Jong-In over her best friend. She took his side and defended him against rumors. When he was fired from his job, she didn't accuse him or judge him, just listened and helped him see the lesson. When he failed his entrance exam, she didn't let him spiral, but helped him study, calmed his nerves, made him eat and sleep. She was his best friend, his sister.

That's why a romantic relationship was out of the question. He couldn't lose her, and she couldn't lose him. They were family! And that's how it would stay.

Taking a deep breath, he threw away any lingering traces of romantic love and knocked on the door.

Su-Bin answered, her eyes swollen and red. He could smell the alcohol. He stepped straight toward her and held her in his arms, swaying her gently back and forth.

She buried her face between his shoulder and chin, nestling her lips against his neck. Her warm breath tickled his skin. They held each other, wrapped in silence, in history.

Jong-In squeezed her tight, and she snuggled closer, her lips kissing his neck. He closed his eyes, breathing hard, his heart pounding. *What's happening?*

Su-Bin kissed him again. His skin tingled, and his body stiffened. He swallowed, unsure if this was real.

She kissed him more, sliding her leg in between his to press against him. Jong-In didn't move, he knew she could feel him. His adrenaline surged and his organ grew.

She kissed and kissed. His body trembled and his mind raced. *How should I react?* Su-Bin was drunk. He wouldn't take advantage of her.

She laid her hand on his chest, standing straight, looking him in the eyes. He saw her gaze was expressive, reflecting surprise and realization. "I love you," she whispered.

Jong-In drew back. He was dreaming. These encounters had always been dreams. Her round, vulnerable, innocent eyes tugged at his soul. This was the moment. He'd been wishing for this. Parting the curtain that hid his heart, Jong-In revealed the depth of his emotions. Placing his hands on her cheeks, he professed, "I love you! So much."

She moved her hand to the back of his neck and pulled him close, parting her lips.

Soft—two petals of ecstasy. Heat—moist, intoxicating breath. The anticipation of suckling love drew him closer to her lips, causing the liquids in his body to move at dangerous speeds.

When they finally kissed, pungently sweet smells of perfumed pheromones gushed into the air. His long-suppressed emotions clamored to be released. Seventeen years of pent-up desire, closely regulated, were now on the verge of a cataclysmic eruption, as countless nights of this dream now became a reality. She was finally wanting him, acknowledging him as more than a friend. Would they become lovers? Would he be able to breathe in her scent every night and hold her in his arms every morning? The hope, the image, the yearning, filled Jong-In to the brink of combustion.

The moment her tongue touched his, an electrical storm thundered through his existence, exceeding the pressure limits of his organ. A violent hail of emotions bombarded him with such force that his release was seismic, causing his body to convulse.

Su-Bin placed Jong-In's head on her shoulder, stroking his hair. "You are a very good actor," she whispered, tickling his ear. "All these years, and you've never said anything."

Jong-In tried to raise his head. He was so embarrassed. All he could think to do was bow and ask forgiveness.

Su-Bin held him firmly. "How have you managed your emotions? Why did you do that?"

Jong-In stopped trying to move. He melted into her arms, digesting chemicals that his body had never processed before.

Nibbling his ear, Su-Bin whispered, "Let's take a shower. I need you. We can do this all night long."

The following day, Su-Bin stood in front of her office door, greeting team members as they entered Moon Law and Associates. *Is Min Yun going to show?* The question sat at the back of her throat, like bitter acid she couldn't swallow.

The doors opened. Su-Bin tensed—then relaxed.

Seo-Ah stepped inside, offering a greeting and a polite bow. "Is it true that Brandon is leaving us?" she asked.

"Yes," Su-Bin replied, her eyes still fixed on the door, hoping Min wouldn't come.

"It's a shame. He was such a good teacher. Who will replace him?"

Su-Bin didn't answer. Her mind was clouded. How had Yoona convinced her to invite Min back? The door opened and her chest tightened. *Whew, not Min.*

"I'm sorry," Seo-Ah said, bowing as she stepped away. "I didn't mean to bother you."

Blinking, Su-Bin forced herself to look away from the entrance. "No, Seo-Ah—you're fine. There's ... a lot on my mind right now."

"Of course," Seo-Ah replied. "May I get you anything?"

The door opened again, drawing Su-Bin's gaze. Min Yun waltzed in with a cocky smile and the air of a superstar. He waved and offered a slight bow like nothing had happened.

Su-Bin recoiled in disgust. She slipped inside her door and pressed her back against the wall. Her hands went to her temples, and she took a second to catch her breath.

Brandon passed her door, deep in conversation with a bald man sporting a black braided goatee and a tattoo that curled from his ear down around his neck. He was the scariest man she'd ever seen. Who was he? Why was Brandon with him? Su-Bin placed her hand over her heart to calm the flutter of nerves.

420

Peering around the corner, she watched as Min muttered something to Brandon as they passed, but Brandon didn't acknowledge him.

Su-Bin eased back into her hiding place and knocked the back of her head against the drywall. *I should say goodbye.* She nodded. *I need to say goodbye.* Rushing to the door, she caught a glimpse of the car as it turned the corner. Brandon was gone.

Her shoulders slumped as she exhaled. A hollow ache settled in the center of her chest. Why did it hurt so much not to say goodbye? He was a sexual predator. And yet, Yoona's cryptic words from the night before had implied Brandon was innocent. Was he innocent?

Min's voice slithered through the halls of the building, making her stomach curdle. She had to know the truth. Turning on her heels, she marched to HR.

"Did you call and verify Brandon's employment history?" she asked in a harsh tone.

They had. He came highly recommended.

Su-Bin reviewed Brandon's résumé. The Thai school where he had taught was called Streemanda, and the headmistress listed was Sister Atchara. Those names were the same ones in Min's video.

Min's videos.

Something about them made her uneasy. The edits and the theatrical satisfaction in Min's delivery felt staged. And her entire understanding of what was said came from a translator Min had hired. What had Sister Atchara actually said in that video? She wondered what any of the women had actually said.

Su-Bin ordered her HR department to find translators for Thai, Spanish, and Japanese. Forty-five minutes later, she was rewatching the videos with her own interpreters.

The Thai interpreter watched the video clip of Min and Sister Atchara and began to laugh. "Oh, my! They aren't even talking about the same thing. The man asked a question about Brandon, but the translator asked about the flood that damaged the school. The Sister is explaining how the water rose to the second floor. This video is not a translation or even an interpretation; it's a fabricated story."

Going to the next clip with the young woman and the baby, the interpreter said, "Again, two completely different stories. The young woman says Brandon was a great teacher. Then when asked about her baby, she explains that she had sex with her boyfriend when they were drunk, and she ended up getting pregnant. She's working with her mom." Turning to Su-Bin, the translator asked, "Who gave you this? It's slander. This Brandon guy could totally sue."

The Spanish translator was confused as well. "The woman is talking about an earthquake and destruction done to the city, not Brandon."

The Japanese translator said that Brandon was a loving husband and that the death of her daughter, Hina, and her grandchild, Jaime, had been awful for everyone.

Su-Bin felt terrible. Now that she knew the truth—that the woman and child in the photo she'd shoved in his face were really his wife and son—everything clicked. His haunted look hadn't been guilt; it had been grief. She needed to find Brandon and apologize.

Turning her thoughts to Min, she couldn't believe he had spent all that time, money, and effort to slander someone. He was crazy. If he'd stoop that low to win her back, then what would he do to free her mother? Su-Bin was certain Min would propose marriage after her mother's release. And he'd do anything to make that happen.

Slander. The word echoed in her mind. Dr. Kim was suing her firm for slander—because Min had accused him of being a suspect in her father's murder.

A cold wave of dread ran through her. "Oh, no." Had Min framed Dr. Kim? The hard lump in her chest was telling her yes.

Su-Bin took out her phone and called the private detective used by her firm. She needed eyes on Min—everywhere he went, everything he did. After hanging up, the sick feeling in her stomach only deepened. What else had Min lied about?

Her thoughts jumped to the photos of the different knives. Her mother had identified one without hesitation. *The* knife. Not a similar knife, not the same type—the exact one.

Looking at the time, Su-Bin hurried to her office. She was due in court but had a few minutes to spare. She pulled up the photo of the knife on her computer. The unicorn symbol on the handle stared back at her. Min had claimed it was a popular brand. Opening an internet browser, she typed: "unicorn brand EDC folding knife." Scrolling through the search results, she couldn't find a knife that resembled the one her mom had identified.

She tried, "Unicorn symbol EDC folding knife." Still nothing.

She opened a different browser. Again, nothing.

Her heart dropped.

With trembling fingers, she dragged the photo into the search bar for a reverse image search.

No results. Not a single match. Her throat tightened. This knife wasn't part of any product line. It wasn't a stock photo or anywhere on the internet. She was afraid to put words to what this meant.

Su-Bin closed her computer and cleared her mind. She couldn't think about this now; she had to leave for court.

It was three in the afternoon when Matthew finished helping Brandon pack and clean his apartment. After taking his things to the car, Brandon signed the forms at the apartment office and paid the early termination fee. Then they stopped to eat.

"This place makes the best beef bone soup in all of Seoul," Matthew said. He tilted the bowl and slurped. "Excited about training? You're moving up to the big leagues."

"Not as much as I thought I would be," Brandon responded.

"Isn't this what you wanted?"

Brandon took a second before trying to explain. He felt conflicted and uneasy about Yoona's abilities. She was unbelievably strong. Her powers were unnatural, something out of a sci-fi movie. It scared him. "Yoona's power is... I don't know. She's—"

"She's a beast," Matthew interjected.

"She got inside my mind, and I—"

"I told you she would."

"Yes, but this feels like a mistake."

"Good. It means you're ready."

Brandon sighed, then took a spoonful of soup. Matthew wasn't going to let him walk out of training. "Yoona has made me aware of everything happening in my body. I can feel my liver cleaning my blood. It's not natural."

"You're rattled. I get it. But we need you. More of these battles are coming." Matthew scowled. "This fucking traitor in our government is going to burn. The day Yoona discovers this guy is the day I ensure hell is unleashed upon him."

"I'm sure you'll get that opportunity," Brandon said.

"Here's hoping." Matthew took a shot of soju. "Welcome to the war, soldier." He glanced out the window. "We better get going. I need to deliver you to the temple before dark."

"Can we swing by Su-Bin's house? I want to say goodbye," Brandon said.

"Sure."

They drove to Su-Bin's home. Brandon sat in his seat, looking at the front gate.

Matthew asked, "Having second thoughts?"

"No. Just feeling nervous."

"You guys had a little romance, uh?"

"A little," Brandon responded. Then corrected himself, "Yes, we did. She's special to me."

"Go," Matthew urged.

He stepped out of the car and slowly made his way past the gate to the door. What would he say? How would she receive him? He looked back at Matthew, who shooed him with a wave of his hand. Brandon knocked.

Su-Bin called out in Korean. He responded, "It's Brandon."

The door opened, and she stood there, smiling. "Brandon."

"Hi. We didn't get a chance to say goodbye."

"Come in."

Entering, he saw Jong-In in the living room. Brandon smiled and waved. Jong-In responded in kind.

"Sit for a moment," Su-Bin said. "I have something I want to give you." She headed for her bedroom.

"How's your arm? It looks pretty bad," Jong-in said.

"It's healing quickly," he replied, though that was an understatement. Since he could now direct his body's resources with precision and stimulate rapid cellular regeneration, the healing process had been accelerated far beyond normal.

"That's a relief." After a moment of silence, Jong-in said, "Su-Bin told me you were once married."

With a deep breath, Brandon nodded. "That's right. We had a son, but they both passed away."

"I'm so sorry."

"It was a few years ago. I'm comfortable talking about it, if you would like to hear the story."

Jong-In hesitated. "Only if you're sure… I don't want to pry."

Brandon smiled. "You're a good man, Jong-In. Talking about this helps me heal, so thank you for listening." Taking a breath, Brandon felt relieved that he was now able to tell the story without walls crumbling down.

"We were walking together in Seoul, and I was assaulted. My wife had propped our son on her shoulder and tripped backwards. They both hit the cement. The assailants fled; I was unconscious. It was late at night and by the time they received medical treatment, it was too late."

"I can't even imagine."

Su-Bin returned with a small box. "I wanted to apologize for my rash behavior and give you this gift. Something to remember me by."

"No, no. You don't have to."

"It'll mean a lot to me if you take it. Every time I see that it's missing, I'll remember you with fondness."

"I … I don't have anything for you," he stammered.

"You do. Accepting this is your gift to me."

"Shall I open it now?"

"No. There's a note in the box."

"Thank you."

Su-Bin hugged Brandon. "I'm sorry I was angry with you."

"I think you had good cause."

"Not really, no. But you were so calm and understanding about my feelings. It was a welcome change from other men I've dated in the past. You are a good man."

Brandon bowed. "*Kamsahamnida, jinjja cheongsam gochughae.*" *Thank you for the compliment.*

Jong-In stood and gave Brandon a hug. "It was nice meeting you. Stay in touch." Then Jong-In backed up and held Su-Bin's hand.

With a warm smile, Brandon said, "Good for you. You two are perfect for each other."

They saw Brandon to the door and said goodbye.

The temple dorm was a large single room. Matthew laid Brandon's bags next to his sleeping mat.

"The floor is nice and warm," Brandon said.

"It's the Korean traditional heating system called *ondol*. The smoke from the kitchen fire flows under the raised floor." Looking at the mat and then back at Brandon, Matthew asked, "Are you going to be okay sleeping on this? How are your arm and shoulder feeling?"

"They're much better." Brandon held it out, moving it slowly around.

"Damn! You heal quick. But, still, I'll see if I can get you some extra pillows."

"Thanks."

Brandon scanned the furniture-less room, which was pleasant to be in. The wooden support beams stuck out from the bare tan walls. Six eight-foot windows could be opened, acting as doors, or closed, covered by wooden shutters. The ceiling had three levels—the outer level, mid level, and center level, rising to a point. Small windows in each part allowed for light, and the logs and wooden beams that supported the roof gave the room its natural beauty.

Brandon's sleeping mat was one of eight. A pillow and a blanket lay on top of the folded mats, and next to them sat a small box containing a toothbrush, a brown bottle of peroxide, a box of baking soda, a bottle of water, a diary, and a book—philosophy in one, medical in another, and metaphysics in a third. There was nothing else in the room.

Returning with extra pillows, Matthew told Brandon, "Your bags are going to be stored in a small building next to the maintenance shed. You're not allowed any personal items here. There are clean towels and fresh robes for you to change into at the bathroom entrance. Are you sure you're ready for this?"

"I am."

Matthew gathered Brandon's bags.

"Wait. Let me open the present Su-Bin gave me first."

"Sure."

Brandon removed the small box from the side pouch of his bag and opened it. Inside was a large golden ring laden with gems.

"Wow. Look at that," Matthew exclaimed.

Unfolding the note, Brandon read:

Dear Brandon,

I want to thank you for your honesty, for connecting with me, and for the special time we had together. This ring belonged to my father. Your image of him is one of goodness and love. I want you to keep that idea alive. As for me, that ring represented something else. Now that it's gone, the empty place where it sat reminds me that he had love in his heart for me and that you have experienced it. That is the most precious and valuable gift I could ever have. I wish you the best of luck in your training with Yoona and hope that our paths will cross again.

Love, Su-Bin.

Matthew whistled. "Wow ... that's not just a thank-you note, that's..." His voice trailed off.

Brandon stared at the note, tears forming in his eyes. "She turned a symbol of pain into a memory of love," he said. "This note is the rewriting of her story."

"And you're a part of it," Matthew said.

Folding the note, Brandon let out a slow breath. He returned it to the box and placed it in his bag. "I'm ready."

Matthew gave him a hug, wished him luck, and carried away his bags.

The next two days were spent meditating and reading. His instructor, a Korean woman with greying dark hair and eyes that held unseen forces, guided him in generating and controlling energy. Healing became the focus of that training, and they spent hours repairing the damage to his arm and shoulder in preparation for his physical work.

On the third day, Yoona came to instruct the students. The morning started, as always, with meditation and stretching. Brandon's arm, although weak, had a wide range of movement. The students were called to the courtyard, where they stood in formation, ready to learn.

"Today, we begin martial arts training," Yoona said. "Not for combat, but for awareness. A Shaman must learn to listen—to your body, your energy, and your feelings." Yoona moved down the line, meeting each student's gaze. "Shamans anticipate movement and intention without fear. Read emotion and prepare for its force without absorbing it. We must notice shifts and judge their threat. Through martial arts we learn these skills while gaining balance, finding peace, and cultivating a calm presence."

Brandon wished he had learned these skills before his encounter with Bellevue. But curating these abilities would take years to become second nature.

Yoona faced the class instructor. They bowed and began a sparring demonstration. The instructor moved, throwing forward punches. Yoona glided to her left, avoiding the hits, then landed a jab to the ribs. As they continued fighting, Yoona projected her awareness. The students were able to feel her balance and control. Brandon inched closer, observing the fight not only with his eyes, but through Yoona's connection. Her weight was centered. She perceived every shift from her opponent and acted before the instructor advanced. Yoona was reading intent and exploiting aggression while maintaining composure.

When the fight ended, the instructor paired students to practice what they had just experienced.

Yoona left the field and came over to Brandon. "Are you ready to become a master?"

Brandon pointed at himself. "Me?"

"Yes, I am going to implant my martial arts knowledge directly into your brain. Come."

She led him into the building. There, she handed him a stick and instructed him to bite down.

Brandon turned the stick in his hand, staring at it. "I need to understand something first."

Yoona stood, calm and patient. Brandon wished he had rehearsed this, because he wasn't sure how to begin. He was angry. He had seen her kill a man. He had shot two himself, and she hadn't stopped him. His thoughts kept circling one question: if she could incapacitate someone, why kill at all? He took a sharp breath and started with, "When we first met, you asked me if I desired justice as a detective. I told you no." He turned his gaze from the stick to meet her eyes. "If I am to judge you by your own standards, then I believe you desired justice for those men at the raid."

Yoona's expression was unreadable. If he had upset her or insulted her, he couldn't tell.

"I'm not going to assume I understand. Please explain further."

"All right," Brandon said. "The men you killed on the ship and the two that I shot. Why did they have to die? You have the power to drop a person to their knees. They were unarmed. Why didn't you tell me they were no longer a threat?"

Yoona nodded. "When I helped you make the shield, what happened to your body?"

"I couldn't move."

"You took the energy your body required and pushed it into a defensive force. I needed to do that while battling ten men with machine guns. I needed a shield and the ability to move. Dark energy gave me that ability. I killed that man, so I could stay alive. As for the two you shot, I merely knocked the wind out of them with a concentrated blast. I bought you seconds to gain the upper hand. When those men recovered, they would have killed you. You made the right decision to shoot them."

Brandon's gaze went back to the stick, his anger shifting toward comprehension. Yoona had given him seconds, and he was now alive to judge her for it.

"Those men knew the risk when they signed on with that organization," she said. "They were ready to kill. My intervention was never about justice, only safety and time to act. There was no 'right' way to do that."

"How do you make a decision when there is no 'right'?"

"Now you know why I trust you." She pointed to the stick. "Are you ready?"

He kneeled on the floor and put the stick into his mouth. Yoona stood behind him, placed her hands on the sides of his head, and leaned forward, touching her forehead to the back of his head. She entered his mind.

You have expanded your awareness nicely, Yoona said. *Your control has increased tenfold. Your progression is perfect.* She rubbed his temples with her fingertips and added, *The implanting of skills is extremely painful. Are you ready?*

Brandon nodded.

Yoona's presence pressed in upon his thoughts. His brain throbbed, his muscles twitched, and his eyes burned. Brandon clenched his teeth hard against the stick. Then the real pain came. Yoona ripped and tore—into memories, cognitive processing, and reflexes. A deep guttural scream thundered from his throat as tears as big as gumdrops rolled down his cheeks. His jaw locked, the wood splintered, and the taste of sap seeped into his mouth.

His mind had become a battleground, assaulted by raw knowledge and experiences that rained in from Yoona's connection. The pressure, building from the unnatural insertion of knowledge, pushed against the bone plates in his head. Brandon felt them separating, his brain seemingly swelling through the cracks. His breath came in ragged gasps, each inhale a struggle.

Then came etching. Yoona's phantom touch needled tissue, each puncture producing a shockwave that rippled through his nervous system. The relentless, craze-inducing taps assaulted his senses, magnifying every sound and touch. The world around him slowed. In the distance, a tiny circle of light hit the wall. Specks of dust in the luminous cylindrical ray floated in suspended animation. He was seeing—

Scorching heat blinded him. Molten iron flowed through the crevices of his brain. His flesh turned crimson and sweat poured down his face in rivulets. The stick crumbled into tiny bits as trickles of blood dripped from his ears.

Yoona released him.

Brandon dropped to the floor like a sack of flour. His bloodshot eyes stared into a void, unfocused and distant. For several seconds, he didn't move. He lay there, breathing.

When he finally moved, he placed his palms on the floor and noticed the wood beneath had distinct grooves. He felt vibrations—the students outside were moving in unison, and Yoona shifted her weight to her left foot.

He blinked and the room came into focus. He was seeing depth, angles, spacing—things he'd never noticed or thought about before. In a quick, smooth motion, he rolled to his hands and knees. His balance adjusted automatically, and his weight stayed center without thought. He felt different. Alive. Stronger and faster than he'd ever imagined. The connection between his mind and his body had improved.

"Shall we see what you can do?" Yoona asked.

Brandon sprang to his feet. They made their way to the courtyard, where the students had transitioned from sparring to synchronized actions.

The instructor spoke in a calm voice as the students shifted their weight and lifted their knees. Their movements were smooth and purposeful like a fluid dance.

"Build your spiritual energy and expand it outward. Merge with the world around you. Allow energy to ebb and flow, in, around, and through you. Feel the power stored in rocks. Connect with the plants and the soil. Touch the currents of the wind and the sun. Your strength lies in life itself, in each observable moment, in the here and now. In that awareness, find bliss: the pulse of spiritual energy. This is the way of a Shaman. This is how we see people in their true form—as souls. This is how we communicate with our ancestors, view the future, and induce visions."

Brandon joined the others in the movements. He grew the light inside him and expanded it outward, encompassing the entire courtyard. He could sense each student, every individual presence, as if they were extensions of his own being.

Yoona gave a light clap, and the students gathered around. "I will give a private lesson to anyone who can land a strike on Brandon."

The students circled him. Brandon set his feet and raised his hands. This stance carried memories—centuries of combat and discipline Yoona had etched into his nervous system. Her truths were now his: training with her father in the hills of China, battling rebel monks during the fall of the Tang Dynasty, grappling with a Himalayan guardian in a brutal struggle for control of Shogu-La Pass. Spins, kicks, and dodges weren't techniques learned in a classroom, but lived experiences he remembered.

Bending his knees, he was ready to strike or defend at a moment's notice. A sly smile crept over his face. "I know kung fu." He motioned with his fingers for the others to come test him.

As the students closed in, Brandon's movements became a blur of precision and power. He sidestepped a sweeping kick with a fluid twist of his torso, driving a powerful counterstrike into his opponent's midsection. He leaned back, a high punch just missing his nose. With a quick pivot, he responded with a sharp elbow to the attacker's ribs. The *crack* evoked a moan of empathy from the others. Another student lunged, but Brandon blocked the incoming punch, grabbed his assailant's arm, and spun her around, delivering swift, rapid jabs to the kidneys.

The remaining students hesitated. Their eyes communicated their thoughts as they angled for an advantage. Brandon saw it all and adjusted accordingly. He danced around them, dodging and weaving with the agility of a seasoned fighter. He ducked under a high kick and swept his leg out, sending a fighter crashing to the ground. With a sudden burst of speed, he closed the distance between himself and another, landing a kick to the chest.

When the last student conceded, Yoona ended the class and sent them to meditate.

The next morning, following meditations and stretching, Yoona asked Brandon to walk with her. "There is more that I need to teach you," she said.

They crossed a small stone bridge spanning a stream and followed the path into the forest toward the clearing where students often meditated.

"How is your mind and body responding to your new abilities?" Yoona asked.

Answering this question was tricky. He wasn't exactly sure how to name what he was experiencing. Heightened perception came to mind. The forest had never been so alive to him before. He noticed everything—the bird hopping across a branch, the mayfly quietly drifting to the leaf to rest, the smell of pine resin, the different types of bark. New awareness also topped the list. The forest listened. The path they walked had history. Stillness granted invisibility, while movement drew attention. His body instinctively reacted to motion, making him feel jittery, yet he was focused and aware, which made him calm. He glanced at Yoona and said, "Like my body already knows what to do, and my mind needs to catch up."

"Good. If I had the luxury of time, I would let you grow into your new abilities."

"Are you rushing my development because of what happened at the port?"

They stepped over gnarled roots that twisted across the trail and began to hike up the slope.

"We are leaving for Lake Valley soon," Yoona said. "A disturbance will happen there, creating a string of events that will take us to Washington, D.C. There, I will learn who the corrupt Shaman is."

"What kind of disturbance?"

"I don't know yet."

They came to a stairway made of rocks laid into the hillside and started climbing.

Brandon found navigating the steps to be a lot simpler than he had imagined, so he continued with the conversation. "What are you teaching me today?"

"How to leave your body," Yoona responded.

"Leave my body?"

"Yes. I gave you mastery of martial arts yesterday because you need total bodily awareness and control before separation is possible."

"How does separation work?" Brandon asked.

"Normally, through physical conditioning. When your body operates at peak performance, you begin to understand that your physical form is an instrument you inhabit. That realization creates the separation. Then you simply step out of your body and move as pure energy. But if you leave without full control of your body, it will shut down."

They reached the top of the stairs and entered the clearing. It was a round, well maintained grassy area surrounded by trees.

Brandon spun around, taking in the warm sun. "I'm going to leave my body here?" he asked. "What will happen to it?"

"Your subconscious will take over," Yoona responded.

"If my soul is pure energy, won't it dissipate in the sunlight?"

"No. Your soul is tethered to your body. And today we'll begin stretching that tether."

Tethered. Brandon pictured his soul leashed to his body like a dog to its owner. He followed Yoona to the center of the clearing. "What is the purpose of leaving my body?"

"To know your true self. To learn how to manipulate energy."

"I thought I was already learning how to manipulate energy."

Yoona smirked, then sprang into the air and floated toward a tree. She planted her foot on the trunk and pushed off, soaring higher. In the treetops, she danced along the branches, then drifted through the air like a gossamer scarf taken by the wind.

Brandon let out a slow breath.

She landed without a sound and gave a small, acknowledging nod.

"I understand now. This is different than spiritual energy."

"Having lived as pure energy, I can manipulate the energies my body creates—thermal, bioelectric, chemical, and magnetic. I can expel them, giving me push, while simultaneously attracting them, giving me pull." She demonstrated by slowly rising a meter off the ground and then softly landing. "This ability is only possible once you've traveled outside your body. And you can only do that after you have total control."

"If you can manipulate the energy around you, why did you need dark energy? Why not just use the heat from the sun to create your shield? Then you could still move and fight while protecting yourself."

Yoona lifted a hand and gestured to her surroundings. "Pine trees, sunlight, wind, soil, nuts—direct energy, stored energy, and kinetic energy. We cannot use this power without processing it first." She bent over and picked up an acorn.

"This is a battery. We must first digest it, then convert the energy into something we can use."

She moved toward him and placed her hand on his chest. "Energy manipulation always starts within you. The energy inside your body is already aligned. When you made the shield, you compressed and pushed what was already yours." She cupped her hand and scooped it as if drawing water from a stream. "The energy around us must first be drawn in, converted, and aligned with yourself. That takes time. A shield doesn't allow for time."

"How is that different from what you just showed me?"

"I demonstrated exchange. Push and pull. Flow. To draw power from the environment, you must first understand that power. So, I will teach you how to leave your body to gain that knowledge."

"Will the other students learn how to step outside their bodies?"

Yoona shook her head. "Not likely. To take complete control of one's own body is a daunting task. It requires years of work. Those who dedicate themselves may achieve the ability, but very few ever do. There have been rare individuals who have the innate capacity, but in this age of distraction, I haven't encountered one in over a decade. Those who do master the skill become Circle members."

Yoona pointed to a slender branch on the ground. "The final and possibly most difficult skill you will learn is telekinesis, although it is a bit of an anomaly. There are those who can perform the ability without understanding the rules." She opened her palm, and the stick floated straight into her grasp. "The mechanics involve extending your soul outward, containing the object within your field, and aligning its energy with yours. Its difficulty lies in knowing how to manipulate energy while stretching part of your soul outside yourself. In order to learn this, you must first exist as pure energy." She handed him the stick.

Brandon stared at it and swallowed. He accepting the stick, placed it in his mouth, and knelt. Sweat was already beading on his brow.

Min Yun arrived home after work with one thought on his mind: time to free Su-Bin's mother. He and her mom had already discussed how he would propose marriage. It would be during the dinner party celebrating Hye-Kyoung's release from prison. Su-Bin's mother was overjoyed with Min's plans—thrilled that her daughter would marry such a wonderful man.

With rubber gloves in hand, Min went to his tool shed, retrieved a shovel, and ventured into his garden, where a row of *mugunghwa* flowers, also known as the Rose of Sharon—the South Korean national flower—had bloomed. He carefully dug up the third plant, revealing a tin that had once held traditional Korean sweets called *hangwa*, crafted from nuts, fruits, and honey. He opened the tin and admired the contents. Lifting the item, he let it dangle from his fingers. "Time to relocate you somewhere the police are sure to find you," he murmured to the necklace as its sparkle released his dark secret.

Lake Valley, Oregon

Collapsing Ascension

The school board meeting was full of concerned parents, teachers, and community members gathered to discuss the final details of the school year. Leah Davenport sat two rows back, her hands fidgeting with her outlined proposal.

She kept glancing at her notes as the meeting progressed. As topics shifted from summer classes to next year's curriculum, Leah would sit forward to show engagement, then lean back to calm her nerves. Finally, the chairperson called for public comments.

Leah rose from her chair and shuffled into the aisle. Her heartbeat played against her raw nerves, steady and relentless. As she moved toward the microphone, she rubbed her palms against the sides of her jeans. *This has to work. I didn't bend all those minds to have it end here.*

Summoning strength from her core, Leah found her alter ego, the voice that had emerged with the intake of dark energy. She reached the podium, cleared her throat, and began. "Good evening, esteemed members. My name is Leah Davenport, and I am here to advocate for justice, healing, and the return of sacred land to its rightful owners."

The room filled with hushed comments and awe-filled whispers. "Oh, my God, do you know who that is?"

"I heard she's an angel, sent to heal us."

"It's her, the one in the news."

The air crackled with enthusiasm as all eyes turned to Leah.

"The land I speak of holds a history stained with tragedy and sorrow. It was once home to the proud Sukiya Nation, until they were brutally massacred, and their grounds stolen from them." The room remained captivated.

She hardened her gaze and put power behind her words. "Two city officials have recently been charged with corruption related to the sale of this land. Dr. Lynn Mathis, a respected medical professional, has tirelessly advocated for the closure of the Center due to health concerns. The string of abductions and tragedies associated with this land cannot be ignored."

She paused, her gaze sweeping across the members in front of the room. "This land has caused immeasurable pain and trouble for our city. The Sukiya Nation have continued to insist the land be returned, and I believe the time to make amends, to right the wrongs of our past—and return what was taken—has come." Her resolve strengthened as she mentioned her grandfather. "Bill Stillen, a man known for his integrity and compassion, will be attending my graduation ceremony. It is during this event that I ask for permission to hold a formal protest. With downtown being flooded by people fighting for different causes, it is at graduation, with the eyes of the world upon us, that we can make a statement that cannot be ignored."

Murmurs rose in the audience.

Leah's impassioned plea continued. "As graduates, we are entrusted with the responsibility of shaping our future and the world. This protest is not just a statement but a testament to the values instilled in us by the Lake Valley School District. It shows that our voices matter, that our thoughts and opinions are respected and valued. Allowing us to peacefully protest at graduation reflects positively on the school board and our educational system, showcasing our commitment to fostering critical thinking and civic engagement."

Leah's allotted time closed. "Thank you for giving us the chance to be heard. I implore you to allow us to stand together—as students, as a community, as voices for what is right." She took her seat to a round of tentative applause.

One of the school board members, a woman with a firm demeanor, addressed Leah. "We appreciate your passion and the importance of your cause. We respect your opinions and understand your concern for the land and the native community. However, I must note that this issue falls outside the purview of the school district. The matter requires city-wide deliberation and decision-making. While we admire your initiative and commitment, allowing a protest of this nature on school grounds would be inappropriate and could set a precedent that we cannot endorse."

A second school board member interjected, "Leah, we appreciate the clarity and conviction of your presentation. This is clearly a matter of significance, and we will take it under advisement. The board will discuss your request further and reconvene after the break to issue a formal decision."

The room buzzed, and the chairperson called for order. Public remarks continued.

As they went on with new business, Leah found herself conflicted. The possibility of a favorable outcome, of winning permission for the protest, tantalized her. Yet, the fear of losing, of facing another devastating rejection, gnawed at her resolve. The pull to take matters into her hands was strong. She had the power to sway the board's decision by force, ensuring a yes vote. She knew the dangers of such manipulation, but the urge gripped her. She wondered how slippery the fall into corruption would be. Using her powers for personal gain was against the rules, but this wasn't for her. This was for the community at large. She had the ability to right an injustice a century in the making and would do so.

She clenched her fists, grappling with this choice. *I've already used my abilities to influence others.* She had manipulated Eric to win Barb a prom date, her father to calm his anxiety, and her classmates to get volunteers. She hadn't felt any negative repercussions from that. She wanted to believe this, could easily allow herself to believe this, but she recognized the entitlement, the need to win, and the pull to have her way. Power clawed at her insides, and she knew it was precisely because she *had* used her powers inappropriately.

This land issue, however, had real implications, and she couldn't allow the board to reject her.

When the time came, she made her way to each member and connected with them, reaching into their minds. She erased objections and strengthened the arguments that had resonated. And when the meeting reconvened, Leah was given permission to hold her protest.

A reporter stopped Leah as she left the building and asked for a statement. Taking the opportunity, Leah reiterated what she had said during the meeting. Uncle Tim and Roy would approve. Her father and grandfather? She wasn't so sure. Tomorrow's headline would read: "Leah Davenport: From Divine Hero to Advocate, Wins School Board Battle."

As Leah drove home, her car speaker announced, "Call from Cindy. Would you like to answer it?"

Leah sighed. Cindy had probably heard about the school board meeting and wanted all the juicy details.

Her car speaker beeped, reminding her of the incoming call.

Stopping at the light, Leah considered answering. Cindy's cheery voice and bubbly persona would shift Leah into school mode, where she exuded joy and became everyone's friend. It would be a welcome reprieve from her current self-doubt as she was questioning her motivations and purpose. Light conversation and giggles would be therapeutic.

"Yes," Leah said, accepting the call.

Cindy's voice shot through the speaker, laced with pleading panic. "Leah? Oh, thank goodness. Leah, please, I need you. My mom's in the hospital. She was complaining about stomach pain and stood to go to the bathroom when she became weak and dizzy. She collapsed on the floor." Cindy was crying. "You have to come."

"Of course. I'm on my way. Which hospital are you at?"

"Mercy."

Leah gripped the wheel tighter and turned the corner, speeding towards the hospital. When she arrived, she swerved into an empty parking spot and hurried to the entrance. She phoned Cindy. "I'm here. Which room are you in?"

"Two-seventeen."

The hospital doors slid open, and Leah stopped cold, prickled by unseen energy. The feeling intensified into a sharp stab that jabbed her chest, making it difficult to breathe. *Death*. She could smell it. The unique burnt aroma triggered the memory of shard-glass fingers. Her muscles tensed and quivered as if trying to tear free from her bones. The visceral reaction caused both pain and insatiable cravings. Wrapping her arms across her chest and holding onto her shoulders, Leah tried to refocus as she continued forward, one step at a time.

Moving along the halls, the smell of hospital disinfectants replaced the sticky residue of a transcendence. Leah came to room 217 and found Cindy holding her mom's hand. Approaching, she calmed her mind and built her spiritual energy.

"Leah, please. You have to help her. I can't—" Cindy broke down in tears.

"I'll try." Leah went to the bed, held the woman's hand, and leaned over her, stroking her hair. Cindy's mom opened her eyes and Leah connected. She searched the woman's mind for the cause of her sickness. Leah saw that she ate lots of meat, dairy, and snack foods, including too many donuts. She didn't exercise much and watched a lot of TV. Leah went deeper and learned that the woman's heart was tired and her blood had trouble flowing.

But the reason she was here now was because of her digestive tract.

Releasing the woman's hand, Leah said, "She's going to be fine. It's digestive issues. But if she doesn't make significant changes to her diet and daily routines, she's going to continue to have problems. Her heart and blood pressure are not good."

"Can you heal her?" Cindy asked.

Leah shook her head and lowered her voice. "I am not what you think I am. I don't have divine powers. Your mom needs to make better health choices."

Cindy's lips began to move, but Leah had gone stiff and didn't hear what she was saying. A soul had touched her and began to communicate. *My wife is in the next room. Can you comfort her?*

The spirit left, and Leah let out a slow breath. "Cindy, give me a minute. I'll be right back."

Leaving 217, Leah stepped to the next door and peered through the window. She saw a woman holding a man's hand, crying.

The soul touched Leah and said, *I can't move on. The entrance to the other side is closed. My wife needs to release me.*

Leah tapped on the door and entered.

The woman wiped her eyes and said, "Are you from his work? He didn't make it."

Staring at the woman, Leah contemplated the reason she was learning to manipulate energy. Was it for situations like these, to help people heal? To help with closure, and comfort both those who had passed and those who were left behind to struggle with the loss—or for a higher cause? If Mr. Anderson was correct and she was going to become the most powerful person in the world, then helping individuals felt like a waste of her talents. She had just turned the school board! Could she really be an architect of world peace? But here, at this moment, her actions felt noble, right. Where was her calling?

Sitting with the woman, Leah gazed into her eyes and rubbed her back, connecting. She sent soothing and comforting emotions while placing the thoughts, *I'm going to be okay*, and *He's in a good place*, into her mind. After a few minutes, the soul thanked Leah and transcended.

A black, potent aroma permeated the air. Leah thirsted for its power. She wanted it. Needed to feel it flowing and stimulating her insides. Rising from her seat, she stumbled towards the door and ran down the hall at a frenzied pace. She bumped into a tall man in nurse scrubs, who put a firm hand on her shoulder. "Slow down, miss!" The order broke through Leah's delirium.

A gurney surrounded by nurses and doctors rushed past her. "Heart attack. He needs open-heart surgery. Elliott, you're going to be okay." At the end of the hall, a shocked man held his hands over his mouth.

Leah saw an exit and burst through the hospital doors, panting for fresh air.

Her phone buzzed. Leah lifted it. Barb had texted: "You okay?"

Leah returned her phone to her pocket and headed to her car. The pinball tone of her phone sounded as she unlocked her doors. Uncle Tim was calling. Reaching into her pocket she turned it off. Her emotions were still too raw.

Ten o'clock the next morning, Mr. Anderson sat at the upstairs window of his rented room, three houses down from Leah's. Through the slates of the blinds, he watched Leah and Jared hop into Tim's truck. Walt and Mari—Jared and Tim's parents—were arriving that afternoon, and from the sound of things, there'd be lunch, maybe even a long sit-down at the hotel.

This was the window Mr. Anderson needed.

He slipped out the back door and moved down the street with casual confidence, then cut through a neighbor's yard and through the side gate to Leah's house. This time, the back door was locked. Crouching, Mr. Anderson placed the palm of his hand against the lock and manipulated the energy around it. After a moment of concentration, the lock clicked open.

The inside of the house carried Leah's scent—the faint smell of soap and perfume. Mr. Anderson moved from room to room, retrieving each tiny piece of tech like a thief securing valuable treasure. Bill Stillen had confirmed he would attend the graduation party, but if his security team swept the house and found a bug, he might not come. Leah needed to speak with him—to convince her grandfather she belonged at Extended Life. These bugs threatened to cancel his visit, so Mr. Anderson had to make sure he found them all.

The last device was beneath Leah's desk. Mr. Anderson swept the house a final time using a RF scanner, finding one more under the picture frame. With a sigh of relief, he exited through the back door. The lock clicked behind him.

The morning of graduation, Leah printed the names of the refugees taken from Misty's camp and put the paper in her pocket. Then she drove to meet her grandfather Bill at the Royal Crest Hotel and Spa. At the front entrance, a valet opened Leah's door and offered his hand as she exited. Inside the hotel, she met a security guard, who led her to her grandfather's luxury suite.

"Leah!" Bill exclaimed. "It's so good to see you. You have no idea how worried I've been. Come, give me a hug."

Leah bounced into his outstretched arms and wrapped her arms around his broad chest. Finding a sense of security and comfort in his embrace, her stress eased, and a tear formed in her eye.

Her grandfather, usually boisterous and firm, showed a rare moment of tenderness as Leah began to cry. "You're safe now," he murmured in a gruff voice.

Leah gripped him tighter, allowing herself to be vulnerable. She missed him—the luxury, the comfort, the safety. Not all of it, but here, in his arms, she missed enough of it.

"Now, now, come now," he said, rubbing her back. "We have lots to discuss. Let's eat before our food gets cold." Bill raised his hand, and a maid hurried away. He pulled back, looking at Leah's tear-stained face, and wiped her eye with his thumb.

Her grandfather offered a faint smile, and Leah returned it. With a deep breath, she remembered why she was here and took this moment to connect with him. But the connection failed.

"Let's sit," he said.

Leah took his hand, and they walked out onto the private balcony. Before she dropped his hand, Leah looked him in the eyes and attempted to connect again. Once more, it failed.

They sat down to a table set with china and silver. Leah unfolded her napkin and laid it on her lap. Pastries and muffins, watermelon, grapes, kiwi and strawberries, freshly squeezed orange juice, water, and coffee lay in reach. The maid returned with scrambled eggs, bacon, spinach and sausage omelets, and crêpes.

Leah reached for the omelet but froze mid-reach. Her grandfather was staring at her—his gaze locked and hardened with suspicion. His eyes flicked between hers, like he was trying to decide who she really was. She returned his stare without saying anything.

"Leah," he began in a firm tone. "You tried to connect with me. Twice."

Leah nodded, feeling a little guilty and a bit surprised, though she shouldn't have been. Mr. Anderson did say he would teach her how to stop a connection, a skill she still hadn't learned—despite having been connected to twice without permission.

Bill continued, "Connecting is not something to be taken lightly. Its ability allows one to gather information."

His pause let Leah know he had taken her attempts to connect as a possible attack, or at the minimum, a violation of etiquette and protocol.

"What exactly were you trying to accomplish by connecting with me?" His words hung in the air, the underlying question clear: *are you a thief, a spy, or is this something else?*

Leah hated this feeling, the lack of control unnerving her. She was on the defense, unsure of how to turn the tables. Recalling Mr. Anderson's intrusion into her own mind, Leah steadied her breathing and met her grandfather's gaze head-on, the firmness in her voice matching his. "Grandpa Bill. We both know the importance of strength and control. I understand your concerns perfectly well. After all, my own privacy was violated as a way for you to evaluate my worth to your company."

Bill's brow furrowed. "Really? By whom?"

"Mr. Anderson. Do you know him?"

Bill nodded and reached for the coffee. He poured himself a cup, added a splash of cream, and a spoon of sugar. "I'm sorry you had to experience that."

Leah was about to speak when Bill held his hand up to stop her. He let the silence hang. His glare seemed to dissect her every movement as he gathered clues and information. She didn't shy away, refusing to be intimidated.

"Who taught you to connect?" he asked.

Leah let out an exasperated sigh. *This question again?* Shaking her head, she grinned. "What do you know about the supernatural world?"

The question simmered as Bill sipped his coffee. He cleared his throat and said, "I've seen a few things ... things that defy logic and science, like connecting." Leaning forward, a slight scowl formed, and he emphasized, "Who taught you?"

"My abductor," she answered. "A spectral entity. A ghost my boyfriend knew. It took Dad, and when I attempted to save him, It abducted me."

Bill straightened. "You were abducted by a ghost?" The words came out as if he were testing how they sounded.

"Of sorts, yes. My abilities were awakened when the ghostly energy surrounded me. To answer your question honestly, I taught myself. I'm not a spy or a thief. I'm not working for anyone. My attempts to connect with you were to learn more about Extended Life and what the company does."

"You could have asked." Bill leaned back, tapping the arms of his chair with his fingers as he took in her explanation. "Your abilities," he said in a measured yet curious tone, "Father Joseph referenced those in the newspaper article. Your divine powers."

"Yes. And that's why Mr. Anderson connected to me, to learn the extent of my abilities and to recruit me. Your company wants to hire me."

Leah served herself an omelet and a blueberry muffin.

Bill sipped his coffee. "So, what did my company offer you?"

"Seven hundred thousand a year, a house, a car, my dad's old job back, positions for my friends, and to pay for us all to relocate."

Bill gave a full belly laugh. "That's quite an offer."

"Your recruiter told me I could become the most powerful person on the planet, calling me a 'magnificent individual with special talents.' He appreciates my ability to talk with the press and my knowledge of cultures."

An incredulous chuckle rose, lightening the mood and brightening the colors around them. "'Special talents.' Do you even know what Extended Life does?"

"Do *you* know what Extended Life does?" Leah retorted.

Bill tapped his plate with his fork. He took a breath to speak, but this time Leah was the one to silence him, raising her hand and shaking her head. His face reddened, and he expanded his chest as if to assert his dominance.

"According to the file I was given," Leah said, "your company uses nanotechnology to reinvigorate human cells. They've developed 'smart blood' that enhances the immune system and muscle performance. You have a contract with the government to treat soldiers and politicians. You also offer the treatment to important magnates of society."

"That's right. So what exactly do you see yourself doing in this company?"

"Grandpa, please. This conversation started because you were able to stop me from connecting. The truth is, I don't know what your company does, but I know it involves taking refugees and using them as guinea pigs before you kill them."

Bill's eyes widened and he slammed his hand on the table. "That's a serious accusation! The FBI has already investigated those baseless claims—"

"At least twenty missing or dead," Leah shouted, waving the paper she printed in his face. "From a refugee camp in India."

Her grandfather ripped the paper from her hands and scanned it. After a moment, he placed the paper on the table and sipped more of his coffee. Then he reached for a strawberry. "It's true that we have hired refugees," he said in a calm, steady voice. "It's a win-win for everyone. But we don't harm them; we give them new identities. This is to protect them and us. This way they aren't targets. The technology Extended Life has developed is extremely valuable."

"Why list them as dead or missing?"

"Anonymity. Keeps everyone safe."

Leah really wished she could connect to her grandfather. She harbored doubts about his explanation. "What does Extended Life do that requires anonymity?"

"Exactly what you said we do, extend people's lives. It's a technology that is worth billions with a capital B. Corporate espionage is a very real threat. I believed you had been abducted as a plan to get to me. That's why I had insisted on bodyguards."

"Tim did a great job. And with my new abilities, I can take care of myself."

"Why don't you explain to me a bit more about your abilities?"

"What do you know about Shamans and Banishers?"

"They're fortune tellers, talk with the dead, superstitious, and cryptic. The chief strategist of Extended Life is a Banisher."

"And they manipulate energy; my talents lie there."

Bill nodded. "I, myself, don't understand it. Twenty years ago, I about choked to death with laughter after hearing a presentation about individuals who could extend their life through energy manipulation. But then that person connected to me and spoke directly into my mind while searching my memories. Are you saying you are able to extend your life span?"

Leah opened her mouth and then closed it. "I don't... I wasn't aware of that ability. Mr. Anderson said he would train me."

"I see," her grandfather said.

"So that's how your company works?" Leah asked. "You find energy manipulators to go into people's bodies and stimulate their cells?"

"I was told it was a combination of energy and technology. Something to do with the way talismans are made. The plants are manipulated as they grow, after harvest, and again once they've been turned into cream."

"And you believe that?"

"What I believe is that I charge the government seventy-five million dollars for a single treatment and the ultra-rich five hundred million. There's no shortage of customers, just product."

"How much of that is profit?"

He smiled, his eyes holding a knowing glint, but Bill offered no verbal response.

"So, my position in the company will be to manipulate these plants?"

"I'm not involved in the day-to-day operations of the company, so I won't speculate. However, if you do accept the position, I will insist you attend Columbia University."

"Are you asking me to work with your company?"

"I trust my advisor, and apparently, she sees something in you. I shouldn't be surprised; your parents were quite the couple. A little stubborn and unruly, though."

"Grandpa, can you at least try to get along with them? Just for today and tomorrow night. For me."

Bill smiled and nodded. "About your graduation present."

"Please, Grandpa. No need. Seriously. My trust fund is more than enough, not to mention my college tuition."

"I'm glad you think so, because I don't know what I'm giving you yet. But I'm keeping my eye open."

Leah thought about her Audi. He had given her that car for her sixteenth birthday. She really didn't need stuff, but what she did need was a favor. "We need to talk about graduation tomorrow."

Bill grinned. "My security team has already briefed me about the protest. I'm proud of you."

Breathing easier, she asked, "Could you give a statement?"

"I can do that. Tell me what the protest is about."

Leah proceeded to tell him the story of Bellevue. She started with how the house had manipulated Dan's family. Then came the fire, the abductions, the need for love, the priest—and how his body was in a coma, but his soul was in the house... how she'd saved him, and how she had escaped. She told him that the cycle was ready to repeat because the building was alive. The land needed to be returned to the Sukiya Nation.

Bill listened intently, fascinated and intrigued, showing signs of surprise but not disbelief. "That's quite a story. The authorities spun a very different account, and you didn't mention any of this when we spoke on the phone."

"How could I have? I was struggling to understand it myself."

"I see why my company took interest in you. Welcome to Extended Life. I'm positive you'll make an exceptional addition to the team."

"I still need to think about it, and I want to talk with Mom and Dad first. Mr. Anderson said he'd schedule a meeting so we can all sit down together."

"All right. I'll make sure he sets that up."

After breakfast, her grandfather showed her to the door. He kissed the top of her head and said, "You have my number; use it. Anytime, for any reason."

Leah nodded. "I won't call unless it's important."

"Anytime. For any reason," he repeated with emphasis. "I'm never too busy for you."

With a wide grin, Leah said, "Thanks. I love you."

He gave her another hug, saying, "I'll see you later today."

The school waited, and so did the storm she was about to stir.

After his granddaughter left, Bill had lots to contemplate. First and foremost, this land and the building Leah talked about—a goldmine! The market was vast for those who wanted experiences with the spiritual world, or the opportunity to communicate with an ancestor. This was an investment he had to make.

Next, learning that Leah had been captured by a ghost, could communicate with It, and wielded the same power as Ruth, meant Leah could replace Ruth—the same way Ruth had replaced his beloved partner.

He missed Ruth Jones, the woman who had helped him build Extended Life. Her death had shaken him more than he had realized. Extended Life—the whole company model, the promise to clients that they could live to 120 or 125 in perfect health—had hinged on her. When she died, despite every medical report showing she was strong and capable, it had nearly ruined the company, until her protégé appeared, bearing the same name and the same powers, insisting her mentor had instructed her to assume the same position. At the time, Bill found himself hoping she could keep the company afloat. She has done more than that, but he has never trusted her.

He unfolded the paper with the list of refugees and read the names. *Twenty.* What he had told Leah was true, for the few individuals he knew about. But twenty from one camp? And there were other camps from which Ruth had taken refugees. What *was* his company doing? Leah couldn't have revealed her abilities at a better time.

Then there was the issue of invading Leah's mind. What was Ruth after? Bill began to fume. There was so much he didn't know or understand, most likely by design. It was time to call Ruth and have a real heart-to-heart.

His phone rang. It was Ruth. Damn, crazy Banisher and her psychic abilities. If she wasn't making him the richest man on the planet, he'd have nothing to do with her.

Answering, he stated in a calm, flat tone, "You have some explaining to do."

"Many of the refugees were sick, Bill. There's nothing to be done about that. We needed workers. Your company is expanding rapidly, and the medicines we make are labor intensive. I've told you this before."

"How many refugees do you have working for us? And how did twenty of them die?"

"I've told you; we give them new identities."

"Twenty!?"

"A few were sick. They brought a virus with them, and in their weak conditions, some did die."

"I am ordering an audit. This sneaking behind my back has become unacceptable and needs to be addressed immediately."

"Yes, yes. And as for your granddaughter, Mr. Anderson's connection was to ensure her safety. While shadowing Leah, he saw her potential, which is why we need her."

"Her potential—to do what exactly?"

"Manipulate energy," she snipped back. "She'll double our productivity."

"You're telling me my granddaughter is able to extend an individual's life? How?"

"Through the same methods I've mastered, Bill. Rituals, channeling. Leah can do this."

Bill smiled. Leah would be running the company in no time.

"Make an appointment with Jared," Ruth continued, "for the morning following her party. Mr. Anderson will lead that meeting; all you need to do is agree. Your granddaughter is extremely special, and others are trying to recruit her, so be nice and make sure she's coming to New York within the week. I expect you can do that."

Ruth's tone rubbed Bill the wrong way. This whole operation had been fishy from the start. He was in the dark, and now that questions were being asked, he didn't like it. "I know you're up to something."

"Count the money, Bill. Life holds great value for those who have wealth."

"Expect a team within the week. I'm also making a personal visit to inspect the grounds and speak with the employees."

"As you wish."

He hung up the phone, dread coating his insides. He wasn't in control. With a grunt, he dialed his secretary. "Prepare an investigative team to audit Extended Life. I want them to go through everything."

"Yes, sir. I'll assemble a team right away."

"Also, gather the acquisition team. I want to meet with them after lunch today."

Acknowledge the Theft!
Take Responsibility
Make Reparations
Return Stolen Sacred Lands
Accept the Consequences
Improve Relations Between Our Peoples
Make Our World a Better Place

Protest posters lined the terrace leading to the school where a demonstration table had been set up. Leah's grandparents, Walt and Mari, were working the table. They had flown in from Wisconsin and were here for the week. Barb and Lyla walked together, holding signs and marching with others, while Ploy, Nong, and the remaining students carried petition forms for parents to sign. Leah stared at her classmates, happy they were feeling the pride she wasn't allowing herself to experience. She was watching for angry parents, keeping an open and clear mind so she could intervene before a scene erupted.

The last couple she encountered had red, irritated faces. They had bullied straight toward her, intending to tell her, "How dare you ruin our son's graduation with this silly protest! What does any of this have to do with school?" The bystanders looked uncomfortably at each other, but before the couple opened their mouths, Leah touched them, looked into their eyes, and sent them happily on their way. She felt strength and power flowing through her. With every manipulation that defused opposition and convinced parents to sign petitions, she ensured that the media saw unanimous support. She relished the control, confident that this was the best way to achieve a smooth and peaceful protest that garnered widespread backing. She smiled, ignoring the warning in the back of her mind. She couldn't listen. Not now.

The news anchor started his broadcast near the street, instructing his cameraman to get a wide view of the area. He talked about the controversial school board decision to allow the protests, then found Leah.

The broadcaster asked, "Why did you decide to protest this issue at graduation?"

Leah smiled. She was prepared. Roy had tutored her well, and she drew on one of their practiced responses. Tapping into her alter ego—the composed, unflinching personality that lent her an articulate, mature voice—she began.

"As we leave this institution and step into society, we will, inevitably, make mistakes. That is part of being human. We may accidentally strike a parked vehicle or unlawfully take another person's possession without consent. When those moments occur, the path forward is clear: we must acknowledge the error, accept responsibility, embrace the consequences, and learn from our mistakes. That is how individuals grow—and that is how communities thrive.

"As graduates, we are held to that standard. We are expected to live with integrity, accountability, and a willingness to evolve. We are asking Lake Valley to do the same. This protest is not about blame—it is about correction. About restoring what was taken. About modeling the very principles we are taught to uphold."

Leah glanced at the small crowd that had gathered to watch. Many had lifted their phones.

"What is the mistake that Lake Valley made?"

"We stole sacred land from the Sukiya Nation. The facts are clearly documented. We've acknowledged the injustice. I am not here to entertain justifications rooted in timing, ownership, or historical context. What I expect to hear is a commitment to take responsibility—and a plan to return the land."

"Does your decision to protest for the return of sacred lands stem from your abduction at the Center?"

"My abduction opened my eyes to the quiet horrors that surround us. People have come to me—some desperate, some hopeful—believing I might be able to help. They've shared stories of cancer, chronic illness, failing hearts. I see their pain, but I cannot heal their bodies.

"What I can do is speak for the Sukiya Nation. Their suffering may not look the same, but it is no less urgent. It is the pain of unresolved injustice. Over a century ago, our ancestors massacred their families and seized their land. That act is not a relic of the past—it echoes into the present. The stolen land is a living wound, a thorn buried deep in the heart of a people." Leah looked directly into the camera. "If we are to heal as a community, that thorn must be removed."

Barb pushed her way to the front of the crowd. Leah smiled, glad her friend was here.

"Leah, your grandfather is the founder and CEO of a multinational corporation with several subsidiary companies. He's made the Forbes list of richest people in the world several times. It seems to me you could advocate for any number of important issues. Why this one?"

"My grandfather has championed several causes through his foundation. For me, this issue is about injustice. The blatant theft of the land and the belligerent refusal to return it sends a clear message that the Native people don't matter. We saw that in *Worchester v. Georgia* (1832), when the Supreme Court ruled in favor of the Cherokee Nation, affirming their sovereignty and rights to their land. Despite this, the U.S. government refused to acknowledge their legal victory, and the same pattern of dismissal has occurred here. That is unacceptable."

Several in the crowd clapped.

"In order to truly be one nation where people live in harmony, we must hold ourselves to the principles we claim to stand for—a nation of laws, not of social status. The law must apply equally to everyone, and every institution. The crime has been established. Now we must atone and make reparations."

The reporter hesitated, clearly choosing his next words. "The sacred land in question is currently owned by Jenny Oh, a U.S. citizen who legally purchased the land. Her business is very popular among Lake Valley residents. How do you propose the land be returned to the Sukiya Nation?"

The microphone inched closer. "First of all, the city illegally annexed the land and sold it without proper notice. Two officials have been charged in connection with this unlawful act. The city must repurchase the land, de-annex it, and formally transfer the title to the Sukiya tribe. It's really not that difficult."

Gasps and murmurs drew the reporter's attention away from Leah.

"It's him!" a woman exclaimed in awe.

Leah stepped to the side to get a clear look. Her grandfather's limo, flanked by two security trucks, glided to a stop.

"Thank you for your time," the newsman said and hurried toward the motorcade.

In a cabin on the other side of the lake, Uncle Tim, Big Steve, and Nate listened to Leah's interview while assembling explosive devices.

"Holy crap, Tim," Big Steve said, eyes glued to the screen. "Your niece is fantastic. She doesn't sound like an eighteen-year-old at all. Sounds more like a politician running for Congress."

Tim shrugged, a faint smile tugging at his lips. "She's had private schooling and tutors for a big chunk of her life. This is exactly what I expected."

"I'm serious. She's going to make it easier for us to get the signatures we need."

Sighing, Tim looked up from the explosive device he was assembling. His eyes were pleading for quiet. "I agree. Can I concentrate here?"

"What's wrong, Tim? You don't feel like blowing off your arm today?"

Tim glared at Big Steve. "Not funny." He returned to his work.

Nate jumped in, "Has Jared told you where we need to place these?"

"I didn't exactly tell him what we were doing," Tim confessed.

"Why not? Your brother's an architect. And if he knows about the water spirit, what's the problem?"

"I'm not sure he would accept the extreme action we're taking."

"What about his girlfriend, Nong? She's also an architect," Big Steve suggested.

"If I didn't tell my brother, I'm not going to tell her. Besides, I know a thing or two about buildings. Don't worry," Tim held.

"So, tell me the plan again," Big Steve insisted.

Tim stopped what he was doing and sighed.

"I want to hear it again," Big Steve said. "Talking through it helps us find the weak spots."

"Turn off the television," Tim said. The screen went dark, the room went quiet, and Tim laid out the plan in his mind before speaking. "The Education Center has four security guards on its payroll. If one of them gets sick or has vacation time, the building hires a guy from Manned Up Security. Dylan got a job at the company two weeks ago. We sent the evening guy food laced with a laxative, along with a note from the Education Center, thanking him for his hard work. He called in sick the next day, and Dylan got the assignment. He rigged the computer system to crash tomorrow evening. With the cameras off, we can go in after the security guard locks up at eight o'clock and place the explosives. Then we break the gas line as we leave. I'll stay behind, keeping watch to make sure the place stays empty, while everyone else returns to their alibis. If Nate doesn't hear from me by 9:30, he'll detonate the bombs."

"Dylan will be a suspect! With all our noise and protesting, his connection will implicate us. We're going to get caught," Big Steve complained.

"We have solid alibis. There's nothing at our houses, nothing to lead them here. We play it cool, cooperate fully. We'll be fine. This isn't our first time under the microscope."

"I know. But it seems a bit too simple. I feel like we're missing something."

Officer Choi watched Leah's interview. The news feed showed her shaking hands with parents who were agitated. But after she talked with them, they walked away smiling, and some even signed the petition. He knew what she was doing and that meant he had to step in. He wondered when her formal assessment would happen and how long it would be until she was brought into the community and mentored properly.

Choi's wife called him from Korea. "What's wrong, honey? I can feel your anxiety. You have me worried."

"I'm okay. I've finally found the energy manipulator, but she's a young woman, still in high school. And she's abusing her power."

"And you don't want to confront her."

"No, I don't. She's grown quite powerful very quickly. My aunt doesn't want me to interfere with her progress, but the kid is using her powers to manipulate people. I'm not comfortable with that. This isn't the first time I've disagreed with Yoona, and I'm starting to question her judgment."

"You're worried about the young girl."

"She's traveling a dangerous path. If she doesn't change her direction, she'll be forced to transcend before she's had a chance to live. Other members of the Circle won't be as forgiving, especially with a corrupt Shaman currently climbing to power."

"Maybe it's time you use your best judgment and do something."

"Yeah, thank you for the push." With a deep exhale, he said, "So, how are things there? Is my mom treating you well?"

"Your mom is a saint. We're doing very well. But it's late. I'm going to try and get some more sleep. If you're going to send me any more emotions, they better be loving ones."

Choi chuckled, "Yes, dear. I love you too. I'll call you later."

Jared opened the refrigerator door and pulled out two bell peppers—one red and one yellow—a habanero pepper, and a stalk of oregano before opening the dry bin and snatching a sweet onion and a garlic bulb. His mom, Mari—a tall, thin woman with a kind smile and watchful eyes—opened and drained cans of black and kidney beans.

"I can't believe she's all grown up," Mari commented.

Jared looked at Leah who played Uno with Ploy in the living room. "She has a wonderful future ahead of her," he said. He glanced at Nong who was talking to his dad before he started cutting vegetables.

Mari set the leftover turkey on the counter and pulled chunks from the carcass, placing them in a bowl.

Jared moved from the peppers to the onion.

Mari placed her hand on Jared's arm, her wrinkled skin a pale white, so different from Jared's freckled, sun-warmed forearm. "Why don't you move back home?"

Jared paused his cutting of the onion. He heard the plea in his mom's words.

"Your dad and I aren't getting any younger, and we'll need someone to take over the shop."

Jared set down the knife and faced his mom.

Her eyes glistened. "Your abduction was challenging for us. Not knowing what had happened..." Her voice cracked and she paused. "I couldn't go through that again."

Jared pulled her into his arms and gave her a hug.

Mari continued, "Having you back home would mean everything to us. Leah's moving on to new adventures, and when she comes home to visit, I'd get to see her. You kids being so far away..." She let out a sigh. "We're missing moments together."

"I hear you, Mom. I do. But I just got my life back on track."

Mari squeezed his arm and went to the stove. She heated olive oil, then tossed in the peppers.

Jared finished chopping the onion and handed her the cutting board.

Mari chuckled.

"What is it, Mom?"

"I was just thinking about the girl who pulled a camera out from under her robes and started taking photos of the audience."

Giggling came from the living room. "Another Draw Four!" Leah gasped. "How many of those do you have?"

Ploy snickered. "I call the color ... green."

Walt had the ballgame on and watched while chatting with Nong. His lanky, fragile frame, bald head, and grey whiskers only made Nong's graceful, petite build and flowing black hair stand out more. The Mariners were playing the Athletics, with the score 5-2 at the bottom of the seventh.

"You and Jared seem to have a good connection," Walt remarked with a friendly and warm tone.

"We do," Nong replied with a smile. "He's understanding and kind, has vision, and is talented. I see us growing quickly."

Walt stroked his chin. "You mean the architectural firm?"

"Yes. We've been open for a week and already have one client, and we're currently in talks with two others. Jared and I make a great team."

"Do you see your partnership evolving beyond the business aspect?" Walt asked.

Nong gave a playful smile. "Are you wondering if you'll be meeting my parents anytime soon?"

Walt chuckled. "Well, you know, these things do pique my curiosity. Your parents live in the area?"

"They do, yes. They had Ploy while I was away."

Walt's expression turned thoughtful. "I guess this is home for you then, or would moving be an option? A change of scenery, a fresh start."

"What's on your mind, Walt?" Nong's gentle gaze pierced his eyes.

Walt made a fist and set it on the arm of the sofa with purpose. "Right." With a nod and a smile, he said, "We have a long-standing, successful business in Green Bay. Mari and I are getting old, and this whole ordeal that happened with you, Jared, and Leah aged us quicker than we would have liked. We're hoping Jared would move back home and take over the shop. We have some savings and could help the two of you buy a house."

Nong lifted her hand to stop him. "I get it. Have you two thought about moving out here with Jared and Tim?" The question hung between them. "I grew up in Dearborn, Michigan, and I can honestly say, I don't think I could move back to the Midwest. The winters and summers are brutal. The tornadoes and thunderstorms... No. Ploy is starting middle school, and her friends are here. My parents live here. My business is starting to take root, and I own four different properties. Why don't you consider joining us? I could rent you one of the houses I own," she suggested. "They're beautiful homes in an upscale neighborhood located on the mountain. You'd be very comfortable."

Jared walked in and announced that dinner was about ready. He asked for Leah and Ploy to clean up and for Nong and Walt to set the table.

Moving into the dining room, Nong continued, "Lake Valley itself has so much to offer." The enthusiasm in her voice was strong. "The weather is fantastic year-round, with mild winters and pleasant summers. The mountains are close for skiing and hiking, the lake is great for boating and swimming, the ocean is only a few—"

"Okay, okay." Walt laughed. "You've given us something to consider."

Once the table was set and everyone seated, they said grace and then dished up.

"You are so brave, Leah," Nong said. "I don't think I would've organized a protest to take place during my graduation ceremony."

"You would have if you had been captured by a confused, love-hungry animal," Leah returned.

"Touché," Nong responded.

Ploy gushed, "I thought the protest was fun. Most of the people were nice, and I got twelve signatures on my paper." Turning to Leah, she added, "I liked how you calmed the angry people and made them walk away. It was like magic."

Nong smiled. "Yes, she did a good job."

"Are you excited to start school in the fall?" Mari asked.

"What would you think if I were to work in one of Grandpa Bill's companies in New York?" Leah asked. "He's insisting I still attend university, but it'd be Columbia instead of Stanford."

Ploy blurted, "No, Leah! You were so happy to go to Stanford."

Jared asked, "Did Bill offer you a job this morning?"

"He did with Extended Life. He offered Barb a position, too, and said you could have your job back, if you wanted it." She quickly added, "They're meeting with us the day after tomorrow to discuss it."

Jared put his elbows on the table and leaned forward with a frown.

"Is this something you want, Leah?" Walt asked.

"School is challenging and a lot of fun," Nong said. "I'd hate for you to miss out on the full experience because you were working. There's no need for you to do both."

In an angry tone, Jared asked, "Why is Bill all of a sudden interested in hiring you? Does he know about your connecting?"

Mari tilted her head and eyed Leah. "Are you one of those influencers?"

Leah gave her father a hard stare. "No, Grandma. He's talking about a skill I learned earlier." Holding her father's gaze, she added, "We'll talk about this later."

There was a pause in the conversation, and Ploy, oblivious, took the opportunity to ask, "What kind of games are you going to have at your graduation party?"

Jane sat with Craig and Olivia at a quiet dinner table. Her gaze stayed on her daughter's defiant scowl. The earlier visit to the Education Center had left Jane shaken. Olivia's interaction with the building and the unsettling realization that her pretend friend could penetrate Jane's thoughts were deeply disturbing. The warnings from the stranger, Tim, the rumors about that place, and recent tragic events only heightened her fears. Olivia's outburst confirmed Jane's worst fears—that something malevolent had seeped into her daughter.

"Olivia, eat your peas," Jane demanded.

Throwing her fork across the room, Olivia yelled, "Why do you have to control everything I do? I want to go back to art class. I want to see Bella."

"Bella isn't real," Jane spat.

"She's real to me!" Olivia shouted, storming out of the room.

"Olivia!" Jane demanded, but Craig put his hand on her shoulder.

"Just let her calm down," Craig said gently.

Olivia stomped up the stairs, yelling, "I hate you!"

Jane sighed deeply, unsettled by Olivia's changed behavior and overwhelmed by a powerful sense that something was very wrong. An imaginary friend was supposed to be just that—imaginary, something that could follow Olivia everywhere. Yet, Bella was confined to the Education Center, a place that felt increasingly sinister.

Craig took her hand and said, "Jane, I see how much Olivia's been struggling since we pulled her from the art center. I know you had your reasons, and I respect that. But given how much she thrived there and how unhappy she is now, do you think it might be worth reconsidering our decision? Maybe there's a way to address your concerns while still letting her go back."

Jane looked at Craig, her eyes reflecting her turmoil. "Craig, if Bella were a true imaginary friend, Olivia could play with her anywhere—in her room, at school, outside. But Bella is only present at the Education Center, and that place—it scares me. I felt something! I saw Olivia interacting with the building as if it were alive. She read my mind." Jane turned her head away, stealing a moment to collect her thoughts. "All the crazy things in the news—abductions, priests falling into comas, and police officers being tricked. There are rumors about toxic waste, drug testing, and ghosts. The stranger's warnings, my friends' concerns—everything points to something dangerous there. I can't let Olivia go back, no matter how unhappy she is. It just doesn't make sense to put her at risk like that."

Craig nodded. "I'll go online and see if we can enroll her somewhere else—Anne's art lab downtown, the library. I think the museum offers workshops for kids. There has to be an art-based summer camp."

"That would be great. Can you talk to her about those options? I'll lose my temper."

"Of course. I'll sit down with her after I get some information."

After a pleasant evening of dinner, games, and watching baseball, Leah's grandparents were the first to leave, followed shortly by Nong and Ploy. Once the goodbyes were said, Leah helped her dad clear the table and wash the dishes. They worked side by side, and Leah kept glancing at her father, relieved his depression had passed. Being kidnapped by Bellevue had turned out for the best.

When the kitchen was tidy and the last dish was put away, Leah exchanged a warm smile with her dad before heading to her room. The house felt calm and peaceful, a perfect atmosphere for her to dive back into her training. Sitting on her bed, she heard the hum of her computer and went to shut it down but saw she had an email. Checking it, she read what Misty had written.

Subject: Spiritual Rituals for the Dead?

Dear Leah,

I am a doctor. I have never believed in ghosts or spirits. I don't believe in an afterlife. I am struggling to understand what happened to my brother and your friend. I don't know how you obtained private information about my father's conversation with me, but you implied you can talk with ghosts. I'm having a hard time believing that. After talking with people here who hold such beliefs, I'm willing to consider the possibility. I'm curious if you, and they, have similar rituals to communicate to those who have died. To be honest, I doubt I'll ever hear from you again. Although

I do hope for news about what happened to the refugees who were taken and pray it's not what I believe it to be.

Misty.

Leah hit reply. The curser blinked in the subject line like an impatient mother tapping her foot. She didn't know what to tell Misty. She hadn't been able to connect with Bill, but she could see her grandfather didn't know the truth. Closing down the computer, she decided to meditate.

Moving to the middle of her room, she mentally explored her body in preparation for stretching.

For the next half hour, she felt like a track star, bending and pulling her limbs. She immersed herself in the elasticity of her body, feeling the tiny tears and hearing the little pops as she leaned and pushed further. Separating her consciousness from her body, Leah observed her muscles as if they were alien objects, her hands running along the taught bands. She envisioned plucking the tissue and hearing the sweet vibrations. When she finished, her soul felt light. She wanted to float away.

Leah reviewed the martial arts exercises. She bent her knees slightly and moved around the room, kicking and punching the air. As she practiced, her movements became a dance. She lost herself in her rhythm, feeling like she could fly. Her body was warm, her blood flowed freely and easily. She jumped to and from the bed, grabbed the back of the chair and lifted her body up into the air. Spinning and dancing, she lost herself in the moment. After pushing herself off the wall, Leah landed with a backward roll on the floor. She was free. No stress. No worries. No wants or desires. There was nothing she needed to do or think about. Panting, she laid on the floor, catching her breath.

Her mind and emotions were as quiet as a windless winter morning after a new snowfall. In this blissful state, the boundaries of her consciousness began to expand. Energy flowed all around her. She could feel its song vibrating her soul, lifting her up. It felt spectral.

Letting go, Leah's spirit rose. She looked down at her body and glanced around her room. She floated to the window, going right through it.

"Good evening, Mr. Davenport."

Leah saw Dan at the front door with a bouquet of flowers. She drifted to him.

"My exams? Oh, they went well. I finished the semester with a 3.7 GPA."

"That's great!" Jared said. "Have you decided on a major yet?"

"I'm going into criminal justice."

"Good for you," Jared said. "Is Leah expecting you?"

Leah's soul was between them now and she looked back and forth from one to the other. Neither of them had any idea she was there. She went close to Dan, putting her hand on his cheek, but it passed through him.

Dan's brow furrowed. He touched his temple, then glanced at Jared with an edge of concern. "Is Leah alright?"

"She's fine. Come on in."

Leah saw Dan's ideas for her graduation party. Karaoke in one room, video games in the next, a card table for euchre and Texas Hold 'Em, grilling burgers and brats outside, horseshoes, badminton, and the ladder toss game.

She pressed, engaging with his emotions, finding...

Fear. *She's slipping away.*

Hope. *There's still a chance we can be together.*

Exclusion. *Why hasn't she connected to me?*

Guilt. *Am I not worthy? Did I do something wrong?*

Love. *Nothing feels right without her.*

Leah pulled her hand back. Dan was hurting. Worried he'd lose her. *Why didn't I connect with him? I could have, the night we laid together. But I wasn't ready. Prom night? No, because Paul was attached to me. Afterwords? Too much chaos.*

"Can I get you something to drink? You look a little pale."

"Yes, please. Water is fine." Dan sat down. "It's Leah. I—"

"She's in her bedroom." Jared said filling a glass at the kitchen sink. "I imagine you've been stressed like the rest of us."

"Life has been challenging. Are you sure she's okay?"

Jared handed Dan the water. "Is Leah okay?" he repeated. "There's a lot happening in her life."

That's an understatement, Leah thought as she hovered near Dan. She spoke to him, hoping her words could be heard. *You never blamed me. Even now, I don't feel blame. Thank you for giving me space. I don't want to lose you. You are worthy.*

Dan drank the water, then placed his hand over his heart.

Jared held out his hand. "Here, I'll take the glass."

Dan handed it to him.

"You feeling alright?" Jared asked.

"I've missed Leah. Barb's told me she's been going through a lot."

Barb's voice echoed through Leah: *Dan misses you. You've been ... distant.* Leah had wanted to defend herself, but Barb stopped her. *Oh, he knows. You don't have to explain.*

Leah spoke to Dan again, seeing that her words touched him, even if he wasn't able to hear them. *I believed her. I had to because it meant I wasn't doing anything wrong. But now, I understand that my distance hurt you. I'm sorry.*

"Leah's..." Jared's voice trailed off. "You should speak to her yourself. She's grown quite a bit." He went back into the kitchen, asking, "Do you want me to call her?"

"If you don't mind, I'll go to her. We were going to plan for her party."

"Go ahead. And, Dan? I'm glad you're here."

Leah followed Dan down the hall. He tapped on the door. The vibration hit her body and Leah's soul snapped back into place. She felt groggy and stumbled to the door. Dan stood in front of her with a tulip and hyacinth flower bouquet.

"Congratulations. The yellow is for success and joy, and the purple is for accomplishment. I hope you like them. They smell so sweet—like you."

"Oohh. Thank you," Leah said, taking the flowers. "Come in."

He entered, rubbing his hands on his thighs. "I have some ideas for your party tomorrow."

Leah set the flowers on the shelf, turned to Dan, and wrapped her arms around him.

"What's wrong?" he asked.

"We need to talk." She took his hand and led him to the bed.

"If it's about you going away for college, I don't want to have that conversation yet. We've got the summer, and can hang like before … when we were lost inside Bellevue—free and together." He paused. "Can we do that?"

Leah kissed him on the cheek. "Of course. I want the same thing."

"You do?"

"Yes. I want you in my life. Not just when it's convenient or when I need help, but always."

"What about college?" Dan objected. "Long distance relationships aren't easy. And you're going to meet—"

Leah put her finger over his lips. "Distance isn't a problem if we're connected."

Dan's face brightened. "I was hoping you'd teach me how to connect." He held out his hands.

Leah grinned and shook her head. "We're not going to connect like that," she said, placing both hands on his chest. "I need something deeper. More intimate."

Dan's smile faded and a question formed in his eyes. "Are you sure? We haven't been together that long."

"We've been together through Bellevue, the FBI, Paul..." Leah leaned in, putting her ear over his heart. It was racing. "I trust you," she said.

"I trust you too," he whispered.

She sat on the bed and pulled Dan to join her. "I have grown," she said. "In every way but one. My mind has expanded, and my powers have awakened. I've guided souls, walked in pure energy, and bent minds. But there is one part of me I have yet to discover."

Leah stared deep into Dan's eyes, twirling a strand of hair with her finger. Her body warmed and she became aware of each breath. "To become what I'm meant to be, to unlock my full potential as an energy manipulator, I need to experience everything this body is capable of doing. I need to understand the pathways to energy that meditation, or prayer, or even soul-walking can't create. I need to tap into creation itself."

She placed his hand on her waist, her heart joining his in rapid motion.

"I'm choosing you because you see me. Because you've waited for me. Because you've never tried to take—only understand. And now, I'm ready to step forward—as a woman, as an energy manipulator."

She inched closer, resting her head on his shoulder. "Will you do this with me? Join me in manifesting my true self—my true powers?" Looking up, she asked, "Dan ... will you connect with me in this way?"

His body was trembling. He held her gaze, then nodded.

Leah placed her hand on his cheek and connected. Her essence wound into his mind where she placed the words, *I love you.*

You're here. Dan's thoughts entered her mind. *I felt you earlier, while I was talking with your dad.*

Leah's eyes widened. *When did you learn telepathy?*

I didn't. But this is how Bell and I used to talk.

This is amazing, Dan. I can feel you inside me. And I love it. Leah pulled him close and pressed her lips to his. Then she pushed forward, sending him onto his back.

What about your dad? he asked.

We can make all the noise we want here. Keep your mouth closed and he won't hear a thing. She pulled his shirt up, over his head and ran her hands across his shoulders. *Oh, so perfect.*

I heard that, Dan said.

Your body is amazing.

Her insides stirred. Closing her eyes, she focused on her emotions. This moment wasn't only about them; it was also about understanding her energy, her body. It was about biology.

Leah tracked the chemistry, analyzing the chemicals that were bursting from within: her adrenal and pituitary glands, her gut, her hypothalamus, and her brain. The explosions thundered, chaining their way through every nerve, aligning her entire being to experience this sacred moment. Straddling Dan, she locked eyes with him and then met his lips.

Their kiss, felt twice over through their connection, reverberated between them. They were interconnected, hearts thrumming in unison, each feeling what the other felt—the smooth curve of her lips, her gentle pressure, the trembling of her mouth. Every touch, every move, every press, was experienced in stereo. And Leah learned. Their passionate exchanges were creating a blueprint for the origin of her power.

Dopamine lit up their brains, a wildfire of craving, and a waterfall of pleasure. She needed him, was driven to take him, her nerves amplified to experience him.

Adrenaline—the spark plug—had their hearts racing and muscles tense. She was alive in a way she had never been before. Her body quivered as his fingers traced her collarbone, like live wires sparking heat.

Endorphins produced euphoria. His squeezes and love bites sent ripples of ecstasy through her, forcing a moan.

Oxytocin—the bonding hormone—stitched their souls together like thread through silk. Her hands ran through his hair, and she was unable to let him go. They floated as one, in a magical realm of togetherness.

They quickly removed their clothes and pressed their bodies together. His hands caressed her breasts. His mouth was warm and moist. They moved in a fluid motion, rolling, rubbing, and grasping.

Leah's breaths came in short, heavy beats. Dan paused before entering.

Not waiting for the question, she pleaded, "Yes!" and pulled him closer.

He entered, and Leah winced. The pinch made her gasp, and her body tensed.

They started slow, each thrust hitting just right. She felt the endorphins kick and the adrenaline rush, dulling the discomfort and intensifying the pleasure. The high was so powerful, she couldn't see straight. Her toes curled. Her calves clenched. She arched her back, body pulsating. Gripping his shoulders, she whimpered, *holy shit...* Her chest swelled, pressure strained against her ribs, her ears, into the soft places beneath bone. Dan drove harder—*yes!* Teeth set. The surge, the roar, the kick...

A violent wave gushed—stripping away all the tightness and strain. Cleaning. Cool. Sweat coated her skin, beaded on her eyelashes. Leah was forever changed.

She lay in Dan's arms, in their shared skin, with their shared breaths. Serotonin flooded her system. She was content. She had tapped into the sacred power of creation and attained the fullness of womanhood—the final key to her transformation, to becoming an energy manipulator.

Seoul, Korea

<u>Triumph and Turmoil</u>

Su-Bin felt a dull glob of emotion lodged in her upper chest between her lungs and her throat. She tried to identify the emotion—a mix of anger, frustration, stress, and worry all balled up in a gooey mess. She gave that mucilaginous feeling a name: Min Yun.

Pulling into a parking space, Su-Bin studied the sign on the wall of the office building: "Darkness to Light Private Investigators." Dae-Su Ryu had offered his services the day she opened Moon Law and Associates' doors for business. Of all the investigative services she used, his team was the best.

Looking at the time, Su-Bin hurried to the door. Dae-Su Ryu had called her the night before, saying, "We need to meet first thing tomorrow morning. I have some photos you need to see."

"Min Yun?"

"Yes, ma'am."

She was patting herself on the back for her decision to have him followed, and her curiosity about what the private eye had found now dwarfed the gelatinous mess in her chest. Su-Bin entered, seeing Dae-Su on the phone. She greeted Hwan-Jin, who had been a theater major. His explanation for working with Dae-Su lived in Su-Bin's memory: "Acting on stage or in front of a camera pales to the intensity and demands of acting in real time, for a real purpose. I'll never go back." Su-Bin recognized the man sitting at the computer as Dae-Su's hacker. There were two men absent, Dae-Su's "professional stalkers." Dae-Su had arrested both of them for the crime when he worked as a detective with the police department.

"Ms. Moon, thank you for coming," Dae-Su said, ushering her into his office. "We need to act fast."

"Why? What did you find?"

He motioned for her to sit and opened a manila folder full of photographs. Flipping through them, Dae-Su told her the story they showed.

"Last night, Dr. Kim was sitting on his back deck enjoying an evening drink when a delivery driver rang his bell. As Dr. Kim went to answer the door, you can see Min climb over the wall, cross the yard, and climb the deck. Meanwhile, Dr. Kim talked with the driver and fumbled for his ID, which the driver had to scan. Min walked through the open back door and placed something in the vase on the fireplace. Then, while the doctor was signing the delivery scanner, Min walked back out the rear door. You can see the doctor closing the front door and carrying a case of *soju* into the kitchen. Min crossed the lawn and retreated back over the wall."

"What did he put in the vase?"

"Hwan-Jin went over there this morning." Dae-Su flipped the next photo to show a necklace.

Su-Bin's face paled. She stood and stumbled backward. Then her face turned a brilliant red. Min had her father's necklace this whole time. *He* had killed her father! He was the reason her mother was in prison. And she, herself, had slept with ... that repulsive pile of shit.

Dae-Su continued, "Min Yun just left the courthouse with a detective. They have a search warrant for Dr. Kim's home."

Su-Bin couldn't think. Her insides burned. Her skin crawled. She wanted to shoot Min Yun dead. Pound the life out of him with a mallet. Dig his eyeballs out with a spoon. Su-Bin crumpled the photo as her hands curled into fists.

"We can take him down," Dae-Su said. "The evidence we have is enough to arrest him while they investigate. We've got him."

"I want to be there when they do. I want to see the look on his face when he discovers I know. I want him to look at me as the police handcuff him."

"Let's go. We'll talk to the captain at the station. When they return from the search, Min will be arrested."

Sitting in an interrogation room, Su-Bin and Dae-Su talked with Captain Cheo Yong. Su-Bin explained her father had been murdered and her mother imprisoned for the crime, but that she was innocent. She told him why she had hired Min Yun, that they dated and broke-up. She detailed how he had framed Brandon and the doctor, which is why she had him investigated. Dae-Su talked about his stakeout and showed the captain the photos from last night. When they finished talking, the captain radioed his team.

"Have you found anything?"

"We found the necklace and the emergency medical EDC folding knife with the white unicorn."

"Where was the necklace found?"

"In a vase on the mantle of the fireplace."

Su-Bin whispered, "Don't tell them yet. Wait until they return."

"Bag it. Bring it in."

"We're not finished with the search."

"I don't think you'll find anything else. Come back, and bring the lawyer with you."

"Yes, Sir."

"May I call the press?" Su-Bin asked. "I want his arrest to be public."

"Be my guest," the captain said. "I understand sweet revenge."

Min felt a rush of pride as he pulled up to the police station. Reporters were ready to take statements, and Min was already daydreaming about making love to Su-Bin after they watched the evening news together.

He stepped out of the car, smiling and waving as the photographers took his photo. Because he was basking in his own glory, it took him several moments to register the questions being asked.

"Did you kill Ki-Tae Moon?"

Min's expression slowly turned to confusion. Looking around, he saw Su-Bin glaring at him as two officers approached, informing him that he was under arrest for obstructing justice and for the murder of Ki-Tae Moon. They told him he had a right to stay silent and put him in cuffs. He couldn't believe what was happening.

Did Su-Bin really know what he had done? How? It wasn't possible. But here he was, handcuffed, being escorted into the station by two officers. He found Su-Bin in the crowd. She was smiling, savoring the moment.

He pleaded, "I was only protecting you from your father! Your mother wasn't supposed to go to prison. I'm sorry. I love you!"

His anguish seemed to strengthen Su-Bin's pleasure. She looked at him as if he were a disgusting worm squirming to escape the hot sun.

Five weeks later, as Su-Bin waited outside the prison for her mom, she thought about Yoona. How had she known what would happen? Yoona had directed Su-Bin as if she were the star of a new blockbuster hit, and Su-Bin wasn't sure if she should feel grateful or angry. If Yoona had known all this time, why didn't she just tell her that Min was her father's murderer?

Su-Bin reached for Jong-In's hand. "Thank you for coming with me."

"This is a huge moment for you," Jong-In responded, squeezing her hand.

The gate to the prison door clicked and Su-Bin's heart froze, tears stinging her eyes. The door swung open, and her mother stood, blinking against the sunlight. Su-Bin ran to her. "Momma."

The day after Min Yun was arrested, in a temple outside of Seoul, Brandon sat on his sleeping mat, meditating before starting his day. The temple instructor entered the room and informed the students that they would be communicating with a soul. Each student was to counsel the soul assigned to them and help it transcend before the morning meal.

Brandon built the glowing light in his core, the way Yoona had taught him, and extended it to fill the room. He saw several souls hovering near the instructor. The students formed a line, and as the instructor moved to each person, she motioned for a soul to touch the student in front of her. The souls then waited with the students for instructions.

When the instructor reached Brandon and a soul touched him, he was flooded with emotions of regret and sadness. Memories of phone calls from home to the soul's office played through his mind. Brandon saw that the soul had missed special events and occasions that were important to his family. Then the visions stopped.

"Take what you have learned from the soul and make a talisman, one that represents the soul you just met," the instructor said.

With pencil and paper in hand, Brandon thought back to the first talisman he had painted—Bellevue—composed of Chinese, Egyptian, and Celtic symbols. He remembered what Yoona had taught him: it wasn't the symbols themselves that held power, but the energy and meaning he infused into them.

He focused on the soul that had touched him—the missed birthdays, the voice messages, the desperate effort to provide. The words *presence, regret,* and *hope* formed in his mind.

Brandon let his spiritual energy flow through him, into the pencil as he drew:

—a circle, symbolizing family, togetherness, and the soul's longing to return;

—a spiral, to show motion, the endless work cycle that pulled the soul away;

—a square standing on its point, embodying duty and commitment;

—sun rays, for the enduring glimmer of hope;

—and a single tear, etched at the base, for regret.

The energy flowed into the paper, giving him his talisman.

After Brandon finished, he invited the soul into his body. Twenty minutes later, Brandon held the talisman in front of him, drawing the soul out before it transcended.

Sitting on his sleeping mat, Brandon journaled the experience. This was the second soul that had attached to him, so he compared this encounter with the day he had communicated with Bellevue. Both of the souls had fought to control his mind, but unlike his time with Bellevue, this soul hadn't found any hidden secrets or unresolved pain to hold. The other difference was in how they communicated. This soul didn't speak English, and Brandon couldn't speak Korean, so they relied on memories, emotions, and visions. The soul had been a father of three and had worked long hours. He had missed out on his children's upbringing and wanted to possess Brandon in order to spend quality time with his kids, since he was robbed of that time by the demands of his company and of society in general.

Brandon didn't share the soul's sentiment that it had been robbed. The soul had seen its children grow, establish successful careers, and find love. Brandon felt jealous. His son had died at the early age of one. Brandon told the soul to be grateful that it hadn't had to live through losing a child. The soul felt better after the exchange, understanding that in the eyes of others, his life had been a good one. It left Brandon and transcended.

In guiding the soul toward gratitude, Brandon found a flicker of peace—not in what he had, but in what he could give.

In the peaceful calm of the temple's main hall, Yoona meditated while sitting on a patterned carpet in front of a Buddha statue. The sweet fragrance in the air emanated from a smoking incense stuck in the sand at the base of the altar. Placing her fingertips on the floor, Yoona melded with the energy flowing through this convergence point and connected with the other twenty-two members of the Circle.

This meeting, held every other month, was to discuss the ripples of events and the locations of those causing them. With members located throughout the world, they could collectively create an image of the world's population that appeared to Yoona as nondescript, gray figures. Among them were scattered dots of varying shades of pink and red. These represented individuals with the ability to manipulate energy, ranging from faint, barely discernible hues to deep, intense crimson for the most skilled.

As the members linked telepathically one by one, an image of the world and its citizens coalesced in Yoona's mind. She focused on Lake Valley and recognized the dots representing Choi and Leah. Surrounding them were representations of doctors, counselors, religious leaders, and sales representatives. However, what caught Yoona's attention was the prominent red dot—a designation the Circle had given to the corrupt Shaman's helper—now residing within Lake Valley. Yoona didn't know the identity. But seeing that this individual was after Leah meant that they had an opportunity to discover who this person was.

Taking a moment before the meeting started, Yoona addressed Circle member Nehio Mah-seet, a Native American medicine man, who was near Lake Valley. "Elder Nehio, I need your assistance with an urgent matter," she began. "A situation is unfolding in Lake Valley involving a young recruit named Leah Davenport. She has been courted by the corrupt Shaman, and your presence and expertise are crucial in helping uncover this person's identity. Watcher Choi can assist you. Additionally, would you guide her through the meditations to cleanse her soul?"

Yoona sensed the elder bowing. "Moodang Yoona, you honor—" Nehio was silenced by a loud pop. Every member's attention snapped to the sound, known within the Circle as a disturbance, originating from Lake Valley. Ripples of energy surged across the globe, and when the shockwave reached each member, it forced a psychic vision of the future upon them.

Yoona found herself standing in the halls of the White House, facing a dark figure cloaked in shadows. Her hair was wrapped in a samurai bun, and she held a staff. "How I have waited for this time to come," the woman snarled.

Yoona gathered the ambient energy in the room, drawing it from the warmth of the windowpanes, the carpet, the light, and the very air itself.

the woman raised her staff and flicked a switch. Three sharp metal blades sprang forth from the handle, each extendin two feet until they converged at a lethal point. The blades locked into place, forming an imposing sword. Activating the second switch caused the weapon to hum as arcs of blue electricity raced along the metal, crackling and sparking with raw power. The electricity danced across the surface, illuminating the edges with a brilliant, pulsating light, turning the once cold metal into a weapon of sheer, electrified energy.

Secret Service agents rounded the corner, their eyes widening as they took in the sight of the crackling, electrified sword in the woman's hand. Instinctively, they raised their guns. "Drop..." one of them started, but paused as if he knew the weapon was too volatile. He took a steadying breath and commanded, "Shut it down!"

In a fluid motion, she spun the sword around her body. The blue electricity crackled as it formed a protective field around her. The agents opened fire, but their bullets ricocheted off the energy field and embedded into the walls and ceiling. Drawing energy from her sword, she unleashed bolts of electricity from her hand, striking the men down.

Yoona frantically searched for the souls, intending to harness their transcendent energy and amplify her power. However, the woman's sword acted as a hypnotic allure and drew the souls to it like flies to an electrified trap.

Facing Yoona, the woman let out a maniacal laugh. She ran forward, closing the distance between them, then thrust her blade forward. The electricity disrupted Yoona's shield, and her sword went straight into Yoona's chest. "That's for erasing my father from existence!" she declared, turning to the twenty-two others sharing the vision. "I'm coming for each and every one of you. The Circle's reign of power has come to an end."

Yoona severed her connections with the others and cut the ties that had bound her to the Circle members. The discussions and debates were pointless. She had seen versions of this vision before and knew her path. Death did not concern her; she would find another body. However, this version of the vision unsettled her. The weapon wielded by the corrupt Shaman was unlike anything she had encountered—an enigmatic device that drew souls directly towards it, an ominous threat that could give this Shaman unprecedented control over Yoona's essence. How could she counter such a weapon? What measures could she take to ensure that her soul, upon death, would not be ensnared by this malevolent sword staff?

What mattered now was swift and decisive action. The mystery of this weapon could wait. Yoona sprinted to find Brandon. He was eating breakfast.

"It's time to go. We must leave immediately."

Lake Valley, Oregon

Fateful Decisions

At seven o'clock in the evening, wearing a cowboy hat and bright red flannel shirt, Big Steve strolled across the parking lot and entered the Family Fun House. He took off his hat as he purchased tokens, making sure the camera saw his face, and then returned the hat to his head and walked into the gaming room. He had made a point to come twice a week since the meeting in Tim's basement and planned to keep coming for the next two to establish a pattern. Sitting at a machine, he played for half an hour before going into the restroom. Inside, he switched his hat and shirt with another man and promptly left the establishment. The man in the bathroom, sporting Big Steve's cowboy hat and bright flannel shirt, went back to the machine and resumed playing.

Big Steve drove to the the Education Center. The building closed at 7:30, and he was meeting the others there at eight. Once the explosives were set, he would return to the Family Fun House and meet the man in the restroom again at 9:15. Wearing his hat and flannel shirt, Big Steve would order a hotdog and make sure the camera saw his face.

Big Steve parked his car in the apartment complex across the street from the Center and waited. At 7:52, the night guard locked the doors and drove away. Big Steve made his way around the building to where it butted against the hillside. When Tim and Nate arrived, they broke the window and climbed inside.

What are you doing here? Big Steve stopped, confused by the thought he just had. *Are you a thief? There is nothing of value here.*

"I'm having some really weird thoughts," Big Steve said.

"Me too," Nate agreed.

"That's the water spirit," Tim said. "Don't listen to it."

At 8:05, Officer Choi arrived at Leah's house. The sign in the yard and the cars parked out front told Choi that he had come during her graduation party. He thought about turning back but decided to congratulate her and make an appointment to talk later.

Outside her front door, he was met by a security guard. "Sorry, no weapons."

Choi returned to his car and secured his belt. Once inside the house, he heard a Korean pop song, "Congratulations" by Eric Nam, coming from the speaker in the backyard. Purple and yellow balloons and streamers hung from the ceiling. He smelled the burgers and brats on the grill. Stepping through the back door, he recognized Barb, Dan, and Ploy, who were playing horseshoes with their friends. Jared and Walt were setting up bug lamps and tiki torches, as the sun began to set. Leah's mom, Stacy, her grandmother, Mari, Tim's wife, Patty, and Grandma Carol were tending the fire pit, enjoying drinks. Nong and Bill were chatting while hitting crochet balls. Leah saw Officer Choi and bounced over.

"Hi," she said, smiling. "Do you want a hamburger? My uncle Tim cooked them."

Taking another glance at the party, Choi didn't see her uncle anywhere. "No, thank you. I came to congratulate you and wish you success at Stanford. You are still planning to attend in the fall, right?"

"I'm not sure. I might be attending Columbia instead."

"New York City. Your mom lives there."

"Her business office and apartment are there, yes."

"Cool."

An awkward silence rose between them. Over at the horseshoe pit, Dan cheered, celebrating his ringer and high-fiving his teammates. A new rhythm rolled over the party—canga-style drums, handclaps, and a soft guitar playing a syncopated riff that Choi couldn't ignore.

"Ooh. I like this," he said, moving his shoulders with the music.

"Ricky Martin—Pégate," Leah said.

"Nice party song."

Leah pulled Choi closer to the house and away from the others. "I'm still curious about this disturbance. What is it?" she asked. "Your wife was scared, and you sent her to Korea to avoid it."

Choi exhaled and nodded. *How do I address this?* He feared Leah was possibly the one to spark the disturbance, and may have already set events in motion when she manipulated others tied to the protest. He wanted to set a time for them to sit and talk. He hoped to look at her future again, walk through the meditations she needed to perform, and set hard boundaries for her.

Leah continued, "If you sent your family away, then it's something serious. Maybe I should ask my grandpa to fly us all to Fuji."

Choi grinned. "That would be fun." Placing a hand on Leah's shoulder, he said, "Actually, I was hoping you could shed some light on what this disturbance might be." Since Leah was powerful, maybe she had seen what was to come. "Have you had any visions?"

"One," Leah said. "But it was about Bellevue."

He asked her about it, and she explained how she had felt a pull to go to Diamond Creek and warn Judy about the house.

Choi frowned. "Your vision means the disturbance has something to do with Bellevue." He brought his hand to his chin. "But that can't be. Bellevue transcended."

Leah shook her head. "No. Bellevue *is* the Education Center."

Choi raised an eyebrow. "*Is* the Education Center?"

"The building is alive. I told Agent Bruce Duchovny."

"What?" Choi took a step back. He couldn't believe what she was saying. "Alive? You must mean possessed. But the priest who had come to exorcise Bellevue from the building said It wasn't there."

"Choi. The building is alive. Go talk with It."

"If what you're saying is true, then..." He glanced at the mountain in Bellevue's direction. *How?* was the only thought that came to him. He knew the land sat on a nexus, a perfect location for a temple. "Do you mean the spirit is suspended between realms? Anchored to this world through the Education Center while existing in the afterlife?"

"I don't think so. I think It's alive. The building is a living entity."

Choi had no idea how that could be true, but he couldn't ignore her vision. "Will you come with me to the Center and help me understand what's happening there?"

Her lips parted, but she just stared at him. Then words trembled out. "No, I'm not ready."

"Your abilities suggest otherwise. And I could really use your help here."

"I ... I can't," she voiced. "Are you sure the disturbance has something to do with Bellevue?"

"We'll soon find out. Yoona is coming to Lake Valley." Choi paused for a beat, wondering how Leah would take the information he was about to give. "When she arrives, she'll assess you. And if you're as strong as I believe you to be, she'll offer you an apprenticeship."

Leah gave a nervous smile. "I have so many questions, but we need to talk about this another time. It's my graduation party."

"Tomorrow afternoon, then. I'll call before I come over."

Leah nodded and motioned to the food. "Hungry?"

"Leah, there's one more thing we need to talk about. I saw your protest on TV and noticed you were manipulating people. I cannot stress enough how dangerous that path is. It's forbidden for a reason, and the consequences are harsh. Have you read the manual in its entirety?"

"I did," she said.

"Manipulating a government body to achieve a desired goal is among the worst ways to abuse your power. That needs to stop. There are meditations for purifying your soul near the back of the book. Look at them tonight, and then we'll meditate together after our meeting tomorrow."

"Okay."

Choi patted Leah's shoulder. "Welcome to the Circle. My aunt will make it official when you meet her. I'm looking forward to seeing how powerful you become." Leah didn't look too happy about the news. Choi added, "Don't get too excited."

He straightened and gave a reassuring nod. "I'm going to say hi to your dad, Nong, and your uncle before I go. We'll talk again tomorrow." Scanning the yard, he asked, "Where is Tim, by the way?"

Leah shrugged. "In the house, maybe. I'll go check."

Choi meandered over to the croquet course. He introduced himself to Bill and greeted Nong, but they were talking business, so Choi slipped away to grab a burger. Where was Tim? Something was amiss. His mysterious behavior at his house the other day and now his disappearance from Leah's party didn't sit well with him. He glanced in Bellevue's directions, his gut slowly turning upside down.

At 8:35, Uncle Tim was securing an explosive to a support beam when Leah's text message dinged his phone: "Where are you? Officer Choi is here and wants to talk with you."

Bellevue's panicked voice cut in, *The police know what you're doing. Stop!*

"Shut up! Nobody knows anything," Tim retorted.

Does Leah know what you're doing? Jared? They don't, do they?

"Shut up!"

Tim's phone rang. It was Stacy. "Where'd you go?"

"I forgot Leah's present. I ran back to the house to grab it."

"All right, hurry back. There's an officer here to talk with you."

Go. Bellevue pleaded. *Take your things and go. Let me live in peace.*

Tim stood and hurried to the other room, but as he approached the door, it slammed closed. *You forgot your things!* Tim opened the door and went into the next room where Big Steve and Nate were securing devices. "There's a police officer at Leah's party. I have to bail."

"We know," Big Steve said. "Our spider senses are telling us everything."

"You can't leave us here with this ghost!" Nate blustered.

"I have to go, or my alibi is shot," Tim exclaimed.

"Who's going to stay behind to keep an eye on the building before it blows?" Big Steve asked.

Tim exhaled. "We gotta do this. We can't back out now. Set the last explosives and go." Tim's body deflated, and his eyes dripped with apologies. "Sorry! I have to leave."

Please. Don't do this. It's not right. I don't want to die. Not like this!

Tim ignored the pleas, climbed out the window, and ran down the trail to Miley. As he drove, he reminded himself not to speed, run any lights, or have an accident. He had to take the same route back that he had taken to get there, to avoid the traffic cameras. The last thing he needed was to be caught on film near the Education Center tonight.

At 8:57, Tim pulled up to the house, removed the present he had stashed behind the seat, and headed inside.

"Hey! He made it back," Jared cheered.

Tim walked coolly and collectedly up to Leah. "I ran home quick to grab this."

Leah hugged her uncle, "Thank you."

After a bit of chatter, Tim spotted Officer Choi and approached him. "How are you doing? Enjoying my burgers?"

"They're really good."

"I mix the spices in the night before," Tim said.

Choi finished chewing and then said, "I want to discuss Leah. Did you know about the book she's reading?"

Tim raised his eyebrows. "She reads lots of books. Both her and her father are avid readers. Have you seen her bookshelves?"

Choi nodded. "Yes, I noticed. Quite the collection. But there was one in particular that caught my attention." He took a second to study Tim's reaction. "A training manual."

Tim's face remained neutral, but his posture shifted. "Leah's always had eclectic tastes."

Choi leaned in and lowered his voice. "The author of that book is coming to town soon and will need Leah's help."

Tim frowned. "With what?"

"Leah is powerful. Very powerful. The author of the book she's reading is the head of an organization that protects the citizens of this world."

Tim chuckled. "They're doing a bang-up job. How many wars are happening now?"

"Which is why she needs Leah. I need you to talk to her sometime this week and help her understand that her abilities are meant for a higher purpose. Leah has untapped potential, and with the right guidance, there's no limit to what she could achieve."

Tim nodded. "Sure, I'll talk to her."

As Choi and Tim chatted, Bill approached Leah.

"I've been thinking about Mr. Anderson's offer to you. I support it and want to officially offer you a position at Extended Life." He put his arm around Leah. "I need you to learn everything you can." He lowered his voice. "I want you to take over."

Leah pulled at a strand of her hair. "We have a meeting set for tomorrow morning at eleven. We'll discuss it then."

"Yes, but we'll meet before Mr. Anderson joins us. I've talked with Nong and have hired her firm."

Leah took a second to register what he meant. "You've hired my dad?" she asked, a smile forming. "How about my friend Barb? Will you hire her too? Mr. Anderson said her talents were valuable."

"Of course. Anything else?"

"Get my boyfriend into Columbia. I want us to study together."

"I'll see what I can do."

"Okay," she said, nodding.

"Good, good," Bill declared, patting her back.

Choi came over and interrupted to reconfirm his appointment. "Tomorrow?"

Sighing, she said, "Tomorrow." She finished the sentence in her thoughts. *I'll tell you, sorry, I'm heading to New York.*

At 9:22, Choi started his cruiser and pulled into the street. His radio crackled to life with a call from dispatch, directing him to check out another party situation. Apparently, the neighbors were concerned about kids jumping off the roof into a pool. Shaking his head with a wry smile, Choi chuckled at the insane things teenagers did. At 9:24, as Choi was plotting the route to the party location, a second call came over the radio, alerting all officers to a break-in at the Education Center, with reports of a strong gas odor.

Bellevue!

At 8:57, while Tim was entering Leah's party with present in hand, Craig Rose stepped into his living room to talk with his wife, Jane.

"Olivia didn't come down for dinner. It's bedtime. Do you want to check on her and see if she wants a snack before lights out?"

"Sure." Jane went upstairs and knocked on her daughter's bedroom door. "Olivia?" No answer. "I'm coming in." Opening the bedroom door, Jane froze. The floor was littered with crumpled papers, scattered art supplies, and stuffed animals. The window was wide open, and Olivia was nowhere to be seen. She screamed, "No! Craig! Craig! Olivia's gone!"

Jane stared at the crumpled papers on the floor, grinding her teeth. Her daughter had been trying to draw the Bellevue House. Olivia had run away to the Education Center to see her imaginary friend, Bella.

Jane's husband rushed outside. "The lattice is broken. She climbed out the window," Craig called.

Running to her husband, Jane swore, "Damn it. You're too soft with her!"

"Where do you think she went?" Craig asked.

Handing the car keys to her husband, she said, "To the Education Center. Let's go."

As Craig drove, Jane fumbled with her phone, her fingers hovering over the 9-1-1 dial screen. "Drive faster," she urged.

It was 9:18 when they arrived at the Center. Jane rushed to the entrance while Craig went around the building to the right. As Jane went to the left, she heard her husband shouting for her. She doubled back and found him climbing through a broken window.

"I can smell gas," he said. "Call 9-1-1."

Jane did and talked with the operator. "Yes, We're at the Education Center. We think our daughter broke a window and climbed inside. We can smell gas."

Craig waited for his wife to finish the call, so he could pull her up and through the window.

"The police are on the way. They told us not to go in, but to wait by the street."

"I'm having strange thoughts," Craig said. "I'm going to look for Olivia." He rubbed his forehead. "Why don't you go wait for the police?"

Jane headed back toward the parking lot but paused at the large windows of the Art room. She pressed her forehead against the glass and framed her face with her hands to peer inside, hoping to catch a glimpse of her daughter. She saw a tiny red-light blinking.

At 9:20, Bill took the karaoke microphone and gave a speech about hard work, perseverance, and resilience. Tim put his arm around his wife and kissed her forehead. In a few minutes, he would announce they were expecting. Everything would be perfect. The Education Center would be gone, and the ghost wouldn't be able to hurt anyone else. The land would surely be returned to the tribe, and he could find some peace from his recurring nightmares. As 9:20 became 9:26, his heartbeat raced faster. Four minutes to go.

Leah laid a hand on his shoulder, whispering, "Is something wrong. Are you feeling alright?"

"Oh," Patty grunted. She placed her hand on her belly.

"Babe, you okay?" Tim asked.

She paused a moment, then said, "Yeah. It's nothing."

Leah pressed, "Tim, I've got a bad feeling."

Bill concluded his speech with an announcement. "I'm buying the Education Center and the land."

Tim's stomach drop.

"I have a meeting with the Sukiya tribe next week, and we'll discuss plans for them to manage the property. It's my intention, with the help of Nong's company, to rebuild the Bellevue House."

"Oh, shit," Tim gasped. He fumbled for his phone. The time read 9:29. With fingers shaking, he tapped at the numbers to unlock it, desperately trying to dial Nate before 9:30, the scheduled time for the bombs to detonate.

As Tim hit the contacts list, and Bill announced Leah's employment, Patty yelled out in pain. All eyes turned on her. She reached out for Tim's support, knocking his phone to the ground.

"No!" Tim shouted, falling to his knees and snatching it.

Blood ran down Patty's leg. She clutched her abdomen and fell next to Tim. "The baby!" she cried out.

"You're pregnant?" Stacy exclaimed. "Jared! Come help."

Mari held Patty's hand and ordered, "Walt, go start the car."

Leah clutched her chest. "I feel … something tearing," she gasped.

Boom! A distant rumble thundered. Heads turned to see a brilliant fireball rising into the sky, followed by billowing smoke.

"Tim! Help me!" Stacy shouted.

Tim stared in shock.

Mari and Stacy supported Patty, helping her towards the house as the others stared at the red glow and black smoke coming from Bobcat Mountain.

Jared grabbed Tim by the collar with one hand and a handful of hair with the other. In a low, graveled voice, he demanded, "Did you just blow up the Education Center?"

Tim's dazed stare went through him. His mouth opened and hung like a window on a broken hinge. "I did," he whispered. "I had to."

"You fucking idiot! Bellevue will be a ghost again."

Olivia walked along the trail, nearing the Education Center, when she heard the loud explosion and saw a billowing ball of flames rising above the trees.

"Bella!" she screamed, running toward the building. She rounded the turn in the trail and stopped short in front of the smoking rubble of the Education Center.

"Bella?" she called. "Bella?!" Her knees wobbled, and tears ran down her cheeks. "Bella!" Olivia cried.

She stumbled around the building, sobbing. Small fires burned in the ruin, and the dust and smoke hurt her lungs. She could hear sirens approaching and looked to see the flashing lights. She couldn't them. Then she noticed a woman lying on the ground in the rocks and debris. It kind of looked like her mom.

The sirens grew louder, their lights now visible. Olivia crept warily toward the woman lying on the ground when a form suddenly began to take shape right in front of her. The ghostly glow grew and grew. Olivia watched in amazement as a giant house finally appeared—the very house she had drawn in art class, the one that had been on display—the house her teacher had called the Bellevue House.

"Bella?"

Witness Bellevue's dramatic metamorphosis in the next book of the Ascension series: *A Haunting Redemption*.

Acknowledgements

Help is always appreciated, sometimes more than you realize.
Thank you for helping those in your life who need it.

Anne Topp and Jared Bancroft
Andrea, Tayweadah, Tasanaht, Ging, Raychel, Steve, Damien Oz, Abram Oz,
Corah Goelzer, Mir-Yashar, Cutter Letang, Aaron, Kerry Sirotta, Eric Levintski,
Meek, Shannon Elam

Beta Readers on Fiverr
Kimberly @kimberlysj, Kate @kslove35, Jennell B. @jennellbrown

Vonnie—follow her @ www.goodreads.com/vonniew

A big thank you to Melissa Chandler, Dylan Hagans, Eric Lehr, and Kara
Nguyen. Your support helped bring this book into the world